ELEPHA

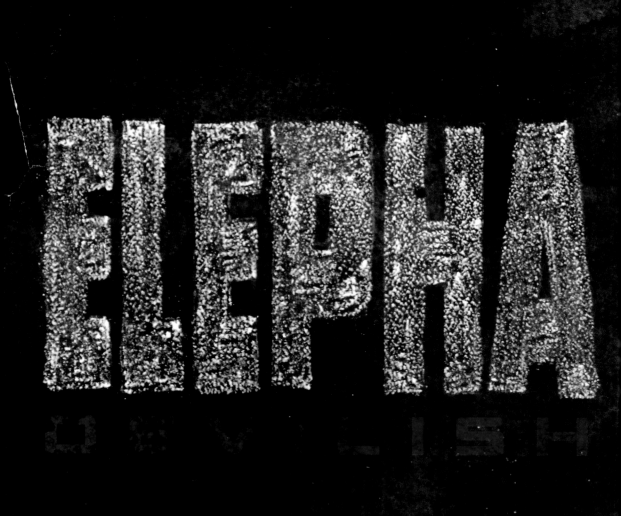

NTMEN

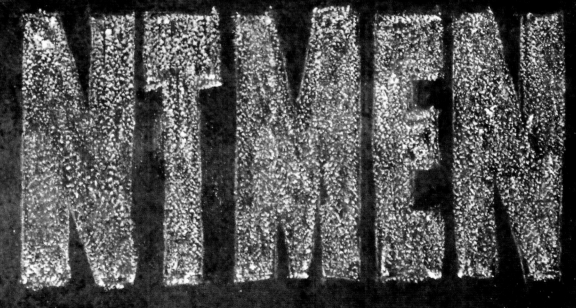

STORY & LETTERING
RICHARD STARKINGS

ARTWORK
AXEL MEDELLIN
SHAKY KANE

COVER ART
BOO COOK

J.SCOTT CAMPBELL
with NEI RUFFINO
KEU CHA
IAN CHURCHILL
ED McGUINNESS

COLOR
AXEL MEDELLIN
GREGORY WRIGHT

DESIGN
J.G. ROSHELL
of COMICRAFT

COO
ROBERT KIRKMAN

CFO
ERIK LARSEN

President
TODD McFARLANE

CEO
MARC SILVESTRI

Vice-President
JIM VALENTINO

Publisher
ERIC STEPHENSON

Sales & Licensing Coordinator
TODD MARTINEZ

PR & Marketing Director
JENNIFER DE GUZMAN

Accounts Manager
BRANWYN BIGGLESTONE

Administrative Assistant
EMILY MILLER

Marketing Assistant
JAMIE PARRENO

Events Coordinator
SARAH DELAINE

Digital Rights Coordinator
KEVIN YUEN

Production Manager
TYLER SHAINLINE

Art Director
DREW GILL

Design Director
JONATHAN CHAN

Production Artists
MONICA GARCIA
VINCENT KUKUA
JANA COOK

SISOHPROMATEM
THIS MAN, THIS MONSTER

"ONE MORNING, WHEN GREGOR SAMSA WOKE FROM TROUBLED DREAMS, HE FOUND HIMSELF TRANSFORMED INTO A GIGANTIC INSECT."

IF YOU HAD TO STUDY Franz Kafka's METAMORPHOSIS at high school as I did, you'll be familiar with the story of Gregor Samsa, the travelling salesman who wakes one morning to find himself transformed into a giant cockroach. As Gregor comes to terms with his condition, his family becomes concerned when they discover he has locked himself in his room. Inevitably, Gregor has to open the door and is greeted with dismay and disgust by his parents and sister, causing him to withdraw from them even more.

Disgust eventually becomes an awkward form of acceptance as Gregor's family struggle to take care of him and keep him hidden from their boarders. Despite their efforts, Gregor manages to scuttle out of his room when he hears his sister's enchanting violin recital, and the family's shame and embarrassment is exposed.

Previously dependent on Gregor's income, the family have been struggling financially and, now that most of their time is spent worrying about and taking care of him, his sister insists that they would be better off without him. Tragically, Gregor's father agrees with her, and Gregor, who can still hear his family even though his raspy insect voice cannot be understood by them, scuttles sadly back to his room and dies.

Gregor's family, greatly relieved from the burden of their shame and loathing, move to the countryside and get on with their lives, seemingly forgetting Gregor and his ordeal altogether.

For the past couple of years the sentence, "I, Hieronymous Flask, awoke one morning to find myself transformed into a normal human being," called out from my subconscious and demanded my attention. However, I was inspired not just by Kafka's tale but by a short story written by Kit Reed called SISOHPROMATEM. My roommate at college, Geoff Edkins, adapted the story for a film project which I appeared in, and I never forgot the opening line:

"I, Joseph Bug, awoke one morning to find myself transformed into an enormous human being!"

There is perhaps less to learn from Joseph's story, which was very much a parody of Kafka's disturbing novel, but it contained a scene that shed more light on the original for me. Much like Gregor Samsa, Joseph Bug attempts to communicate with his family -- in this case, a collection of cockroaches behind the toilet -- but ultimately he crushes them under foot in contempt and disgust.

So how would Hip Flask behave if he experienced a similar transformation?

This was the question out of which spiraled the stories in this collection. I've said elsewhere that I always enjoyed Ben Grimm's dilemma in THE FANTASTIC FOUR story, "This Man This Monster," by Stan Lee and Jack Kirby... that dilemma being: does Ben's girlfriend, the blind sculptress, Alicia Masters, love the man or the monster he has become, the Thing?

Living in Los Angeles for the past 23 years, it has been my fortune to get to know -- and develop friendships with -- a number of veterans of the wars in Vietnam and the Gulf. They count themselves amongst the lucky ones -- they came back in one piece and maintained jobs, relationships and families. But it isn't uncommon to see disabled vets by the side of the road with a cardboard sign asking for food. Many motorists turn to look away or wind up

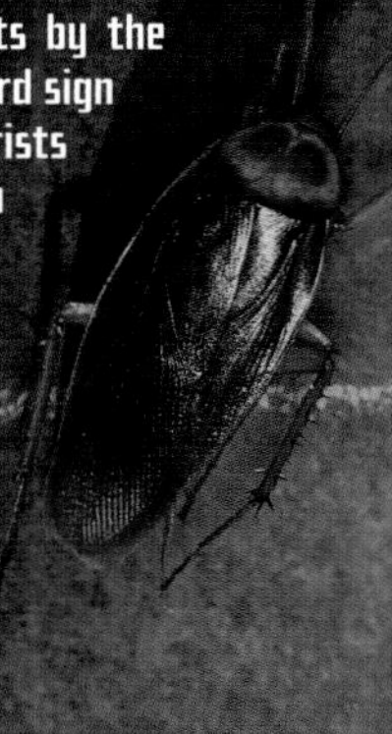

their windows fearfully. One man near my home, whose sign notified us that he had cancer, would stagger up and down the middle of the off ramp asking for food... I remember his skin was red and raw from sunburn, or perhaps an injury my limited experience couldn't imagine.

Why is it we look away? What is it that frightens us about the wheelchair-bound vet with worn clothing, long hair and a faraway look in his eye? We are encouraged to support our troops, but how many of us actively support our soldiers when they come home shell-shocked, physically wounded or emotionally scarred?

Recently I visited one of my buddies in the VA hospital in Westwood. It was an eye-opening experience. I had never seen so many vets -- some my age, some older or younger -- in wheelchairs, on crutches, perhaps with one leg, perhaps with none... or with injuries to the face or burns on their body.

I'm told that modern, technologically advanced body armor and current wartime surgical facilities have enabled soldiers to survive injuries that would have easily killed them 20 or 30 years ago. This means that even more soldiers return from tours of duty very much less than they were before they were sent overseas. They, and those that came back physically intact, have, thanks to technologically advanced weapons and 'smart' bombs, seen more suffering and more terrible injuries to combatants and innocent civilians than ever before.

Amongst the vets that I have known, one has experienced a PTSD related nervous disorder possibly caused by exposure to Agent Orange, another had to fight cancer when he returned from Vietnam as a young man in his twenties, thanks to exposure to radioactive materials where he was stationed. A friend who fought in the Navy in the first Gulf war lost her husband in a firefight... she has Do Not Resuscitate on her ID, hoping that she can move on from this life quickly and enjoy the next one should she be involved in an accident. Recently her lung collapsed and she drove herself to the VA hospital where she technically died on the surgeon's table -- and was resuscitated. I have another friend, a civilian, who was 12 years old when her childhood friend was killed in front of her during wartime. She is not treated as a veteran but carries the same scars nevertheless.

Each of these friends have struggled with various addictions, but ultimately come to terms with the fact that there is not enough whiskey, wine, narcotics or marijuana in the world to numb the pain they were caused to experience.

War changes people. Those that have witnessed it can't unsee the things they have seen or forget the traumas they endured. They have undergone their own metamorphosis and we must not expect them to scuttle under their beds to die, we must try to understand their transformation, because ultimately it affects us all whether we like it or not. And we must constantly question the reasoning of those who compel nations to send their young men and women to war.

I have only visited the VA hospital a couple of times, but my friends are reminded of their sufferings, and those of their comrades, every time they need to go there for medical treatment... or just help with sleeping, or pain management, or anger management, or psychiatric help based on the recommendation of a friend or family member. Some of my friends have created valuable lives for themselves through Buddhist practice, others have created a cynical shell around lives much like Gregor Samsa in Kafka's allegorical tale, others have lost their grip on reality and, unable to cope in society, bounce back and forth between treatment centers and halfway houses.

I didn't know that I would be writing a comic book with themes that included racism, miscegenation and post traumatic stress disorder when I created ELEPHANTMEN 17 years ago, and I have no answers to offer here. I am only sure of a couple of things...

No one wins in a war. Neither Monsters, nor Men.

And the cockroaches will outlast us all, no matter how many we crush underfoot!

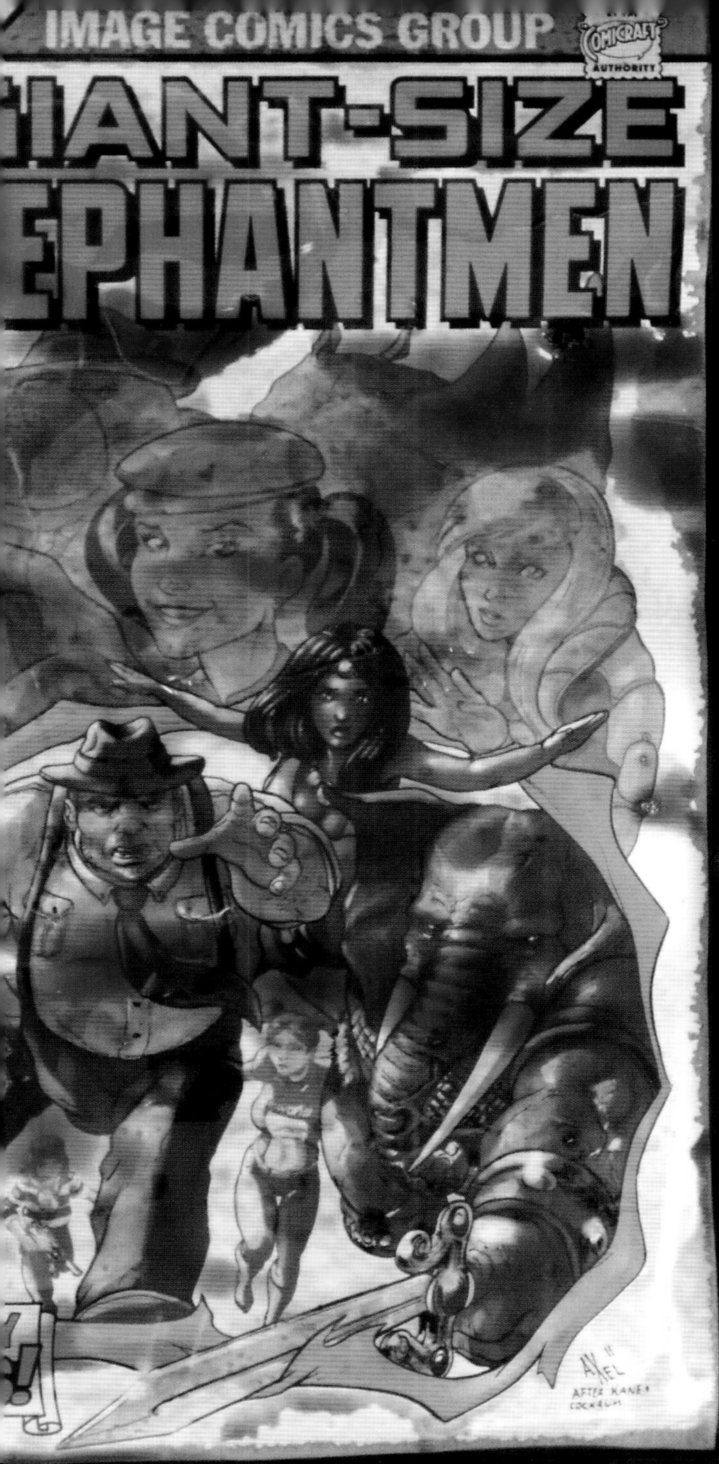
IMAGE COMICS GROUP
COMICRAFT AUTHORITY
IANT-SIZE
EPHANTMEN
AXEL '11
AFTER KANE + COCKRUM

"THERE ARE TWO TRAGEDIES IN LIFE. ONE IS NOT TO GET YOUR HEART'S DESIRE. THE OTHER IS TO GET IT."

GEORGE BERNARD SHAW
MAN AND SUPERMAN

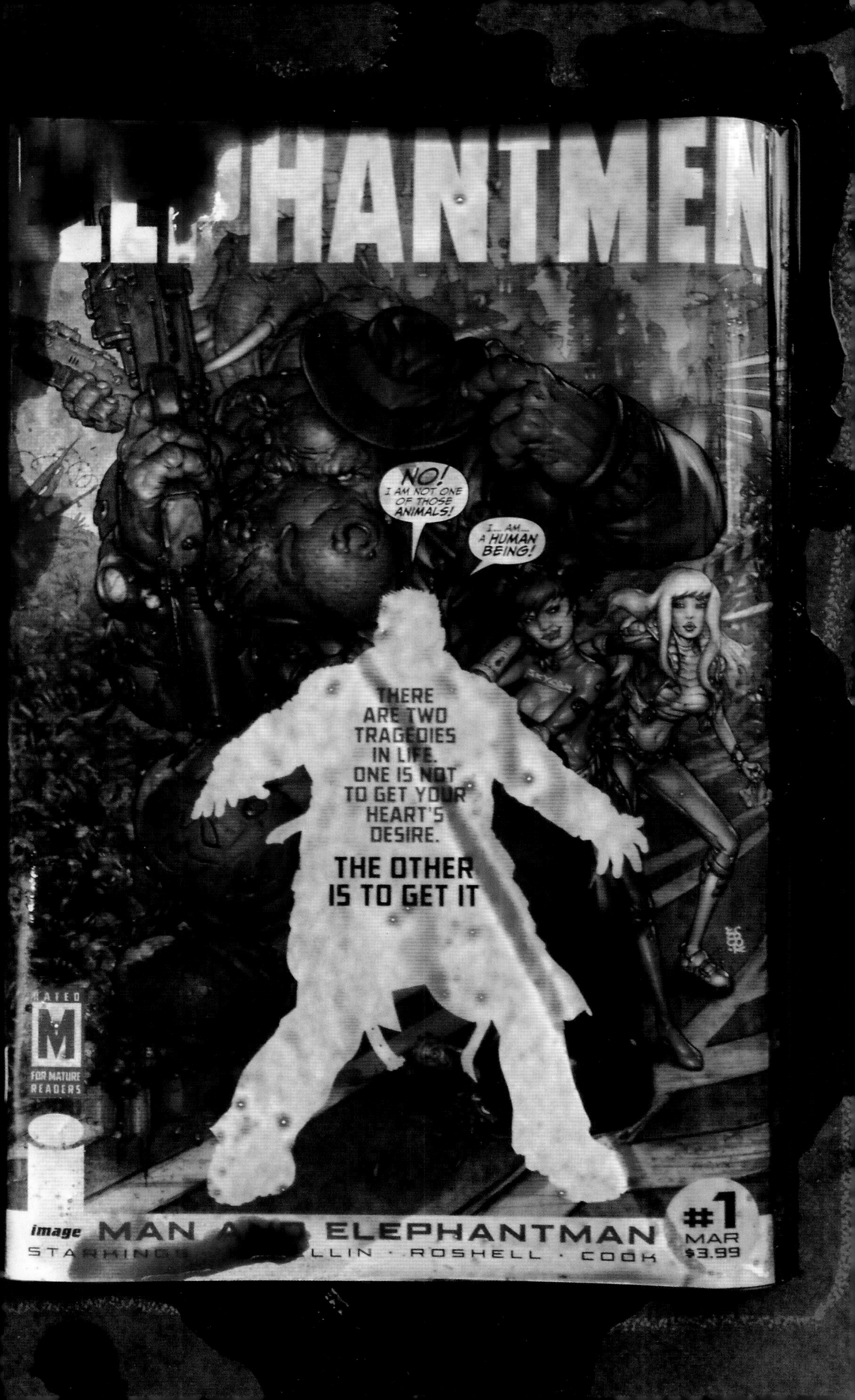
PHANTMEN
NO! I AM NOT ONE OF THOSE ANIMALS!
I... AM... A HUMAN BEING!
THERE ARE TWO TRAGEDIES IN LIFE. ONE IS NOT TO GET YOUR HEART'S DESIRE.
THE OTHER IS TO GET IT
RATED M FOR MATURE READERS
image
MAN
ELEPHANTMAN
STARKINGS
LLIN · ROSHELL · COOK
#1
MAR
$3.99

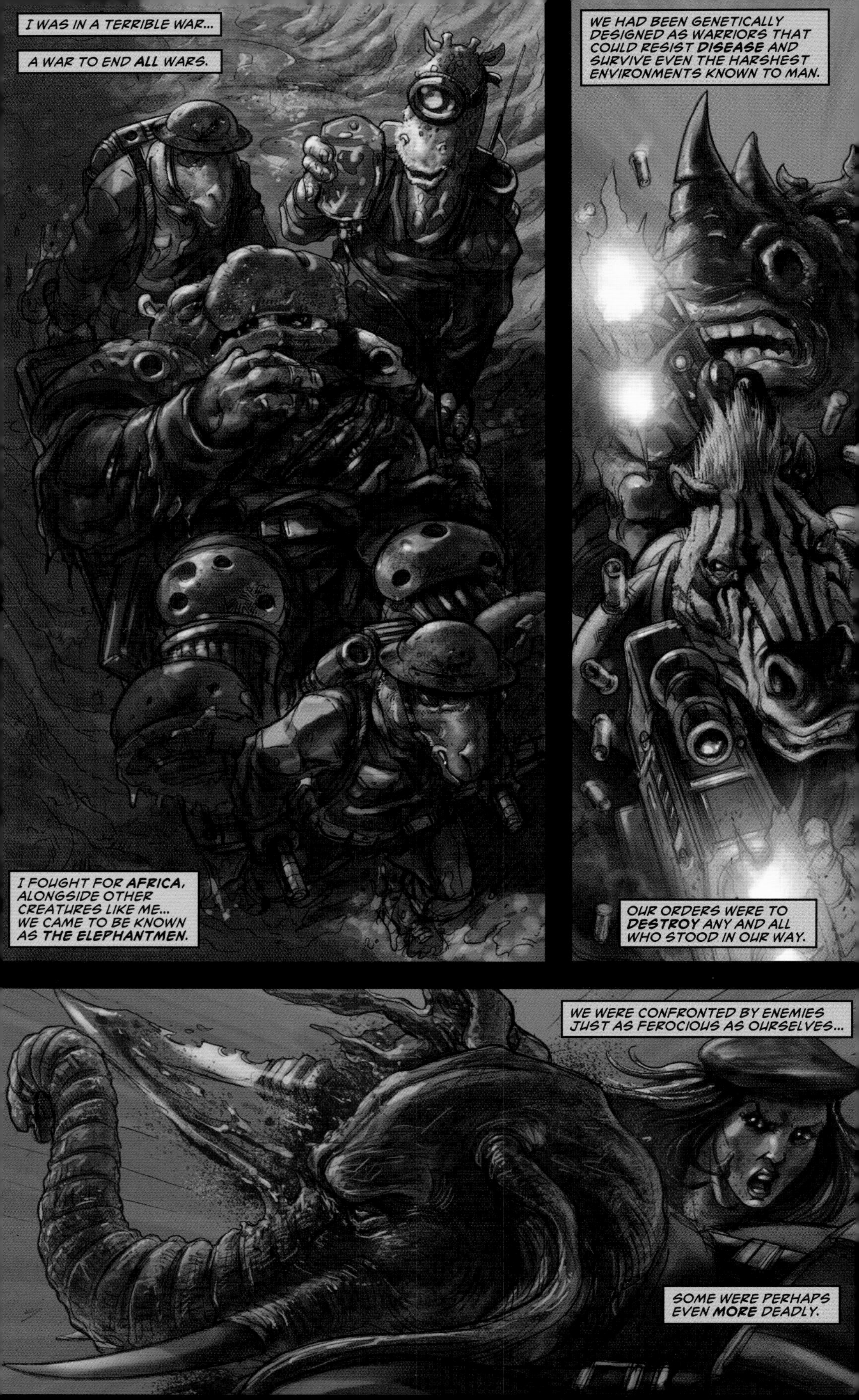
I WAS IN A TERRIBLE WAR...
A WAR TO END ALL WARS.
I FOUGHT FOR AFRICA, ALONGSIDE OTHER CREATURES LIKE ME... WE CAME TO BE KNOWN AS THE ELEPHANTMEN.
WE HAD BEEN GENETICALLY DESIGNED AS WARRIORS THAT COULD RESIST DISEASE AND SURVIVE EVEN THE HARSHEST ENVIRONMENTS KNOWN TO MAN.
OUR ORDERS WERE TO DESTROY ANY AND ALL WHO STOOD IN OUR WAY.
WE WERE CONFRONTED BY ENEMIES JUST AS FEROCIOUS AS OURSELVES...
SOME WERE PERHAPS EVEN MORE DEADLY.

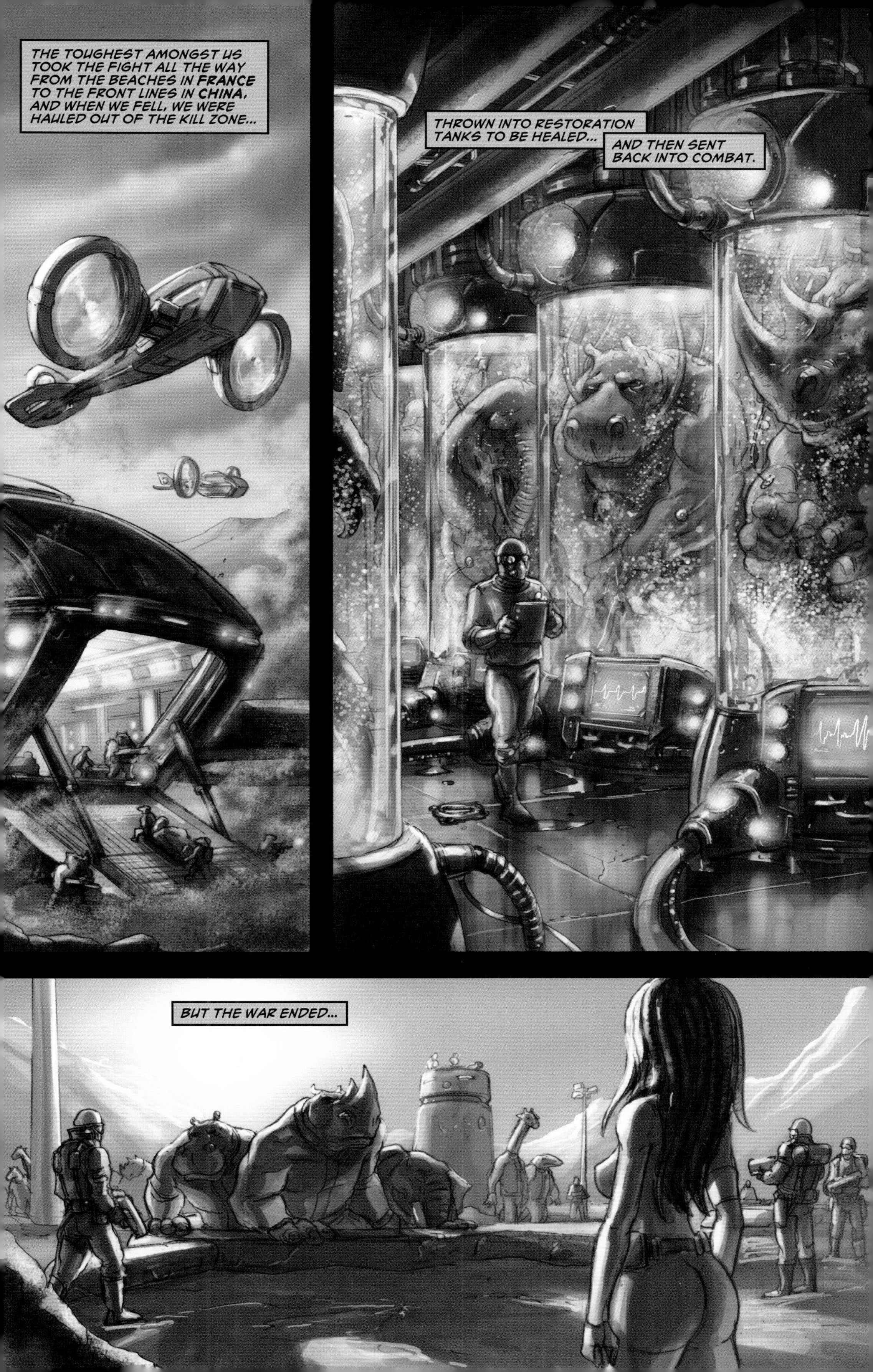
THE TOUGHEST AMONGST US TOOK THE FIGHT ALL THE WAY FROM THE BEACHES IN FRANCE TO THE FRONT LINES IN CHINA, AND WHEN WE FELL, WE WERE HAULED OUT OF THE KILL ZONE...
THROWN INTO RESTORATION TANKS TO BE HEALED...
AND THEN SENT BACK INTO COMBAT.
BUT THE WAR ENDED...

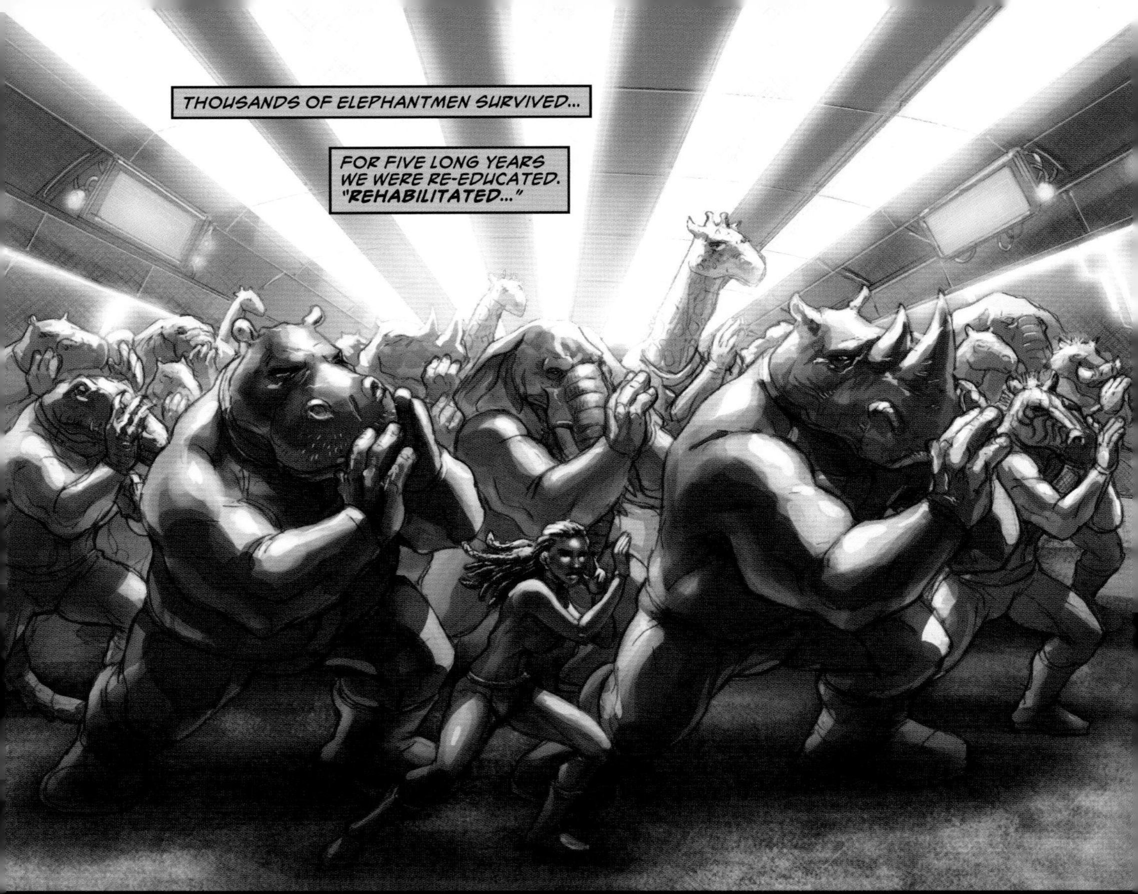
THOUSANDS OF ELEPHANTMEN SURVIVED...
FOR FIVE LONG YEARS WE WERE RE-EDUCATED. "REHABILITATED..."

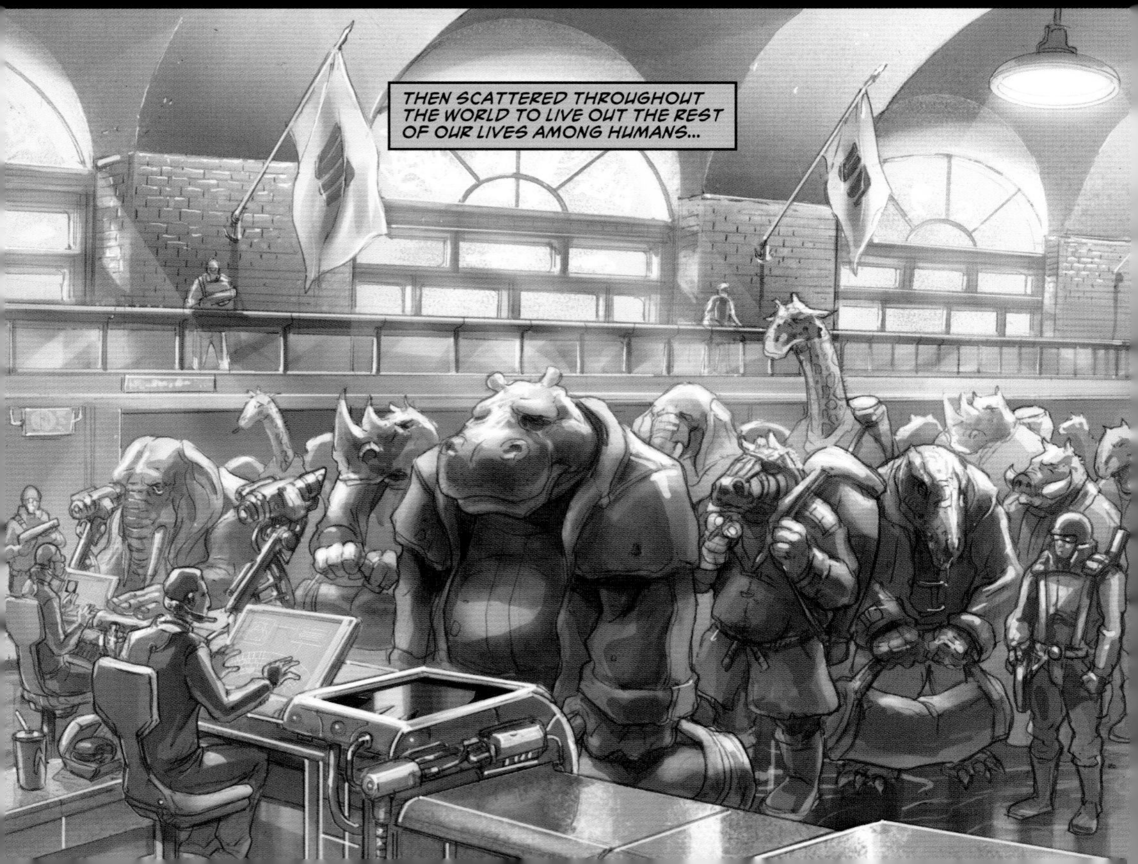
THEN SCATTERED THROUGHOUT THE WORLD TO LIVE OUT THE REST OF OUR LIVES AMONG HUMANS...

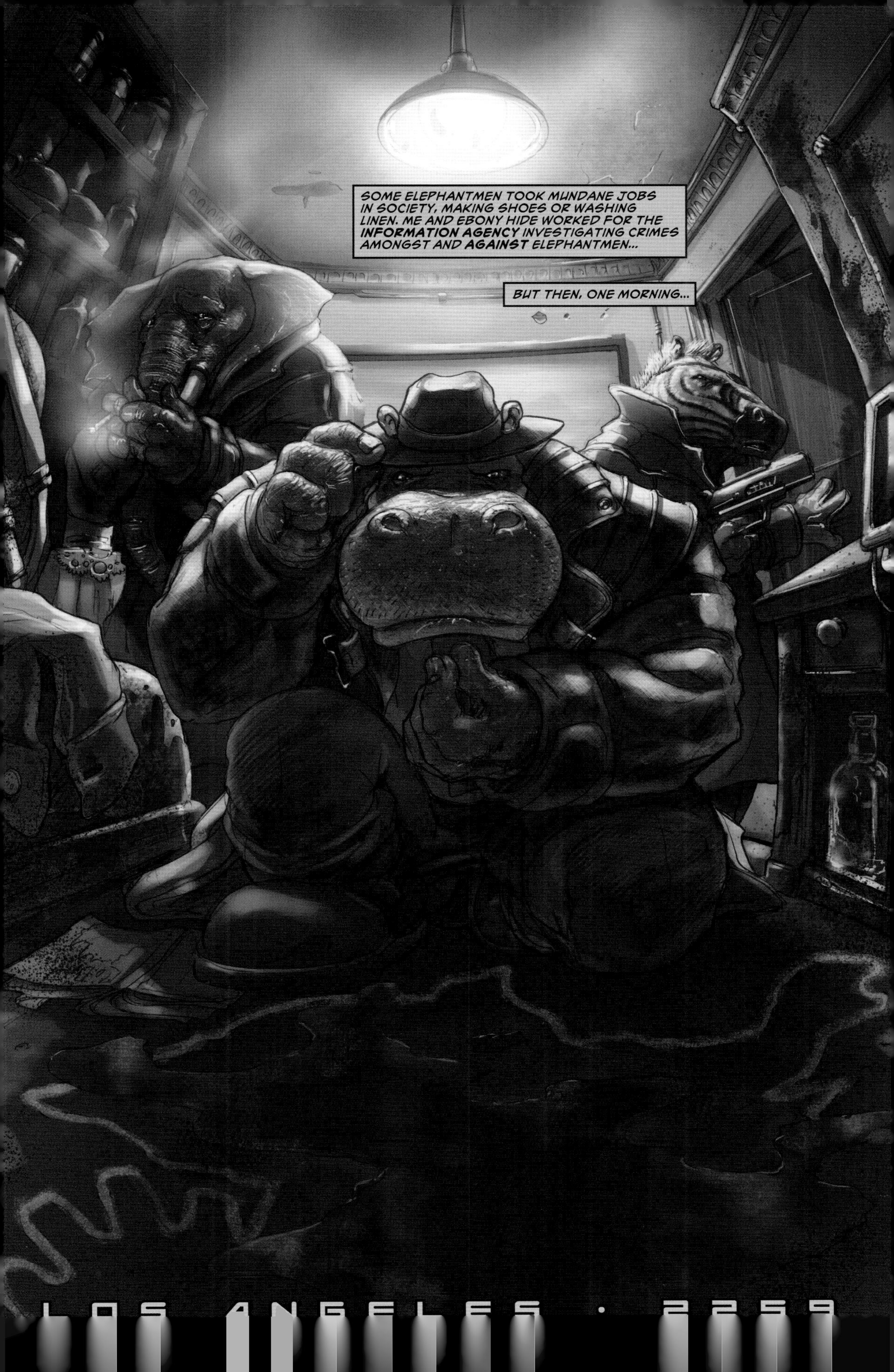
SOME ELEPHANTMEN TOOK MUNDANE JOBS IN SOCIETY, MAKING SHOES OR WASHING LINEN. ME AND EBONY HIDE WORKED FOR THE **INFORMATION AGENCY** INVESTIGATING CRIMES AMONGST AND **AGAINST** ELEPHANTMEN...
BUT THEN, ONE MORNING...
LOS ANGELES · 2259

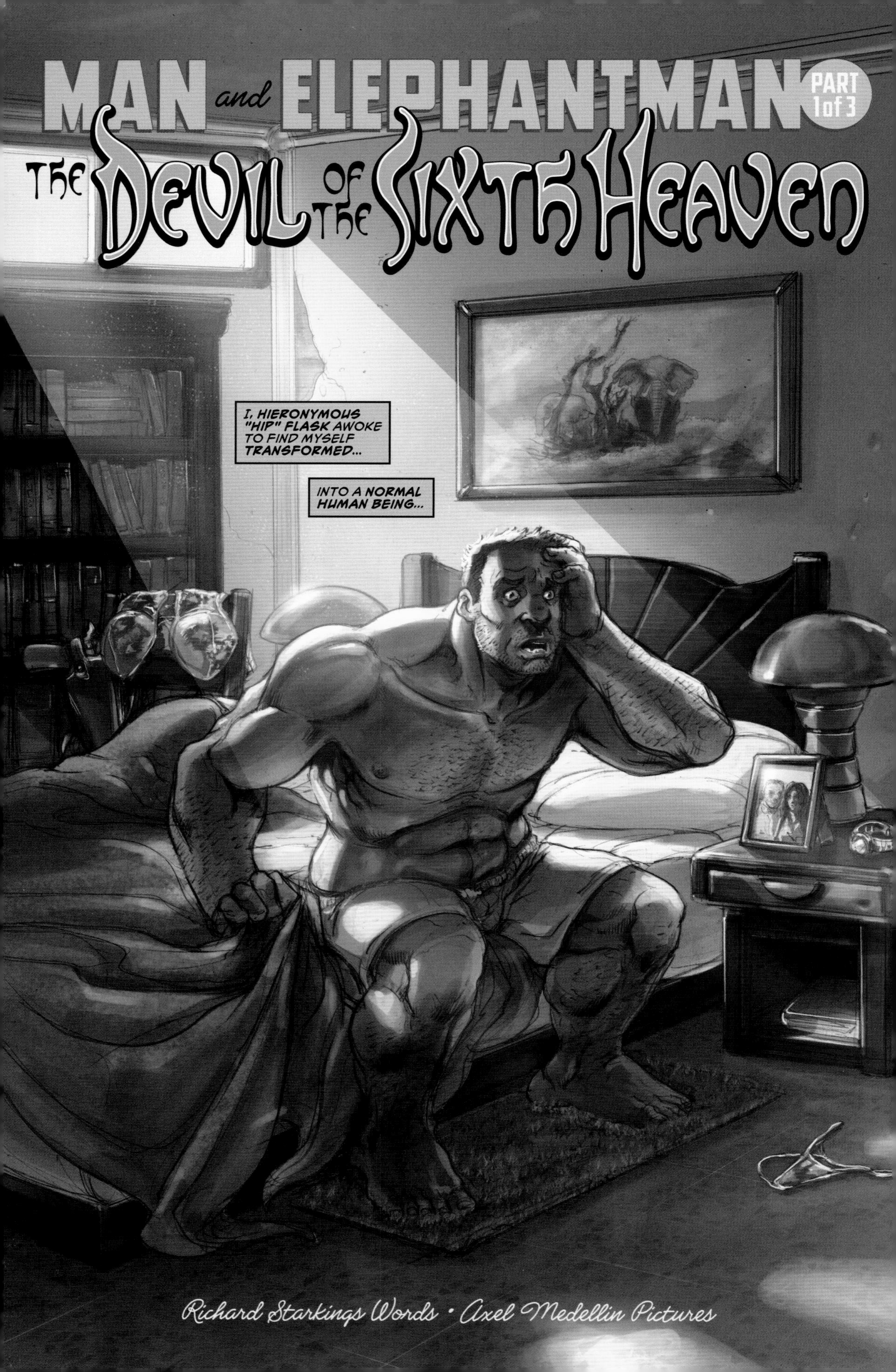
MAN and ELEPHANTMAN
PART 1 of 3
THE DEVIL OF THE SIXTH HEAVEN
I, HIERONYMOUS "HIP" FLASK AWOKE TO FIND MYSELF TRANSFORMED...
INTO A NORMAL HUMAN BEING...
Richard Starkings Words • Axel Medellin Pictures

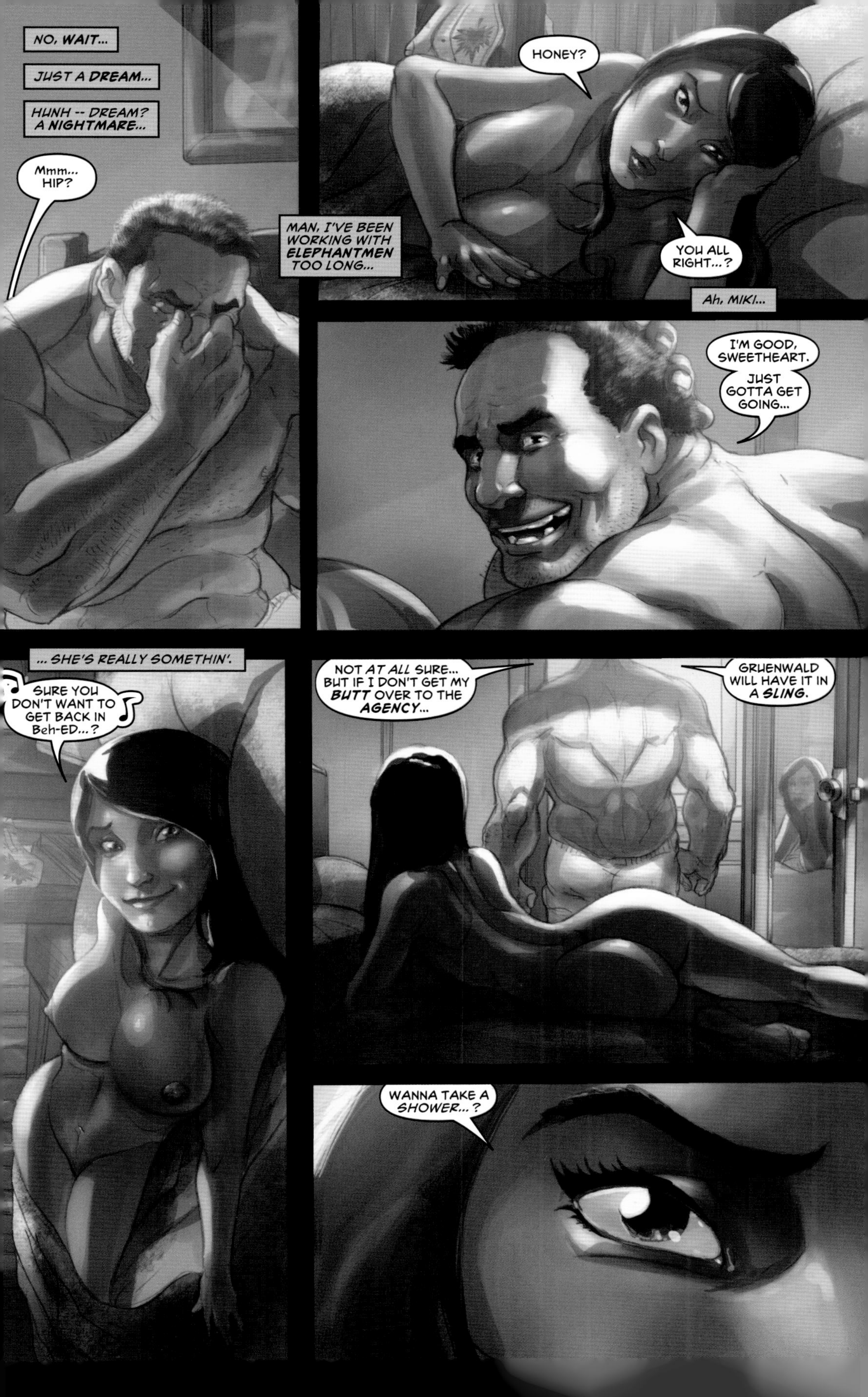
NO, WAIT...
JUST A DREAM...
HUNH -- DREAM? A NIGHTMARE...
Mmm... HIP?
MAN, I'VE BEEN WORKING WITH ELEPHANTMEN TOO LONG...
HONEY?
YOU ALL RIGHT...?
Ah, MIKI...
I'M GOOD, SWEETHEART.
JUST GOTTA GET GOING...
... SHE'S REALLY SOMETHIN'.
SURE YOU DON'T WANT TO GET BACK IN Beh-ED...?
NOT AT ALL SURE... BUT IF I DON'T GET MY BUTT OVER TO THE AGENCY...
GRUENWALD WILL HAVE IT IN A SLING.
WANNA TAKE A SHOWER...?

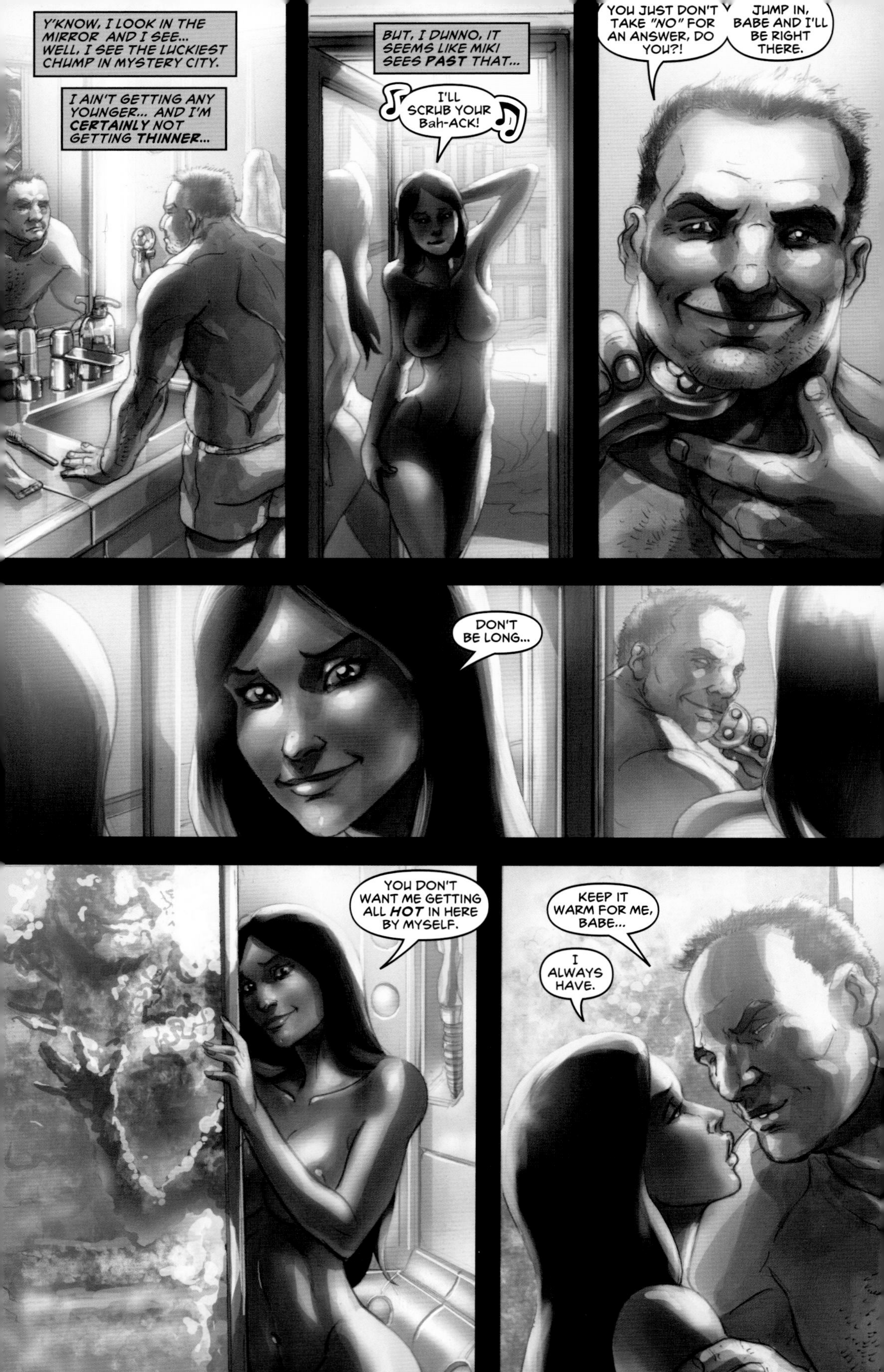

Y'KNOW, I LOOK IN THE MIRROR AND I SEE... WELL, I SEE THE LUCKIEST CHUMP IN MYSTERY CITY.
I AIN'T GETTING ANY YOUNGER... AND I'M CERTAINLY NOT GETTING THINNER...
BUT, I DUNNO, IT SEEMS LIKE MIKI SEES PAST THAT...
I'LL SCRUB YOUR Bah-ACK!
YOU JUST DON'T TAKE "NO" FOR AN ANSWER, DO YOU?!
JUMP IN, BABE AND I'LL BE RIGHT THERE.
DON'T BE LONG...
YOU DON'T WANT ME GETTING ALL HOT IN HERE BY MYSELF.
KEEP IT WARM FOR ME, BABE...
I ALWAYS HAVE.

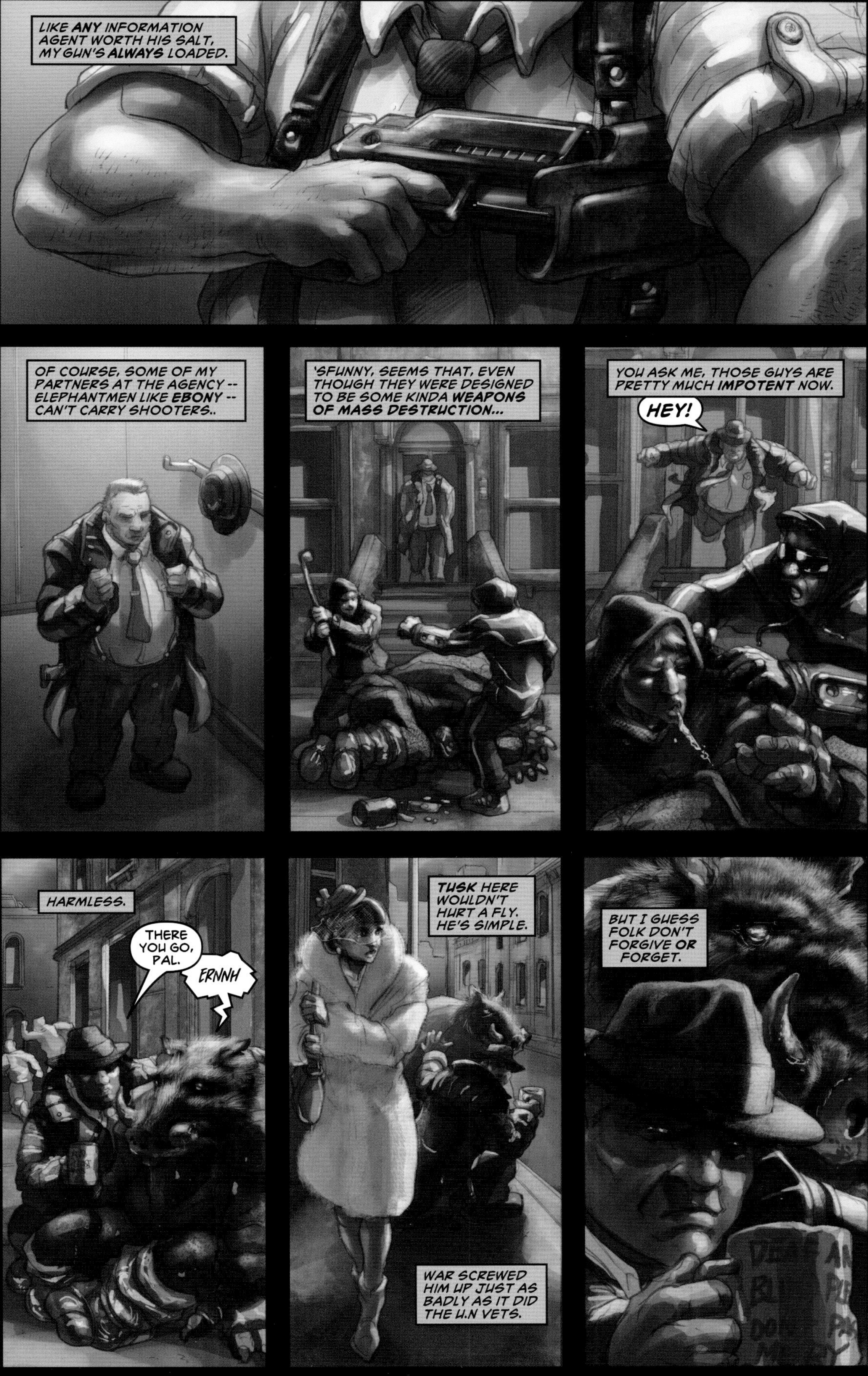
LIKE ANY INFORMATION AGENT WORTH HIS SALT, MY GUN'S ALWAYS LOADED.
OF COURSE, SOME OF MY PARTNERS AT THE AGENCY -- ELEPHANTMEN LIKE EBONY -- CAN'T CARRY SHOOTERS..
'SFUNNY, SEEMS THAT, EVEN THOUGH THEY WERE DESIGNED TO BE SOME KINDA WEAPONS OF MASS DESTRUCTION...
YOU ASK ME, THOSE GUYS ARE PRETTY MUCH IMPOTENT NOW.
HEY!
HARMLESS.
THERE YOU GO, PAL.
ERNNH
TUSK HERE WOULDN'T HURT A FLY. HE'S SIMPLE.
WAR SCREWED HIM UP JUST AS BADLY AS IT DID THE U.N VETS.
BUT I GUESS FOLK DON'T FORGIVE OR FORGET.

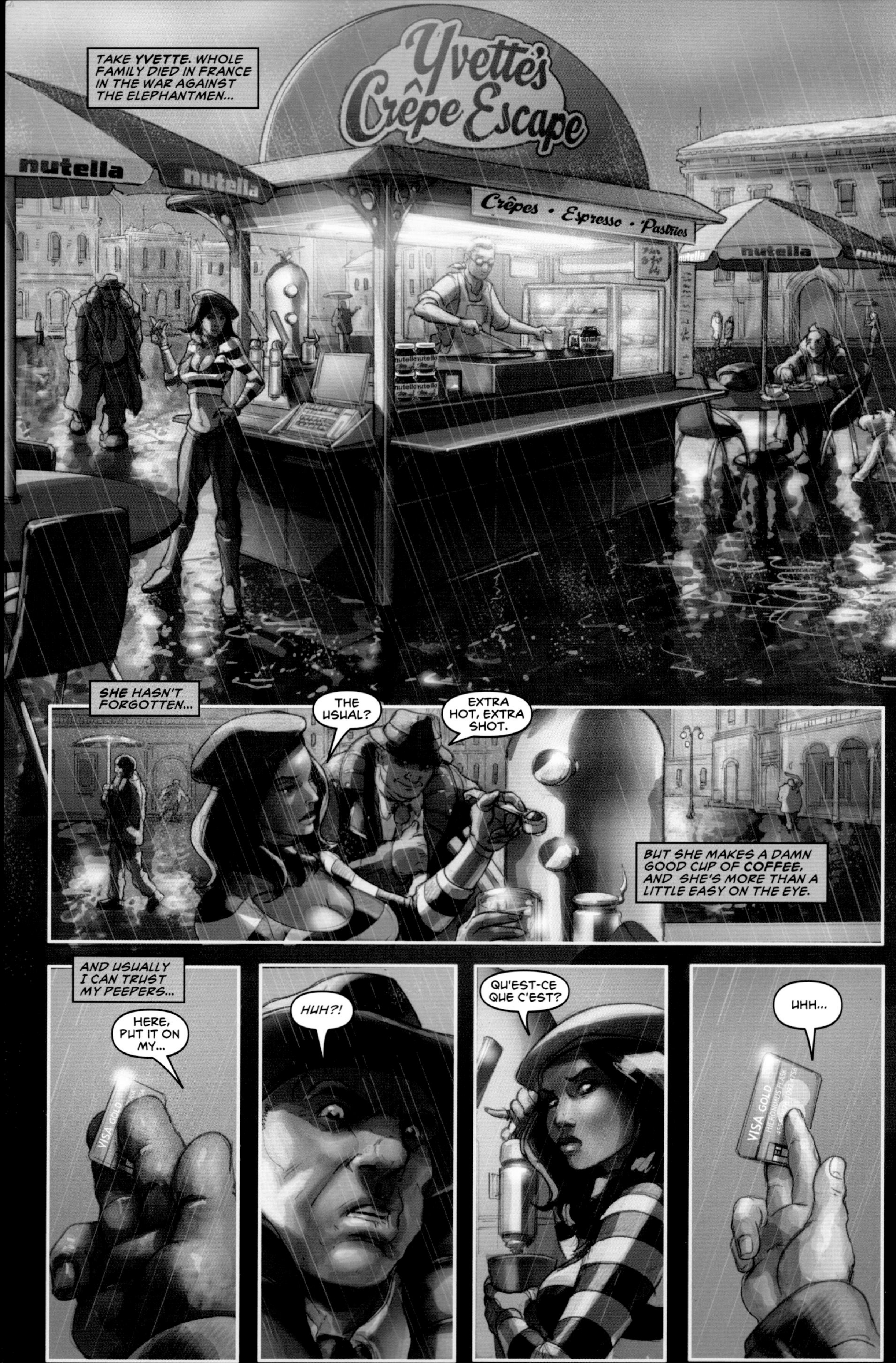
TAKE YVETTE. WHOLE FAMILY DIED IN FRANCE IN THE WAR AGAINST THE ELEPHANTMEN...
Yvette's Crêpe Escape
nutella
nutella
Crêpes • Espresso • Pastries
nutella
SHE HASN'T FORGOTTEN...
THE USUAL?
EXTRA HOT, EXTRA SHOT.
BUT SHE MAKES A DAMN GOOD CUP OF COFFEE, AND SHE'S MORE THAN A LITTLE EASY ON THE EYE.
AND USUALLY I CAN TRUST MY PEEPERS...
HERE, PUT IT ON MY...
VISA GOLD
HUH?!
QU'EST-CE QUE C'EST?
UHH...
VISA GOLD
HIERONYMUS FLASK

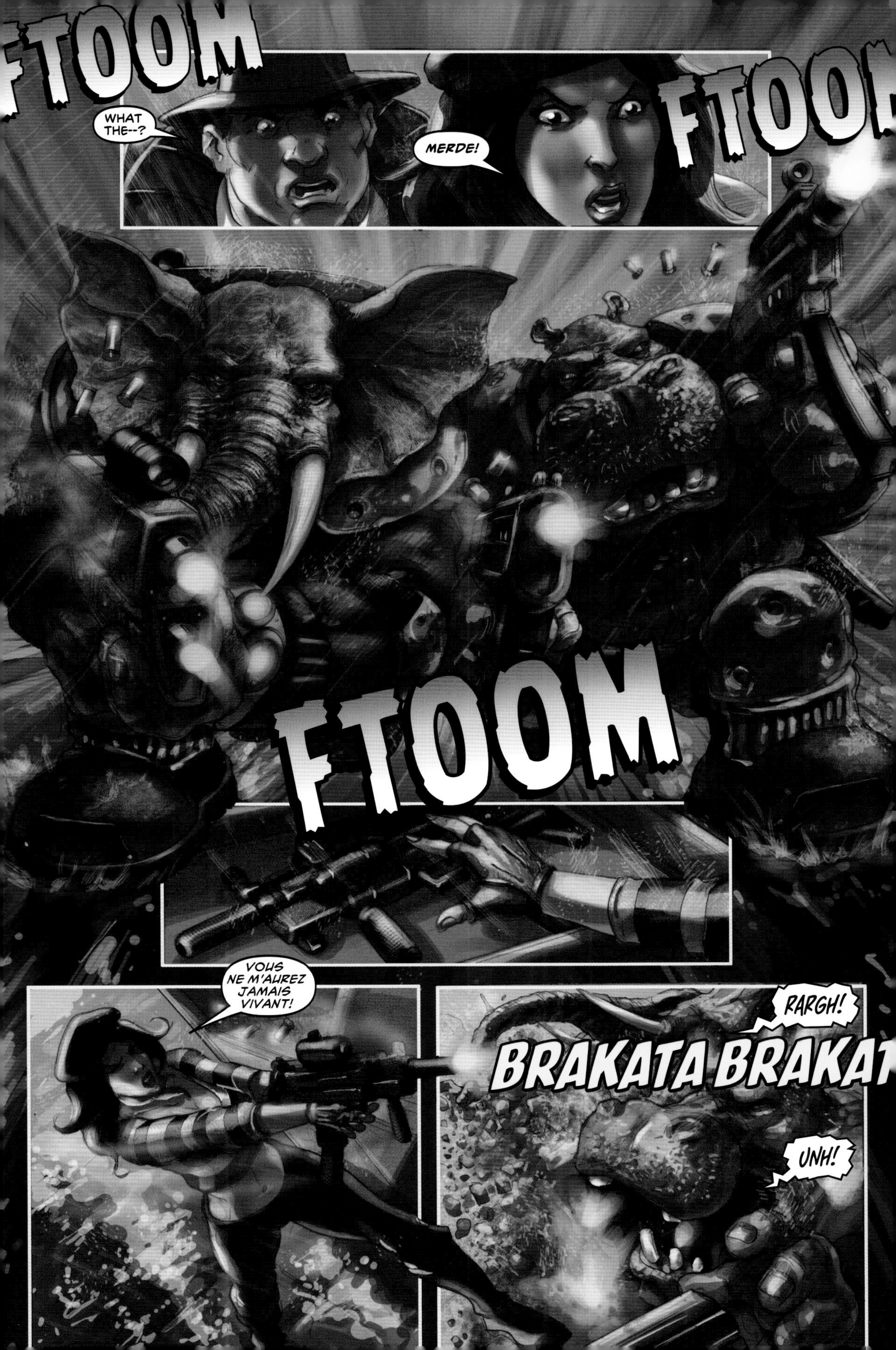
FTOOM
WHAT THE--?
MERDE!
FTOOM
FTOOM
VOUS NE M'AUREZ JAMAIS VIVANT!
RARGH!
BRAKATA BRAKAT
UNH!

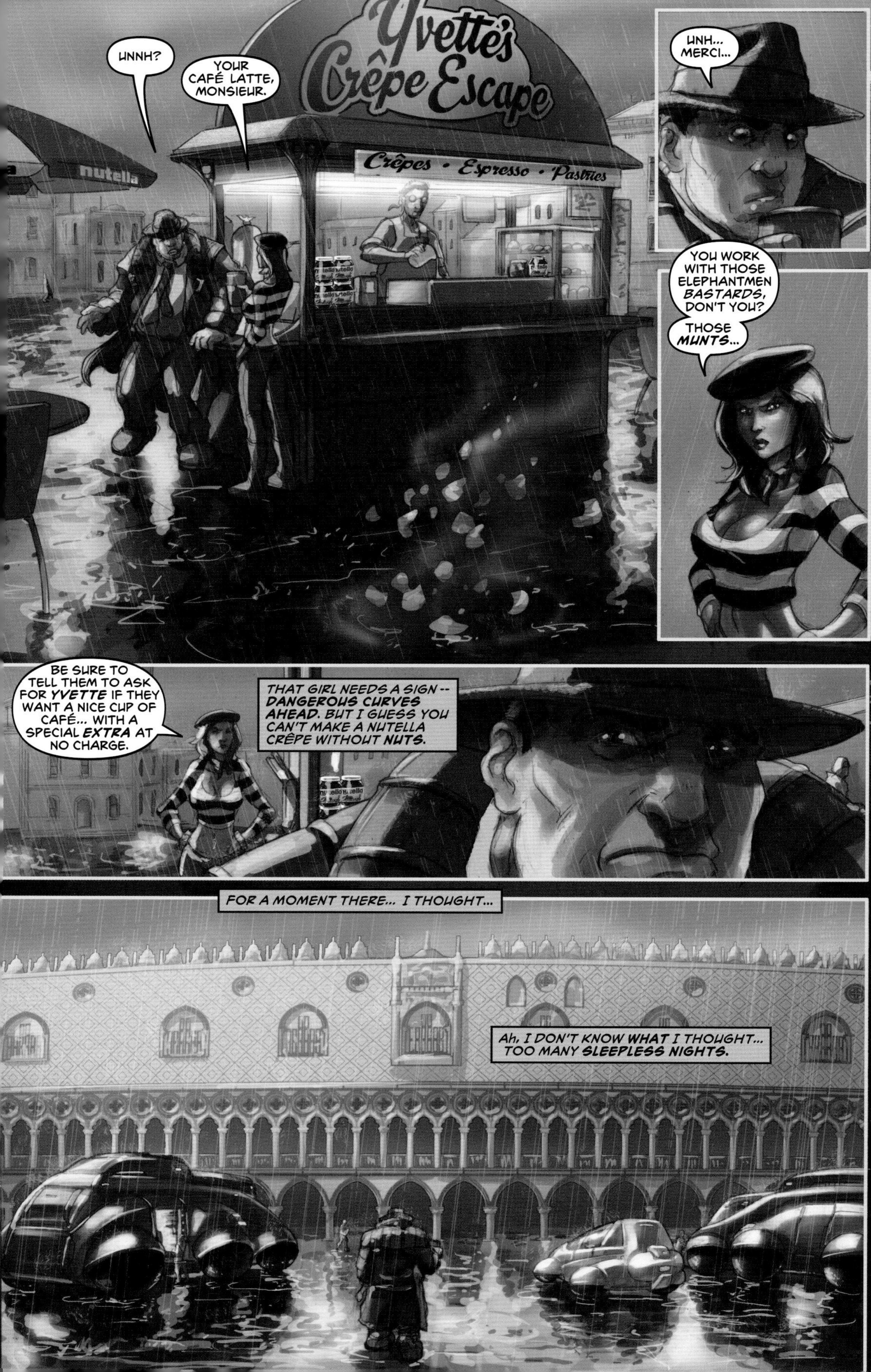
Yvette's Crêpe Escape
Crêpes • Espresso • Pastries
nutella
UNNH?
YOUR CAFÉ LATTE, MONSIEUR.
UNH... MERCI...
YOU WORK WITH THOSE ELEPHANTMEN BASTARDS, DON'T YOU?
THOSE MUNTS...
BE SURE TO TELL THEM TO ASK FOR YVETTE IF THEY WANT A NICE CUP OF CAFÉ... WITH A SPECIAL EXTRA AT NO CHARGE.
THAT GIRL NEEDS A SIGN -- DANGEROUS CURVES AHEAD. BUT I GUESS YOU CAN'T MAKE A NUTELLA CRÊPE WITHOUT NUTS.
FOR A MOMENT THERE... I THOUGHT...
Ah, I DON'T KNOW WHAT I THOUGHT... TOO MANY SLEEPLESS NIGHTS.

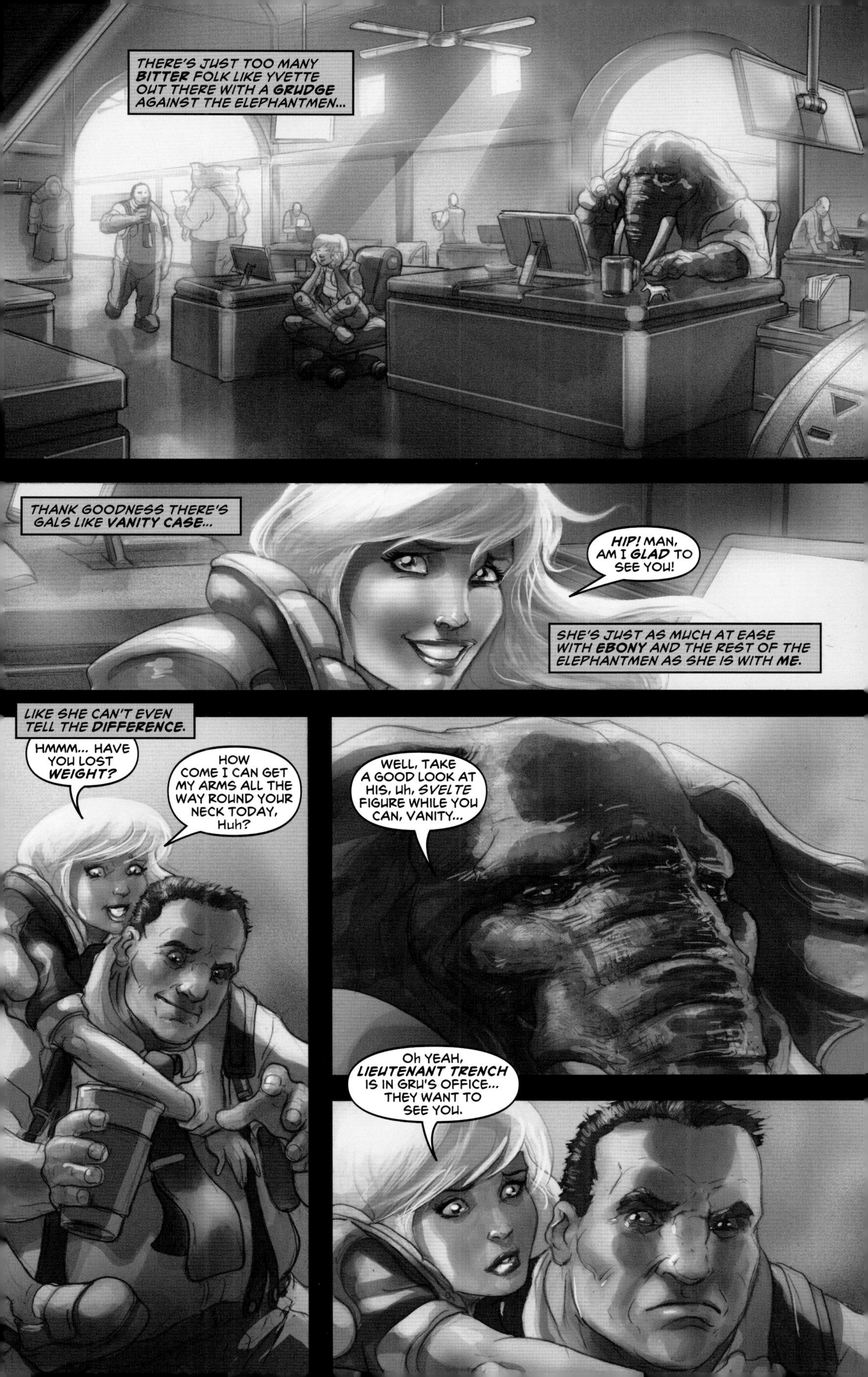
THERE'S JUST TOO MANY BITTER FOLK LIKE YVETTE OUT THERE WITH A GRUDGE AGAINST THE ELEPHANTMEN...
THANK GOODNESS THERE'S GALS LIKE VANITY CASE...
HIP! MAN, AM I GLAD TO SEE YOU!
SHE'S JUST AS MUCH AT EASE WITH EBONY AND THE REST OF THE ELEPHANTMEN AS SHE IS WITH ME.
LIKE SHE CAN'T EVEN TELL THE DIFFERENCE.
HMMM... HAVE YOU LOST WEIGHT?
HOW COME I CAN GET MY ARMS ALL THE WAY ROUND YOUR NECK TODAY, Huh?
WELL, TAKE A GOOD LOOK AT HIS, Uh, SVELTE FIGURE WHILE YOU CAN, VANITY...
Oh YEAH, LIEUTENANT TRENCH IS IN GRU'S OFFICE... THEY WANT TO SEE YOU.

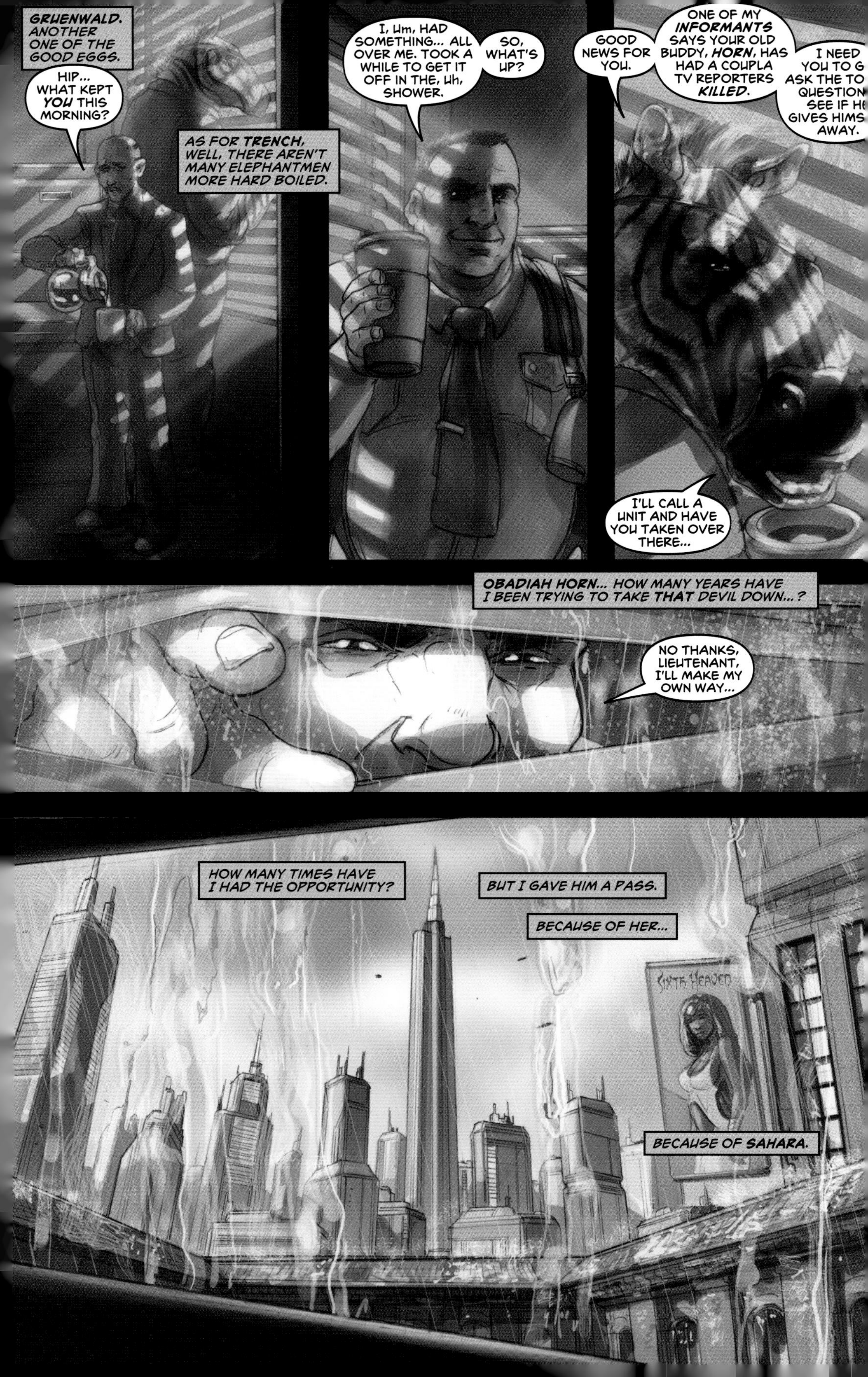
GRUENWALD. ANOTHER ONE OF THE GOOD EGGS.
HIP... WHAT KEPT YOU THIS MORNING?
AS FOR TRENCH, WELL, THERE AREN'T MANY ELEPHANTMEN MORE HARD BOILED.
I, UM, HAD SOMETHING... ALL OVER ME. TOOK A WHILE TO GET IT OFF IN THE, UH, SHOWER.
SO, WHAT'S UP?
GOOD NEWS FOR YOU.
ONE OF MY INFORMANTS SAYS YOUR OLD BUDDY, HORN, HAS HAD A COUPLA TV REPORTERS KILLED.
I NEED YOU TO G ASK THE TO QUESTION SEE IF H GIVES HIMS AWAY.
I'LL CALL A UNIT AND HAVE YOU TAKEN OVER THERE...
OBADIAH HORN... HOW MANY YEARS HAVE I BEEN TRYING TO TAKE THAT DEVIL DOWN...?
NO THANKS, LIEUTENANT, I'LL MAKE MY OWN WAY...
HOW MANY TIMES HAVE I HAD THE OPPORTUNITY?
BUT I GAVE HIM A PASS.
BECAUSE OF HER...
SIXTH HEAVEN
BECAUSE OF SAHARA.

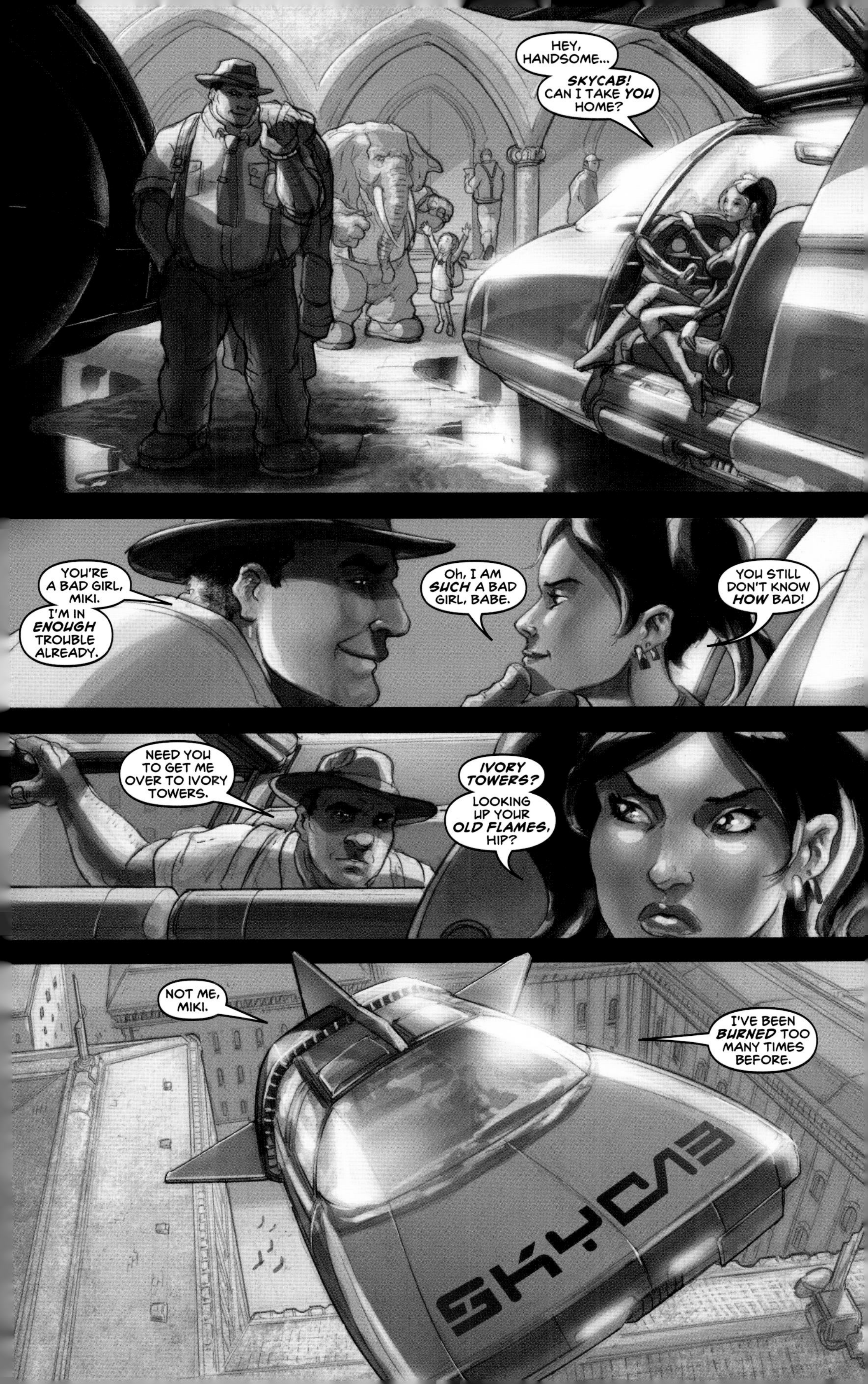
HEY, HANDSOME... SKYCAB! CAN I TAKE YOU HOME?
YOU'RE A BAD GIRL, MIKI.
I'M IN ENOUGH TROUBLE ALREADY.
Oh, I AM SUCH A BAD GIRL, BABE.
YOU STILL DON'T KNOW HOW BAD!
NEED YOU TO GET ME OVER TO IVORY TOWERS.
IVORY TOWERS?
LOOKING UP YOUR OLD FLAMES, HIP?
NOT ME, MIKI.
I'VE BEEN BURNED TOO MANY TIMES BEFORE.
SKYCAB

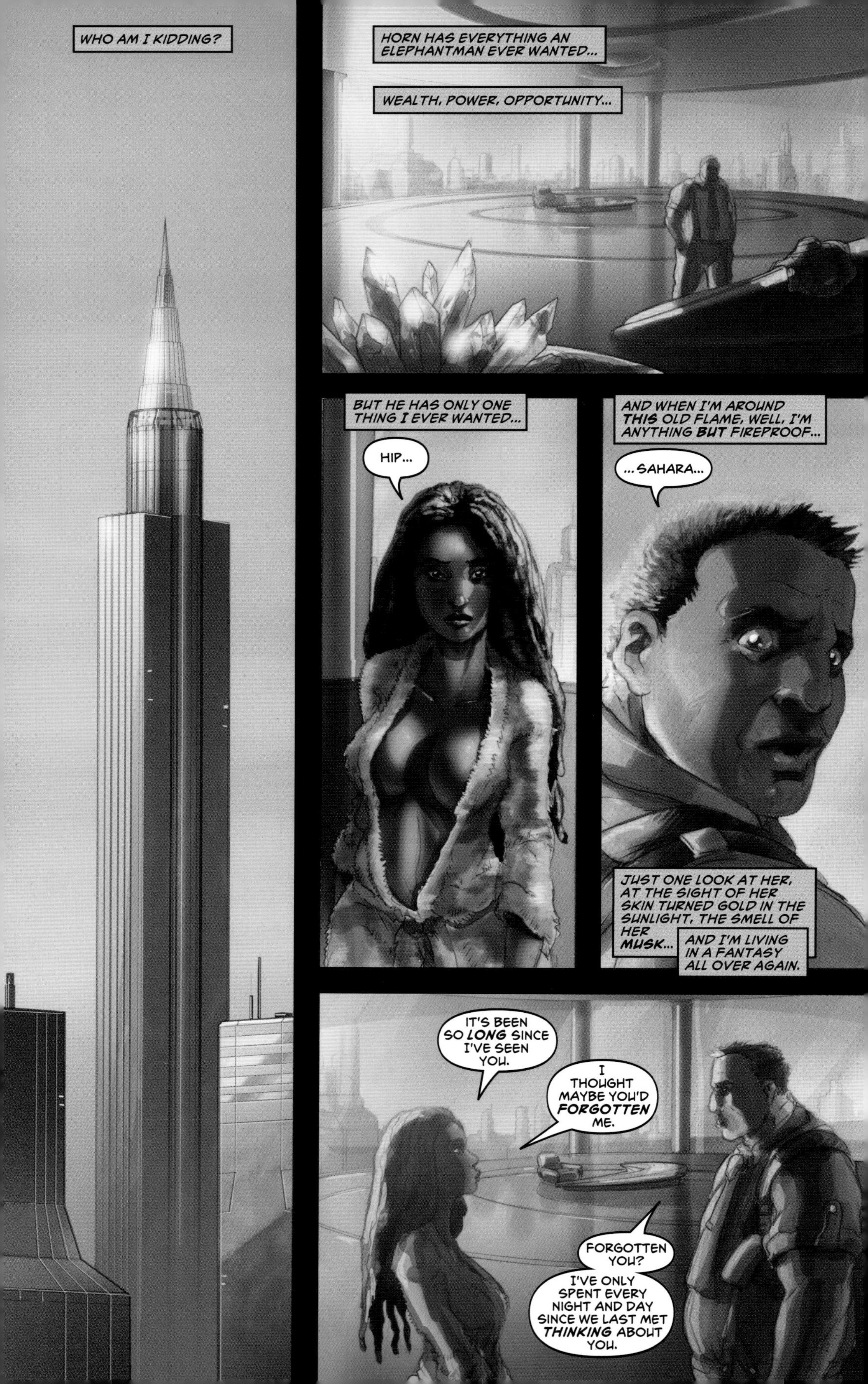
WHO AM I KIDDING?
HORN HAS EVERYTHING AN ELEPHANTMAN EVER WANTED...
WEALTH, POWER, OPPORTUNITY...
BUT HE HAS ONLY ONE THING I EVER WANTED...
HIP...
AND WHEN I'M AROUND THIS OLD FLAME, WELL, I'M ANYTHING BUT FIREPROOF...
...SAHARA...
JUST ONE LOOK AT HER, AT THE SIGHT OF HER SKIN TURNED GOLD IN THE SUNLIGHT, THE SMELL OF HER MUSK...
AND I'M LIVING IN A FANTASY ALL OVER AGAIN.
IT'S BEEN SO LONG SINCE I'VE SEEN YOU.
I THOUGHT MAYBE YOU'D FORGOTTEN ME.
FORGOTTEN YOU?
I'VE ONLY SPENT EVERY NIGHT AND DAY SINCE WE LAST MET THINKING ABOUT YOU.

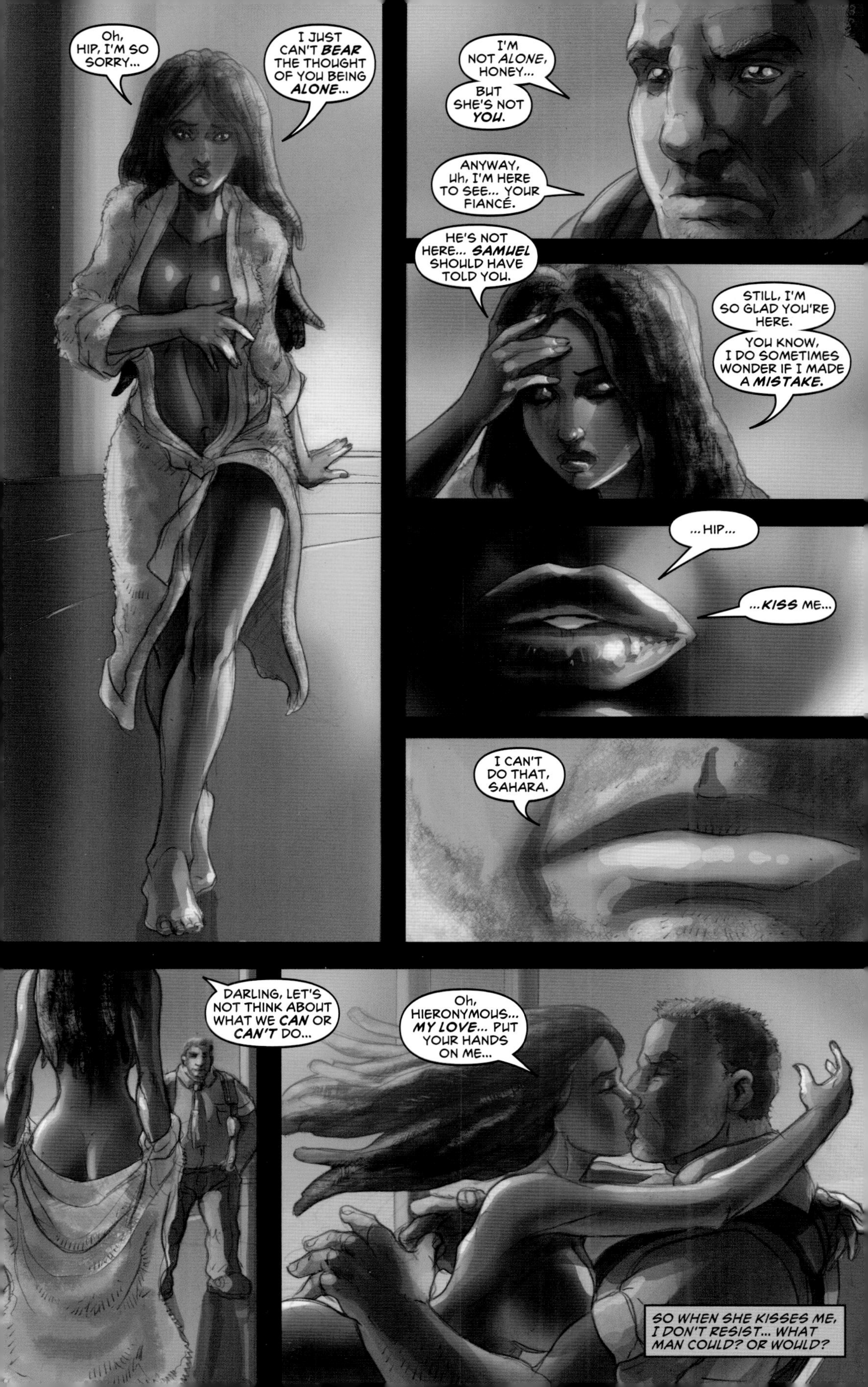
Oh, HIP, I'M SO SORRY...
I JUST CAN'T BEAR THE THOUGHT OF YOU BEING ALONE...
I'M NOT ALONE, HONEY...
BUT SHE'S NOT YOU.
ANYWAY, uh, I'M HERE TO SEE... YOUR FIANCÉ.
HE'S NOT HERE... SAMUEL SHOULD HAVE TOLD YOU.
STILL, I'M SO GLAD YOU'RE HERE.
YOU KNOW, I DO SOMETIMES WONDER IF I MADE A MISTAKE.
...HIP...
...KISS ME...
I CAN'T DO THAT, SAHARA.
DARLING, LET'S NOT THINK ABOUT WHAT WE CAN OR CAN'T DO...
Oh, HIERONYMOUS... MY LOVE... PUT YOUR HANDS ON ME...
SO WHEN SHE KISSES ME, I DON'T RESIST... WHAT MAN COULD? OR WOULD?

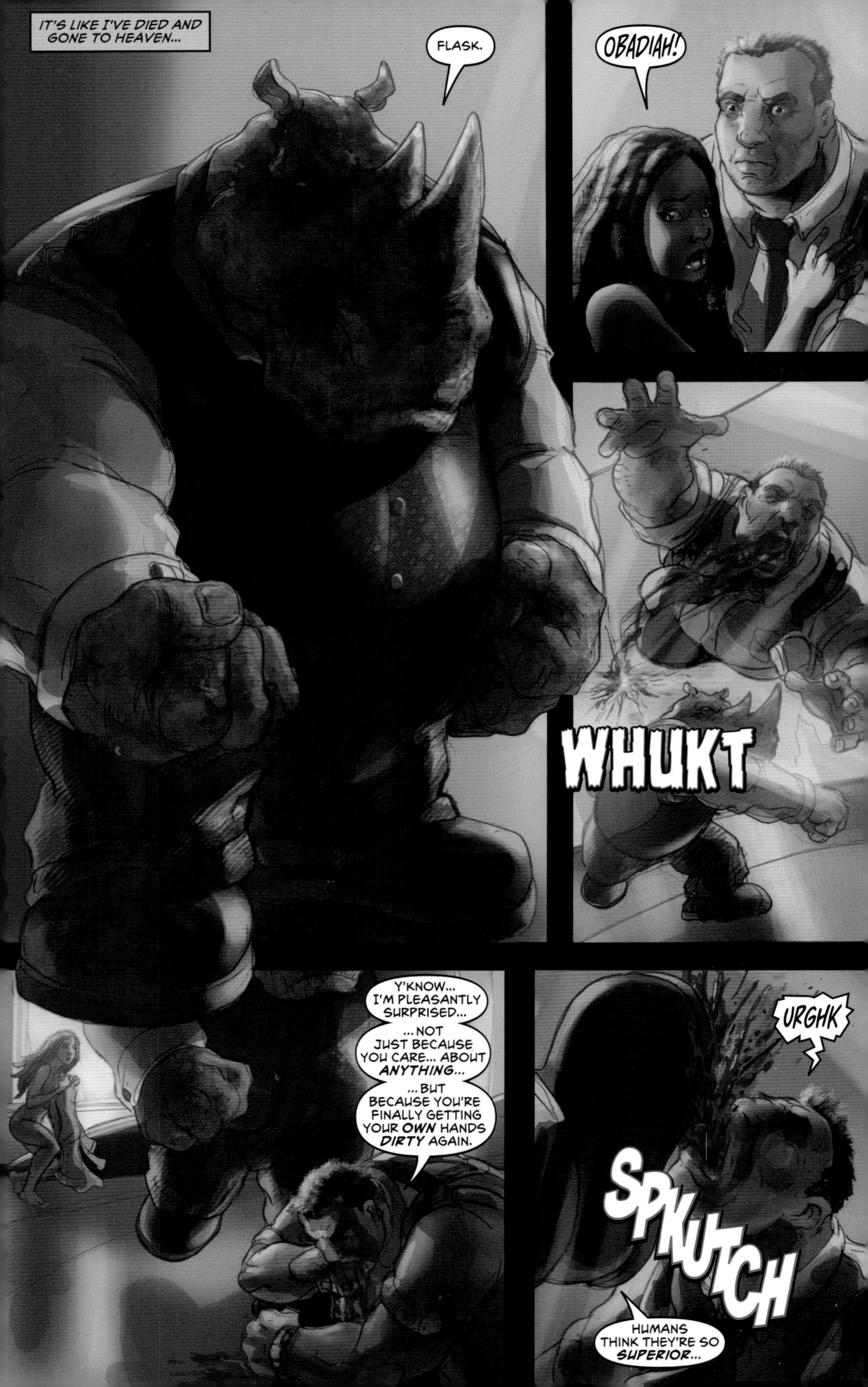
IT'S LIKE I'VE DIED AND GONE TO HEAVEN...
FLASK.
OBADIAH!
WHUKT
Y'KNOW... I'M PLEASANTLY SURPRISED...
...NOT JUST BECAUSE YOU CARE... ABOUT ANYTHING...
...BUT BECAUSE YOU'RE FINALLY GETTING YOUR OWN HANDS DIRTY AGAIN.
URGHK
SPKUTCH
HUMANS THINK THEY'RE SO SUPERIOR...

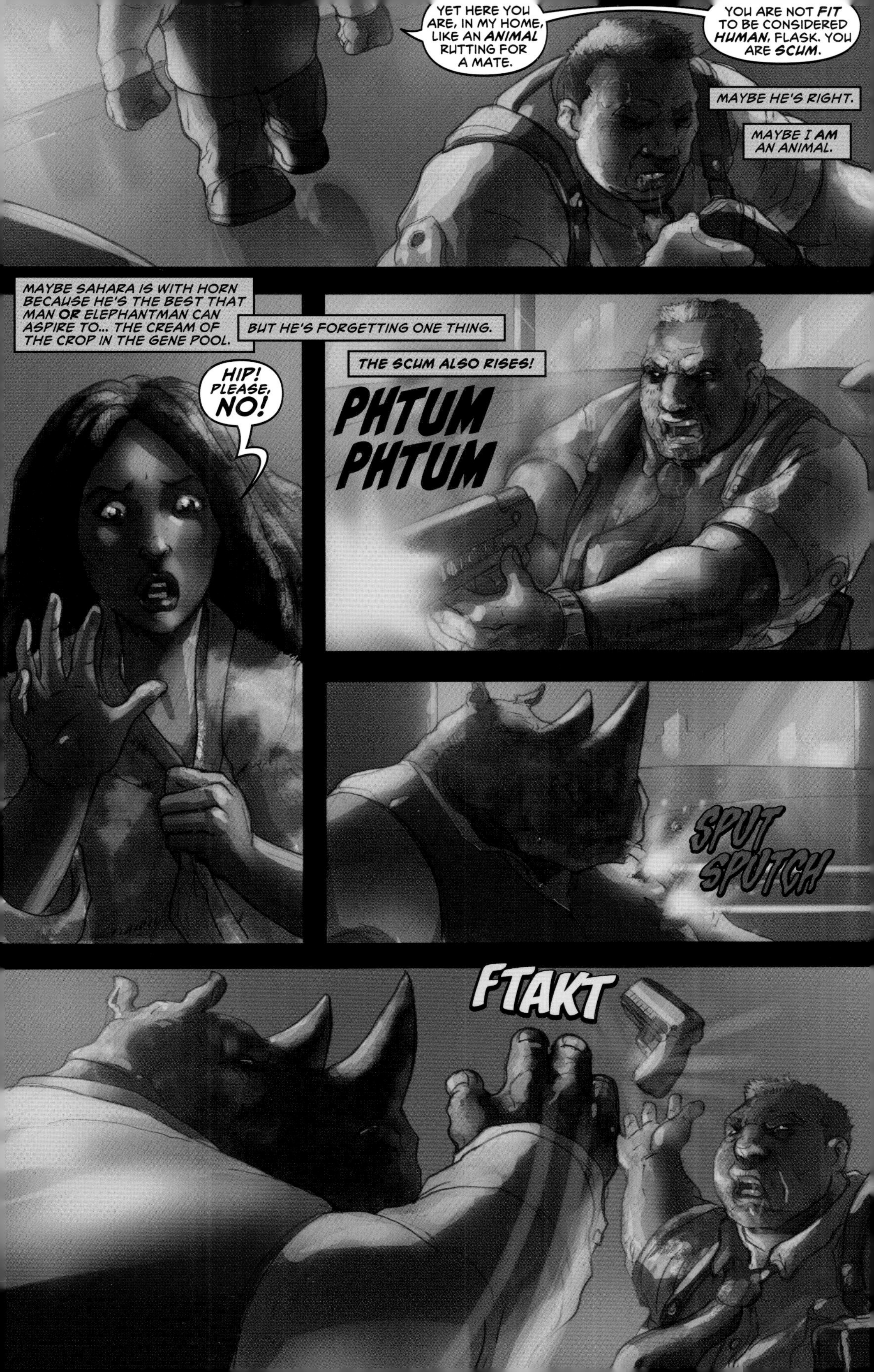

YET HERE YOU ARE, IN MY HOME, LIKE AN ANIMAL RUTTING FOR A MATE.
YOU ARE NOT FIT TO BE CONSIDERED HUMAN, FLASK. YOU ARE SCUM.
MAYBE HE'S RIGHT.
MAYBE I AM AN ANIMAL.
MAYBE SAHARA IS WITH HORN BECAUSE HE'S THE BEST THAT MAN OR ELEPHANTMAN CAN ASPIRE TO... THE CREAM OF THE CROP IN THE GENE POOL.
BUT HE'S FORGETTING ONE THING.
THE SCUM ALSO RISES!
HIP! PLEASE, NO!
PHTUM PHTUM
SPUT SPUTCH
FTAKT

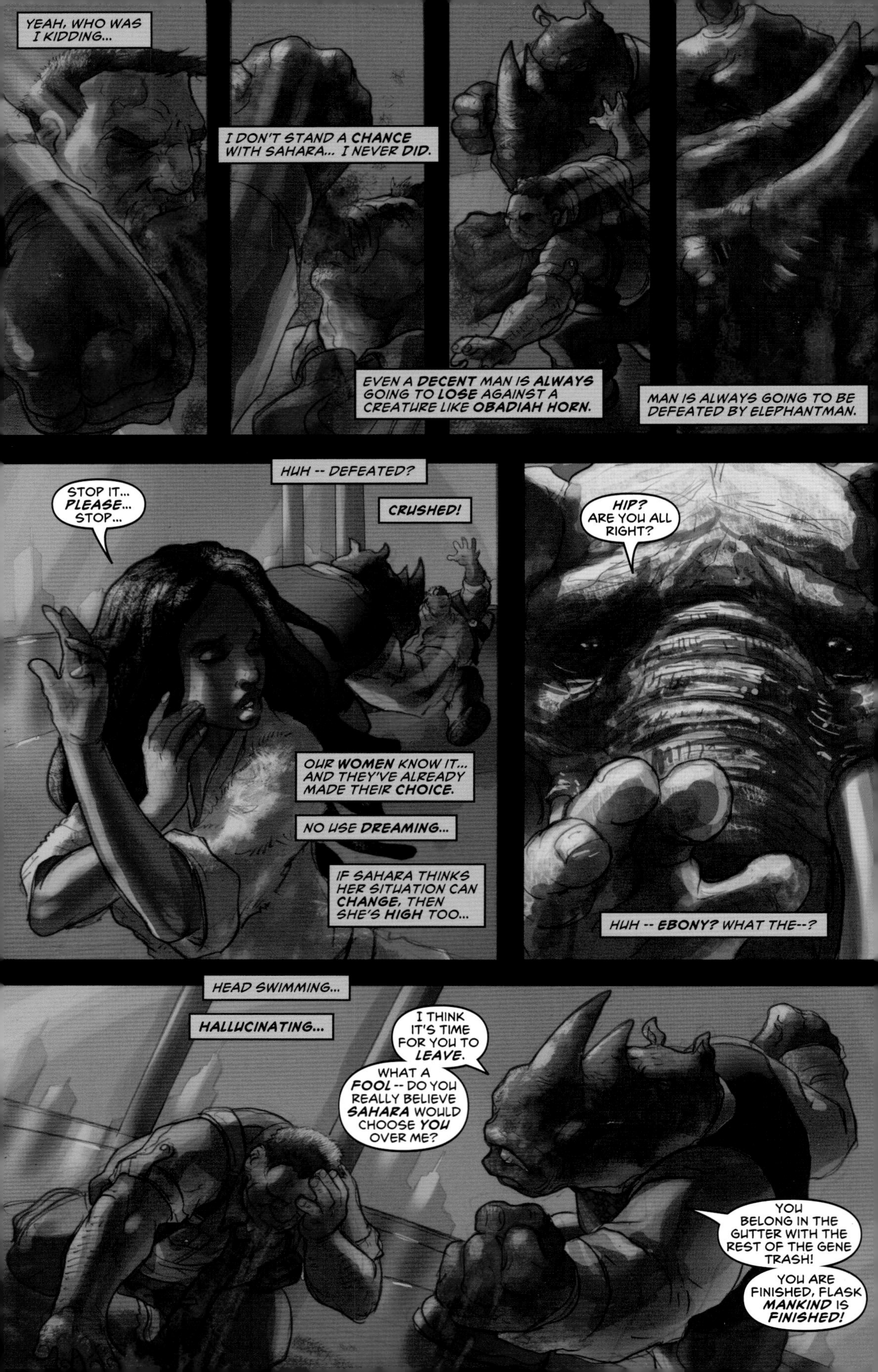
YEAH, WHO WAS I KIDDING...
I DON'T STAND A CHANCE WITH SAHARA... I NEVER DID.
EVEN A DECENT MAN IS ALWAYS GOING TO LOSE AGAINST A CREATURE LIKE OBADIAH HORN.
MAN IS ALWAYS GOING TO BE DEFEATED BY ELEPHANTMAN.
HUH -- DEFEATED?
STOP IT... PLEASE... STOP...
CRUSHED!
OUR WOMEN KNOW IT... AND THEY'VE ALREADY MADE THEIR CHOICE.
NO USE DREAMING...
IF SAHARA THINKS HER SITUATION CAN CHANGE, THEN SHE'S HIGH TOO...
HIP? ARE YOU ALL RIGHT?
HUH -- EBONY? WHAT THE--?
HEAD SWIMMING...
HALLUCINATING...
I THINK IT'S TIME FOR YOU TO LEAVE.
WHAT A FOOL -- DO YOU REALLY BELIEVE SAHARA WOULD CHOOSE YOU OVER ME?
YOU BELONG IN THE GUTTER WITH THE REST OF THE GENE TRASH!
YOU ARE FINISHED, FLASK MANKIND IS FINISHED!

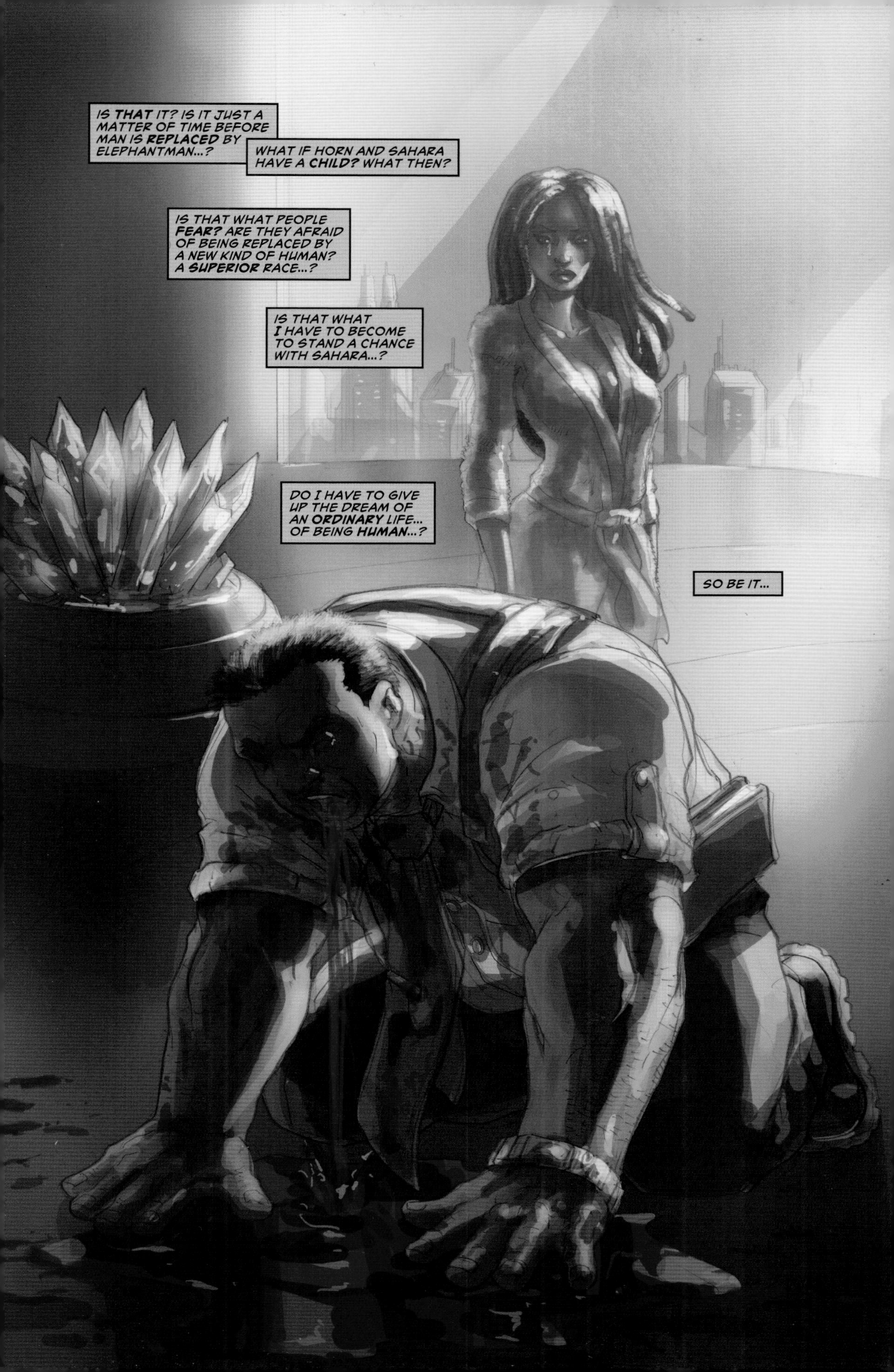
IS THAT IT? IS IT JUST A MATTER OF TIME BEFORE MAN IS REPLACED BY ELEPHANTMAN...?
WHAT IF HORN AND SAHARA HAVE A CHILD? WHAT THEN?
IS THAT WHAT PEOPLE FEAR? ARE THEY AFRAID OF BEING REPLACED BY A NEW KIND OF HUMAN? A SUPERIOR RACE...?
IS THAT WHAT I HAVE TO BECOME TO STAND A CHANCE WITH SAHARA...?
DO I HAVE TO GIVE UP THE DREAM OF AN ORDINARY LIFE... OF BEING HUMAN...?
SO BE IT...

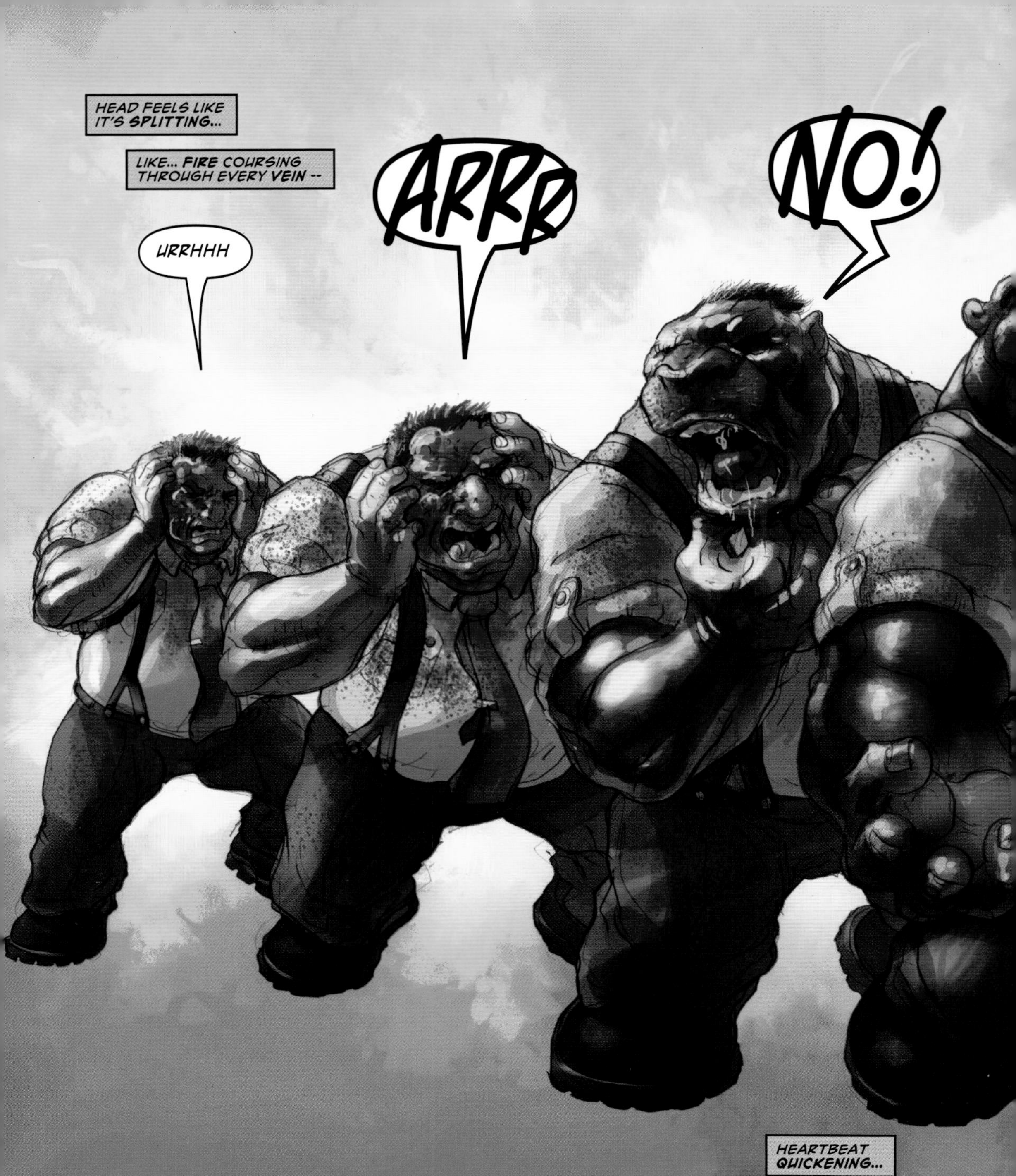
HEAD FEELS LIKE IT'S SPLITTING...
LIKE... FIRE COURSING THROUGH EVERY VEIN --
URRHHH
ARRR
NO!
HEARTBEAT QUICKENING...

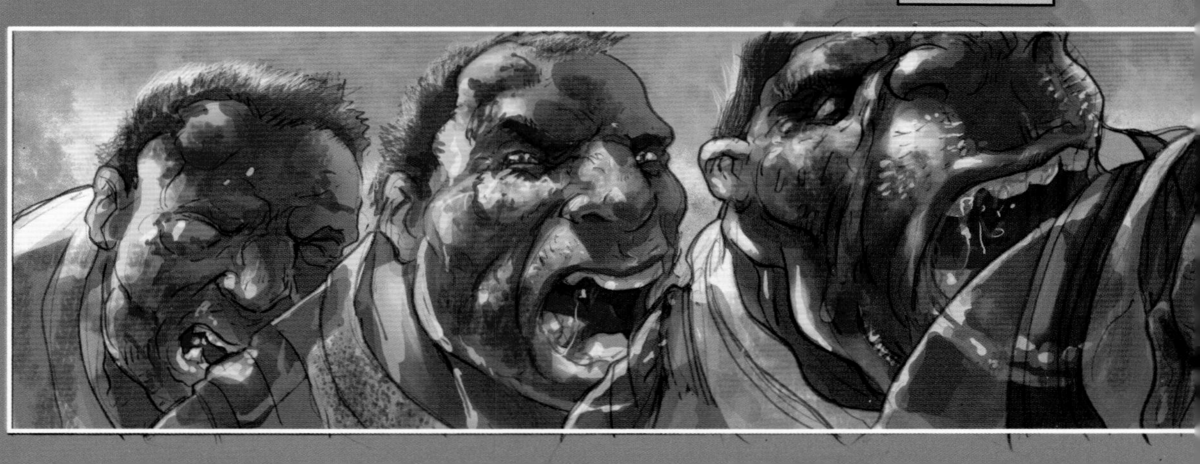

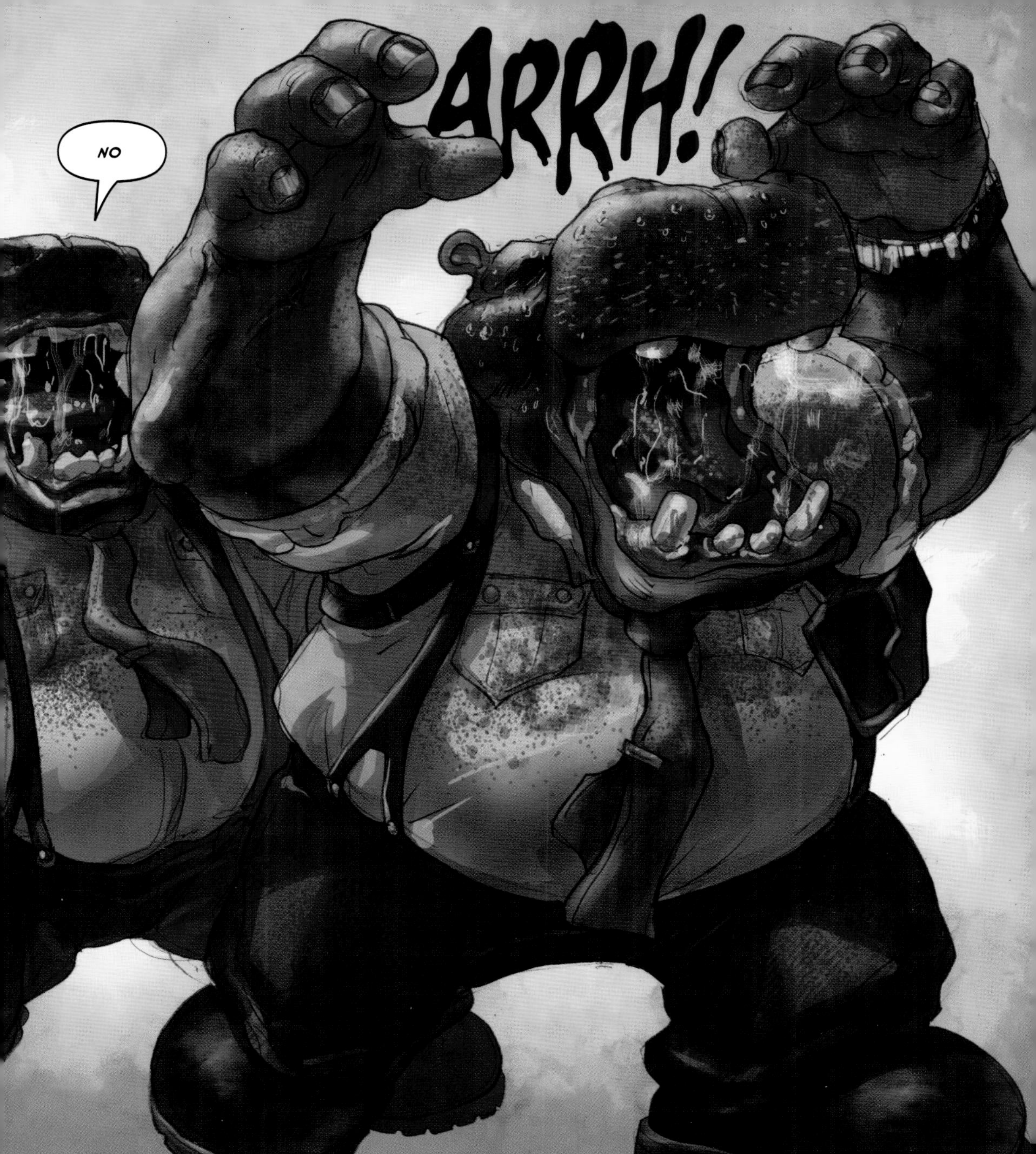
NO
ARRH!

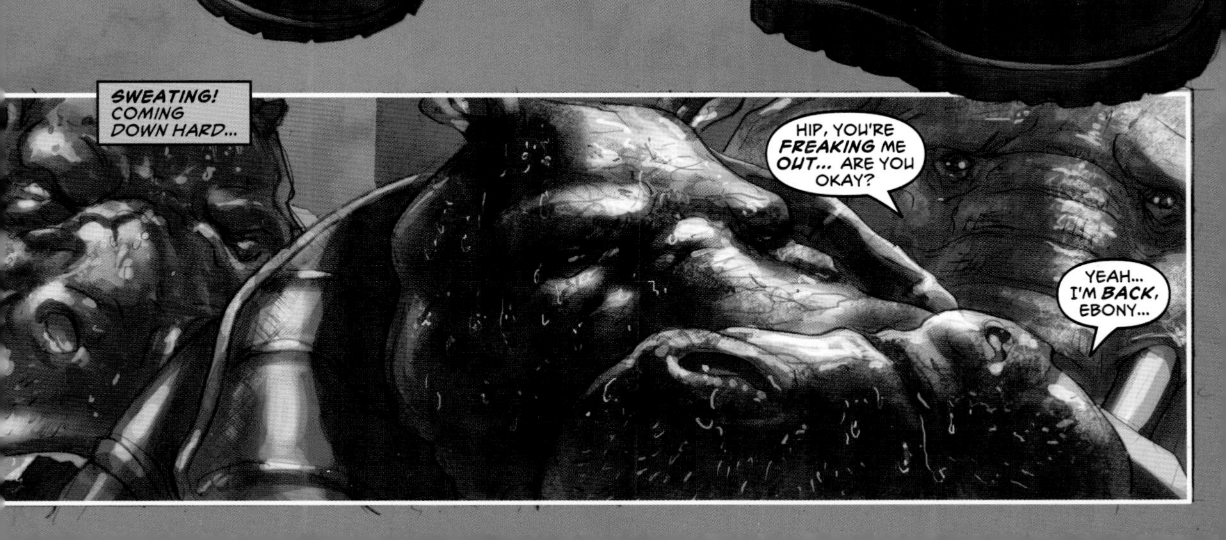
SWEATING! COMING DOWN HARD...
HIP, YOU'RE FREAKING ME OUT... ARE YOU OKAY?
YEAH... I'M BACK, EBONY...

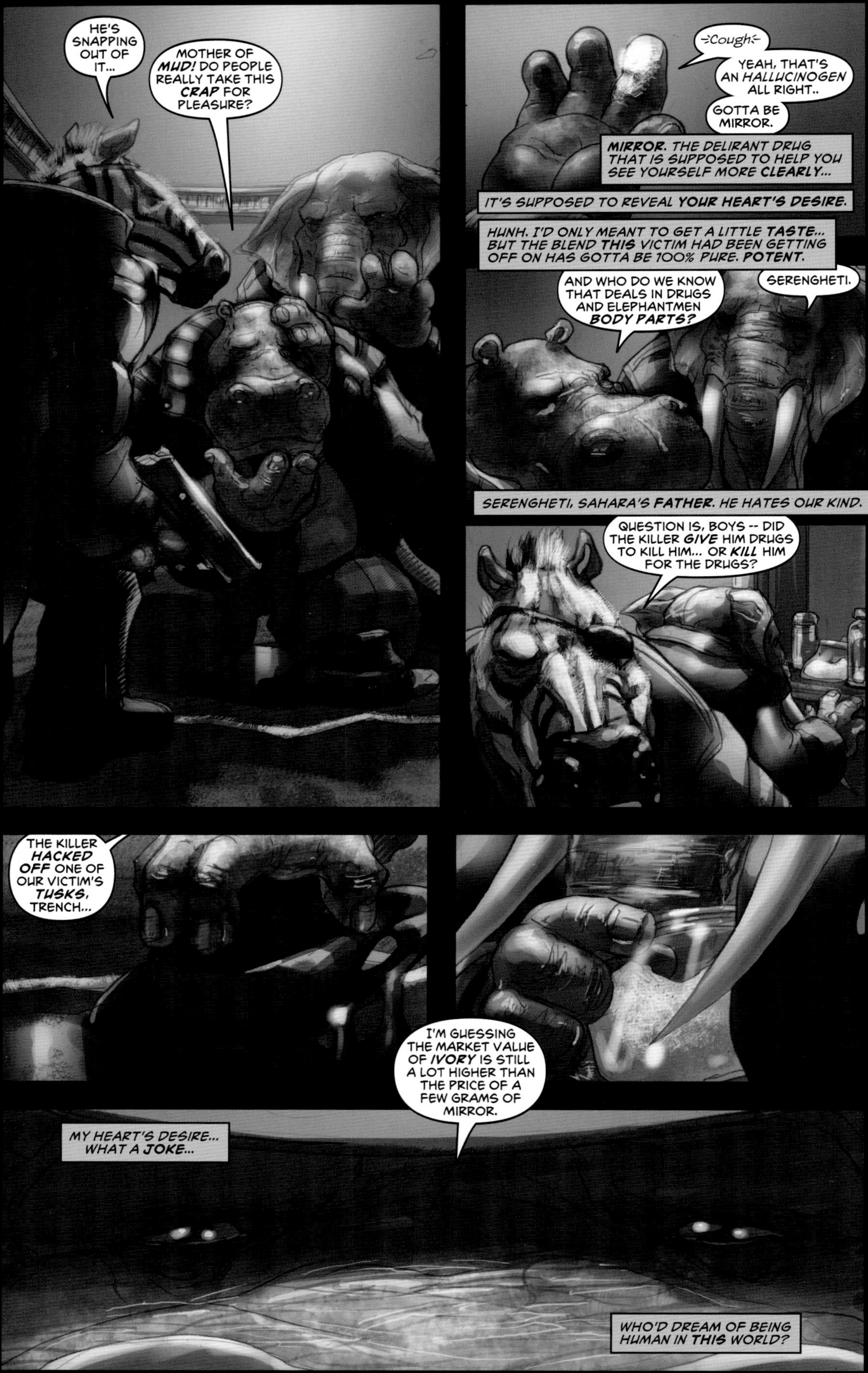
HE'S SNAPPING OUT OF IT...
MOTHER OF MUD! DO PEOPLE REALLY TAKE THIS CRAP FOR PLEASURE?
=Cough=
YEAH, THAT'S AN HALLUCINOGEN ALL RIGHT..
GOTTA BE MIRROR.
MIRROR. THE DELIRANT DRUG THAT IS SUPPOSED TO HELP YOU SEE YOURSELF MORE CLEARLY...
IT'S SUPPOSED TO REVEAL YOUR HEART'S DESIRE.
HUNH. I'D ONLY MEANT TO GET A LITTLE TASTE... BUT THE BLEND THIS VICTIM HAD BEEN GETTING OFF ON HAS GOTTA BE 100% PURE. POTENT.
AND WHO DO WE KNOW THAT DEALS IN DRUGS AND ELEPHANTMEN BODY PARTS?
SERENGHETI.
SERENGHETI, SAHARA'S FATHER. HE HATES OUR KIND.
QUESTION IS, BOYS -- DID THE KILLER GIVE HIM DRUGS TO KILL HIM... OR KILL HIM FOR THE DRUGS?
THE KILLER HACKED OFF ONE OF OUR VICTIM'S TUSKS, TRENCH...
I'M GUESSING THE MARKET VALUE OF IVORY IS STILL A LOT HIGHER THAN THE PRICE OF A FEW GRAMS OF MIRROR.
MY HEART'S DESIRE... WHAT A JOKE...
WHO'D DREAM OF BEING HUMAN IN THIS WORLD?

To Be Continued!

ELEPHANTMEN ™

THE BURDEN OF TYRANNY

RATED **M** FOR MATURE READERS

MAN AND ELEPHANTMAN **#2** OF 3 **#31** MAY $3.99

STARKINGS · MEO... ...SHELL · COOK

"Revolutions have never lightened the burden of tyranny. They have only shifted it to another shoulder."

George Bernard Shaw
Man and Superman

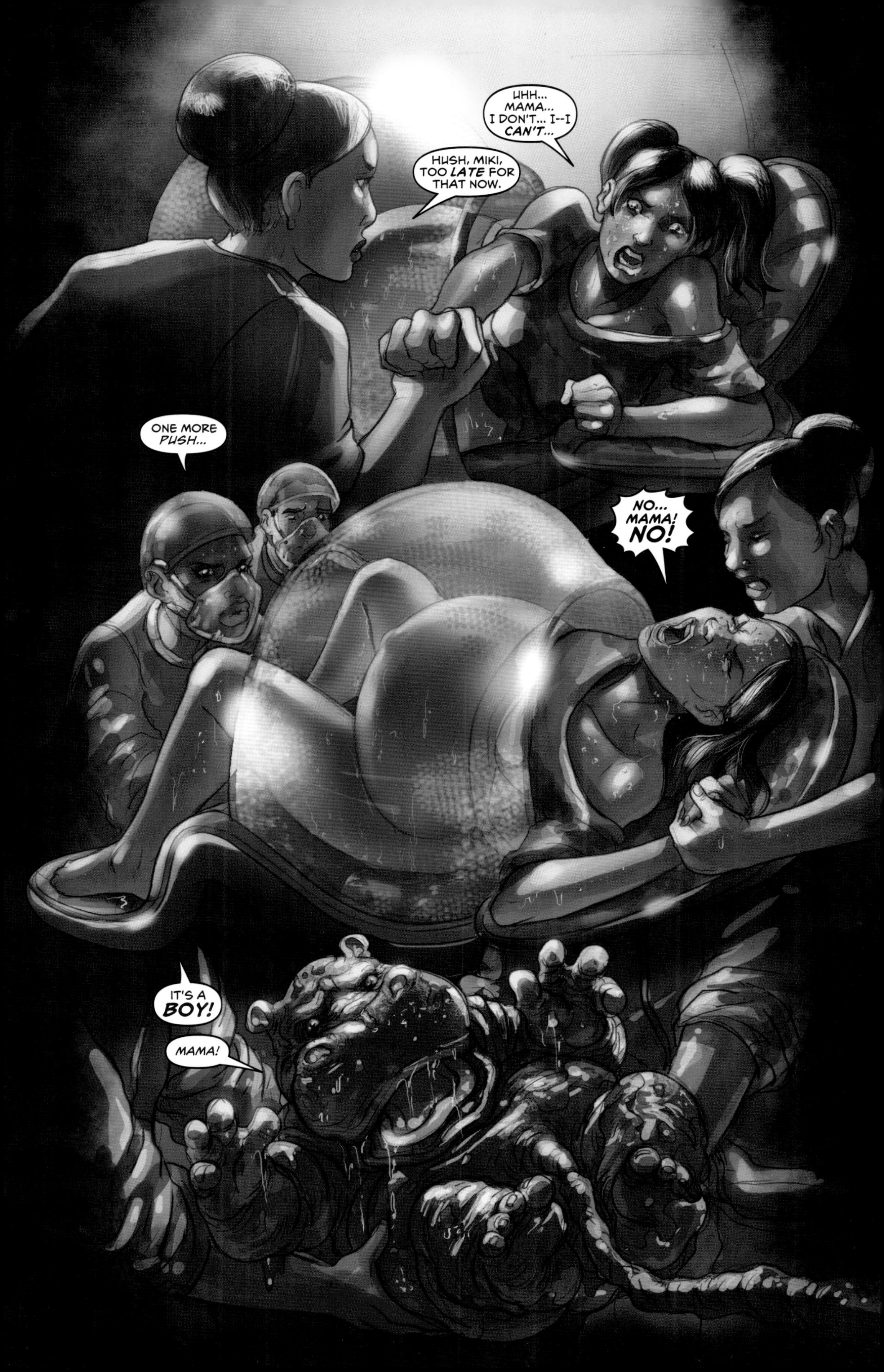
UHH... MAMA... I DON'T... I--I CAN'T...
HUSH, MIKI, TOO LATE FOR THAT NOW.
ONE MORE PUSH...
NO... MAMA! NO!
IT'S A BOY!
MAMA!

MAN and ELEPHANTMAN
PART 2 of 3
A SHIP TO CROSS A SEA OF SUFFERING
HUH?
Richard Starkings Words • Axel Medellin Pictures
Special Thanks to Janet Zucker

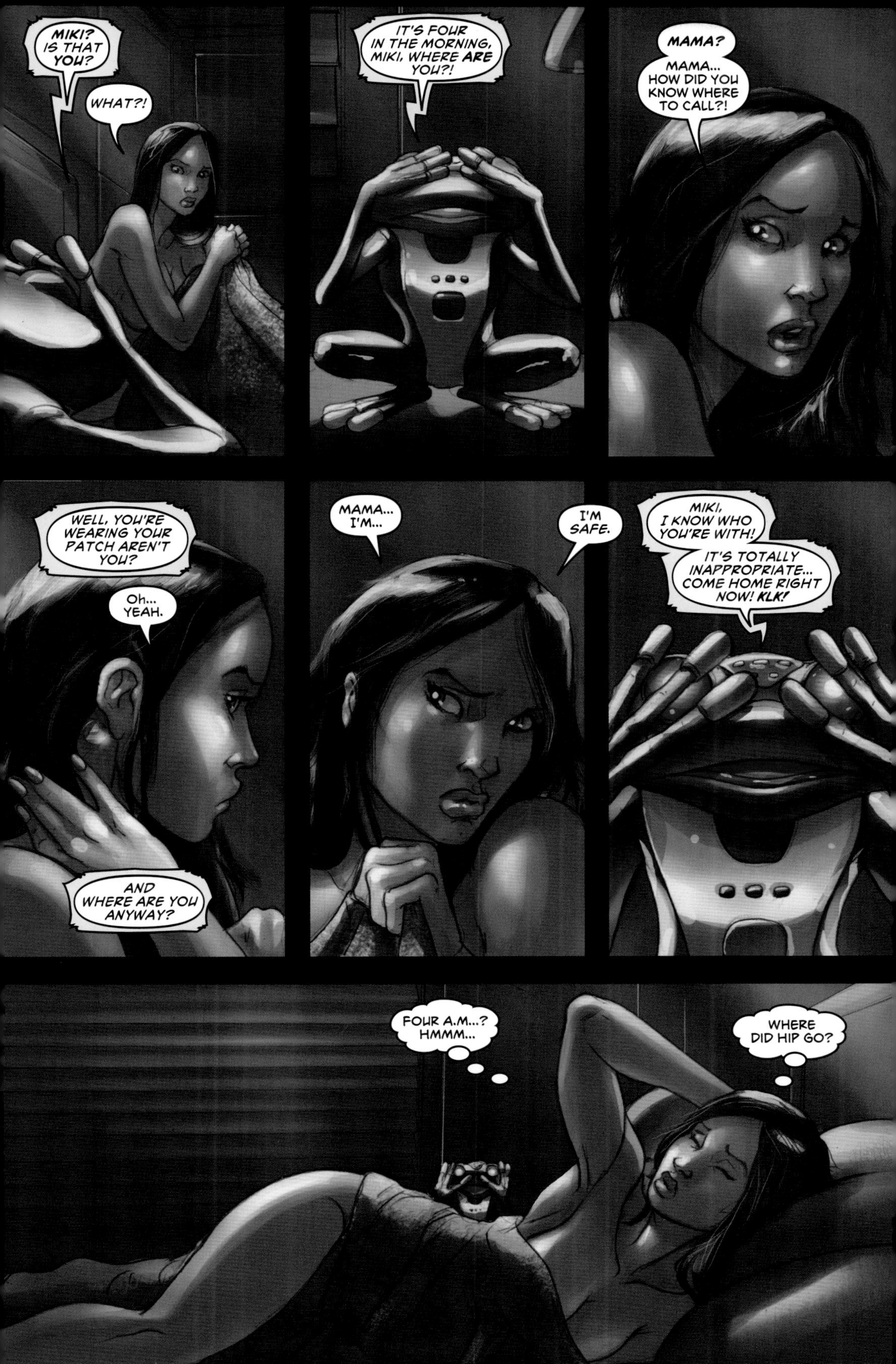
MIKI? IS THAT YOU?
WHAT?!
IT'S FOUR IN THE MORNING, MIKI, WHERE ARE YOU?!
MAMA?
MAMA... HOW DID YOU KNOW WHERE TO CALL?!
WELL, YOU'RE WEARING YOUR PATCH AREN'T YOU?
Oh... YEAH.
AND WHERE ARE YOU ANYWAY?
MAMA... I'M...
I'M SAFE.
MIKI, I KNOW WHO YOU'RE WITH!
IT'S TOTALLY INAPPROPRIATE... COME HOME RIGHT NOW! KLK!
FOUR A.M...? HMMM...
WHERE DID HIP GO?
SANTA MONICA · 2259

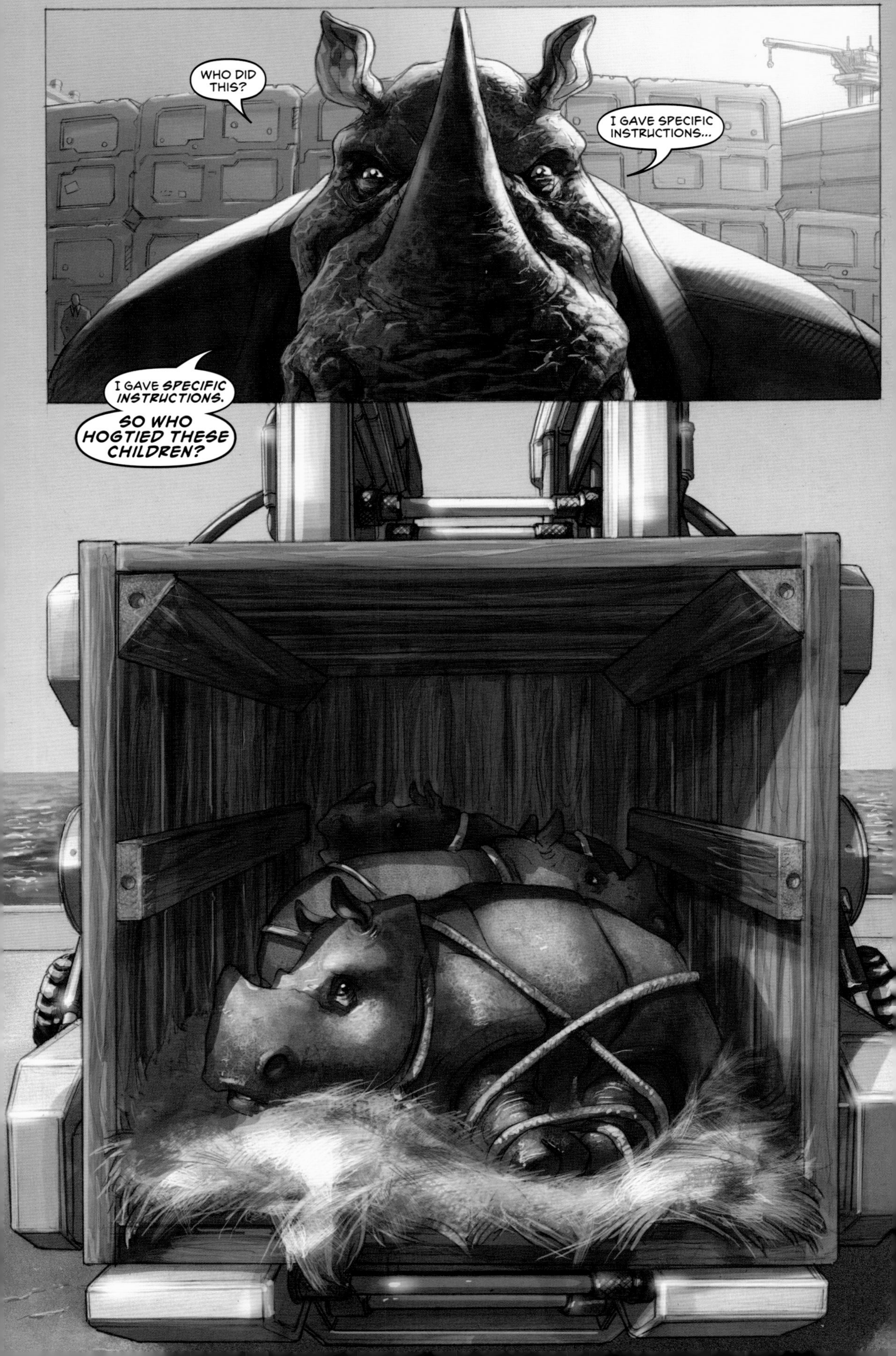
WHO DID THIS?
I GAVE SPECIFIC INSTRUCTIONS...
I GAVE SPECIFIC INSTRUCTIONS.
SO WHO HOGTIED THESE CHILDREN?

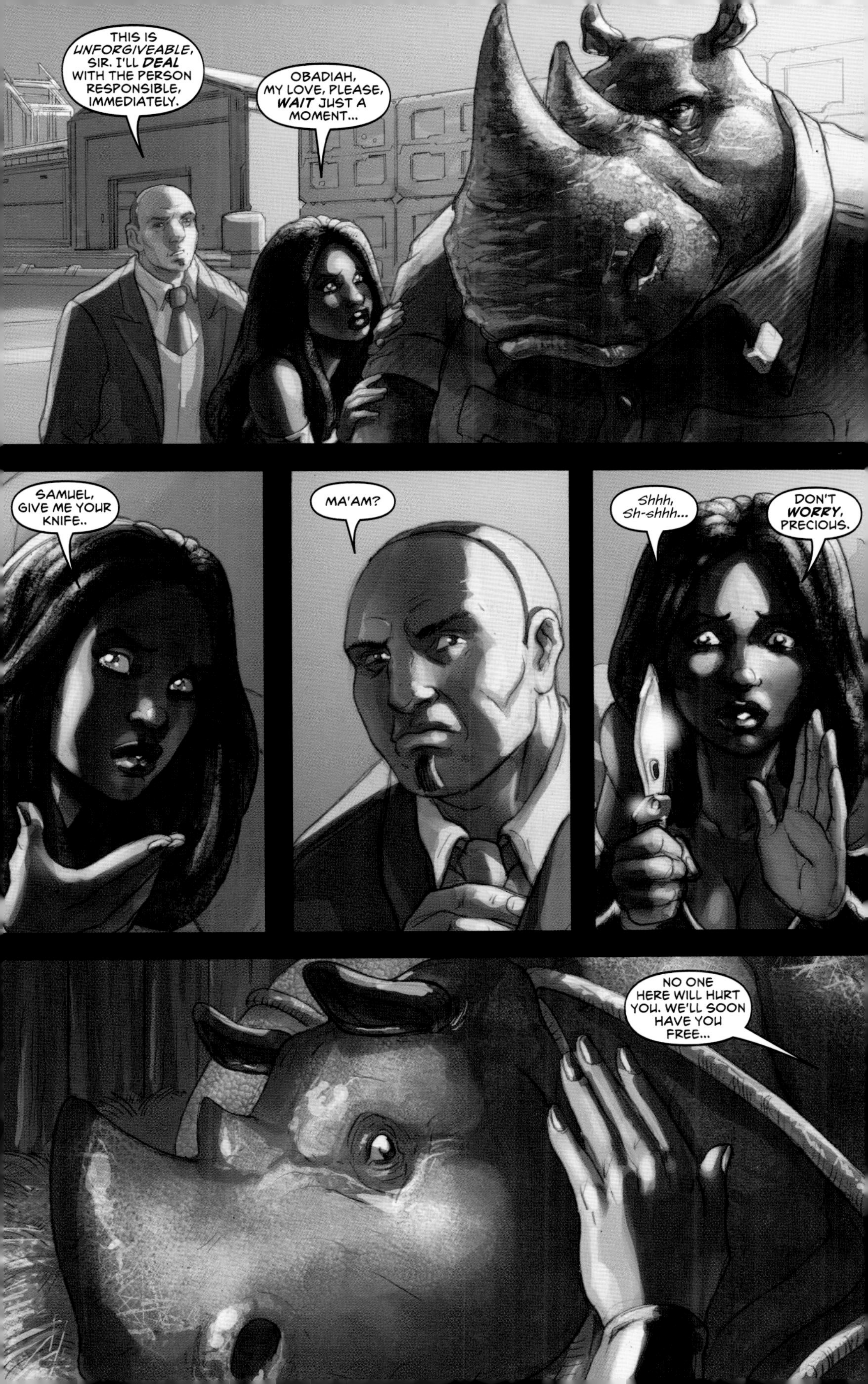
THIS IS UNFORGIVEABLE, SIR. I'LL DEAL WITH THE PERSON RESPONSIBLE, IMMEDIATELY.
OBADIAH, MY LOVE, PLEASE, WAIT JUST A MOMENT...
SAMUEL, GIVE ME YOUR KNIFE..
MA'AM?
Shhh, Sh-shhh...
DON'T WORRY, PRECIOUS.
NO ONE HERE WILL HURT YOU. WE'LL SOON HAVE YOU FREE...

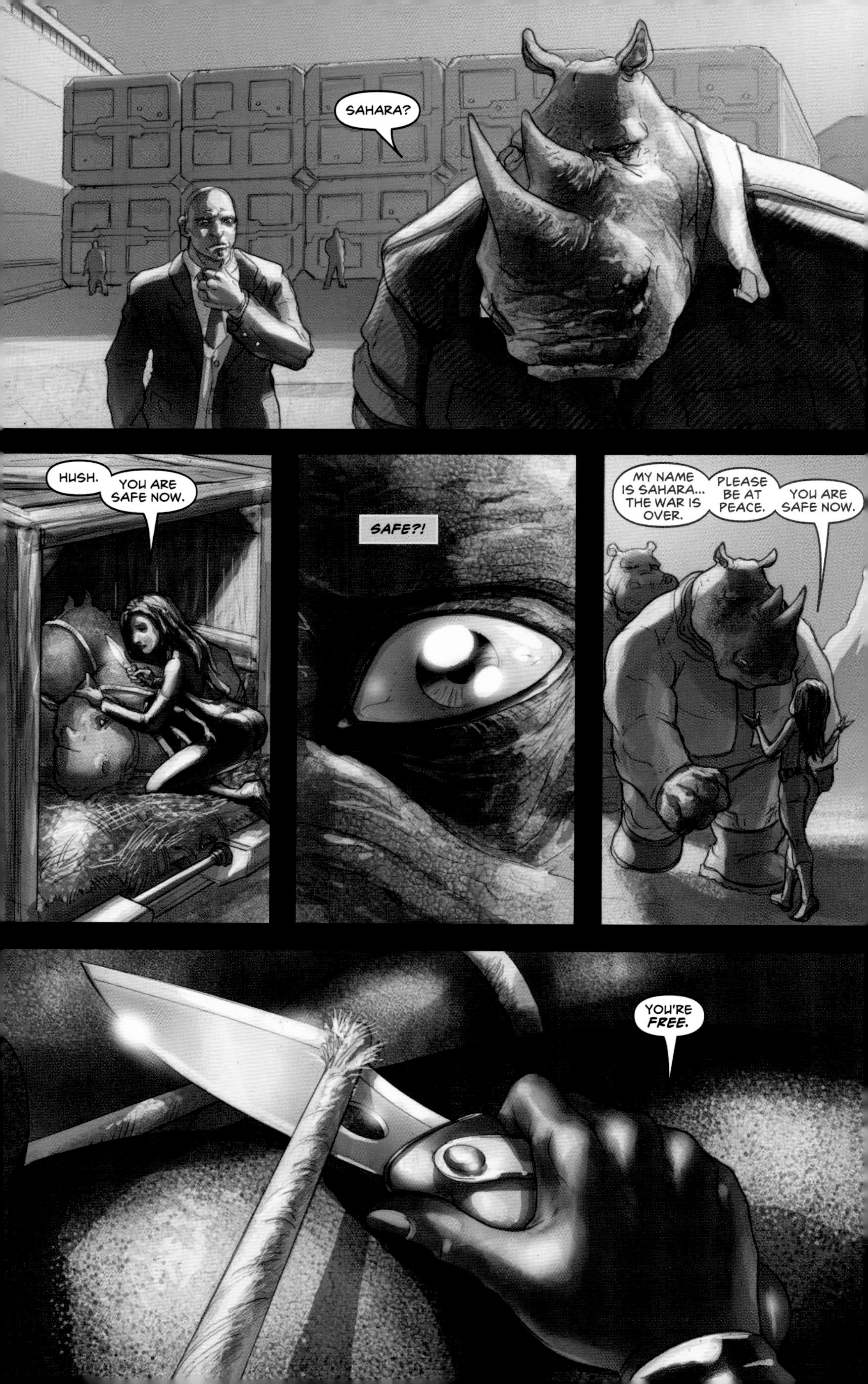
SAHARA?
HUSH.
YOU ARE SAFE NOW.
SAFE?!
MY NAME IS SAHARA... THE WAR IS OVER.
PLEASE BE AT PEACE.
YOU ARE SAFE NOW.
YOU'RE *FREE.*

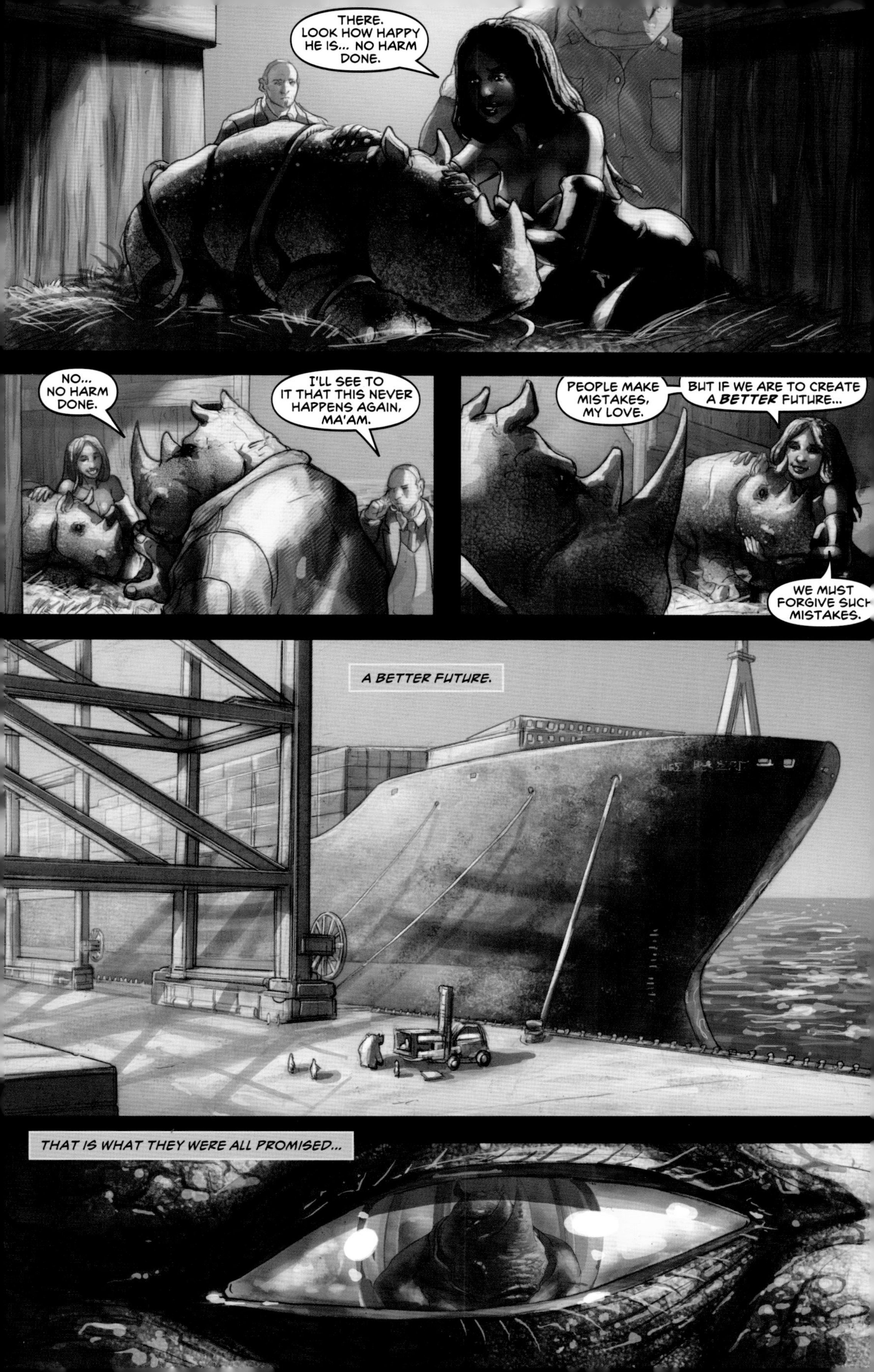
THERE. LOOK HOW HAPPY HE IS... NO HARM DONE.
NO... NO HARM DONE.
I'LL SEE TO IT THAT THIS NEVER HAPPENS AGAIN, MA'AM.
PEOPLE MAKE MISTAKES, MY LOVE.
BUT IF WE ARE TO CREATE A **BETTER** FUTURE...
WE MUST FORGIVE SUCH MISTAKES.
A BETTER FUTURE.
THAT IS WHAT THEY WERE ALL PROMISED...

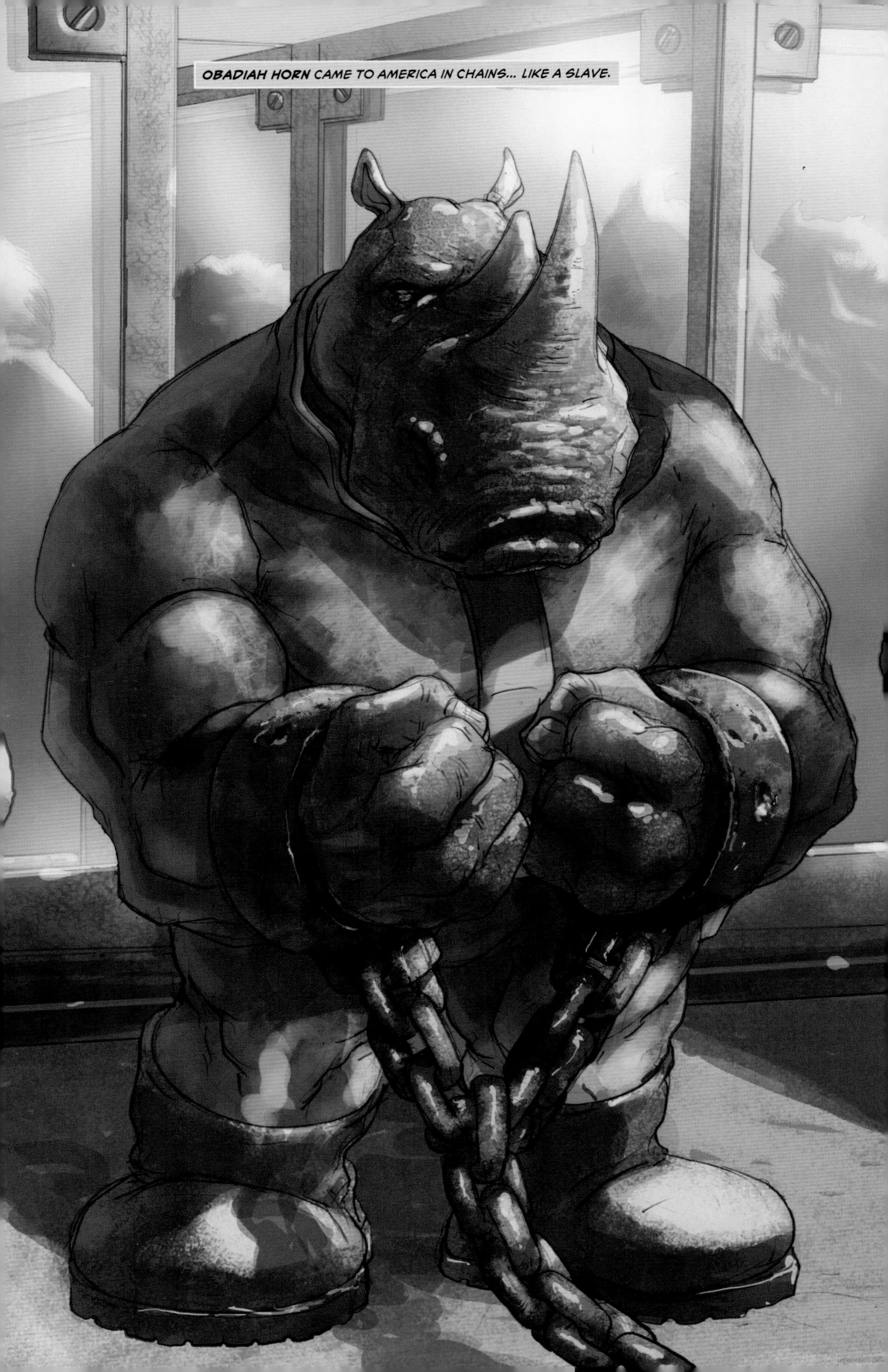
OBADIAH HORN CAME TO AMERICA IN CHAINS... LIKE A SLAVE.

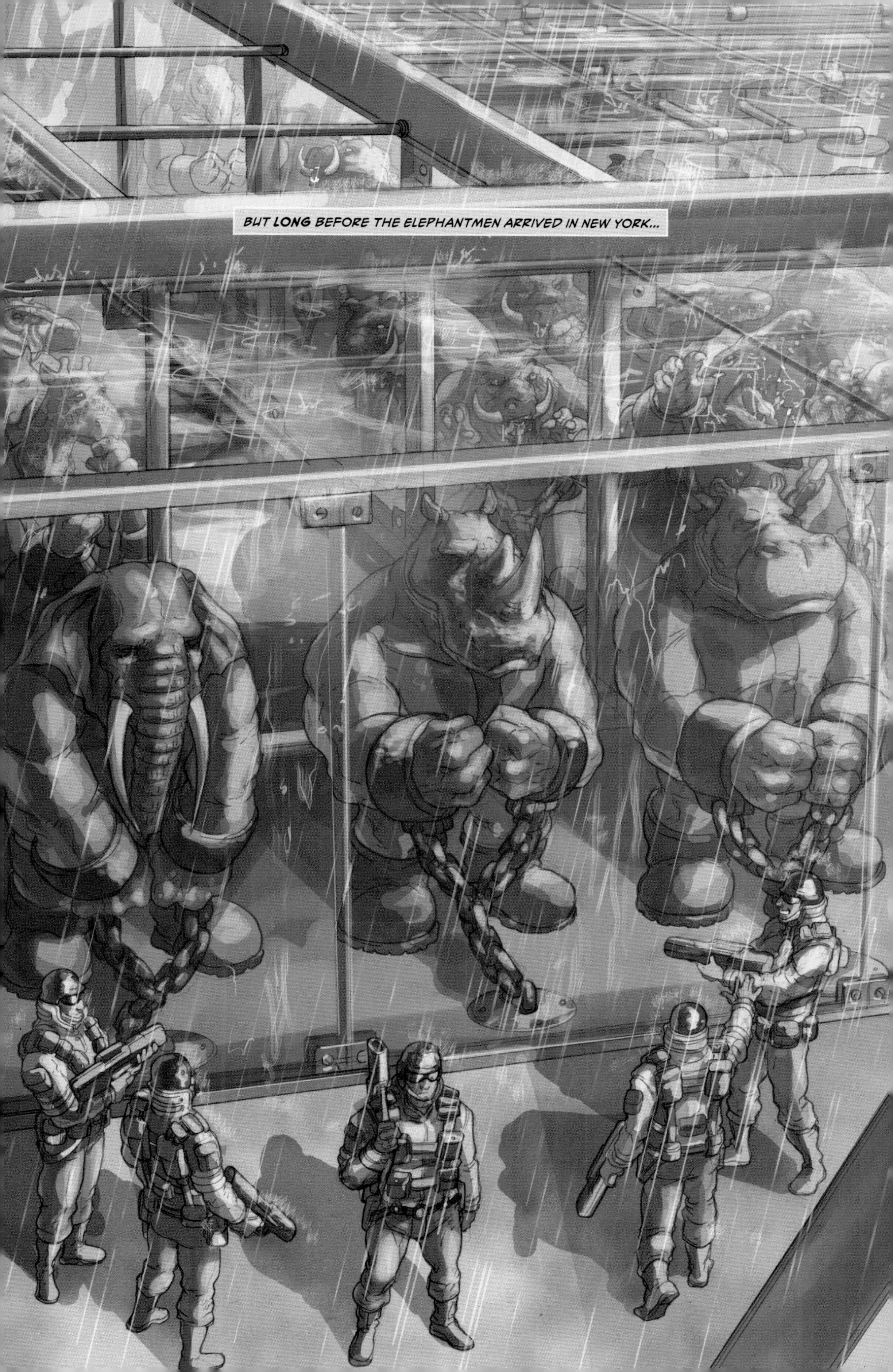
BUT LONG BEFORE THE ELEPHANTMEN ARRIVED IN NEW YORK...

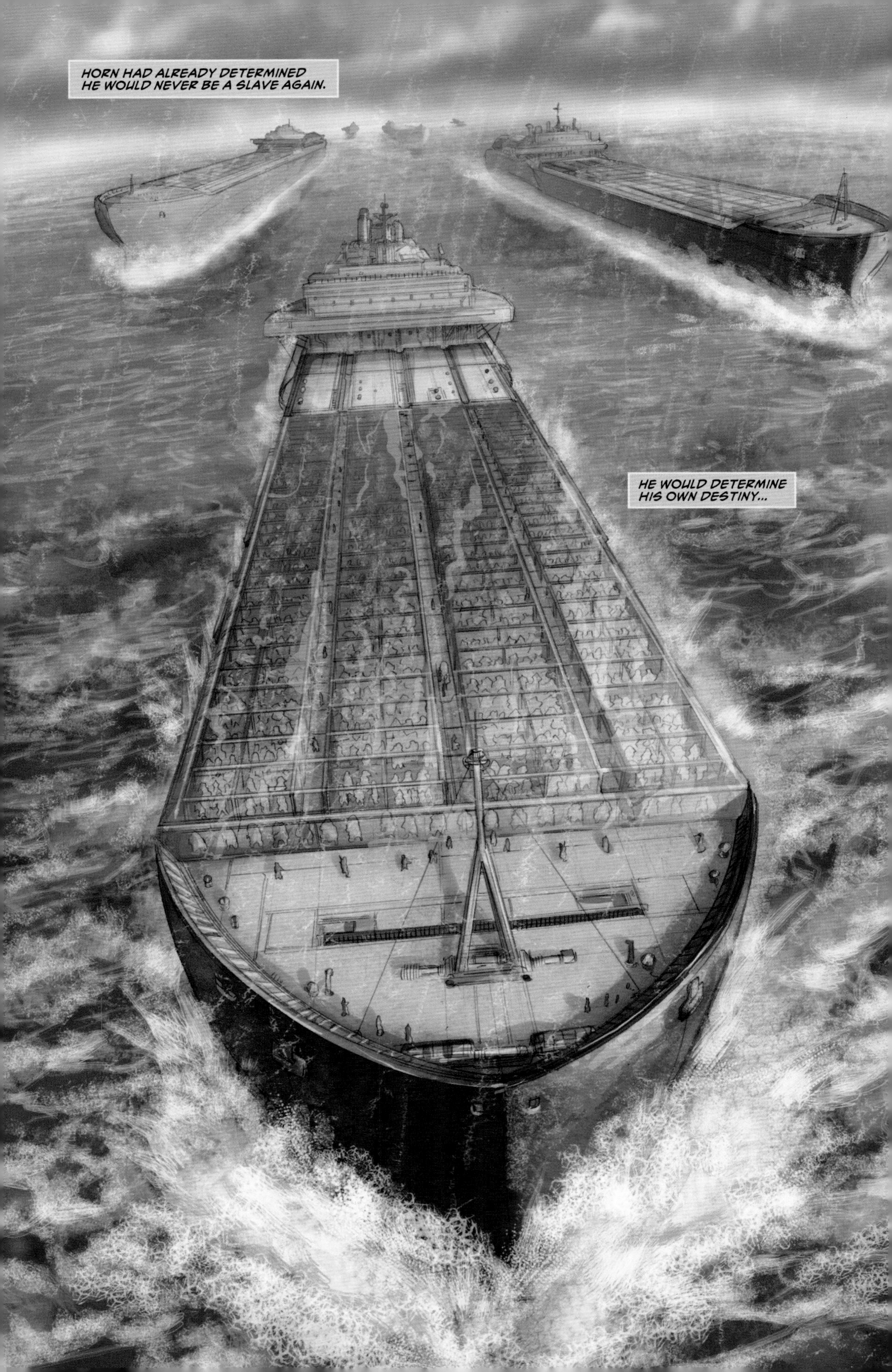
HORN HAD ALREADY DETERMINED HE WOULD NEVER BE A SLAVE AGAIN.
HE WOULD DETERMINE HIS OWN DESTINY...

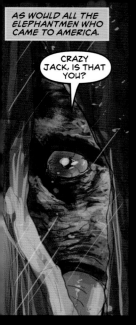

AS WOULD ALL THE ELEPHANTMEN WHO CAME TO AMERICA.

CRAZY JACK, IS THAT YOU?

OF *COURSE* IT'S ME, MATHEUS! LET ME *IN*!

YOU HAVE *MIRROR* WITH YOU, RIGHT?

HAVE YOU GOT *CASH*?

YAH-HA-HAA! *WHOA*, MAN, I NEVER SEEN AN ELEPHANTMAN WITH HIS *TACKLE* OUT BEFORE!

HEY, I CAN WEAR WHATEVER I WANT IN MY OWN HOME.

AN' I LIKE TO BE NAKED WHEN I GET HIGH, YOU GOT A PROBLEM WITH THAT?

UH, NO, I GET IT... IF I WAS HUNG LIKE YOU, I'D BE *SWINGING* IT AROUND ALL DAY TOO.

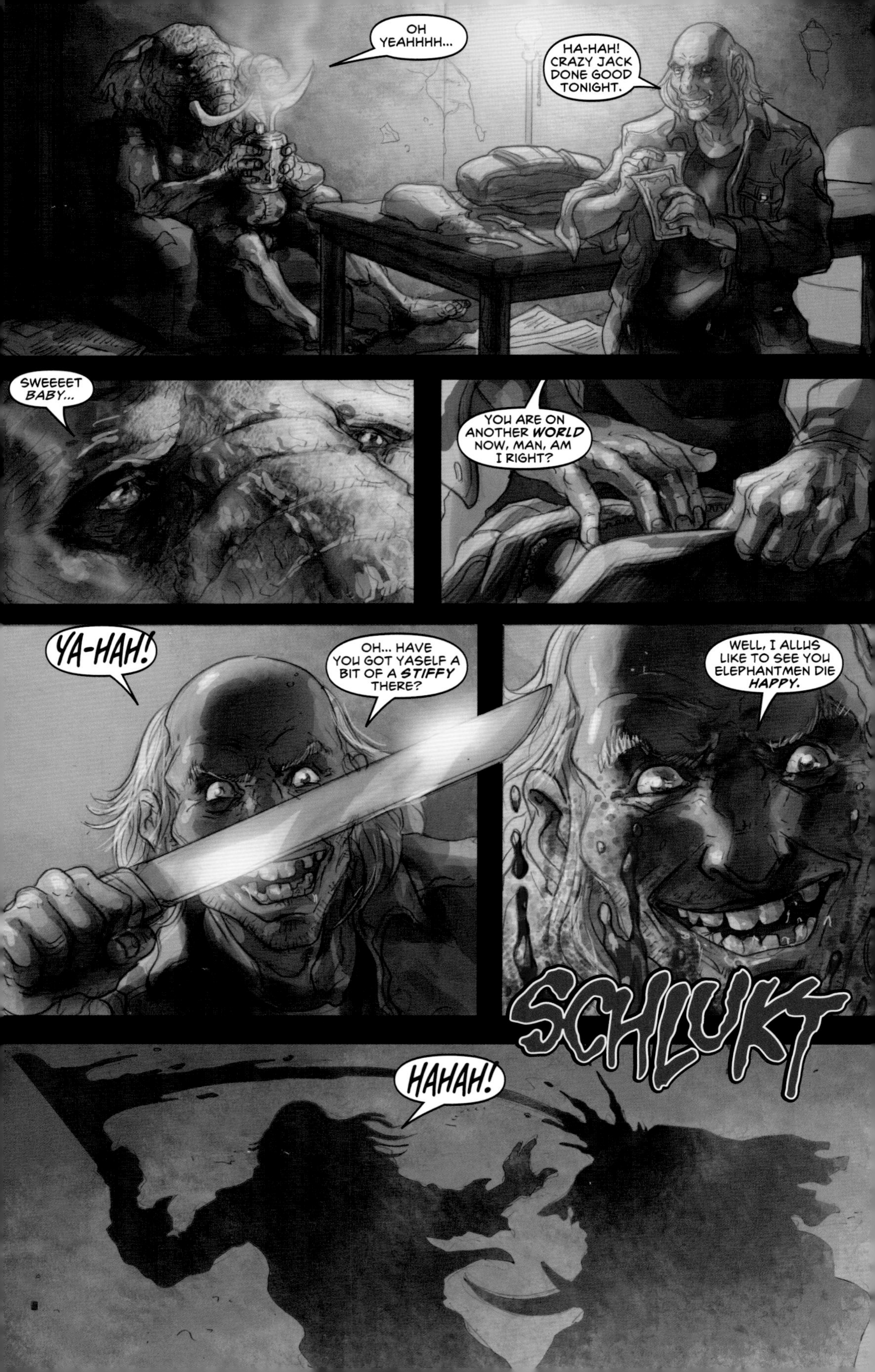
OH YEAHHHH...
HA-HAH! CRAZY JACK DONE GOOD TONIGHT.
SWEEEET BABY...
YOU ARE ON ANOTHER WORLD NOW, MAN, AM I RIGHT?
YA-HAH!
OH... HAVE YOU GOT YASELF A BIT OF A STIFFY THERE?
WELL, I ALLUS LIKE TO SEE YOU ELEPHANTMEN DIE HAPPY.
SCHLUKT
HAHAH!

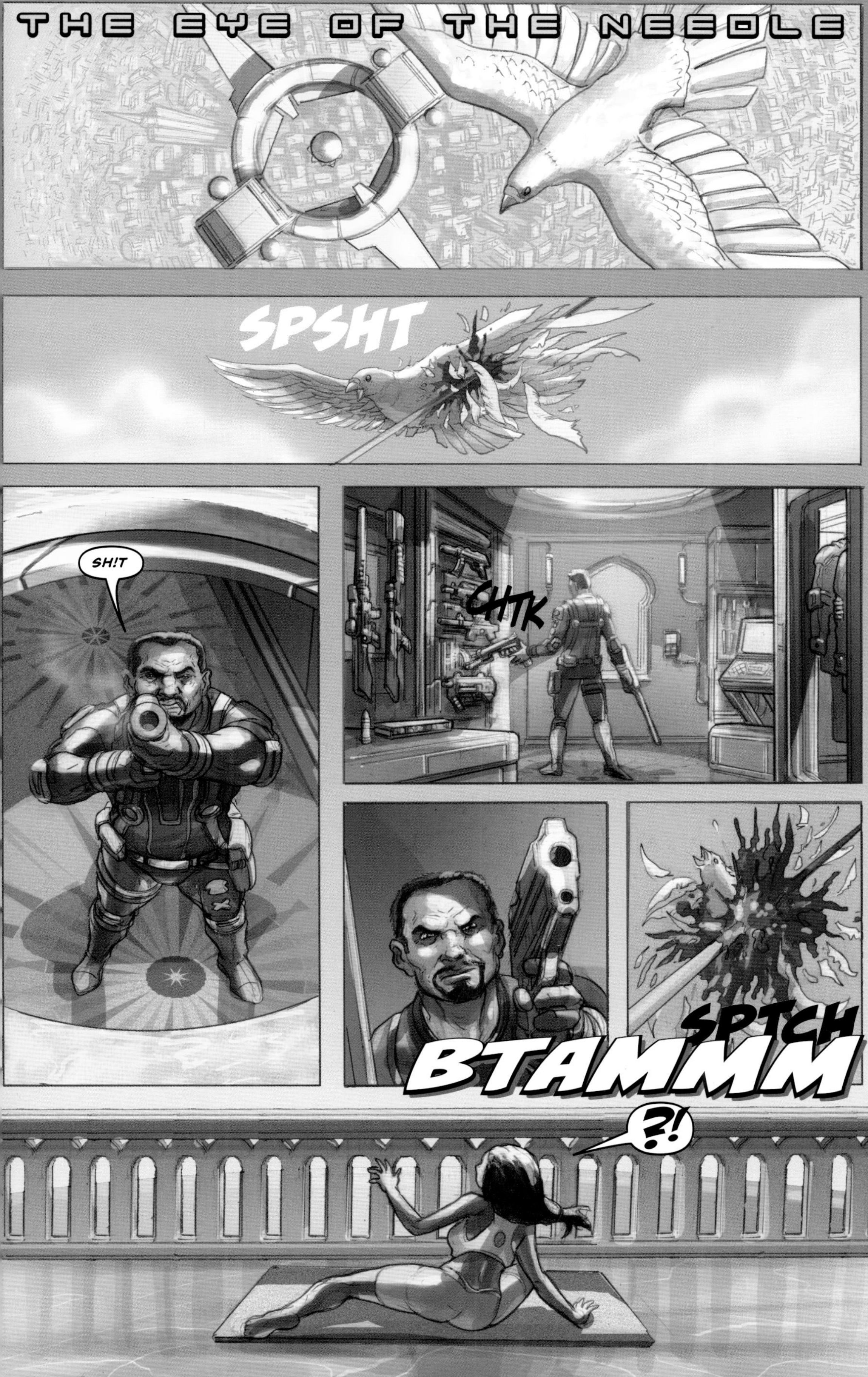
THE EYE OF THE NEEDLE
SPSHT
SH!T
CHTK
SPTCH
BTAMMM
?!

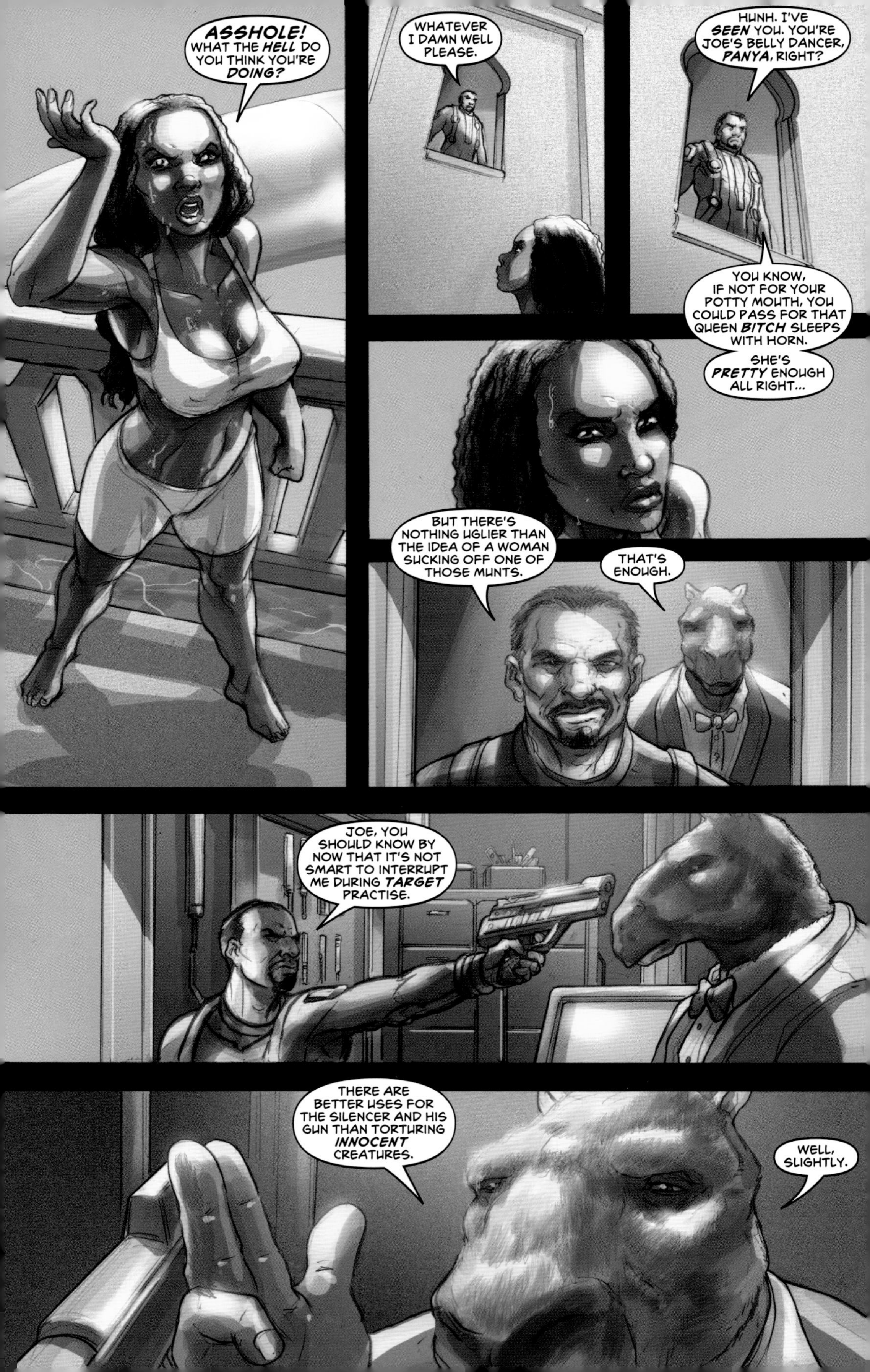
ASSHOLE! WHAT THE HELL DO YOU THINK YOU'RE DOING?
WHATEVER I DAMN WELL PLEASE.
HUNH. I'VE SEEN YOU. YOU'RE JOE'S BELLY DANCER, PANYA, RIGHT?
YOU KNOW, IF NOT FOR YOUR POTTY MOUTH, YOU COULD PASS FOR THAT QUEEN BITCH SLEEPS WITH HORN.
SHE'S PRETTY ENOUGH ALL RIGHT...
BUT THERE'S NOTHING UGLIER THAN THE IDEA OF A WOMAN SUCKING OFF ONE OF THOSE MUNTS.
THAT'S ENOUGH.
JOE, YOU SHOULD KNOW BY NOW THAT IT'S NOT SMART TO INTERRUPT ME DURING TARGET PRACTISE.
THERE ARE BETTER USES FOR THE SILENCER AND HIS GUN THAN TORTURING INNOCENT CREATURES.
WELL, SLIGHTLY.

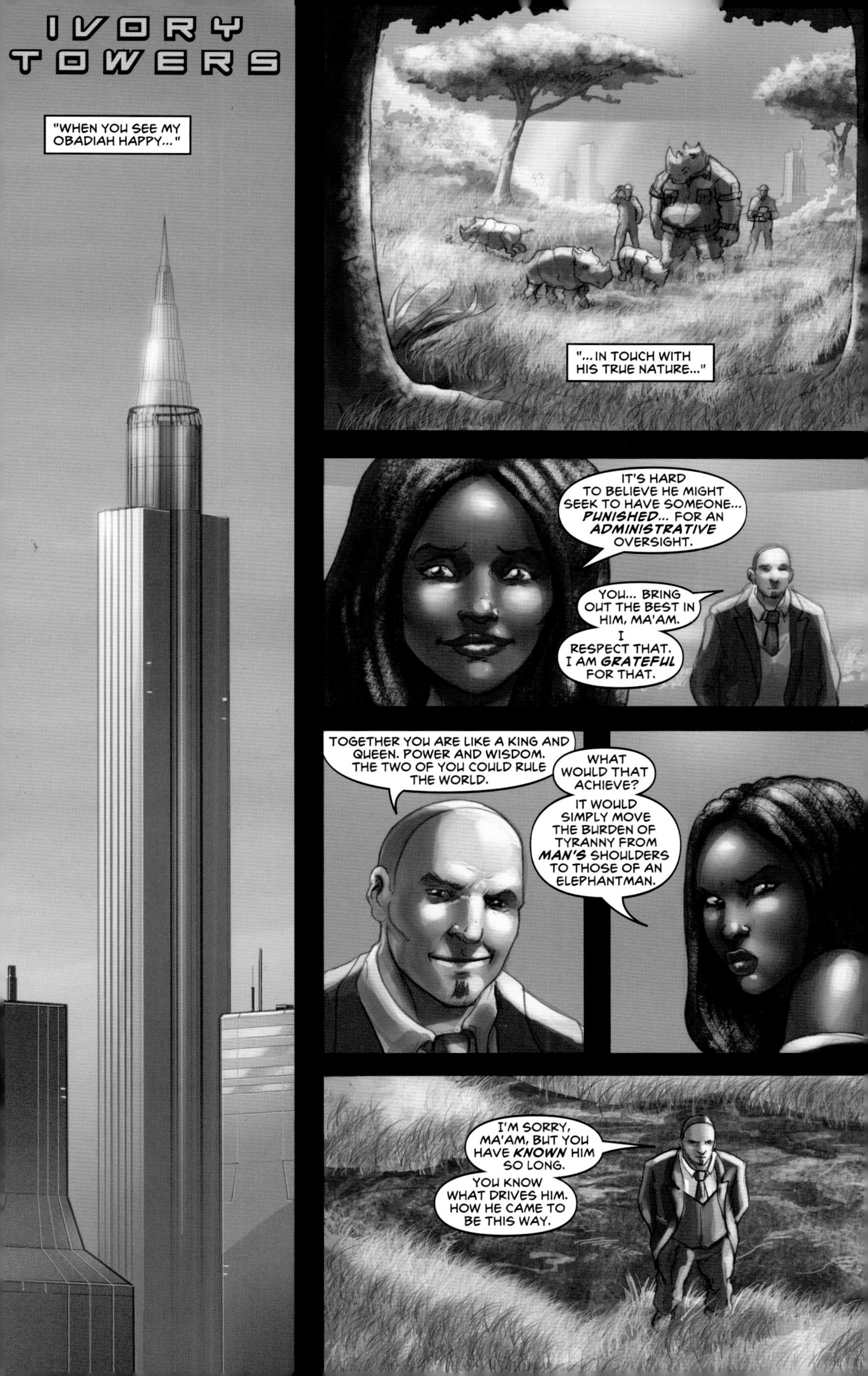
IVORY TOWERS
"WHEN YOU SEE MY OBADIAH HAPPY..."
"...IN TOUCH WITH HIS TRUE NATURE..."
IT'S HARD TO BELIEVE HE MIGHT SEEK TO HAVE SOMEONE... PUNISHED... FOR AN ADMINISTRATIVE OVERSIGHT.
YOU... BRING OUT THE BEST IN HIM, MA'AM.
I RESPECT THAT. I AM GRATEFUL FOR THAT.
TOGETHER YOU ARE LIKE A KING AND QUEEN. POWER AND WISDOM. THE TWO OF YOU COULD RULE THE WORLD.
WHAT WOULD THAT ACHIEVE?
IT WOULD SIMPLY MOVE THE BURDEN OF TYRANNY FROM MAN'S SHOULDERS TO THOSE OF AN ELEPHANTMAN.
I'M SORRY, MA'AM, BUT YOU HAVE KNOWN HIM SO LONG.
YOU KNOW WHAT DRIVES HIM. HOW HE CAME TO BE THIS WAY.

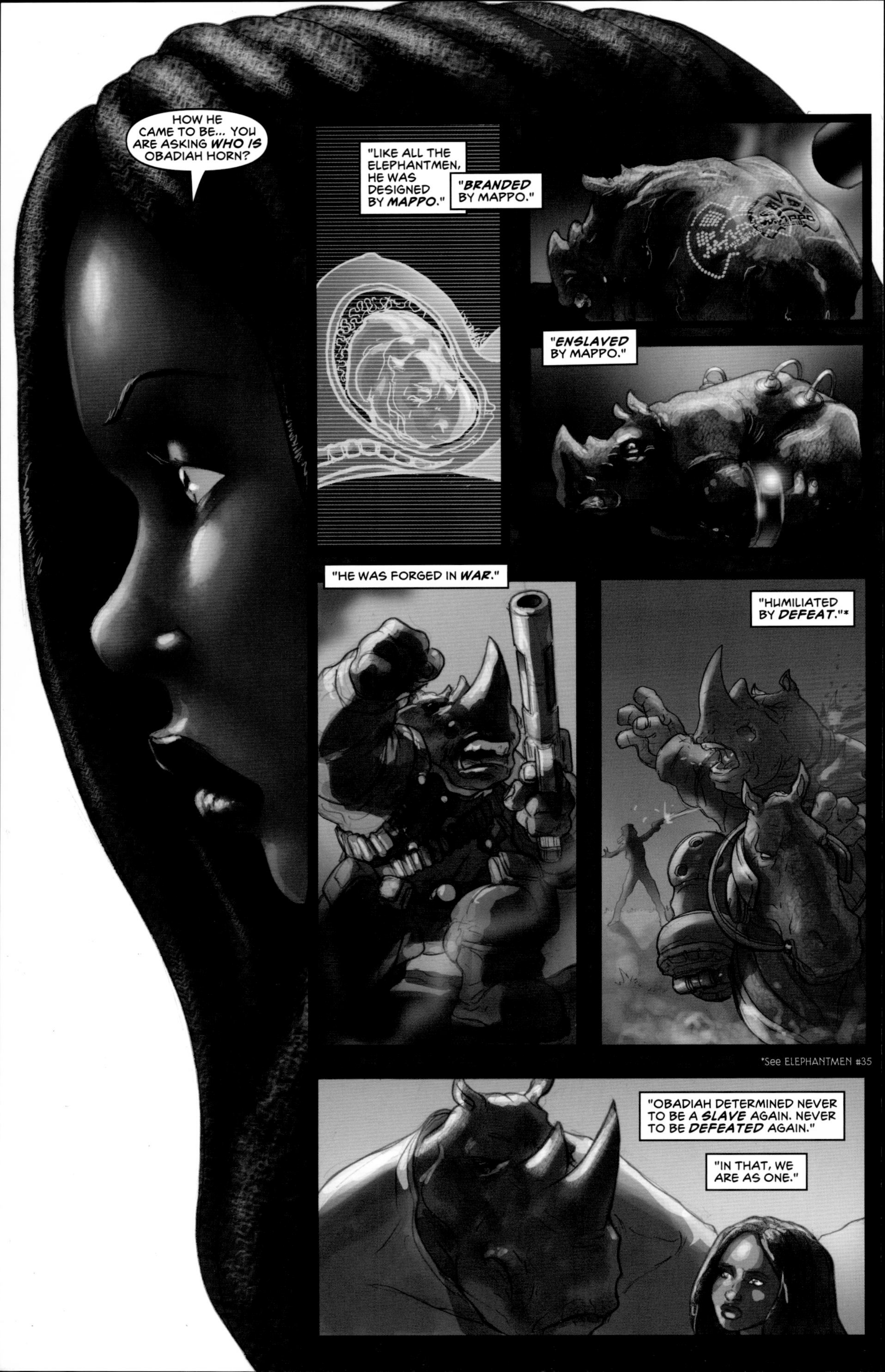
HOW HE CAME TO BE... YOU ARE ASKING WHO IS OBADIAH HORN?
"LIKE ALL THE ELEPHANTMEN, HE WAS DESIGNED BY MAPPO."
"BRANDED BY MAPPO."
"ENSLAVED BY MAPPO."
"HE WAS FORGED IN WAR."
"HUMILIATED BY DEFEAT."*
*See ELEPHANTMEN #35
"OBADIAH DETERMINED NEVER TO BE A SLAVE AGAIN. NEVER TO BE DEFEATED AGAIN."
"IN THAT, WE ARE AS ONE."

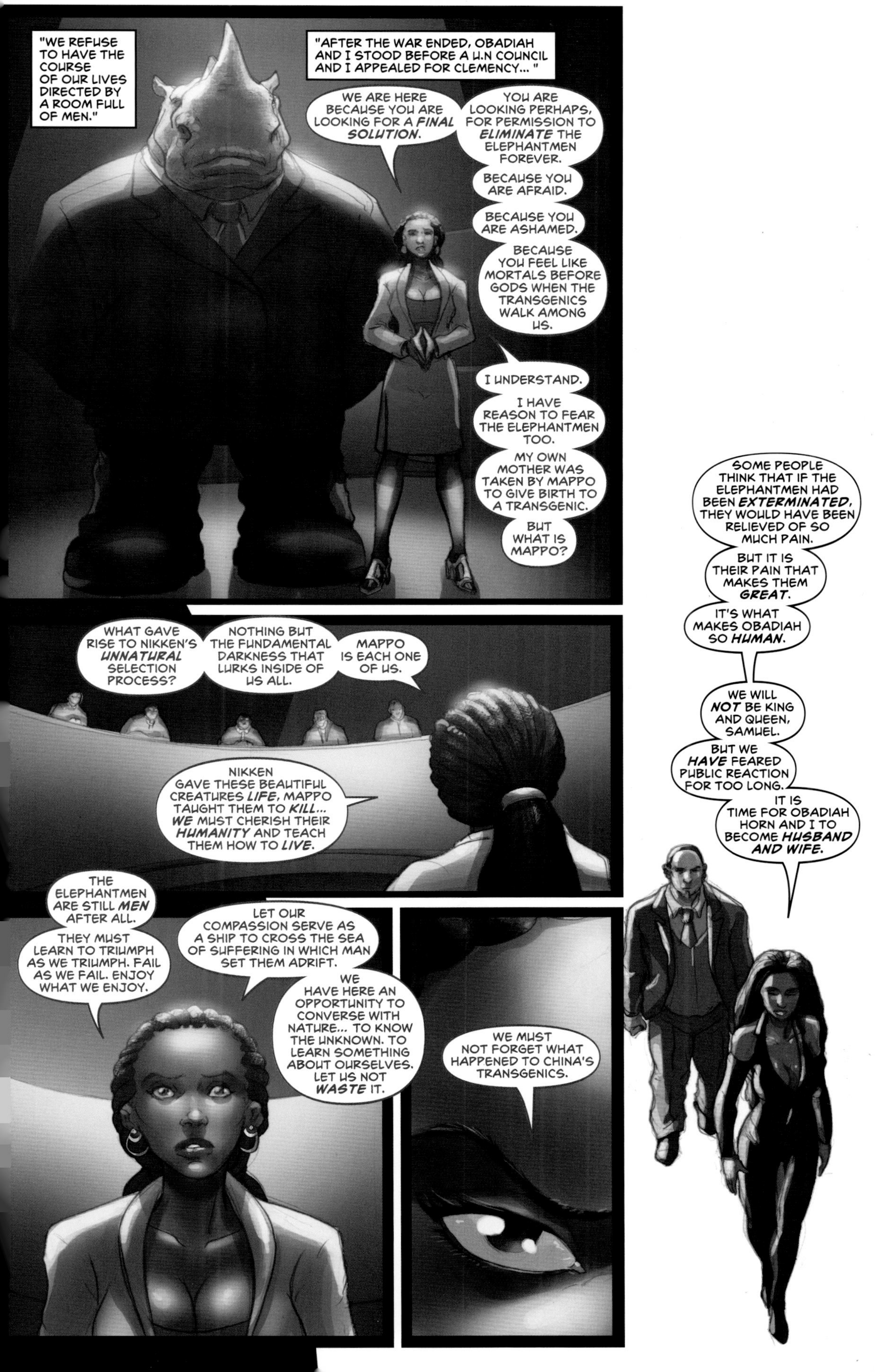

"WE REFUSE TO HAVE THE COURSE OF OUR LIVES DIRECTED BY A ROOM FULL OF MEN."
"AFTER THE WAR ENDED, OBADIAH AND I STOOD BEFORE A U.N COUNCIL AND I APPEALED FOR CLEMENCY... "
WE ARE HERE BECAUSE YOU ARE LOOKING FOR A *FINAL SOLUTION*.
YOU ARE LOOKING PERHAPS, FOR PERMISSION TO *ELIMINATE* THE ELEPHANTMEN FOREVER.
BECAUSE YOU ARE AFRAID.
BECAUSE YOU ARE ASHAMED.
BECAUSE YOU FEEL LIKE MORTALS BEFORE GODS WHEN THE TRANSGENICS WALK AMONG US.
I UNDERSTAND.
I HAVE REASON TO FEAR THE ELEPHANTMEN TOO.
MY OWN MOTHER WAS TAKEN BY MAPPO TO GIVE BIRTH TO A TRANSGENIC.
BUT WHAT IS MAPPO?
WHAT GAVE RISE TO NIKKEN'S *UNNATURAL* SELECTION PROCESS?
NOTHING BUT THE FUNDAMENTAL DARKNESS THAT LURKS INSIDE OF US ALL.
MAPPO IS EACH ONE OF US.
NIKKEN GAVE THESE BEAUTIFUL CREATURES *LIFE*, MAPPO TAUGHT THEM TO *KILL*... *WE* MUST CHERISH THEIR *HUMANITY* AND TEACH THEM HOW TO *LIVE*.
THE ELEPHANTMEN ARE STILL *MEN* AFTER ALL.
THEY MUST LEARN TO TRIUMPH AS WE TRIUMPH. FAIL AS WE FAIL. ENJOY WHAT WE ENJOY.
LET OUR COMPASSION SERVE AS A SHIP TO CROSS THE SEA OF SUFFERING IN WHICH MAN SET THEM ADRIFT.
WE HAVE HERE AN OPPORTUNITY TO CONVERSE WITH NATURE... TO KNOW THE UNKNOWN. TO LEARN SOMETHING ABOUT OURSELVES. LET US NOT *WASTE* IT.
WE MUST NOT FORGET WHAT HAPPENED TO CHINA'S TRANSGENICS.
SOME PEOPLE THINK THAT IF THE ELEPHANTMEN HAD BEEN *EXTERMINATED*, THEY WOULD HAVE BEEN RELIEVED OF SO MUCH PAIN.
BUT IT IS THEIR PAIN THAT MAKES THEM *GREAT*.
IT'S WHAT MAKES OBADIAH SO *HUMAN*.
WE WILL *NOT* BE KING AND QUEEN, SAMUEL.
BUT WE *HAVE* FEARED PUBLIC REACTION FOR TOO LONG.
IT IS TIME FOR OBADIAH HORN AND I TO BECOME *HUSBAND AND WIFE*.

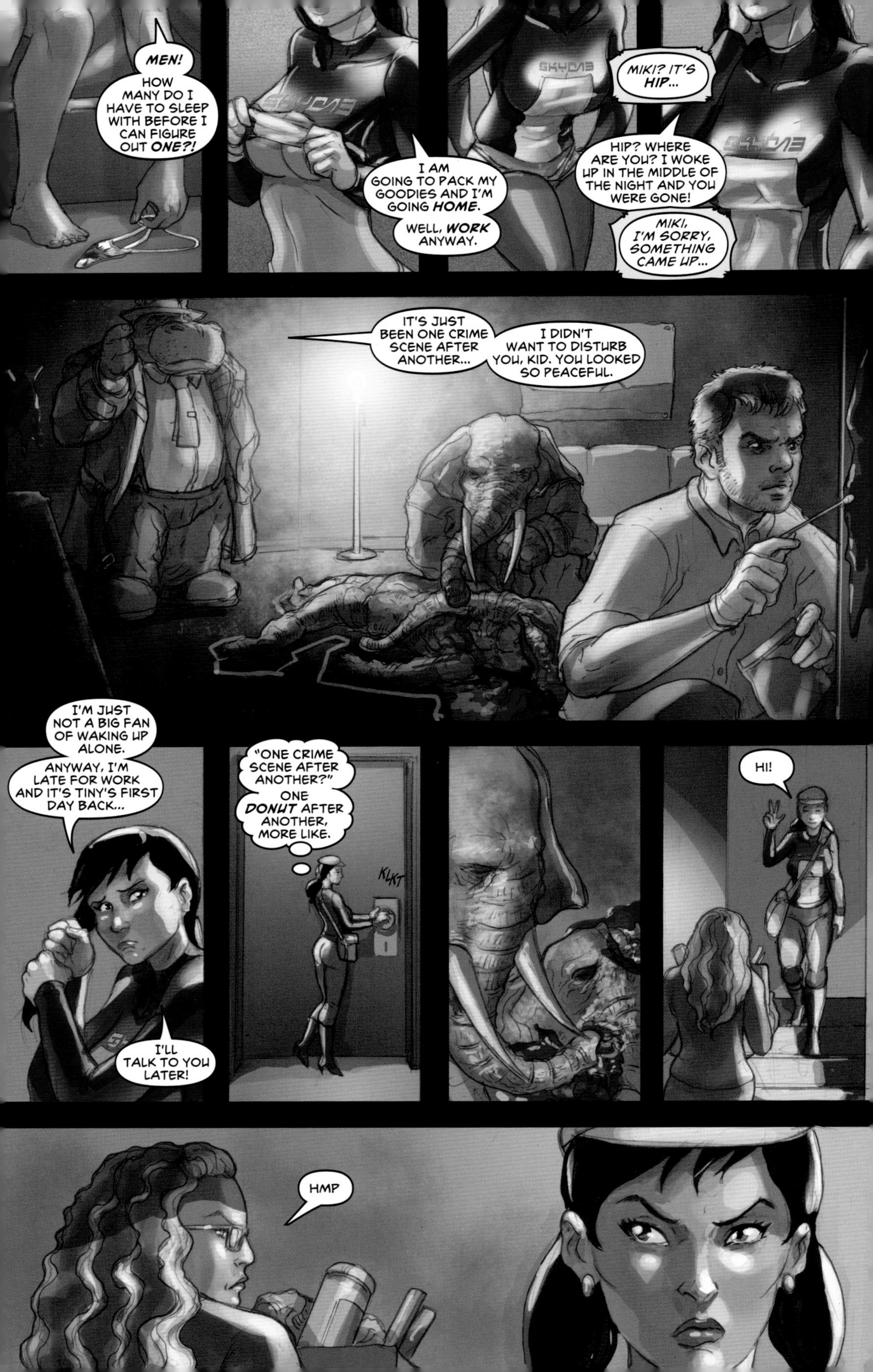
MEN!
HOW MANY DO I HAVE TO SLEEP WITH BEFORE I CAN FIGURE OUT ONE?!
SKYDAB
I AM GOING TO PACK MY GOODIES AND I'M GOING HOME.
WELL, WORK ANYWAY.
MIKI? IT'S HIP...
HIP? WHERE ARE YOU? I WOKE UP IN THE MIDDLE OF THE NIGHT AND YOU WERE GONE!
MIKI, I'M SORRY, SOMETHING CAME UP...
IT'S JUST BEEN ONE CRIME SCENE AFTER ANOTHER...
I DIDN'T WANT TO DISTURB YOU, KID. YOU LOOKED SO PEACEFUL.
I'M JUST NOT A BIG FAN OF WAKING UP ALONE.
ANYWAY, I'M LATE FOR WORK AND IT'S TINY'S FIRST DAY BACK...
I'LL TALK TO YOU LATER!
"ONE CRIME SCENE AFTER ANOTHER?"
ONE DONUT AFTER ANOTHER, MORE LIKE.
KLKT
HI!
HMP

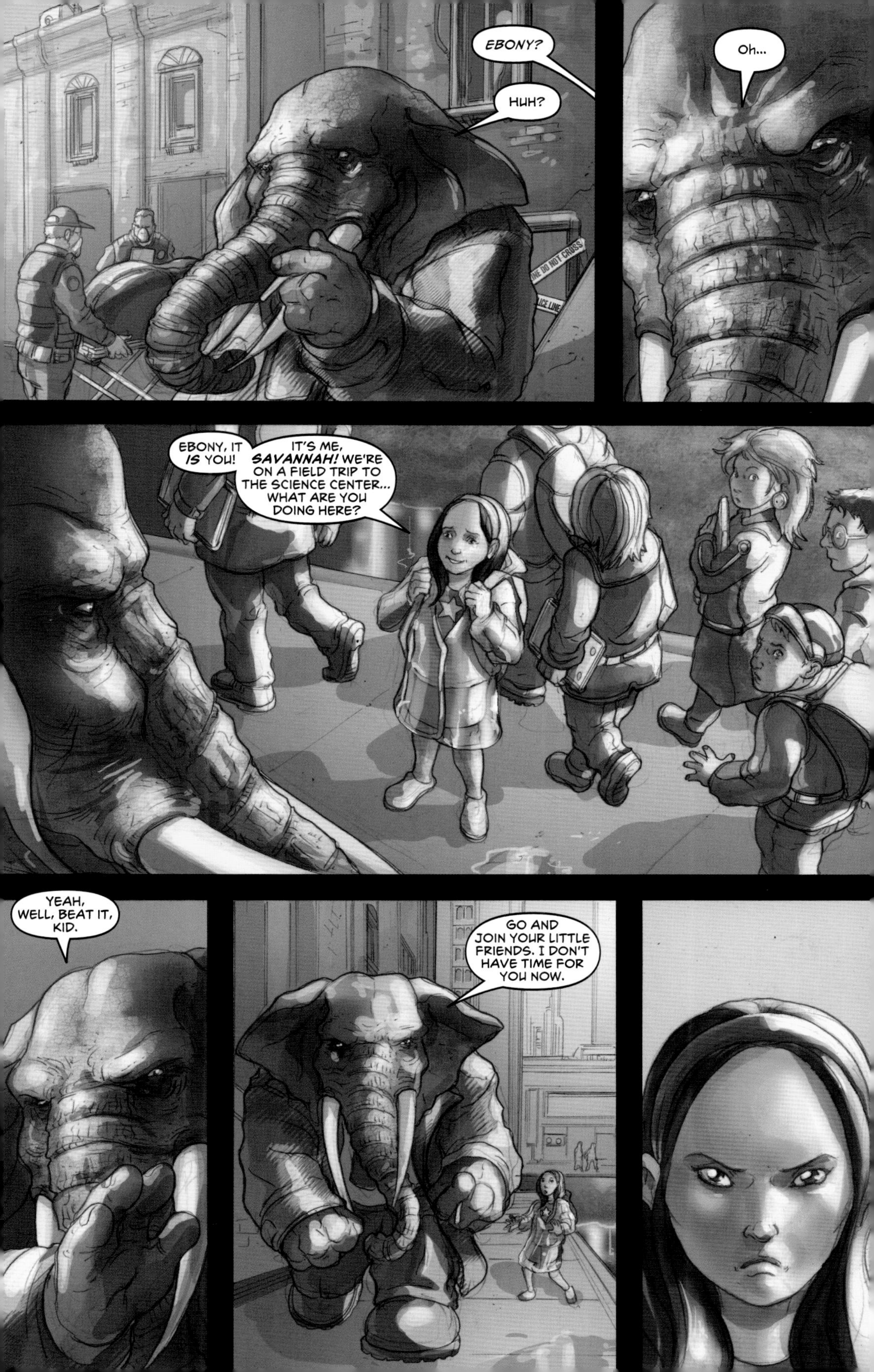
EBONY?
HUH?
Oh...
EBONY, IT *IS* YOU!
IT'S ME, *SAVANNAH!* WE'RE ON A FIELD TRIP TO THE SCIENCE CENTER... WHAT ARE YOU DOING HERE?
YEAH, WELL, BEAT IT, KID.
GO AND JOIN YOUR LITTLE FRIENDS. I DON'T HAVE TIME FOR YOU NOW.

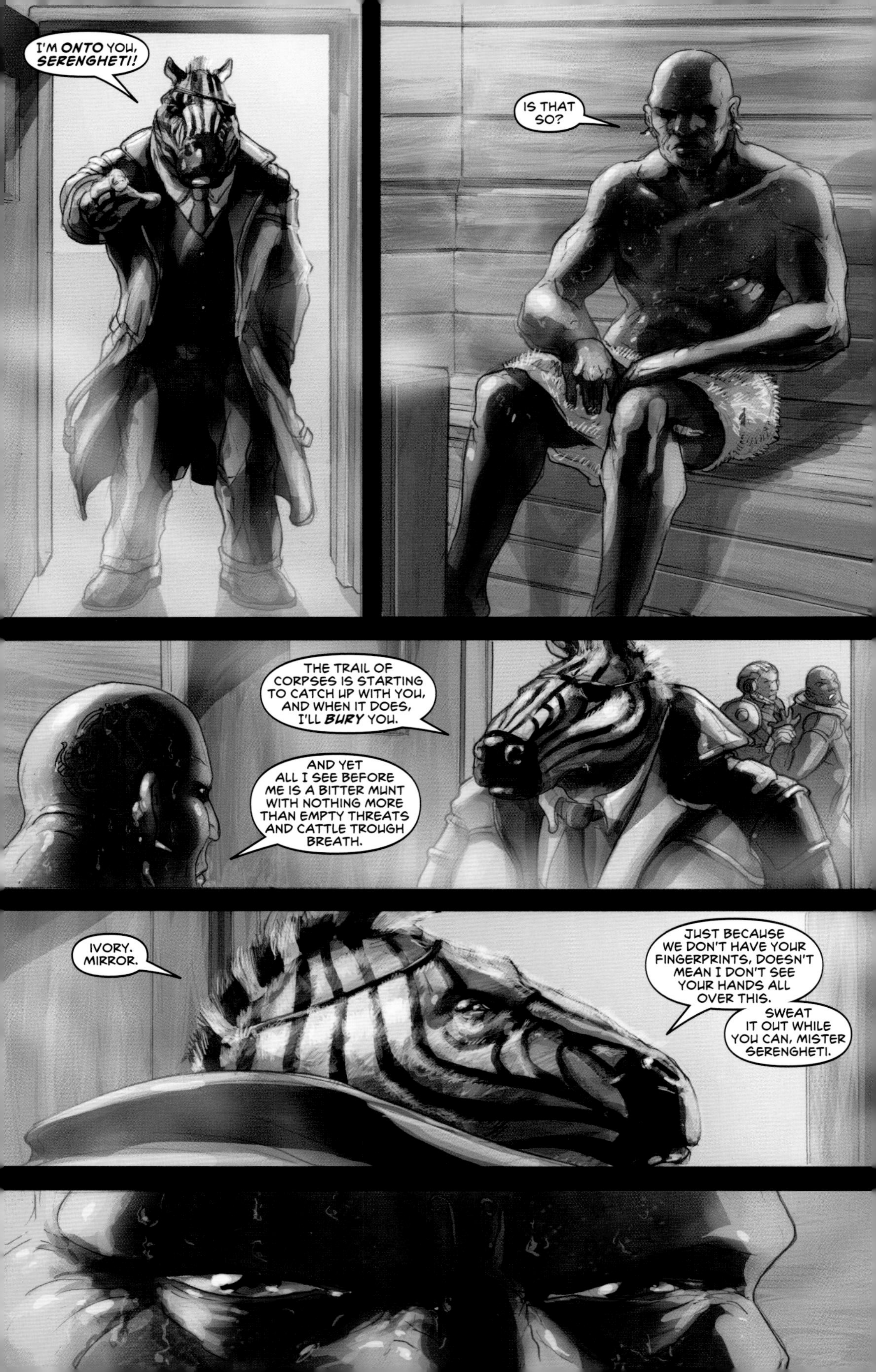
I'M ONTO YOU, SERENGHETI!
IS THAT SO?
THE TRAIL OF CORPSES IS STARTING TO CATCH UP WITH YOU, AND WHEN IT DOES, I'LL BURY YOU.
AND YET ALL I SEE BEFORE ME IS A BITTER MUNT WITH NOTHING MORE THAN EMPTY THREATS AND CATTLE TROUGH BREATH.
IVORY. MIRROR.
JUST BECAUSE WE DON'T HAVE YOUR FINGERPRINTS, DOESN'T MEAN I DON'T SEE YOUR HANDS ALL OVER THIS.
SWEAT IT OUT WHILE YOU CAN, MISTER SERENGHETI.

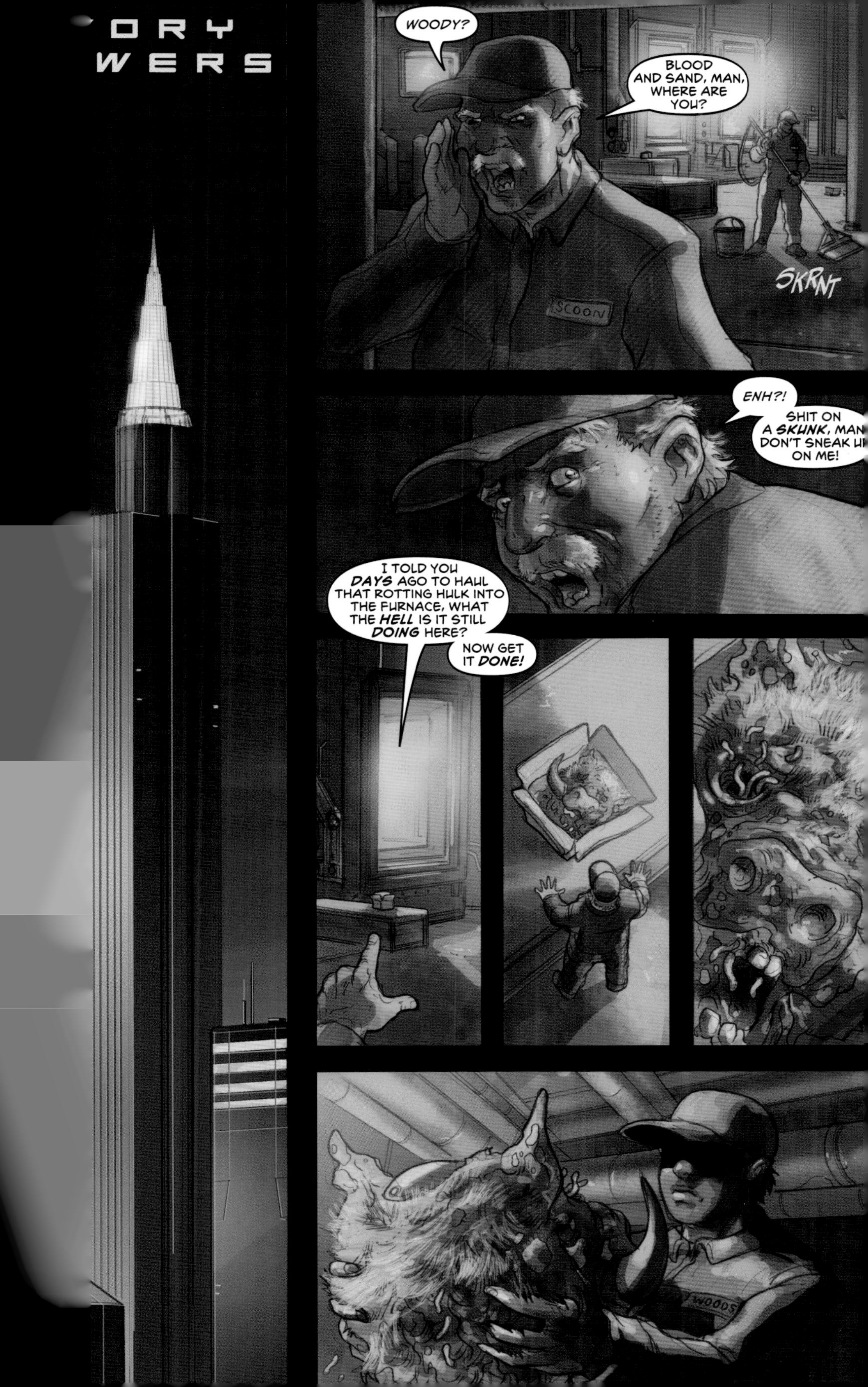
ORY
WERS
WOODY?
BLOOD AND SAND, MAN, WHERE ARE YOU?
SCOON
SKRNT
ENH?!
SHIT ON A SKUNK, MAN DON'T SNEAK U ON ME!
I TOLD YOU DAYS AGO TO HAUL THAT ROTTING HULK INTO THE FURNACE, WHAT THE HELL IS IT STILL DOING HERE?
NOW GET IT DONE!
WOODS

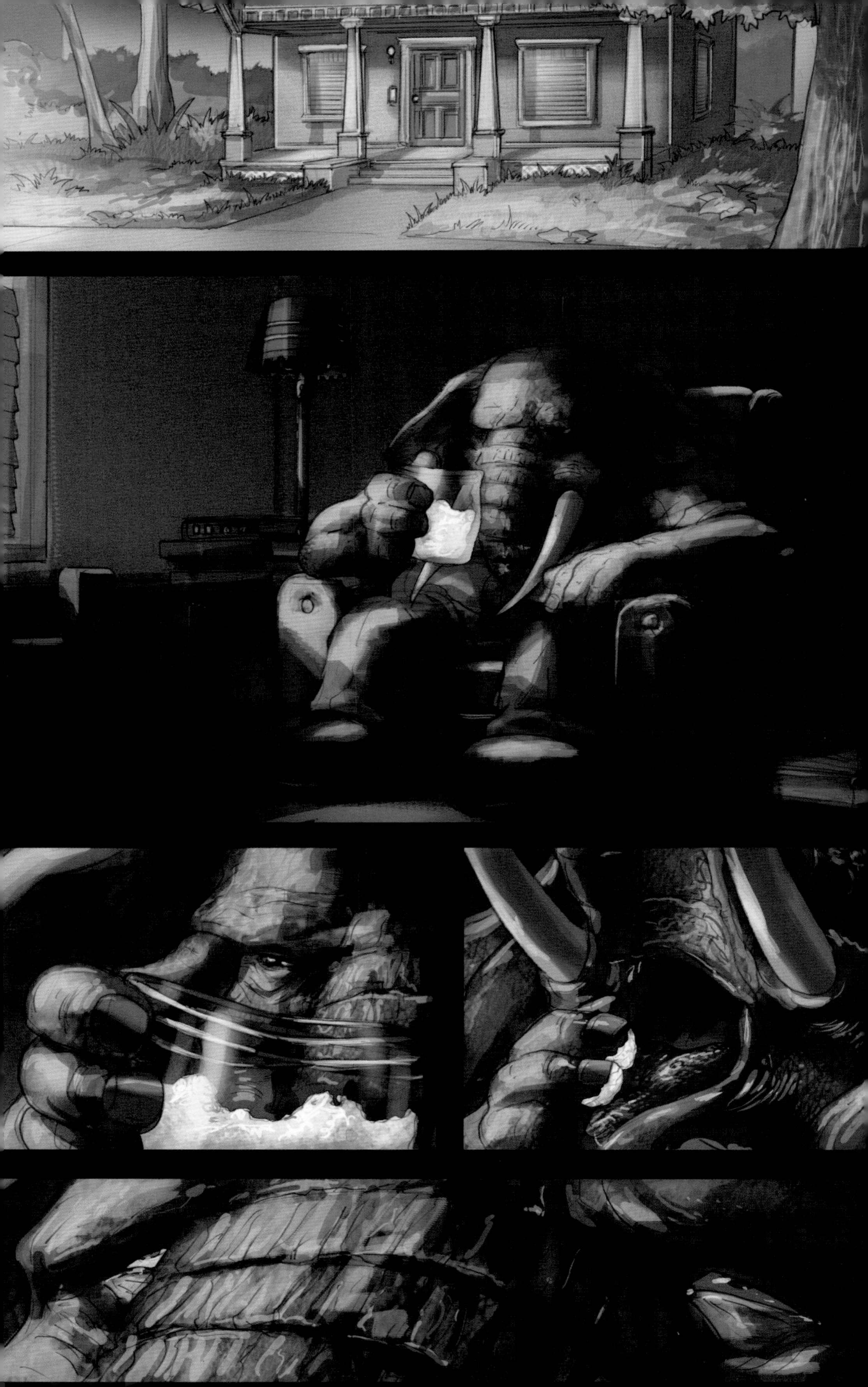

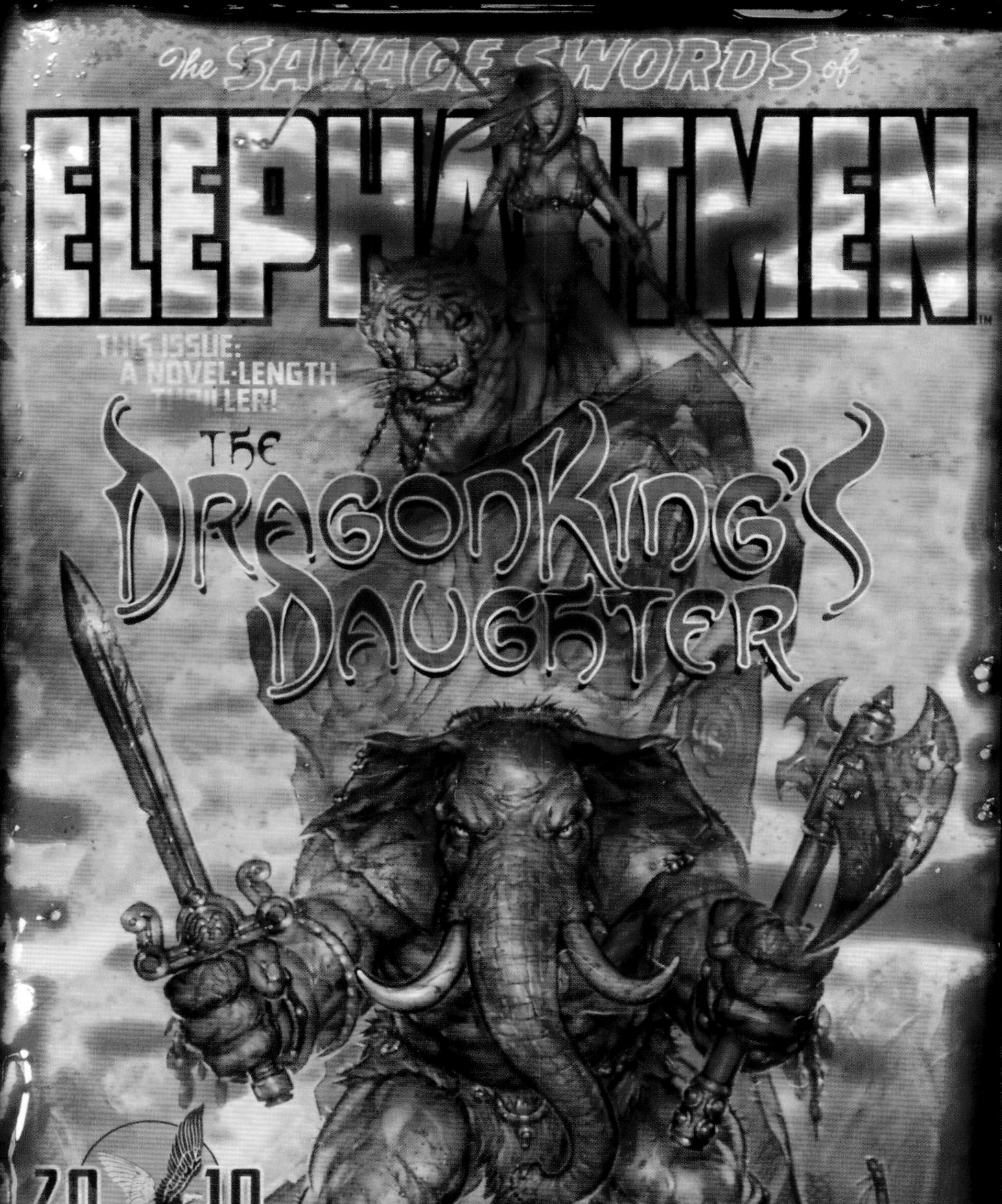

The SAVAGE SWORDS of
ELEPHANTMEN
THIS ISSUE: A NOVEL-LENGTH THRILLER!
THE DRAGONKING'S DAUGHTER
2010 EAGLE AWARD WINNER
Image
MAN AND ELEPHANTMAN
#3 OF 3
#32
JUNE
$3.99
STARKINGS · MEDELLIN · ROSHELL · COOK

"Nobody could stand an eternity of Heaven."

George Bernard Shaw
Man and Superman

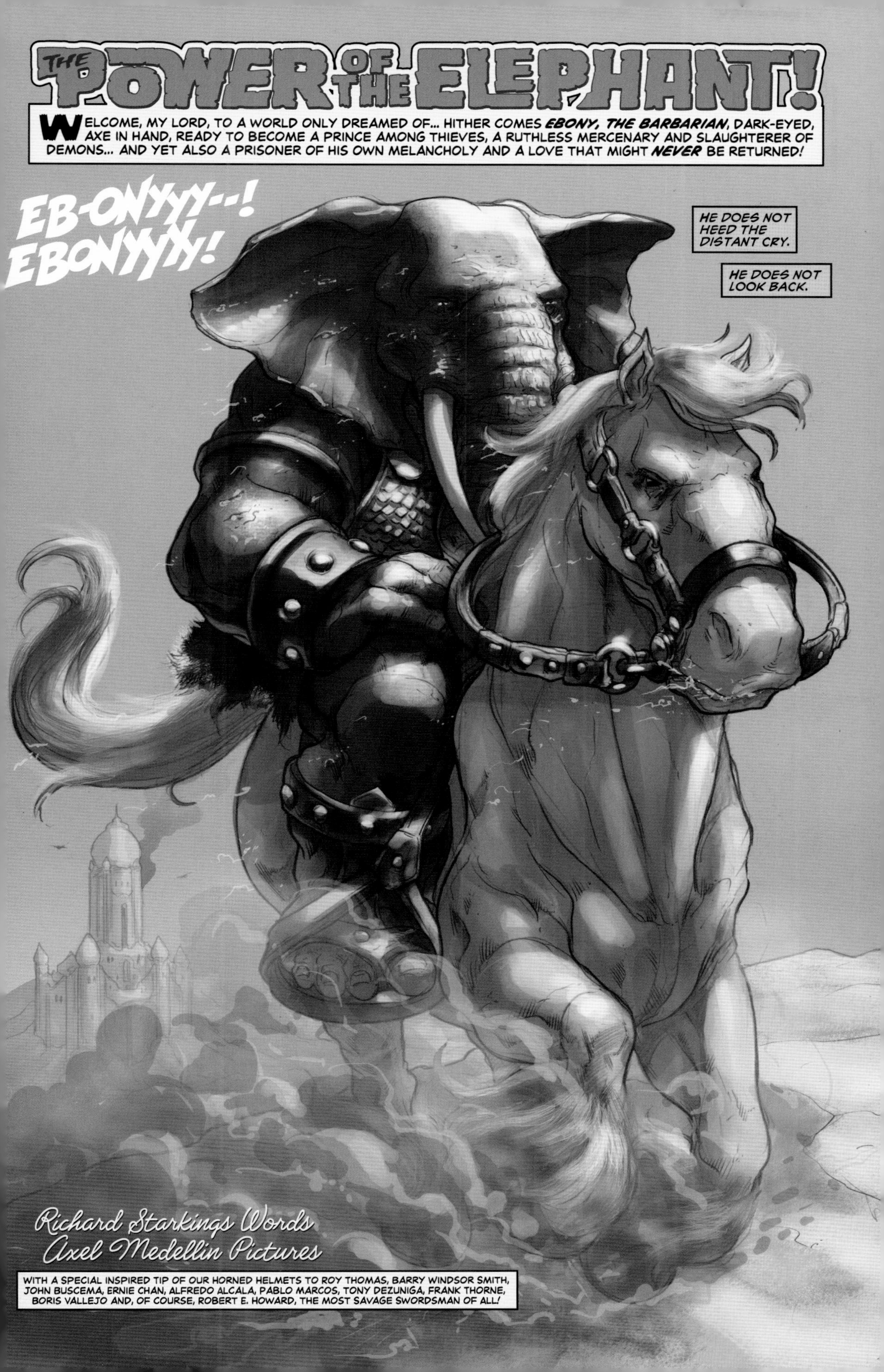
THE POWER OF THE ELEPHANT!
WELCOME, MY LORD, TO A WORLD ONLY DREAMED OF... HITHER COMES EBONY, THE BARBARIAN, DARK-EYED, AXE IN HAND, READY TO BECOME A PRINCE AMONG THIEVES, A RUTHLESS MERCENARY AND SLAUGHTERER OF DEMONS... AND YET ALSO A PRISONER OF HIS OWN MELANCHOLY AND A LOVE THAT MIGHT NEVER BE RETURNED!
EB-ONYYY--! EBONYYYY!
HE DOES NOT HEED THE DISTANT CRY.
HE DOES NOT LOOK BACK.
Richard Starkings Words
Axel Medellin Pictures
WITH A SPECIAL INSPIRED TIP OF OUR HORNED HELMETS TO ROY THOMAS, BARRY WINDSOR SMITH, JOHN BUSCEMA, ERNIE CHAN, ALFREDO ALCALA, PABLO MARCOS, TONY DEZUNIGA, FRANK THORNE, BORIS VALLEJO AND, OF COURSE, ROBERT E. HOWARD, THE MOST SAVAGE SWORDSMAN OF ALL!

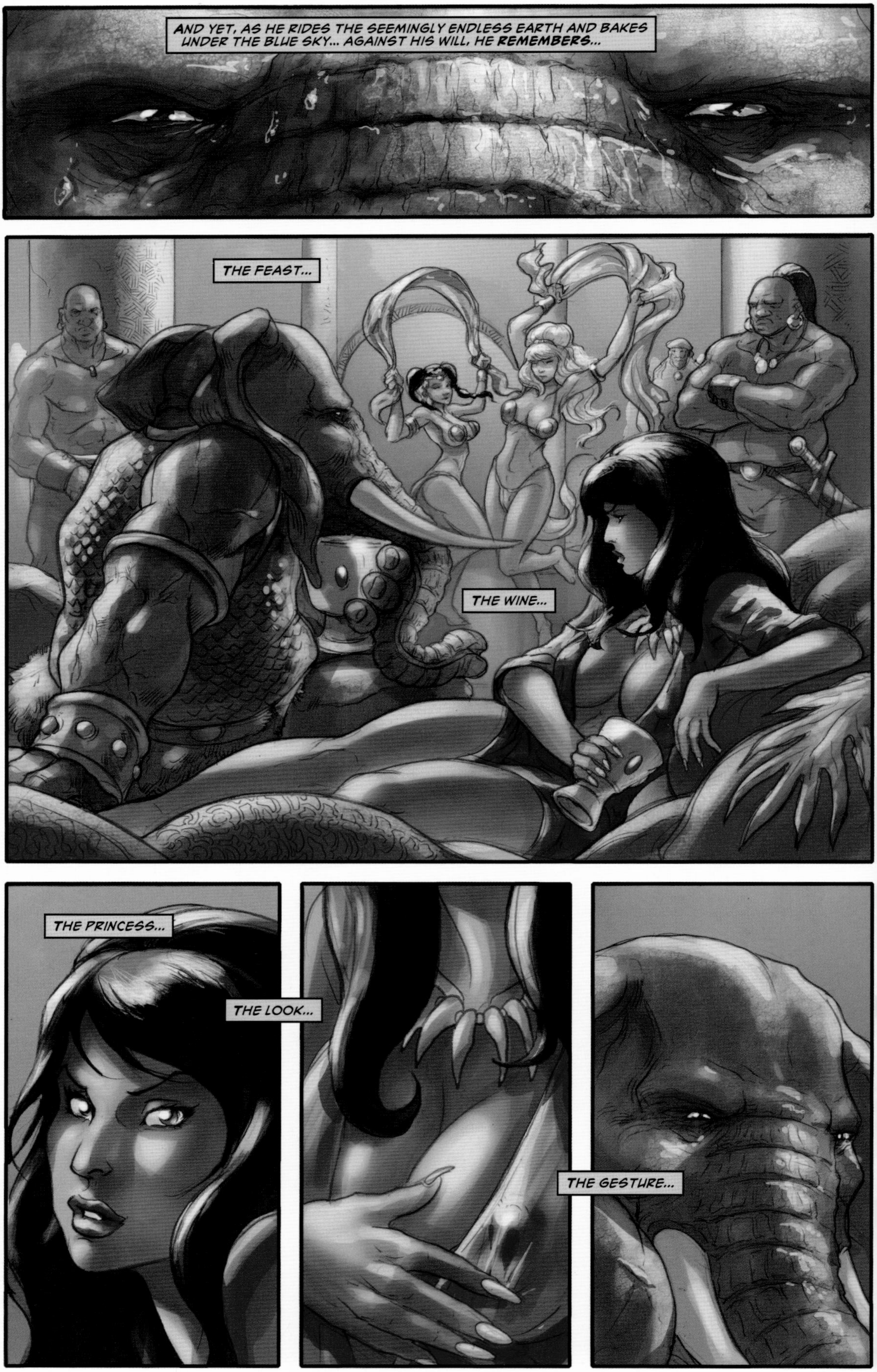
AND YET, AS HE RIDES THE SEEMINGLY ENDLESS EARTH AND BAKES UNDER THE BLUE SKY... AGAINST HIS WILL, HE REMEMBERS...
THE FEAST...
THE WINE...
THE PRINCESS...
THE LOOK...
THE GESTURE...

THE HALLWAY...

THE BEDROOM...

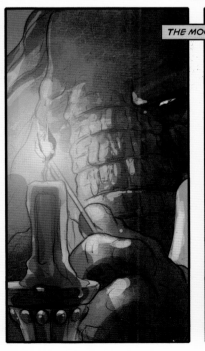

THE MOONLIGHT...

THE KISS...

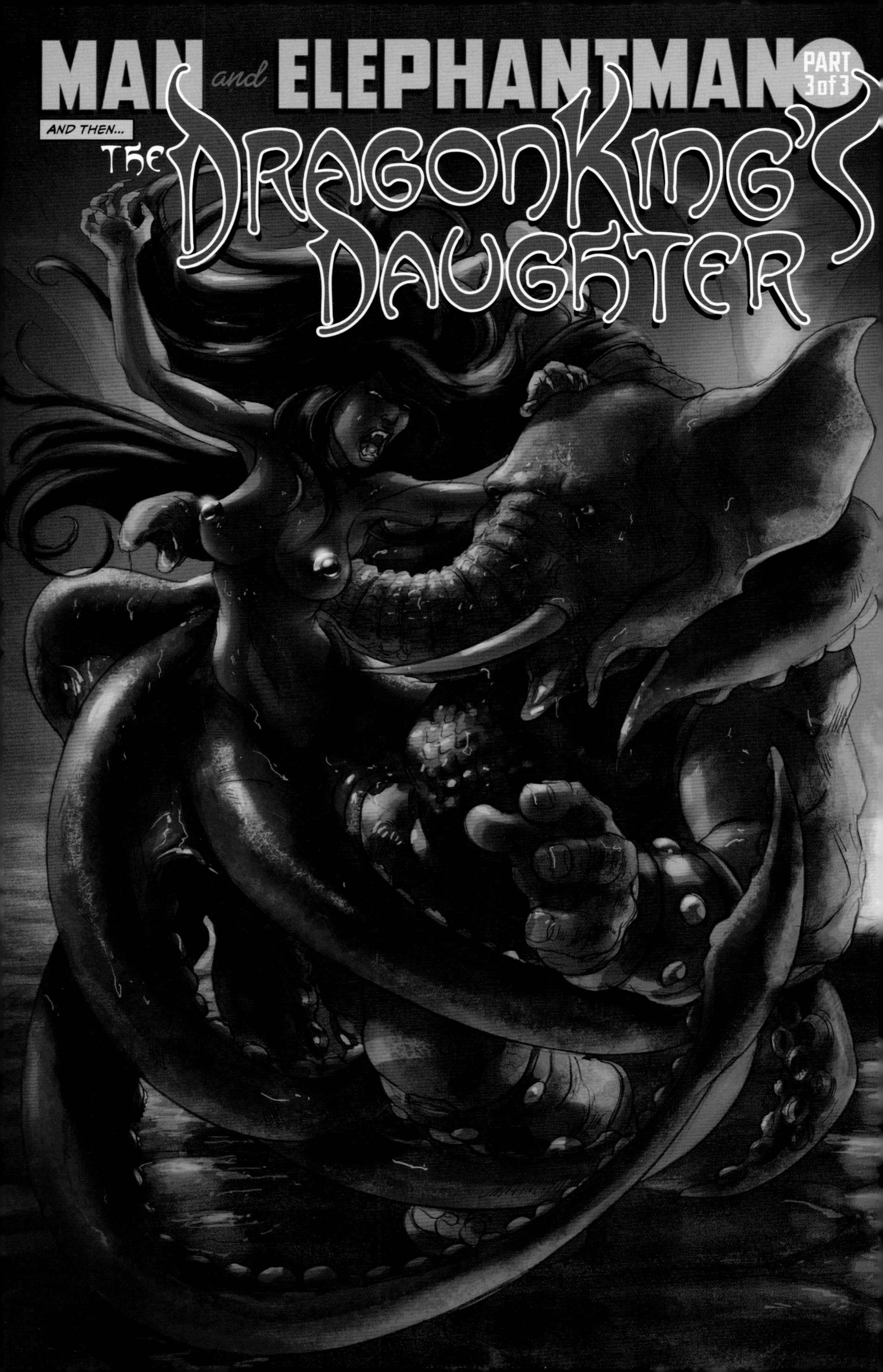
MAN and ELEPHANTMAN
PART 3 of 3
AND THEN...
THE DRAGONKING'S DAUGHTER

He had heard the tales, of course.

Stories of the palace of the divine void...

Of the wizard who inhabited the pavilion of the dark pearl.

A dragon king who commanded both fire and water and could turn the most opulent palace into a burning hell if he so wished...

It was said his daughter moved freely between the waterworld and the human realm promising enlightenment and immortality to any warrior who fell under her spell...

Yes, he had heard all the tales...

Ebony still didn't believe them.

If a creature had a neck, he could strangle it... if it had a heart, he could run his sword through it.

And if it came from some burning hell, or some cold unfathomable place where even sharks felt fear... it could be cast back there, never to return!

Ebony lived only in a world where might equalled right and even the driest thirst could be quenched with the next flagon of mead...

...and lost loves were forgotten by looking into the eyes of the next alehouse wench...

No, he can never go back, no matter how much the voice calls out to him...

He will never venture again across this barren land, this grassy wasteland they call the shamorian... the shamorian...

Hunh, somehow he cannot remember what they call it.

No matter that his heart jumps as the voice calls his name... he must put it out of his mind... a soldier has no time for love... or remembrance....

EB-ONYYY--! EBONYYYY!

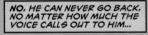

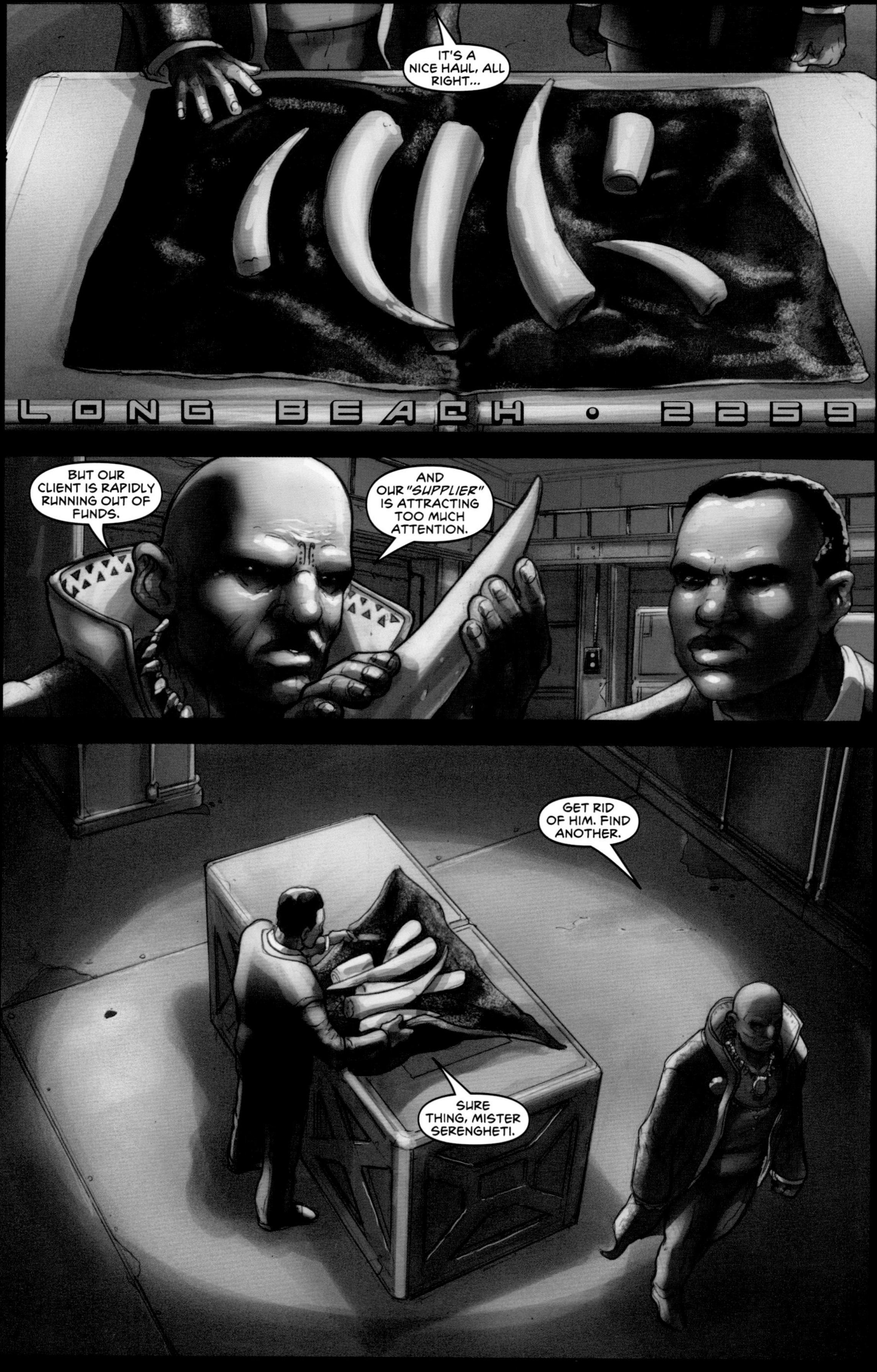
IT'S A NICE HAUL, ALL RIGHT...
LONG BEACH • 2259
BUT OUR CLIENT IS RAPIDLY RUNNING OUT OF FUNDS.
AND OUR "SUPPLIER" IS ATTRACTING TOO MUCH ATTENTION.
GET RID OF HIM. FIND ANOTHER.
SURE THING, MISTER SERENGHETI.

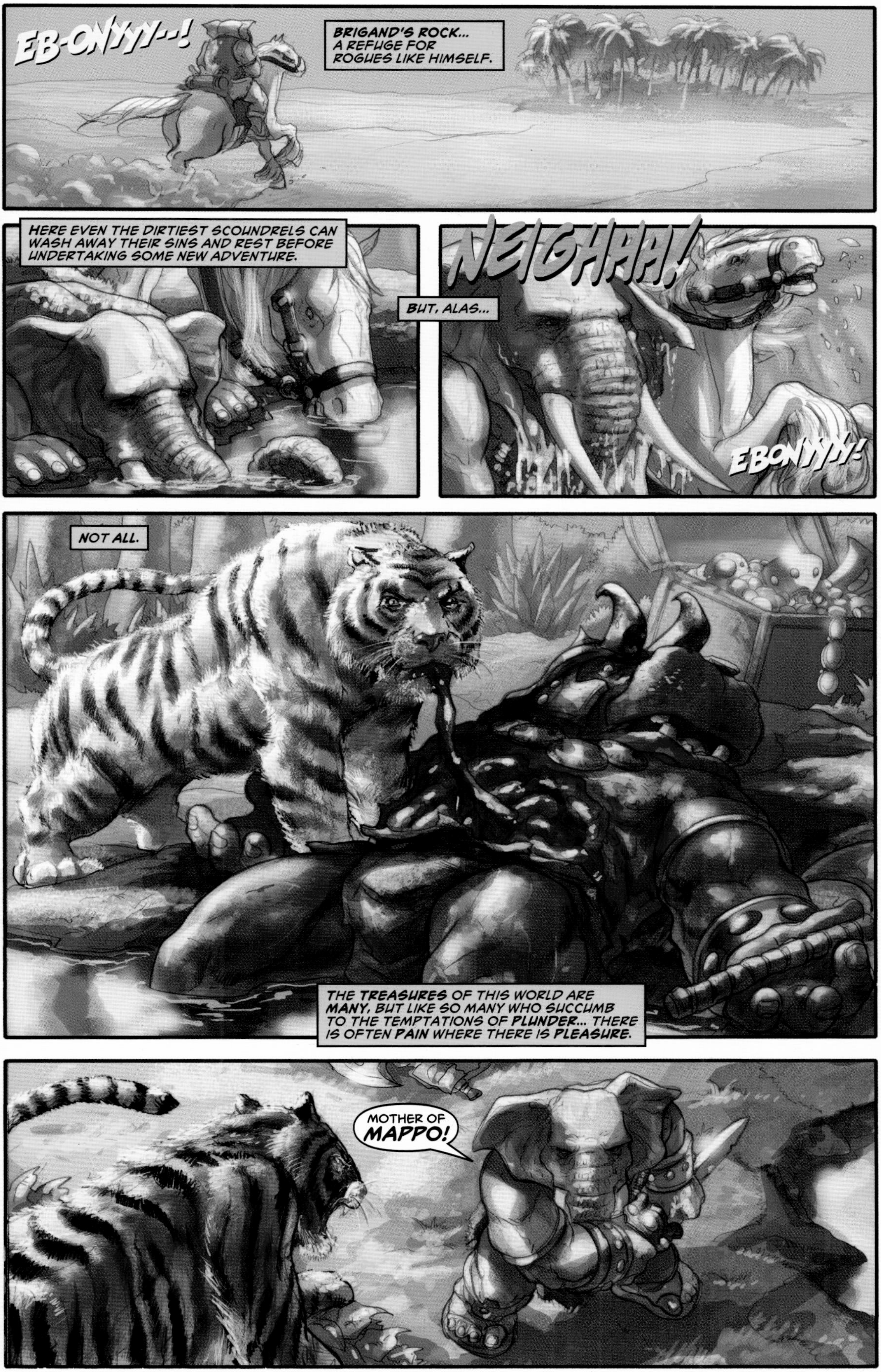
EB-ONYYY--!
BRIGAND'S ROCK... A REFUGE FOR ROGUES LIKE HIMSELF.
HERE EVEN THE DIRTIEST SCOUNDRELS CAN WASH AWAY THEIR SINS AND REST BEFORE UNDERTAKING SOME NEW ADVENTURE.
BUT, ALAS...
NEIGHHH!
EBONYYY!
NOT ALL.
THE TREASURES OF THIS WORLD ARE MANY, BUT LIKE SO MANY WHO SUCCUMB TO THE TEMPTATIONS OF PLUNDER... THERE IS OFTEN PAIN WHERE THERE IS PLEASURE.
MOTHER OF MAPPO!

HOLD!

THESE CATS MEAN YOU NO HARM... LIKE YOU, THEY ARE SIMPLY HERE TO EAT, DRINK AND BE ON THEIR WAY.

IS THAT SO? YET HOW CAN I BE SURE THEY WON'T FEAST ON *ME* NEXT?

YOU DON'T... BUT MY KITTENS PREFER A *SOFT* UNDERBELLY...

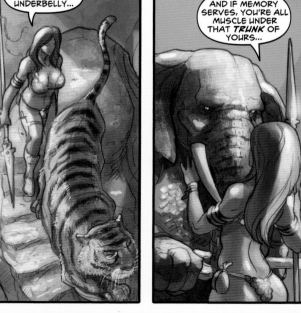

AND IF MEMORY SERVES, YOU'RE ALL MUSCLE UNDER THAT *TRUNK* OF YOURS...

IF *I* RECALL CORRECTLY, LAST TIME WE MET YOU TOOK SOMETHING THAT *BELONGED* TO ME...

SO WERE YOU CALLING ME TO *RETURN* WHAT WAS MINE, VANYA?

CALLING YOU... WHY WOULD *I* HAVE NEED OF A MAN...?

DID YOU THINK YOU MIGHT *ESCAPE* MY DOMAIN?

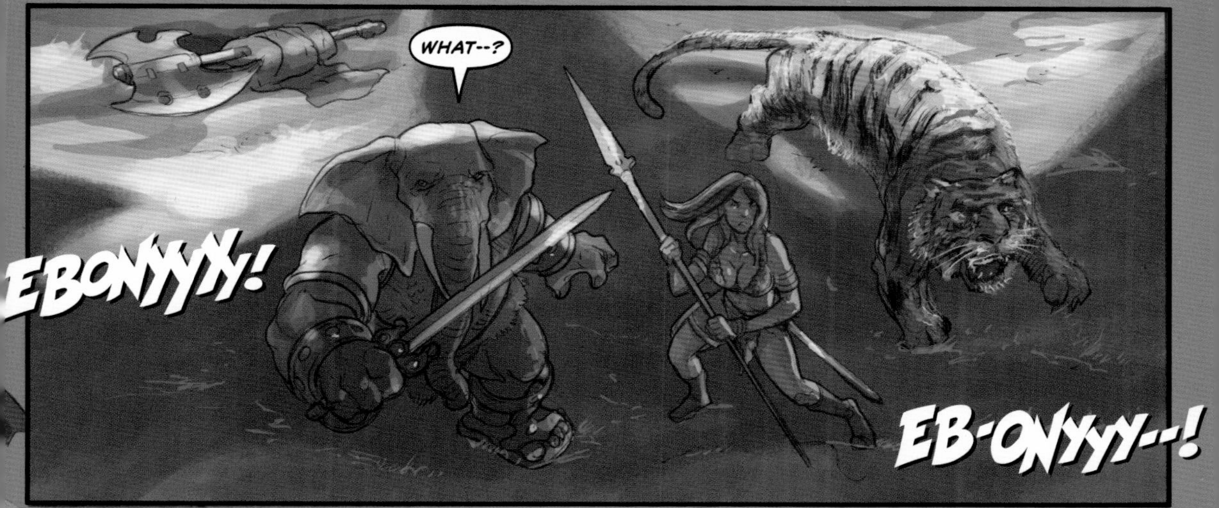
WHAT--?
EBONYYYY!
EB-ONYYY--!
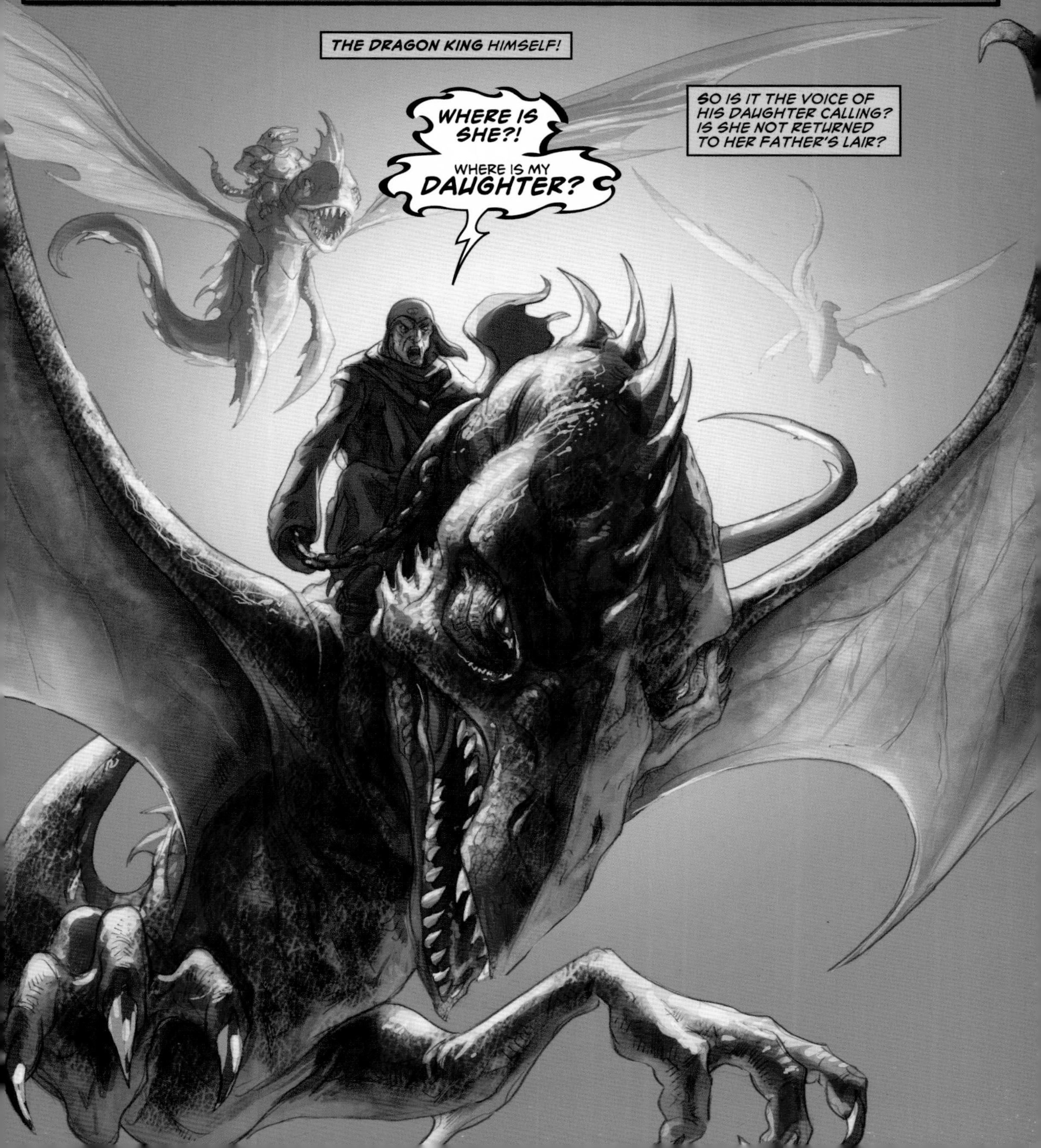
THE DRAGON KING HIMSELF!
SO IS IT THE VOICE OF HIS DAUGHTER CALLING? IS SHE NOT RETURNED TO HER FATHER'S LAIR?
WHERE IS SHE?!
WHERE IS MY DAUGHTER?

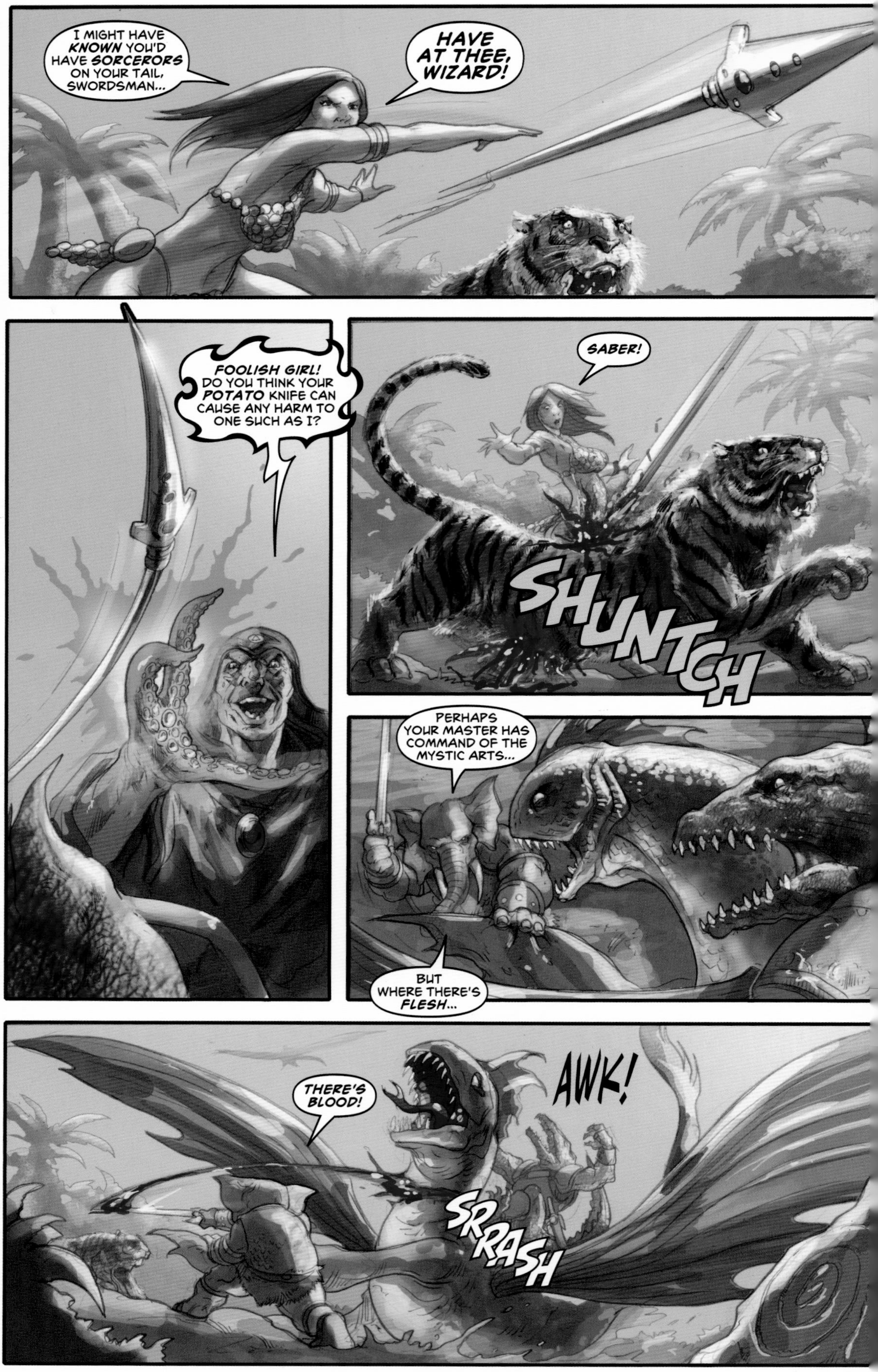
I MIGHT HAVE KNOWN YOU'D HAVE SORCERORS ON YOUR TAIL, SWORDSMAN...
HAVE AT THEE, WIZARD!
FOOLISH GIRL! DO YOU THINK YOUR POTATO KNIFE CAN CAUSE ANY HARM TO ONE SUCH AS I?
SABER!
SHUNTCH
PERHAPS YOUR MASTER HAS COMMAND OF THE MYSTIC ARTS...
BUT WHERE THERE'S FLESH...
THERE'S BLOOD!
AWK!
SRRASH

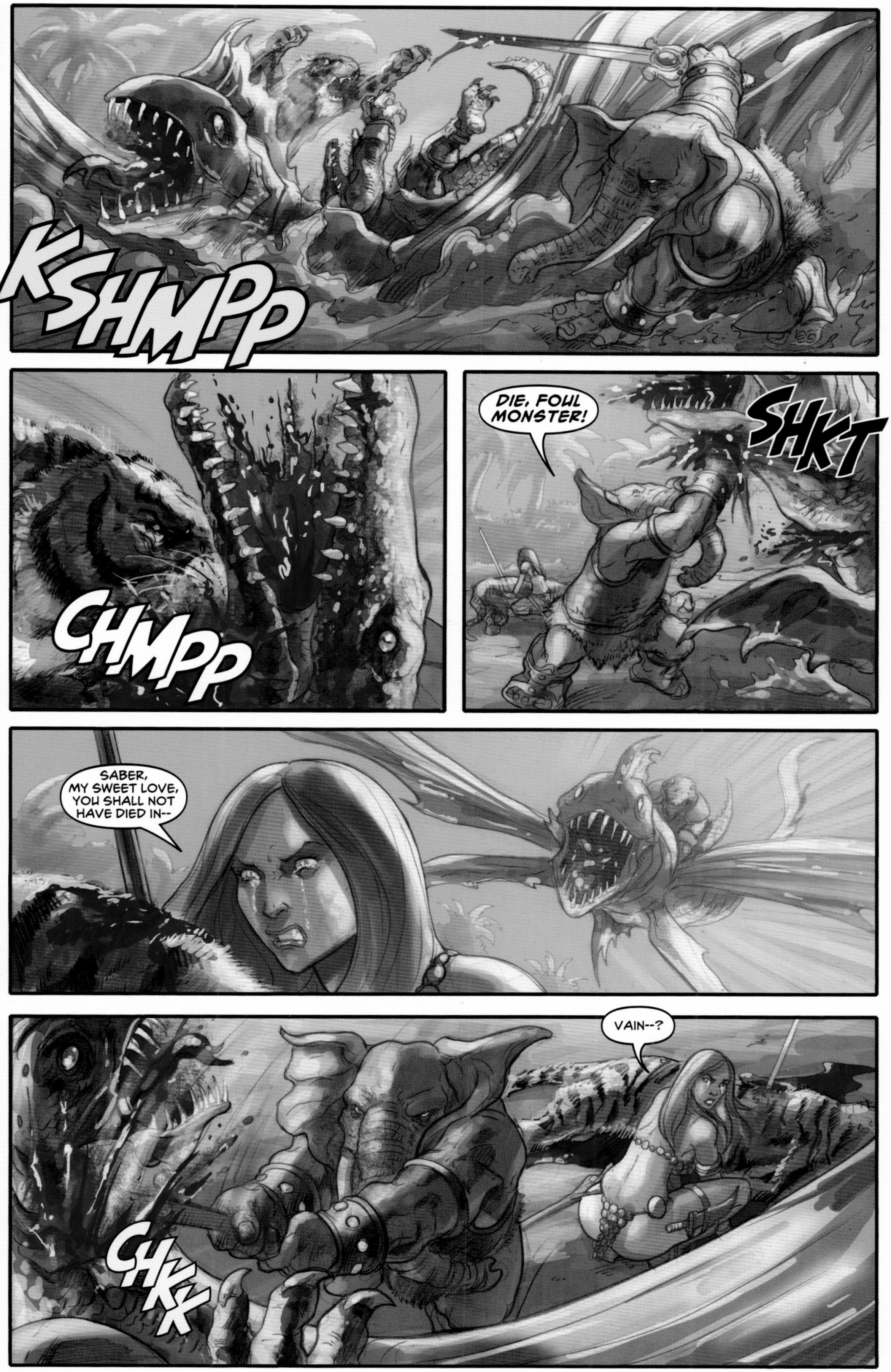
KSHMPP
CHMPP
DIE, FOUL MONSTER!
SHKT
SABER, MY SWEET LOVE, YOU SHALL NOT HAVE DIED IN--
VAIN--?
CHKK

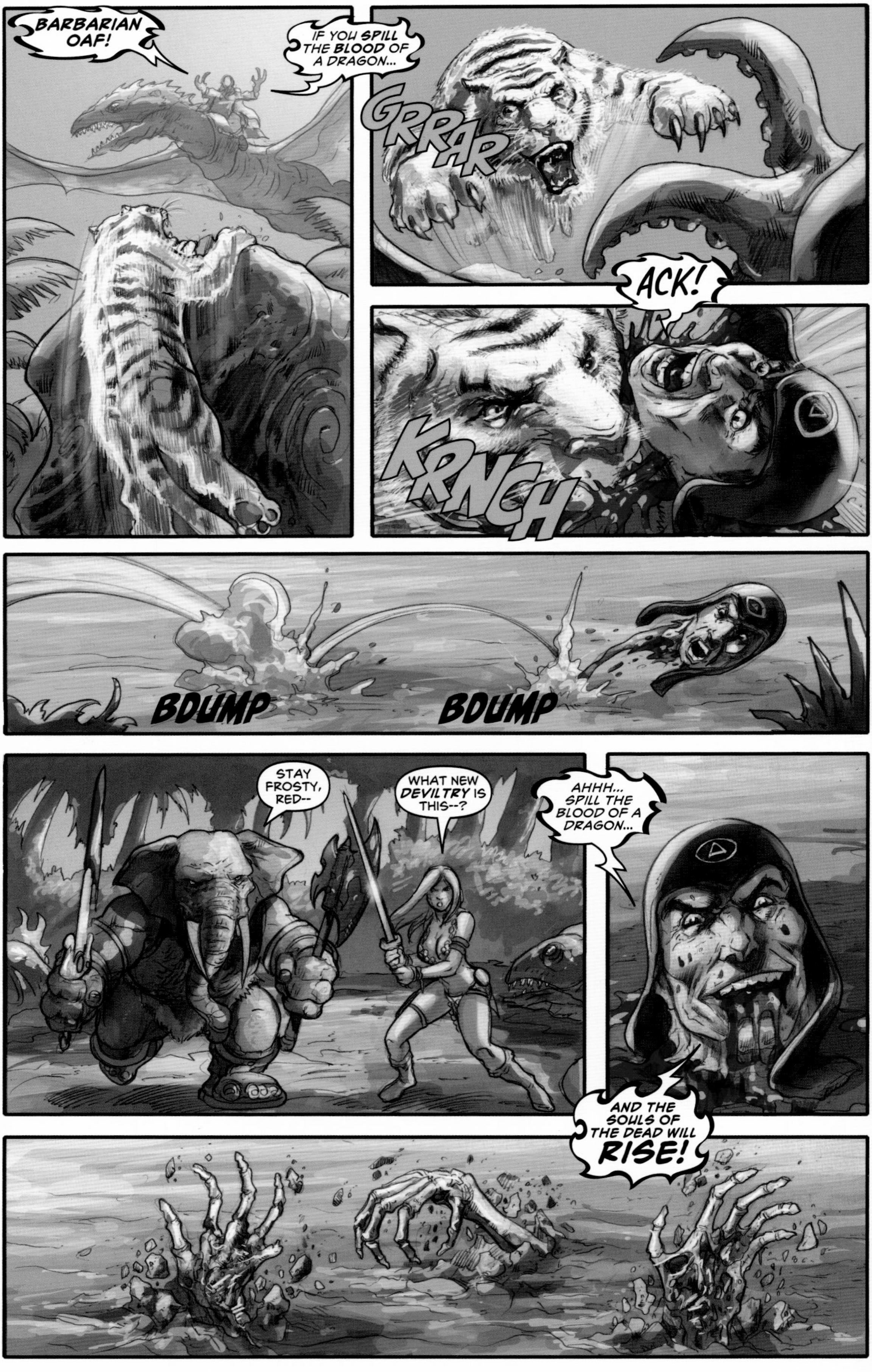
BARBARIAN OAF!
IF YOU SPILL THE BLOOD OF A DRAGON...
GRRAR
ACK!
KRNCH
BDUMP
BDUMP
STAY FROSTY, RED--
WHAT NEW DEVILTRY IS THIS--?
AHHH... SPILL THE BLOOD OF A DRAGON...
AND THE SOULS OF THE DEAD WILL RISE!

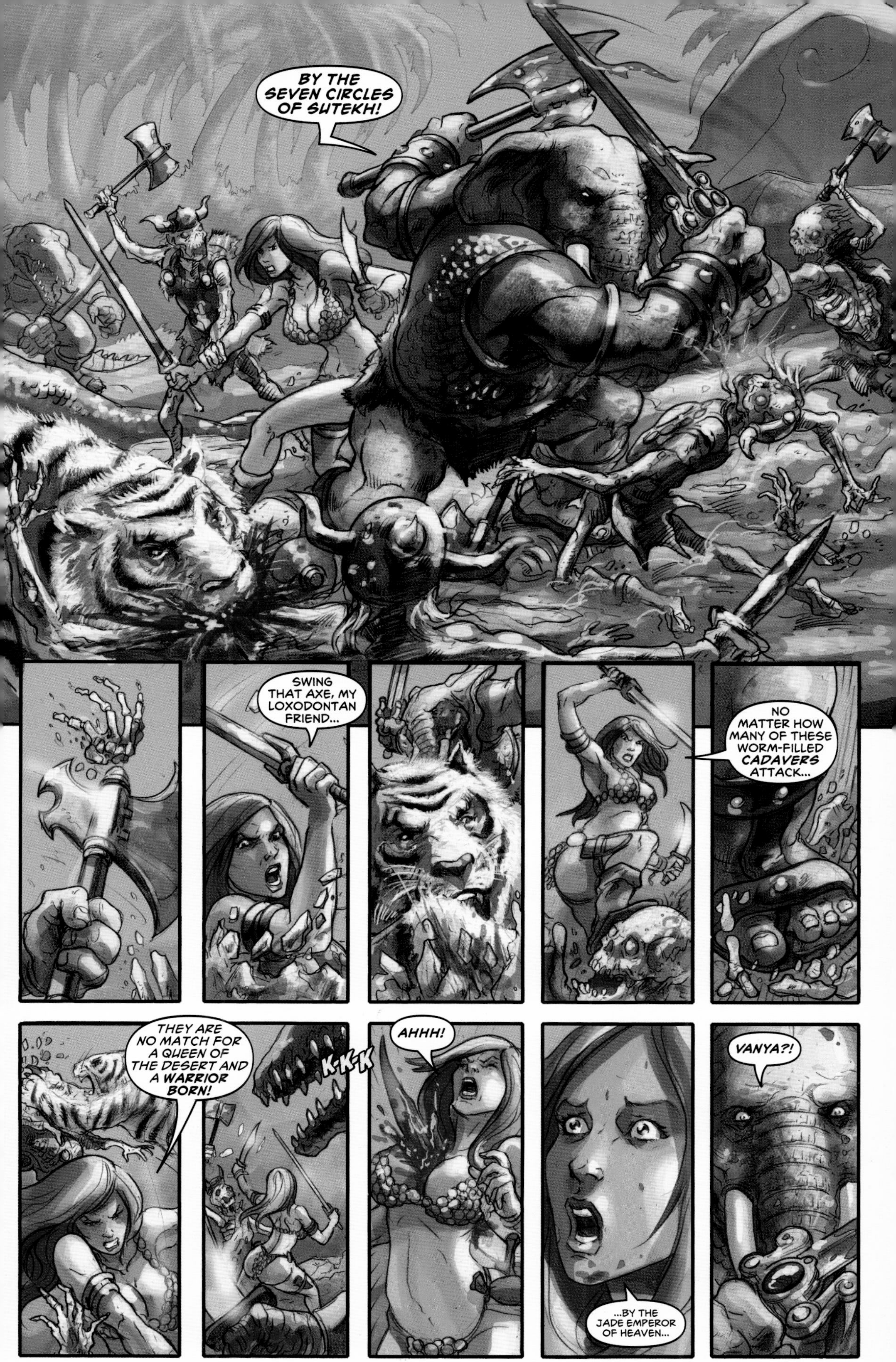
BY THE SEVEN CIRCLES OF SUTEKH!
SWING THAT AXE, MY LOXODONTAN FRIEND...
NO MATTER HOW MANY OF THESE WORM-FILLED CADAVERS ATTACK...
THEY ARE NO MATCH FOR A QUEEN OF THE DESERT AND A WARRIOR BORN!
K-K-K
AHHH!
...BY THE JADE EMPEROR OF HEAVEN...
VANYA?!

GRAR

VANYA... PLEASE... NO...

REMEMBER THIS AS YOUR FRIEND DIES IN YOUR ARMS, MAMMUT...

SWORD WILL *NEVER* DEFEAT SORCERY!

CHMPP

PERHAPS THAT IS SO, WIZARD... BUT TO A PREDATOR, YOU ARE STILL NOTHING MORE THAN PREY.

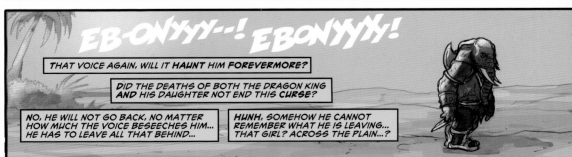

EB-ONyyy--! EBONyyy!

THAT VOICE AGAIN, WILL IT *HAUNT* HIM *FOREVERMORE?*

DID THE DEATHS OF BOTH THE DRAGON KING *AND* HIS DAUGHTER NOT END THIS *CURSE?*

NO, HE WILL NOT GO BACK, NO MATTER HOW MUCH THE VOICE BESEECHES HIM... HE HAS TO LEAVE ALL THAT BEHIND...

HUNH, SOMEHOW HE CANNOT REMEMBER WHAT HE IS LEAVING... THAT GIRL? ACROSS THE PLAIN...?

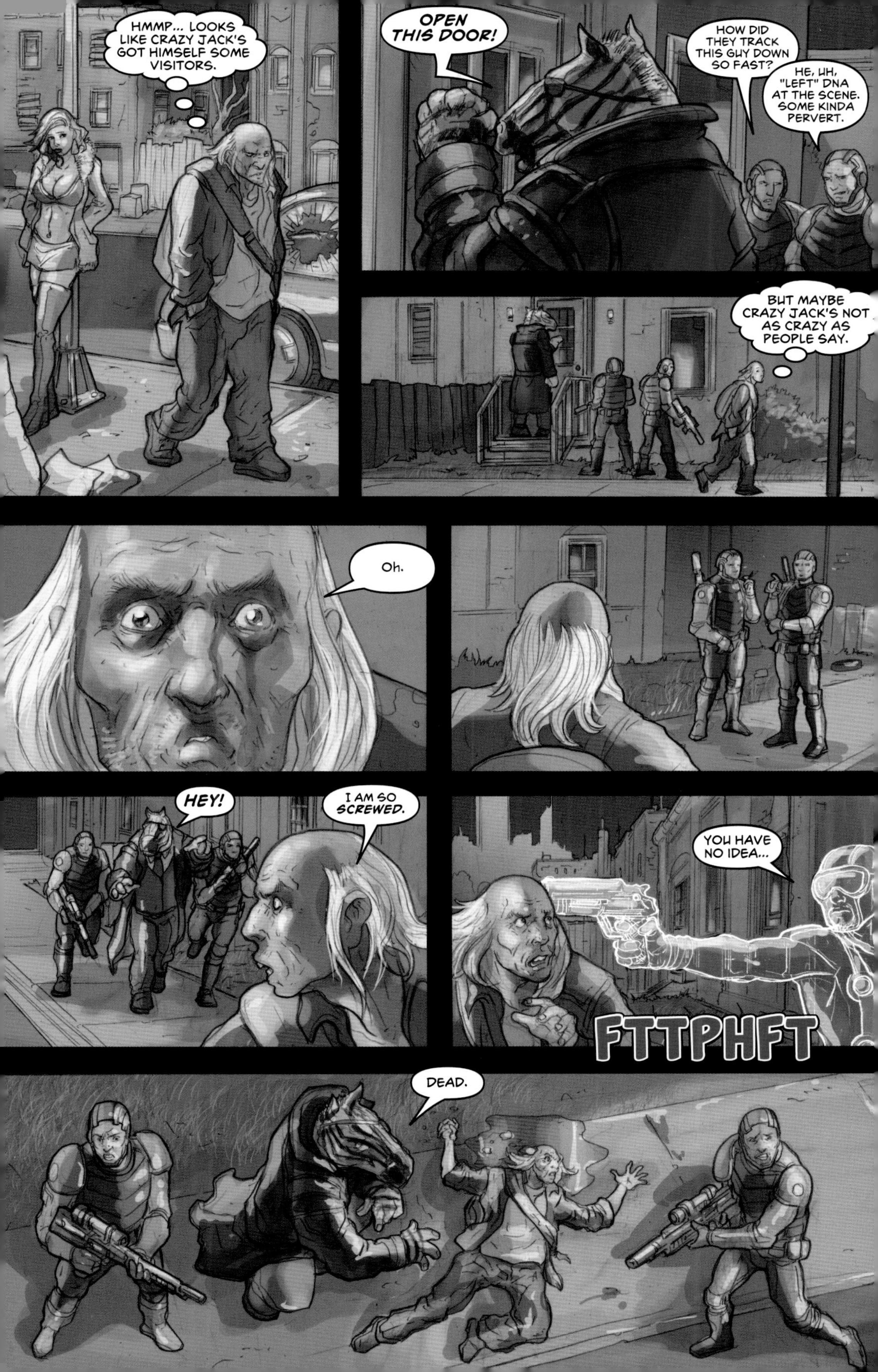
HMMP... LOOKS LIKE CRAZY JACK'S GOT HIMSELF SOME VISITORS.
OPEN THIS DOOR!
HOW DID THEY TRACK THIS GUY DOWN SO FAST?
HE, UH, "LEFT" DNA AT THE SCENE. SOME KINDA PERVERT.
BUT MAYBE CRAZY JACK'S NOT AS CRAZY AS PEOPLE SAY.
Oh.
HEY!
I AM SO SCREWED.
YOU HAVE NO IDEA...
FTTPHFT
DEAD.

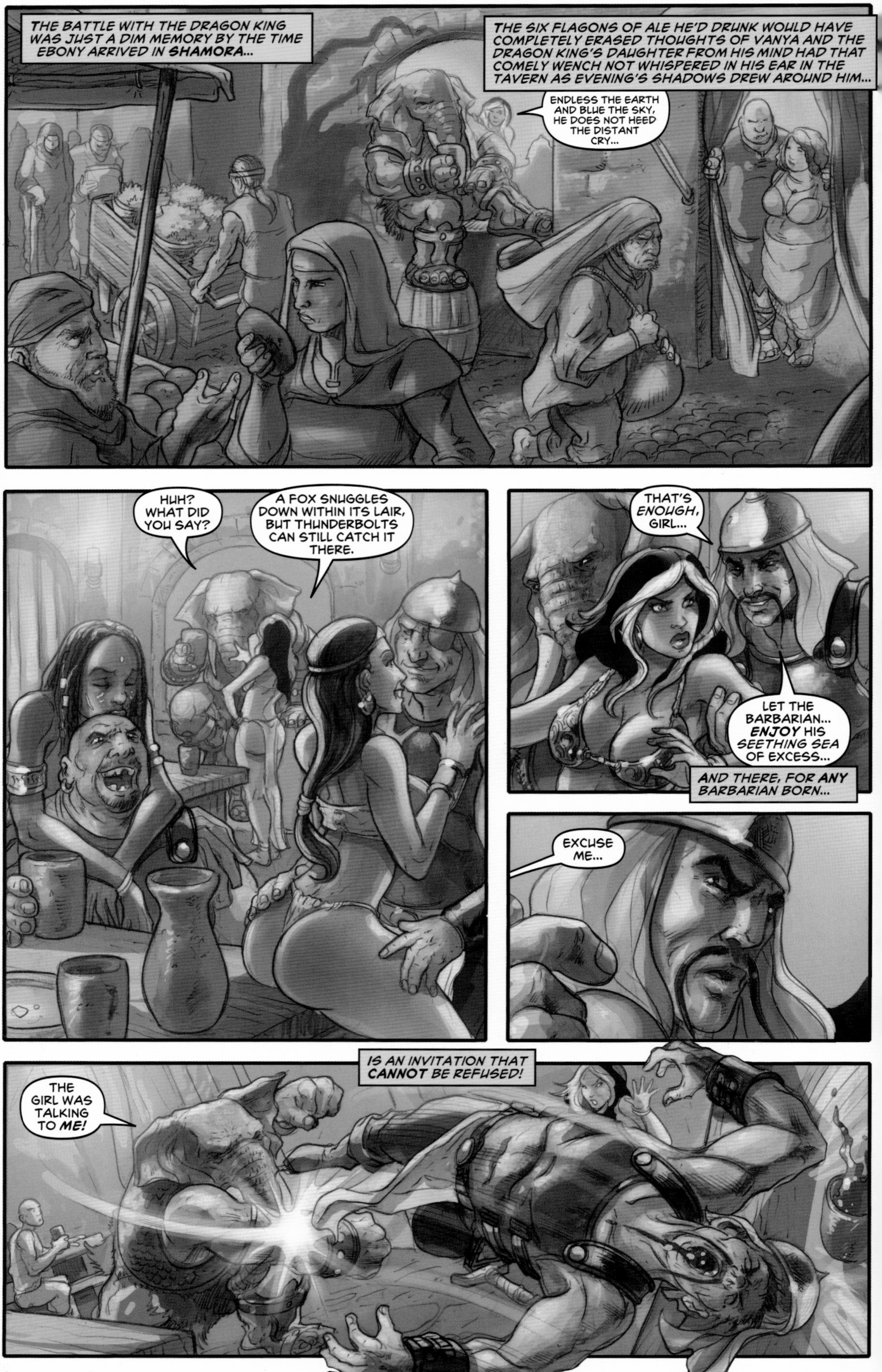
THE BATTLE WITH THE DRAGON KING WAS JUST A DIM MEMORY BY THE TIME EBONY ARRIVED IN SHAMORA...
THE SIX FLAGONS OF ALE HE'D DRUNK WOULD HAVE COMPLETELY ERASED THOUGHTS OF VANYA AND THE DRAGON KING'S DAUGHTER FROM HIS MIND HAD THAT COMELY WENCH NOT WHISPERED IN HIS EAR IN THE TAVERN AS EVENING'S SHADOWS DREW AROUND HIM...
ENDLESS THE EARTH AND BLUE THE SKY, HE DOES NOT HEED THE DISTANT CRY...
HUH? WHAT DID YOU SAY?
A FOX SNUGGLES DOWN WITHIN ITS LAIR, BUT THUNDERBOLTS CAN STILL CATCH IT THERE.
THAT'S ENOUGH, GIRL...
LET THE BARBARIAN... ENJOY HIS SEETHING SEA OF EXCESS...
AND THERE, FOR ANY BARBARIAN BORN...
EXCUSE ME...
IS AN INVITATION THAT CANNOT BE REFUSED!
THE GIRL WAS TALKING TO ME!

THE HEART HAS ALWAYS BEEN A MUSCLE OVER WHICH EBONY HAS NO CONTROL...

BUT, IN A FISTFIGHT...?

IN A FISTFIGHT, EBONY IS ALL MUSCLE AND IN COMPLETE CONTROL!

IF, INDEED, ONE CAN DESCRIBE AN ELEPHANTMAN'S BERSERKER FURY AS BEING UNDER ANY KIND OF CONTROL!

NO MATTER, WHEN EBONY LETS LOOSE HIS ANGER ON HUMANITY...

WHEN THE PENT-UP RAGE OF YEARS OF SLAVERY IS UNLEASHED ON THOSE AROUND HIM... FOR A BRIEF MOMENT HE FEELS A SENSE OF FREEDOM... FREEDOM FROM THE SORCEROUS SCIENCE THAT MADE HIM A STRANGER IN A STRANGER WORLD...

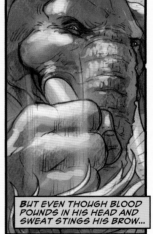

BUT EVEN THOUGH BLOOD POUNDS IN HIS HEAD AND SWEAT STINGS HIS BROW...

STILL THAT VOICE CALLS HIM FROM FAR AWAY...

EBONYYY! EB·ONYYY·!

AND ONCE AGAIN HIS HEART JUMPS AT THE SOUND...

ENOUGH THEN, HE WILL OFFER NO MORE RESISTANCE... SLOWLY, HE TURNS TOWARD THE BECKONING CALL...

EBONYYY!

WHEN WAS IT? WHEN DID HE FIRST HEAR THIS VOICE?

EB·ONYYY··!

WAS IT IN THE CITADEL? IS IT THE VOICE OF THE DRAGON KING'S DAUGHTER CALLING HIM...? NO... NOT HER... IT WAS WHEN HE CROSSED THE GRASSLANDS...

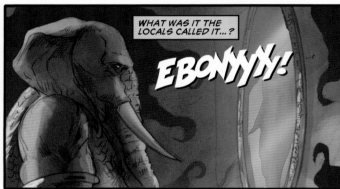

WHAT WAS IT THE LOCALS CALLED IT...?

EBONYYX!

THE SHAMORIAN SLOPES...? NO, NO...

THE SHADED GLADES OF SHAMORA? NO...!

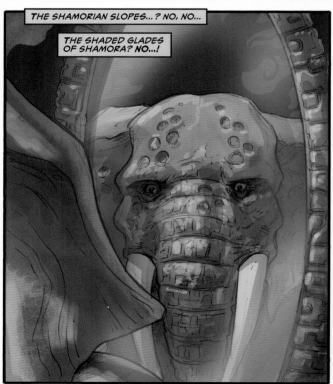

THE SHAMORIAN... SAVANNAH!

EB·ONY!

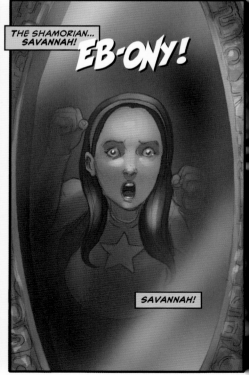

SAVANNAH!

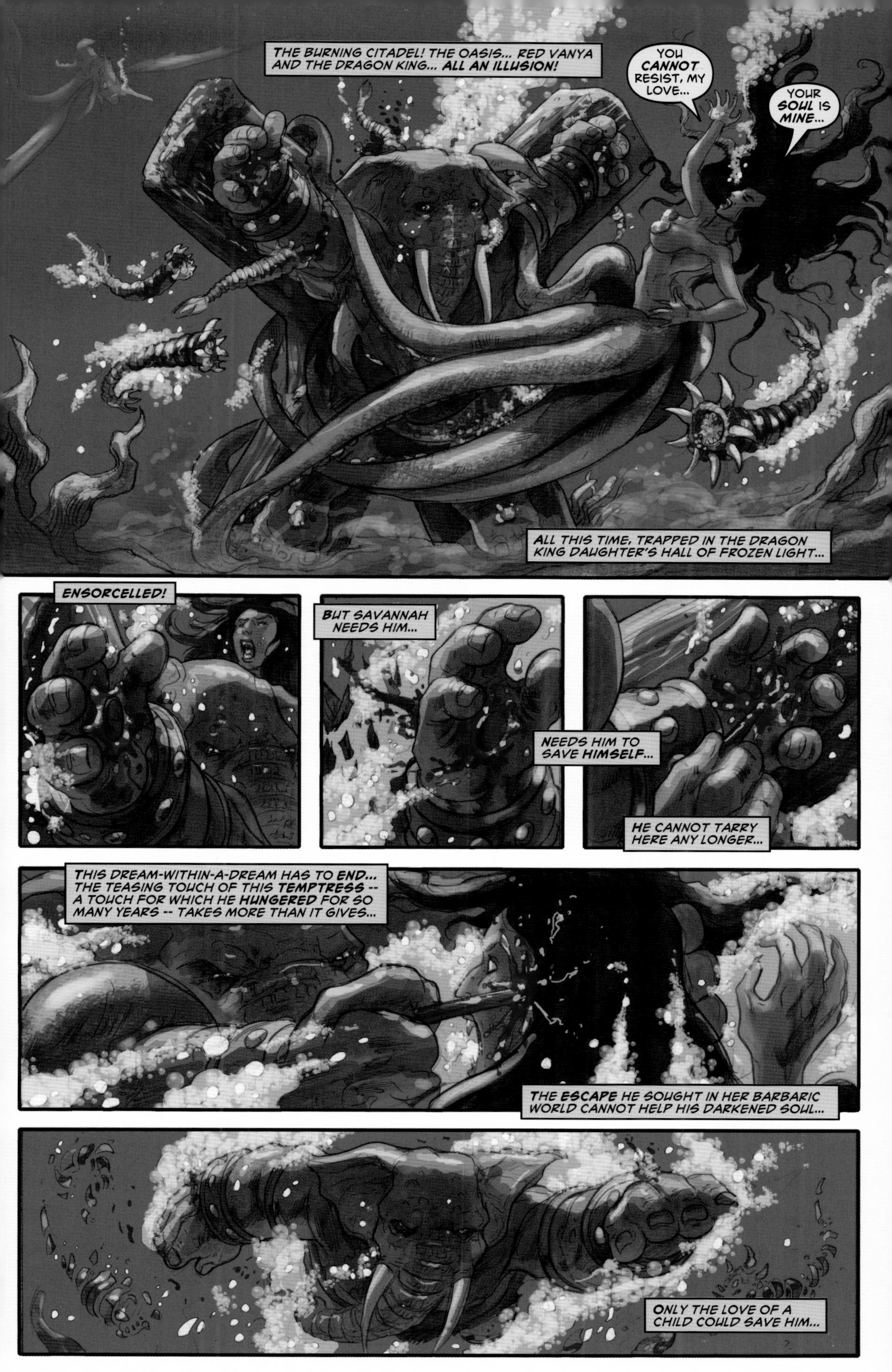
THE BURNING CITADEL! THE OASIS... RED VANYA AND THE DRAGON KING... ALL AN ILLUSION!
YOU CANNOT RESIST, MY LOVE...
YOUR SOUL IS MINE...
ALL THIS TIME, TRAPPED IN THE DRAGON KING DAUGHTER'S HALL OF FROZEN LIGHT...
ENSORCELLED!
BUT SAVANNAH NEEDS HIM...
NEEDS HIM TO SAVE HIMSELF...
HE CANNOT TARRY HERE ANY LONGER...
THIS DREAM-WITHIN-A-DREAM HAS TO END... THE TEASING TOUCH OF THIS TEMPTRESS -- A TOUCH FOR WHICH HE HUNGERED FOR SO MANY YEARS -- TAKES MORE THAN IT GIVES...
THE ESCAPE HE SOUGHT IN HER BARBARIC WORLD CANNOT HELP HIS DARKENED SOUL...
ONLY THE LOVE OF A CHILD COULD SAVE HIM...

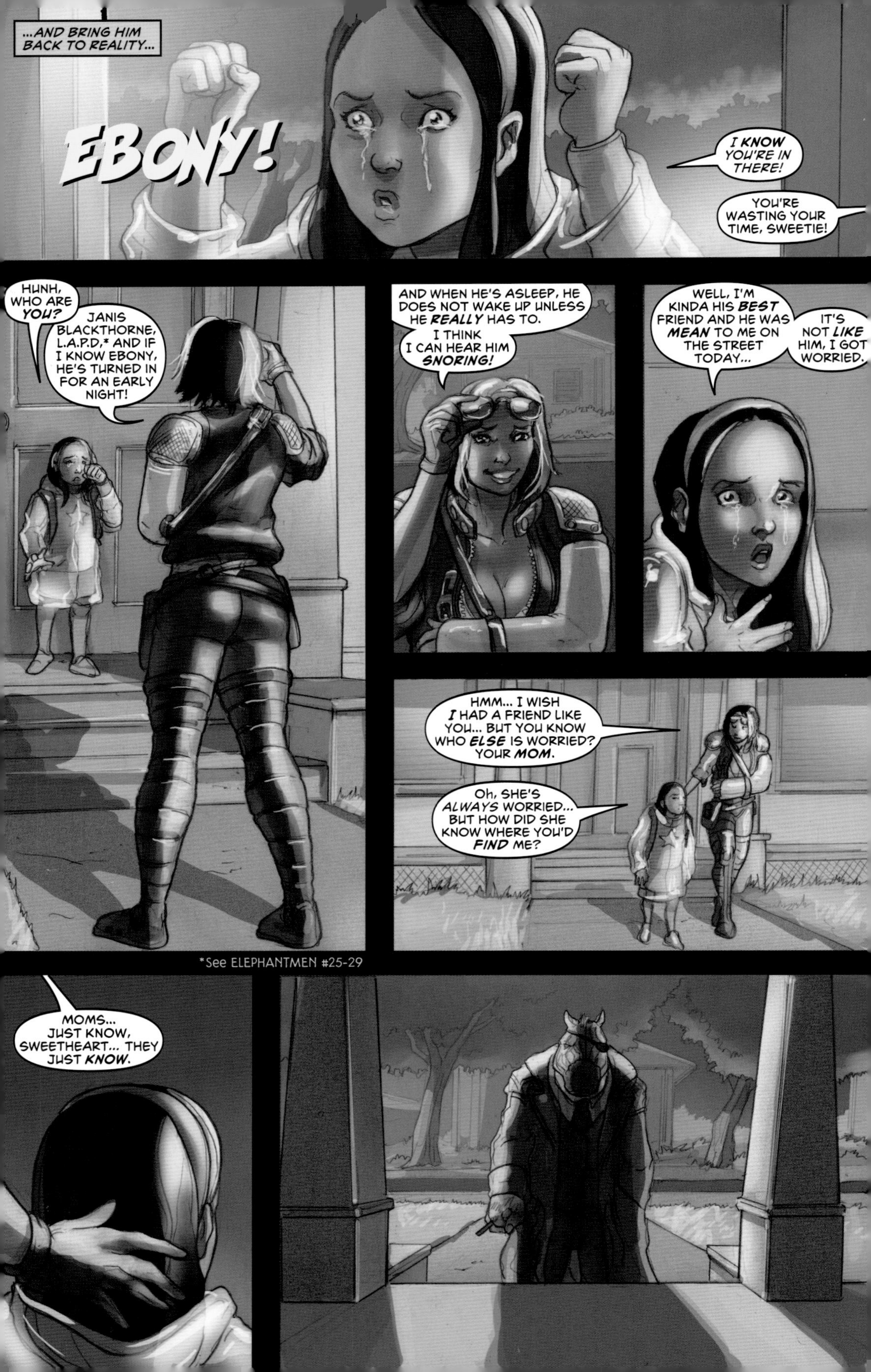
...AND BRING HIM BACK TO REALITY...
EBONY!
I KNOW YOU'RE IN THERE!
YOU'RE WASTING YOUR TIME, SWEETIE!
HUNH, WHO ARE YOU?
JANIS BLACKTHORNE, L.A.P.D,* AND IF I KNOW EBONY, HE'S TURNED IN FOR AN EARLY NIGHT!
AND WHEN HE'S ASLEEP, HE DOES NOT WAKE UP UNLESS HE REALLY HAS TO.
I THINK I CAN HEAR HIM SNORING!
WELL, I'M KINDA HIS BEST FRIEND AND HE WAS MEAN TO ME ON THE STREET TODAY...
IT'S NOT LIKE HIM, I GOT WORRIED.
HMM... I WISH I HAD A FRIEND LIKE YOU... BUT YOU KNOW WHO ELSE IS WORRIED? YOUR MOM.
Oh, SHE'S ALWAYS WORRIED... BUT HOW DID SHE KNOW WHERE YOU'D FIND ME?
*See ELEPHANTMEN #25-29
MOMS... JUST KNOW, SWEETHEART... THEY JUST KNOW.

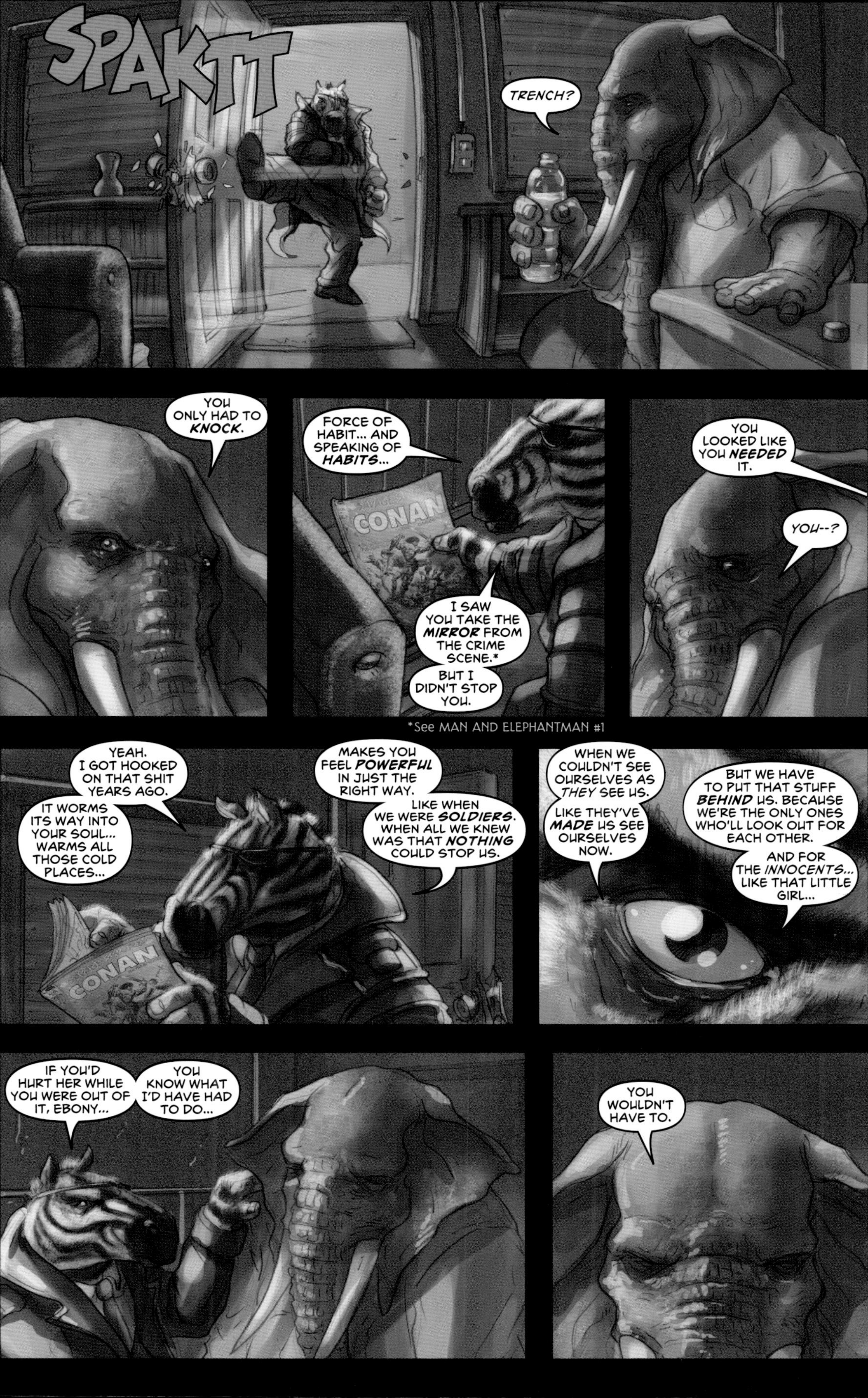
SPAKTT
TRENCH?
YOU ONLY HAD TO KNOCK.
FORCE OF HABIT... AND SPEAKING OF HABITS...
I SAW YOU TAKE THE MIRROR FROM THE CRIME SCENE.*
BUT I DIDN'T STOP YOU.
YOU LOOKED LIKE YOU NEEDED IT.
YOU--?
*See MAN AND ELEPHANTMAN #1
YEAH. I GOT HOOKED ON THAT SHIT YEARS AGO.
IT WORMS ITS WAY INTO YOUR SOUL... WARMS ALL THOSE COLD PLACES...
MAKES YOU FEEL POWERFUL IN JUST THE RIGHT WAY.
LIKE WHEN WE WERE SOLDIERS. WHEN ALL WE KNEW WAS THAT NOTHING COULD STOP US.
WHEN WE COULDN'T SEE OURSELVES AS THEY SEE US.
LIKE THEY'VE MADE US SEE OURSELVES NOW.
BUT WE HAVE TO PUT THAT STUFF BEHIND US. BECAUSE WE'RE THE ONLY ONES WHO'LL LOOK OUT FOR EACH OTHER.
AND FOR THE INNOCENTS... LIKE THAT LITTLE GIRL...
IF YOU'D HURT HER WHILE YOU WERE OUT OF IT, EBONY...
YOU KNOW WHAT I'D HAVE HAD TO DO...
YOU WOULDN'T HAVE TO.

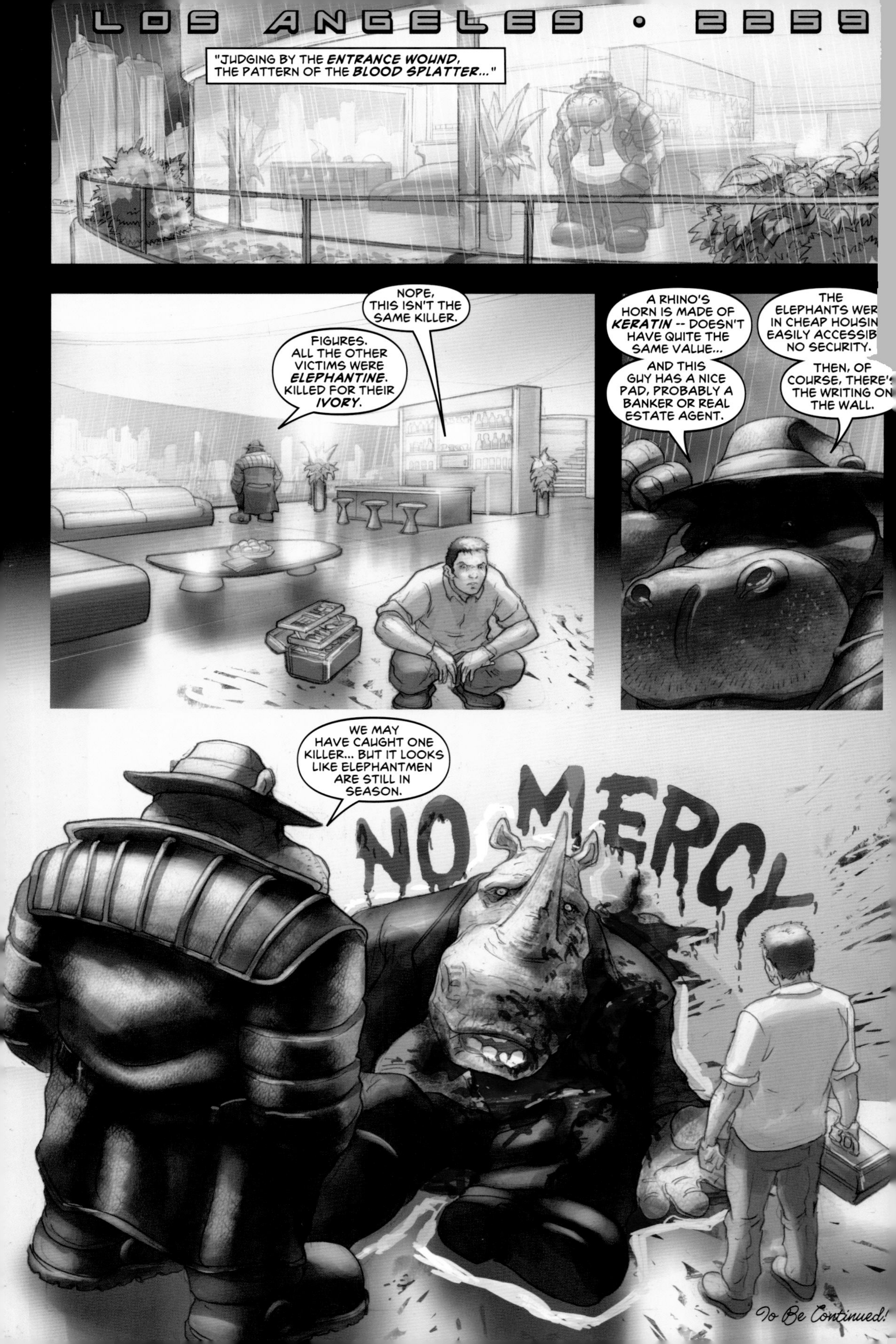

LOS ANGELES • 2259
"JUDGING BY THE ENTRANCE WOUND, THE PATTERN OF THE BLOOD SPLATTER..."
NOPE, THIS ISN'T THE SAME KILLER.
FIGURES. ALL THE OTHER VICTIMS WERE ELEPHANTINE. KILLED FOR THEIR IVORY.
A RHINO'S HORN IS MADE OF KERATIN -- DOESN'T HAVE QUITE THE SAME VALUE...
AND THIS GUY HAS A NICE PAD, PROBABLY A BANKER OR REAL ESTATE AGENT.
THE ELEPHANTS WER IN CHEAP HOUSIN EASILY ACCESSIB NO SECURITY.
THEN, OF COURSE, THERE'S THE WRITING ON THE WALL.
WE MAY HAVE CAUGHT ONE KILLER... BUT IT LOOKS LIKE ELEPHANTMEN ARE STILL IN SEASON.
NO MERCY
To Be Continued!

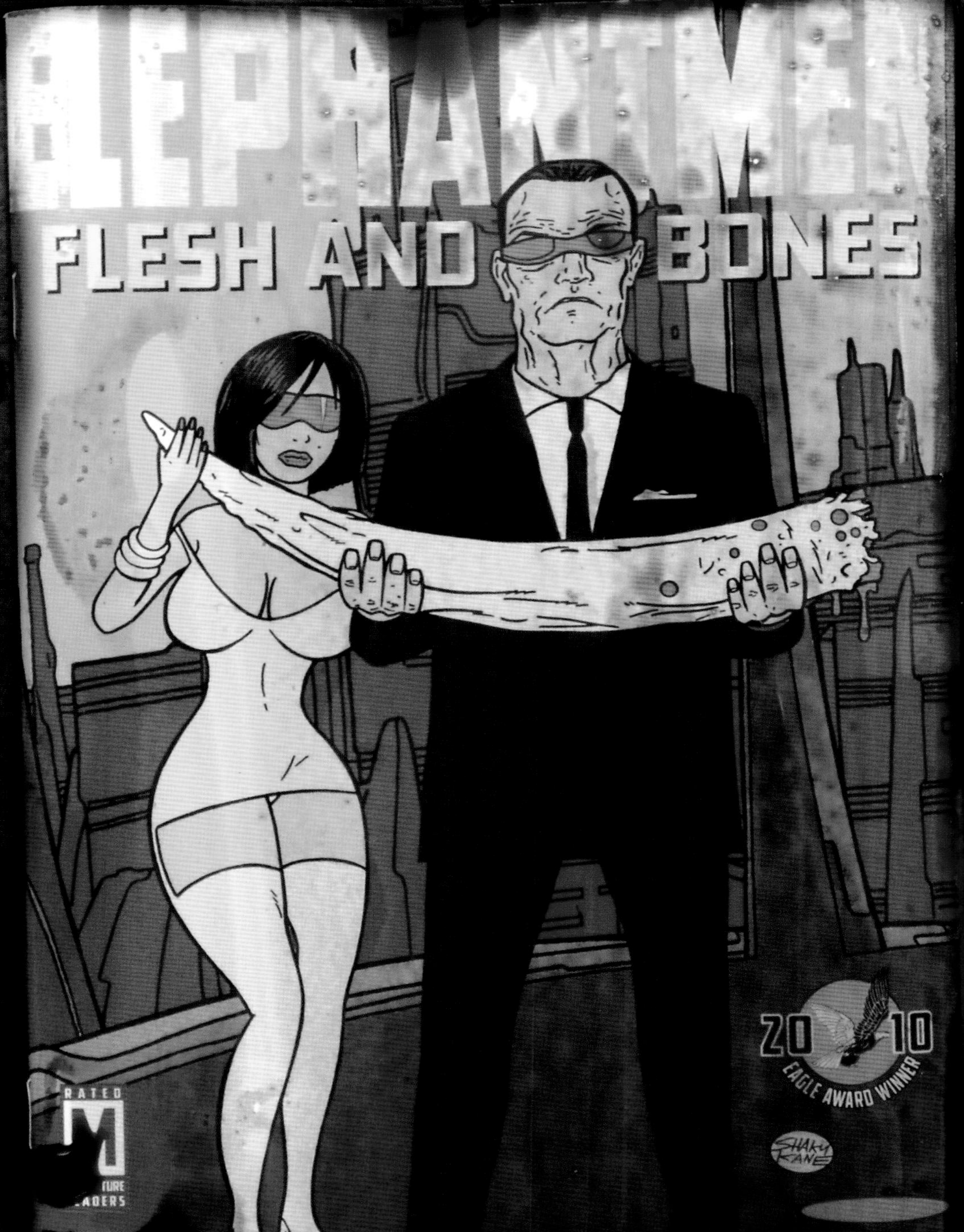

ELEPHANTMEN
FLESH AND BONES
2010
EAGLE AWARD WINNER
SHAKY KANE
RATED
M
#33
JUL
$3.99
MAN AND ELEPHANTMAN
STAR KINGS · EPILOGUE · SHAKY KANE

"WE CUT THE THROAT OF A CALF AND HANG IT UP BY THE HEELS TO BLEED TO DEATH SO THAT OUR VEAL CUTLET MAY BE WHITE; WE NAIL GEESE TO A BOARD AND CRAM THEM WITH FOOD BECAUSE WE LIKE THE TASTE OF LIVER DISEASE; WE TEAR BIRDS TO PIECES TO DECORATE OUR WOMEN'S HATS; WE MUTILATE DOMESTIC ANIMALS FOR NO REASON AT ALL EXCEPT TO FOLLOW AN INSTINCTIVELY CRUEL FASHION; AND WE CONNIVE AT THE MOST ABOMINABLE TORTURES IN THE HOPE OF DISCOVERING SOME MAGICAL CURE FOR OUR OWN DISEASES BY THEM."

GEORGE BERNARD SHAW
MAN AND SUPERMAN

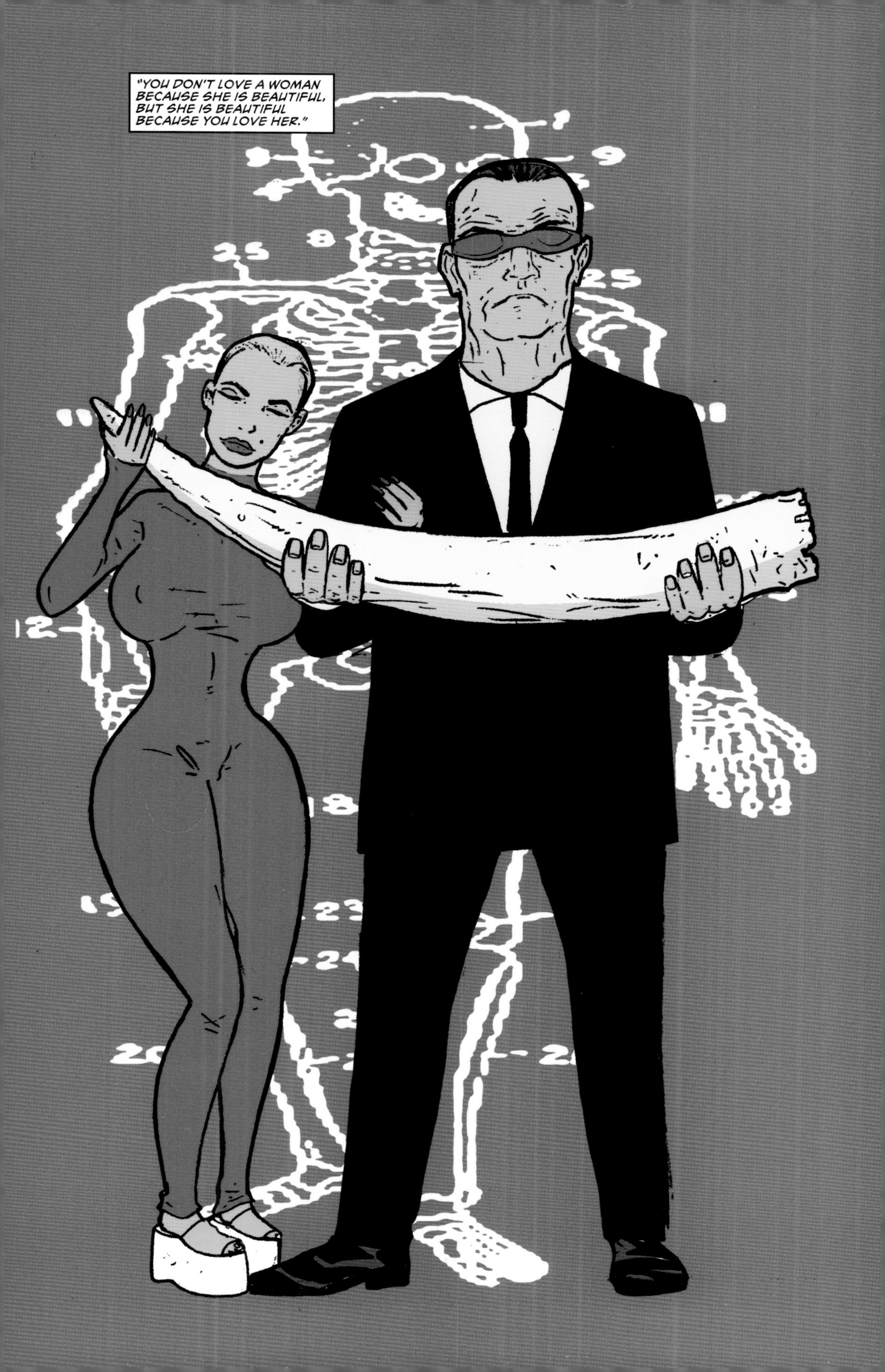
"YOU DON'T LOVE A WOMAN BECAUSE SHE IS BEAUTIFUL, BUT SHE IS BEAUTIFUL BECAUSE YOU LOVE HER."

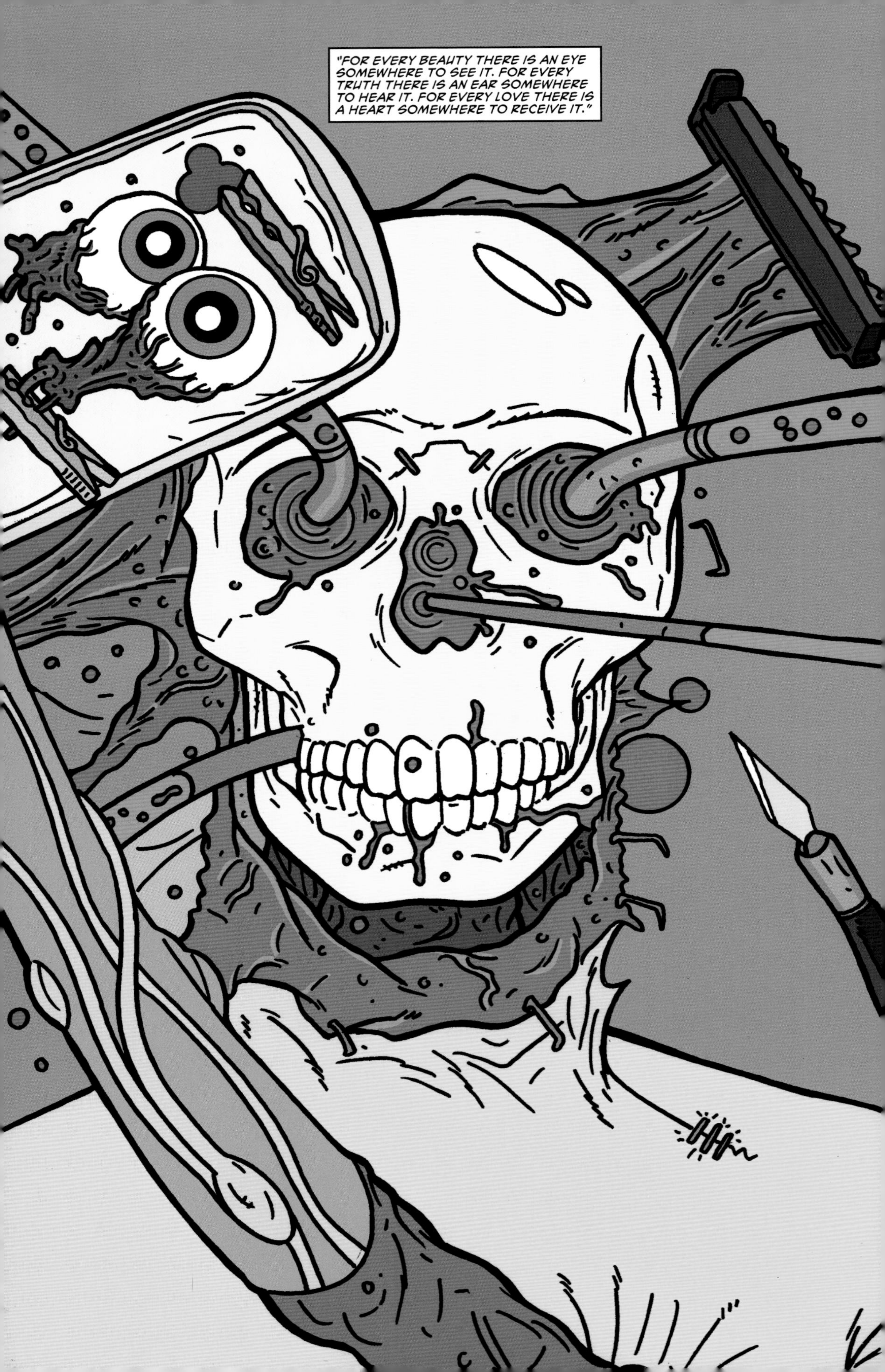
"FOR EVERY BEAUTY THERE IS AN EYE SOMEWHERE TO SEE IT. FOR EVERY TRUTH THERE IS AN EAR SOMEWHERE TO HEAR IT. FOR EVERY LOVE THERE IS A HEART SOMEWHERE TO RECEIVE IT."

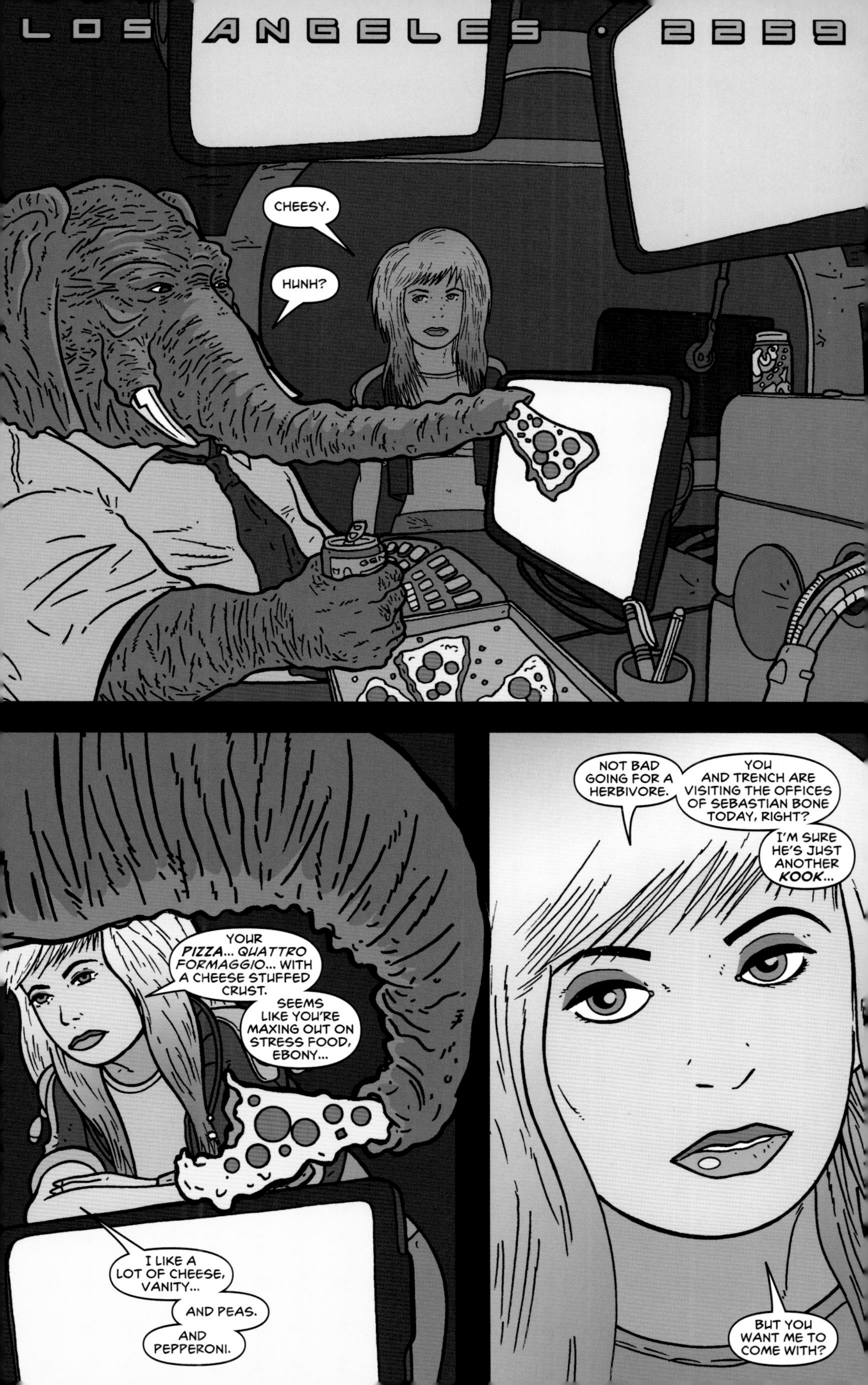
LOS ANGELES · 2259
CHEESY.
HUNH?
YOUR *PIZZA*... *QUATTRO FORMAGGIO*... WITH A CHEESE STUFFED CRUST.
SEEMS LIKE YOU'RE MAXING OUT ON STRESS FOOD, EBONY...
I LIKE A LOT OF CHEESE, VANITY...
AND PEAS.
AND PEPPERONI.
NOT BAD GOING FOR A HERBIVORE.
YOU AND TRENCH ARE VISITING THE OFFICES OF SEBASTIAN BONE TODAY, RIGHT?
I'M SURE HE'S JUST ANOTHER ***KOOK***...
BUT YOU WANT ME TO COME WITH?

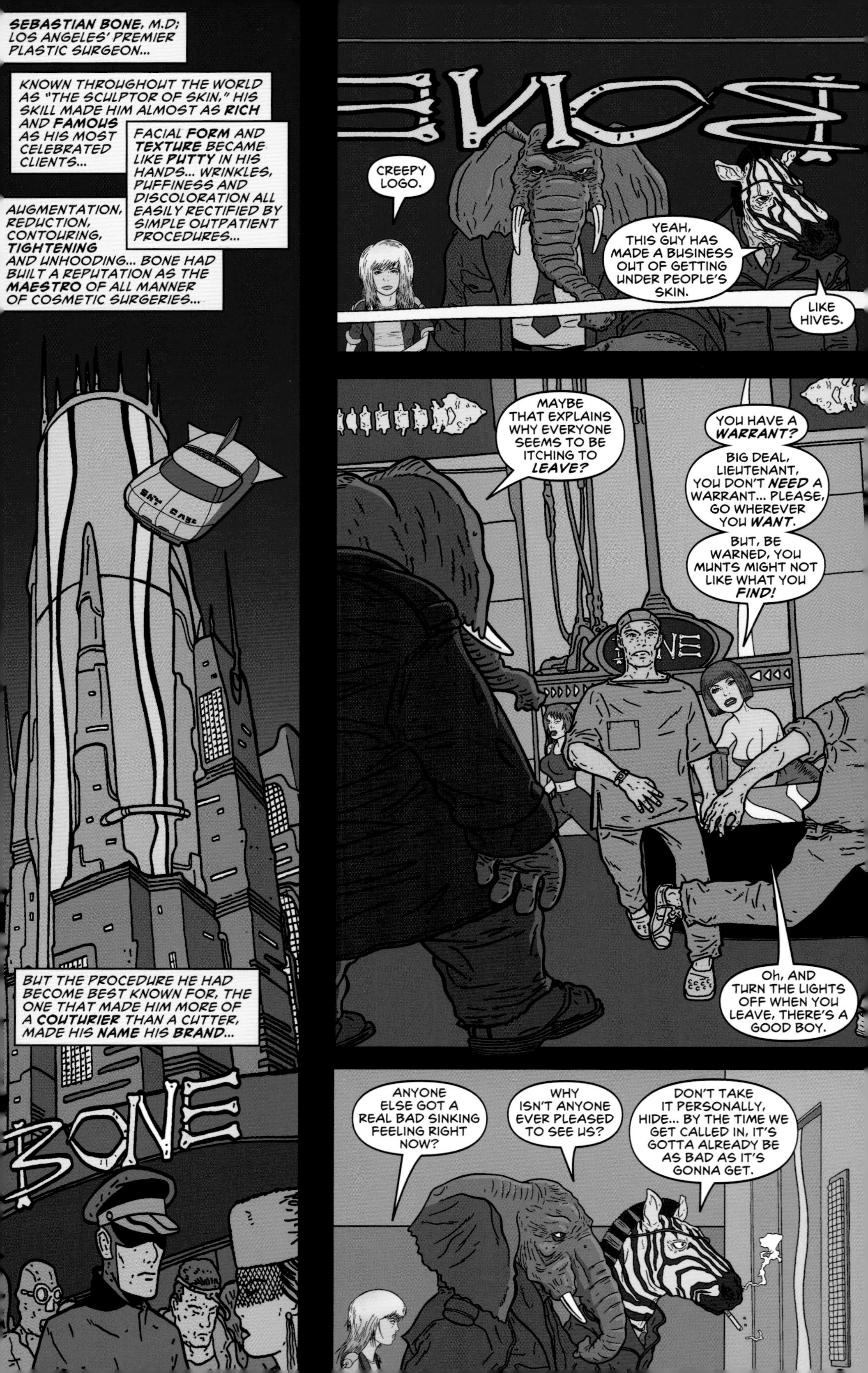
SEBASTIAN BONE, M.D; LOS ANGELES' PREMIER PLASTIC SURGEON...
KNOWN THROUGHOUT THE WORLD AS "THE SCULPTOR OF SKIN," HIS SKILL MADE HIM ALMOST AS RICH AND FAMOUS AS HIS MOST CELEBRATED CLIENTS...
FACIAL FORM AND TEXTURE BECAME LIKE PUTTY IN HIS HANDS... WRINKLES, PUFFINESS AND DISCOLORATION ALL EASILY RECTIFIED BY SIMPLE OUTPATIENT PROCEDURES...
AUGMENTATION, REDUCTION, CONTOURING, TIGHTENING AND UNHOODING... BONE HAD BUILT A REPUTATION AS THE MAESTRO OF ALL MANNER OF COSMETIC SURGERIES...
BUT THE PROCEDURE HE HAD BECOME BEST KNOWN FOR, THE ONE THAT MADE HIM MORE OF A COUTURIER THAN A CUTTER, MADE HIS NAME HIS BRAND...
BONE
CREEPY LOGO.
YEAH, THIS GUY HAS MADE A BUSINESS OUT OF GETTING UNDER PEOPLE'S SKIN.
LIKE HIVES.
MAYBE THAT EXPLAINS WHY EVERYONE SEEMS TO BE ITCHING TO LEAVE?
YOU HAVE A WARRANT?
BIG DEAL, LIEUTENANT, YOU DON'T NEED A WARRANT... PLEASE, GO WHEREVER YOU WANT.
BUT, BE WARNED, YOU MUNTS MIGHT NOT LIKE WHAT YOU FIND!
Oh, AND TURN THE LIGHTS OFF WHEN YOU LEAVE, THERE'S A GOOD BOY.
ANYONE ELSE GOT A REAL BAD SINKING FEELING RIGHT NOW?
WHY ISN'T ANYONE EVER PLEASED TO SEE US?
DON'T TAKE IT PERSONALLY, HIDE... BY THE TIME WE GET CALLED IN, IT'S GOTTA ALREADY BE AS BAD AS IT'S GONNA GET.

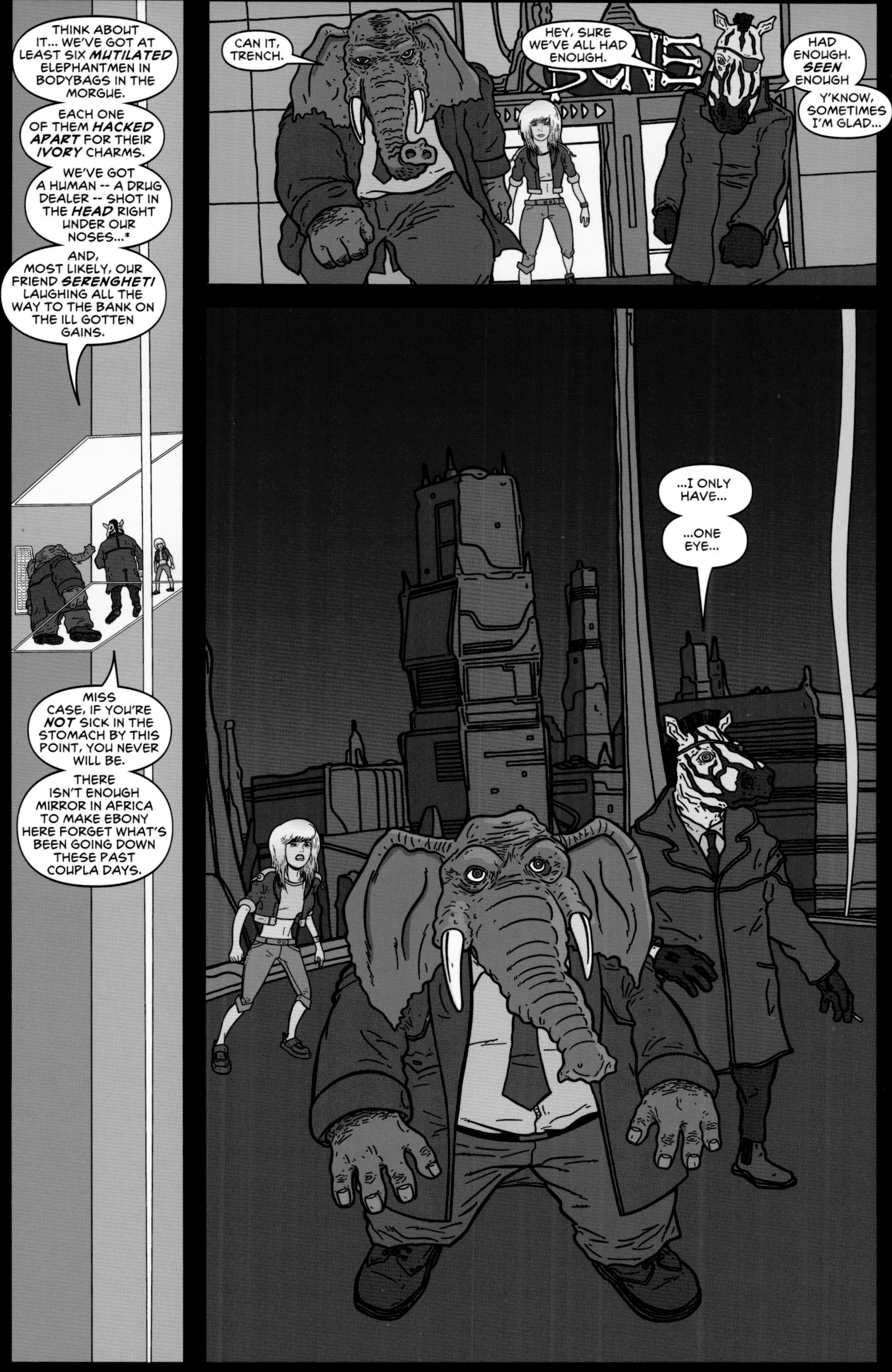
THINK ABOUT IT... WE'VE GOT AT LEAST SIX MUTILATED ELEPHANTMEN IN BODYBAGS IN THE MORGUE.
EACH ONE OF THEM HACKED APART FOR THEIR IVORY CHARMS.
WE'VE GOT A HUMAN -- A DRUG DEALER -- SHOT IN THE HEAD RIGHT UNDER OUR NOSES...*
AND, MOST LIKELY, OUR FRIEND SERENGHETI LAUGHING ALL THE WAY TO THE BANK ON THE ILL GOTTEN GAINS.
CAN IT, TRENCH.
HEY, SURE WE'VE ALL HAD ENOUGH.
HAD ENOUGH. SEEN ENOUGH
Y'KNOW, SOMETIMES I'M GLAD...
MISS CASE, IF YOU'RE NOT SICK IN THE STOMACH BY THIS POINT, YOU NEVER WILL BE.
THERE ISN'T ENOUGH MIRROR IN AFRICA TO MAKE EBONY HERE FORGET WHAT'S BEEN GOING DOWN THESE PAST COUPLA DAYS.
...I ONLY HAVE...
...ONE EYE...

*See ELEPHANTMEN #31-32

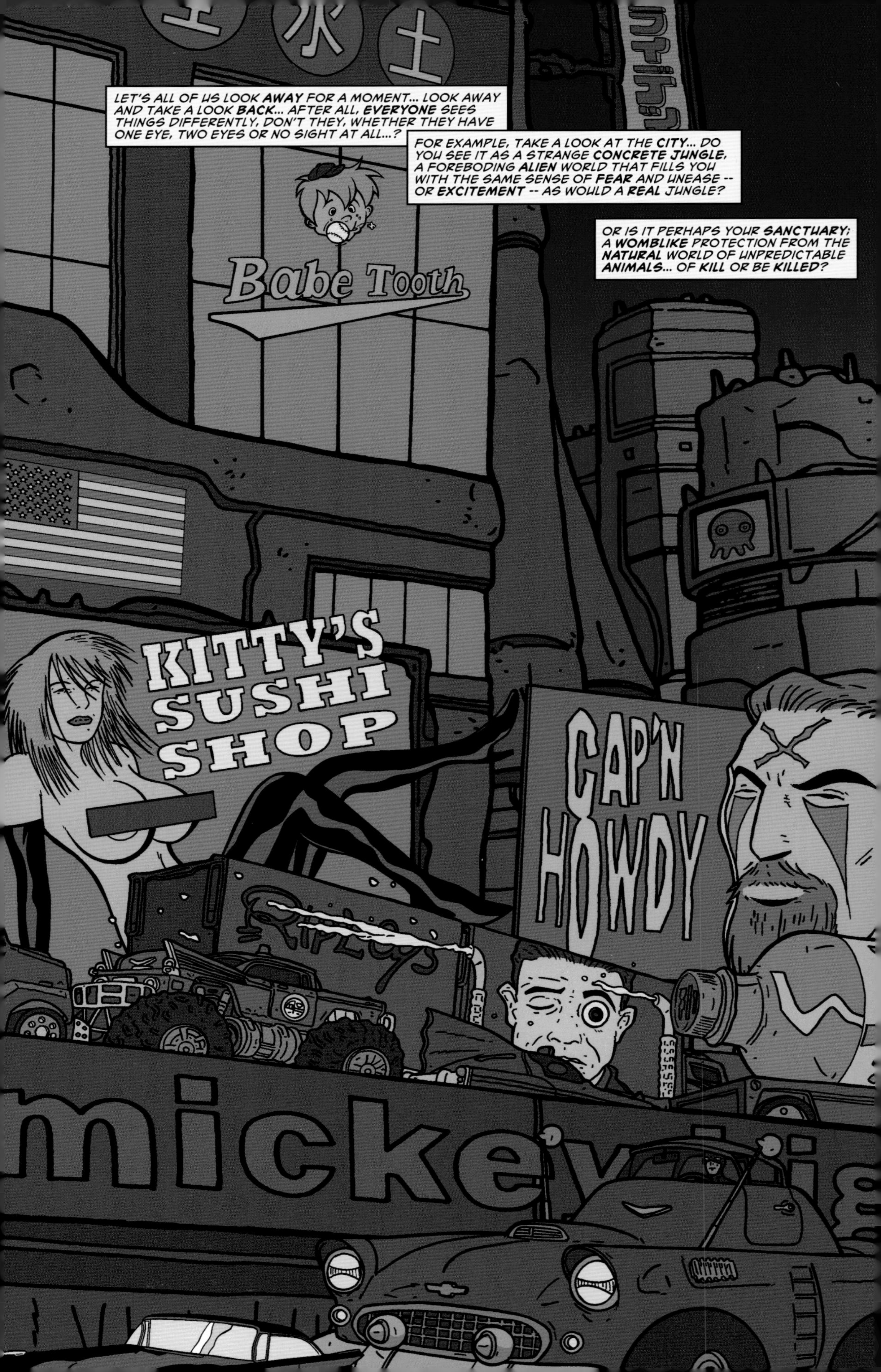
LET'S ALL OF US LOOK AWAY FOR A MOMENT... LOOK AWAY AND TAKE A LOOK BACK... AFTER ALL, EVERYONE SEES THINGS DIFFERENTLY, DON'T THEY, WHETHER THEY HAVE ONE EYE, TWO EYES OR NO SIGHT AT ALL...?
FOR EXAMPLE, TAKE A LOOK AT THE CITY... DO YOU SEE IT AS A STRANGE CONCRETE JUNGLE, A FOREBODING ALIEN WORLD THAT FILLS YOU WITH THE SAME SENSE OF FEAR AND UNEASE -- OR EXCITEMENT -- AS WOULD A REAL JUNGLE?
OR IS IT PERHAPS YOUR SANCTUARY: A WOMBLIKE PROTECTION FROM THE NATURAL WORLD OF UNPREDICTABLE ANIMALS... OF KILL OR BE KILLED?
Babe Tooth
KITTY'S SUSHI SHOP
CAP'N HOWDY
Ripley's
mickey

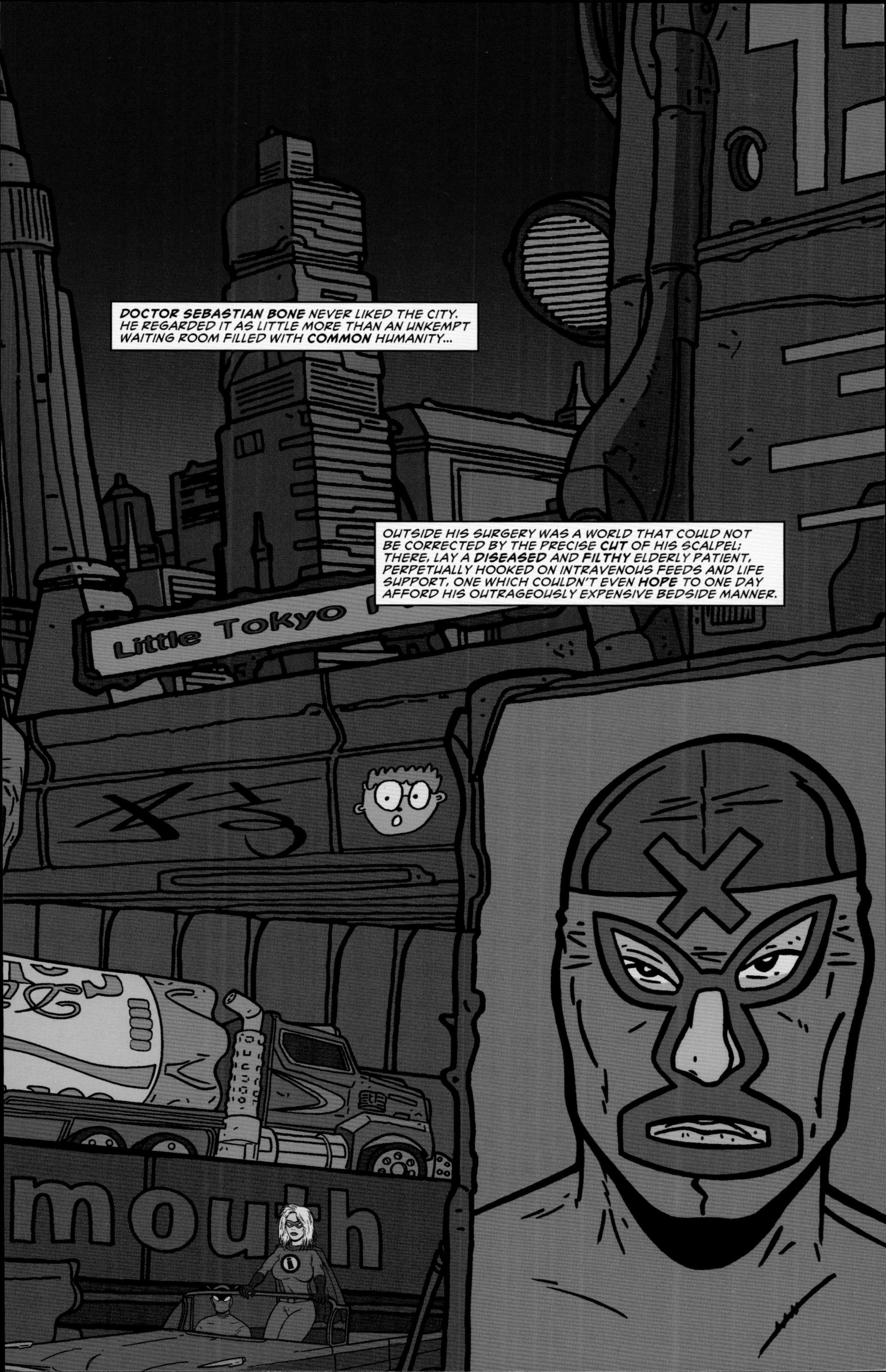
DOCTOR SEBASTIAN BONE NEVER LIKED THE CITY. HE REGARDED IT AS LITTLE MORE THAN AN UNKEMPT WAITING ROOM FILLED WITH COMMON HUMANITY...
OUTSIDE HIS SURGERY WAS A WORLD THAT COULD NOT BE CORRECTED BY THE PRECISE CUT OF HIS SCALPEL; THERE, LAY A DISEASED AND FILTHY ELDERLY PATIENT, PERPETUALLY HOOKED ON INTRAVENOUS FEEDS AND LIFE SUPPORT, ONE WHICH COULDN'T EVEN HOPE TO ONE DAY AFFORD HIS OUTRAGEOUSLY EXPENSIVE BEDSIDE MANNER.
Little TokyO
mouth

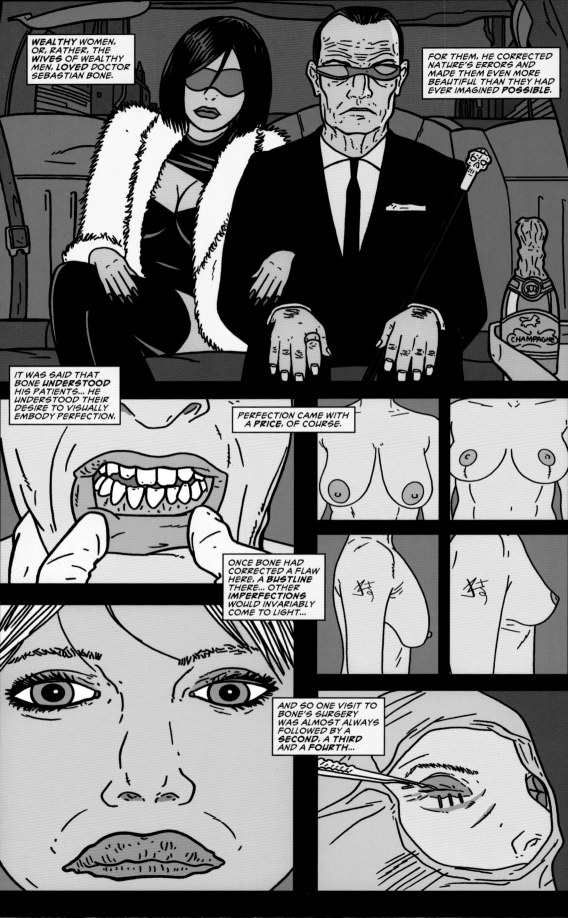

WEALTHY WOMEN, OR, RATHER, THE WIVES OF WEALTHY MEN, LOVED DOCTOR SEBASTIAN BONE.

FOR THEM, HE CORRECTED NATURE'S ERRORS AND MADE THEM EVEN MORE BEAUTIFUL THAN THEY HAD EVER IMAGINED POSSIBLE.

IT WAS SAID THAT BONE UNDERSTOOD HIS PATIENTS... HE UNDERSTOOD THEIR DESIRE TO VISUALLY EMBODY PERFECTION.

PERFECTION CAME WITH A PRICE, OF COURSE.

ONCE BONE HAD CORRECTED A FLAW HERE, A BUSTLINE THERE... OTHER IMPERFECTIONS WOULD INVARIABLY COME TO LIGHT...

AND SO ONE VISIT TO BONE'S SURGERY WAS ALMOST ALWAYS FOLLOWED BY A SECOND, A THIRD AND A FOURTH...

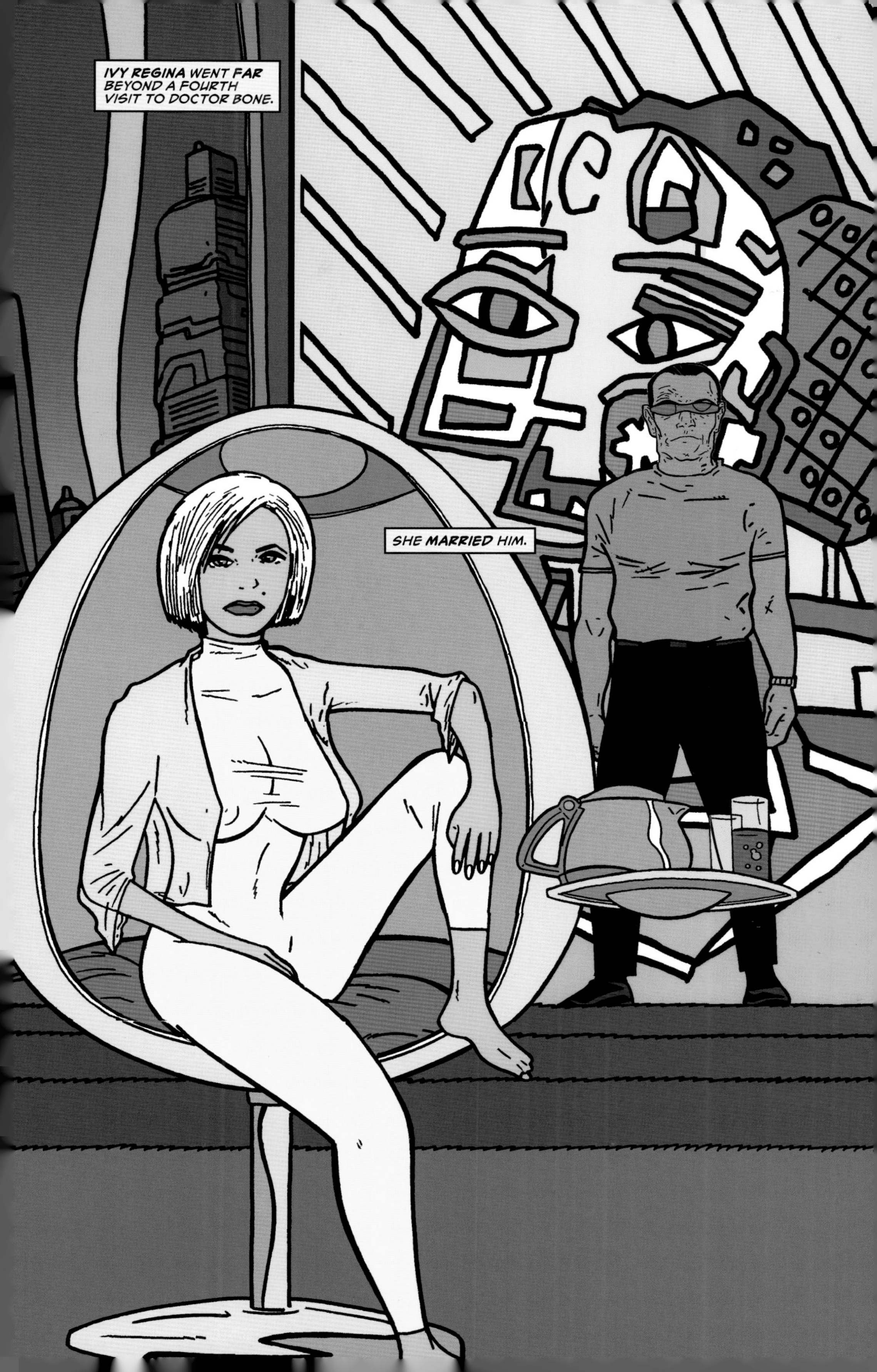
IVY REGINA WENT FAR BEYOND A FOURTH VISIT TO DOCTOR BONE.
SHE MARRIED HIM.

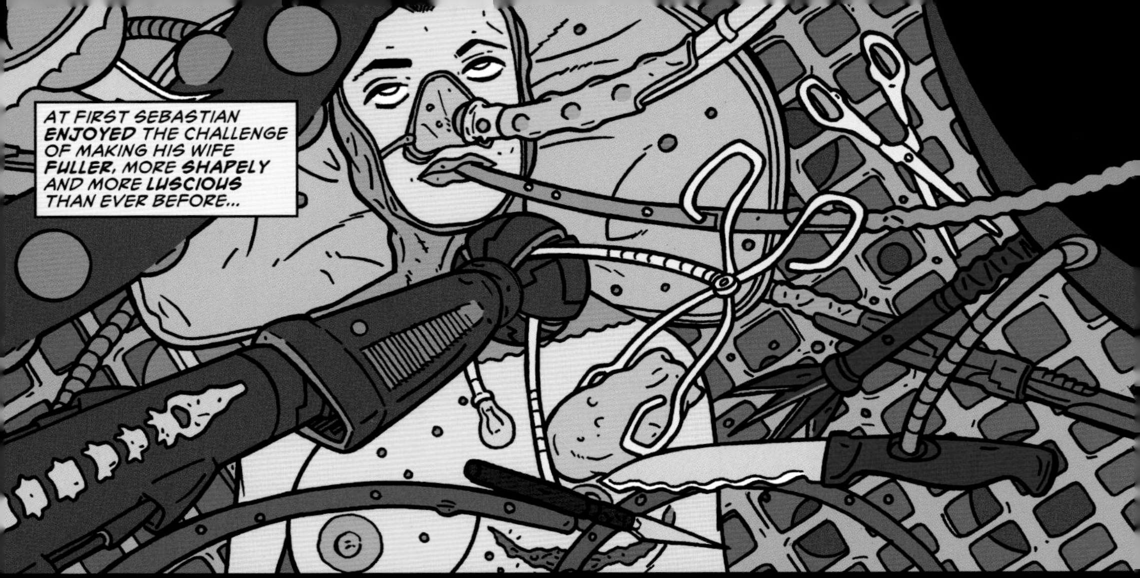
AT FIRST SEBASTIAN **ENJOYED** THE CHALLENGE OF MAKING HIS WIFE **FULLER**, MORE **SHAPELY** AND MORE **LUSCIOUS** THAN EVER BEFORE...

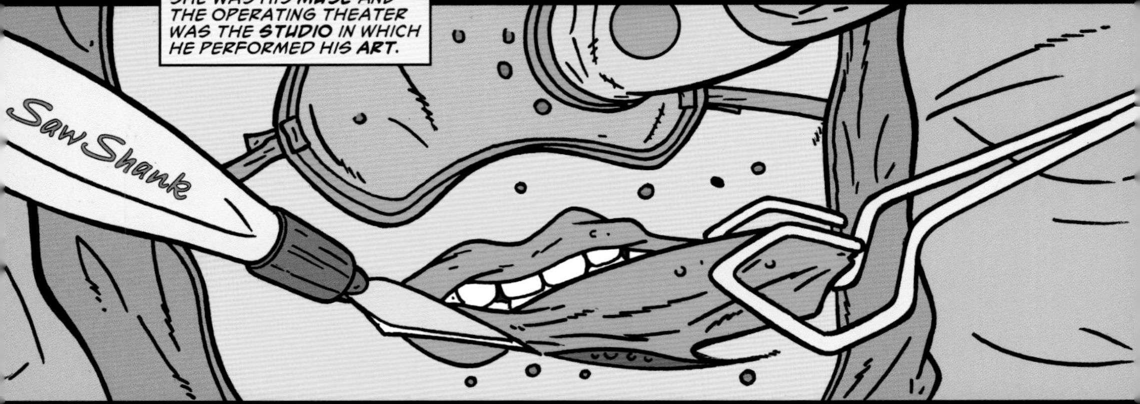
SHE WAS HIS **MUSE** AND THE OPERATING THEATER WAS THE **STUDIO** IN WHICH HE PERFORMED HIS **ART**.
Saw Shank

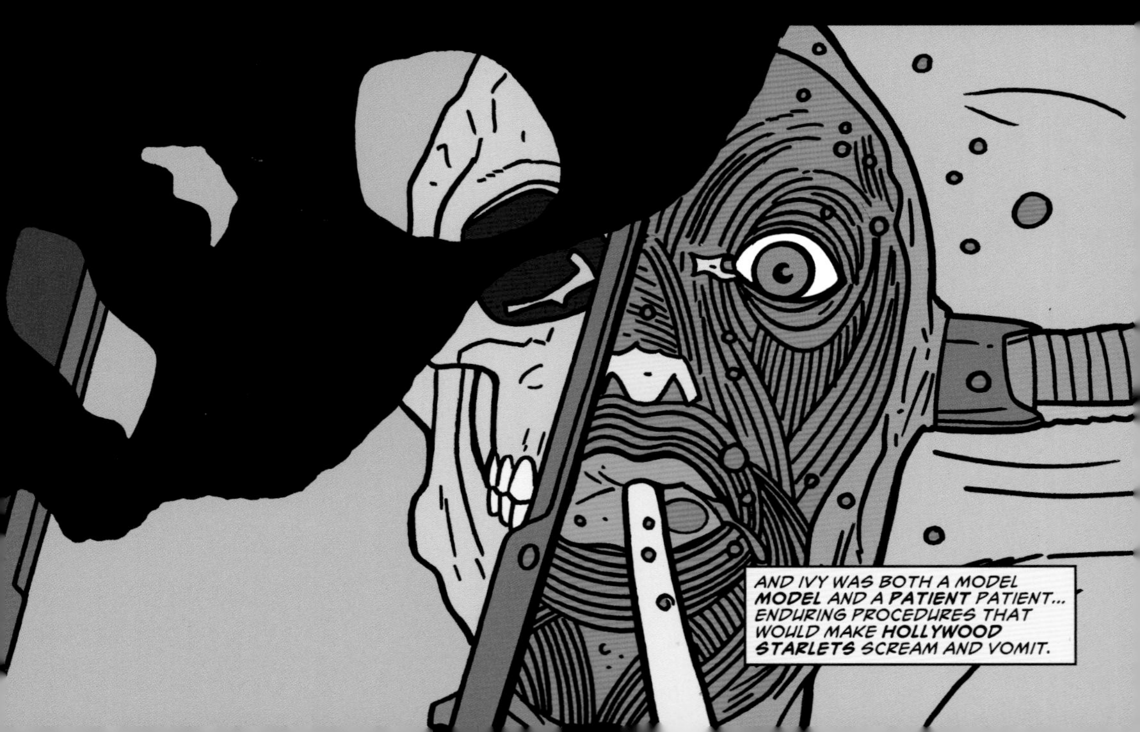
AND IVY WAS BOTH A MODEL **MODEL** AND A **PATIENT** PATIENT... ENDURING PROCEDURES THAT WOULD MAKE **HOLLYWOOD STARLETS** SCREAM AND VOMIT.

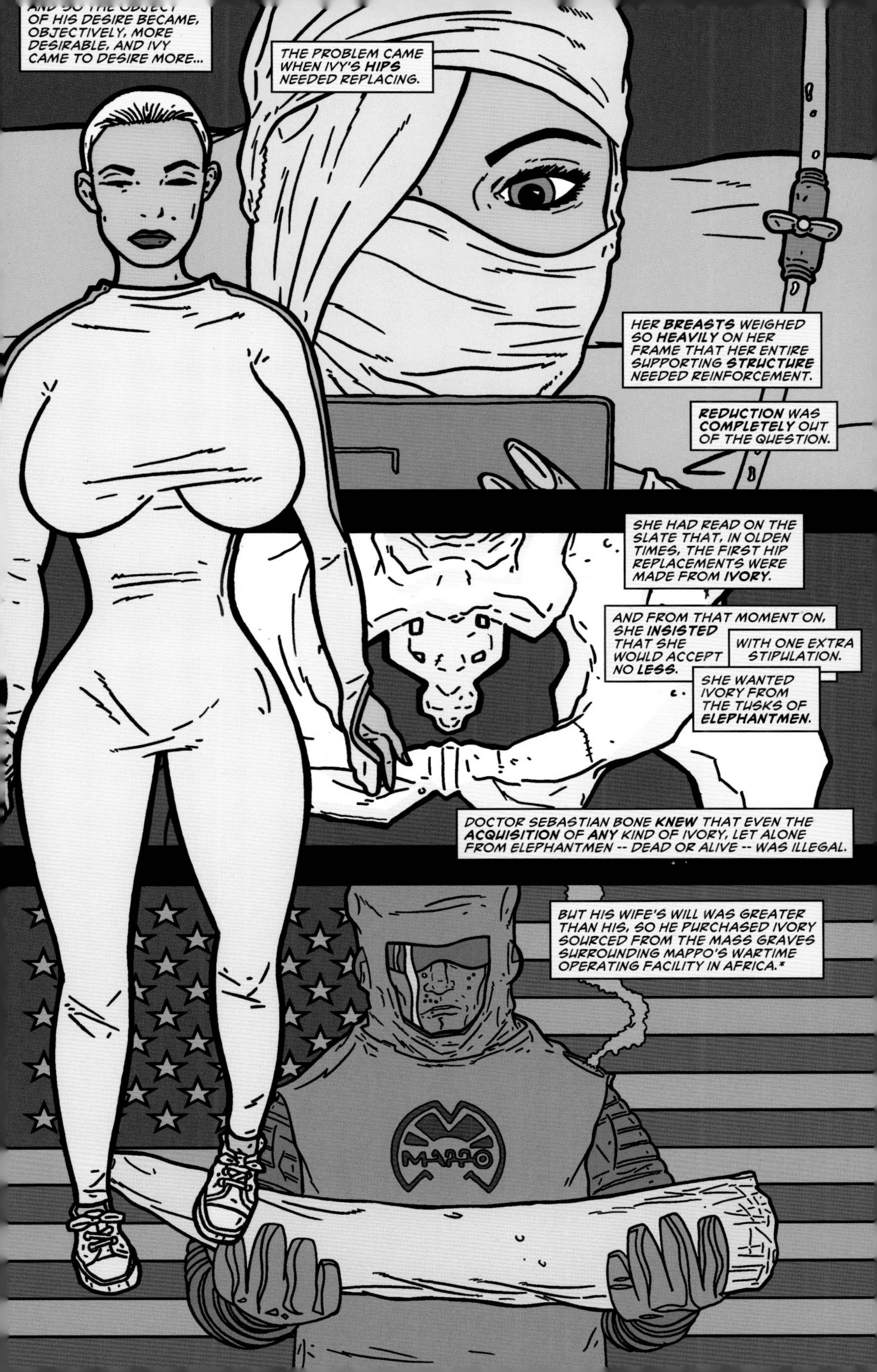
AND SO THE OBJECT OF HIS DESIRE BECAME, OBJECTIVELY, MORE DESIRABLE, AND IVY CAME TO DESIRE MORE...
THE PROBLEM CAME WHEN IVY'S HIPS NEEDED REPLACING.
HER BREASTS WEIGHED SO HEAVILY ON HER FRAME THAT HER ENTIRE SUPPORTING STRUCTURE NEEDED REINFORCEMENT.
REDUCTION WAS COMPLETELY OUT OF THE QUESTION.
SHE HAD READ ON THE SLATE THAT, IN OLDEN TIMES, THE FIRST HIP REPLACEMENTS WERE MADE FROM IVORY.
AND FROM THAT MOMENT ON, SHE INSISTED THAT SHE WOULD ACCEPT NO LESS.
WITH ONE EXTRA STIPULATION.
SHE WANTED IVORY FROM THE TUSKS OF ELEPHANTMEN.
DOCTOR SEBASTIAN BONE KNEW THAT EVEN THE ACQUISITION OF ANY KIND OF IVORY, LET ALONE FROM ELEPHANTMEN -- DEAD OR ALIVE -- WAS ILLEGAL.
BUT HIS WIFE'S WILL WAS GREATER THAN HIS, SO HE PURCHASED IVORY SOURCED FROM THE MASS GRAVES SURROUNDING MAPPO'S WARTIME OPERATING FACILITY IN AFRICA.*
MAPPO

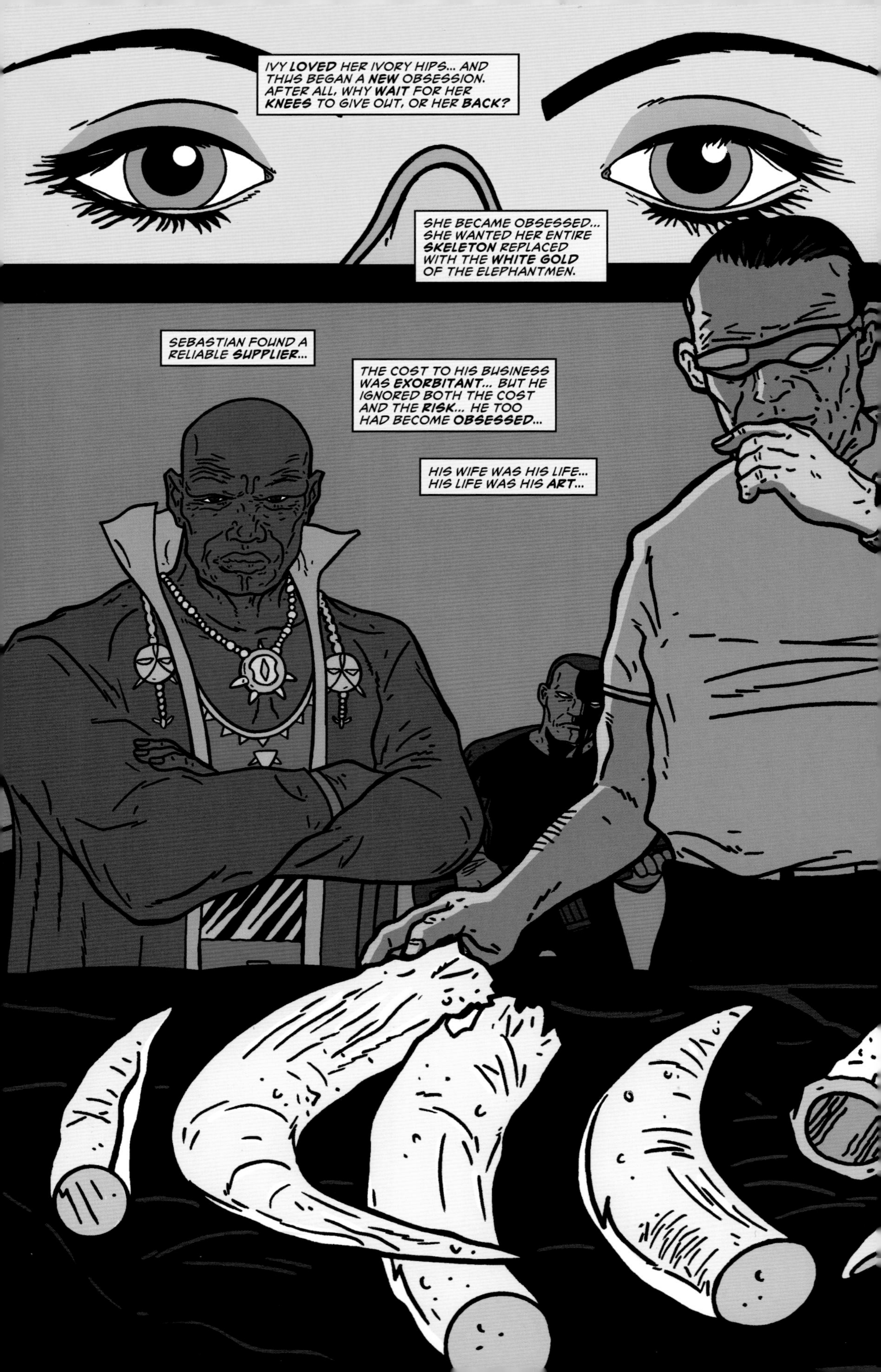
IVY LOVED HER IVORY HIPS... AND THUS BEGAN A NEW OBSESSION. AFTER ALL, WHY WAIT FOR HER KNEES TO GIVE OUT, OR HER BACK?
SHE BECAME OBSESSED... SHE WANTED HER ENTIRE SKELETON REPLACED WITH THE WHITE GOLD OF THE ELEPHANTMEN.
SEBASTIAN FOUND A RELIABLE SUPPLIER...
THE COST TO HIS BUSINESS WAS EXORBITANT... BUT HE IGNORED BOTH THE COST AND THE RISK... HE TOO HAD BECOME OBSESSED...
HIS WIFE WAS HIS LIFE... HIS LIFE WAS HIS ART...

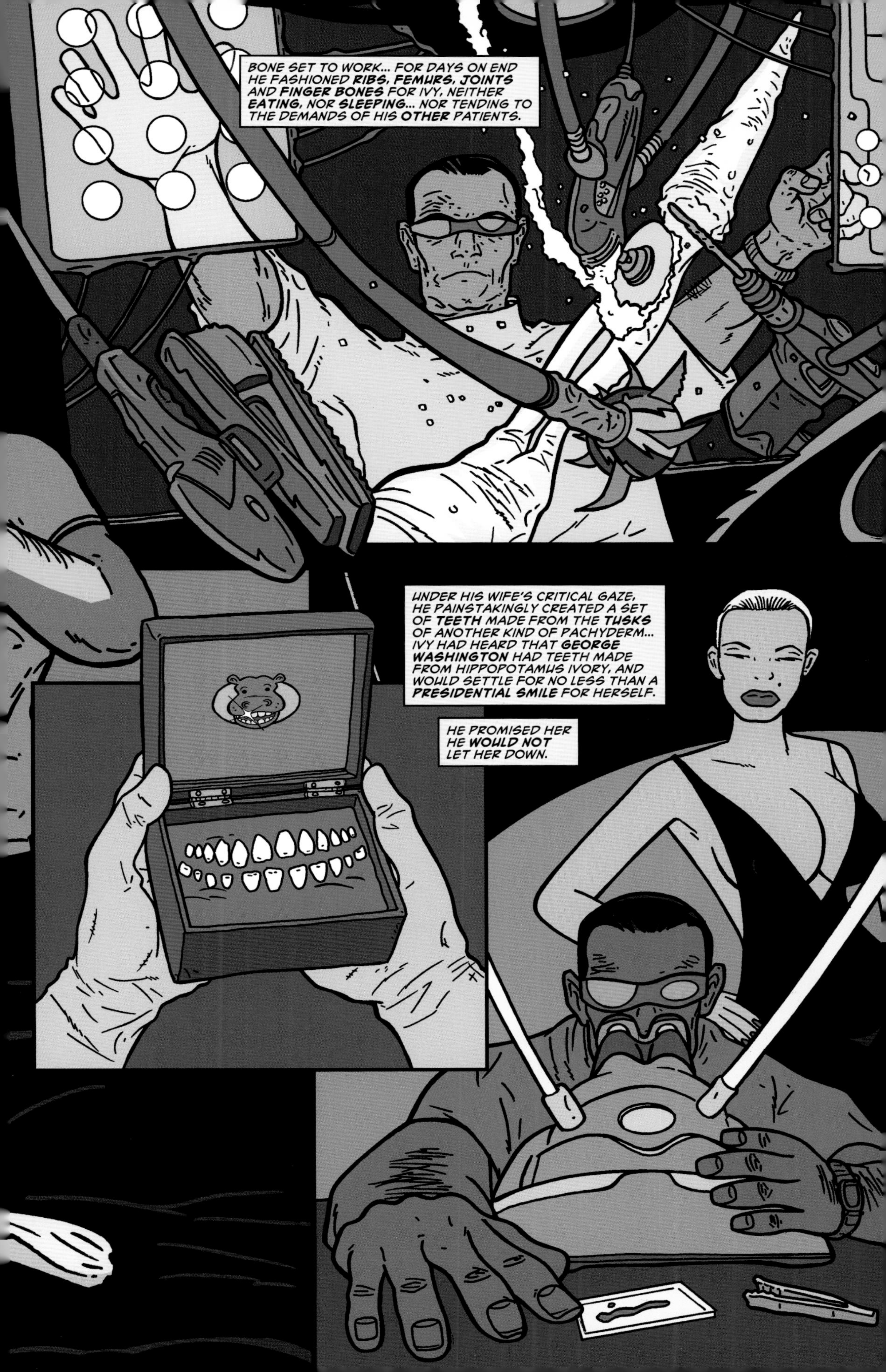
BONE SET TO WORK... FOR DAYS ON END HE FASHIONED **RIBS, FEMURS, JOINTS** AND **FINGER BONES** FOR IVY, NEITHER **EATING**, NOR **SLEEPING**... NOR TENDING TO THE DEMANDS OF HIS **OTHER** PATIENTS.
UNDER HIS WIFE'S CRITICAL GAZE, HE PAINSTAKINGLY CREATED A SET OF **TEETH** MADE FROM THE **TUSKS** OF ANOTHER KIND OF PACHYDERM... IVY HAD HEARD THAT **GEORGE WASHINGTON** HAD TEETH MADE FROM HIPPOPOTAMUS IVORY, AND WOULD SETTLE FOR NO LESS THAN A **PRESIDENTIAL SMILE** FOR HERSELF.
HE PROMISED HER HE **WOULD NOT** LET HER DOWN.

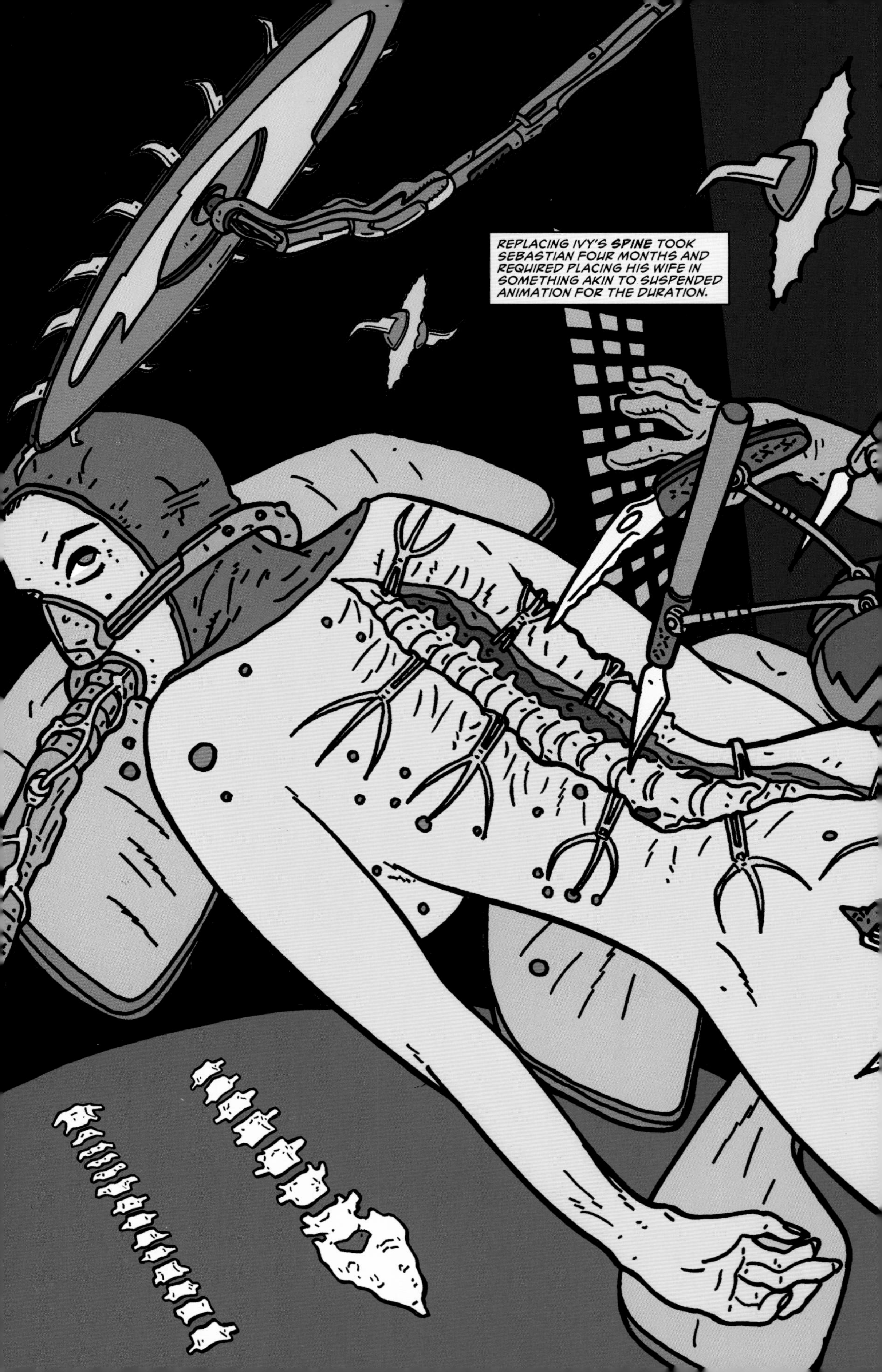
REPLACING IVY'S **SPINE** TOOK SEBASTIAN FOUR MONTHS AND REQUIRED PLACING HIS WIFE IN SOMETHING AKIN TO SUSPENDED ANIMATION FOR THE DURATION.

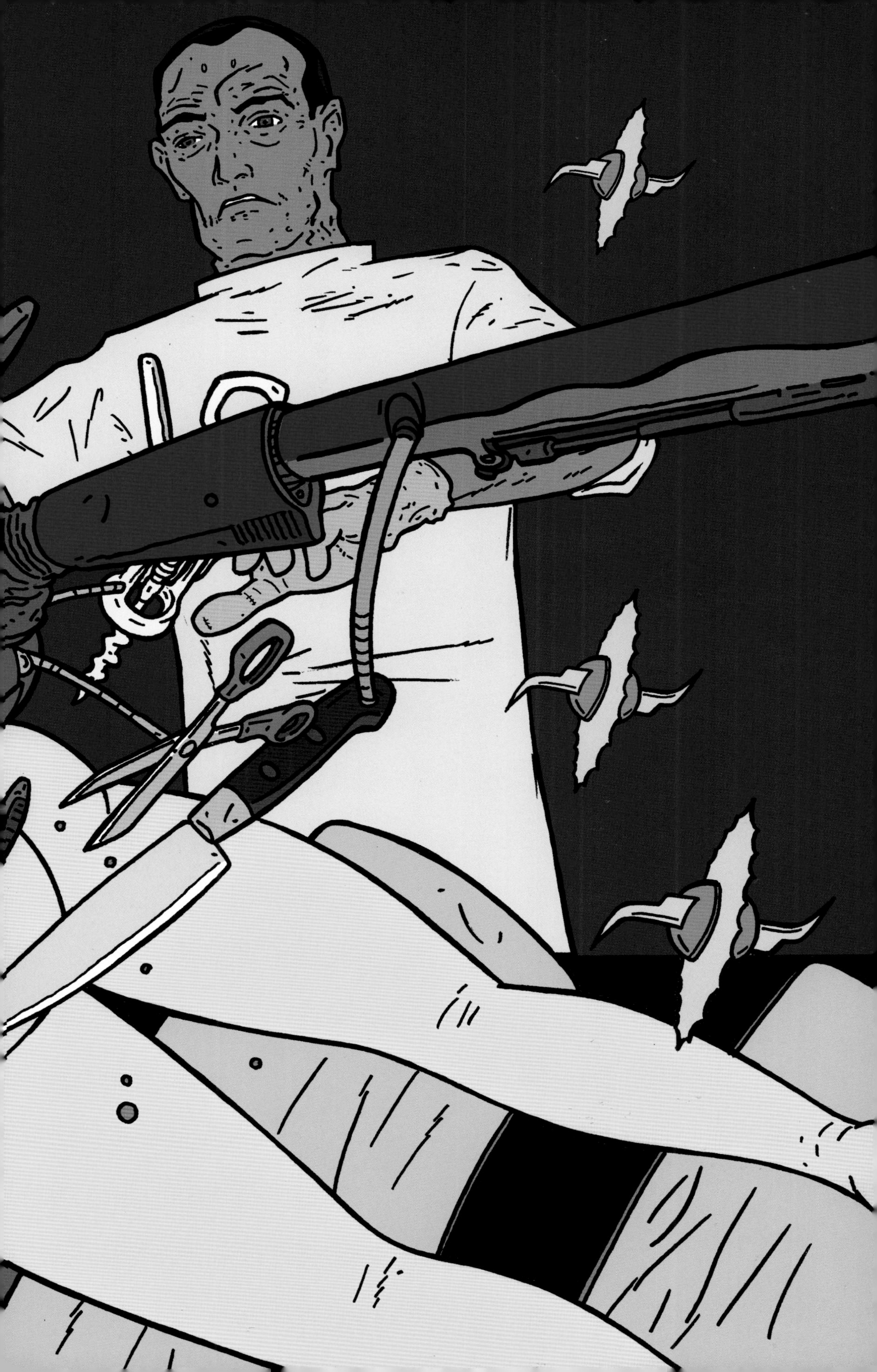

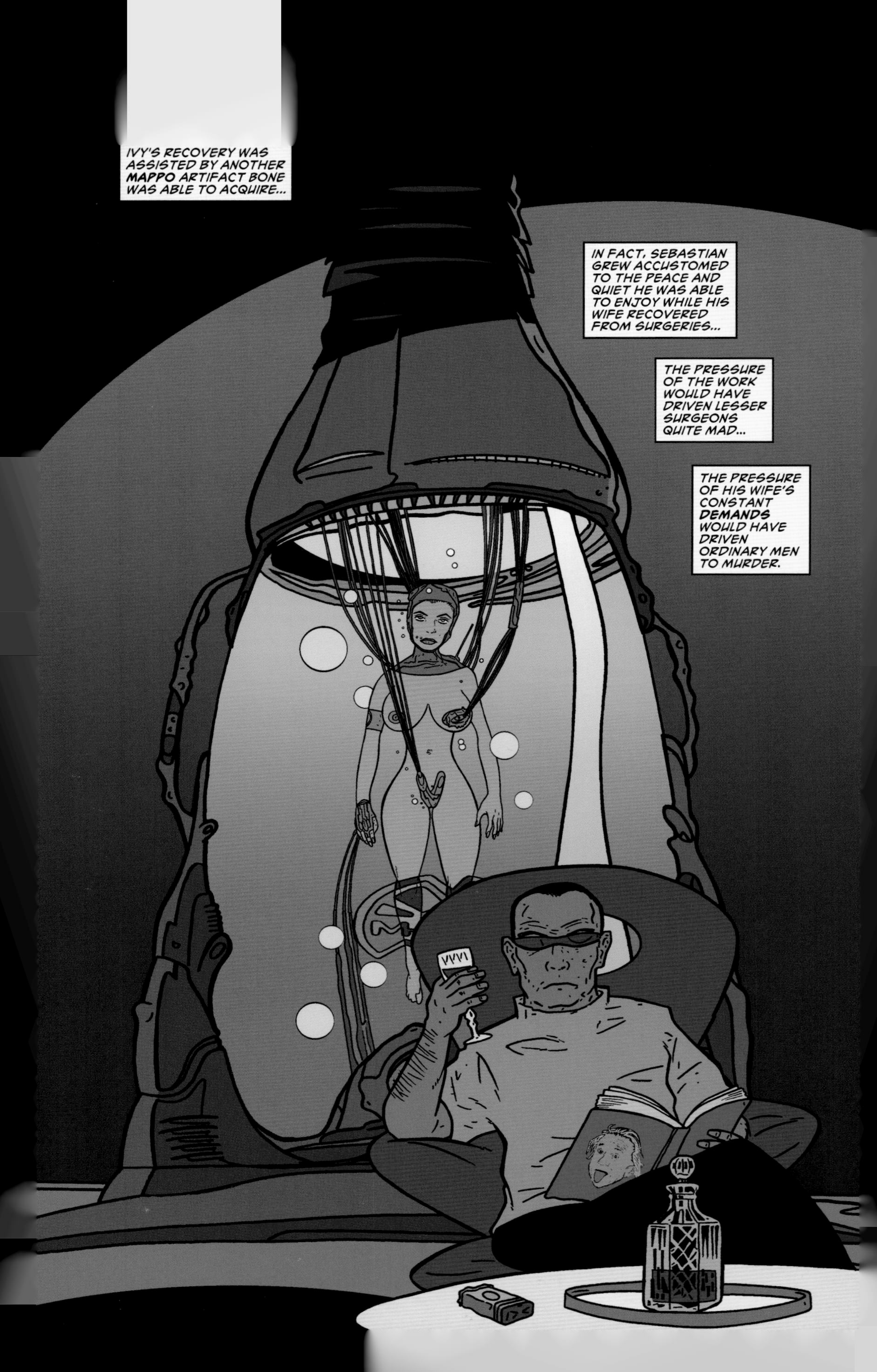
IVY'S RECOVERY WAS ASSISTED BY ANOTHER MAPPO ARTIFACT BONE WAS ABLE TO ACQUIRE...
IN FACT, SEBASTIAN GREW ACCUSTOMED TO THE PEACE AND QUIET HE WAS ABLE TO ENJOY WHILE HIS WIFE RECOVERED FROM SURGERIES...
THE PRESSURE OF THE WORK WOULD HAVE DRIVEN LESSER SURGEONS QUITE MAD...
THE PRESSURE OF HIS WIFE'S CONSTANT DEMANDS WOULD HAVE DRIVEN ORDINARY MEN TO MURDER.

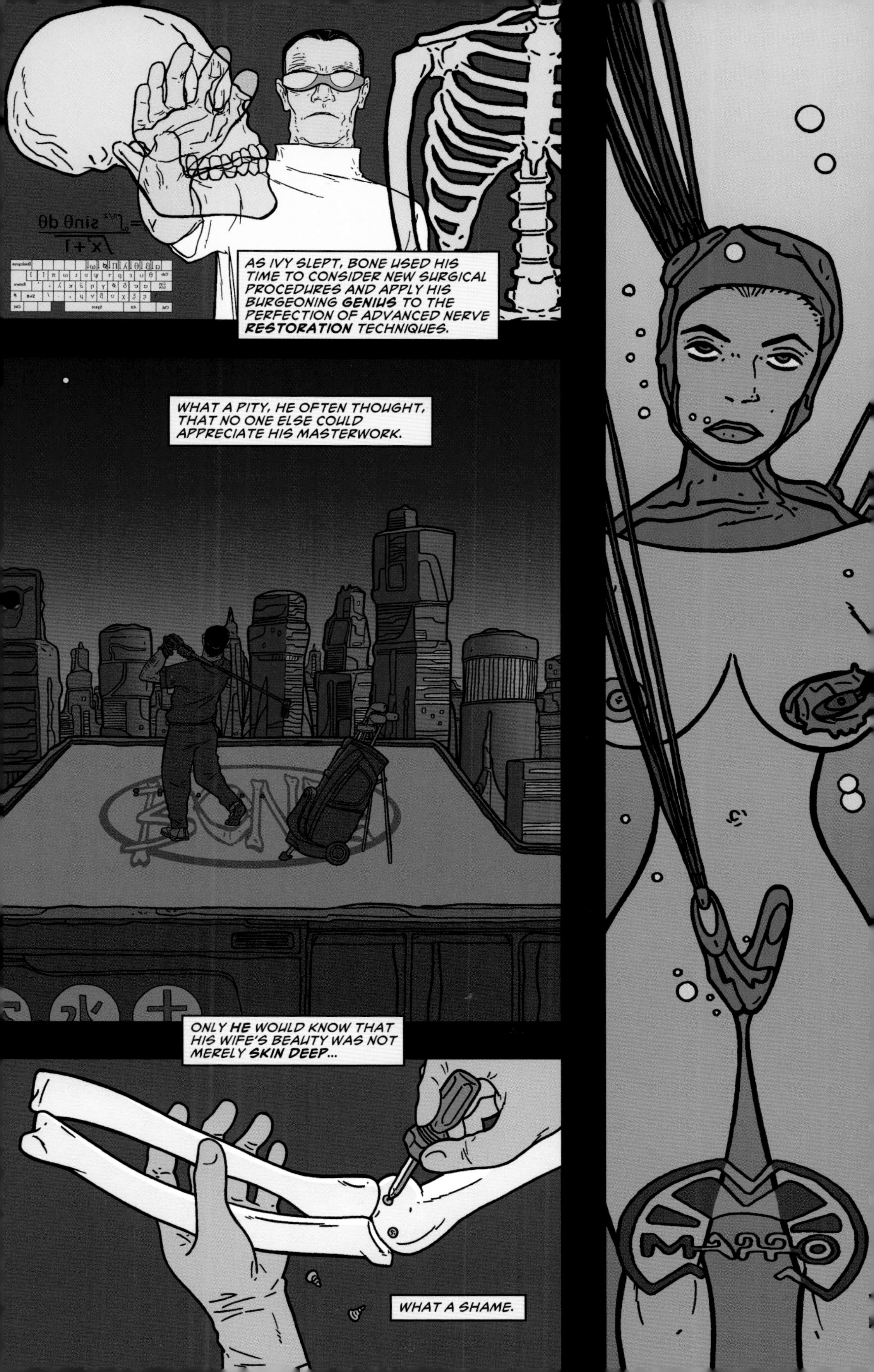
AS IVY SLEPT, BONE USED HIS TIME TO CONSIDER NEW SURGICAL PROCEDURES AND APPLY HIS BURGEONING GENIUS TO THE PERFECTION OF ADVANCED NERVE RESTORATION TECHNIQUES.
WHAT A PITY, HE OFTEN THOUGHT, THAT NO ONE ELSE COULD APPRECIATE HIS MASTERWORK.
ONLY HE WOULD KNOW THAT HIS WIFE'S BEAUTY WAS NOT MERELY SKIN DEEP...
WHAT A SHAME.

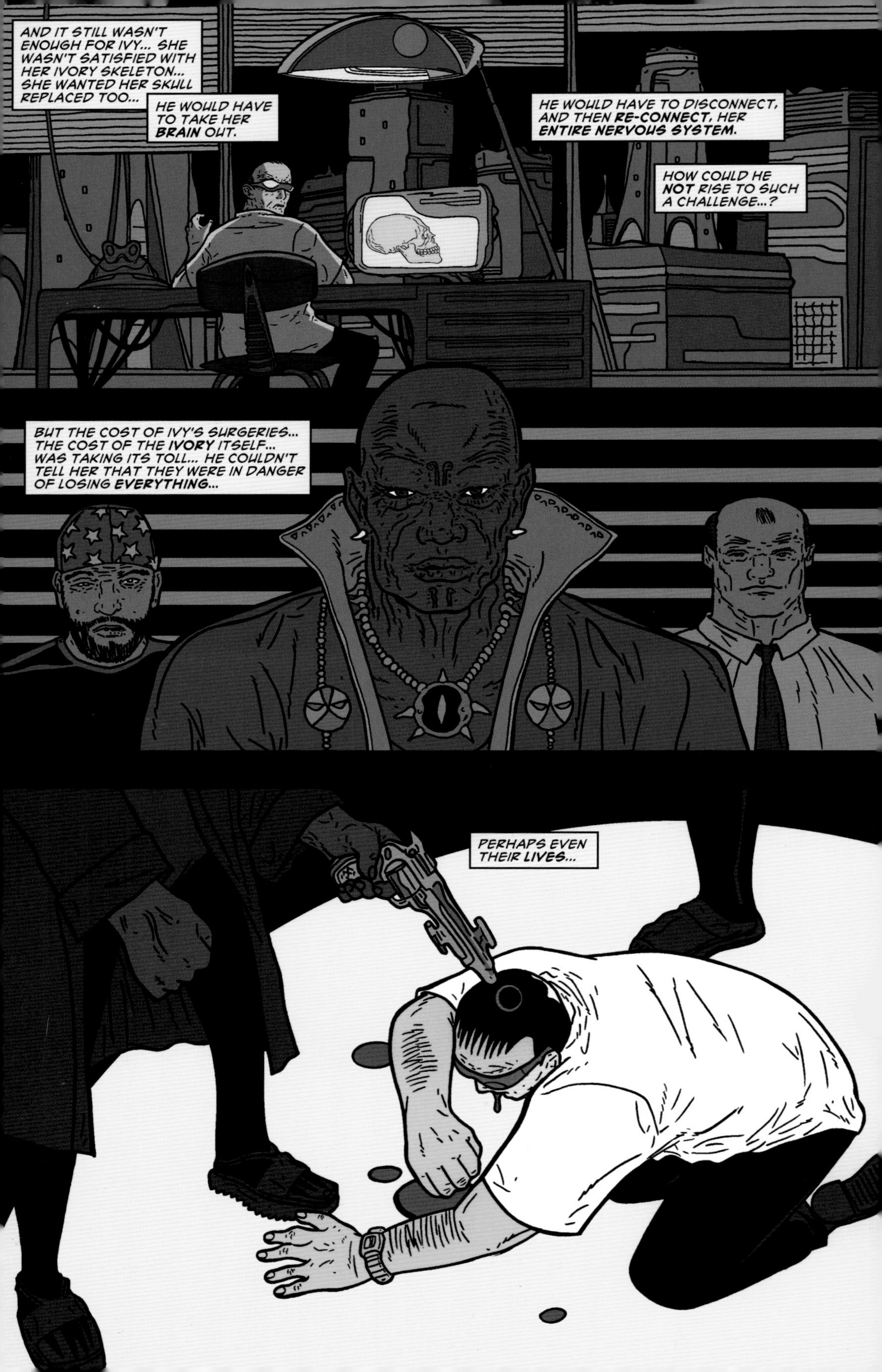
AND IT STILL WASN'T ENOUGH FOR IVY... SHE WASN'T SATISFIED WITH HER IVORY SKELETON... SHE WANTED HER SKULL REPLACED TOO...
HE WOULD HAVE TO TAKE HER BRAIN OUT.
HE WOULD HAVE TO DISCONNECT, AND THEN RE-CONNECT, HER ENTIRE NERVOUS SYSTEM.
HOW COULD HE NOT RISE TO SUCH A CHALLENGE...?
BUT THE COST OF IVY'S SURGERIES... THE COST OF THE IVORY ITSELF... WAS TAKING ITS TOLL... HE COULDN'T TELL HER THAT THEY WERE IN DANGER OF LOSING EVERYTHING...
PERHAPS EVEN THEIR LIVES...

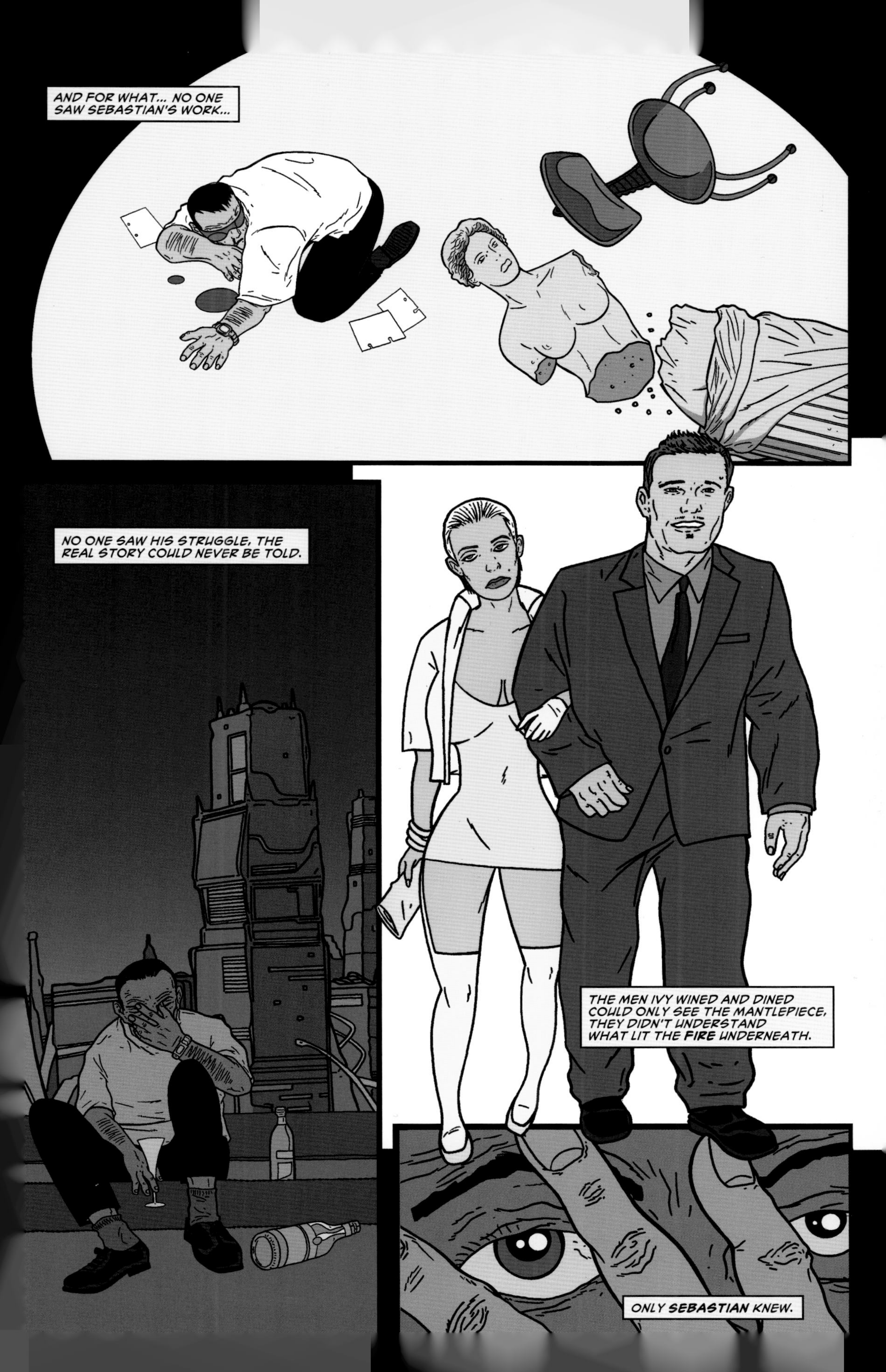
AND FOR WHAT... NO ONE SAW SEBASTIAN'S WORK...
NO ONE SAW HIS STRUGGLE, THE REAL STORY COULD NEVER BE TOLD.
THE MEN IVY WINED AND DINED COULD ONLY SEE THE MANTLEPIECE, THEY DIDN'T UNDERSTAND WHAT LIT THE FIRE UNDERNEATH.
ONLY SEBASTIAN KNEW.

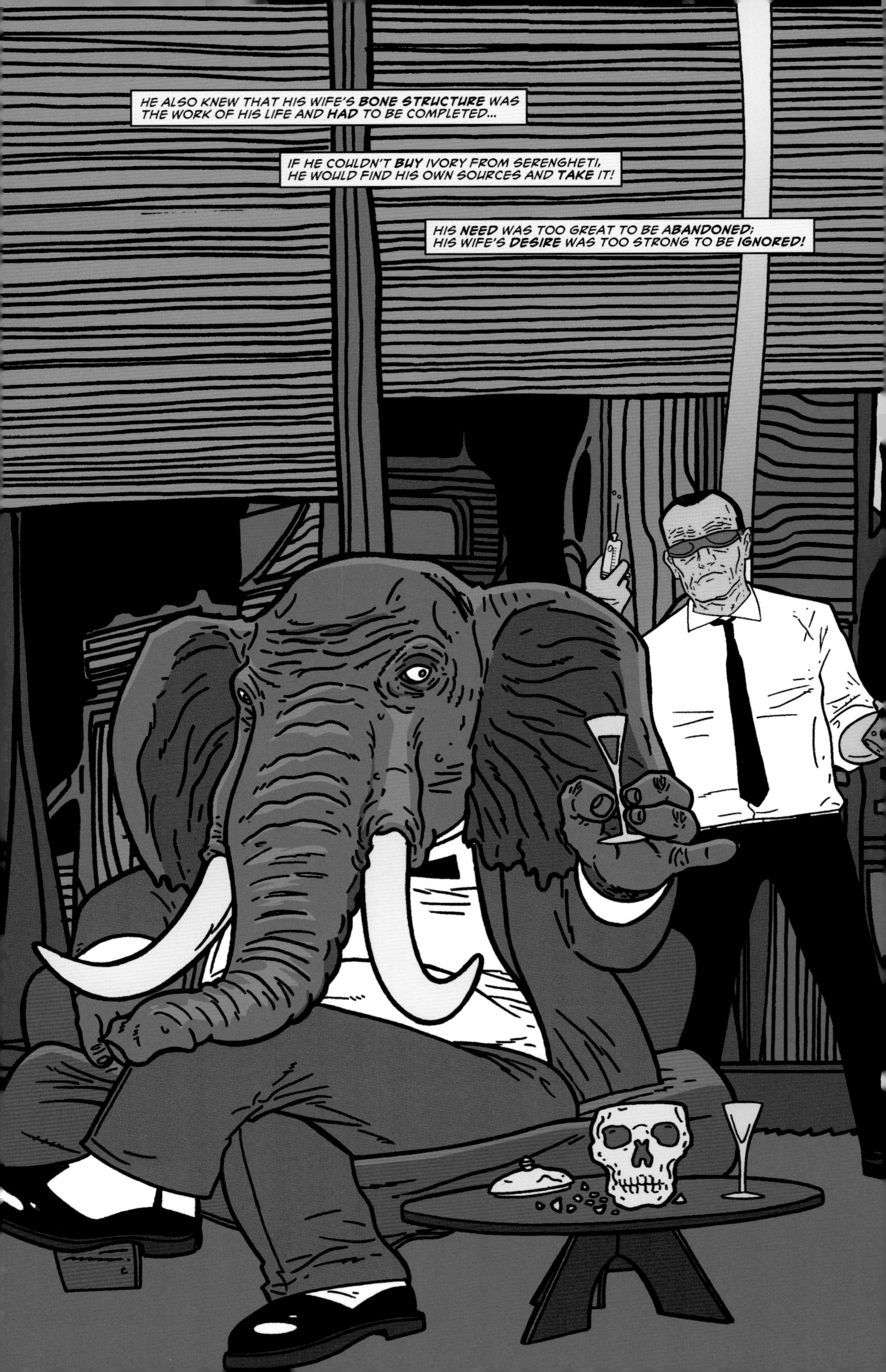
HE ALSO KNEW THAT HIS WIFE'S BONE STRUCTURE WAS THE WORK OF HIS LIFE AND HAD TO BE COMPLETED...
IF HE COULDN'T BUY IVORY FROM SERENGHETI, HE WOULD FIND HIS OWN SOURCES AND TAKE IT!
HIS NEED WAS TOO GREAT TO BE ABANDONED; HIS WIFE'S DESIRE WAS TOO STRONG TO BE IGNORED!

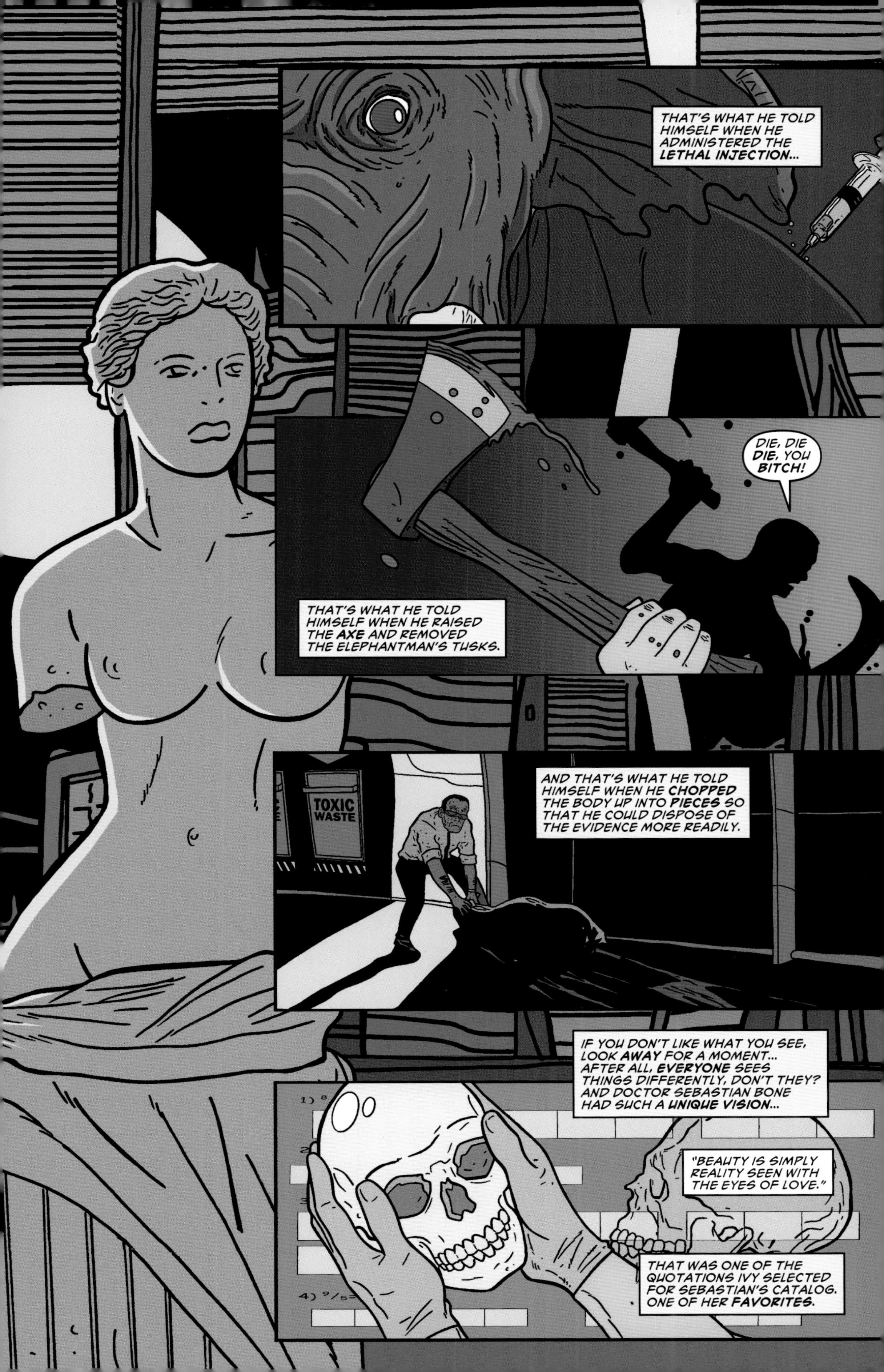
THAT'S WHAT HE TOLD HIMSELF WHEN HE ADMINISTERED THE LETHAL INJECTION...
DIE, DIE DIE, YOU BITCH!
THAT'S WHAT HE TOLD HIMSELF WHEN HE RAISED THE AXE AND REMOVED THE ELEPHANTMAN'S TUSKS.
TOXIC WASTE
AND THAT'S WHAT HE TOLD HIMSELF WHEN HE CHOPPED THE BODY UP INTO PIECES SO THAT HE COULD DISPOSE OF THE EVIDENCE MORE READILY.
IF YOU DON'T LIKE WHAT YOU SEE, LOOK AWAY FOR A MOMENT... AFTER ALL, EVERYONE SEES THINGS DIFFERENTLY, DON'T THEY? AND DOCTOR SEBASTIAN BONE HAD SUCH A UNIQUE VISION...
"BEAUTY IS SIMPLY REALITY SEEN WITH THE EYES OF LOVE."
THAT WAS ONE OF THE QUOTATIONS IVY SELECTED FOR SEBASTIAN'S CATALOG. ONE OF HER FAVORITES.

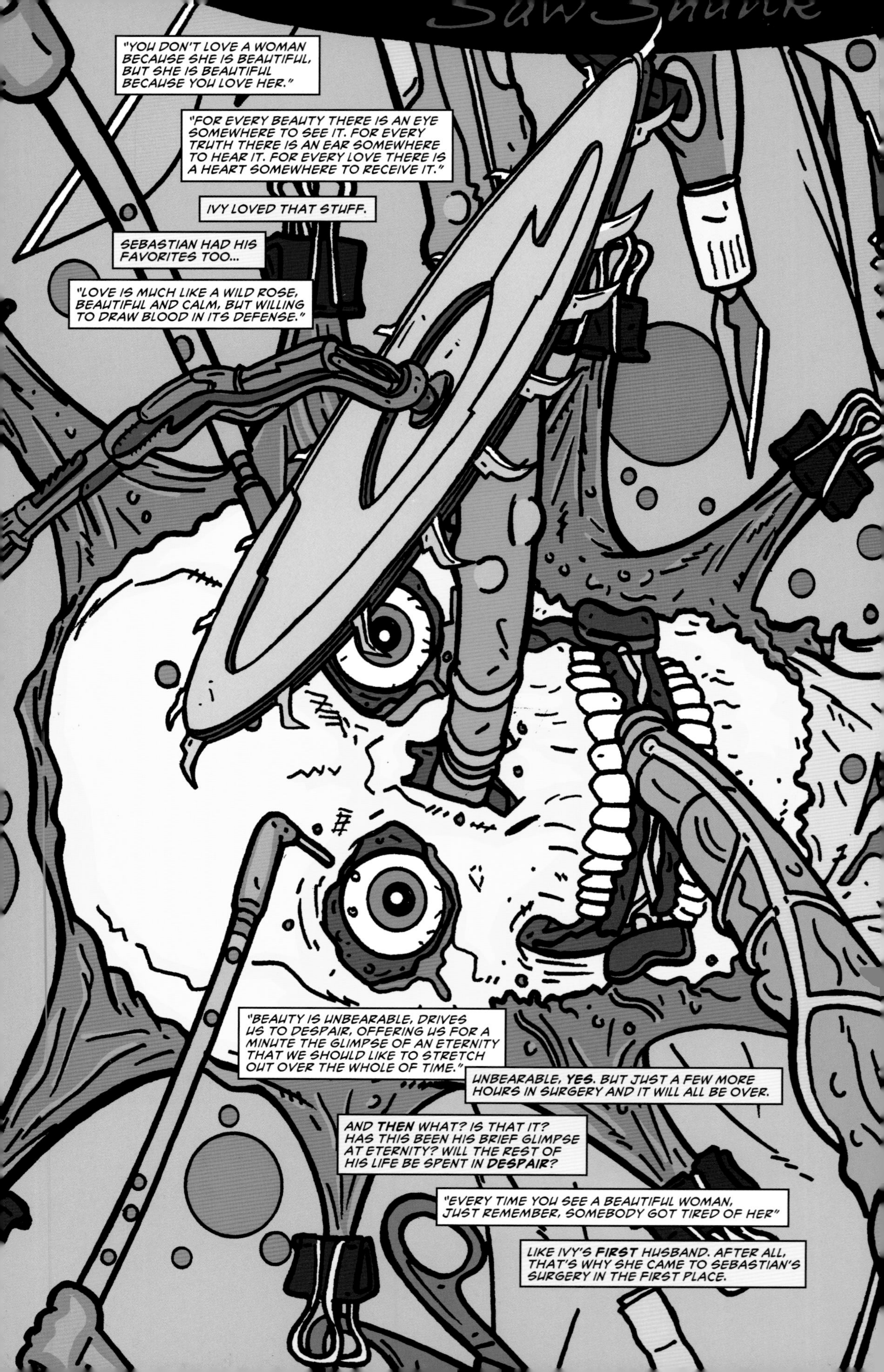
"YOU DON'T LOVE A WOMAN BECAUSE SHE IS BEAUTIFUL, BUT SHE IS BEAUTIFUL BECAUSE YOU LOVE HER."
"FOR EVERY BEAUTY THERE IS AN EYE SOMEWHERE TO SEE IT. FOR EVERY TRUTH THERE IS AN EAR SOMEWHERE TO HEAR IT. FOR EVERY LOVE THERE IS A HEART SOMEWHERE TO RECEIVE IT."
IVY LOVED THAT STUFF.
SEBASTIAN HAD HIS FAVORITES TOO...
"LOVE IS MUCH LIKE A WILD ROSE, BEAUTIFUL AND CALM, BUT WILLING TO DRAW BLOOD IN ITS DEFENSE."
"BEAUTY IS UNBEARABLE, DRIVES US TO DESPAIR, OFFERING US FOR A MINUTE THE GLIMPSE OF AN ETERNITY THAT WE SHOULD LIKE TO STRETCH OUT OVER THE WHOLE OF TIME."
UNBEARABLE, **YES**. BUT JUST A FEW MORE HOURS IN SURGERY AND IT WILL ALL BE OVER.
AND **THEN** WHAT? IS THAT IT? HAS THIS BEEN HIS BRIEF GLIMPSE AT ETERNITY? WILL THE REST OF HIS LIFE BE SPENT IN **DESPAIR**?
"EVERY TIME YOU SEE A BEAUTIFUL WOMAN, JUST REMEMBER, SOMEBODY GOT TIRED OF HER"
LIKE IVY'S **FIRST** HUSBAND. AFTER ALL, THAT'S WHY SHE CAME TO SEBASTIAN'S SURGERY IN THE FIRST PLACE.

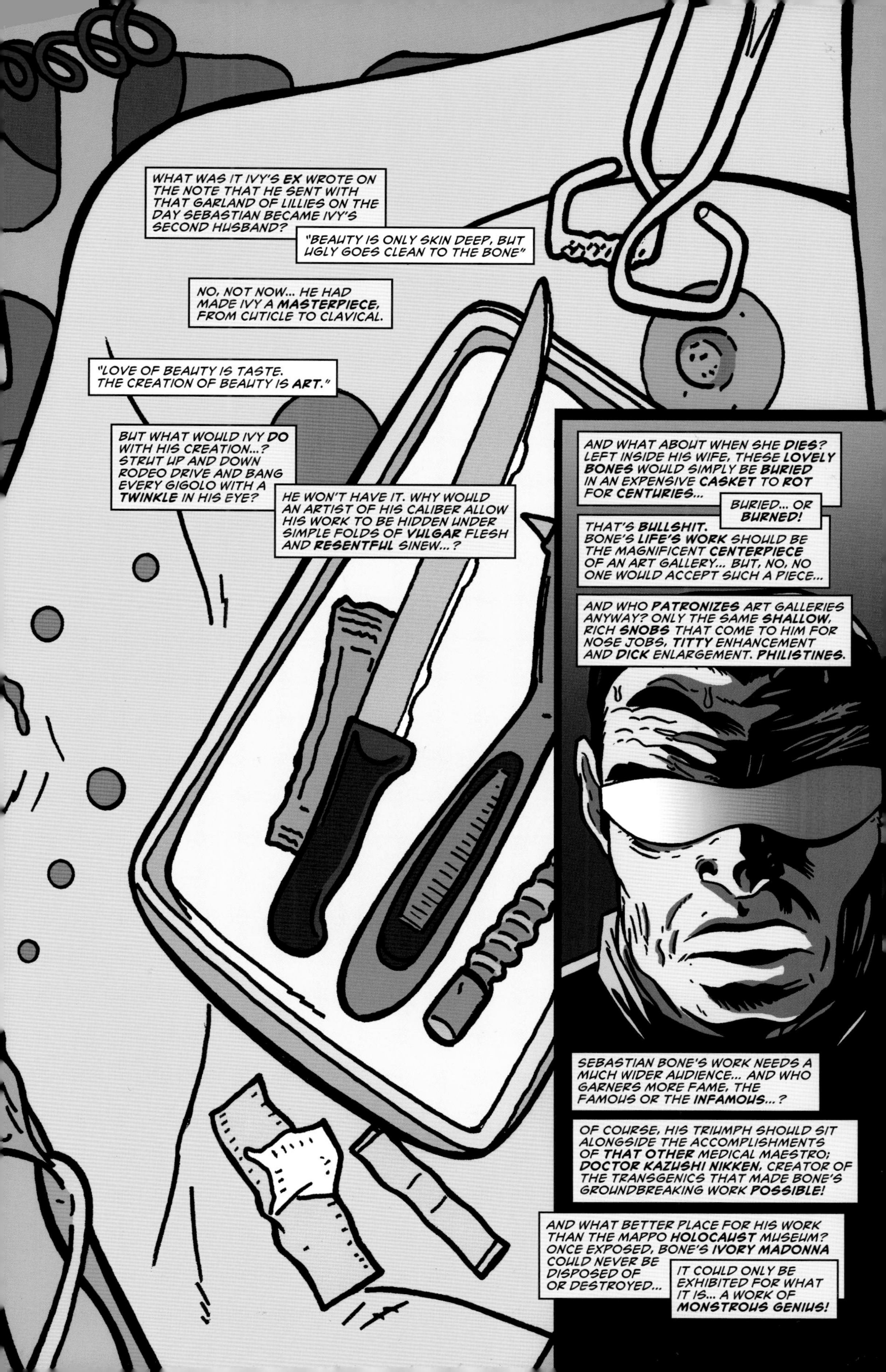
WHAT WAS IT IVY'S EX WROTE ON THE NOTE THAT HE SENT WITH THAT GARLAND OF LILLIES ON THE DAY SEBASTIAN BECAME IVY'S SECOND HUSBAND?
"BEAUTY IS ONLY SKIN DEEP, BUT UGLY GOES CLEAN TO THE BONE"
NO, NOT NOW... HE HAD MADE IVY A MASTERPIECE, FROM CUTICLE TO CLAVICAL.
"LOVE OF BEAUTY IS TASTE. THE CREATION OF BEAUTY IS ART."
BUT WHAT WOULD IVY DO WITH HIS CREATION...? STRUT UP AND DOWN RODEO DRIVE AND BANG EVERY GIGOLO WITH A TWINKLE IN HIS EYE?
HE WON'T HAVE IT. WHY WOULD AN ARTIST OF HIS CALIBER ALLOW HIS WORK TO BE HIDDEN UNDER SIMPLE FOLDS OF VULGAR FLESH AND RESENTFUL SINEW...?
AND WHAT ABOUT WHEN SHE DIES? LEFT INSIDE HIS WIFE, THESE LOVELY BONES WOULD SIMPLY BE BURIED IN AN EXPENSIVE CASKET TO ROT FOR CENTURIES...
BURIED... OR BURNED!
THAT'S BULLSHIT. BONE'S LIFE'S WORK SHOULD BE THE MAGNIFICENT CENTERPIECE OF AN ART GALLERY... BUT, NO, NO ONE WOULD ACCEPT SUCH A PIECE...
AND WHO PATRONIZES ART GALLERIES ANYWAY? ONLY THE SAME SHALLOW, RICH SNOBS THAT COME TO HIM FOR NOSE JOBS, TITTY ENHANCEMENT AND DICK ENLARGEMENT. PHILISTINES.
SEBASTIAN BONE'S WORK NEEDS A MUCH WIDER AUDIENCE... AND WHO GARNERS MORE FAME, THE FAMOUS OR THE INFAMOUS...?
OF COURSE, HIS TRIUMPH SHOULD SIT ALONGSIDE THE ACCOMPLISHMENTS OF THAT OTHER MEDICAL MAESTRO; DOCTOR KAZUSHI NIKKEN, CREATOR OF THE TRANSGENICS THAT MADE BONE'S GROUNDBREAKING WORK POSSIBLE!
AND WHAT BETTER PLACE FOR HIS WORK THAN THE MAPPO HOLOCAUST MUSEUM? ONCE EXPOSED, BONE'S IVORY MADONNA COULD NEVER BE DISPOSED OF OR DESTROYED...
IT COULD ONLY BE EXHIBITED FOR WHAT IT IS... A WORK OF MONSTROUS GENIUS!

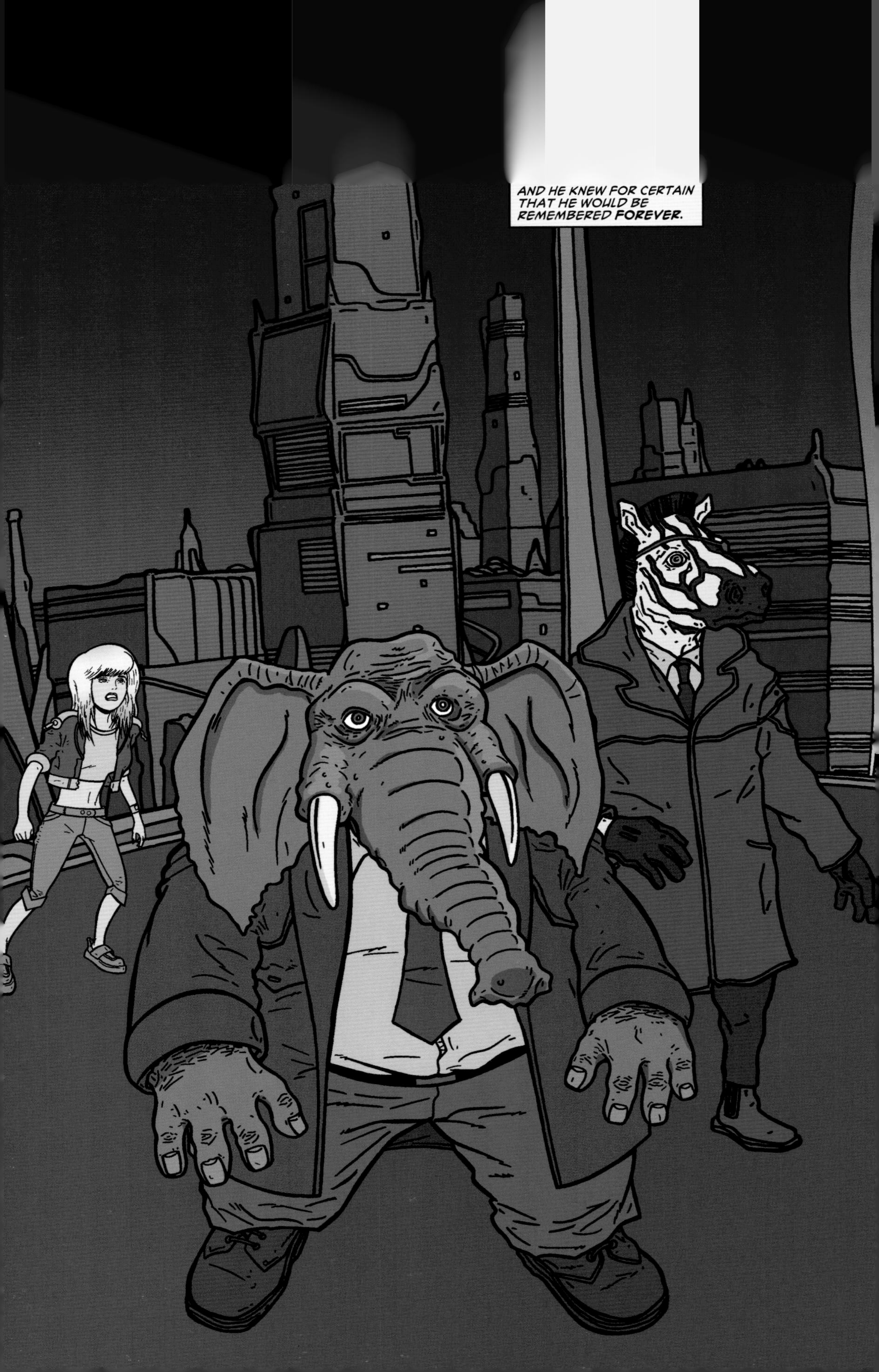
AND HE KNEW FOR CERTAIN THAT HE WOULD BE REMEMBERED FOREVER.

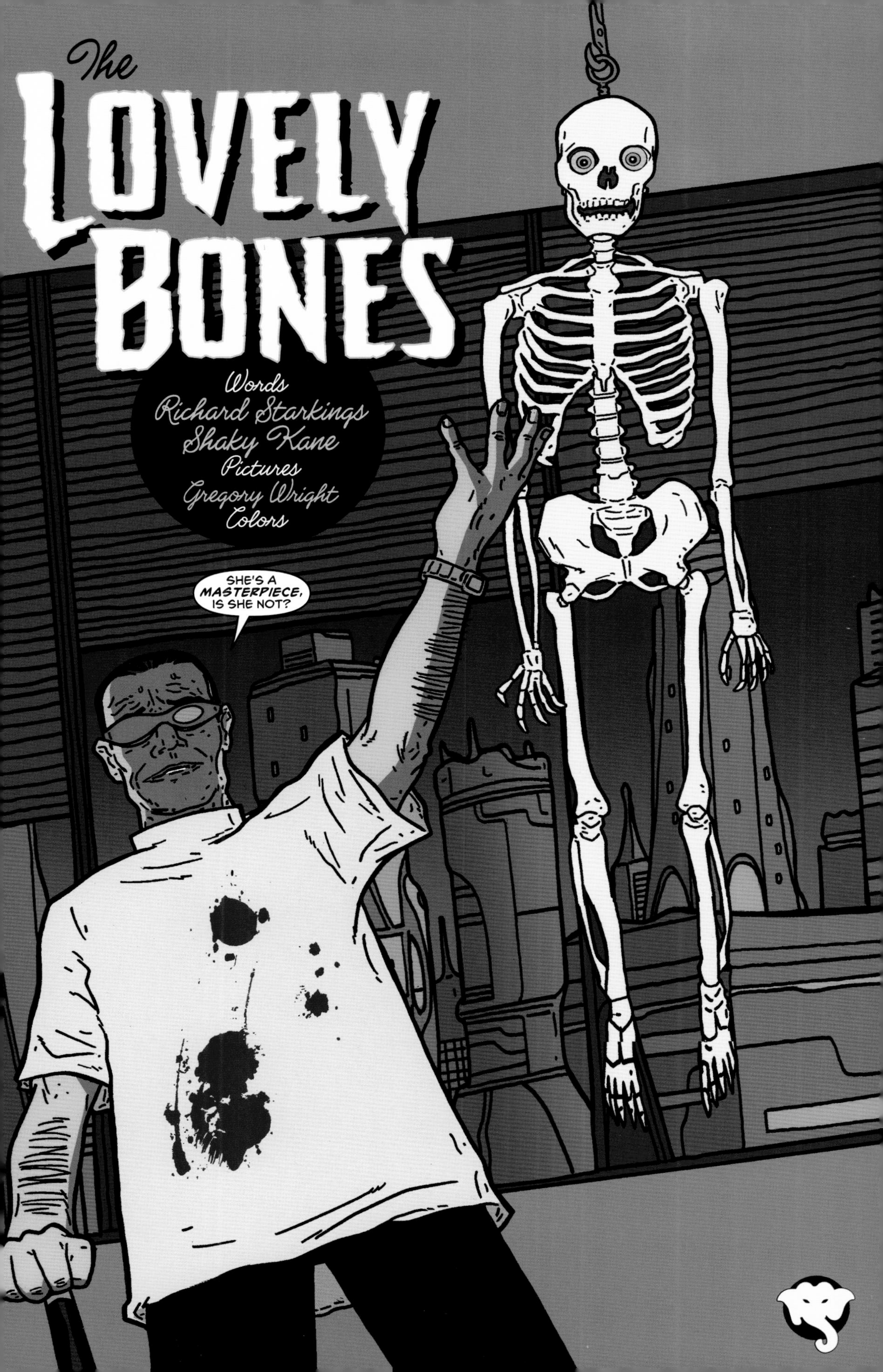
The LOVELY BONES
Words
Richard Starkings
Shaky Kane
Pictures
Gregory Wright
Colors
SHE'S A MASTERPIECE, IS SHE NOT?

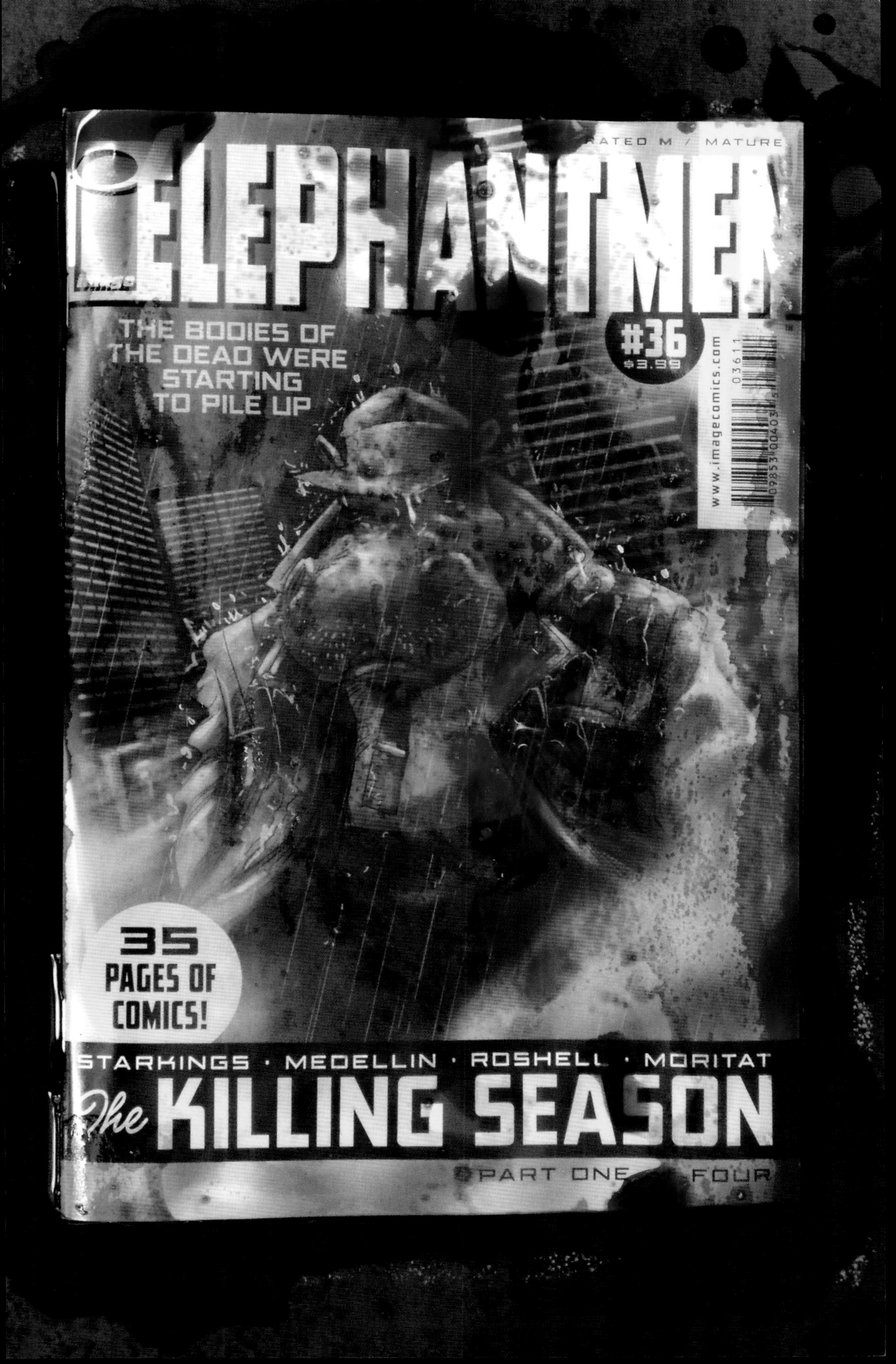
RATED M / MATURE
ELEPHANTMEN
THE BODIES OF THE DEAD WERE STARTING TO PILE UP
#36
$3.99
www.imagecomics.com
35 PAGES OF COMICS!
STARKINGS · MEDELLIN · ROSHELL · MORITAT
The KILLING SEASON
PART ONE
FOUR

"WRITTEN OVER THE GATE HERE
ARE THE WORDS 'LEAVE EVERY
HOPE BEHIND, YE WHO ENTER.'
ONLY THINK WHAT A RELIEF
THAT IS! FOR WHAT IS HOPE? A
FORM OF MORAL RESPONSIBILITY.
HERE THERE IS NO HOPE, AND
CONSEQUENTLY NO DUTY, NO
WORK, NOTHING TO BE GAINED
BY PRAYING, NOTHING TO BE
LOST BY DOING WHAT YOU LIKE.
HELL, IN SHORT, IS A PLACE
WHERE YOU HAVE NOTHING TO
DO BUT AMUSE YOURSELF."

GEORGE BERNARD SHAW
MAN AND SUPERMAN

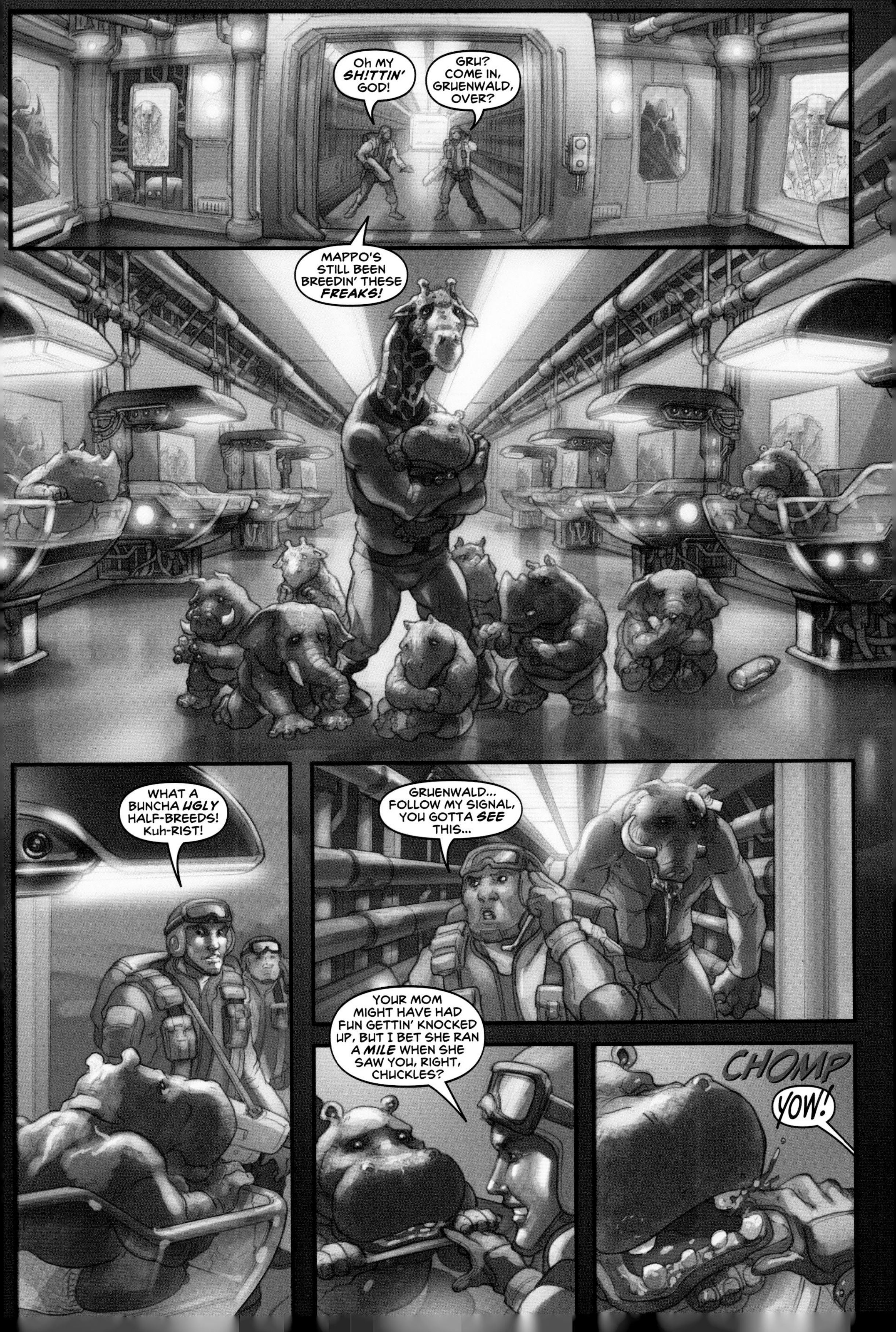
Oh MY SH!TTIN' GOD!
GRU? COME IN, GRUENWALD, OVER?
MAPPO'S STILL BEEN BREEDIN' THESE FREAKS!
WHAT A BUNCHA UGLY HALF-BREEDS! Kuh-RIST!
GRUENWALD... FOLLOW MY SIGNAL, YOU GOTTA SEE THIS...
YOUR MOM MIGHT HAVE HAD FUN GETTIN' KNOCKED UP, BUT I BET SHE RAN A MILE WHEN SHE SAW YOU, RIGHT, CHUCKLES?
CHOMP
YOW!

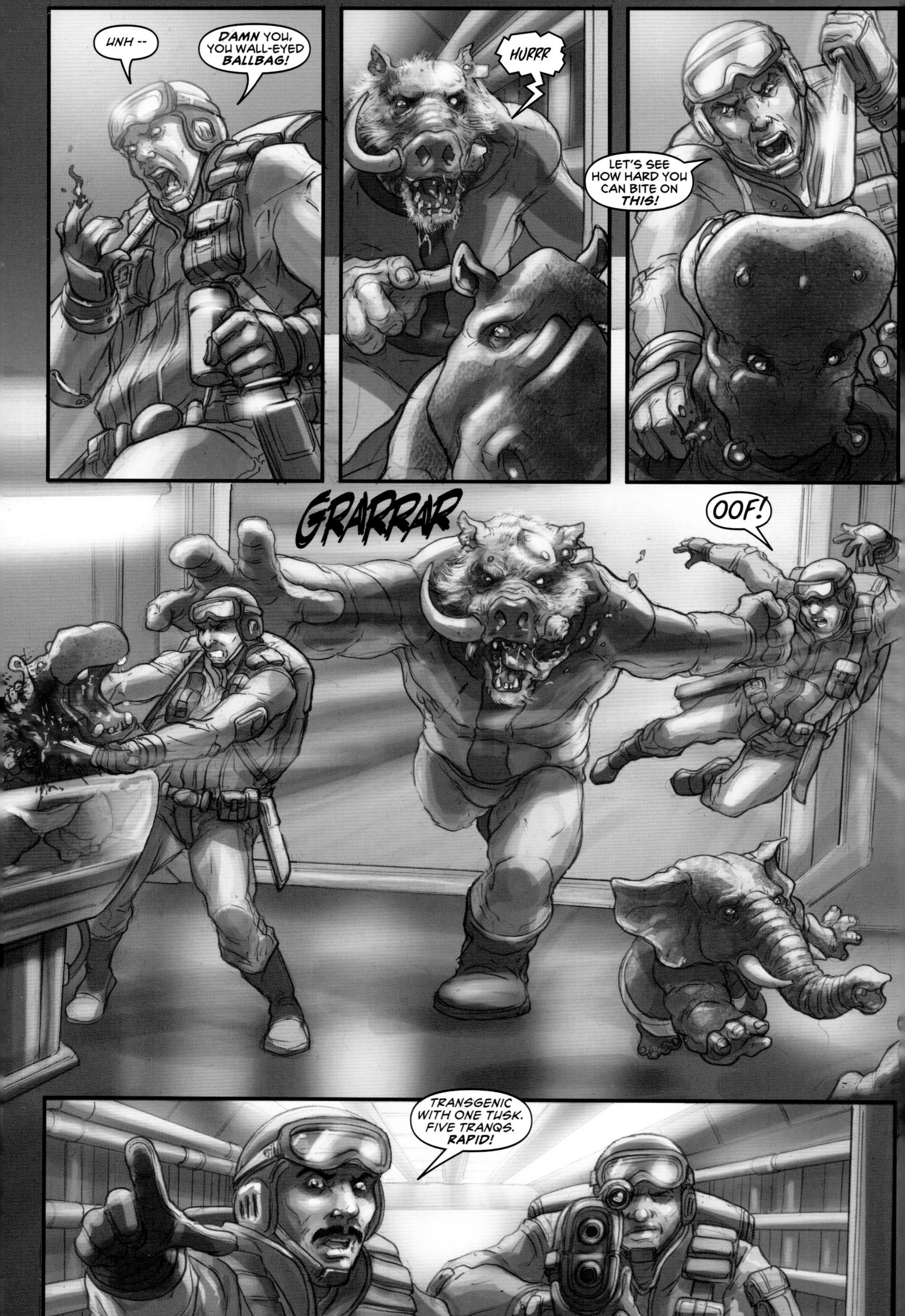
UNH --
DAMN YOU, YOU WALL-EYED BALLBAG!
HURRR
LET'S SEE HOW HARD YOU CAN BITE ON THIS!
GRARRAR
OOF!
TRANSGENIC WITH ONE TUSK. FIVE TRANQS. RAPID!

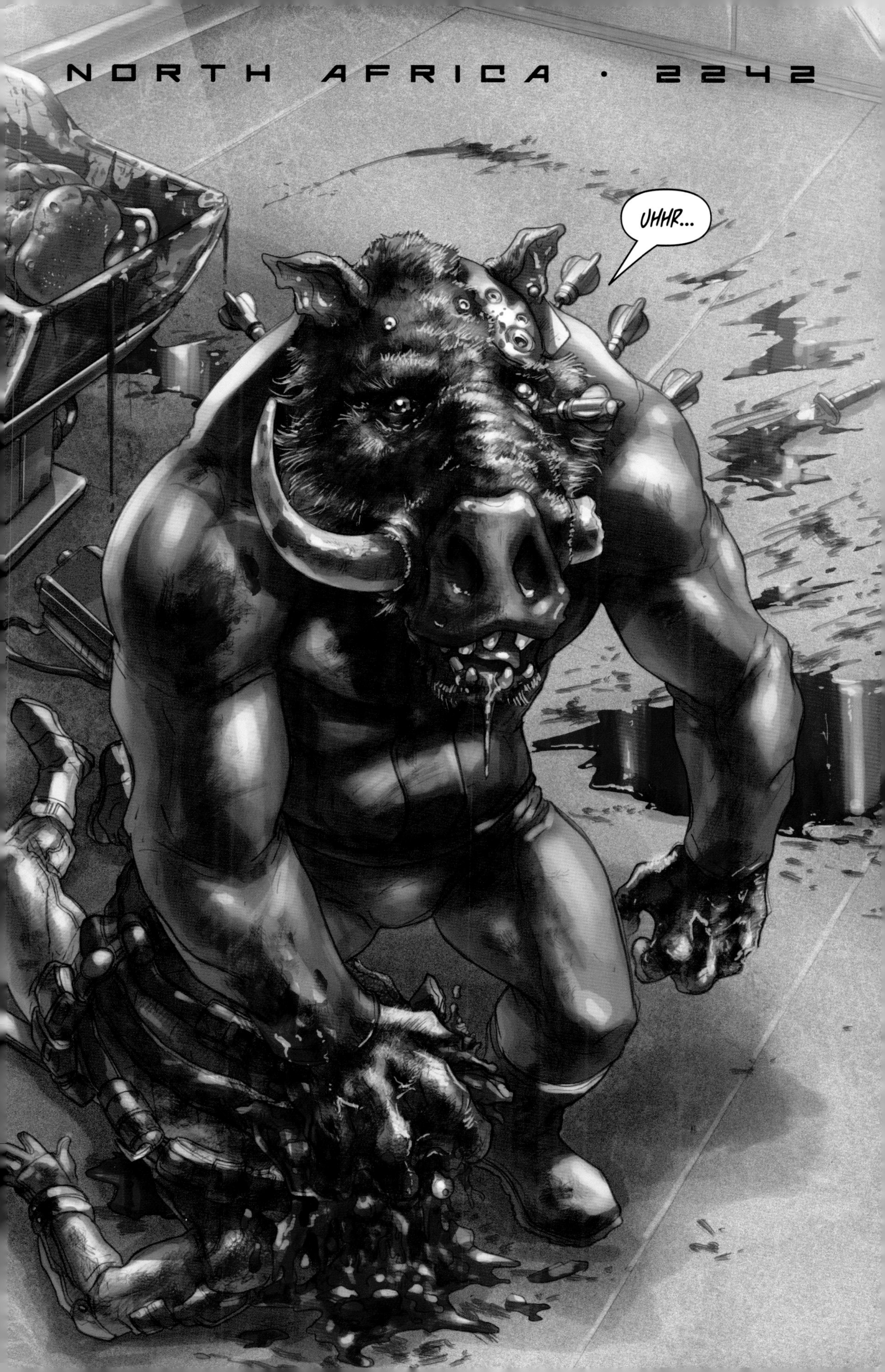
NORTH AFRICA · 2242
UHHR...

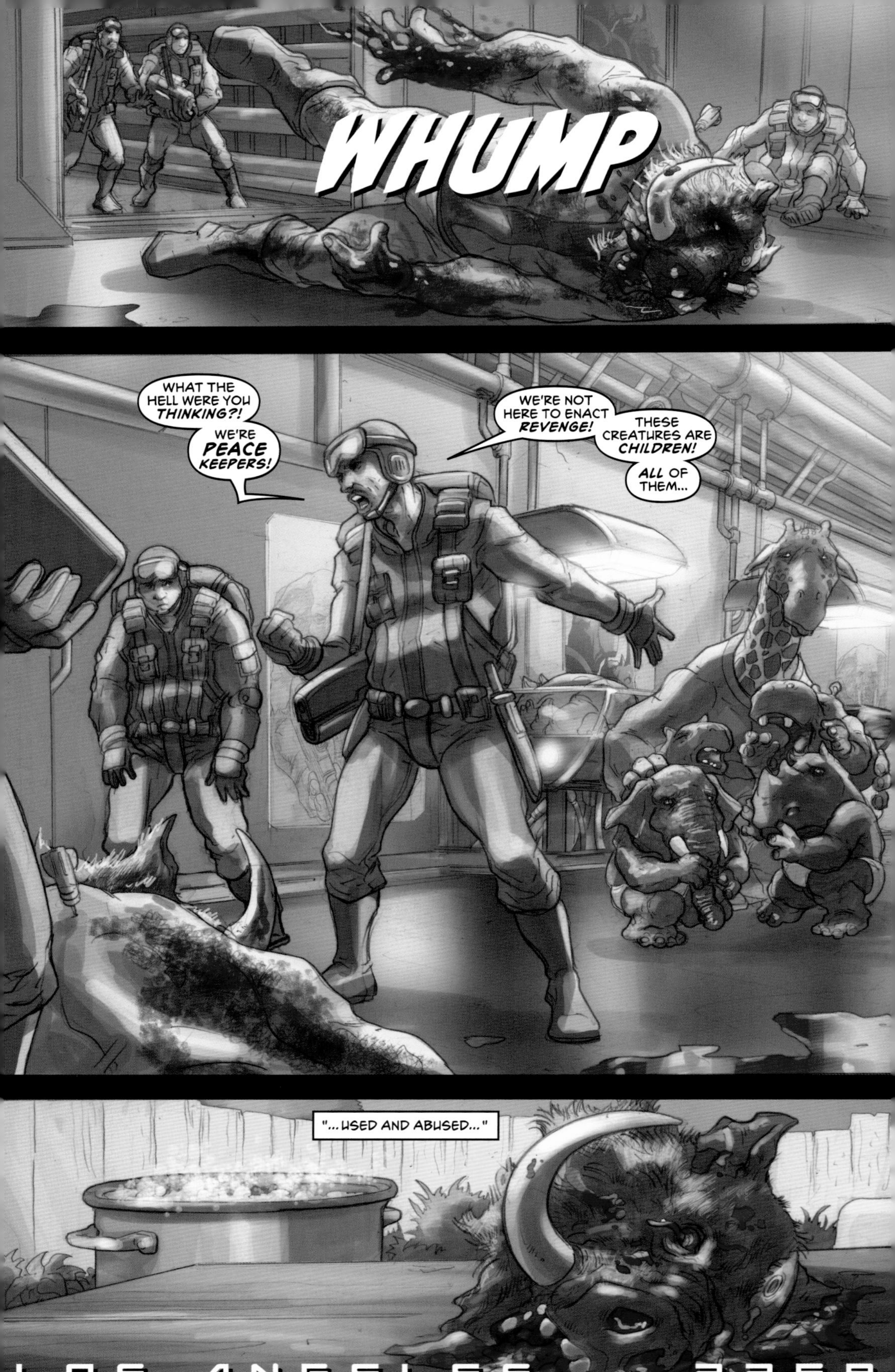
WHUMP
WHAT THE HELL WERE YOU THINKING?!
WE'RE PEACE KEEPERS!
WE'RE NOT HERE TO ENACT REVENGE!
THESE CREATURES ARE CHILDREN!
ALL OF THEM...
"...USED AND ABUSED..."

WHAT *ARE* YOU *STARING* AT, MINNIE?

WHAT'S HE DOING DOWN THERE, *HEY?* YOU KNOW I DON'T *SEE* TOO WELL.

HE'S A *WEIRD* ONE, ISN'T HE?

MIND YOU, SO WAS MY *POOR* JOE.*

ALLUS DOING SOMETHING *SECRETIVE.*

NAUGHTY.

THERE'S A TERRIBLE *SMELL* IN THE AIR, ISN'T THERE? LIKE ROTTEN *VEGETABLES.* DID YOU KILL A *MOUSE* AND LEAVE IT BEHIND THE *DRESSER* AGAIN, Eh, MINS?

*See ELEPHANTMEN #1, 8 & 1

"LOOKS LIKE HE'S *COOKING* SOMETHING, DON'T IT?"

GOVERNMENT HOUSING IS ALL VERY NICE AN' ALL... BUT THEY DON'T FEED US VERY WELL, DO THEY?

I HAVEN'T EATEN A NICE BIT OF MEAT LIKE THAT IN *MONTHS*...

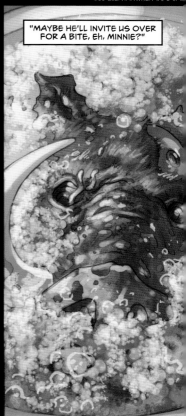

"MAYBE HE'LL INVITE US OVER FOR A BITE, EH, MINNIE?"

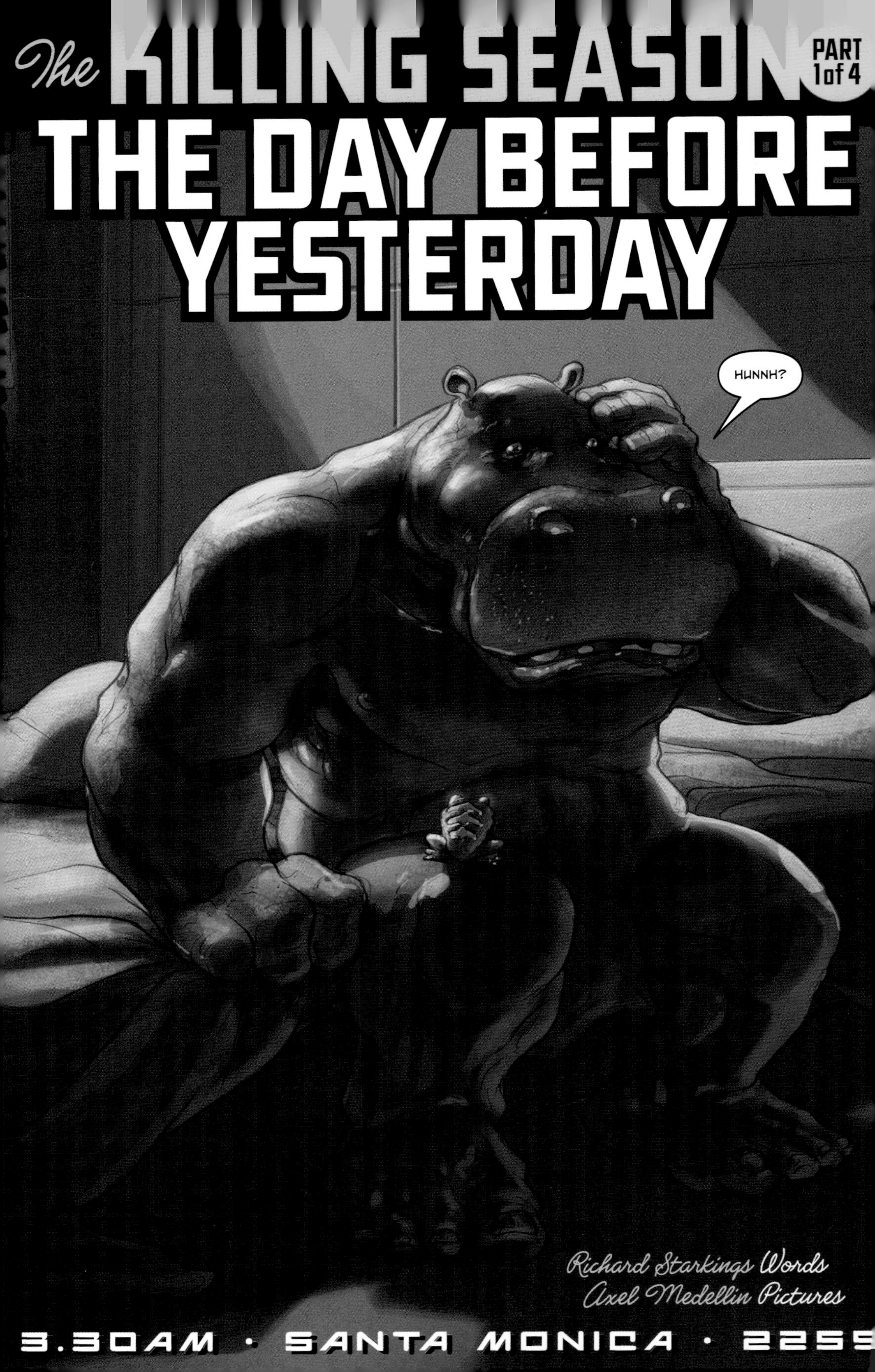
The KILLING SEASON
PART 1 of 4
THE DAY BEFORE YESTERDAY
HUNNH?
Richard Starkings Words
Axel Medellin Pictures
3.30AM · SANTA MONICA · 2255

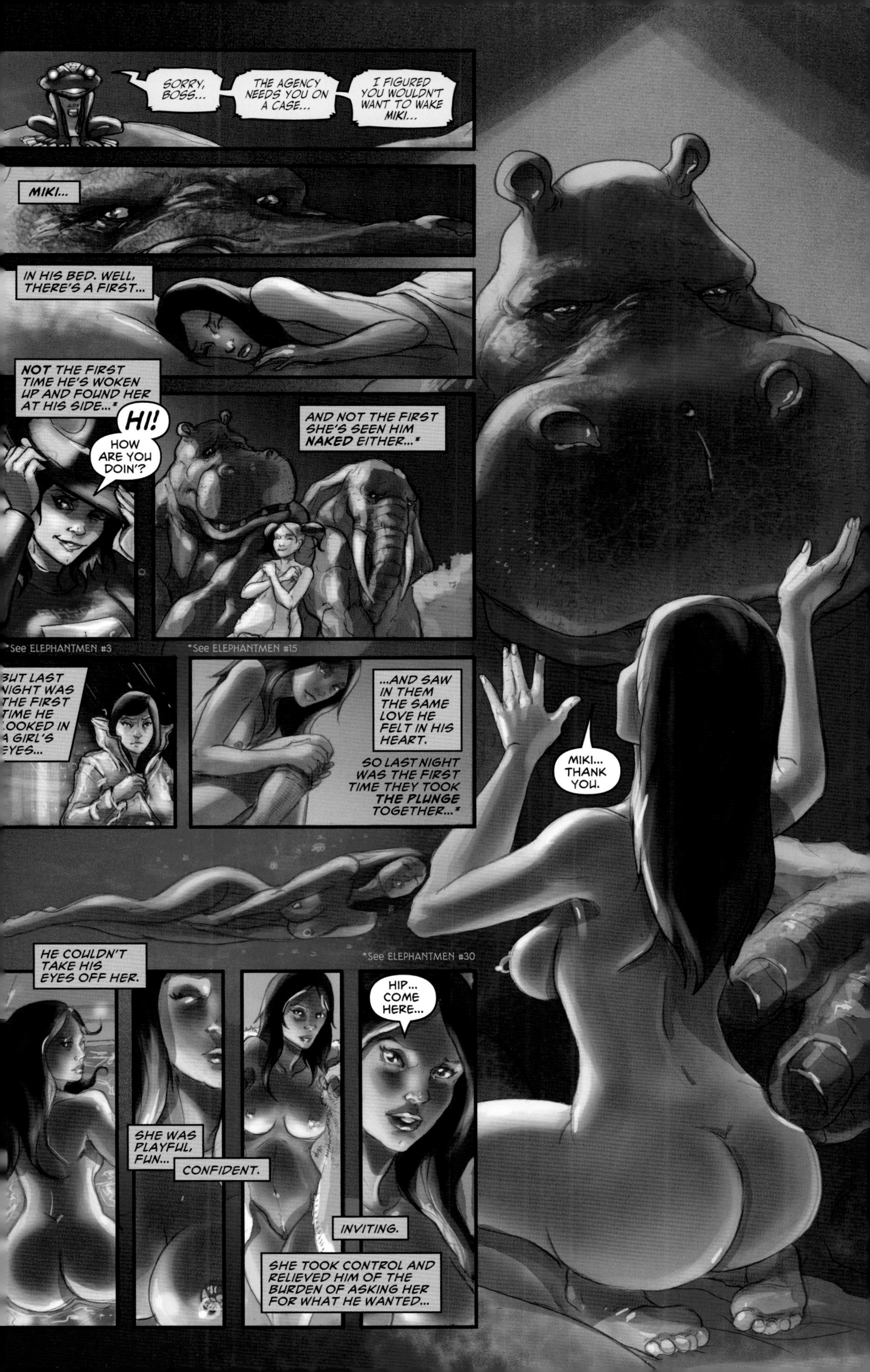
SORRY, BOSS...
THE AGENCY NEEDS YOU ON A CASE...
I FIGURED YOU WOULDN'T WANT TO WAKE MIKI...
MIKI...
IN HIS BED. WELL, THERE'S A FIRST...
NOT THE FIRST TIME HE'S WOKEN UP AND FOUND HER AT HIS SIDE...*
HI! HOW ARE YOU DOIN'?
AND NOT THE FIRST SHE'S SEEN HIM NAKED EITHER...*
*See ELEPHANTMEN #3
*See ELEPHANTMEN #15
BUT LAST NIGHT WAS THE FIRST TIME HE LOOKED IN A GIRL'S EYES...
...AND SAW IN THEM THE SAME LOVE HE FELT IN HIS HEART.
SO LAST NIGHT WAS THE FIRST TIME THEY TOOK THE PLUNGE TOGETHER...*
MIKI... THANK YOU.
*See ELEPHANTMEN #30
HE COULDN'T TAKE HIS EYES OFF HER.
HIP... COME HERE...
SHE WAS PLAYFUL, FUN...
CONFIDENT.
INVITING.
SHE TOOK CONTROL AND RELIEVED HIM OF THE BURDEN OF ASKING HER FOR WHAT HE WANTED...

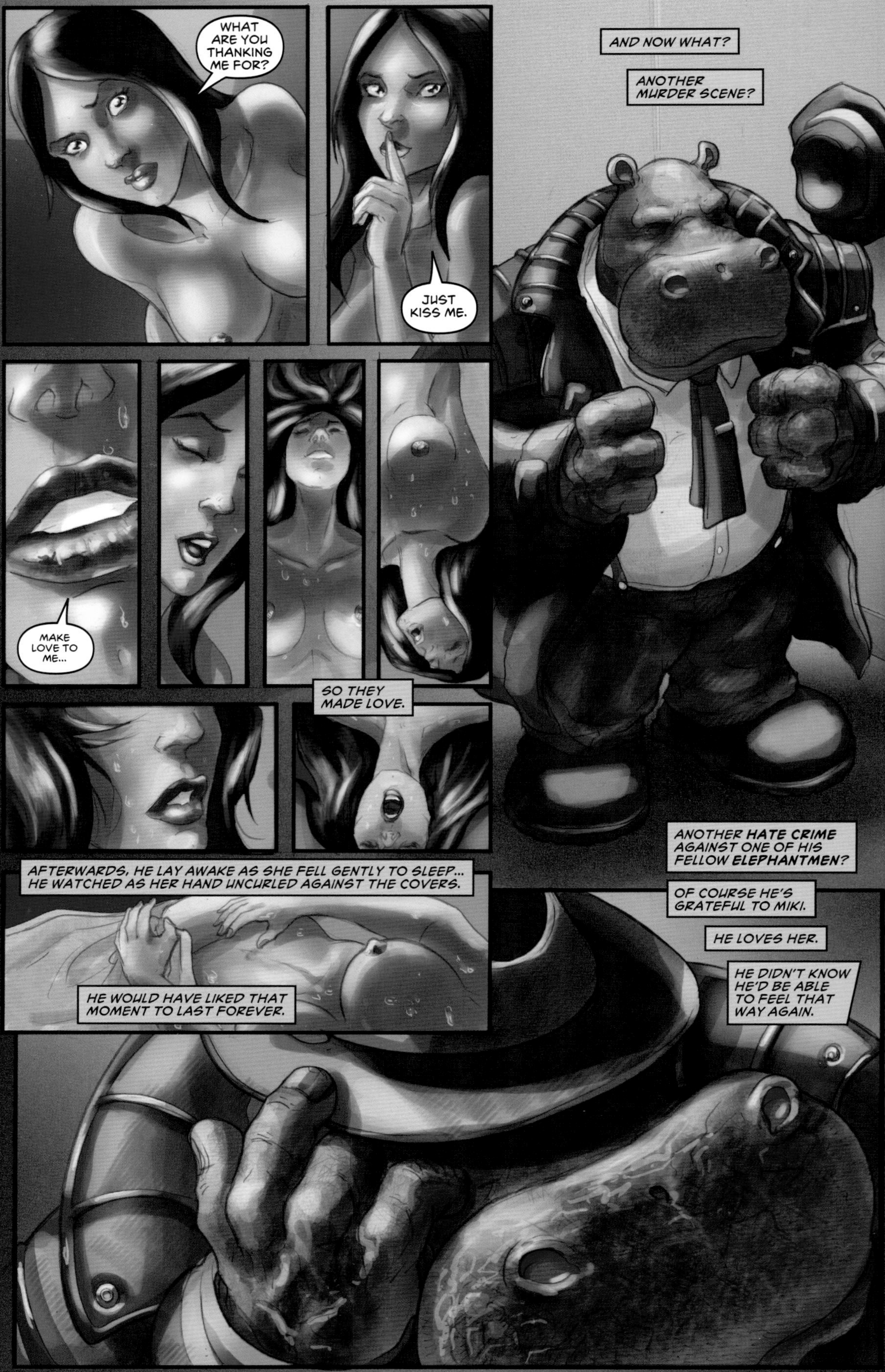

WHAT ARE YOU THANKING ME FOR?
JUST KISS ME.
AND NOW WHAT?
ANOTHER MURDER SCENE?
MAKE LOVE TO ME...
SO THEY MADE LOVE.
AFTERWARDS, HE LAY AWAKE AS SHE FELL GENTLY TO SLEEP... HE WATCHED AS HER HAND UNCURLED AGAINST THE COVERS.
HE WOULD HAVE LIKED THAT MOMENT TO LAST FOREVER.
ANOTHER **HATE CRIME** AGAINST ONE OF HIS FELLOW **ELEPHANTMEN**?
OF COURSE HE'S GRATEFUL TO MIKI.
HE LOVES HER.
HE DIDN'T KNOW HE'D BE ABLE TO FEEL THAT WAY AGAIN.

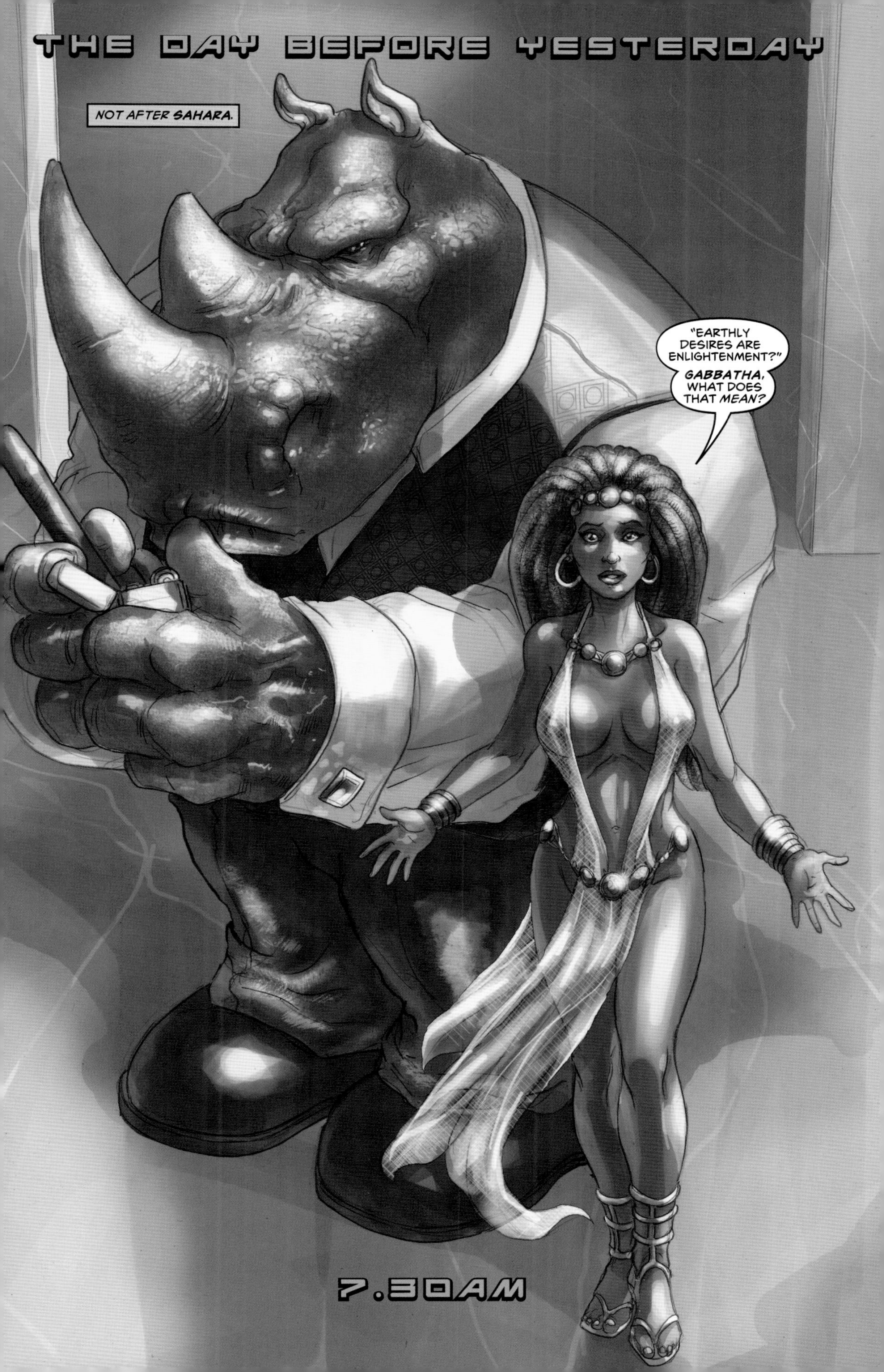
THE DAY BEFORE YESTERDAY
NOT AFTER SAHARA.
"EARTHLY DESIRES ARE ENLIGHTENMENT?" GABBATHA, WHAT DOES THAT MEAN?
7.30AM

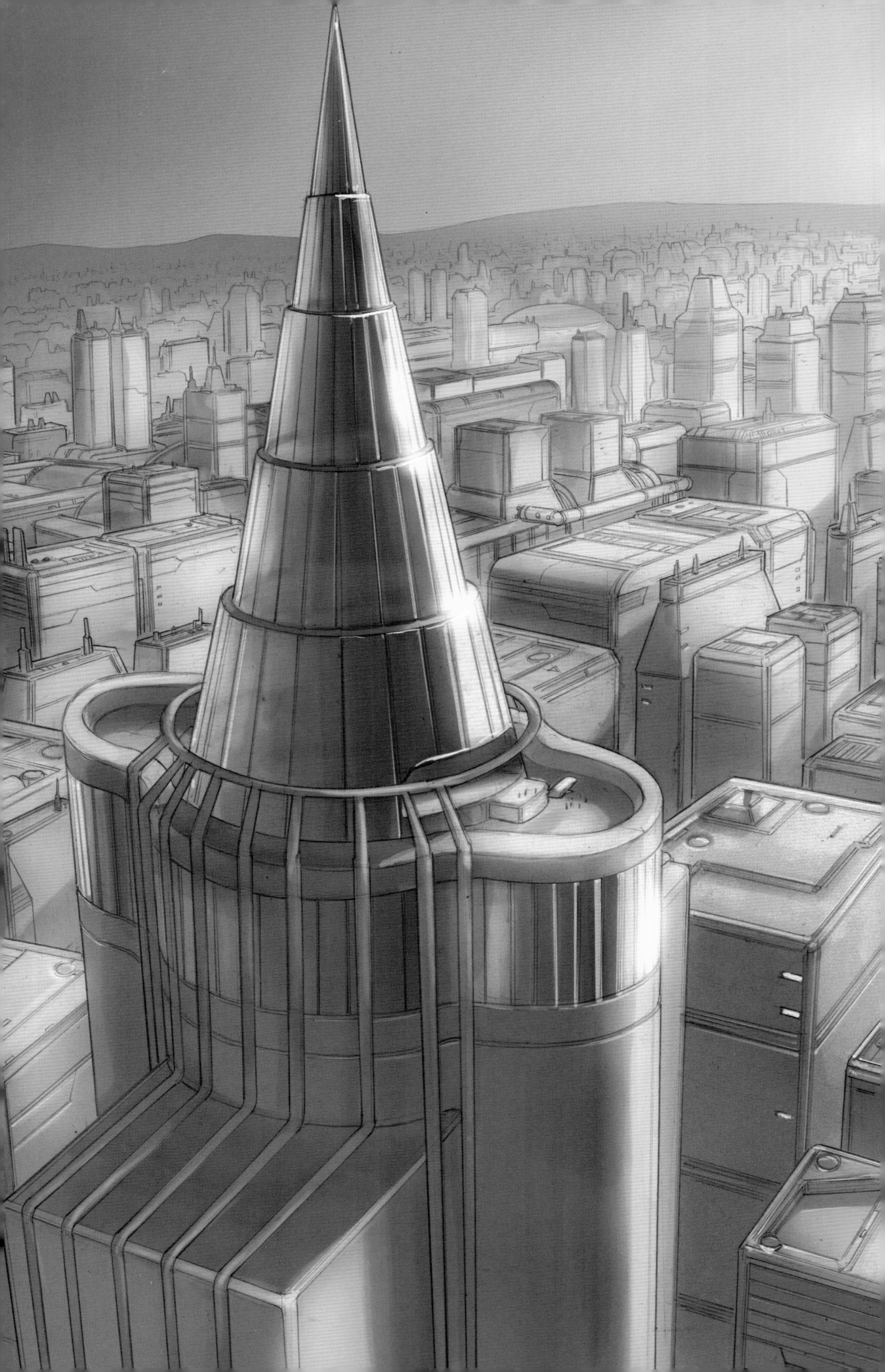

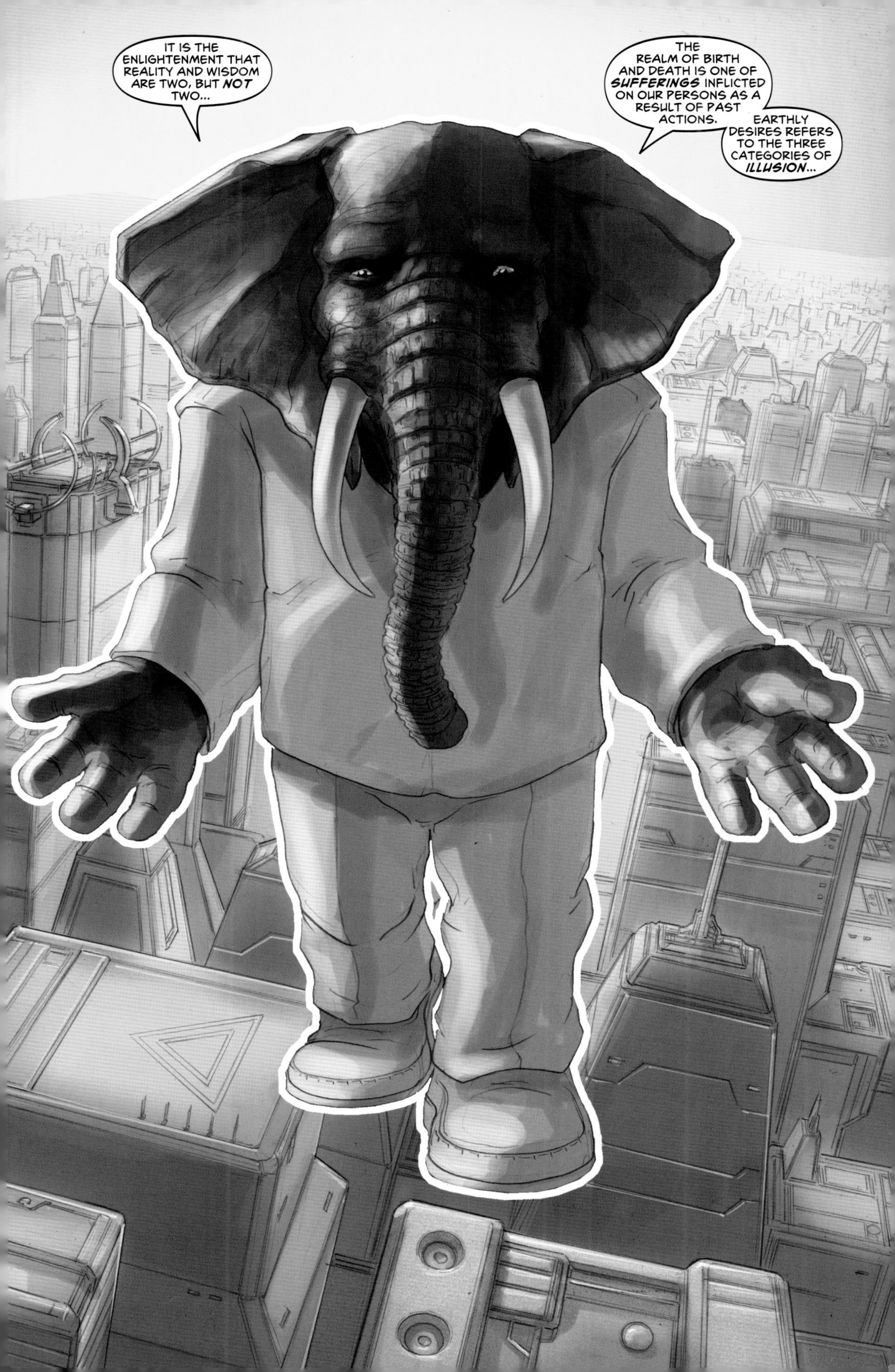
IT IS THE ENLIGHTENMENT THAT REALITY AND WISDOM ARE TWO, BUT NOT TWO...
THE REALM OF BIRTH AND DEATH IS ONE OF SUFFERINGS INFLICTED ON OUR PERSONS AS A RESULT OF PAST ACTIONS.
EARTHLY DESIRES REFERS TO THE THREE CATEGORIES OF ILLUSION...

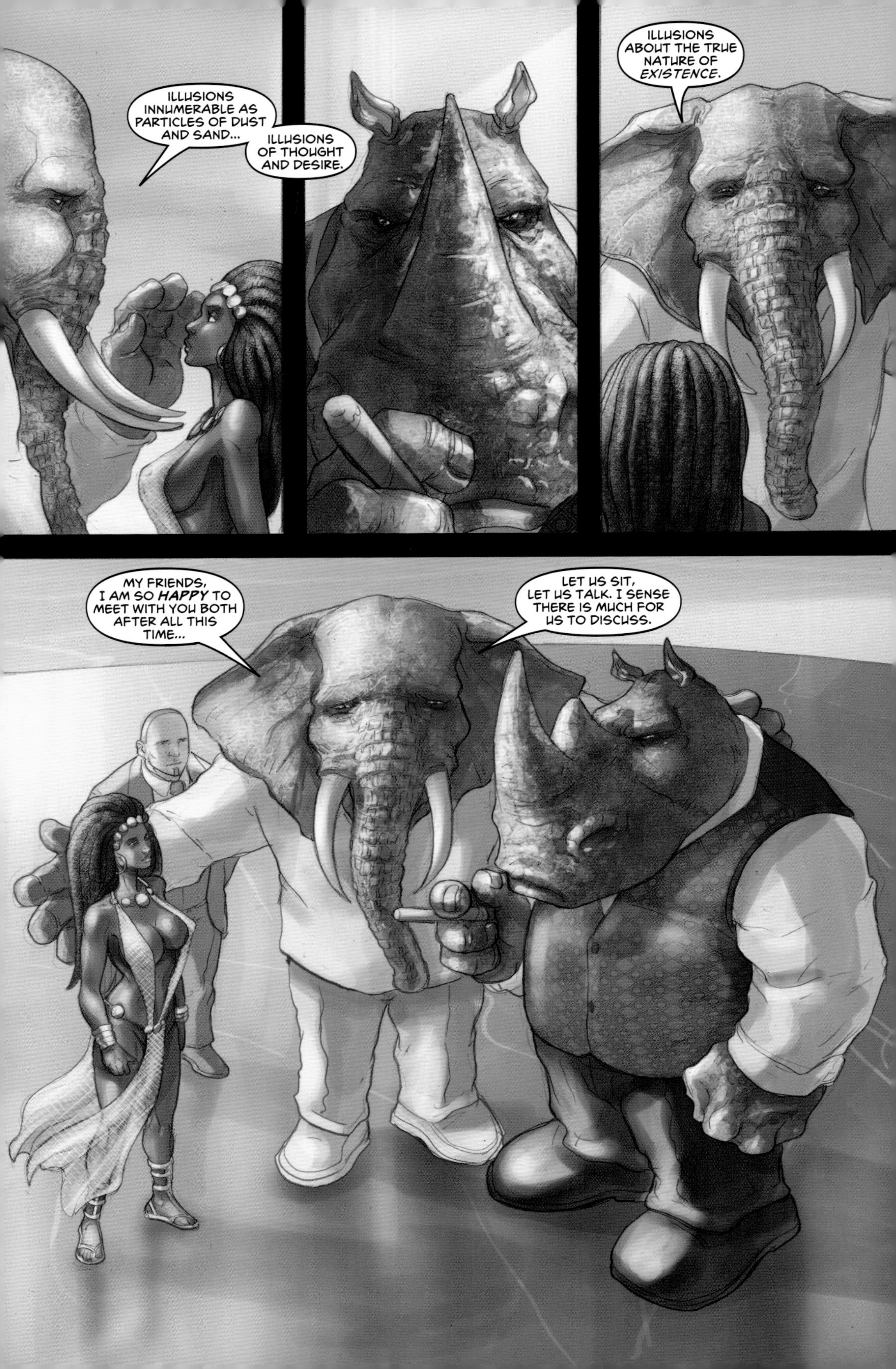
ILLUSIONS INNUMERABLE AS PARTICLES OF DUST AND SAND...
ILLUSIONS OF THOUGHT AND DESIRE.
ILLUSIONS ABOUT THE TRUE NATURE OF EXISTENCE.
MY FRIENDS, I AM SO HAPPY TO MEET WITH YOU BOTH AFTER ALL THIS TIME...
LET US SIT, LET US TALK. I SENSE THERE IS MUCH FOR US TO DISCUSS.

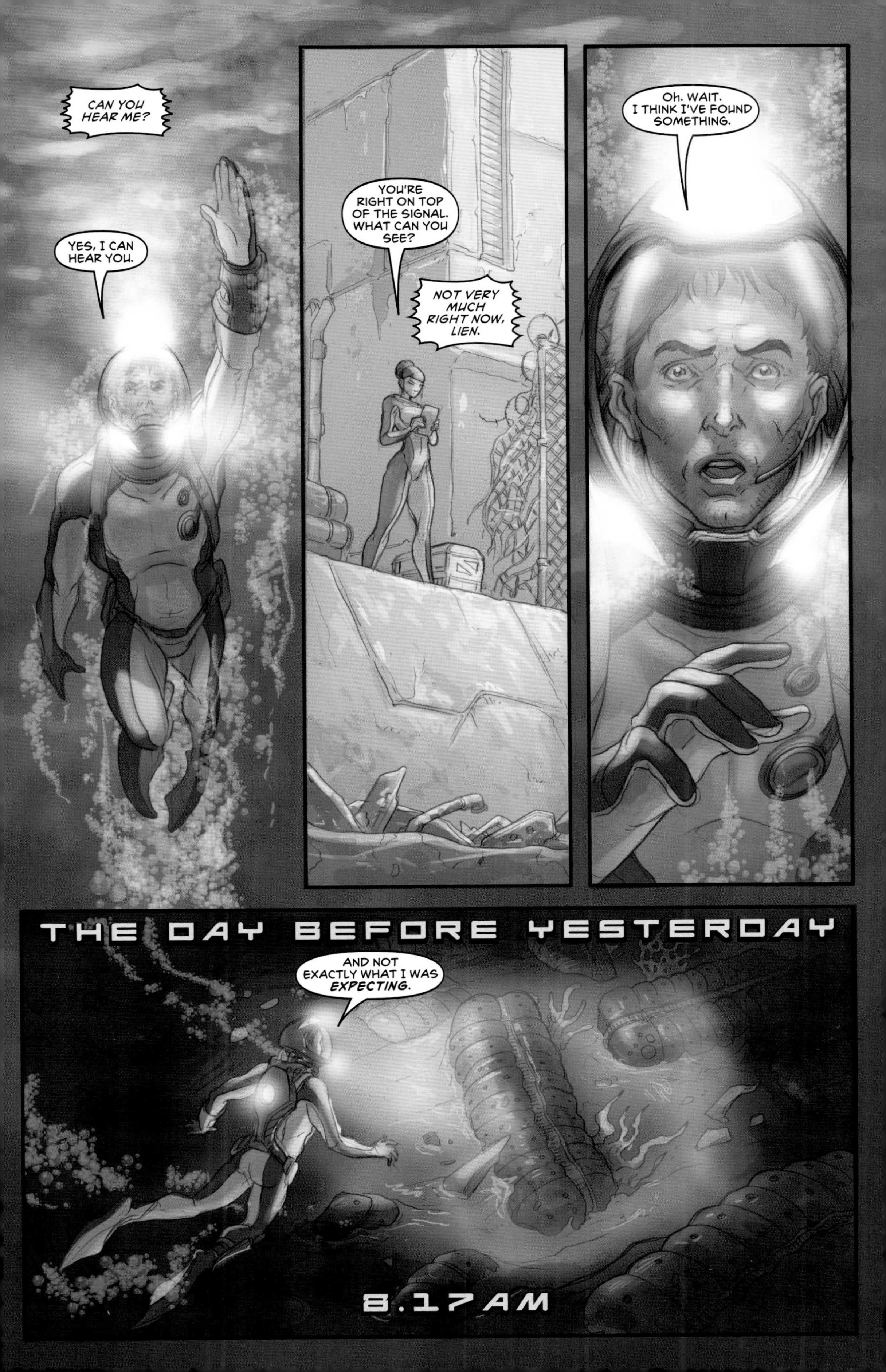
CAN YOU HEAR ME?
YES, I CAN HEAR YOU.
YOU'RE RIGHT ON TOP OF THE SIGNAL. WHAT CAN YOU SEE?
NOT VERY MUCH RIGHT NOW, LIEN.
Oh. WAIT. I THINK I'VE FOUND SOMETHING.
THE DAY BEFORE YESTERDAY
AND NOT EXACTLY WHAT I WAS EXPECTING.
8.17AM

GIVE ME A MINUTE...

SHRRPP

Ohh --

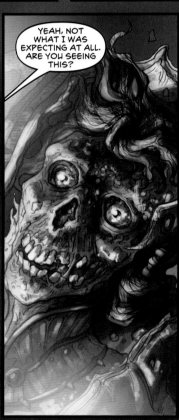
YEAH, NOT WHAT I WAS EXPECTING AT ALL. ARE YOU SEEING THIS?

YES, I SEE IT, MISTER APOSTROPHE... THAT'S A GIRL.

SORRY, HONEY, BUT YOU'RE NOT THE CORPSE I'M LOOKING FOR...

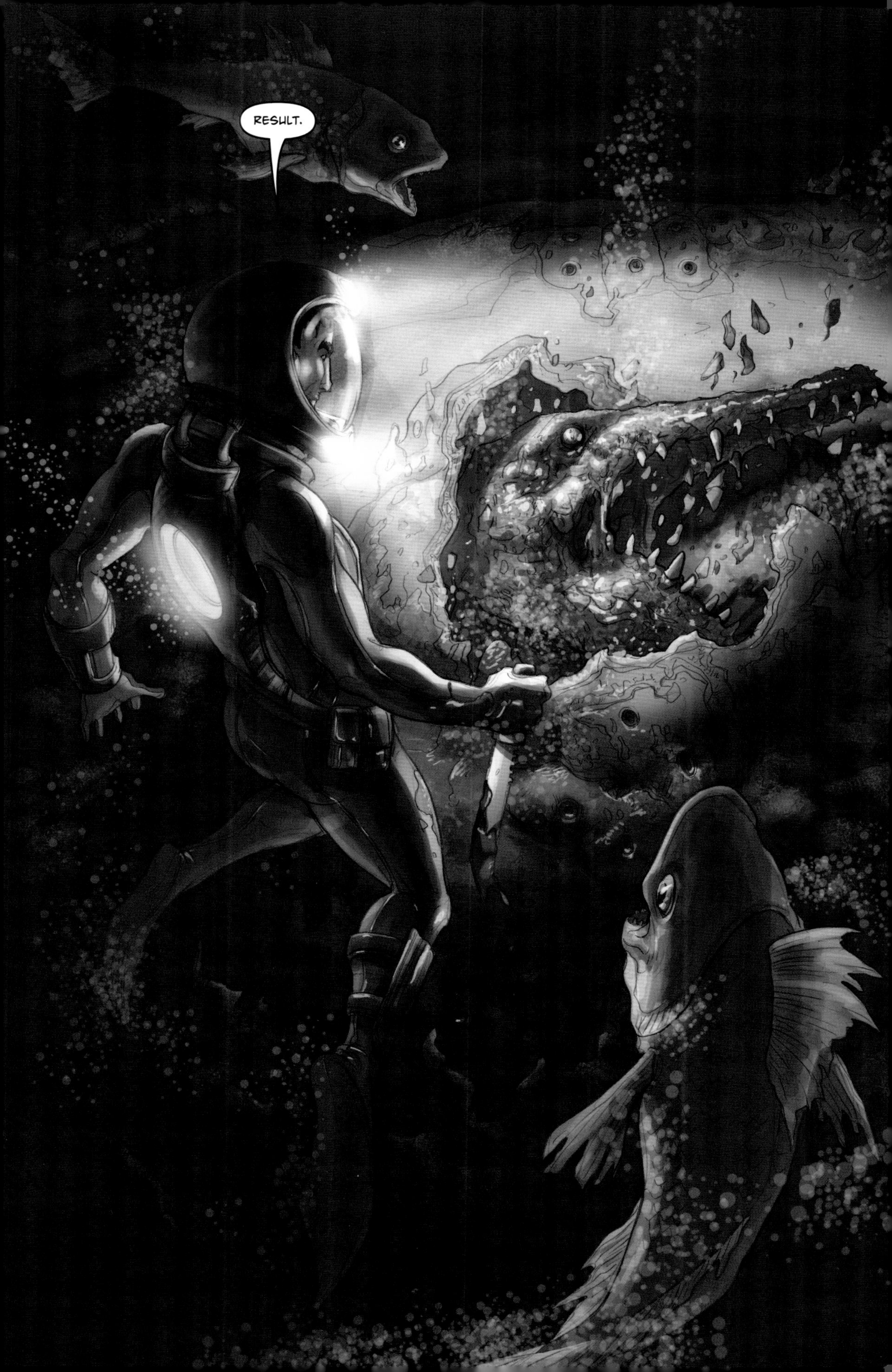
RESULT.

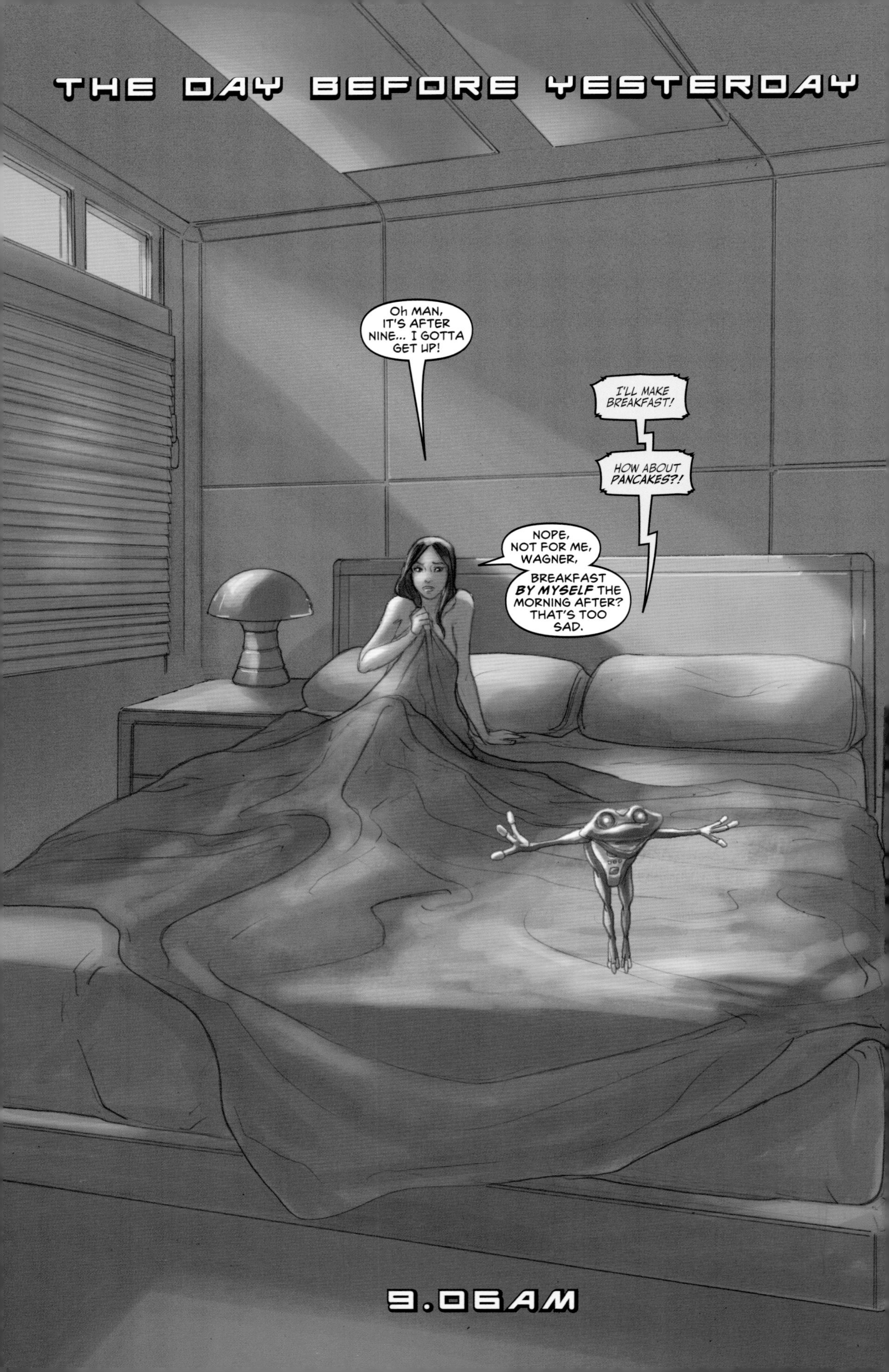
THE DAY BEFORE YESTERDAY
Oh MAN, IT'S AFTER NINE... I GOTTA GET UP!
I'LL MAKE BREAKFAST!
HOW ABOUT PANCAKES?!
NOPE, NOT FOR ME, WAGNER,
BREAKFAST BY MYSELF THE MORNING AFTER? THAT'S TOO SAD.
9.06AM

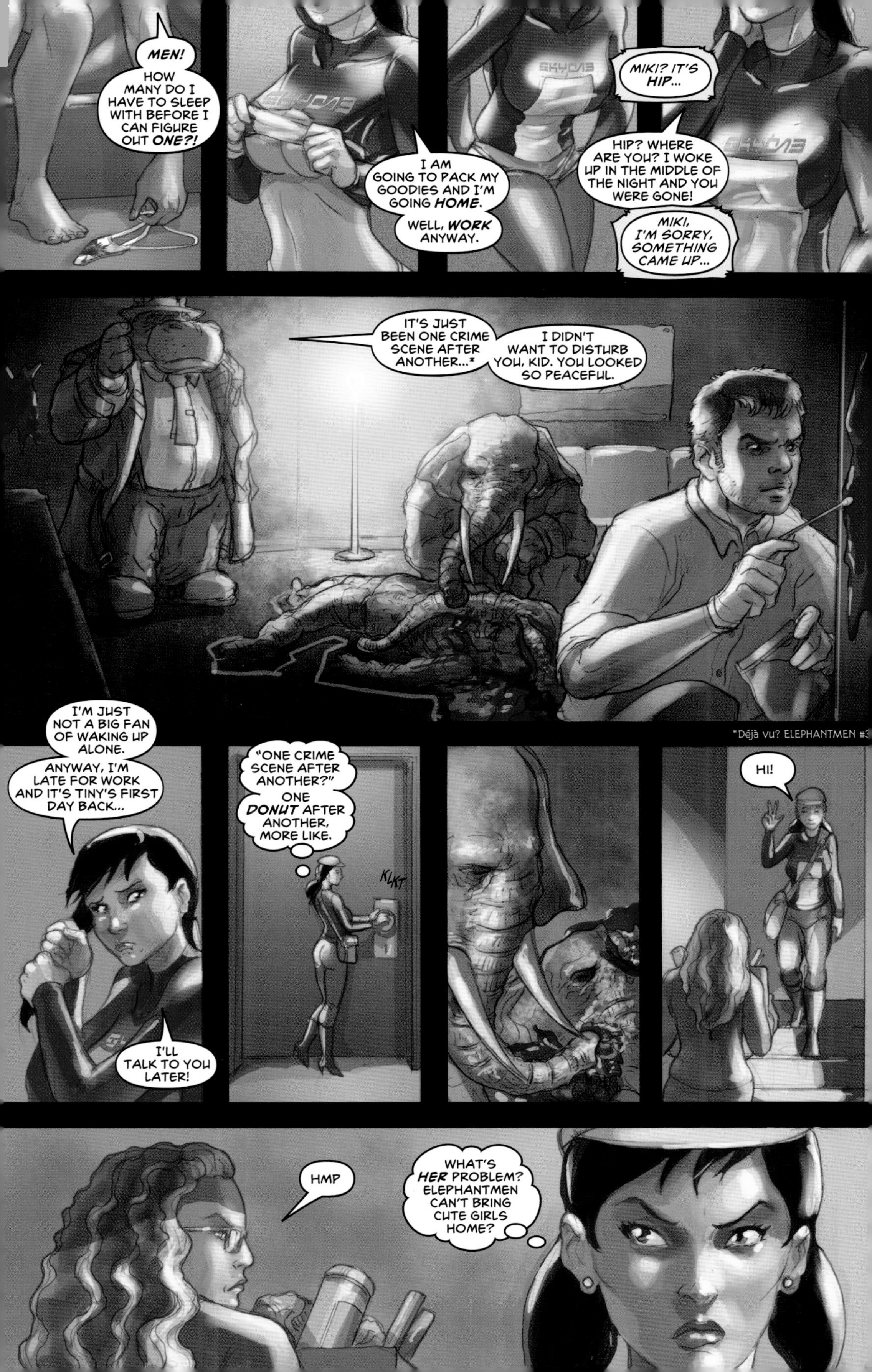
MEN! HOW MANY DO I HAVE TO SLEEP WITH BEFORE I CAN FIGURE OUT ONE?!
I AM GOING TO PACK MY GOODIES AND I'M GOING HOME.
WELL, WORK ANYWAY.
MIKI? IT'S HIP...
HIP? WHERE ARE YOU? I WOKE UP IN THE MIDDLE OF THE NIGHT AND YOU WERE GONE!
MIKI, I'M SORRY, SOMETHING CAME UP...
IT'S JUST BEEN ONE CRIME SCENE AFTER ANOTHER...*
I DIDN'T WANT TO DISTURB YOU, KID. YOU LOOKED SO PEACEFUL.
I'M JUST NOT A BIG FAN OF WAKING UP ALONE.
ANYWAY, I'M LATE FOR WORK AND IT'S TINY'S FIRST DAY BACK...
I'LL TALK TO YOU LATER!
"ONE CRIME SCENE AFTER ANOTHER?"
ONE DONUT AFTER ANOTHER, MORE LIKE.
KLKT
HI!
HMP
WHAT'S HER PROBLEM? ELEPHANTMEN CAN'T BRING CUTE GIRLS HOME?
*Déjà vu? ELEPHANTMEN #3

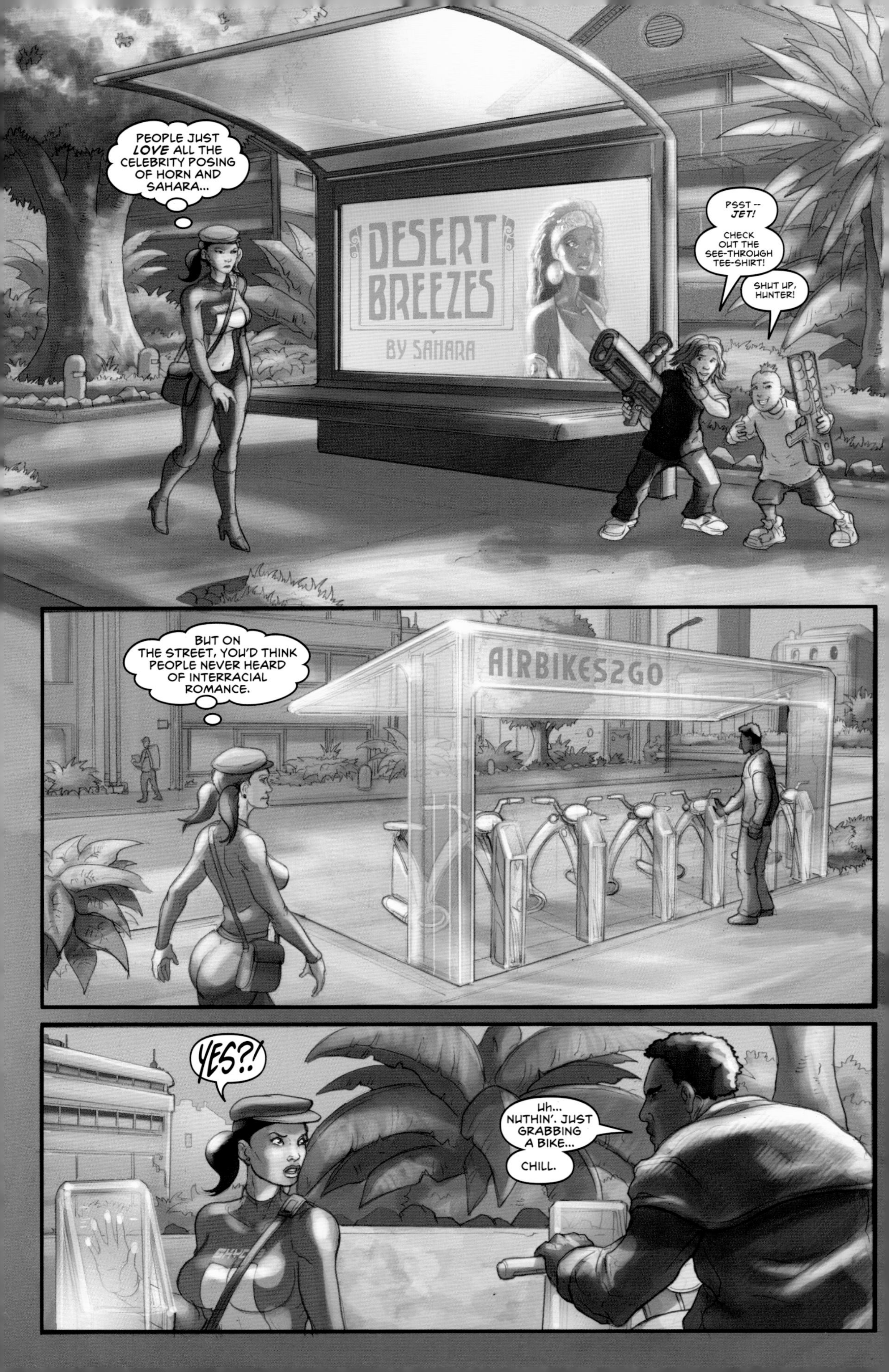
PEOPLE JUST *LOVE* ALL THE CELEBRITY POSING OF HORN AND SAHARA...
DESERT BREEZES
BY SAHARA
PSST -- *JET!*
CHECK OUT THE SEE-THROUGH TEE-SHIRT!
SHUT UP, HUNTER!
BUT ON THE STREET, YOU'D THINK PEOPLE NEVER HEARD OF INTERRACIAL ROMANCE.
AIRBIKES2GO
YES?!
UH... NUTHIN'. JUST GRABBING A BIKE...
CHILL.

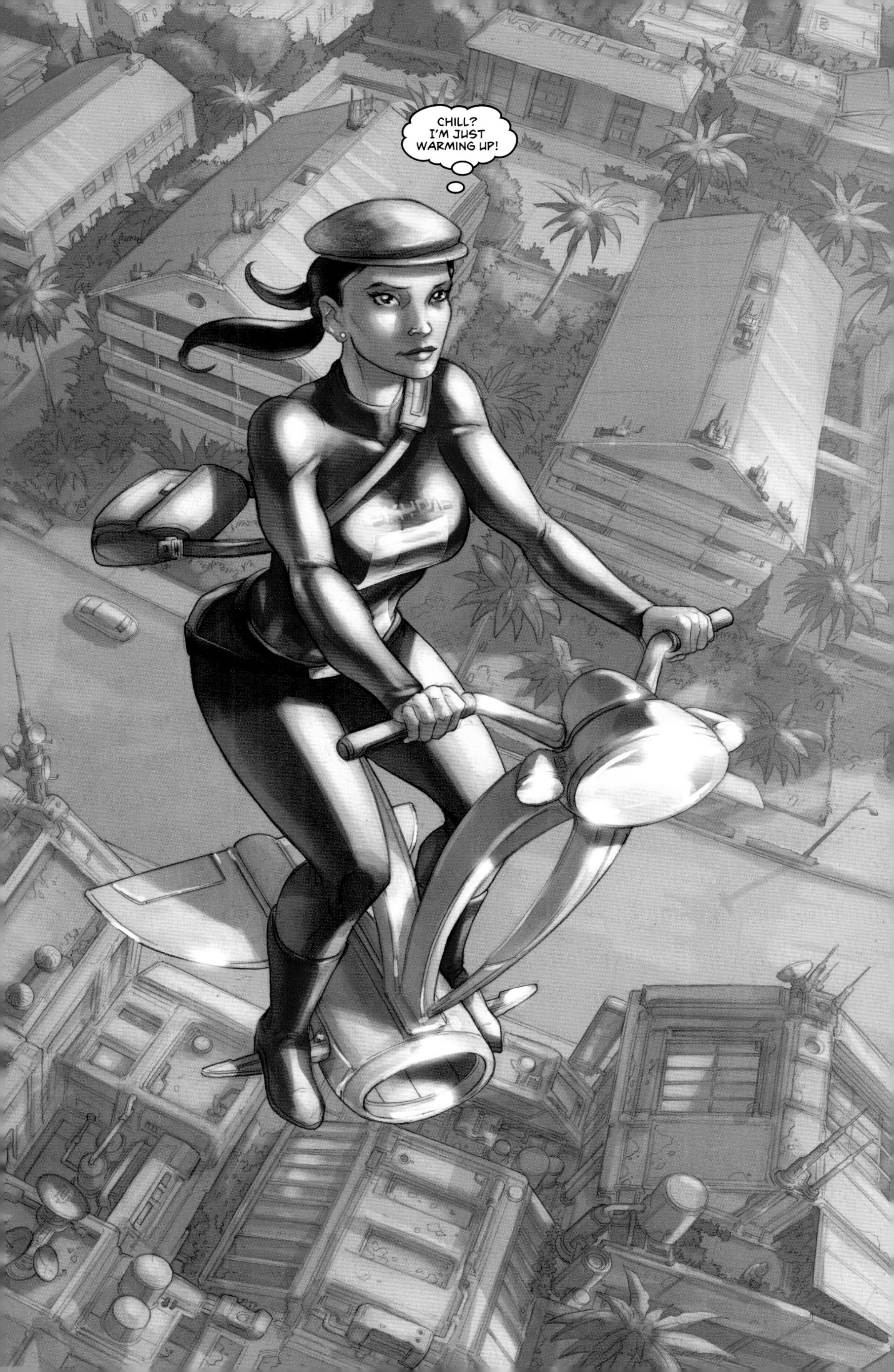
CHILL? I'M JUST WARMING UP!

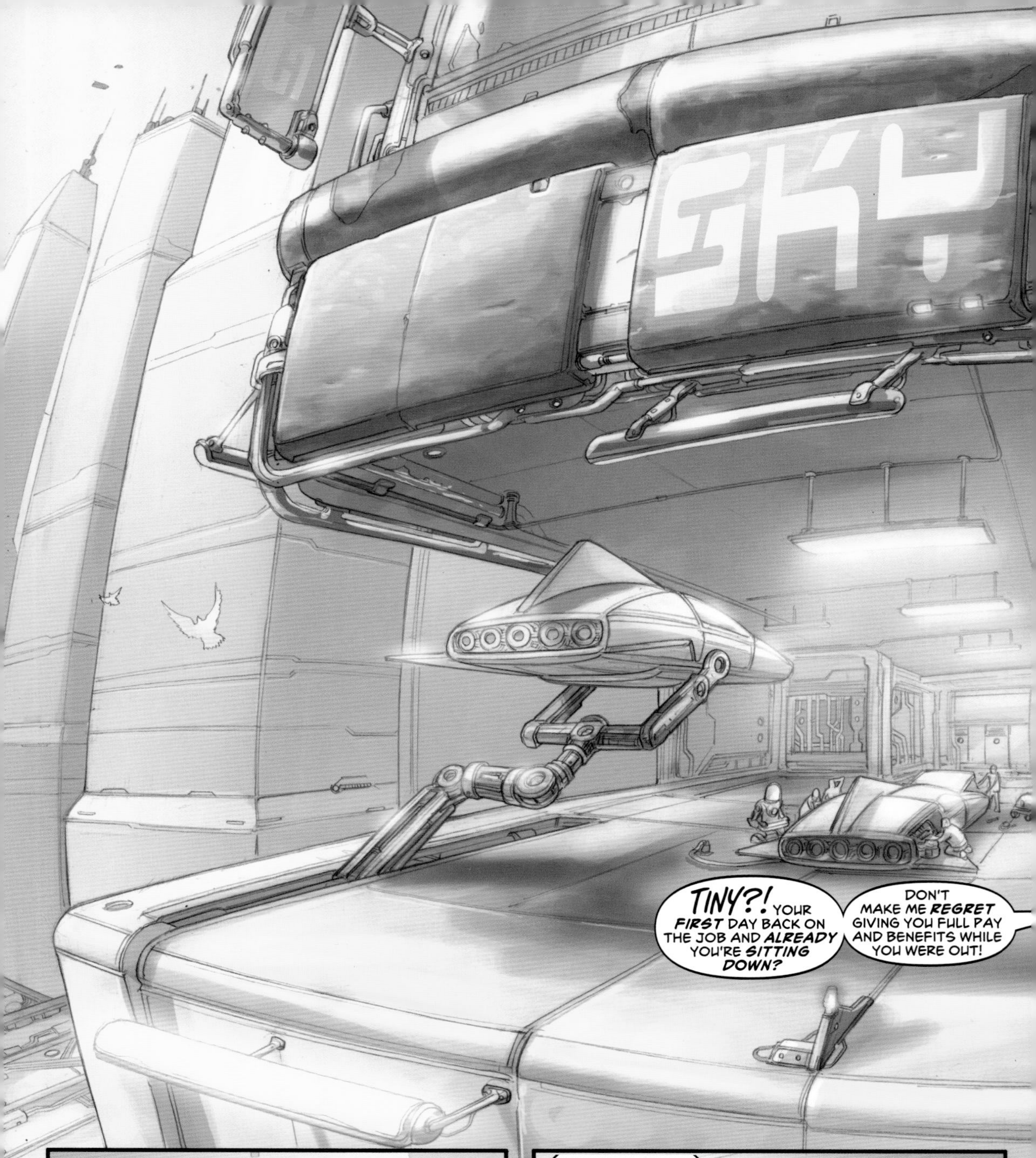
SKY
TINY?! YOUR FIRST DAY BACK ON THE JOB AND ALREADY YOU'RE SITTING DOWN?
DON'T MAKE ME REGRET GIVING YOU FULL PAY AND BENEFITS WHILE YOU WERE OUT!

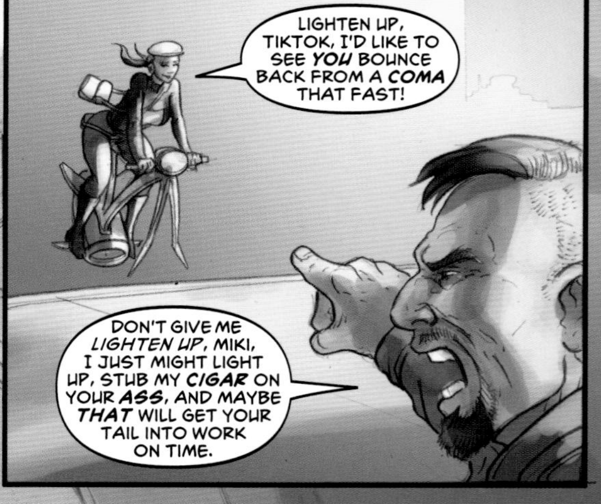
LIGHTEN UP, TIKTOK, I'D LIKE TO SEE YOU BOUNCE BACK FROM A COMA THAT FAST!
DON'T GIVE ME LIGHTEN UP, MIKI, I JUST MIGHT LIGHT UP, STUB MY CIGAR ON YOUR ASS, AND MAYBE THAT WILL GET YOUR TAIL INTO WORK ON TIME.

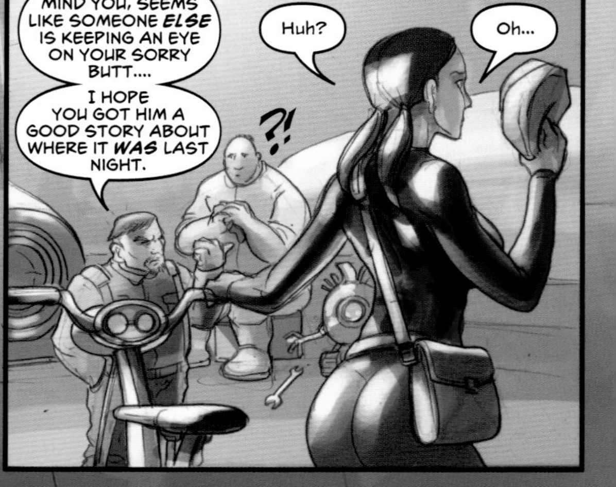
MIND YOU, SEEMS LIKE SOMEONE ELSE IS KEEPING AN EYE ON YOUR SORRY BUTT....
I HOPE YOU GOT HIM A GOOD STORY ABOUT WHERE IT WAS LAST NIGHT.
Huh?
?!
Oh...

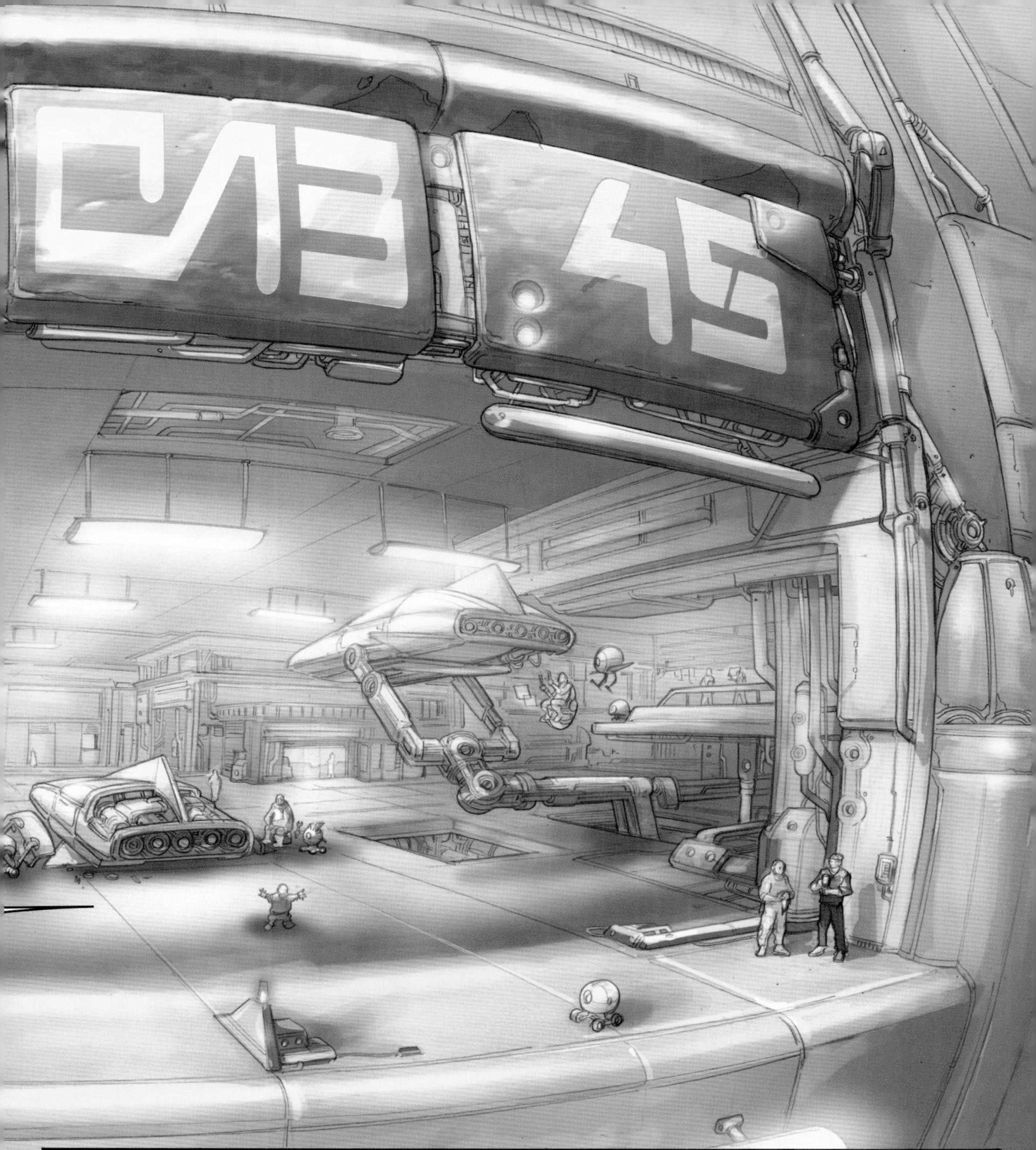

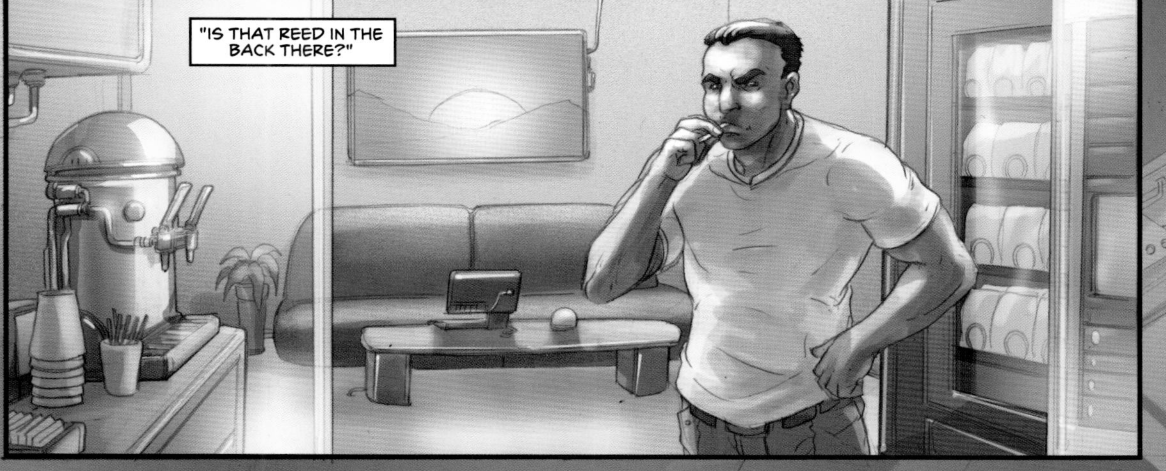
"IS THAT REED IN THE BACK THERE?"

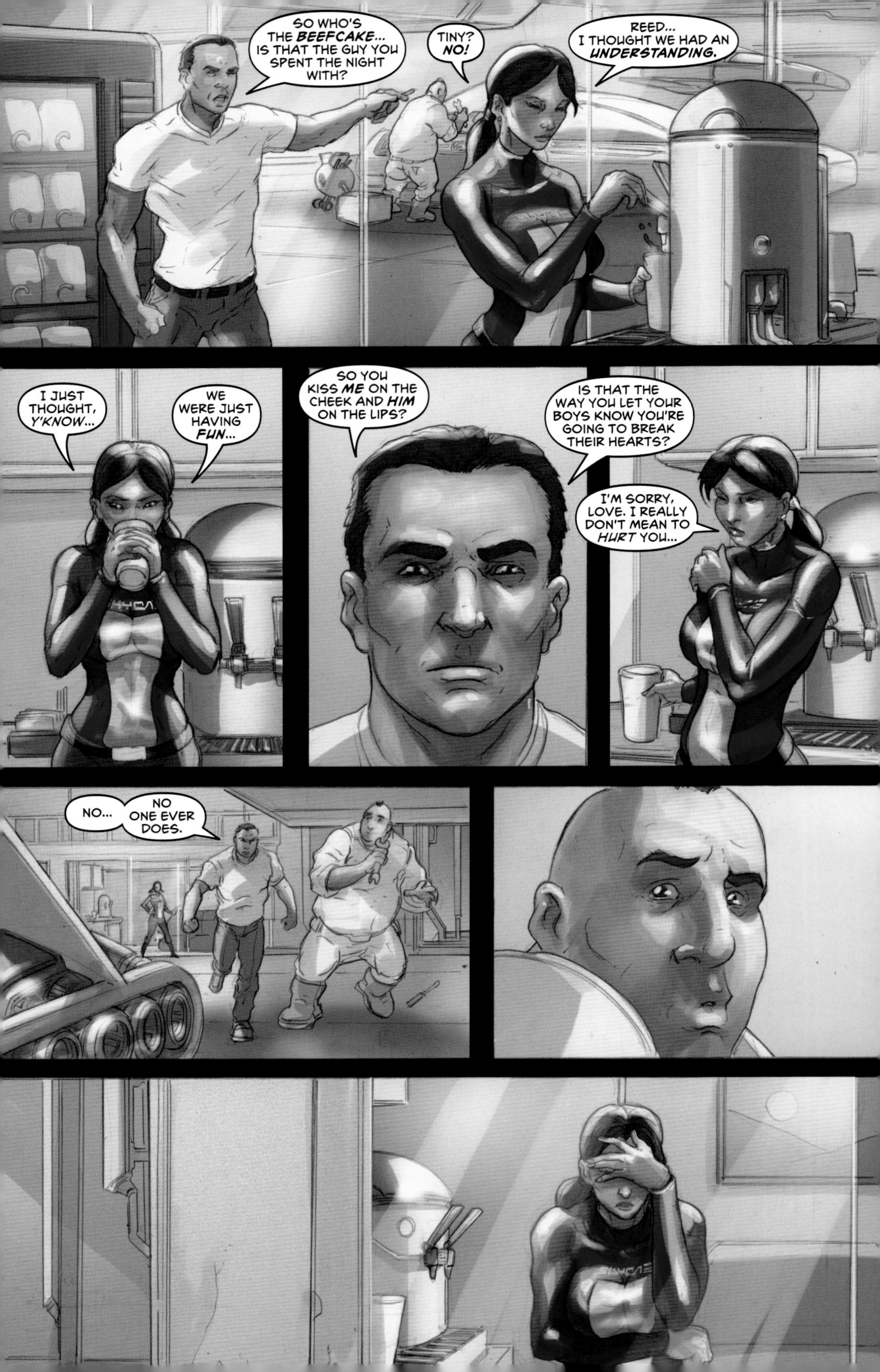
SO WHO'S THE BEEFCAKE... IS THAT THE GUY YOU SPENT THE NIGHT WITH?
TINY? NO!
REED... I THOUGHT WE HAD AN UNDERSTANDING.
I JUST THOUGHT, Y'KNOW...
WE WERE JUST HAVING FUN...
SO YOU KISS ME ON THE CHEEK AND HIM ON THE LIPS?
IS THAT THE WAY YOU LET YOUR BOYS KNOW YOU'RE GOING TO BREAK THEIR HEARTS?
I'M SORRY, LOVE. I REALLY DON'T MEAN TO HURT YOU...
NO...
NO ONE EVER DOES.

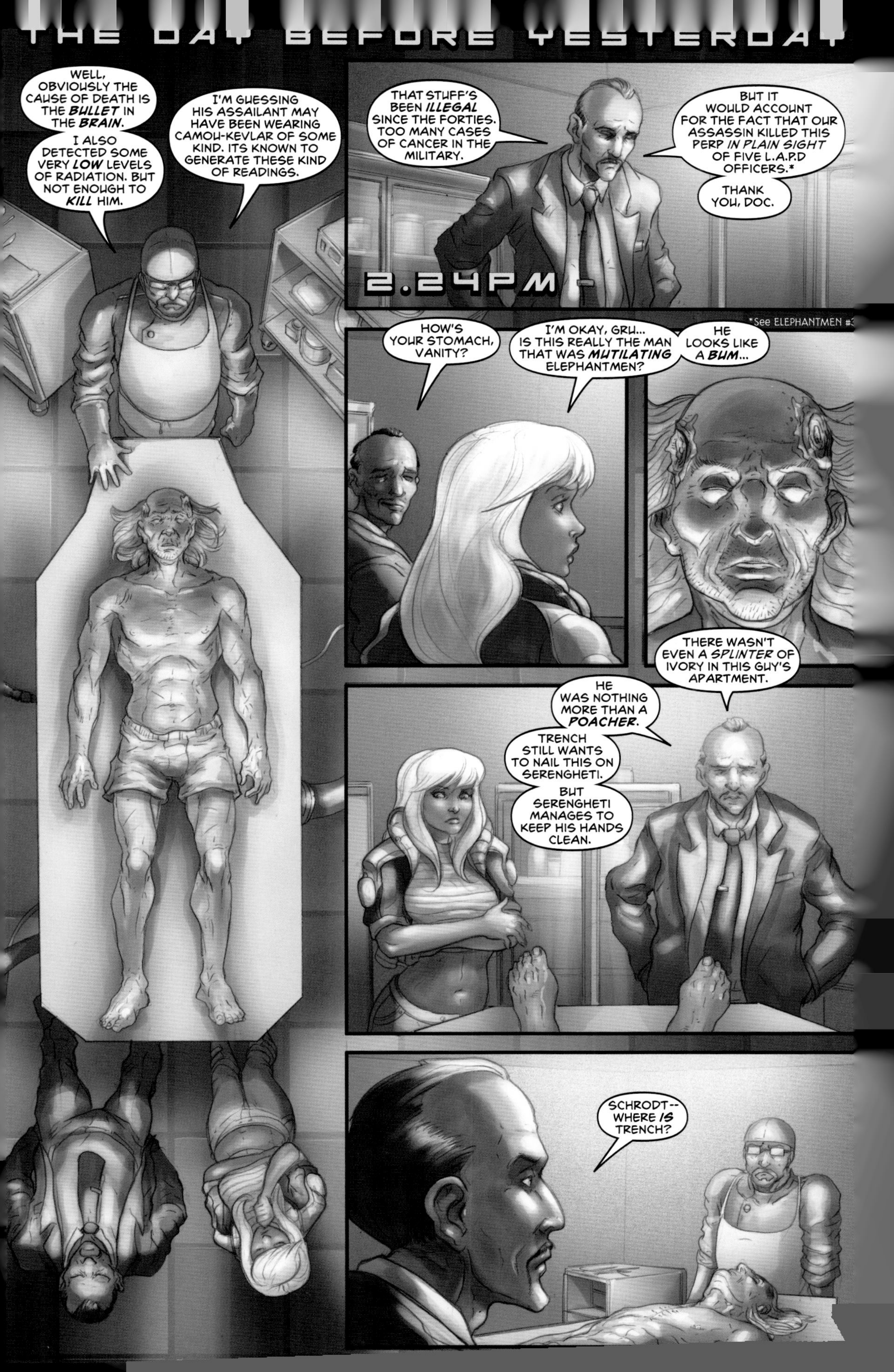
THE DAY BEFORE YESTERDAY
WELL, OBVIOUSLY THE CAUSE OF DEATH IS THE BULLET IN THE BRAIN.
I ALSO DETECTED SOME VERY LOW LEVELS OF RADIATION. BUT NOT ENOUGH TO KILL HIM.
I'M GUESSING HIS ASSAILANT MAY HAVE BEEN WEARING CAMOU-KEVLAR OF SOME KIND. ITS KNOWN TO GENERATE THESE KIND OF READINGS.
THAT STUFF'S BEEN ILLEGAL SINCE THE FORTIES. TOO MANY CASES OF CANCER IN THE MILITARY.
BUT IT WOULD ACCOUNT FOR THE FACT THAT OUR ASSASSIN KILLED THIS PERP IN PLAIN SIGHT OF FIVE L.A.P.D OFFICERS.*
THANK YOU, DOC.
2.24PM -
*See ELEPHANTMEN #3
HOW'S YOUR STOMACH, VANITY?
I'M OKAY, GRU... IS THIS REALLY THE MAN THAT WAS MUTILATING ELEPHANTMEN?
HE LOOKS LIKE A BUM...
THERE WASN'T EVEN A SPLINTER OF IVORY IN THIS GUY'S APARTMENT.
HE WAS NOTHING MORE THAN A POACHER.
TRENCH STILL WANTS TO NAIL THIS ON SERENGHETI.
BUT SERENGHETI MANAGES TO KEEP HIS HANDS CLEAN.
SCHRODT-- WHERE IS TRENCH?

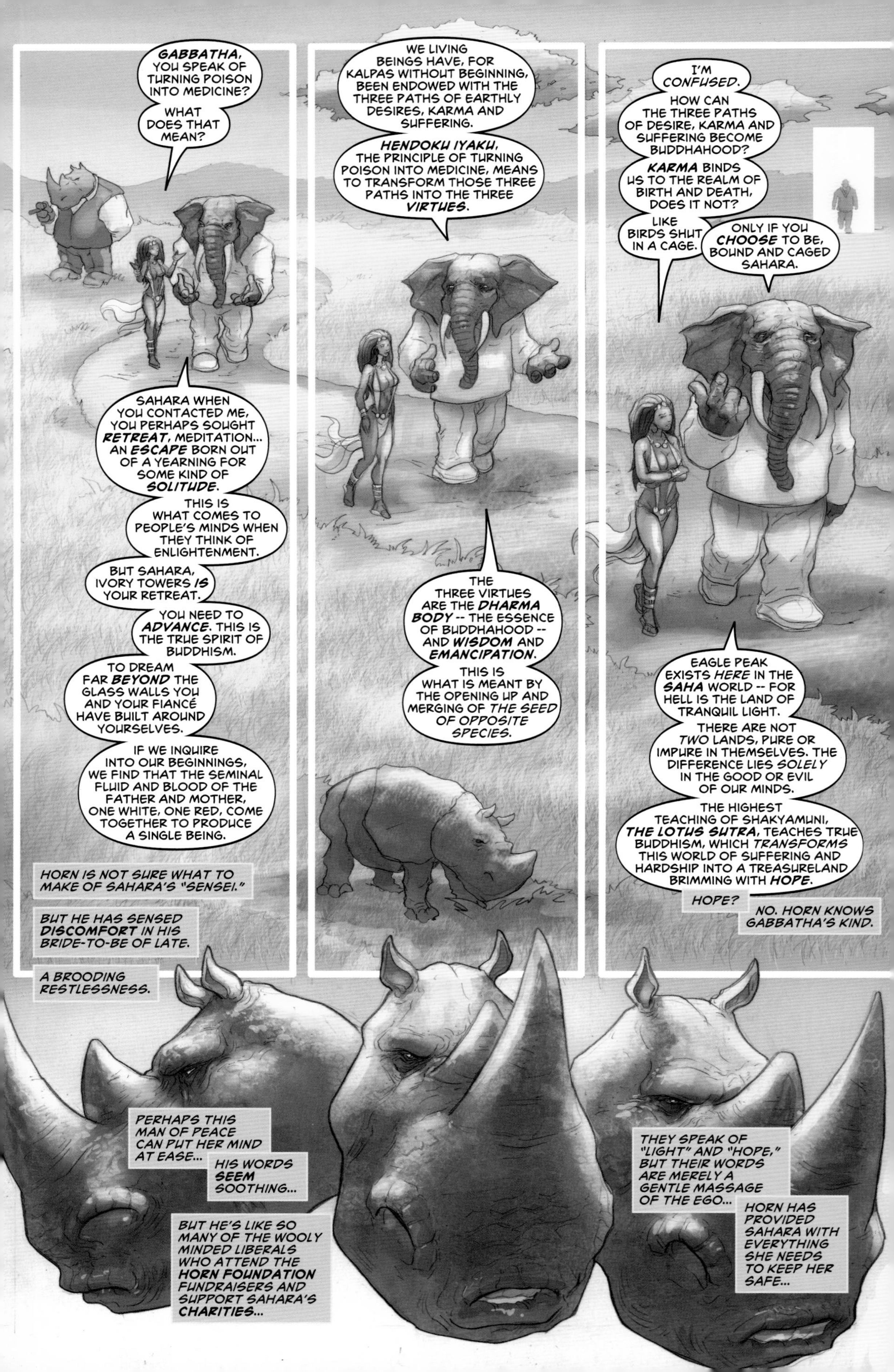
GABBATHA, YOU SPEAK OF TURNING POISON INTO MEDICINE?
WHAT DOES THAT MEAN?
SAHARA WHEN YOU CONTACTED ME, YOU PERHAPS SOUGHT RETREAT, MEDITATION... AN ESCAPE BORN OUT OF A YEARNING FOR SOME KIND OF SOLITUDE.
THIS IS WHAT COMES TO PEOPLE'S MINDS WHEN THEY THINK OF ENLIGHTENMENT.
BUT SAHARA, IVORY TOWERS IS YOUR RETREAT.
YOU NEED TO ADVANCE. THIS IS THE TRUE SPIRIT OF BUDDHISM.
TO DREAM FAR BEYOND THE GLASS WALLS YOU AND YOUR FIANCÉ HAVE BUILT AROUND YOURSELVES.
IF WE INQUIRE INTO OUR BEGINNINGS, WE FIND THAT THE SEMINAL FLUID AND BLOOD OF THE FATHER AND MOTHER, ONE WHITE, ONE RED, COME TOGETHER TO PRODUCE A SINGLE BEING.
HORN IS NOT SURE WHAT TO MAKE OF SAHARA'S "SENSEI."
BUT HE HAS SENSED DISCOMFORT IN HIS BRIDE-TO-BE OF LATE.
A BROODING RESTLESSNESS.
WE LIVING BEINGS HAVE, FOR KALPAS WITHOUT BEGINNING, BEEN ENDOWED WITH THE THREE PATHS OF EARTHLY DESIRES, KARMA AND SUFFERING.
HENDOKU IYAKU, THE PRINCIPLE OF TURNING POISON INTO MEDICINE, MEANS TO TRANSFORM THOSE THREE PATHS INTO THE THREE VIRTUES.
THE THREE VIRTUES ARE THE DHARMA BODY -- THE ESSENCE OF BUDDHAHOOD -- AND WISDOM AND EMANCIPATION.
THIS IS WHAT IS MEANT BY THE OPENING UP AND MERGING OF THE SEED OF OPPOSITE SPECIES.
I'M CONFUSED.
HOW CAN THE THREE PATHS OF DESIRE, KARMA AND SUFFERING BECOME BUDDHAHOOD?
KARMA BINDS US TO THE REALM OF BIRTH AND DEATH, DOES IT NOT?
LIKE BIRDS SHUT IN A CAGE.
ONLY IF YOU CHOOSE TO BE, BOUND AND CAGED SAHARA.
EAGLE PEAK EXISTS HERE IN THE SAHA WORLD -- FOR HELL IS THE LAND OF TRANQUIL LIGHT.
THERE ARE NOT TWO LANDS, PURE OR IMPURE IN THEMSELVES. THE DIFFERENCE LIES SOLELY IN THE GOOD OR EVIL OF OUR MINDS.
THE HIGHEST TEACHING OF SHAKYAMUNI, THE LOTUS SUTRA, TEACHES TRUE BUDDHISM, WHICH TRANSFORMS THIS WORLD OF SUFFERING AND HARDSHIP INTO A TREASURELAND BRIMMING WITH HOPE.
HOPE?
NO. HORN KNOWS GABBATHA'S KIND.
PERHAPS THIS MAN OF PEACE CAN PUT HER MIND AT EASE...
HIS WORDS SEEM SOOTHING...
BUT HE'S LIKE SO MANY OF THE WOOLY MINDED LIBERALS WHO ATTEND THE HORN FOUNDATION FUNDRAISERS AND SUPPORT SAHARA'S CHARITIES...
THEY SPEAK OF "LIGHT" AND "HOPE," BUT THEIR WORDS ARE MERELY A GENTLE MASSAGE OF THE EGO...
HORN HAS PROVIDED SAHARA WITH EVERYTHING SHE NEEDS TO KEEP HER SAFE...

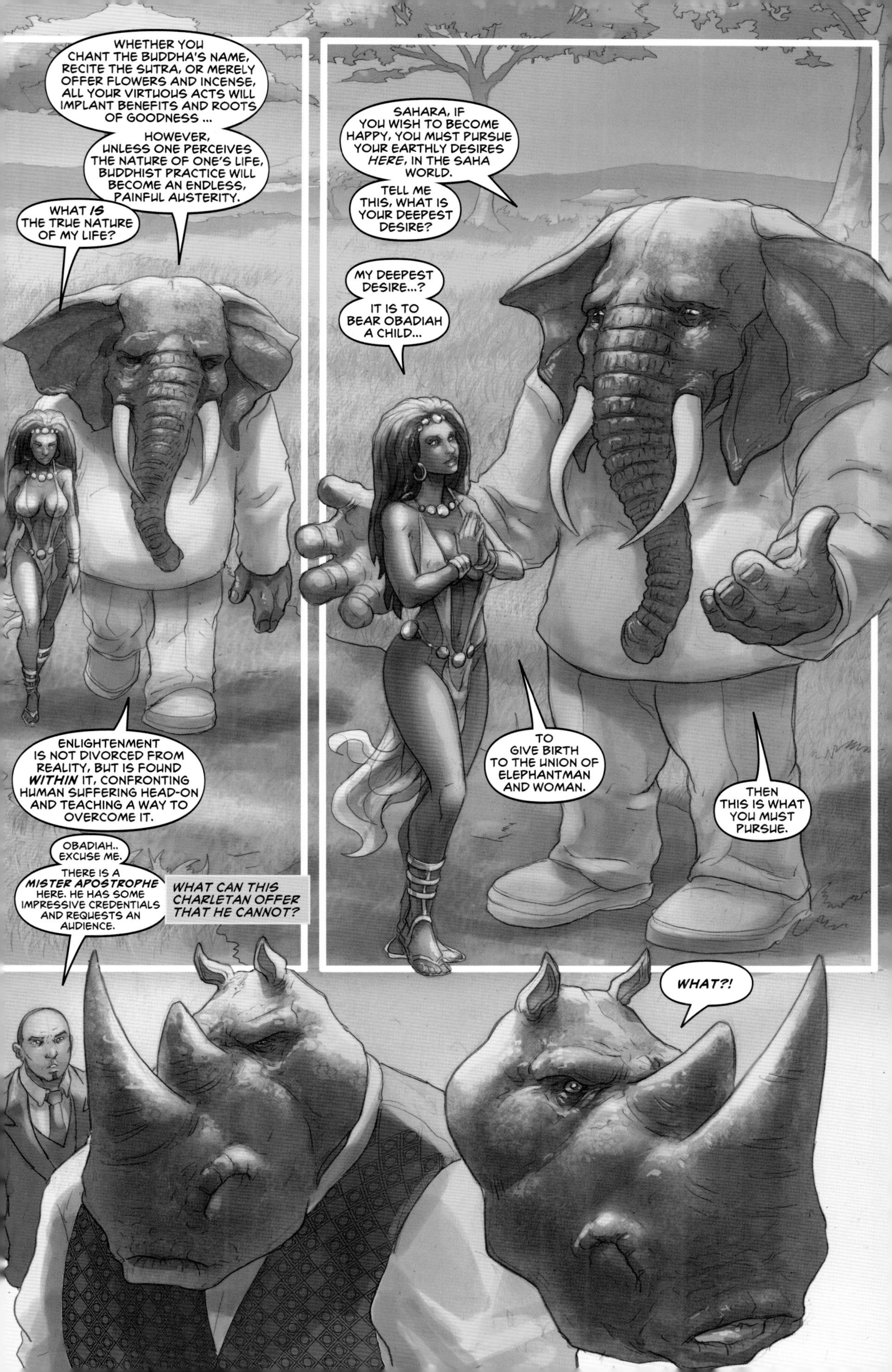
WHETHER YOU CHANT THE BUDDHA'S NAME, RECITE THE SUTRA, OR MERELY OFFER FLOWERS AND INCENSE, ALL YOUR VIRTUOUS ACTS WILL IMPLANT BENEFITS AND ROOTS OF GOODNESS ...
HOWEVER, UNLESS ONE PERCEIVES THE NATURE OF ONE'S LIFE, BUDDHIST PRACTICE WILL BECOME AN ENDLESS, PAINFUL AUSTERITY.
WHAT *IS* THE TRUE NATURE OF MY LIFE?
ENLIGHTENMENT IS NOT DIVORCED FROM REALITY, BUT IS FOUND ***WITHIN*** IT, CONFRONTING HUMAN SUFFERING HEAD-ON AND TEACHING A WAY TO OVERCOME IT.
SAHARA, IF YOU WISH TO BECOME HAPPY, YOU MUST PURSUE YOUR EARTHLY DESIRES *HERE*, IN THE SAHA WORLD.
TELL ME THIS, WHAT IS YOUR DEEPEST DESIRE?
MY DEEPEST DESIRE...?
IT IS TO BEAR OBADIAH A CHILD...
TO GIVE BIRTH TO THE UNION OF ELEPHANTMAN AND WOMAN.
THEN THIS IS WHAT YOU MUST PURSUE.
OBADIAH.. EXCUSE ME.
THERE IS A ***MISTER APOSTROPHE*** HERE. HE HAS SOME IMPRESSIVE CREDENTIALS AND REQUESTS AN AUDIENCE.
WHAT CAN THIS CHARLETAN OFFER THAT HE CANNOT?
WHAT?!

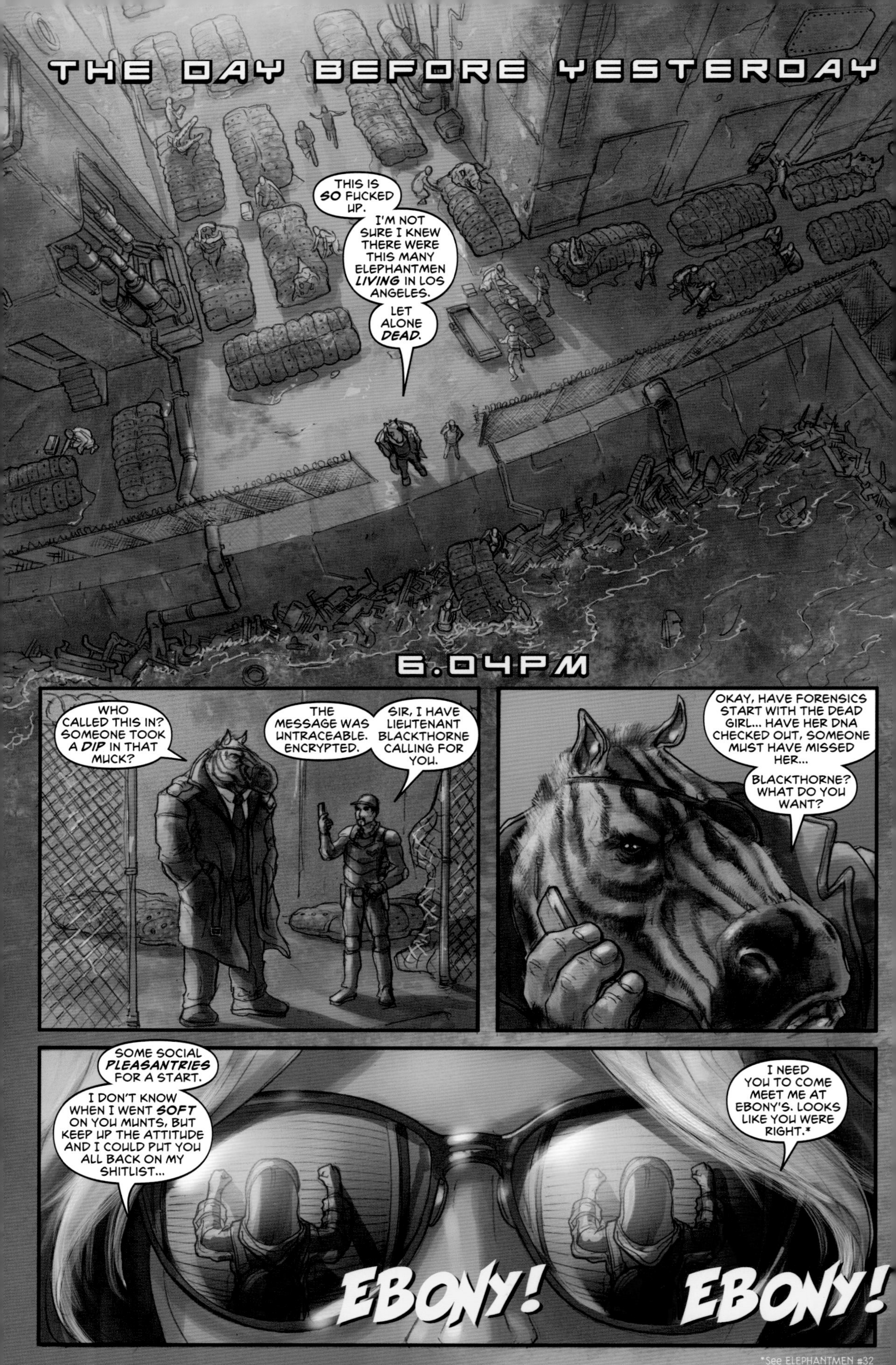
THE DAY BEFORE YESTERDAY
THIS IS SO FUCKED UP.
I'M NOT SURE I KNEW THERE WERE THIS MANY ELEPHANTMEN LIVING IN LOS ANGELES.
LET ALONE DEAD.
6.04PM
WHO CALLED THIS IN? SOMEONE TOOK A DIP IN THAT MUCK?
THE MESSAGE WAS UNTRACEABLE. ENCRYPTED.
SIR, I HAVE LIEUTENANT BLACKTHORNE CALLING FOR YOU.
OKAY, HAVE FORENSICS START WITH THE DEAD GIRL... HAVE HER DNA CHECKED OUT, SOMEONE MUST HAVE MISSED HER...
BLACKTHORNE? WHAT DO YOU WANT?
SOME SOCIAL PLEASANTRIES FOR A START.
I DON'T KNOW WHEN I WENT SOFT ON YOU MUNTS, BUT KEEP UP THE ATTITUDE AND I COULD PUT YOU ALL BACK ON MY SHITLIST...
I NEED YOU TO COME MEET ME AT EBONY'S. LOOKS LIKE YOU WERE RIGHT.*
EBONY!
EBONY!

*See ELEPHANTMEN #32

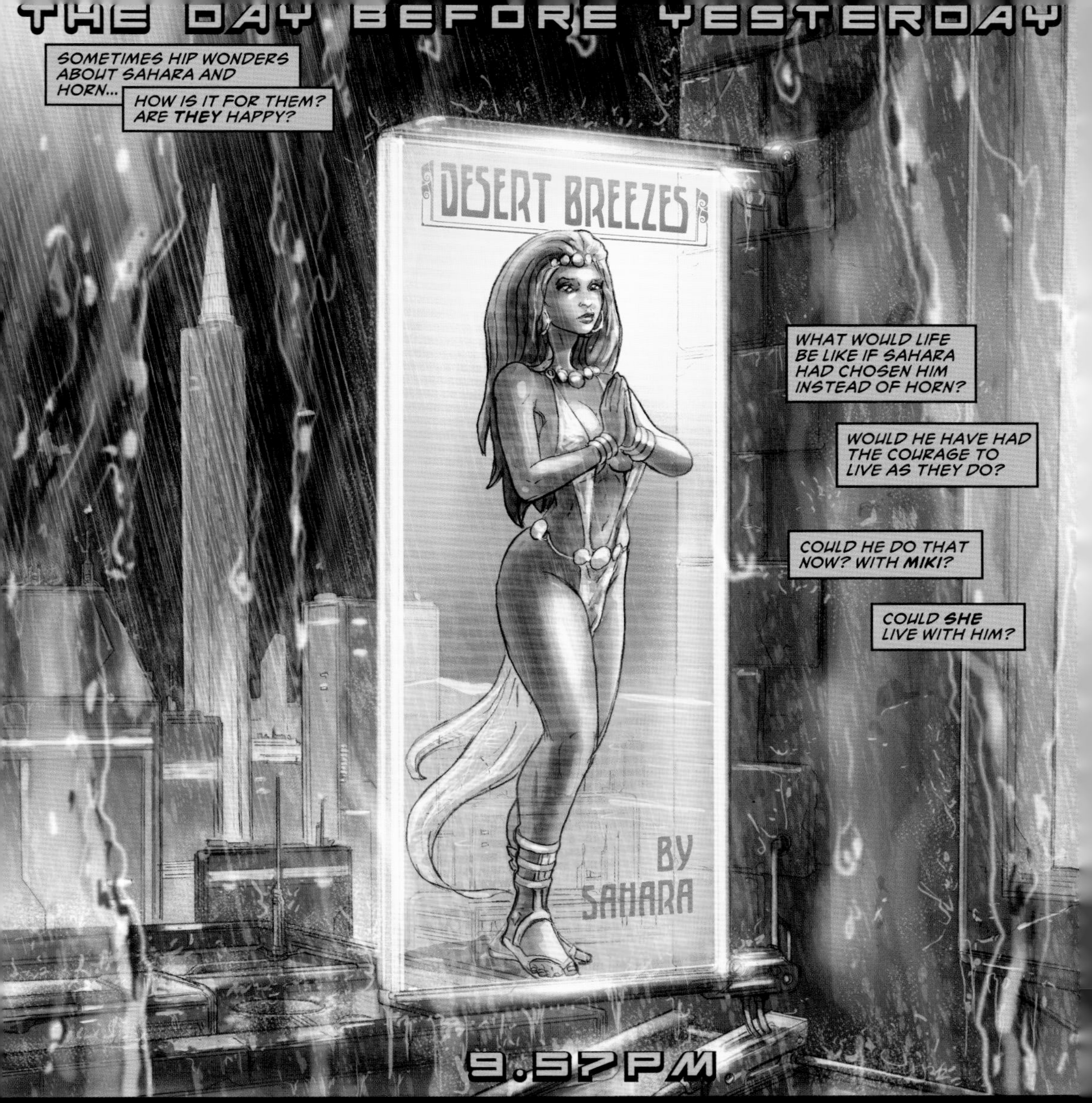
THE DAY BEFORE YESTERDAY
SOMETIMES HIP WONDERS ABOUT SAHARA AND HORN...
HOW IS IT FOR THEM? ARE **THEY** HAPPY?
DESERT BREEZES
BY SAHARA
WHAT WOULD LIFE BE LIKE IF SAHARA HAD CHOSEN HIM INSTEAD OF HORN?
WOULD HE HAVE HAD THE COURAGE TO LIVE AS THEY DO?
COULD HE DO THAT NOW? WITH **MIKI**?
COULD **SHE** LIVE WITH HIM?
9.57PM

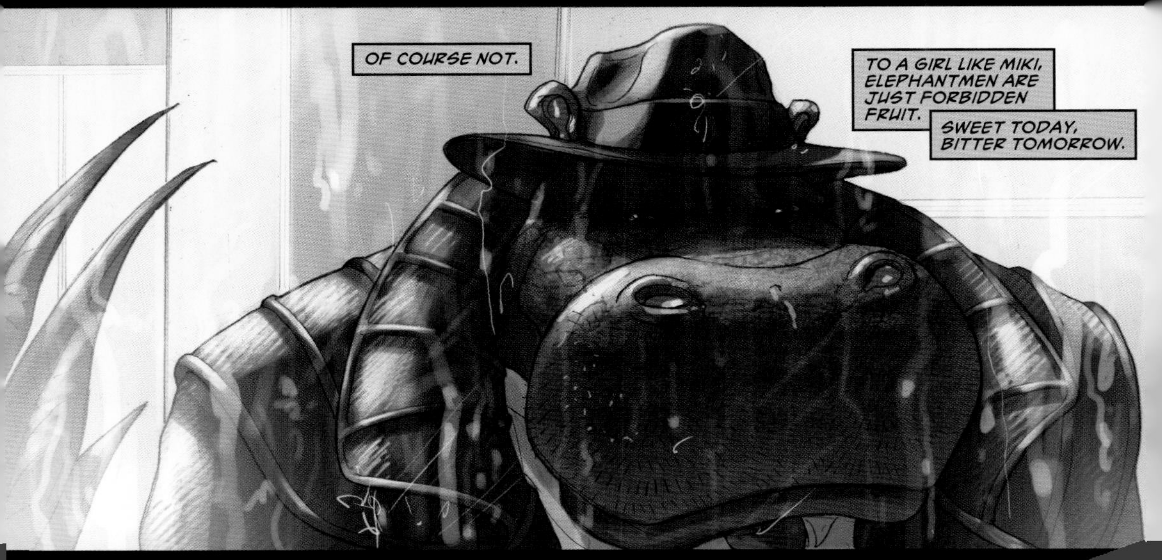
OF COURSE NOT.
TO A GIRL LIKE MIKI, ELEPHANTMEN ARE JUST FORBIDDEN FRUIT.
SWEET TODAY, BITTER TOMORROW.

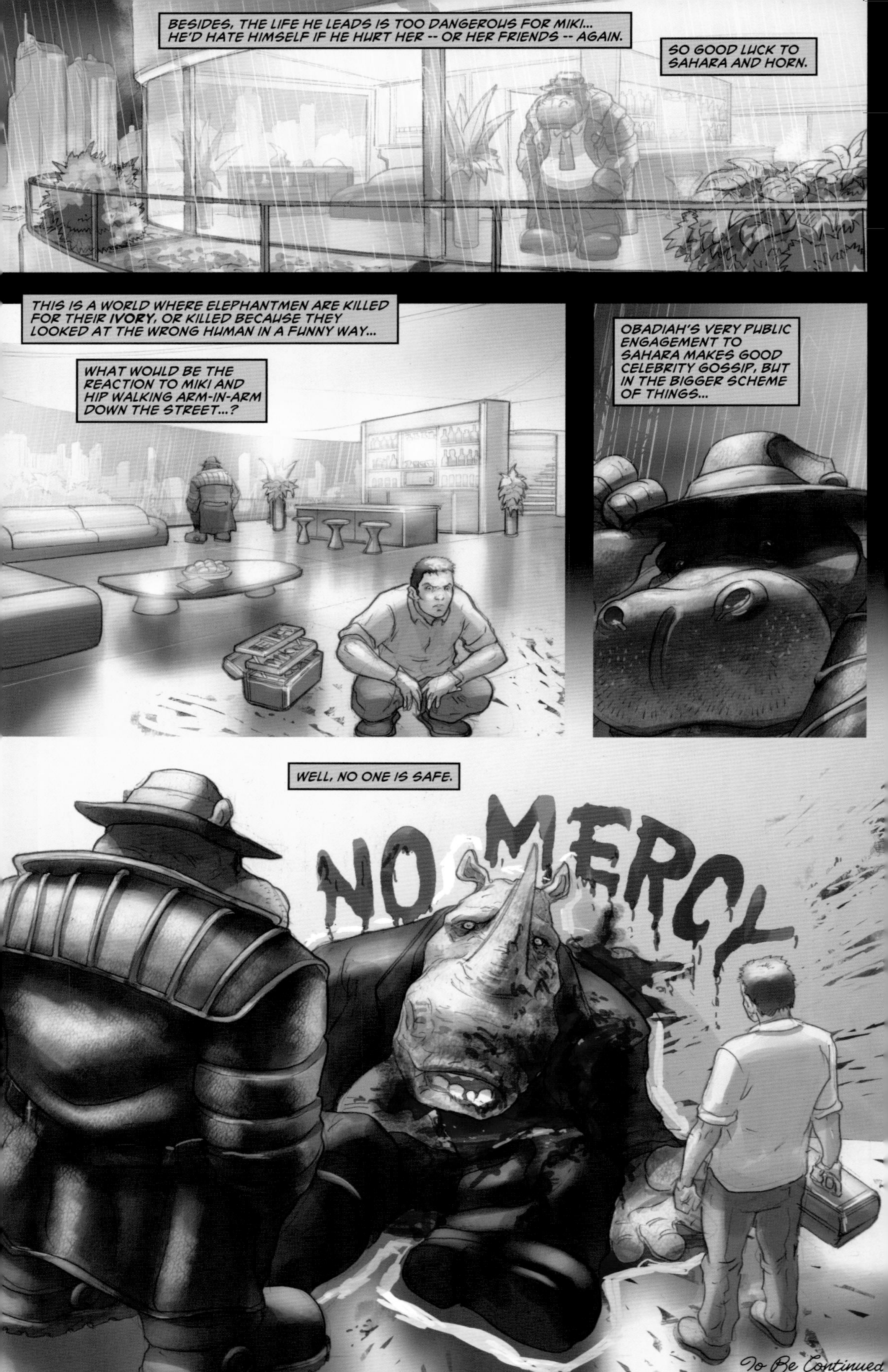
BESIDES, THE LIFE HE LEADS IS TOO DANGEROUS FOR MIKI... HE'D HATE HIMSELF IF HE HURT HER -- OR HER FRIENDS -- AGAIN.
SO GOOD LUCK TO SAHARA AND HORN.
THIS IS A WORLD WHERE ELEPHANTMEN ARE KILLED FOR THEIR IVORY, OR KILLED BECAUSE THEY LOOKED AT THE WRONG HUMAN IN A FUNNY WAY...
WHAT WOULD BE THE REACTION TO MIKI AND HIP WALKING ARM-IN-ARM DOWN THE STREET...?
OBADIAH'S VERY PUBLIC ENGAGEMENT TO SAHARA MAKES GOOD CELEBRITY GOSSIP, BUT IN THE BIGGER SCHEME OF THINGS...
WELL, NO ONE IS SAFE.
NO MERCY
To Be Continued

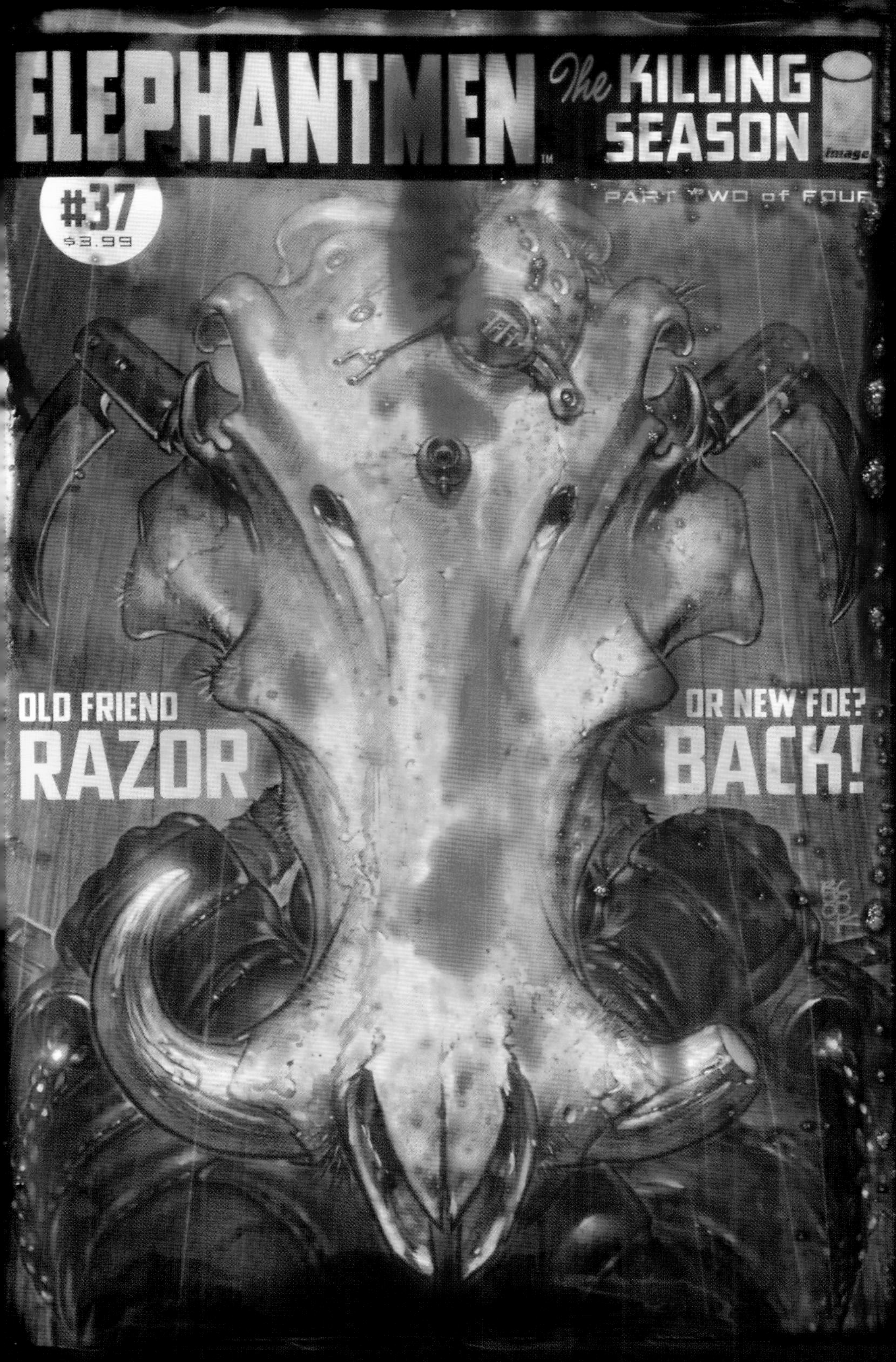
ELEPHANTMEN™
The KILLING SEASON
image
#37
$3.99
PART TWO of FOUR
OLD FRIEND
RAZOR
OR NEW FOE?
BACK!

"CRIMINALS DO NOT DIE BY THE
HANDS OF THE LAW. THEY DIE
BY THE HANDS OF OTHER MEN."
GEORGE BERNARD SHAW
MAN AND SUPERMAN

LOS ANGELES · 2259

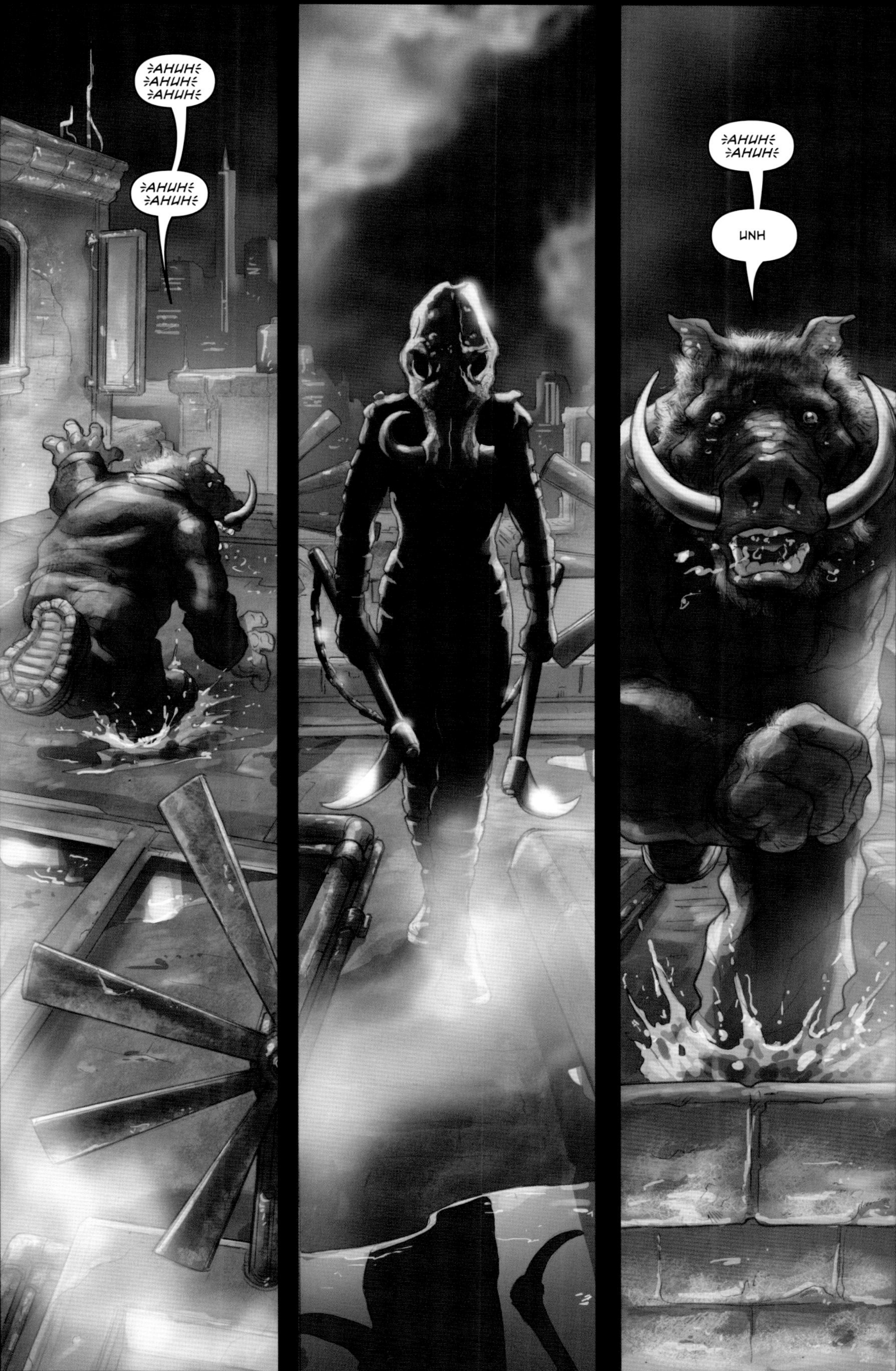

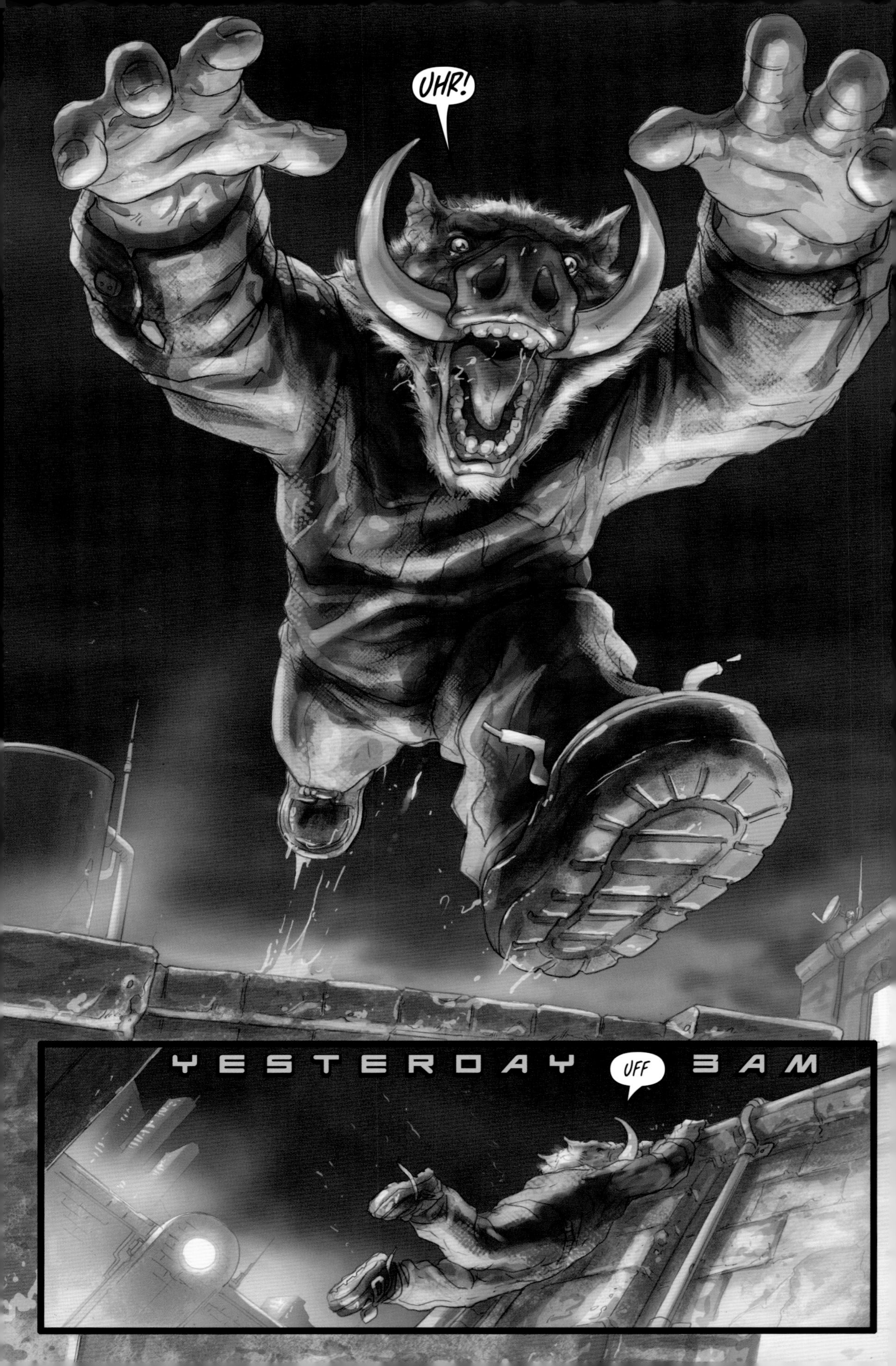
UHR!
YESTERDAY
UFF
3AM

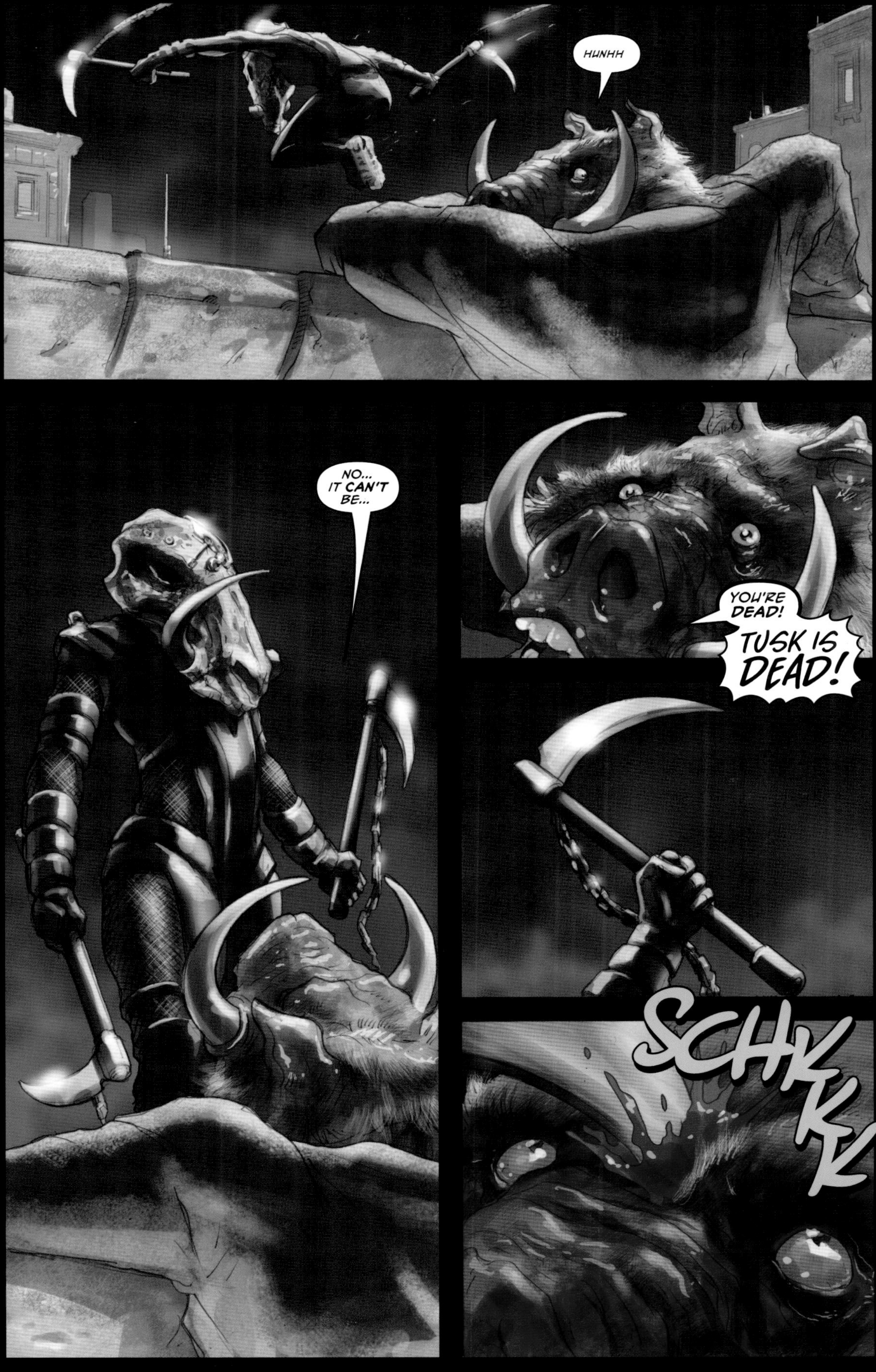
HUNHH
NO... IT CAN'T BE...
YOU'RE DEAD!
TUSK IS DEAD!
SCHKKK

HELL IS THE LAND OF TRANQUIL LIGHT

YESTERDAY · 7.49AM

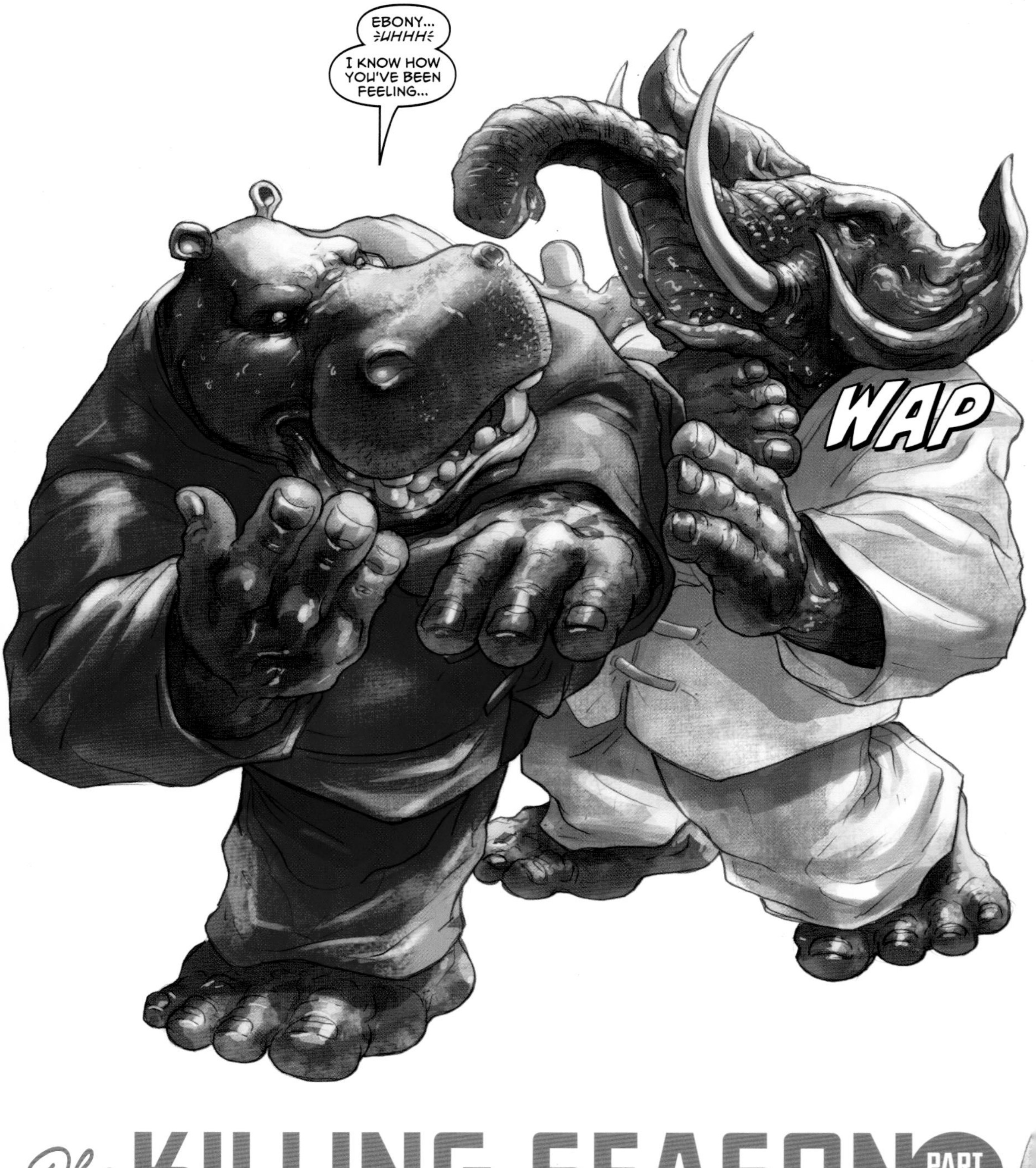
EBONY... UHHH
I KNOW HOW YOU'VE BEEN FEELING...
WAP

The KILLING SEASON PART 2 of 4

Richard Starkings Words · Axel Medellin Pictures

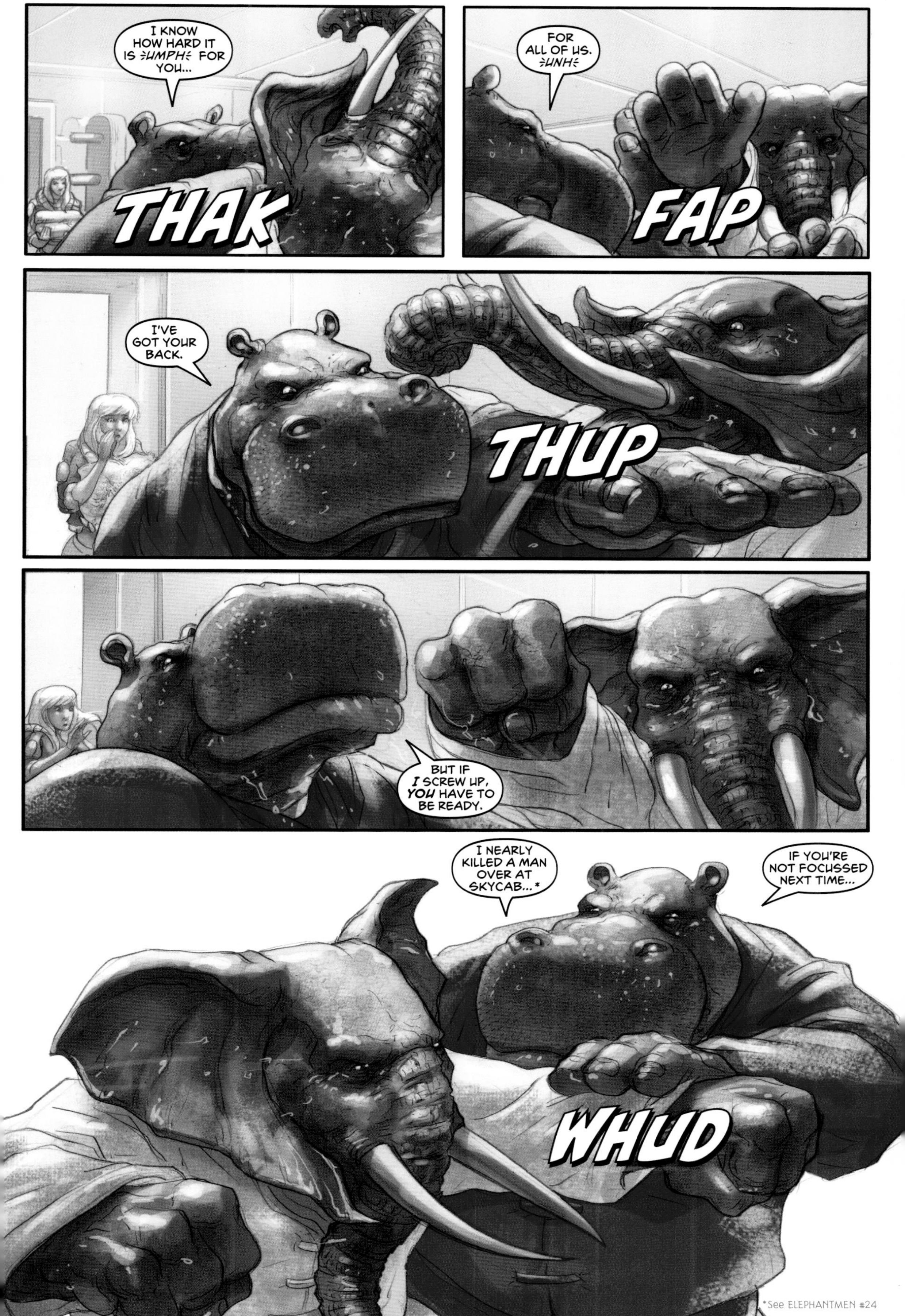
I KNOW HOW HARD IT IS UMPH FOR YOU...
THAK
FOR ALL OF US. UNH
FAP
I'VE GOT YOUR BACK.
THUP
BUT IF I SCREW UP, YOU HAVE TO BE READY.
I NEARLY KILLED A MAN OVER AT SKYCAB...*
IF YOU'RE NOT FOCUSSED NEXT TIME...
WHUD

*See ELEPHANTMEN #24

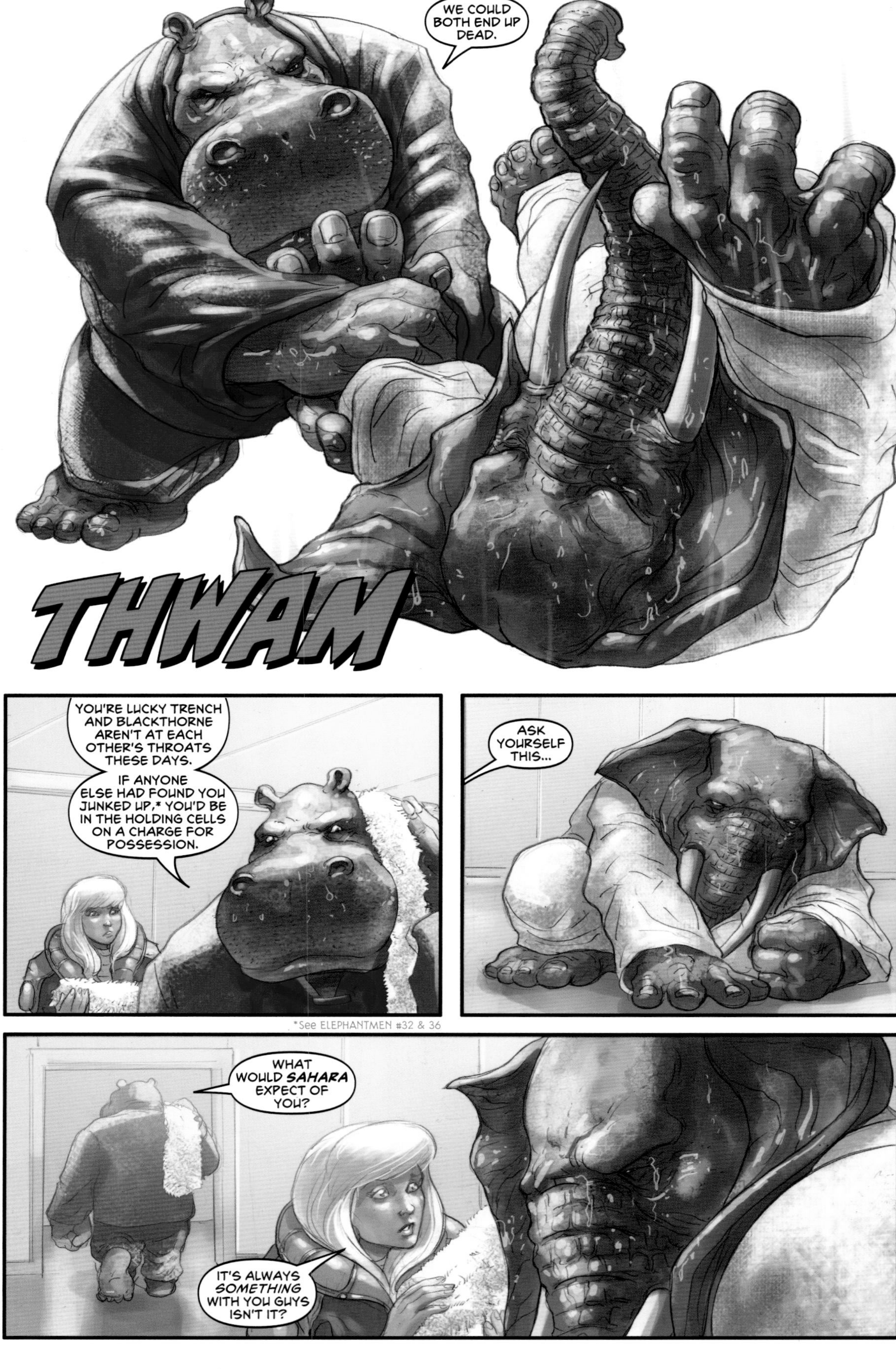
WE COULD BOTH END UP DEAD.
THWAM
YOU'RE LUCKY TRENCH AND BLACKTHORNE AREN'T AT EACH OTHER'S THROATS THESE DAYS.
IF ANYONE ELSE HAD FOUND YOU JUNKED UP,* YOU'D BE IN THE HOLDING CELLS ON A CHARGE FOR POSSESSION.
ASK YOURSELF THIS...
*See ELEPHANTMEN #32 & 36
WHAT WOULD SAHARA EXPECT OF YOU?
IT'S ALWAYS SOMETHING WITH YOU GUYS ISN'T IT?

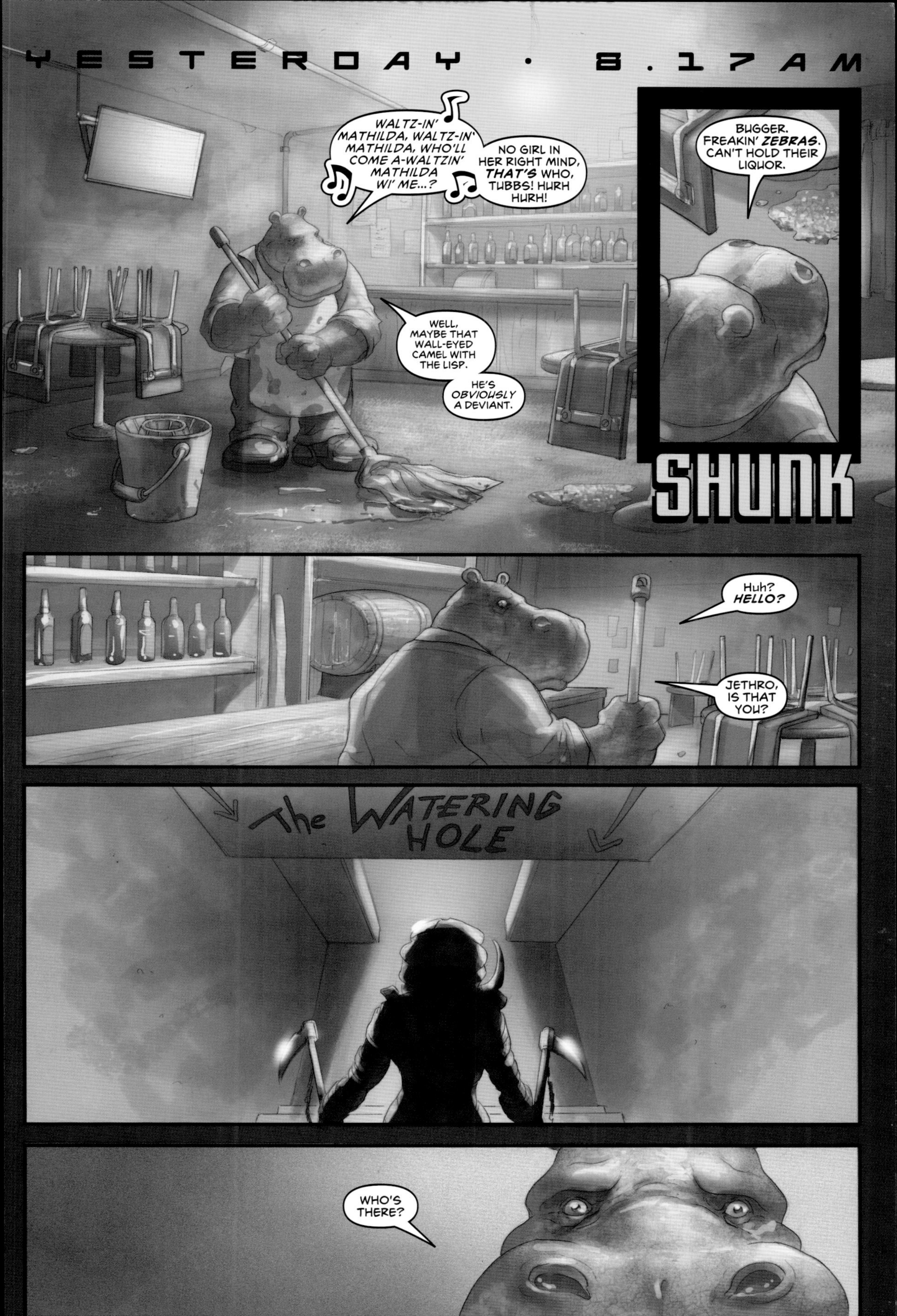
YESTERDAY · 8.17AM
WALTZ-IN' MATHILDA, WALTZ-IN' MATHILDA, WHO'LL COME A-WALTZIN' MATHILDA WI' ME...?
NO GIRL IN HER RIGHT MIND, THAT'S WHO, TUBBS! HURH HURH!
WELL, MAYBE THAT WALL-EYED CAMEL WITH THE LISP.
HE'S OBVIOUSLY A DEVIANT.
BUGGER. FREAKIN' ZEBRAS. CAN'T HOLD THEIR LIQUOR.
SHUNK
Huh? HELLO?
JETHRO, IS THAT YOU?
The WATERING HOLE
WHO'S THERE?

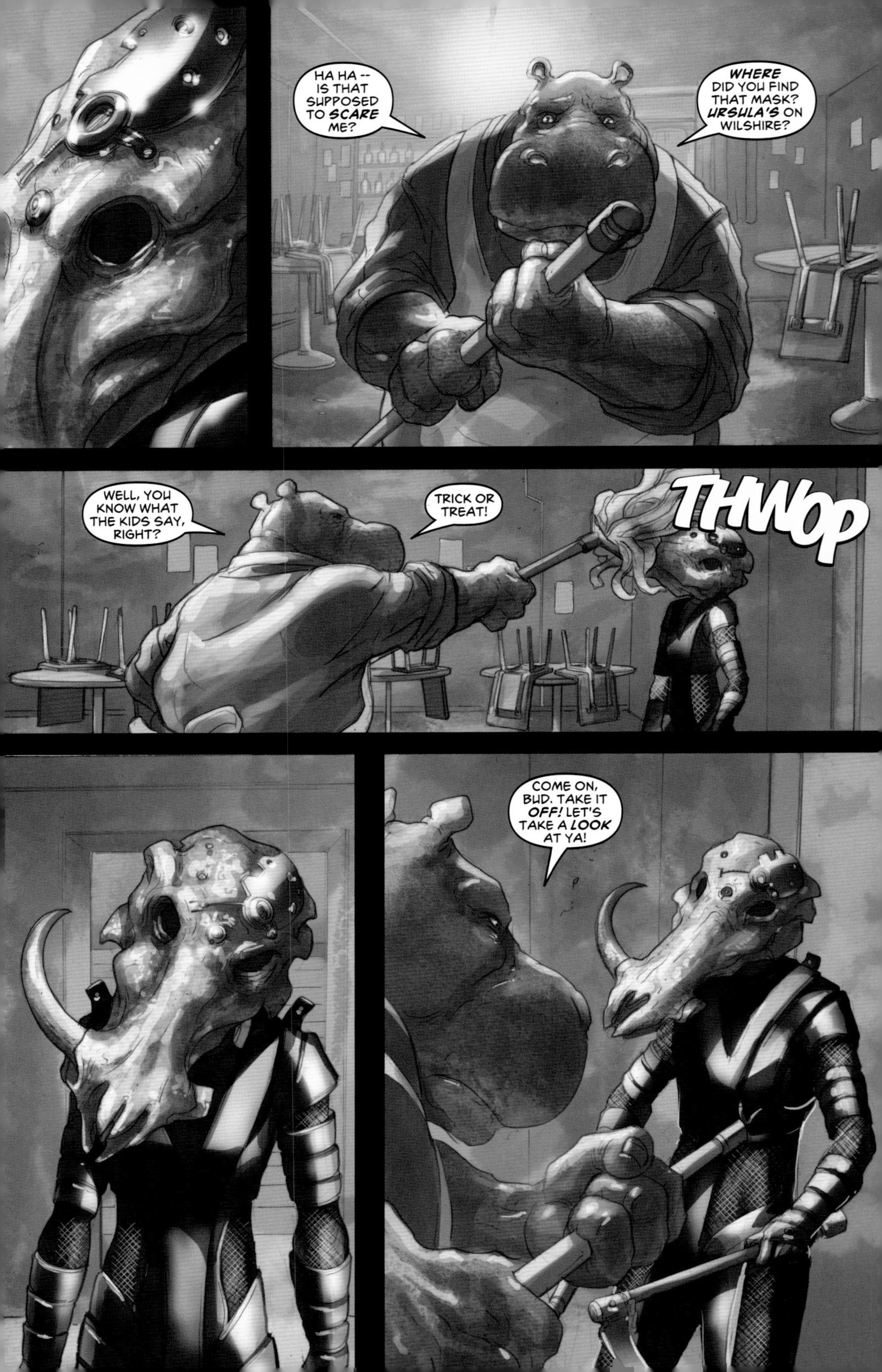
HA HA -- IS THAT SUPPOSED TO SCARE ME?
WHERE DID YOU FIND THAT MASK? URSULA'S ON WILSHIRE?
WELL, YOU KNOW WHAT THE KIDS SAY, RIGHT?
TRICK OR TREAT!
THWOP
COME ON, BUD. TAKE IT OFF! LET'S TAKE A LOOK AT YA!

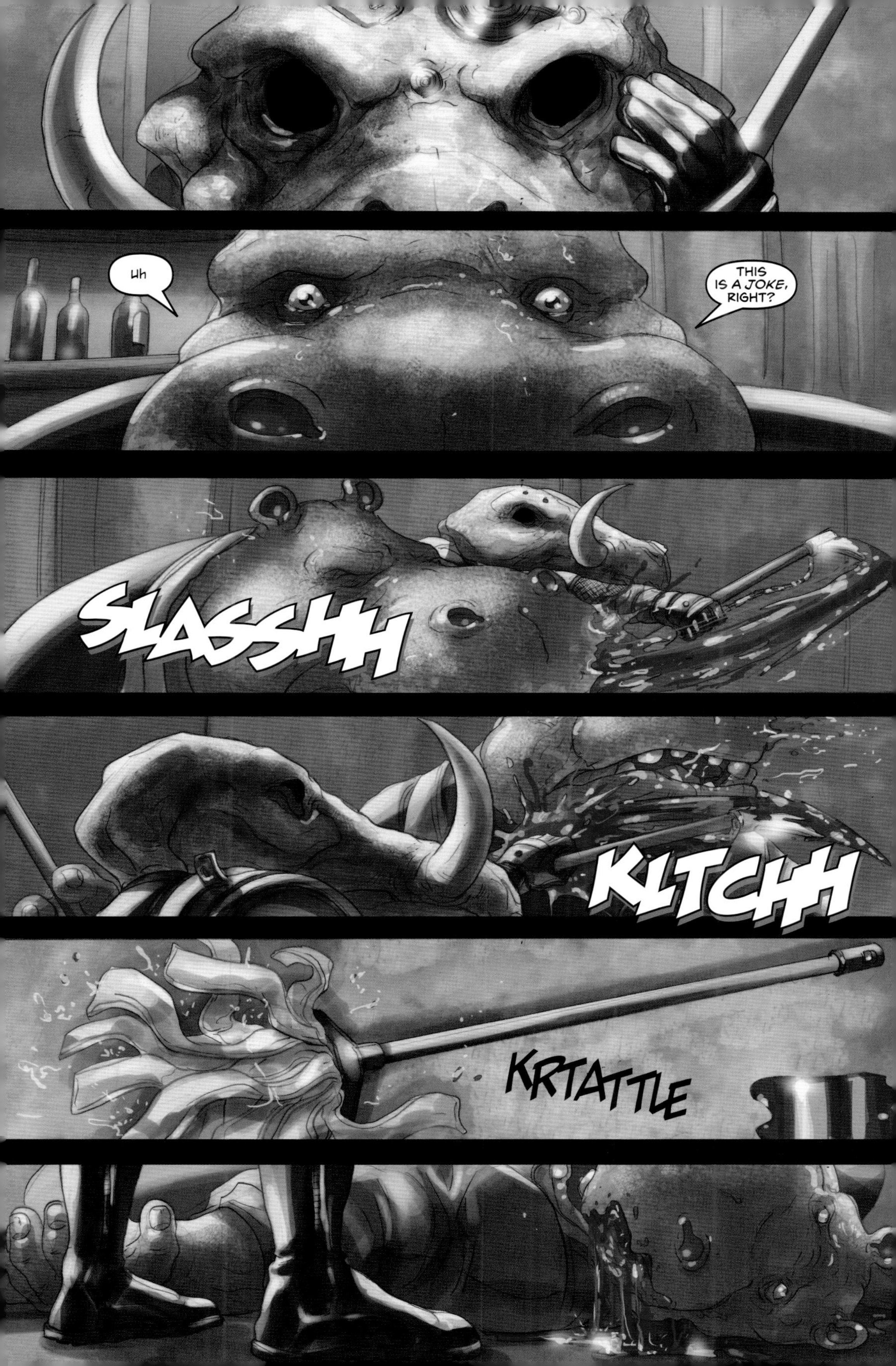
Uh
THIS IS A JOKE, RIGHT?
SLASSHH
KLTCHH
KRTATTLE

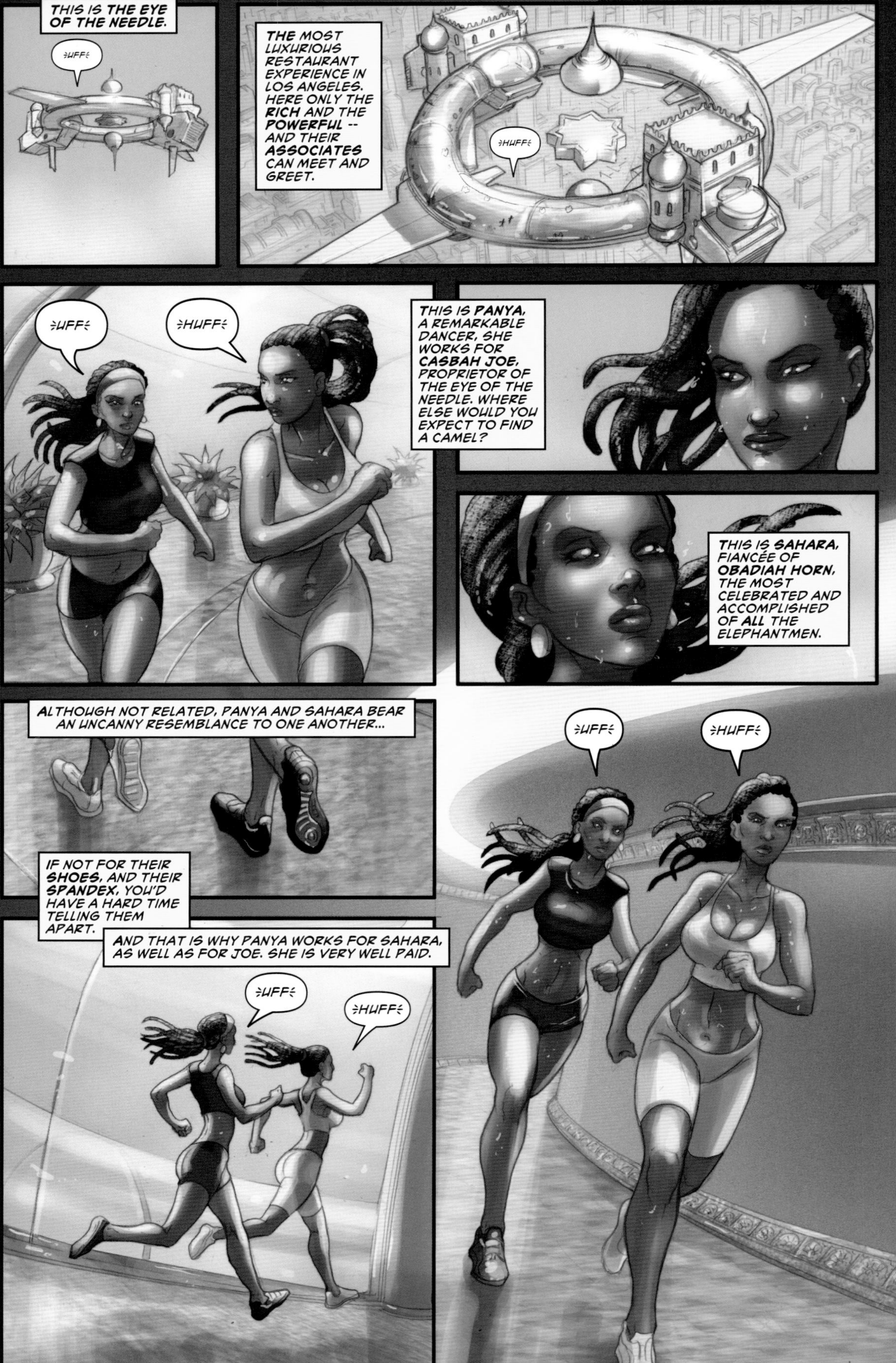
THIS IS THE EYE OF THE NEEDLE.
UFF
THE MOST LUXURIOUS RESTAURANT EXPERIENCE IN LOS ANGELES. HERE ONLY THE RICH AND THE POWERFUL -- AND THEIR ASSOCIATES CAN MEET AND GREET.
HUFF
UFF
HUFF
THIS IS PANYA, A REMARKABLE DANCER, SHE WORKS FOR CASBAH JOE, PROPRIETOR OF THE EYE OF THE NEEDLE. WHERE ELSE WOULD YOU EXPECT TO FIND A CAMEL?
THIS IS SAHARA, FIANCÉE OF OBADIAH HORN, THE MOST CELEBRATED AND ACCOMPLISHED OF ALL THE ELEPHANTMEN.
ALTHOUGH NOT RELATED, PANYA AND SAHARA BEAR AN UNCANNY RESEMBLANCE TO ONE ANOTHER...
IF NOT FOR THEIR SHOES, AND THEIR SPANDEX, YOU'D HAVE A HARD TIME TELLING THEM APART.
AND THAT IS WHY PANYA WORKS FOR SAHARA, AS WELL AS FOR JOE. SHE IS VERY WELL PAID.
UFF
HUFF
UFF
HUFF

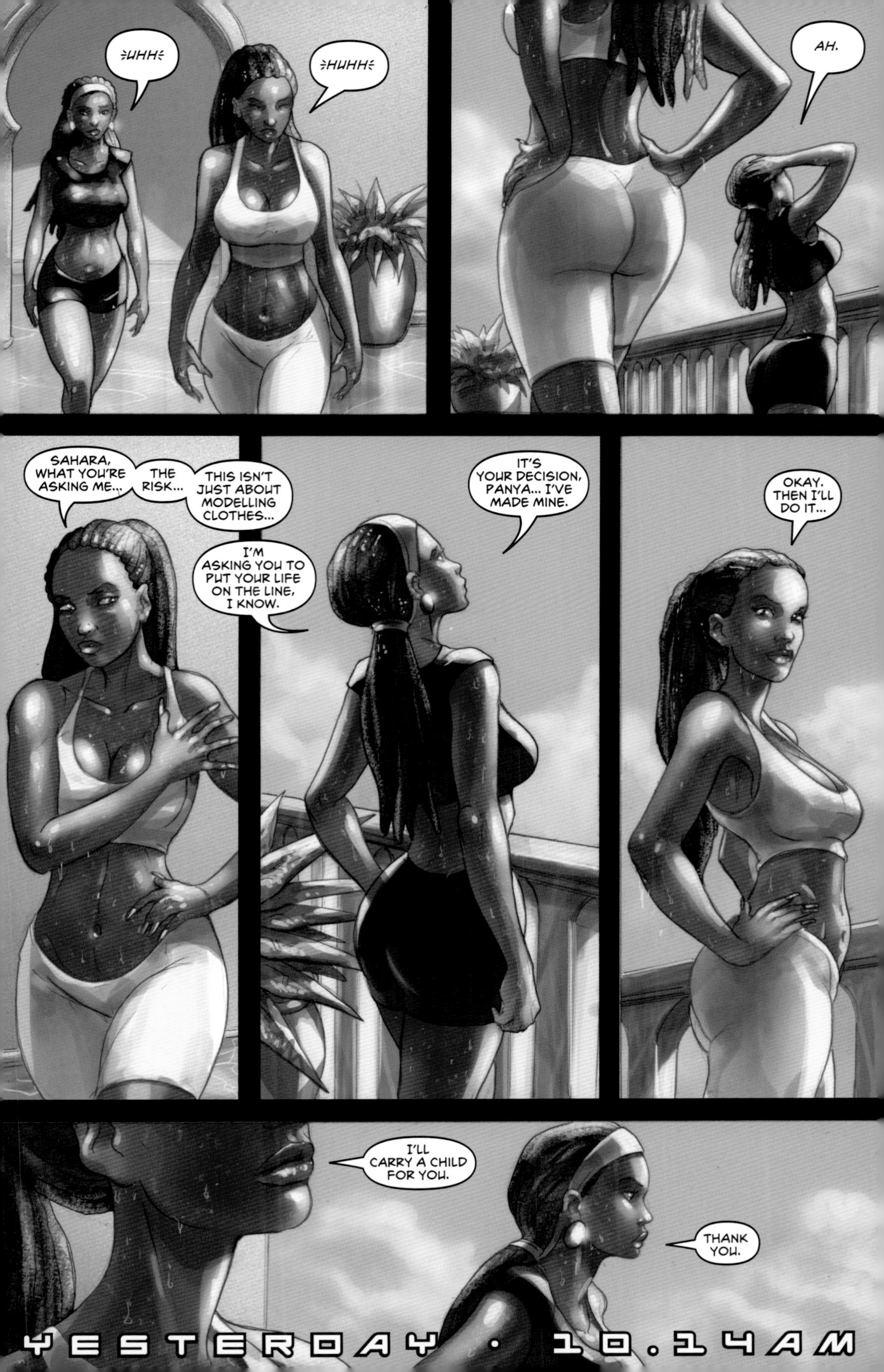

UHH
HUHH
AH.
SAHARA, WHAT YOU'RE ASKING ME...
THE RISK...
THIS ISN'T JUST ABOUT MODELLING CLOTHES...
I'M ASKING YOU TO PUT YOUR LIFE ON THE LINE, I KNOW.
IT'S YOUR DECISION, PANYA... I'VE MADE MINE.
OKAY. THEN I'LL DO IT...
I'LL CARRY A CHILD FOR YOU.
THANK YOU.
YESTERDAY · 10.14AM

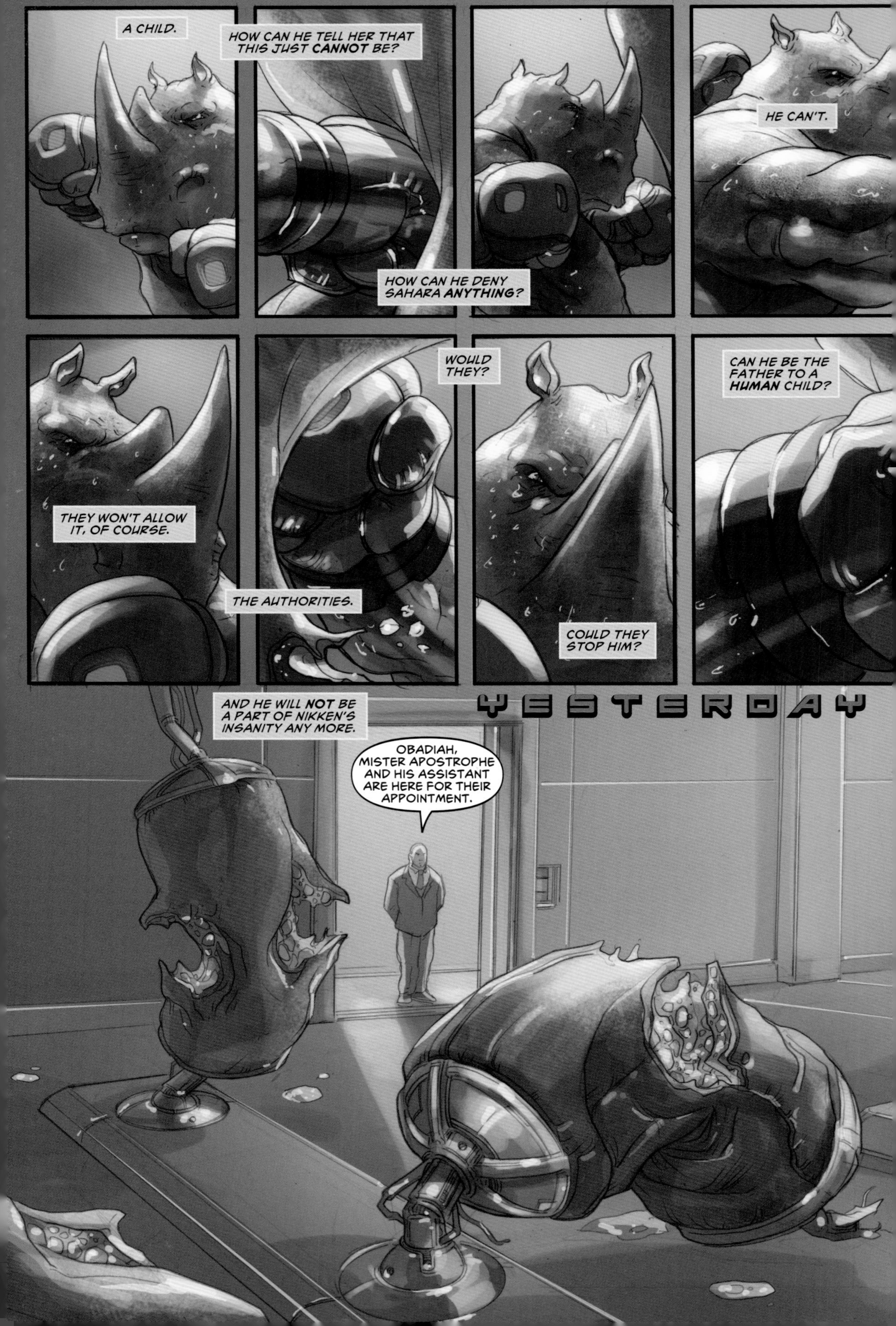
A CHILD.
HOW CAN HE TELL HER THAT THIS JUST CANNOT BE?
HOW CAN HE DENY SAHARA ANYTHING?
HE CAN'T.
THEY WON'T ALLOW IT, OF COURSE.
THE AUTHORITIES.
WOULD THEY?
COULD THEY STOP HIM?
CAN HE BE THE FATHER TO A HUMAN CHILD?
AND HE WILL NOT BE A PART OF NIKKEN'S INSANITY ANY MORE.
YESTERDAY
OBADIAH, MISTER APOSTROPHE AND HIS ASSISTANT ARE HERE FOR THEIR APPOINTMENT.

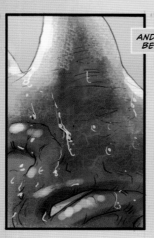

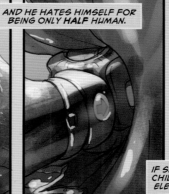
AND HE HATES HIMSELF FOR
BEING ONLY *HALF* HUMAN.

HE LOVES HER
TOO MUCH.

IF SAHARA BEARS HIS
CHILD, AN UGLY HUMAN/
ELEPHANTMEN MUTT...

NEVER.

HE HATES BEING HUMAN
IN ANY WAY AT ALL.

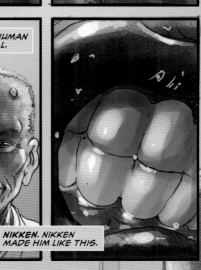

NO.

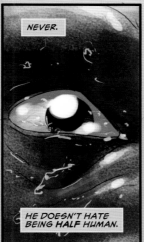
HE DOESN'T HATE
BEING *HALF* HUMAN.

NIKKEN. NIKKEN
MADE HIM LIKE THIS.

11AM

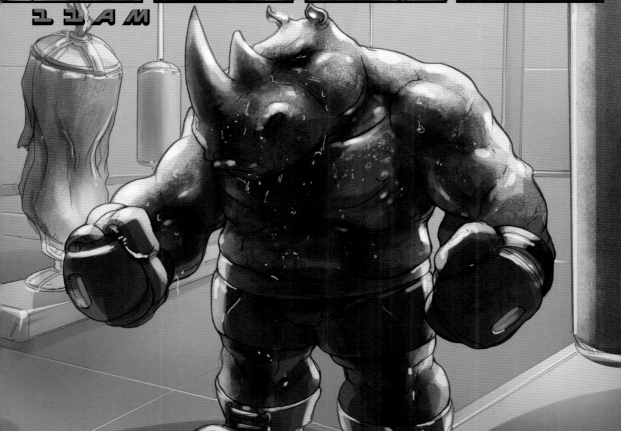

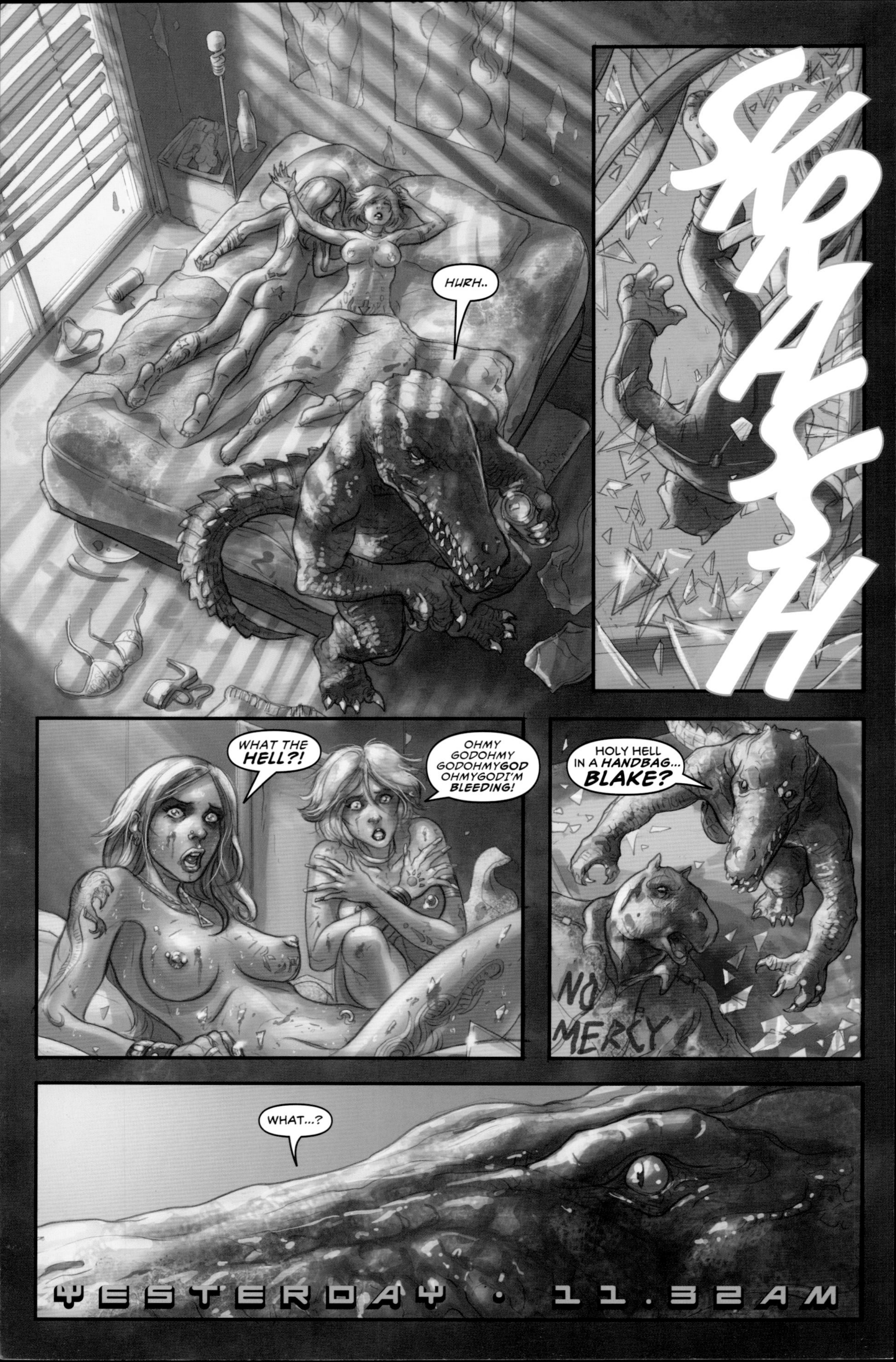
HURH..
WHAT THE HELL?!
OHMY GODOHMY GODOHMYGOD OHMYGODI'M BLEEDING!
HOLY HELL IN A HANDBAG... BLAKE?
NO MERCY
WHAT...?
YESTERDAY · 11.32AM

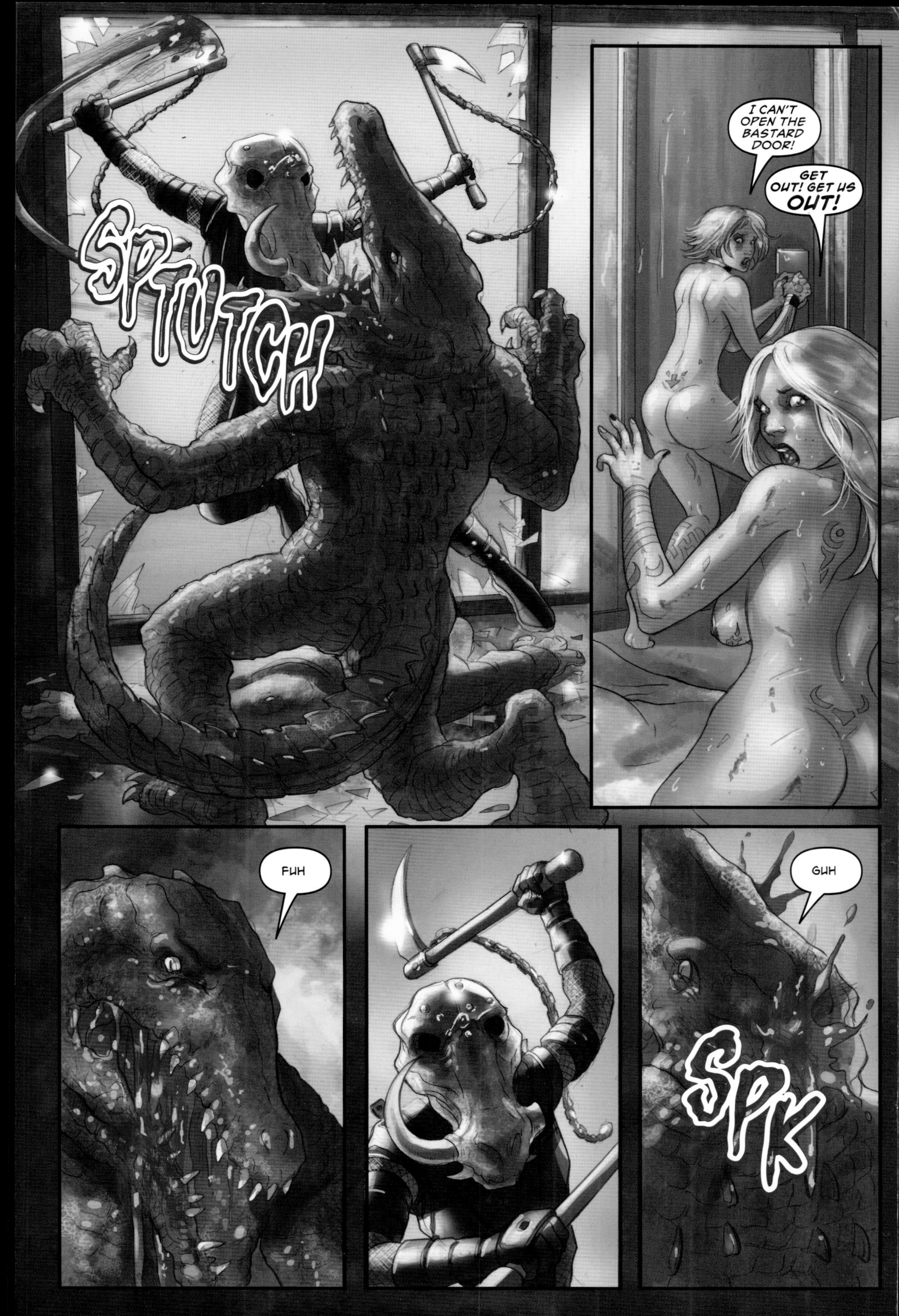
SPTUTCH
I CAN'T OPEN THE BASTARD DOOR!
GET OUT! GET US OUT!
FUH
GUH
SPK

SHMMMPP

NUH-
NUH-NUH

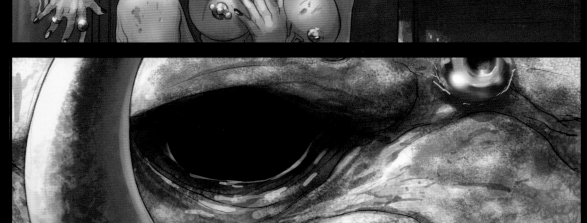

MISTER HORN. THANK YOU FOR SEEING US.

LIEN AND I ARE HERE TODAY BECAUSE THERE'S SOMETHING I THINK YOU SHOULD KNOW...

I THINK THE FIRST THING *WE* NEED TO KNOW IS *WHY* YOU FELT IT WAS NECESSARY TO DELIVER A FESTERING *CORPSE* TO IVORY TOWERS.

Oh, I'M *SURE* MISTER *APOSTROPHE* HAS GOOD REASON FOR REMOVING *EVIDENCE* FROM THE SCENE OF A *CRIME.*

THIS IS ONE OF THE BODIES RECOVERED FROM THE *CANAL* ISN'T IT?*

*See ELEPHANTMEN #36

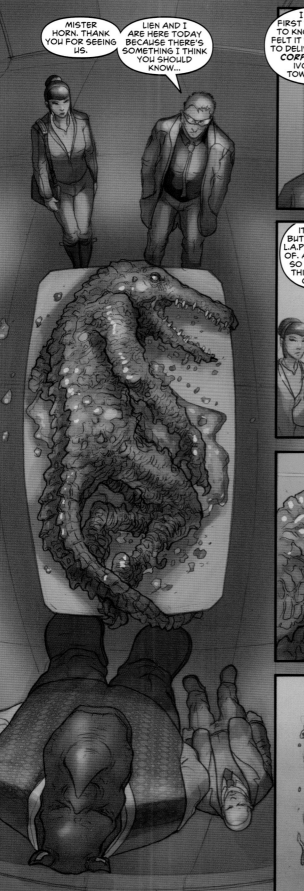

IT IS INDEED. BUT NOT ONE THE L.A.P.D ARE *AWARE* OF. AND HE'S HERE SO YOU CAN SEE THIS WITH YOUR OWN EYES.

I *SEE* A DEAD *MUNT.* I *SMELL* IT. WHAT AM I MISSING?

YOU'RE MISSING THE VERY THING THAT MAKES YOU AND THE CROC HERE MARKEDLY *DIFFERENT...* LIEN?

I'M GUESSING YOU'RE ONE OF THE TRANSGENICS WHOSE *IMPERIUMITE* WAS REMOVED AFTER THE WAR.*

*See ELEPHANTMEN #23-30

YOU WERE ONE OF THE LUCKY ONES.

YES. NOT *ALL* THE IMPERIUMITES WERE REMOVED FROM MAPPO'S SOLDIERS. SOME WERE SIMPLY RENDERED HARMLESS. WHAT OF IT?

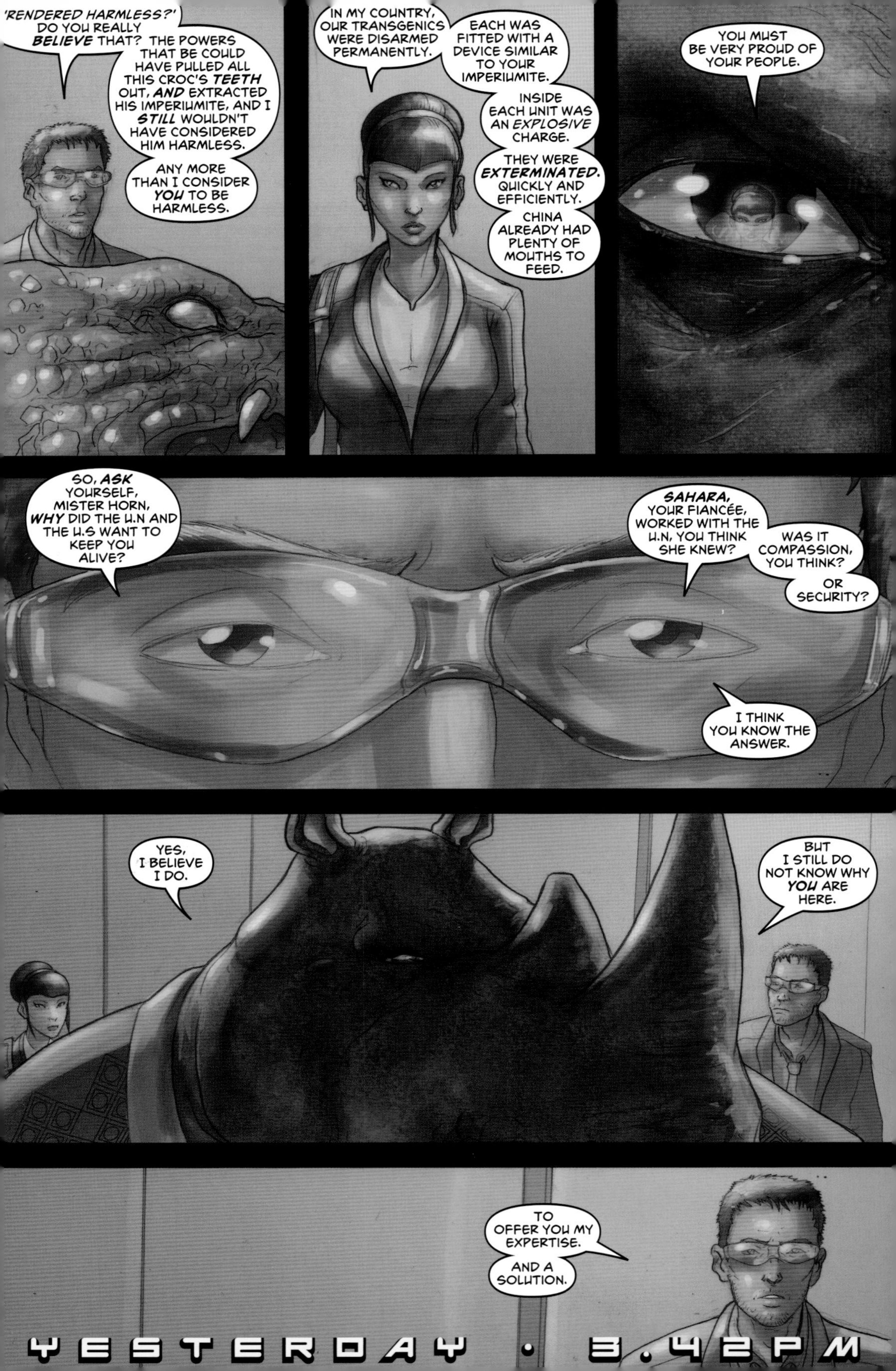
'RENDERED HARMLESS?' DO YOU REALLY BELIEVE THAT? THE POWERS THAT BE COULD HAVE PULLED ALL THIS CROC'S TEETH OUT, AND EXTRACTED HIS IMPERIUMITE, AND I STILL WOULDN'T HAVE CONSIDERED HIM HARMLESS.
ANY MORE THAN I CONSIDER YOU TO BE HARMLESS.
IN MY COUNTRY, OUR TRANSGENICS WERE DISARMED PERMANENTLY.
EACH WAS FITTED WITH A DEVICE SIMILAR TO YOUR IMPERIUMITE.
INSIDE EACH UNIT WAS AN EXPLOSIVE CHARGE.
THEY WERE EXTERMINATED. QUICKLY AND EFFICIENTLY.
CHINA ALREADY HAD PLENTY OF MOUTHS TO FEED.
YOU MUST BE VERY PROUD OF YOUR PEOPLE.
SO, ASK YOURSELF, MISTER HORN, WHY DID THE U.N AND THE U.S WANT TO KEEP YOU ALIVE?
SAHARA, YOUR FIANCÉE, WORKED WITH THE U.N, YOU THINK SHE KNEW?
WAS IT COMPASSION, YOU THINK?
OR SECURITY?
I THINK YOU KNOW THE ANSWER.
YES, I BELIEVE I DO.
BUT I STILL DO NOT KNOW WHY YOU ARE HERE.
TO OFFER YOU MY EXPERTISE.
AND A SOLUTION.
YESTERDAY · 3.42PM

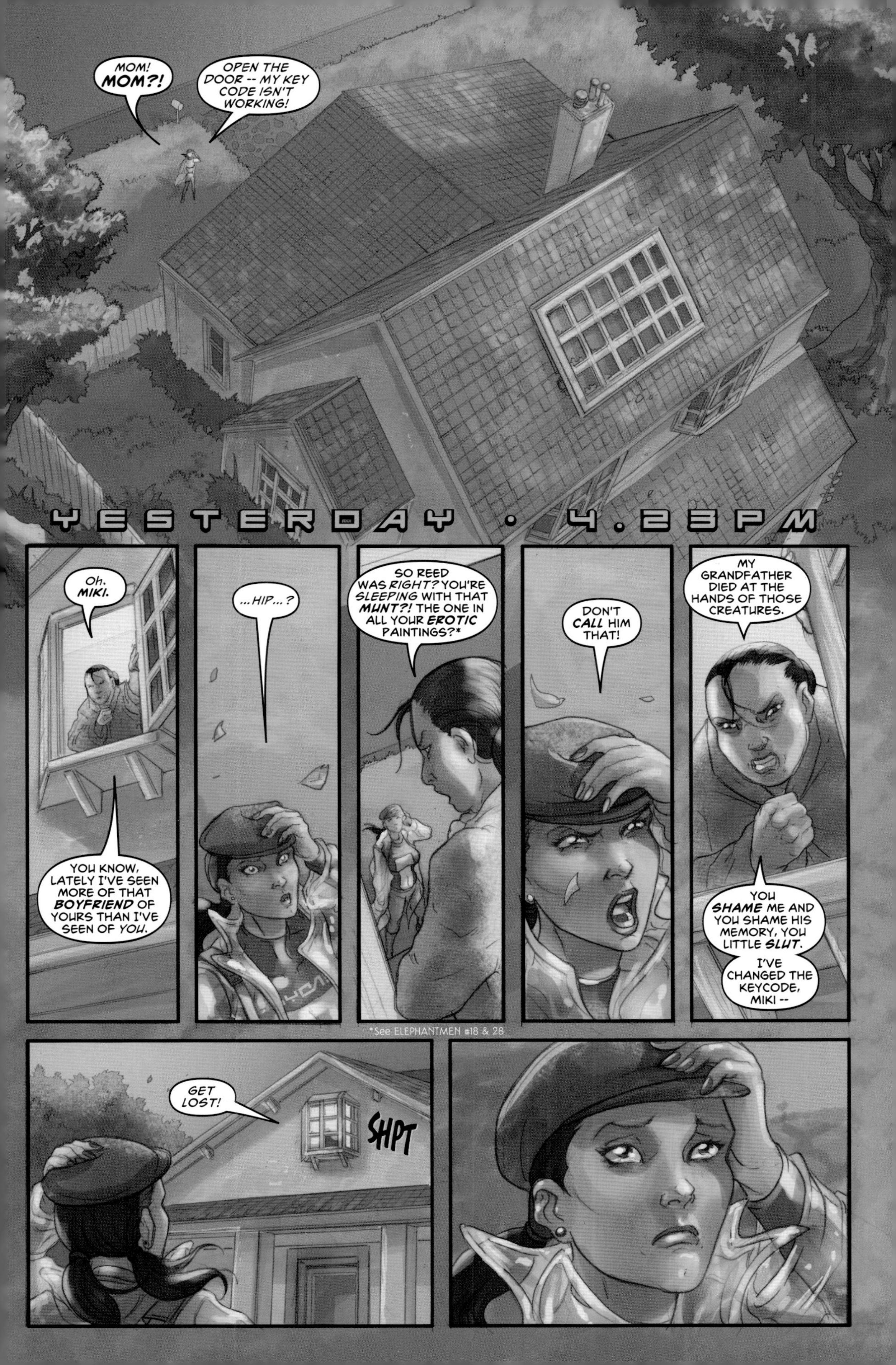

MOM! MOM?!
OPEN THE DOOR -- MY KEY CODE ISN'T WORKING!
YESTERDAY • 4.23PM
Oh. MIKI.
YOU KNOW, LATELY I'VE SEEN MORE OF THAT BOYFRIEND OF YOURS THAN I'VE SEEN OF YOU.
...HIP...?
SO REED WAS RIGHT? YOU'RE SLEEPING WITH THAT MUNT?! THE ONE IN ALL YOUR EROTIC PAINTINGS?*
DON'T CALL HIM THAT!
MY GRANDFATHER DIED AT THE HANDS OF THOSE CREATURES.
YOU SHAME ME AND YOU SHAME HIS MEMORY, YOU LITTLE SLUT.
I'VE CHANGED THE KEYCODE, MIKI --
*See ELEPHANTMEN #18 & 28
GET LOST!
SHPT

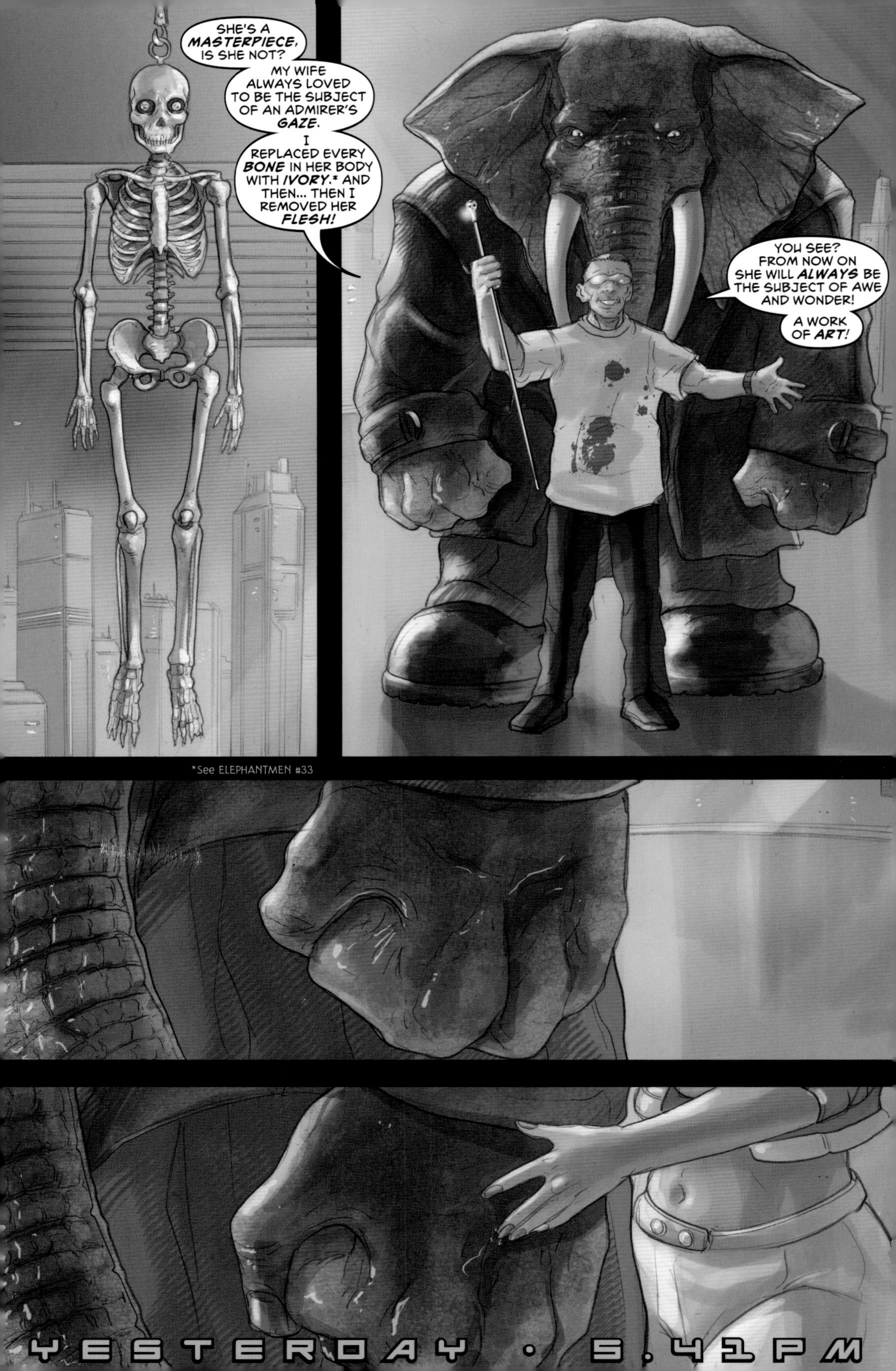

SHE'S A *MASTERPIECE*, IS SHE NOT?
MY WIFE ALWAYS LOVED TO BE THE SUBJECT OF AN ADMIRER'S *GAZE*.
I REPLACED EVERY *BONE* IN HER BODY WITH *IVORY*.* AND THEN... THEN I REMOVED HER *FLESH!*
YOU SEE? FROM NOW ON SHE WILL *ALWAYS* BE THE SUBJECT OF AWE AND WONDER!
A WORK OF *ART!*
*See ELEPHANTMEN #33
YESTERDAY • 5.41PM

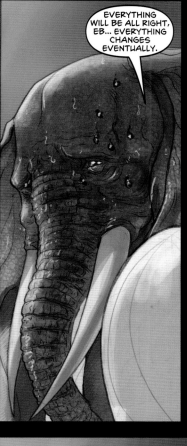

EVERYTHING WILL BE ALL RIGHT, EB... EVERYTHING CHANGES EVENTUALLY.

I KNOW WHAT YOU GO THROUGH EVERY NIGHT, EVERY DAY... I'VE BEEN READING ALL ABOUT P.T.S.D.

IT'S WHAT DOCTORS SAY TO SOLDIERS TO EXPLAIN AWAY THEIR *SHITTY* LIVES.

I CAN GUARANTEE *THIS* DOCTOR WILL LIVE A SHITTY LIFE FROM NOW.

GOOD! I HOPE THEY TOSS THAT *PSYCHO* INTO ISO AND *THROW AWAY THE KEY!*

HOW COME THERE ARE SO MANY FREAKING *WEIRDOS* IN THIS CITY?!

YOU WERE RIGHT, VANITY. I SHOULDN'T HAVE EATEN ALL THAT PIZZA.

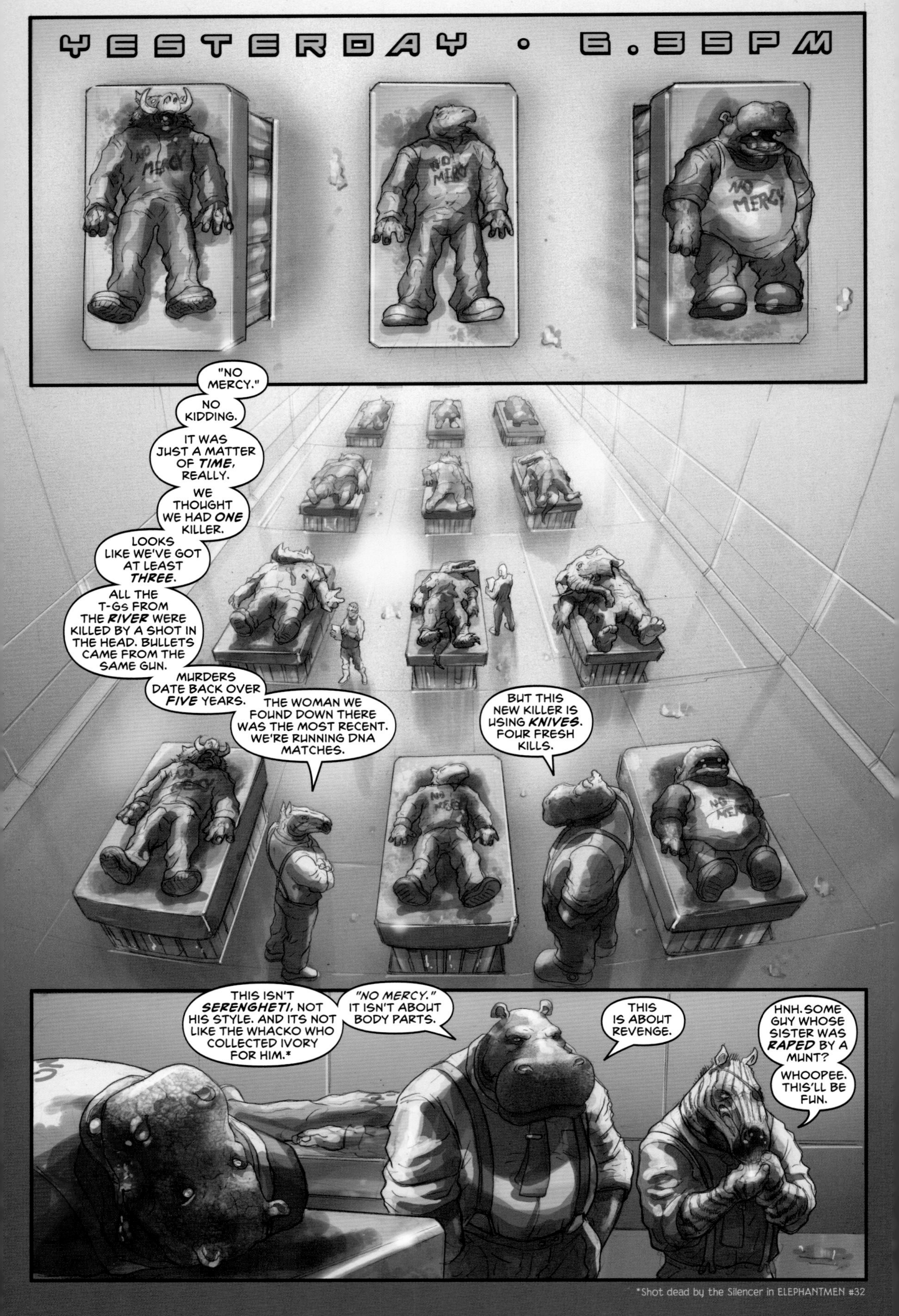

YESTERDAY • 6.35PM
NO MERCY
NO MERCY
NO MERCY
"NO MERCY."
NO KIDDING.
IT WAS JUST A MATTER OF *TIME*, REALLY.
WE THOUGHT WE HAD *ONE* KILLER.
LOOKS LIKE WE'VE GOT AT LEAST *THREE*.
ALL THE T-Gs FROM THE *RIVER* WERE KILLED BY A SHOT IN THE HEAD. BULLETS CAME FROM THE SAME GUN.
MURDERS DATE BACK OVER *FIVE* YEARS.
THE WOMAN WE FOUND DOWN THERE WAS THE MOST RECENT. WE'RE RUNNING DNA MATCHES.
BUT THIS NEW KILLER IS USING *KNIVES*. FOUR FRESH KILLS.
THIS ISN'T *SERENGHETI*, NOT HIS STYLE. AND ITS NOT LIKE THE WHACKO WHO COLLECTED IVORY FOR HIM.*
"NO MERCY." IT ISN'T ABOUT BODY PARTS.
THIS IS ABOUT REVENGE.
HNH. SOME GUY WHOSE SISTER WAS *RAPED* BY A MUNT?
WHOOPEE. THIS'LL BE FUN.

*Shot dead by the Silencer in ELEPHANTMEN #32

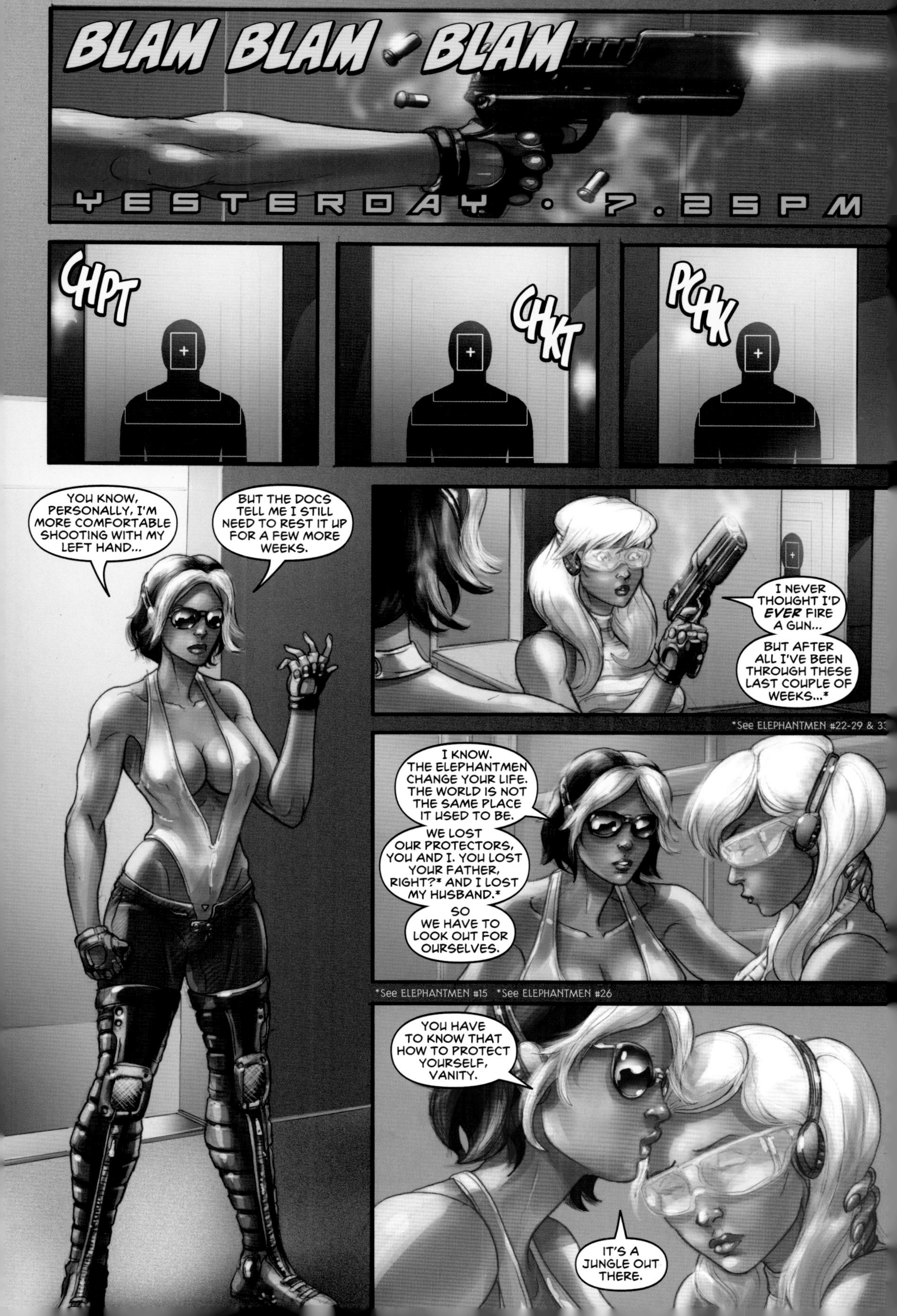
BLAM BLAM BLAM
YESTERDAY • 7.25PM
CHPT
CHKT
PCHK
YOU KNOW, PERSONALLY, I'M MORE COMFORTABLE SHOOTING WITH MY LEFT HAND...
BUT THE DOCS TELL ME I STILL NEED TO REST IT UP FOR A FEW MORE WEEKS.
I NEVER THOUGHT I'D EVER FIRE A GUN...
BUT AFTER ALL I'VE BEEN THROUGH THESE LAST COUPLE OF WEEKS...*
*See ELEPHANTMEN #22-29 & 33
I KNOW. THE ELEPHANTMEN CHANGE YOUR LIFE. THE WORLD IS NOT THE SAME PLACE IT USED TO BE.
WE LOST OUR PROTECTORS, YOU AND I. YOU LOST YOUR FATHER, RIGHT?* AND I LOST MY HUSBAND.*
SO WE HAVE TO LOOK OUT FOR OURSELVES.
*See ELEPHANTMEN #15 *See ELEPHANTMEN #26
YOU HAVE TO KNOW THAT HOW TO PROTECT YOURSELF, VANITY.
IT'S A JUNGLE OUT THERE.

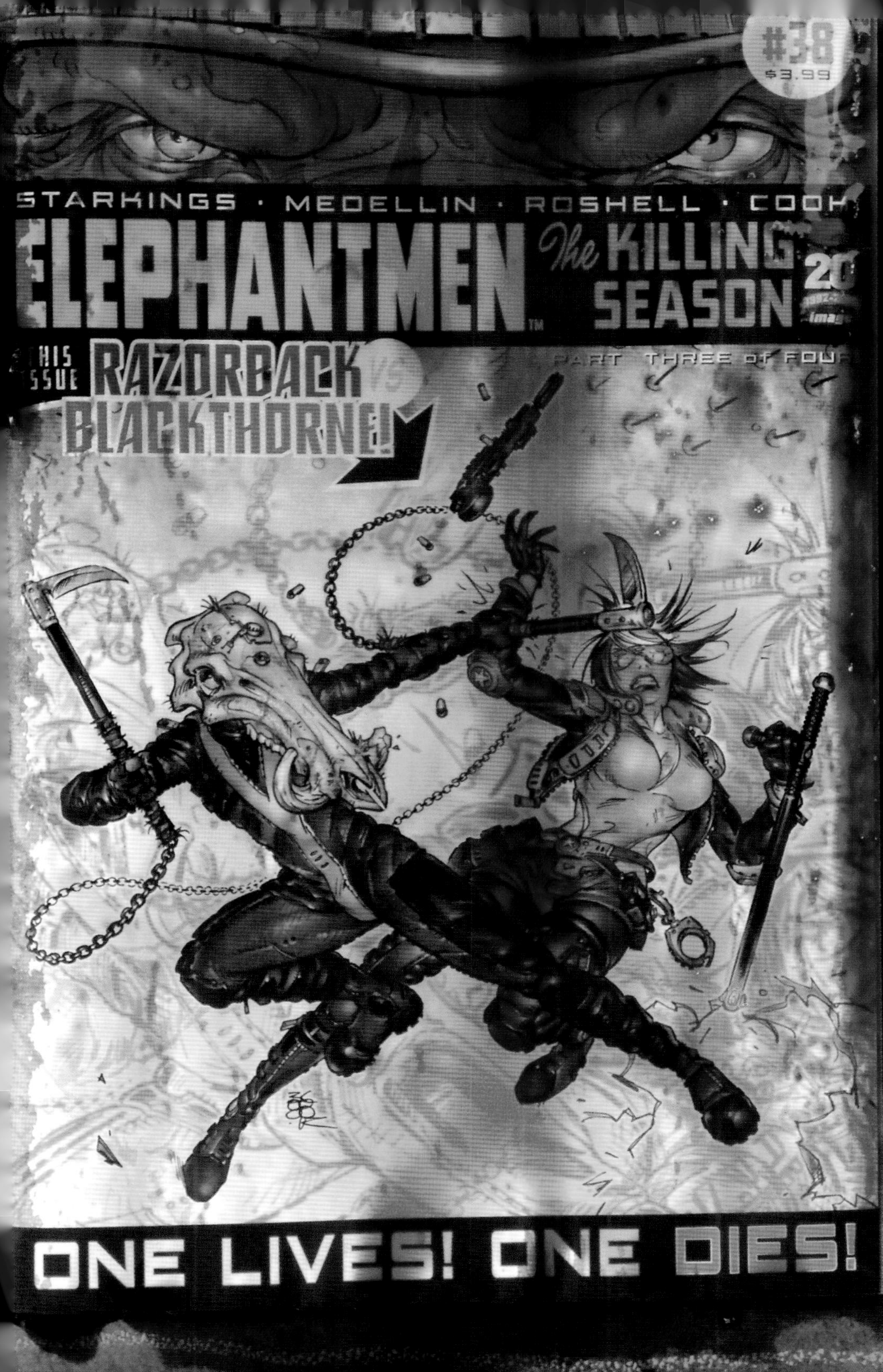
#38
$3.99
STARKINGS · MEDELLIN · ROSHELL · COOK
ELEPHANTMEN
The KILLING SEASON
PART THREE of FOUR
THIS ISSUE
RAZORBACK VS BLACKTHORNE!
ONE LIVES! ONE DIES!

"YOU MAY REMEMBER THAT ON
EARTH - THOUGH OF COURSE WE
NEVER CONFESSED IT - THE DEATH OF
ANYONE WE KNEW, EVEN THOSE WE
LIKED BEST, WAS ALWAYS MINGLED
WITH A CERTAIN SATISFACTION AT
BEING FINALLY DONE WITH THEM."

GEORGE BERNARD SHAW
MAN AND SUPERMAN

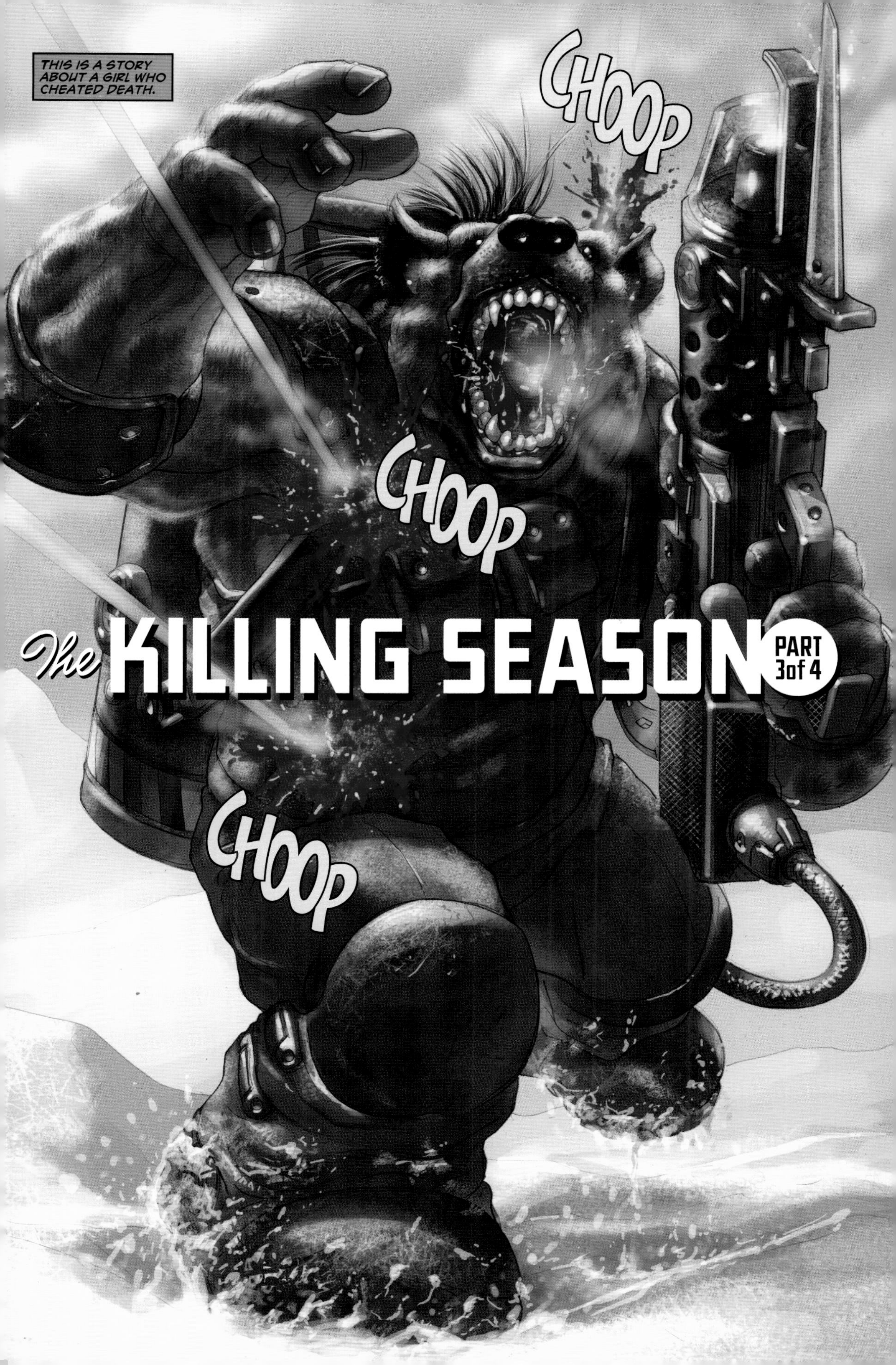
THIS IS A STORY ABOUT A GIRL WHO CHEATED DEATH.
CHOOP
CHOOP
The KILLING SEASON PART 3of 4
CHOOP

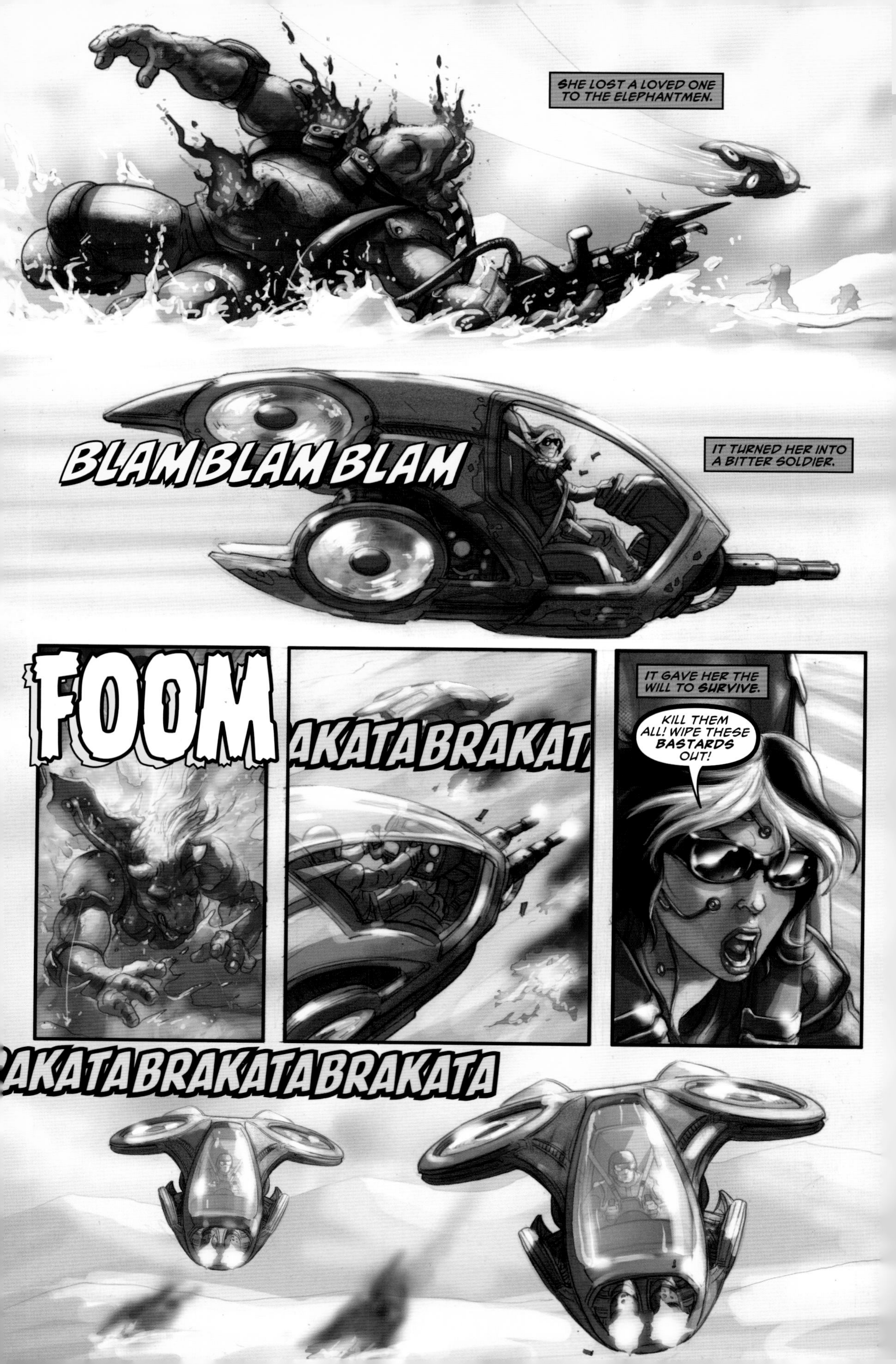
SHE LOST A LOVED ONE TO THE ELEPHANTMEN.
BLAM BLAM BLAM
IT TURNED HER INTO A BITTER SOLDIER.
FOOM
AKATA BRAKAT
IT GAVE HER THE WILL TO SURVIVE.
KILL THEM ALL! WIPE THESE BASTARDS OUT!
AKATA BRAKATA BRAKATA

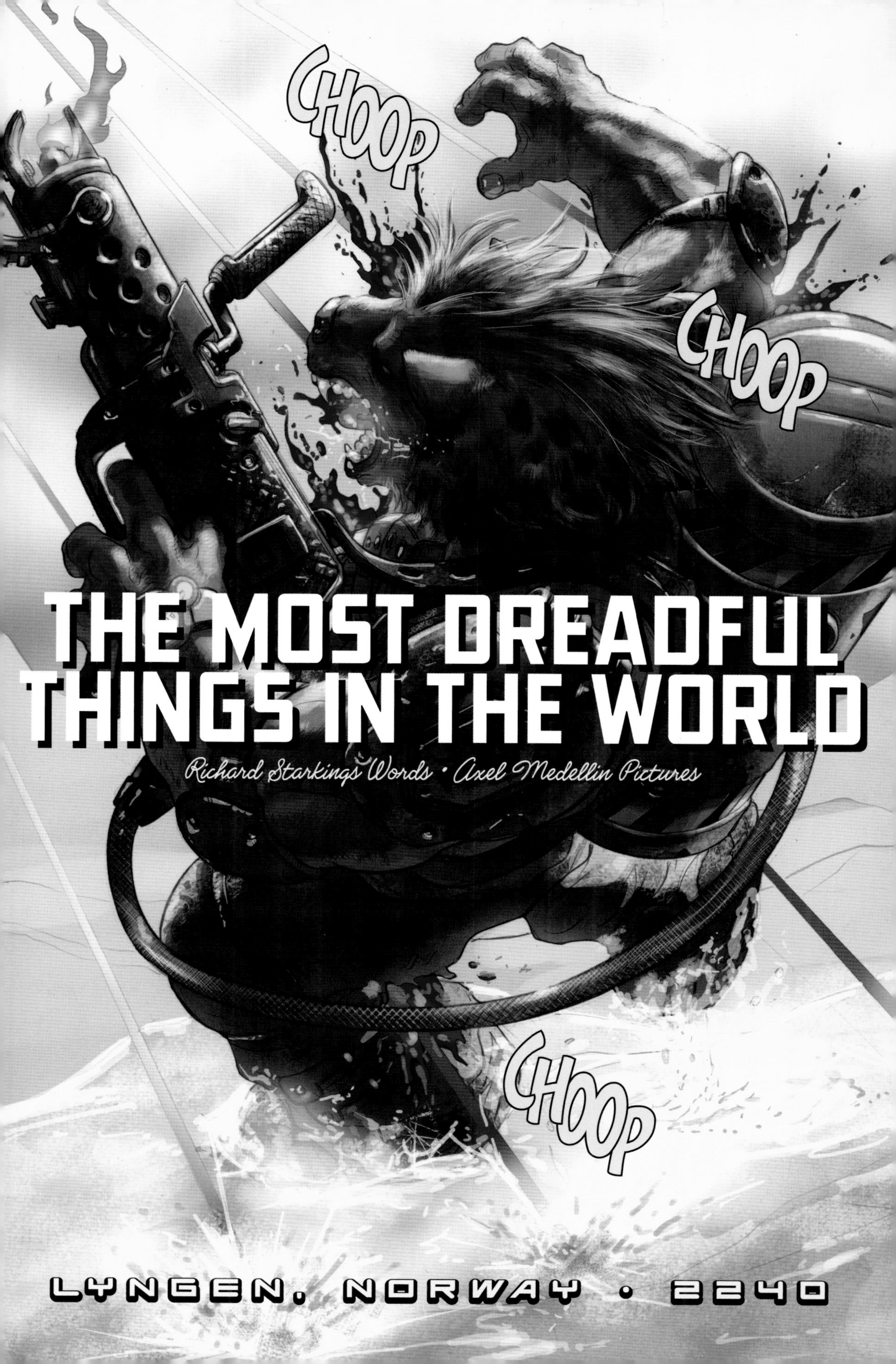
CHOOP
CHOOP
THE MOST DREADFUL THINGS IN THE WORLD
Richard Starkings Words • Axel Medellin Pictures
CHOOP
LYNGEN, NORWAY • 2240

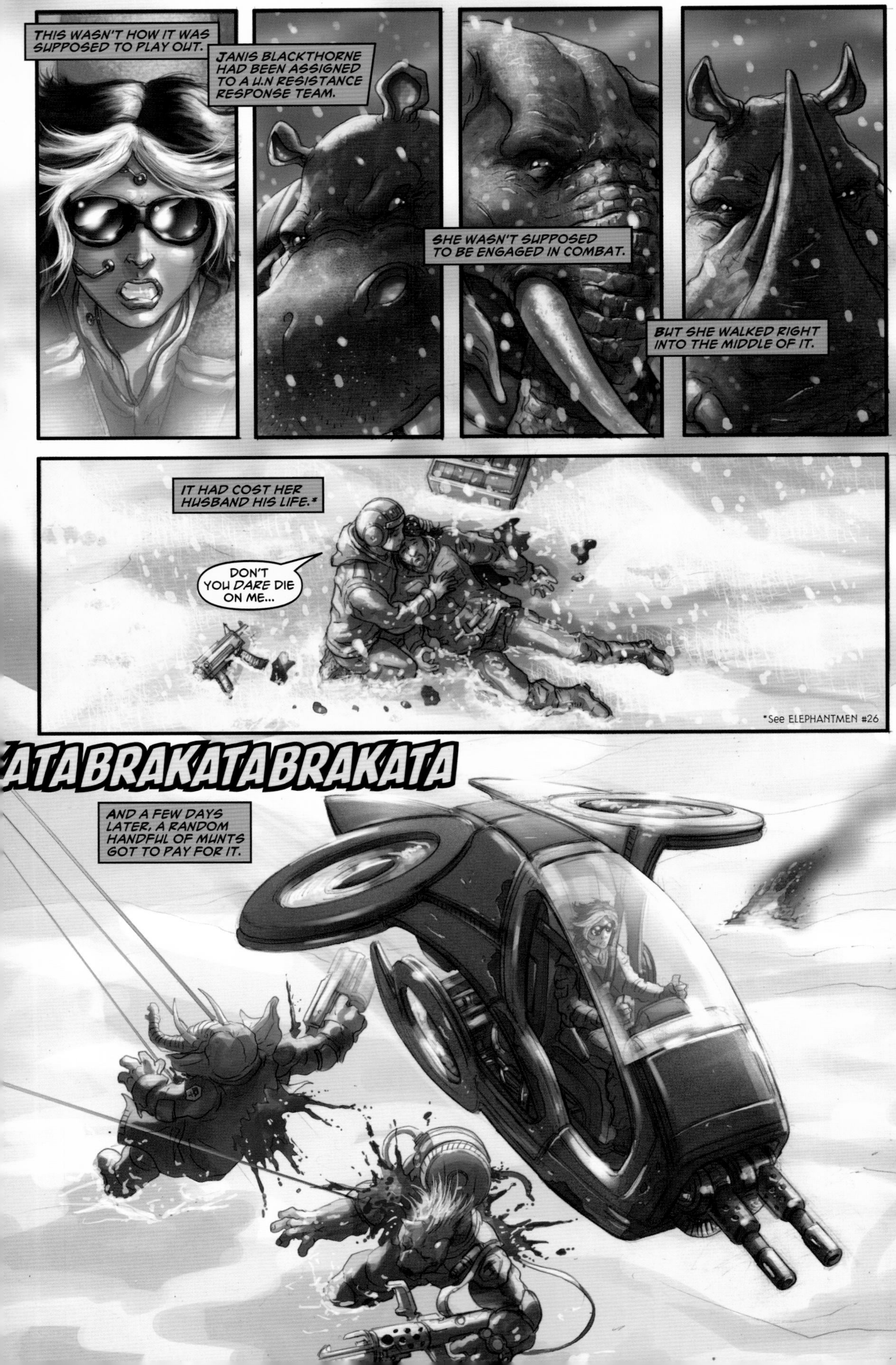
THIS WASN'T HOW IT WAS SUPPOSED TO PLAY OUT.
JANIS BLACKTHORNE HAD BEEN ASSIGNED TO A U.N RESISTANCE RESPONSE TEAM.
SHE WASN'T SUPPOSED TO BE ENGAGED IN COMBAT.
BUT SHE WALKED RIGHT INTO THE MIDDLE OF IT.
IT HAD COST HER HUSBAND HIS LIFE.*
DON'T YOU DARE DIE ON ME...
*See ELEPHANTMEN #26
ATA BRAKATA BRAKATA
AND A FEW DAYS LATER, A RANDOM HANDFUL OF MUNTS GOT TO PAY FOR IT.

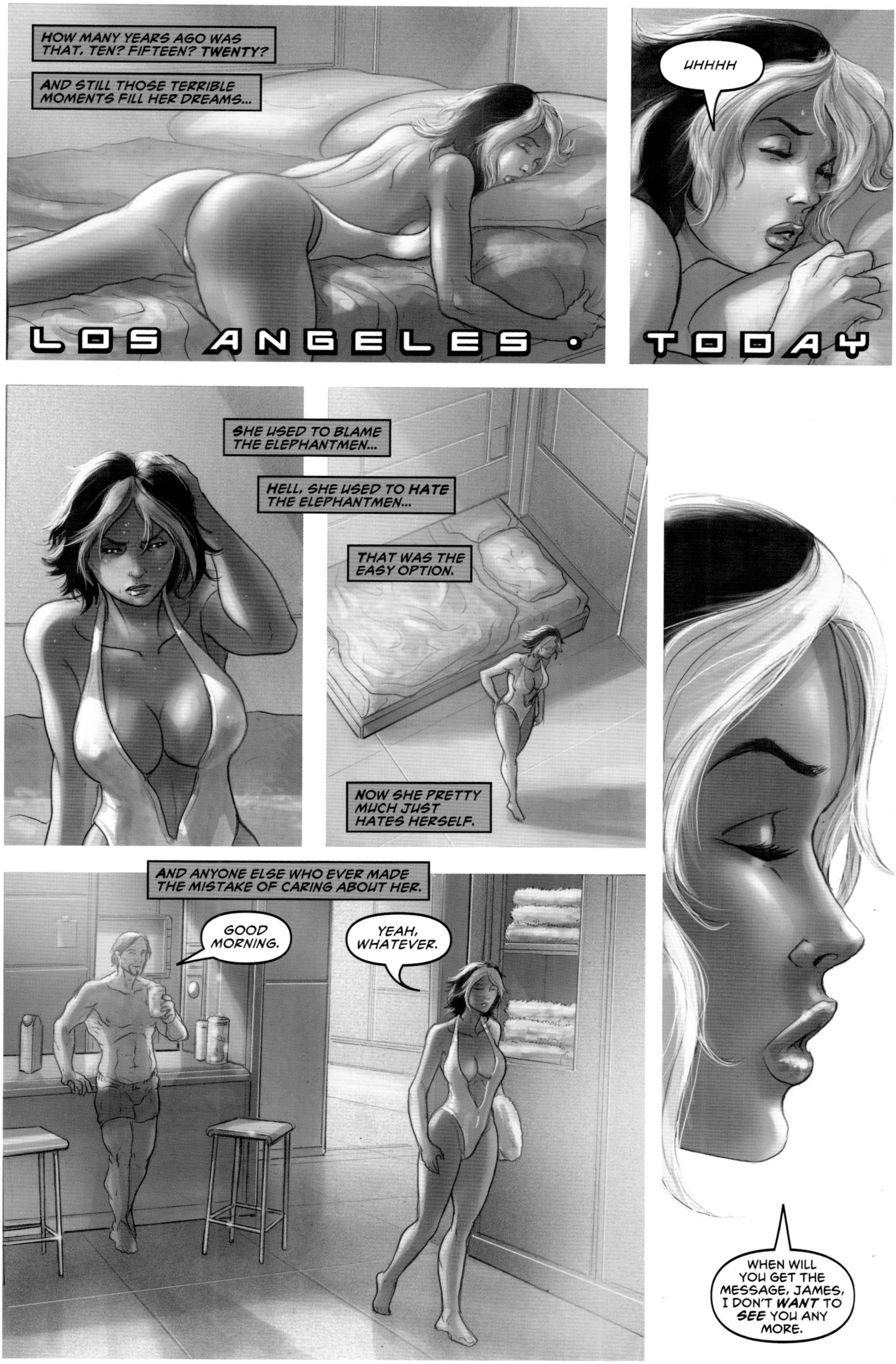
HOW MANY YEARS AGO WAS THAT, TEN? FIFTEEN? TWENTY?
AND STILL THOSE TERRIBLE MOMENTS FILL HER DREAMS...
LOS ANGELES · TODAY
UHHHH
SHE USED TO BLAME THE ELEPHANTMEN...
HELL, SHE USED TO HATE THE ELEPHANTMEN...
THAT WAS THE EASY OPTION.
NOW SHE PRETTY MUCH JUST HATES HERSELF.
AND ANYONE ELSE WHO EVER MADE THE MISTAKE OF CARING ABOUT HER.
GOOD MORNING.
YEAH, WHATEVER.
WHEN WILL YOU GET THE MESSAGE, JAMES, I DON'T WANT TO SEE YOU ANY MORE.

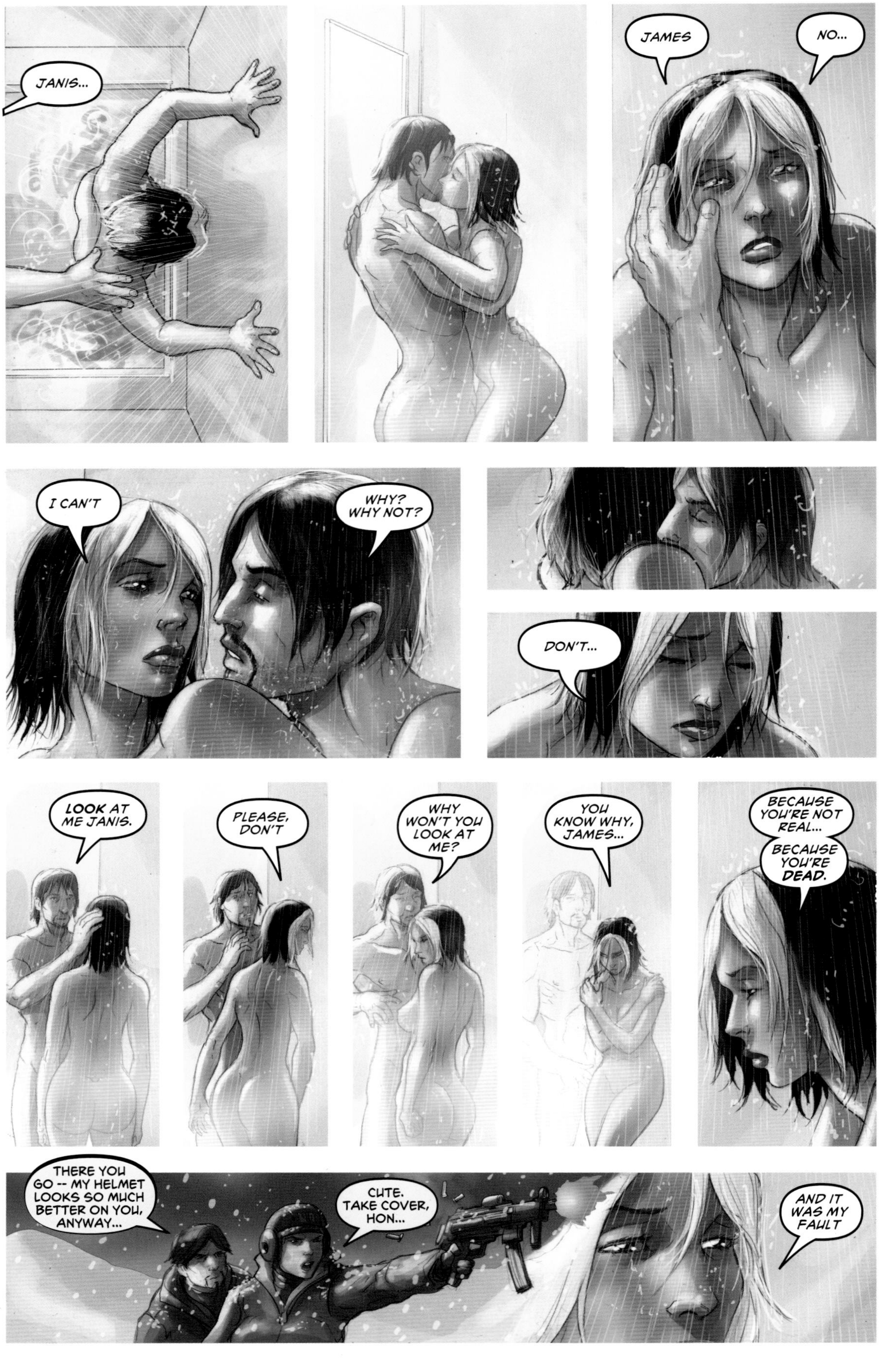
JANIS...
JAMES
NO...
I CAN'T
WHY? WHY NOT?
DON'T...
LOOK AT ME JANIS.
PLEASE, DON'T
WHY WON'T YOU LOOK AT ME?
YOU KNOW WHY, JAMES...
BECAUSE YOU'RE NOT REAL...
BECAUSE YOU'RE DEAD.
THERE YOU GO -- MY HELMET LOOKS SO MUCH BETTER ON YOU, ANYWAY...
CUTE. TAKE COVER, HON...
AND IT WAS MY FAULT

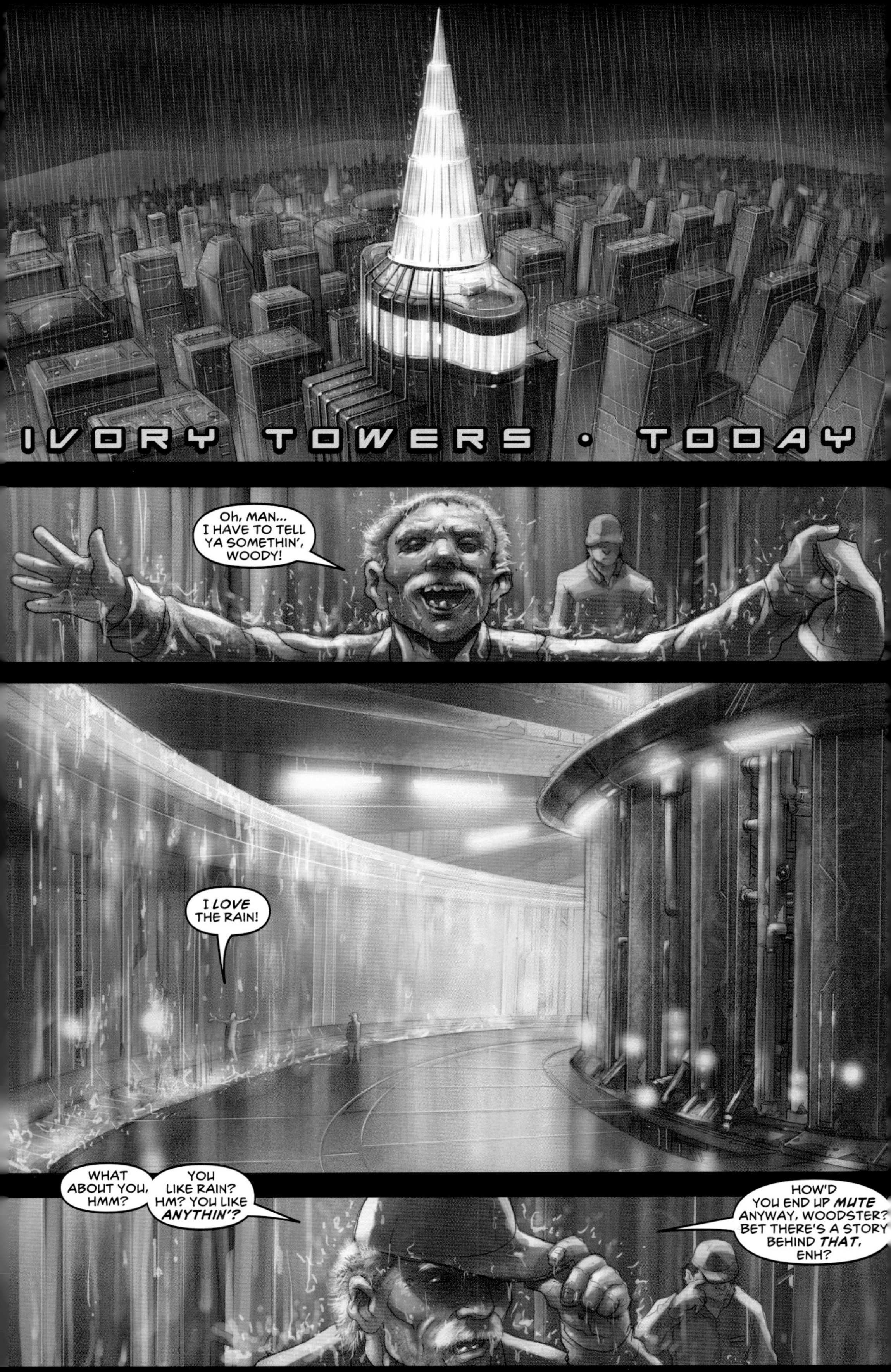
IVORY TOWERS • TODAY
Oh, MAN... I HAVE TO TELL YA SOMETHIN', WOODY!
I LOVE THE RAIN!
WHAT ABOUT YOU, HMM?
YOU LIKE RAIN? HM? YOU LIKE ANYTHIN'?
HOW'D YOU END UP MUTE ANYWAY, WOODSTER? BET THERE'S A STORY BEHIND THAT, ENH?

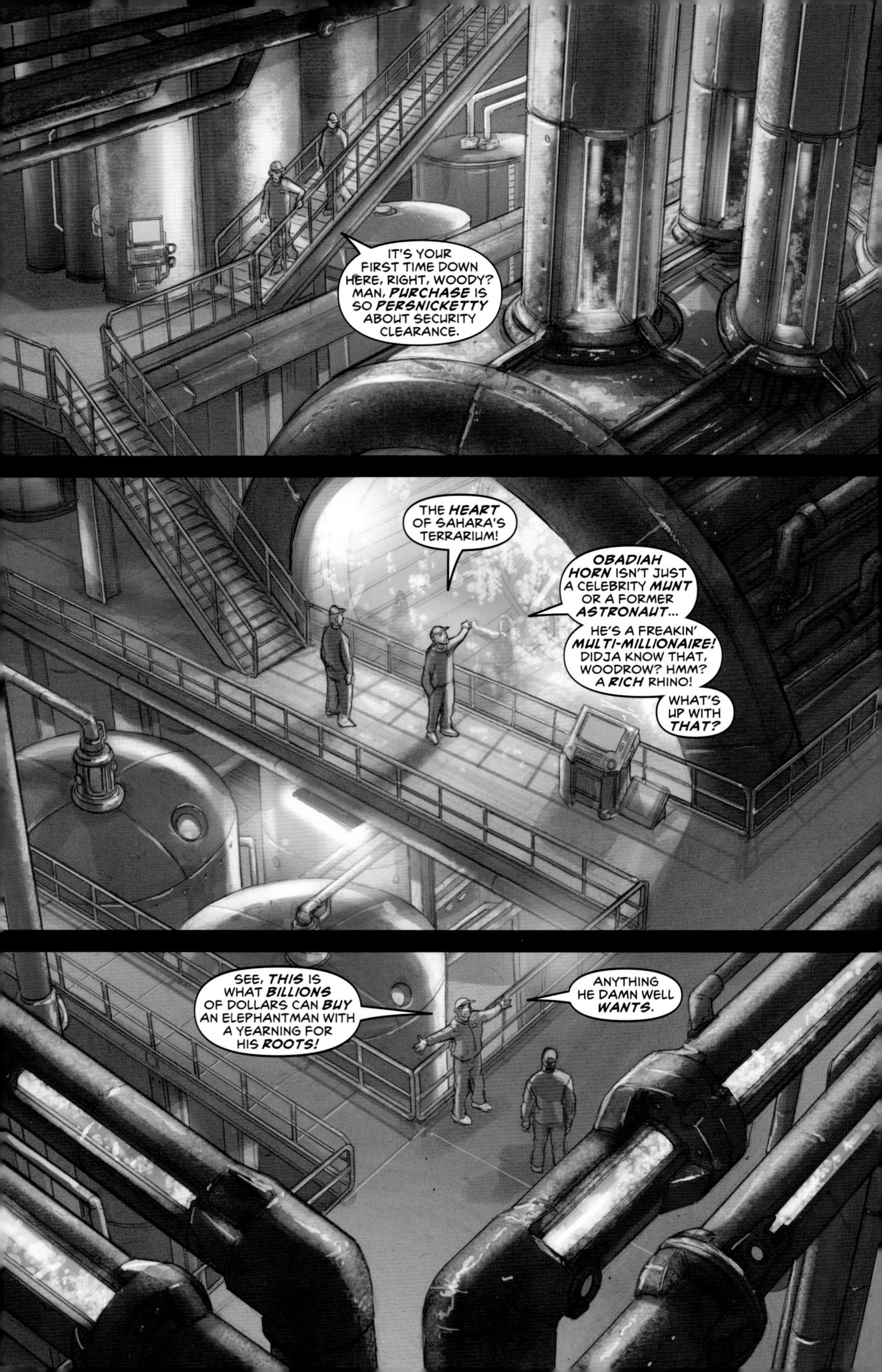
IT'S YOUR FIRST TIME DOWN HERE, RIGHT, WOODY? MAN, PURCHASE IS SO PERSNICKETTY ABOUT SECURITY CLEARANCE.
THE HEART OF SAHARA'S TERRARIUM!
OBADIAH HORN ISN'T JUST A CELEBRITY MUNT OR A FORMER ASTRONAUT...
HE'S A FREAKIN' MULTI-MILLIONAIRE! DIDJA KNOW THAT, WOODROW? HMM? A RICH RHINO!
WHAT'S UP WITH THAT?
SEE, THIS IS WHAT BILLIONS OF DOLLARS CAN BUY AN ELEPHANTMAN WITH A YEARNING FOR HIS ROOTS!
ANYTHING HE DAMN WELL WANTS.

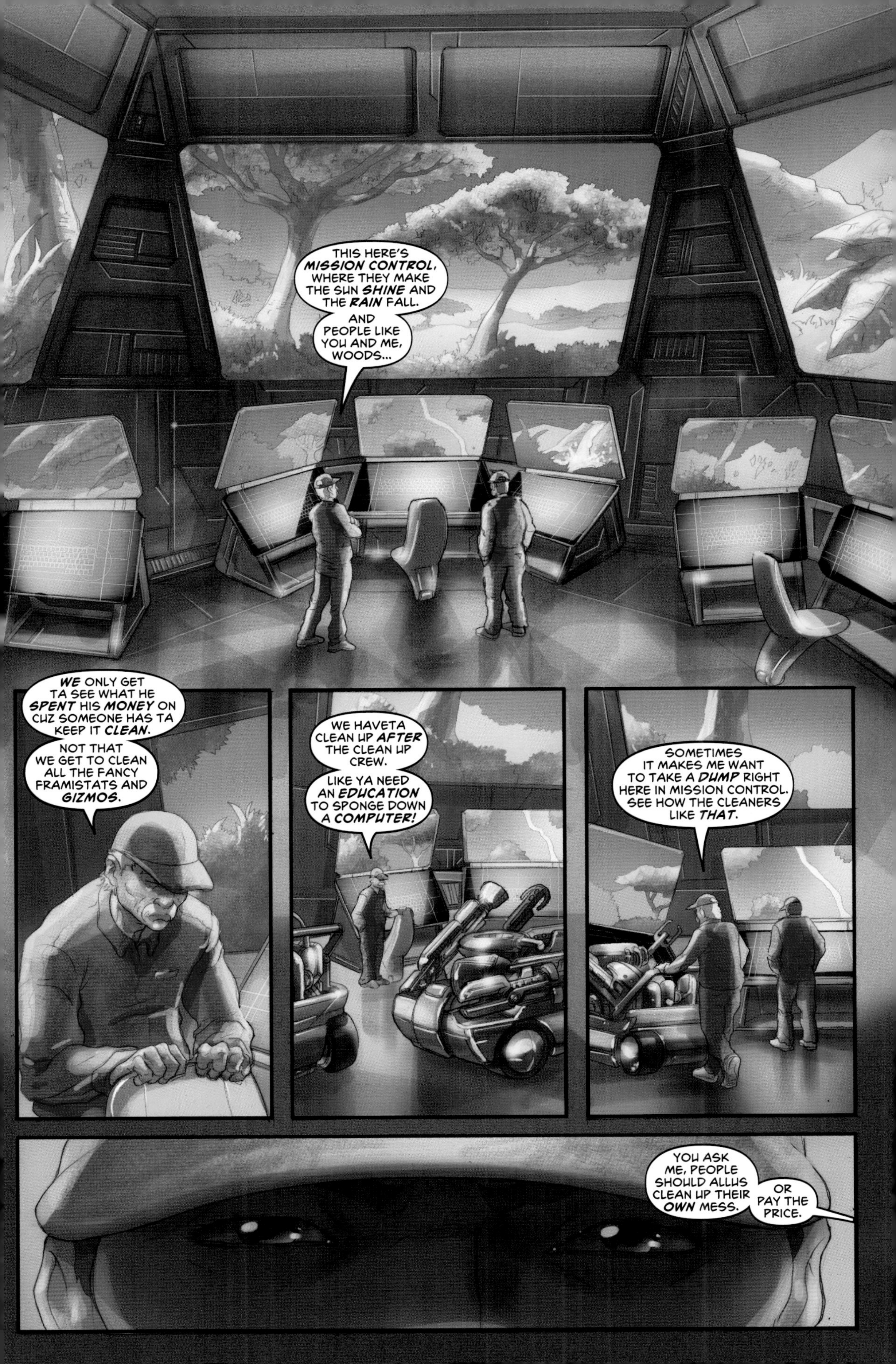
THIS HERE'S MISSION CONTROL, WHERE THEY MAKE THE SUN SHINE AND THE RAIN FALL.
AND PEOPLE LIKE YOU AND ME, WOODS...
WE ONLY GET TA SEE WHAT HE SPENT HIS MONEY ON CUZ SOMEONE HAS TA KEEP IT CLEAN.
NOT THAT WE GET TO CLEAN ALL THE FANCY FRAMISTATS AND GIZMOS.
WE HAVETA CLEAN UP AFTER THE CLEAN UP CREW.
LIKE YA NEED AN EDUCATION TO SPONGE DOWN A COMPUTER!
SOMETIMES IT MAKES ME WANT TO TAKE A DUMP RIGHT HERE IN MISSION CONTROL. SEE HOW THE CLEANERS LIKE THAT.
YOU ASK ME, PEOPLE SHOULD ALLUS CLEAN UP THEIR OWN MESS.
OR PAY THE PRICE.

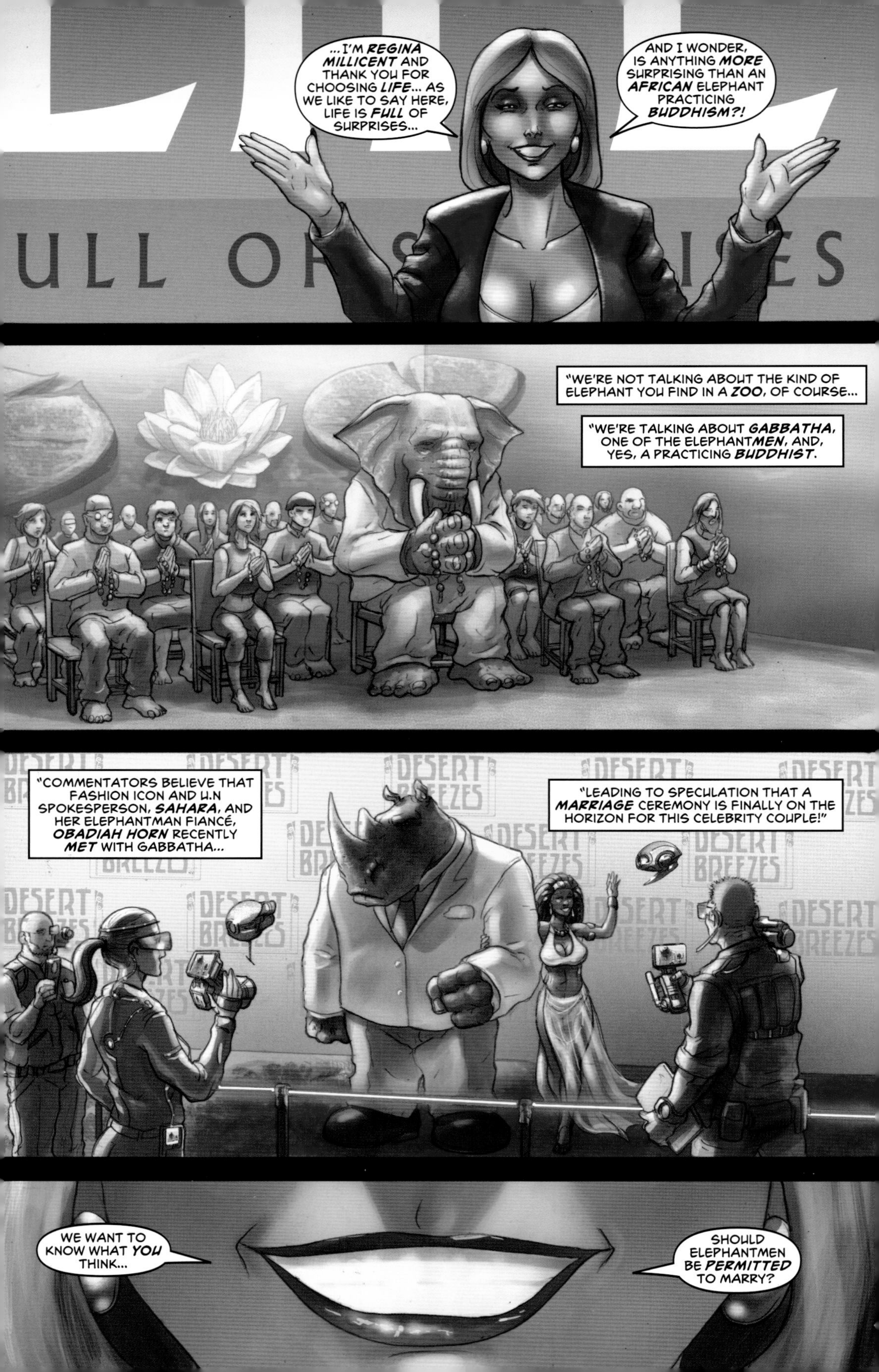
...I'M REGINA MILLICENT AND THANK YOU FOR CHOOSING LIFE... AS WE LIKE TO SAY HERE, LIFE IS FULL OF SURPRISES...
AND I WONDER, IS ANYTHING MORE SURPRISING THAN AN AFRICAN ELEPHANT PRACTICING BUDDHISM?!
"WE'RE NOT TALKING ABOUT THE KIND OF ELEPHANT YOU FIND IN A ZOO, OF COURSE...
"WE'RE TALKING ABOUT GABBATHA, ONE OF THE ELEPHANTMEN, AND, YES, A PRACTICING BUDDHIST.
"COMMENTATORS BELIEVE THAT FASHION ICON AND U.N SPOKESPERSON, SAHARA, AND HER ELEPHANTMAN FIANCÉ, OBADIAH HORN RECENTLY MET WITH GABBATHA...
"LEADING TO SPECULATION THAT A MARRIAGE CEREMONY IS FINALLY ON THE HORIZON FOR THIS CELEBRITY COUPLE!"
WE WANT TO KNOW WHAT YOU THINK...
SHOULD ELEPHANTMEN BE PERMITTED TO MARRY?

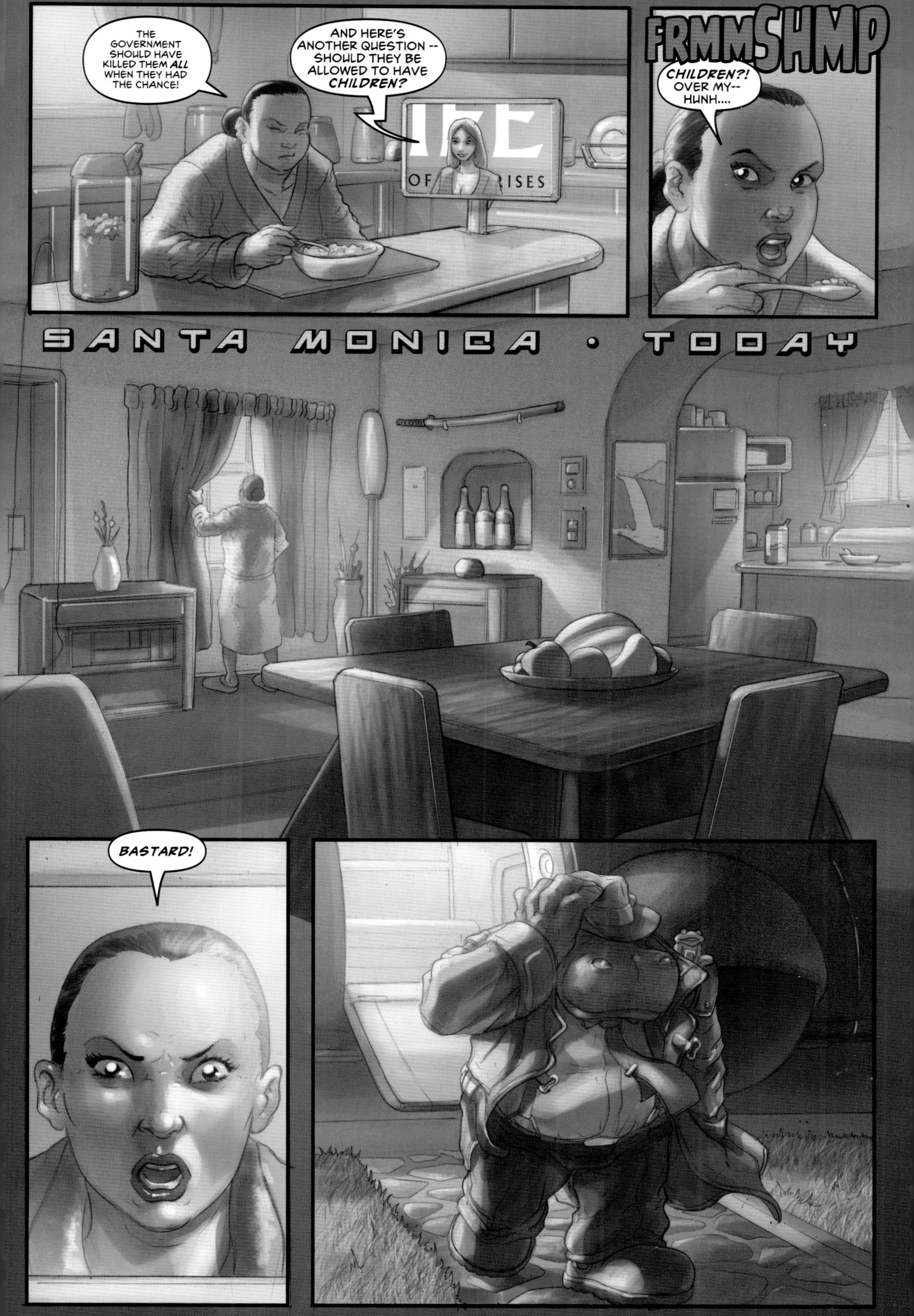
THE GOVERNMENT SHOULD HAVE KILLED THEM ALL WHEN THEY HAD THE CHANCE!
AND HERE'S ANOTHER QUESTION -- SHOULD THEY BE ALLOWED TO HAVE CHILDREN?
FRMMSHMP
CHILDREN?! OVER MY-- HUNH....
SANTA MONICA • TODAY
BASTARD!

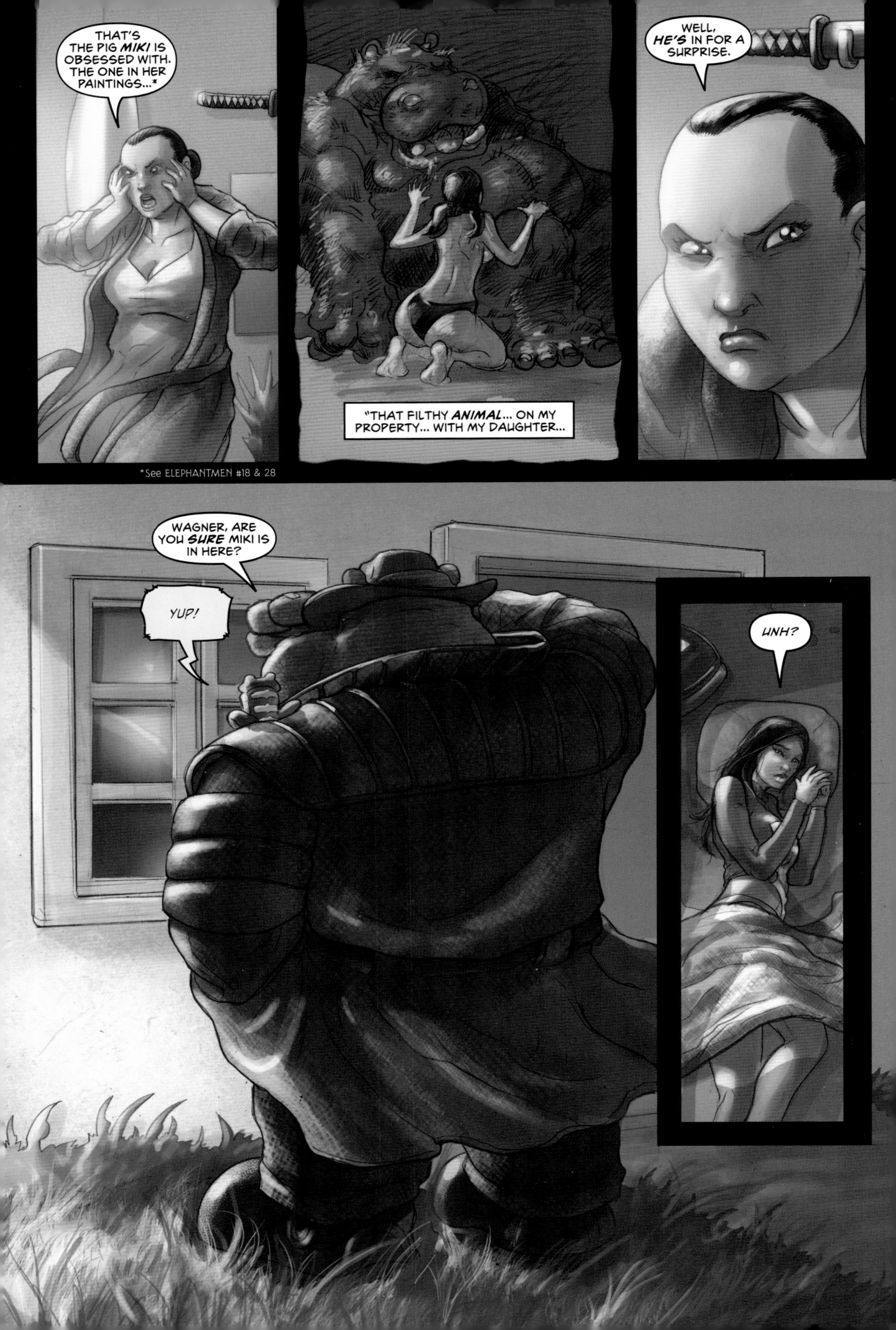
THAT'S THE PIG *MIKI* IS OBSESSED WITH. THE ONE IN HER PAINTINGS...*
"THAT FILTHY *ANIMAL*... ON MY PROPERTY... WITH MY DAUGHTER...
WELL, *HE'S* IN FOR A SURPRISE.
*See ELEPHANTMEN #18 & 28
WAGNER, ARE YOU *SURE* MIKI IS IN HERE?
YUP!
UNH?

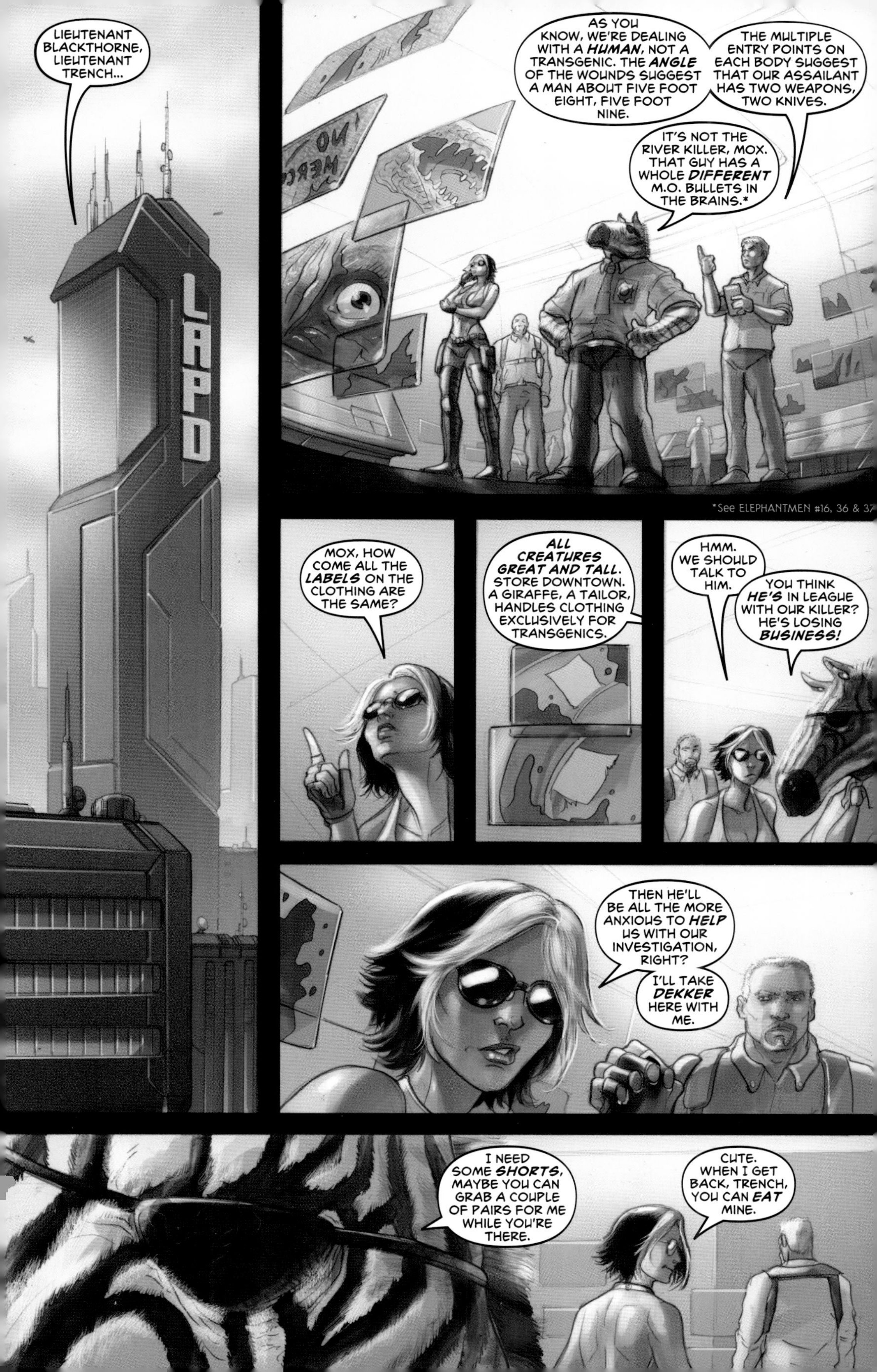
LIEUTENANT BLACKTHORNE, LIEUTENANT TRENCH...
LAPD
AS YOU KNOW, WE'RE DEALING WITH A HUMAN, NOT A TRANSGENIC. THE ANGLE OF THE WOUNDS SUGGEST A MAN ABOUT FIVE FOOT EIGHT, FIVE FOOT NINE.
THE MULTIPLE ENTRY POINTS ON EACH BODY SUGGEST THAT OUR ASSAILANT HAS TWO WEAPONS, TWO KNIVES.
IT'S NOT THE RIVER KILLER, MOX. THAT GUY HAS A WHOLE DIFFERENT M.O. BULLETS IN THE BRAINS.*
*See ELEPHANTMEN #16, 36 & 37
MOX, HOW COME ALL THE LABELS ON THE CLOTHING ARE THE SAME?
ALL CREATURES GREAT AND TALL. STORE DOWNTOWN. A GIRAFFE, A TAILOR, HANDLES CLOTHING EXCLUSIVELY FOR TRANSGENICS.
HMM. WE SHOULD TALK TO HIM.
YOU THINK HE'S IN LEAGUE WITH OUR KILLER? HE'S LOSING BUSINESS!
THEN HE'LL BE ALL THE MORE ANXIOUS TO HELP US WITH OUR INVESTIGATION, RIGHT?
I'LL TAKE DEKKER HERE WITH ME.
I NEED SOME SHORTS, MAYBE YOU CAN GRAB A COUPLE OF PAIRS FOR ME WHILE YOU'RE THERE.
CUTE. WHEN I GET BACK, TRENCH, YOU CAN EAT MINE.

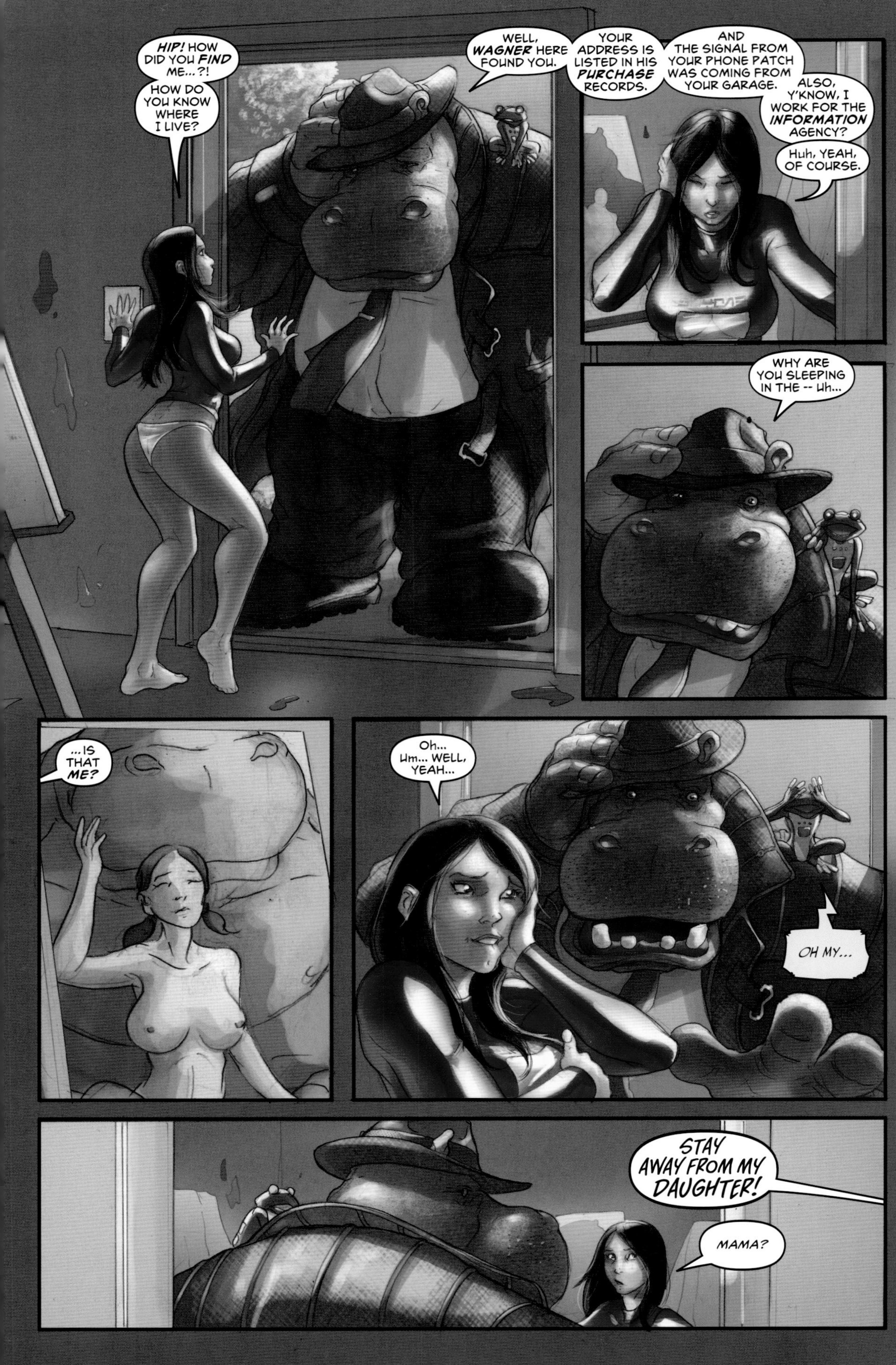
HIP! HOW DID YOU FIND ME...?!
HOW DO YOU KNOW WHERE I LIVE?
WELL, WAGNER HERE FOUND YOU.
YOUR ADDRESS IS LISTED IN HIS PURCHASE RECORDS.
AND THE SIGNAL FROM YOUR PHONE PATCH WAS COMING FROM YOUR GARAGE.
ALSO, Y'KNOW, I WORK FOR THE INFORMATION AGENCY?
Huh, YEAH, OF COURSE.
WHY ARE YOU SLEEPING IN THE -- Uh...
...IS THAT ME?
Oh... Um... WELL, YEAH...
OH MY...
STAY AWAY FROM MY DAUGHTER!
MAMA?

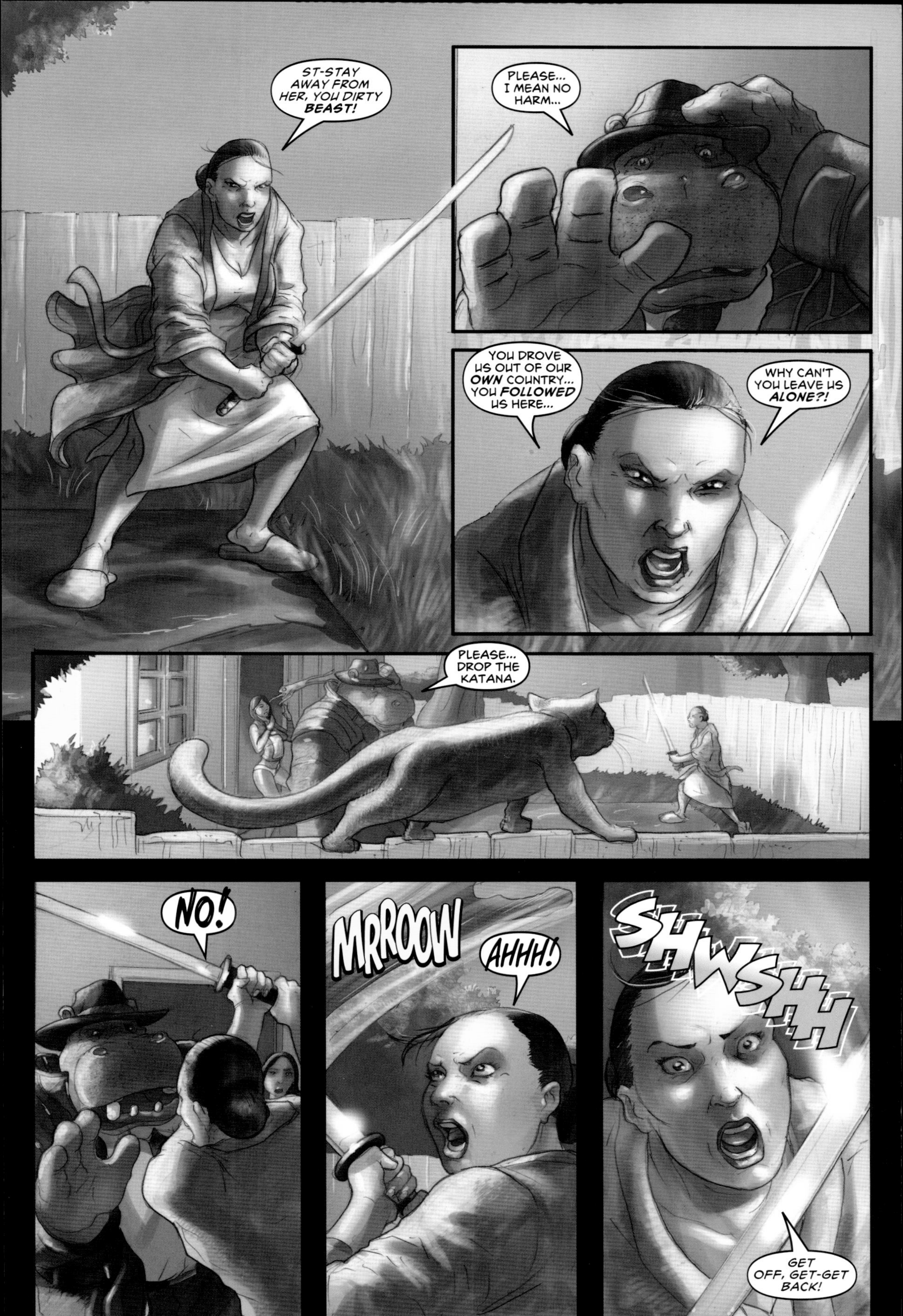
ST-STAY AWAY FROM HER, YOU DIRTY BEAST!
PLEASE... I MEAN NO HARM...
YOU DROVE US OUT OF OUR OWN COUNTRY... YOU FOLLOWED US HERE...
WHY CAN'T YOU LEAVE US ALONE?!
PLEASE... DROP THE KATANA.
NO!
MRROOW
AHHH!
SHWSHH
GET OFF, GET-GET BACK!

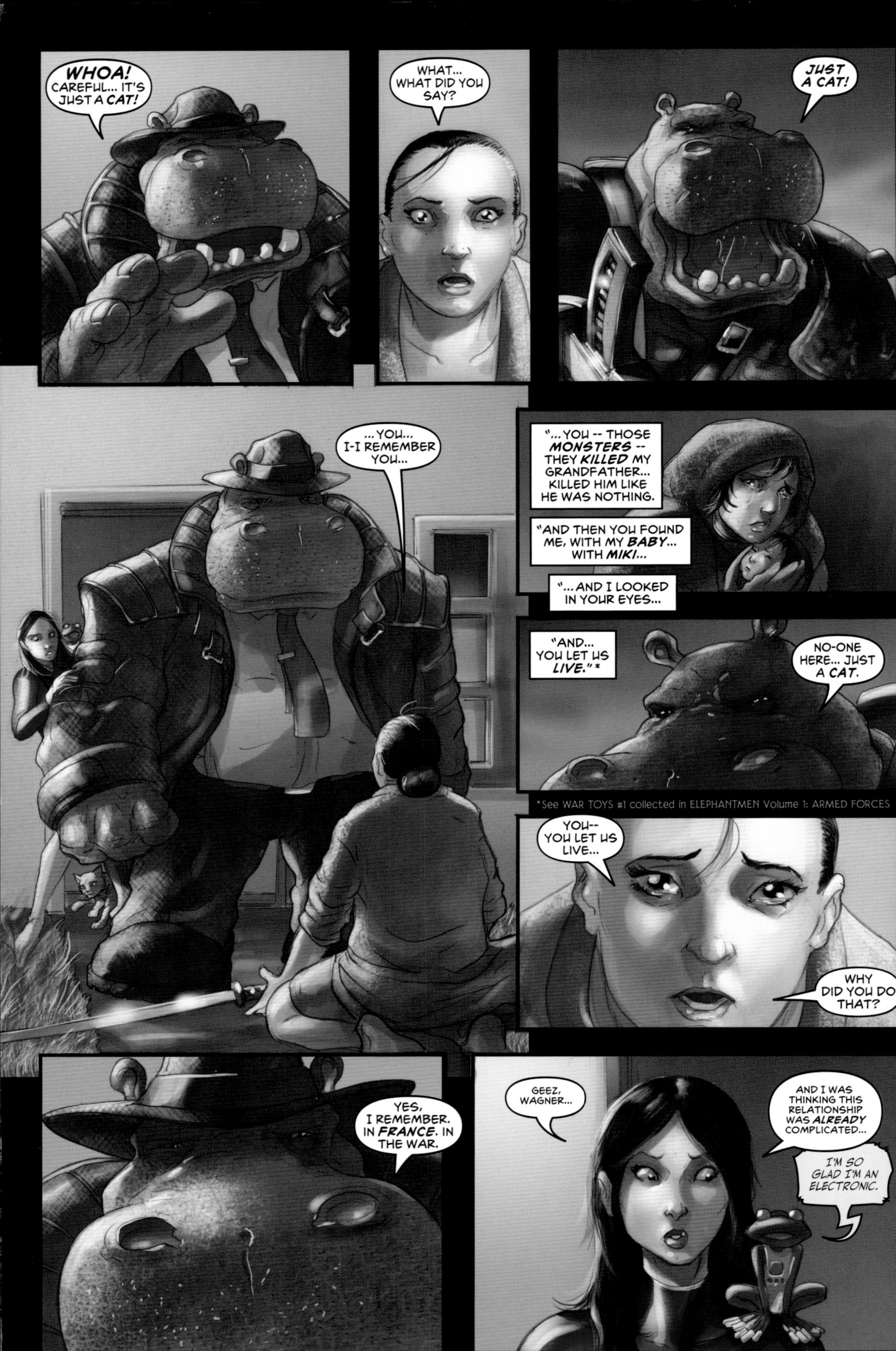
WHOA! CAREFUL... IT'S JUST A CAT!
WHAT... WHAT DID YOU SAY?
JUST A CAT!
...YOU... I-I REMEMBER YOU...
"...YOU -- THOSE MONSTERS -- THEY KILLED MY GRANDFATHER... KILLED HIM LIKE HE WAS NOTHING.
"AND THEN YOU FOUND ME, WITH MY BABY... WITH MIKI...
"...AND I LOOKED IN YOUR EYES...
"AND... YOU LET US LIVE."*
NO-ONE HERE... JUST A CAT.
*See WAR TOYS #1 collected in ELEPHANTMEN Volume 1: ARMED FORCES
YOU-- YOU LET US LIVE...
WHY DID YOU DO THAT?
YES, I REMEMBER. IN FRANCE. IN THE WAR.
GEEZ, WAGNER...
AND I WAS THINKING THIS RELATIONSHIP WAS ALREADY COMPLICATED...
I'M SO GLAD I'M AN ELECTRONIC.

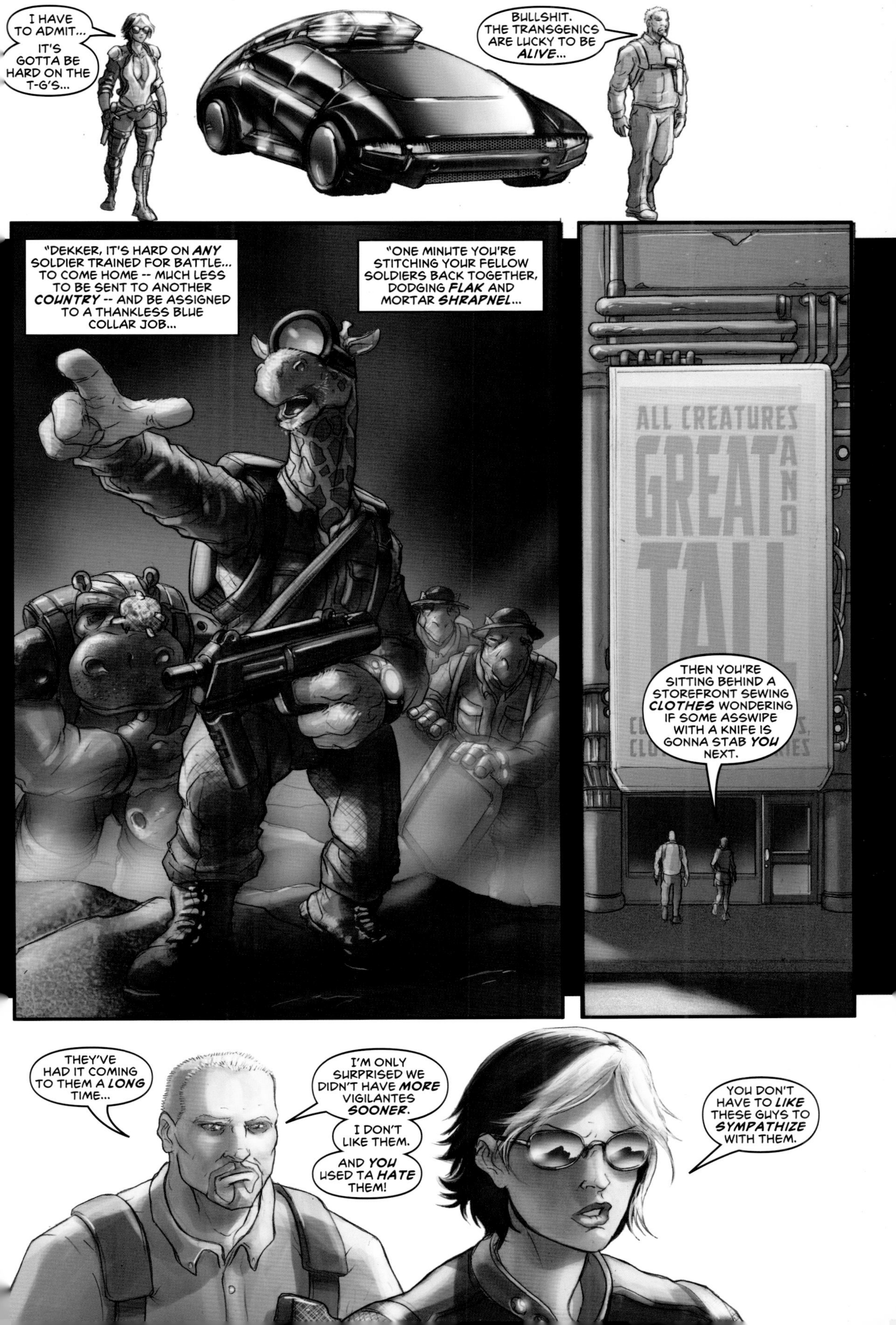
I HAVE TO ADMIT... IT'S GOTTA BE HARD ON THE T-G'S...
BULLSHIT. THE TRANSGENICS ARE LUCKY TO BE ALIVE...
"DEKKER, IT'S HARD ON ANY SOLDIER TRAINED FOR BATTLE... TO COME HOME -- MUCH LESS TO BE SENT TO ANOTHER COUNTRY -- AND BE ASSIGNED TO A THANKLESS BLUE COLLAR JOB...
"ONE MINUTE YOU'RE STITCHING YOUR FELLOW SOLDIERS BACK TOGETHER, DODGING FLAK AND MORTAR SHRAPNEL...
ALL CREATURES GREAT AND TALL
THEN YOU'RE SITTING BEHIND A STOREFRONT SEWING CLOTHES WONDERING IF SOME ASSWIPE WITH A KNIFE IS GONNA STAB YOU NEXT.
THEY'VE HAD IT COMING TO THEM A LONG TIME...
I'M ONLY SURPRISED WE DIDN'T HAVE MORE VIGILANTES SOONER.
I DON'T LIKE THEM.
AND YOU USED TA HATE THEM!
YOU DON'T HAVE TO LIKE THESE GUYS TO SYMPATHIZE WITH THEM.

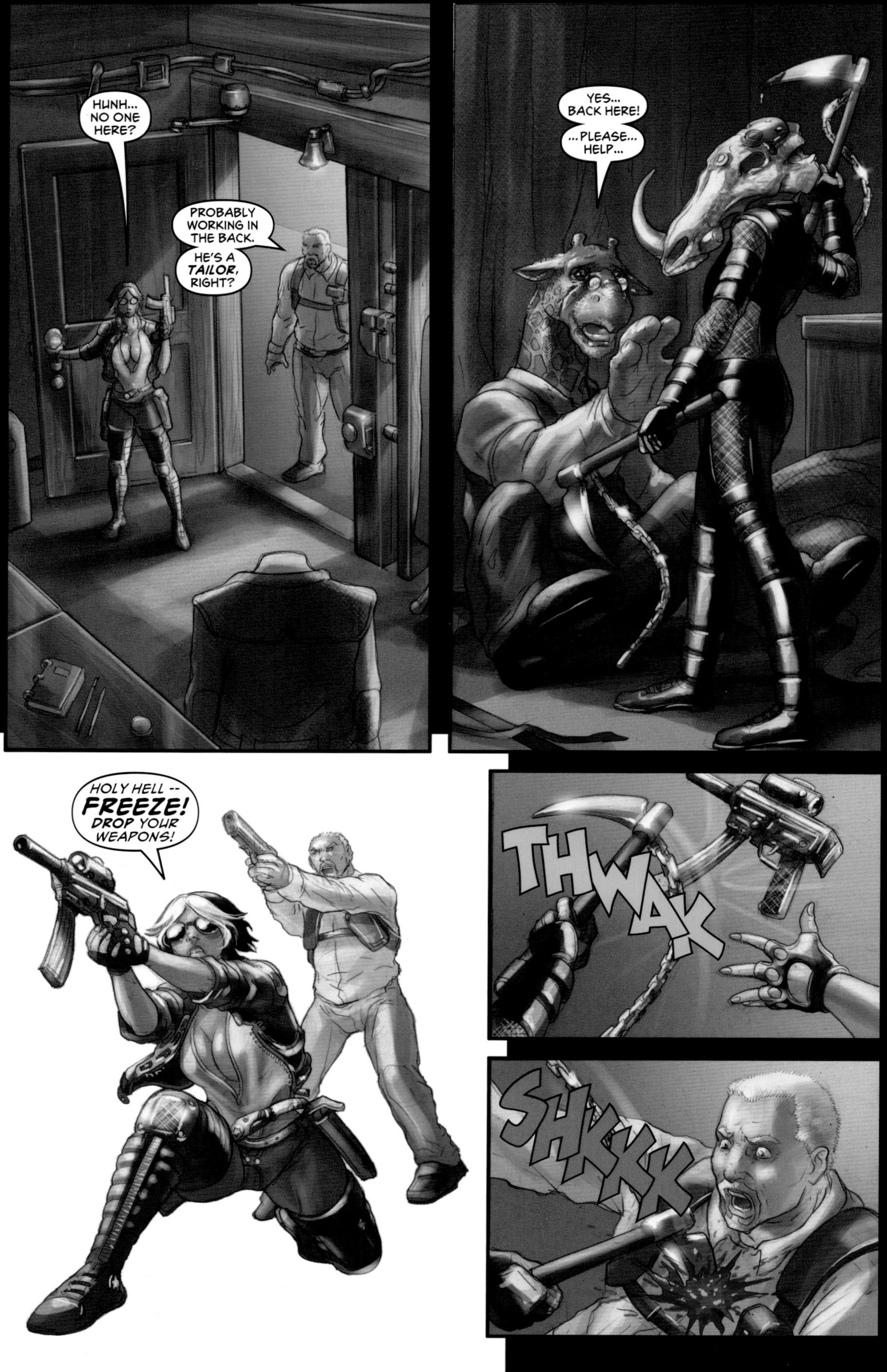
HUNH... NO ONE HERE?
PROBABLY WORKING IN THE BACK.
HE'S A *TAILOR*, RIGHT?
YES... BACK HERE!
...PLEASE... HELP...
HOLY HELL -- **FREEZE!** ***DROP*** YOUR WEAPONS!
THWAK
SHKKK

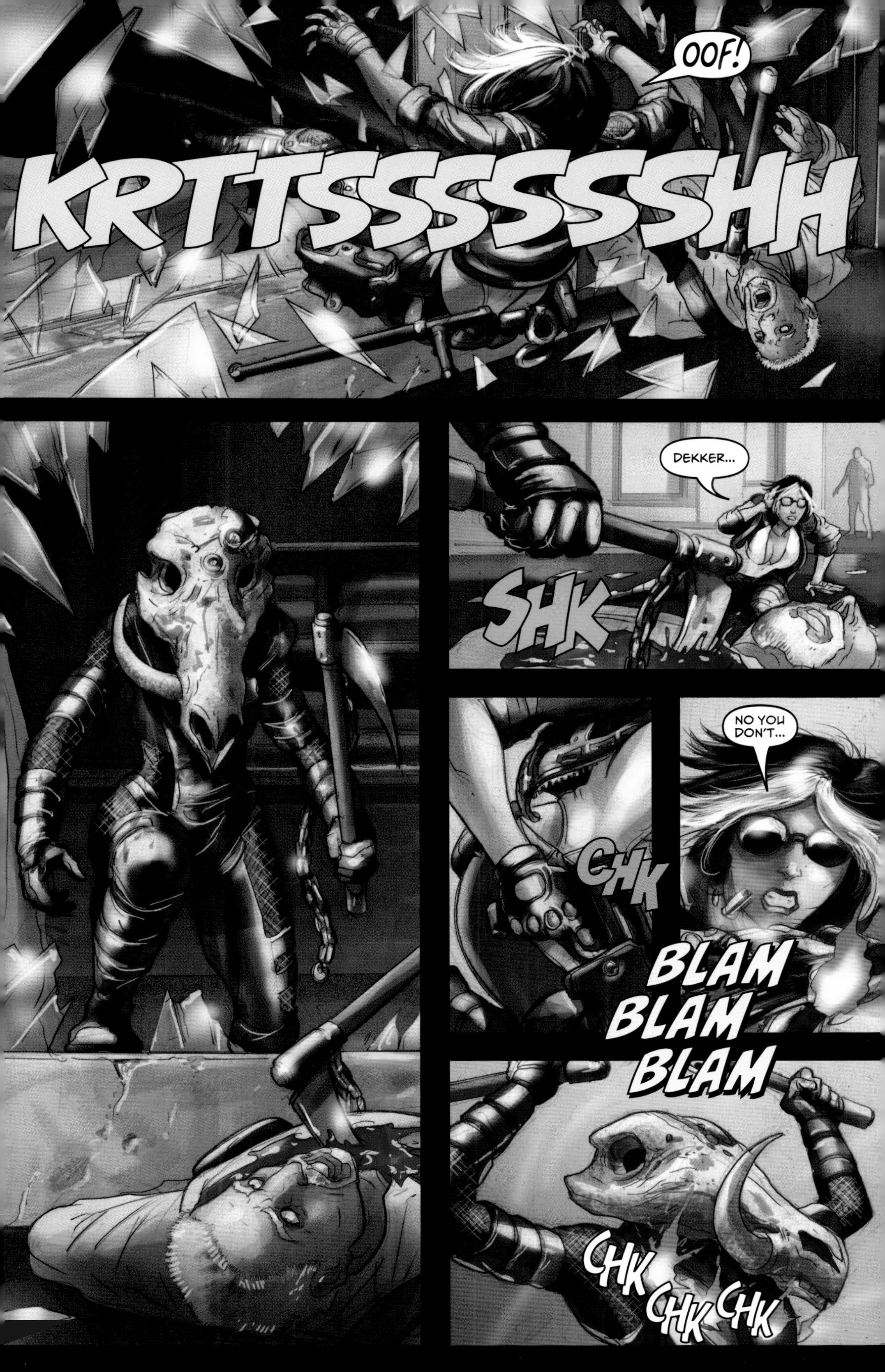
OOF!
KRTTSSSSSSHH
DEKKER...
SHK
NO YOU DON'T...
CHK
BLAM
BLAM
BLAM
CHK
CHK
CHK

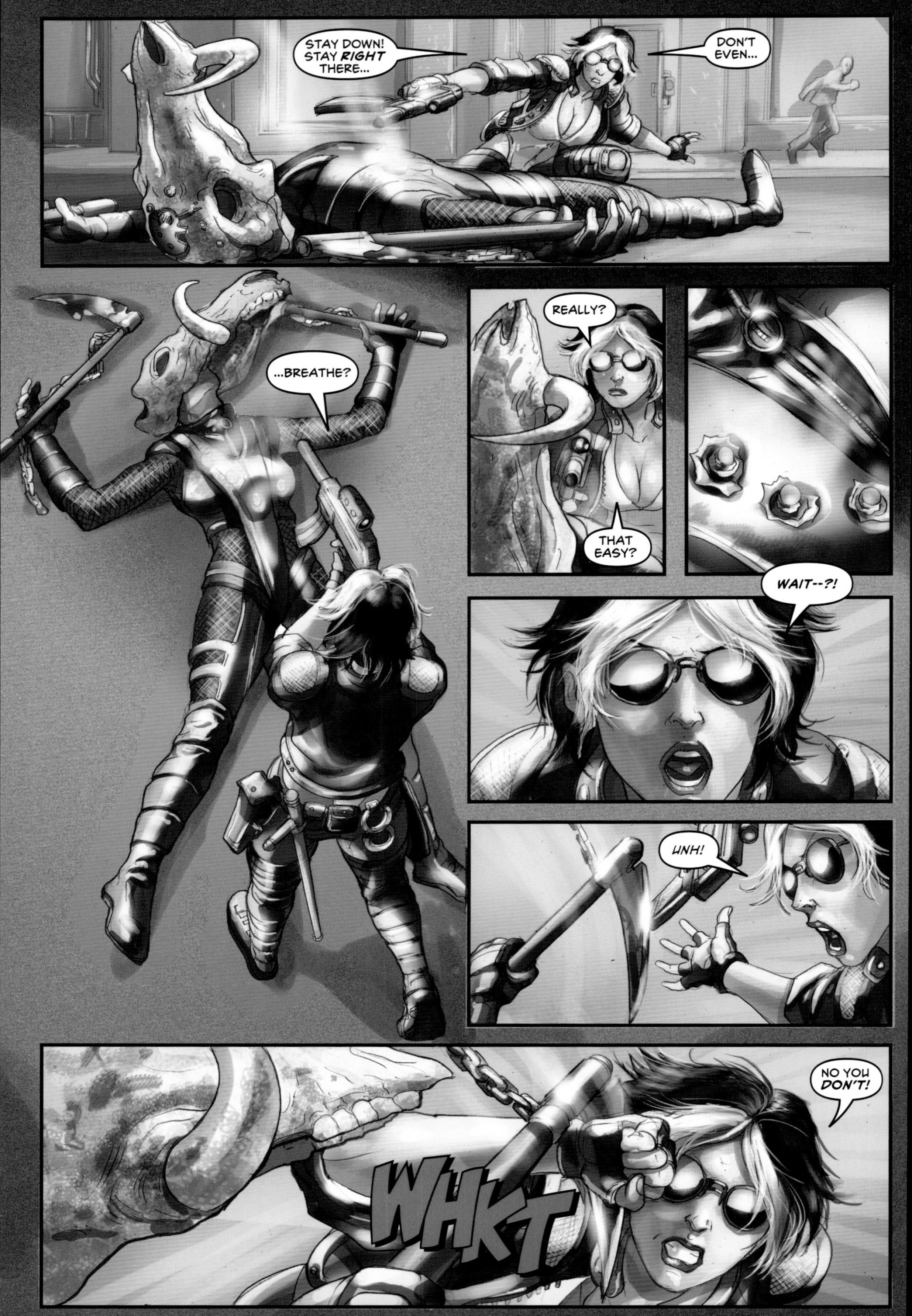
STAY DOWN! STAY RIGHT THERE...
DON'T EVEN...
...BREATHE?
REALLY?
THAT EASY?
WAIT--?!
UNH!
NO YOU DON'T!
WHKT

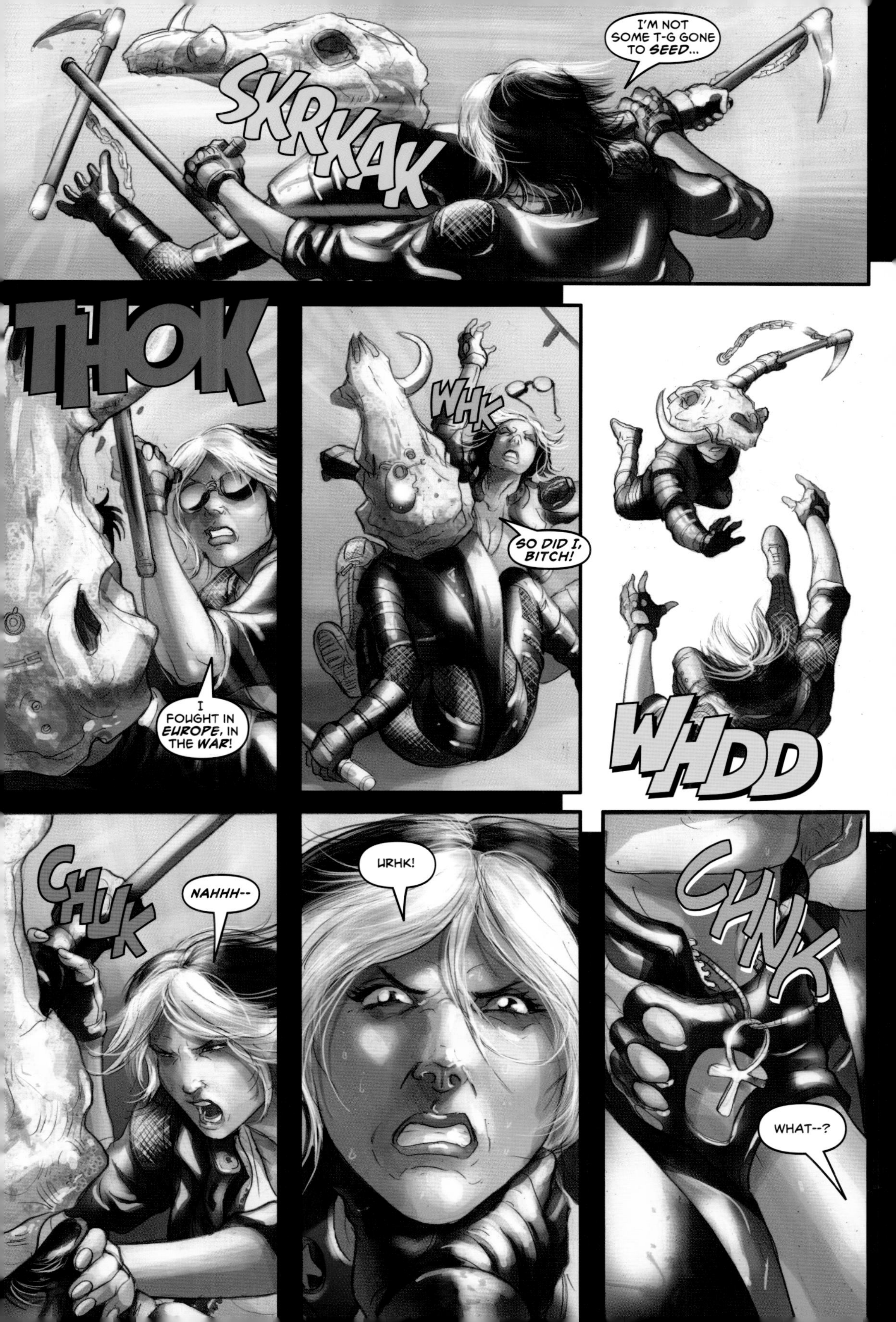
SKRKAK
I'M NOT SOME T-G GONE TO SEED...
THOK
I FOUGHT IN EUROPE, IN THE WAR!
WHK
SO DID I, BITCH!
WHDD
CHUK
NAHHH--
URHK!
CHNK
WHAT--?

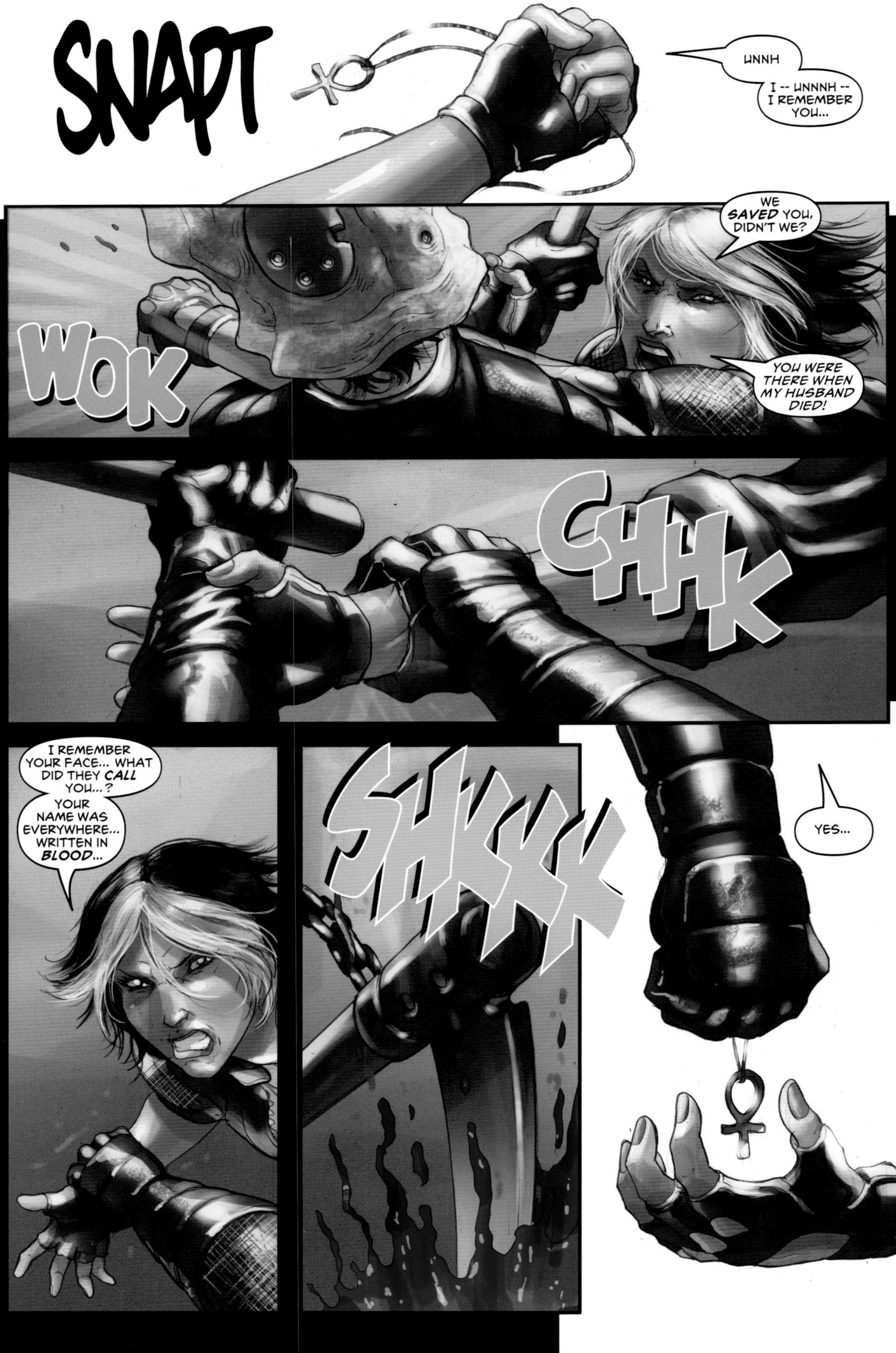
SNAPT
UNNH
I -- UNNNH -- I REMEMBER YOU...
WE SAVED YOU, DIDN'T WE?
WOK
YOU WERE THERE WHEN MY HUSBAND DIED!
CHHK
I REMEMBER YOUR FACE... WHAT DID THEY CALL YOU...?
YOUR NAME WAS EVERYWHERE... WRITTEN IN BLOOD...
SHKKK
YES...

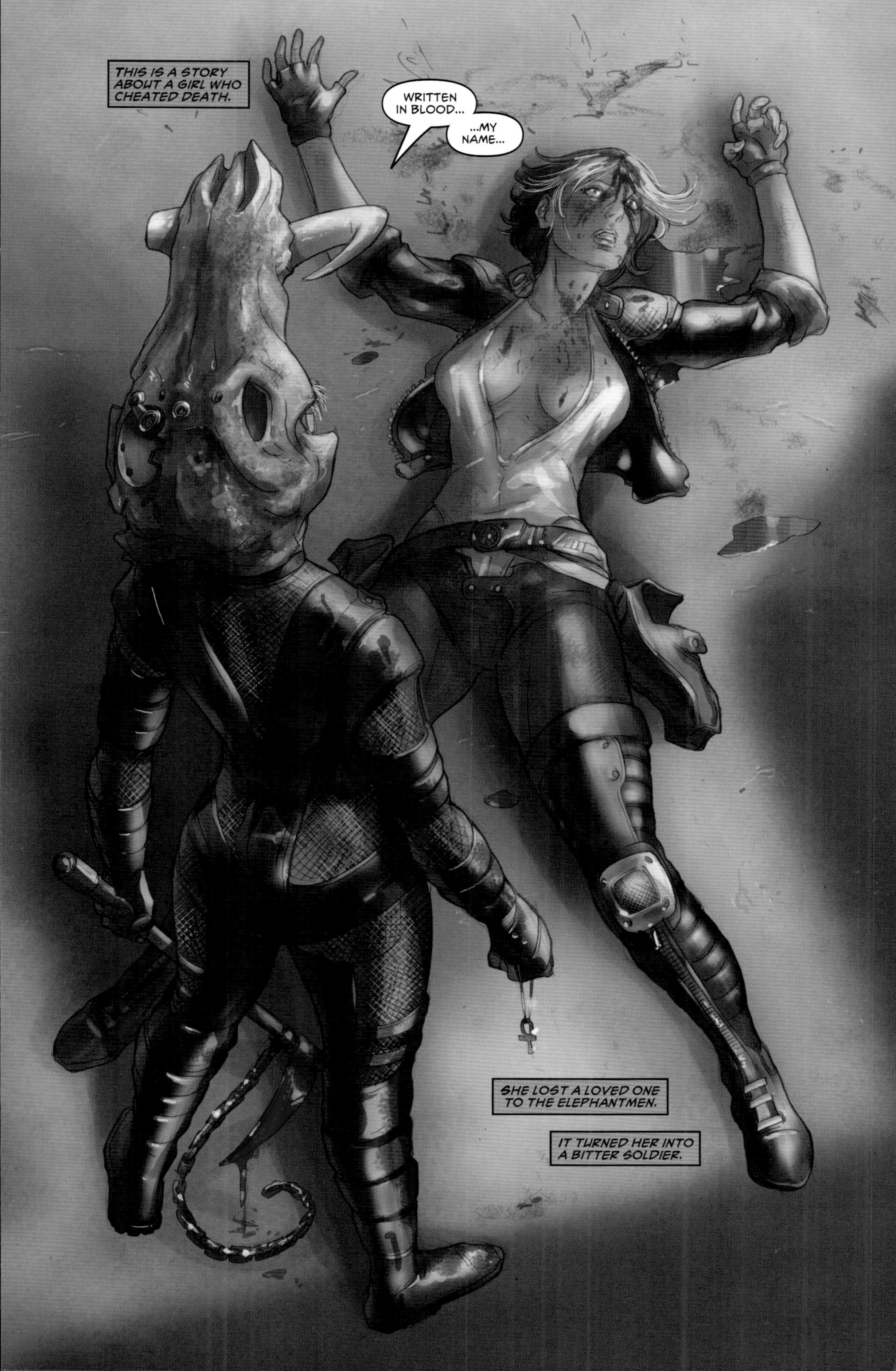

THIS IS A STORY ABOUT A GIRL WHO CHEATED DEATH.
WRITTEN IN BLOOD...
...MY NAME...
SHE LOST A LOVED ONE TO THE ELEPHANTMEN.
IT TURNED HER INTO A BITTER SOLDIER.

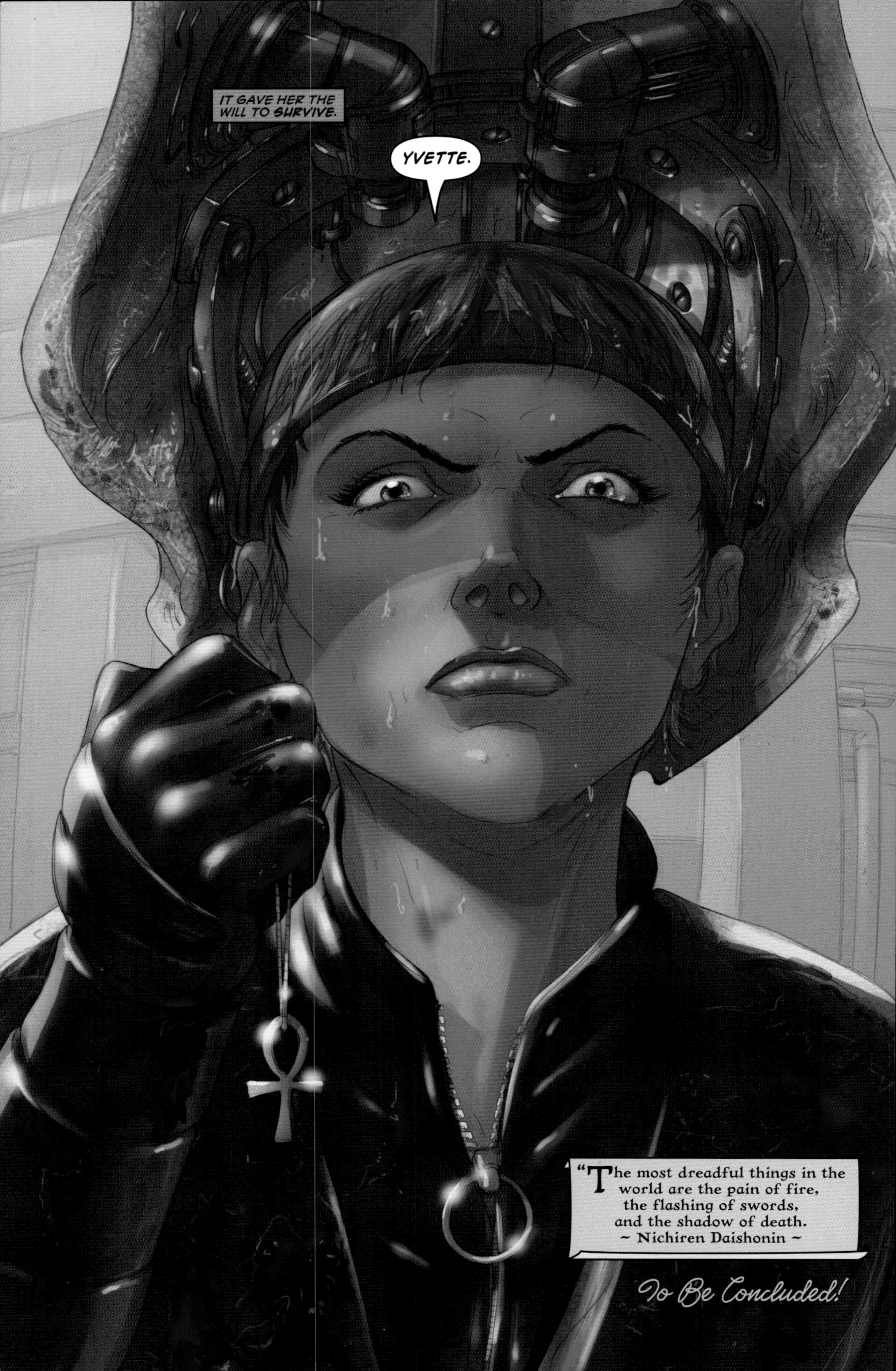
IT GAVE HER THE WILL TO SURVIVE.
YVETTE.
"The most dreadful things in the world are the pain of fire, the flashing of swords, and the shadow of death.
~ Nichiren Daishonin ~
To Be Concluded!

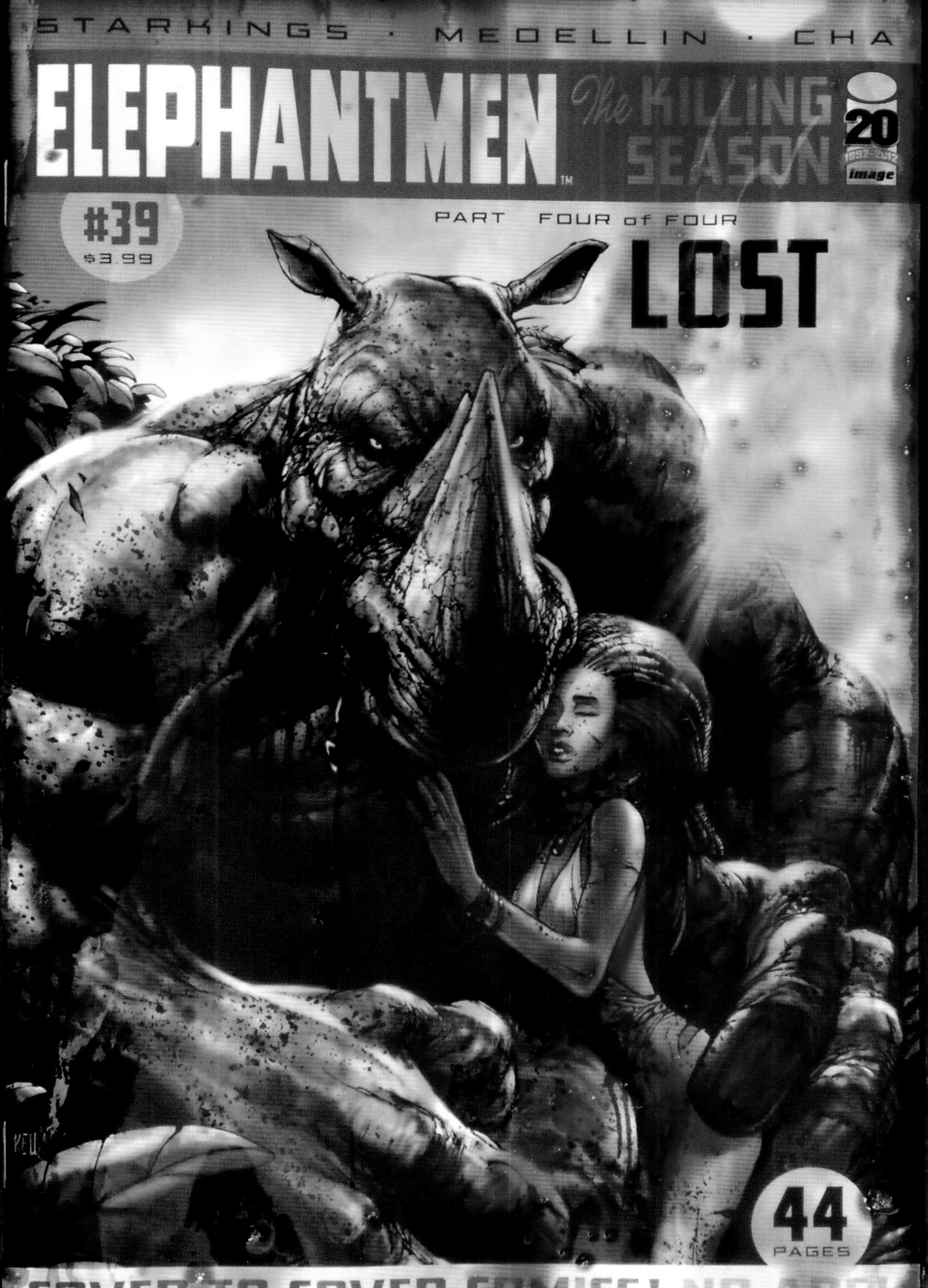
STARKINGS · MEDELLIN · CHA
ELEPHANTMEN™
The KILLING SEASON
20
1992-2012
image
#39
$3.99
PART FOUR of FOUR
LOST
44
PAGES
COVER-TO-COVER COMICS! NO ADS!

"WHEN A MAN WANTS TO MURDER
A TIGER HE CALLS IT SPORT; WHEN
A TIGER WANTS TO MURDER HIM
HE CALLS IT FEROCITY."

GEORGE BERNARD SHAW
MAN AND SUPERMAN

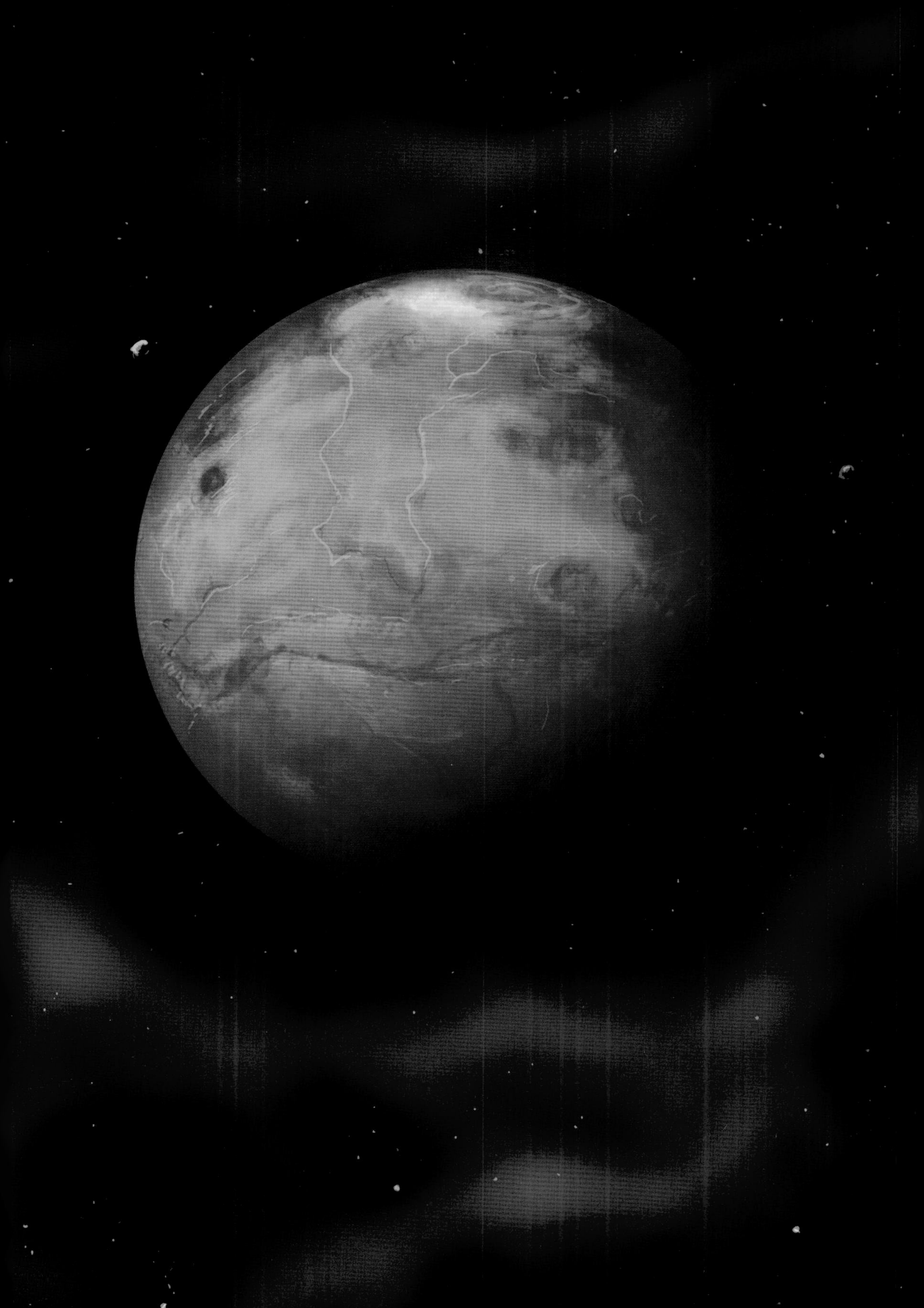

MARS · 2249

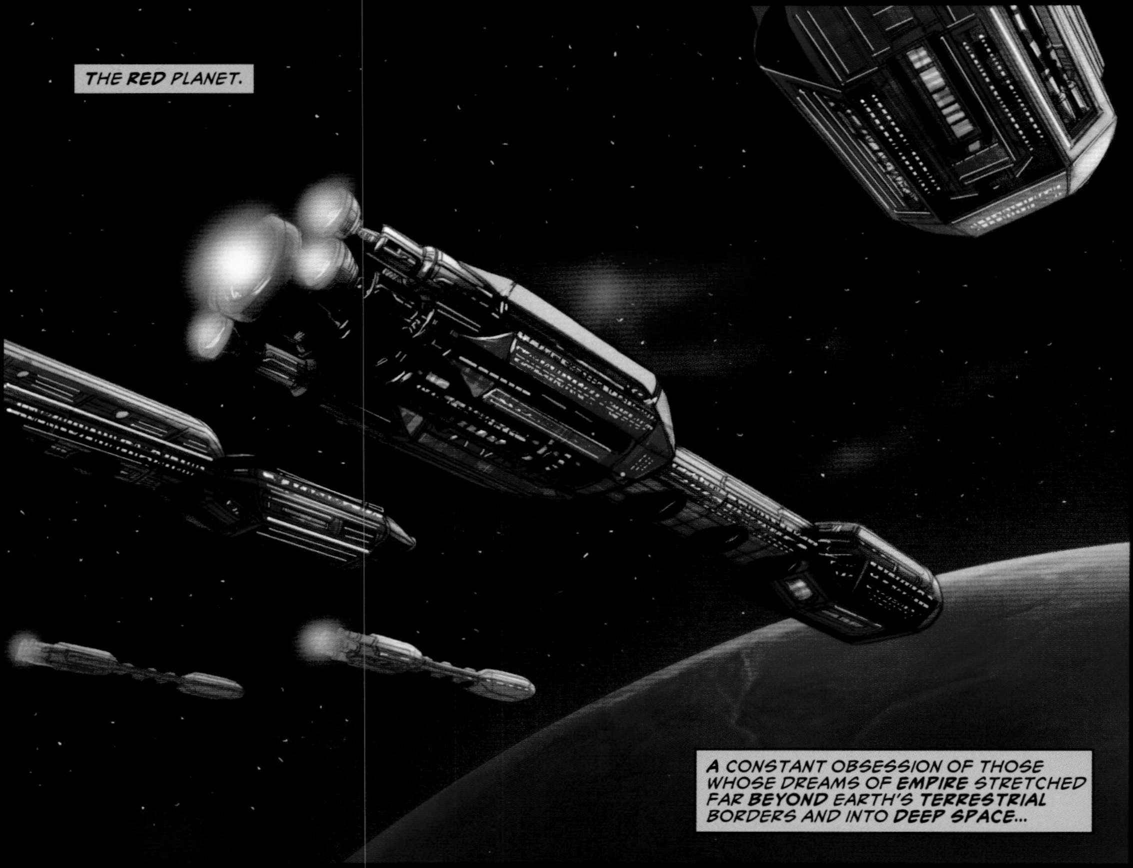
THE RED PLANET.
A CONSTANT OBSESSION OF THOSE WHOSE DREAMS OF EMPIRE STRETCHED FAR BEYOND EARTH'S TERRESTRIAL BORDERS AND INTO DEEP SPACE...

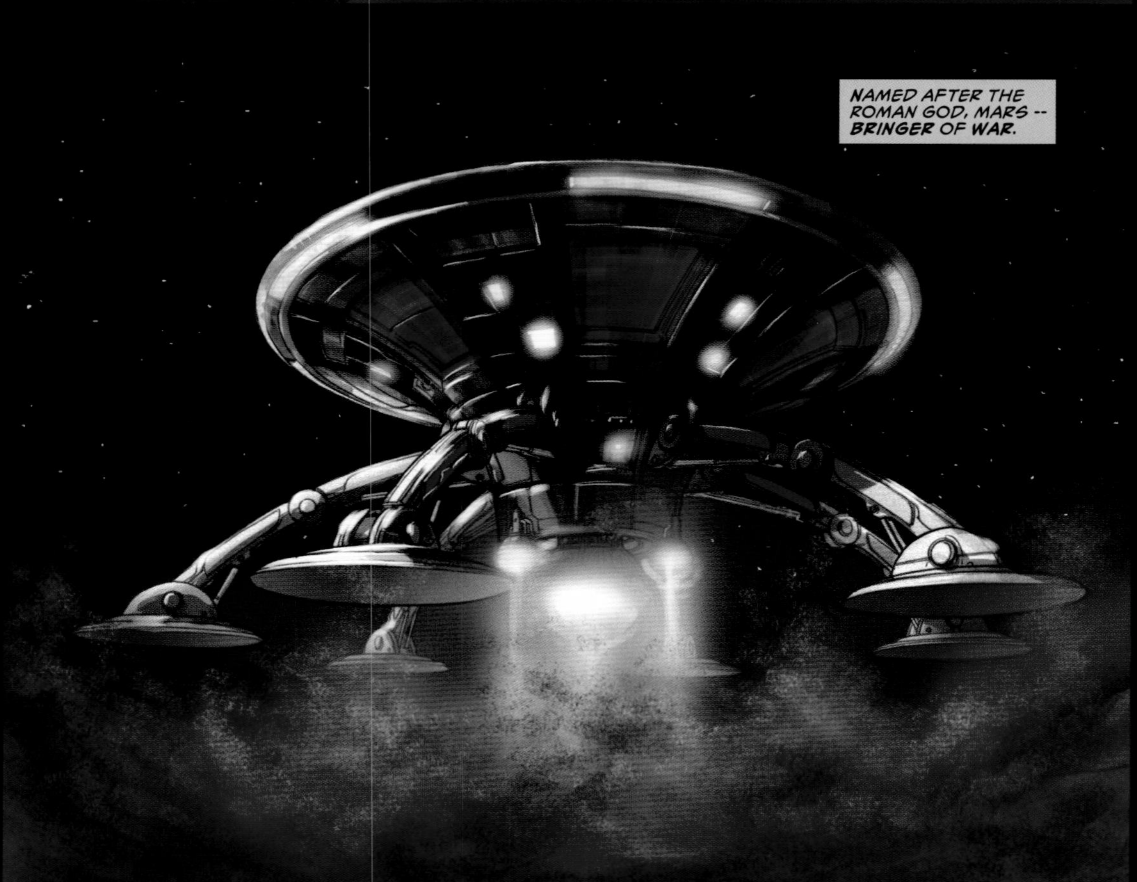
NAMED AFTER THE ROMAN GOD, MARS -- BRINGER OF WAR.

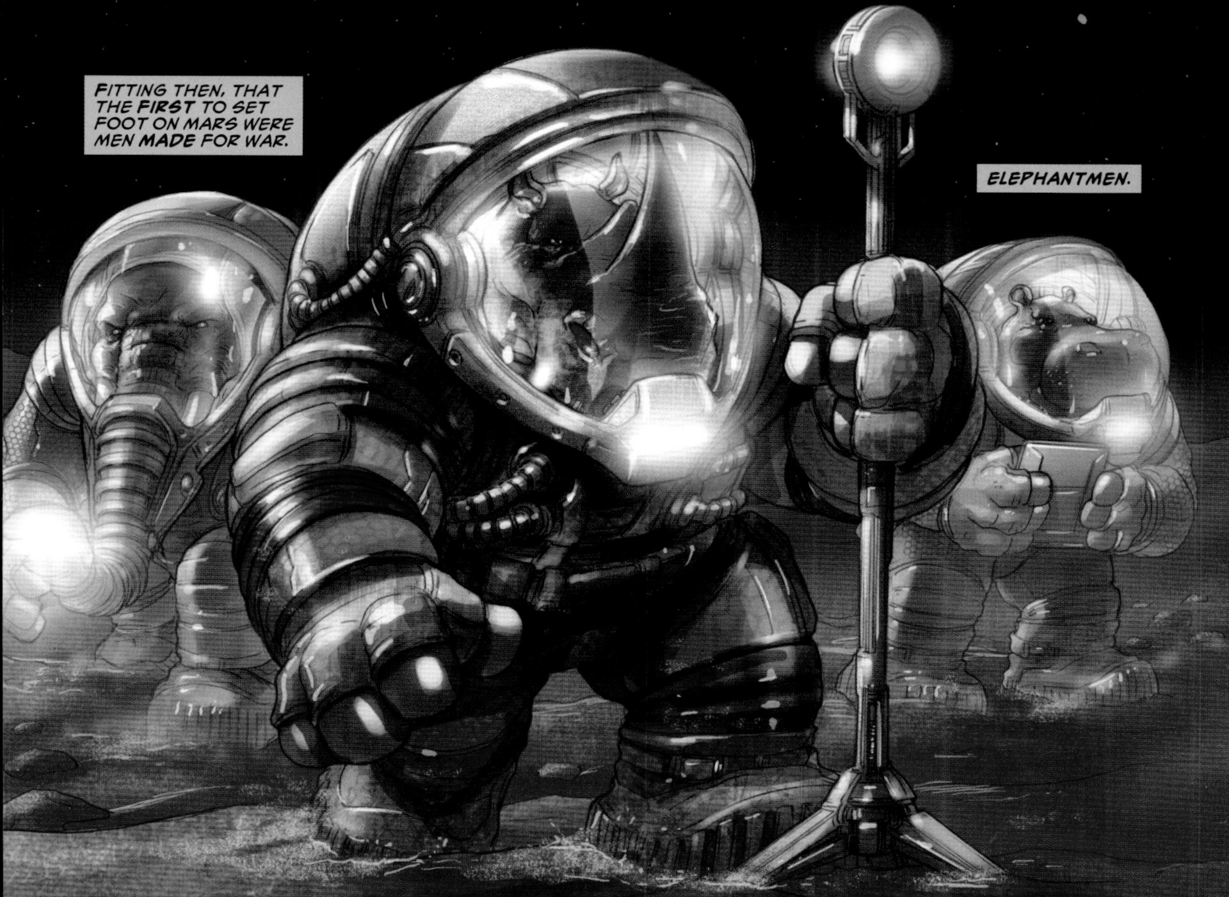
FITTING THEN, THAT THE FIRST TO SET FOOT ON MARS WERE MEN MADE FOR WAR.
ELEPHANTMEN.

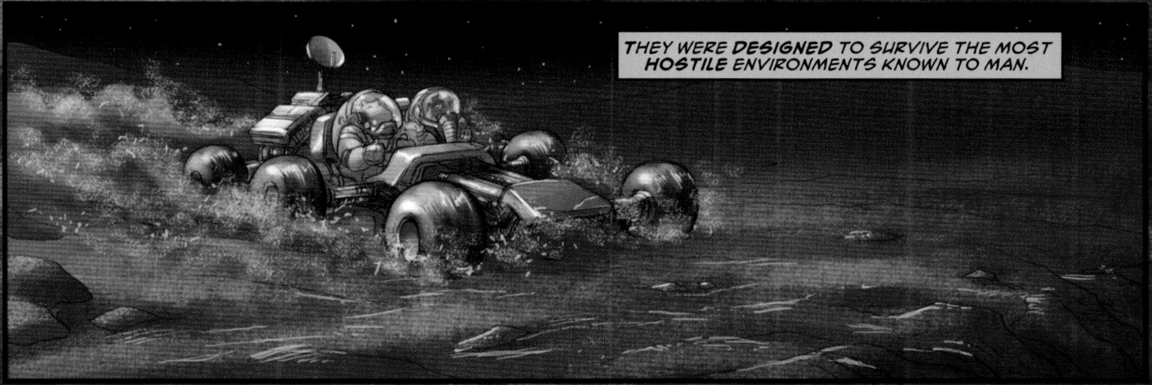
THEY WERE DESIGNED TO SURVIVE THE MOST HOSTILE ENVIRONMENTS KNOWN TO MAN.

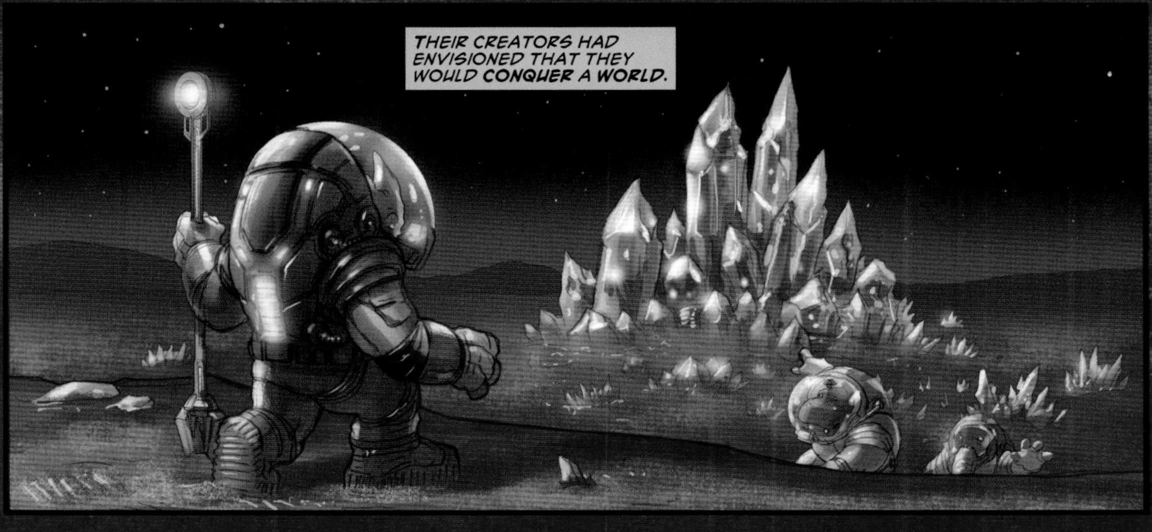
THEIR CREATORS HAD ENVISIONED THAT THEY WOULD CONQUER A WORLD.

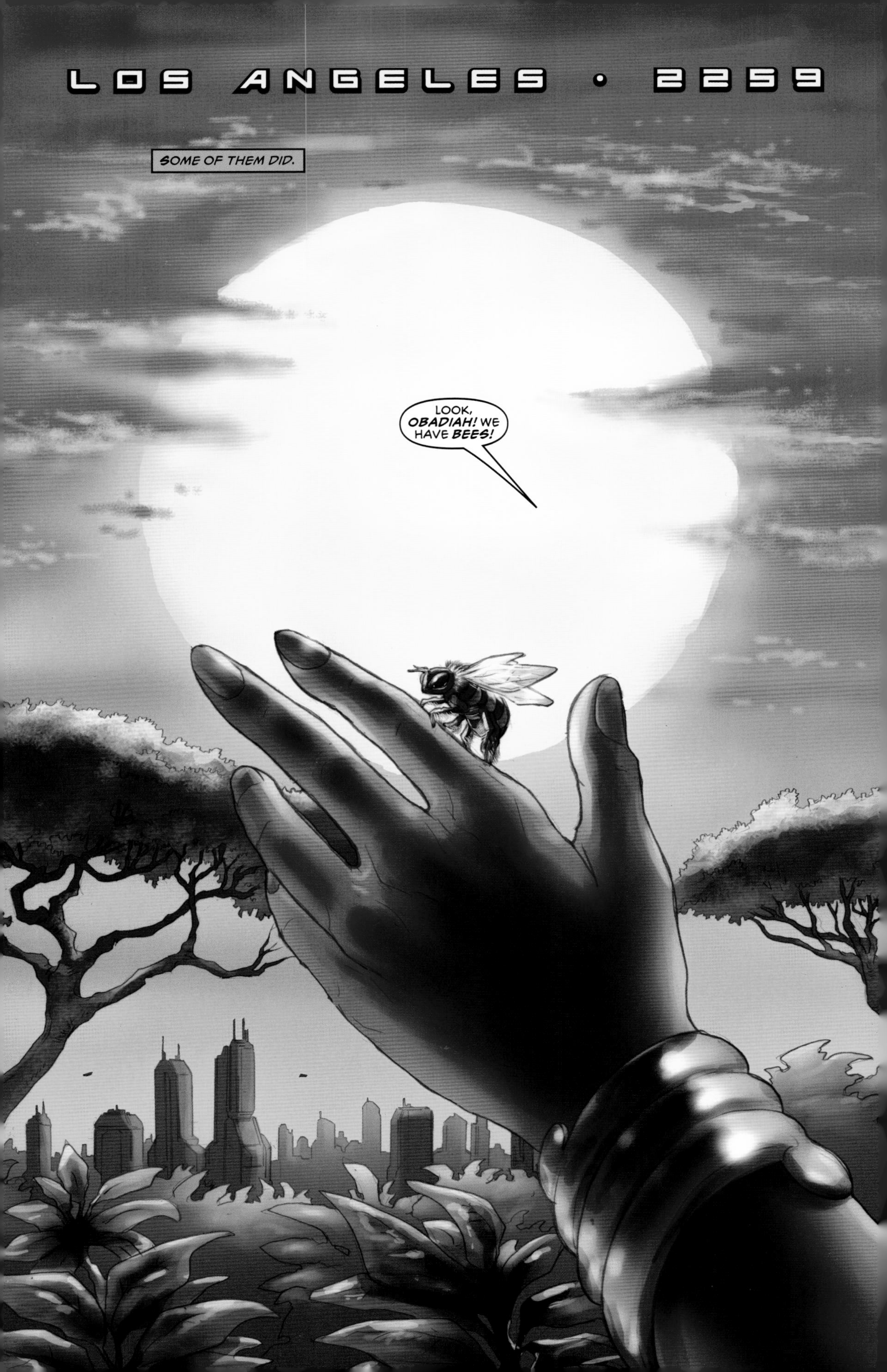
LOS ANGELES • 2259
SOME OF THEM DID.
LOOK, OBADIAH! WE HAVE BEES!

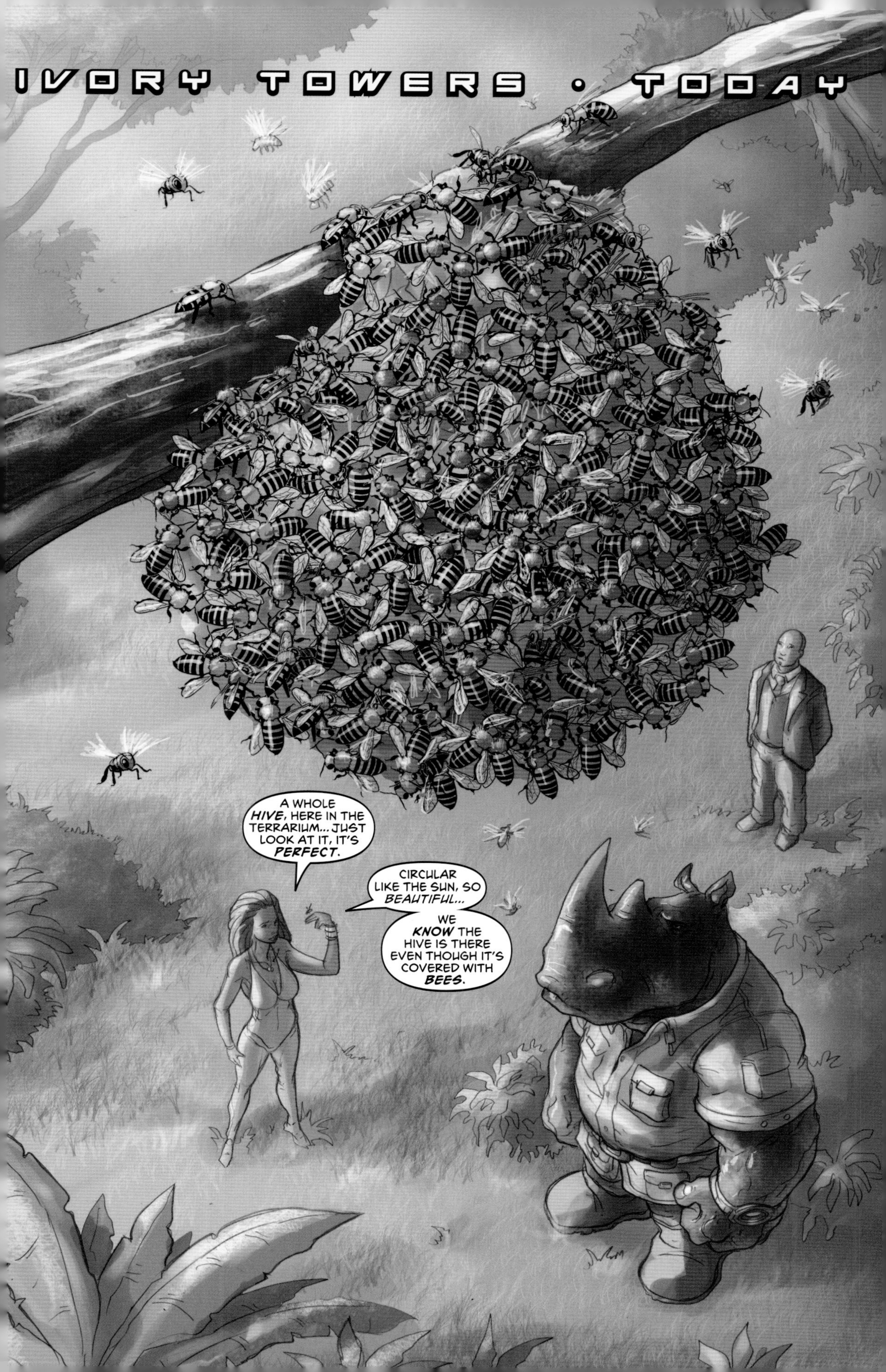
IVORY TOWERS • TODAY
A WHOLE HIVE, HERE IN THE TERRARIUM... JUST LOOK AT IT, IT'S PERFECT.
CIRCULAR LIKE THE SUN, SO BEAUTIFUL...
WE KNOW THE HIVE IS THERE EVEN THOUGH IT'S COVERED WITH BEES.

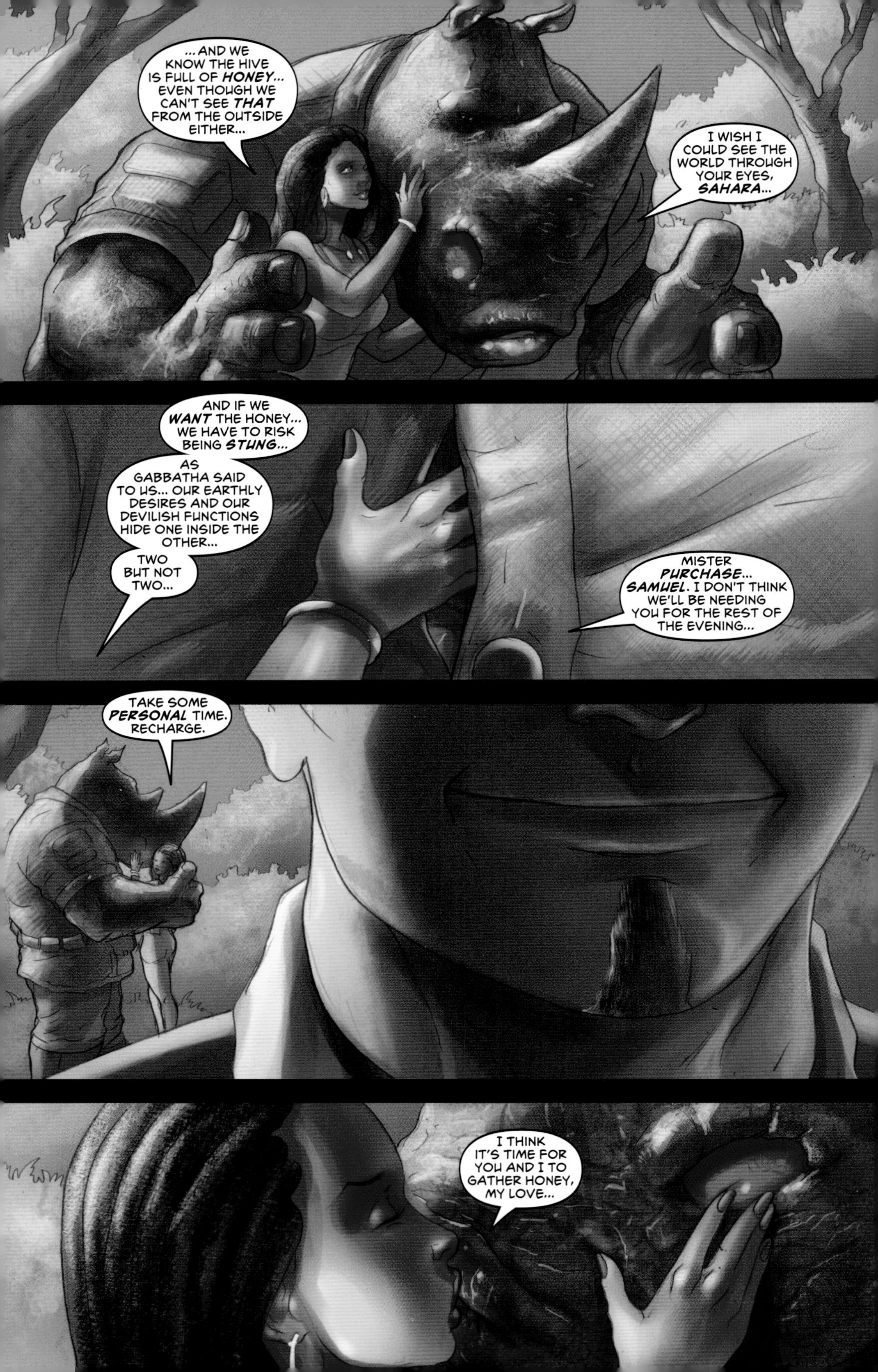
...AND WE KNOW THE HIVE IS FULL OF HONEY... EVEN THOUGH WE CAN'T SEE THAT FROM THE OUTSIDE EITHER...
I WISH I COULD SEE THE WORLD THROUGH YOUR EYES, SAHARA...
AND IF WE WANT THE HONEY... WE HAVE TO RISK BEING STUNG...
AS GABBATHA SAID TO US... OUR EARTHLY DESIRES AND OUR DEVILISH FUNCTIONS HIDE ONE INSIDE THE OTHER...
TWO BUT NOT TWO...
MISTER PURCHASE... SAMUEL. I DON'T THINK WE'LL BE NEEDING YOU FOR THE REST OF THE EVENING...
TAKE SOME PERSONAL TIME. RECHARGE.
I THINK IT'S TIME FOR YOU AND I TO GATHER HONEY, MY LOVE...

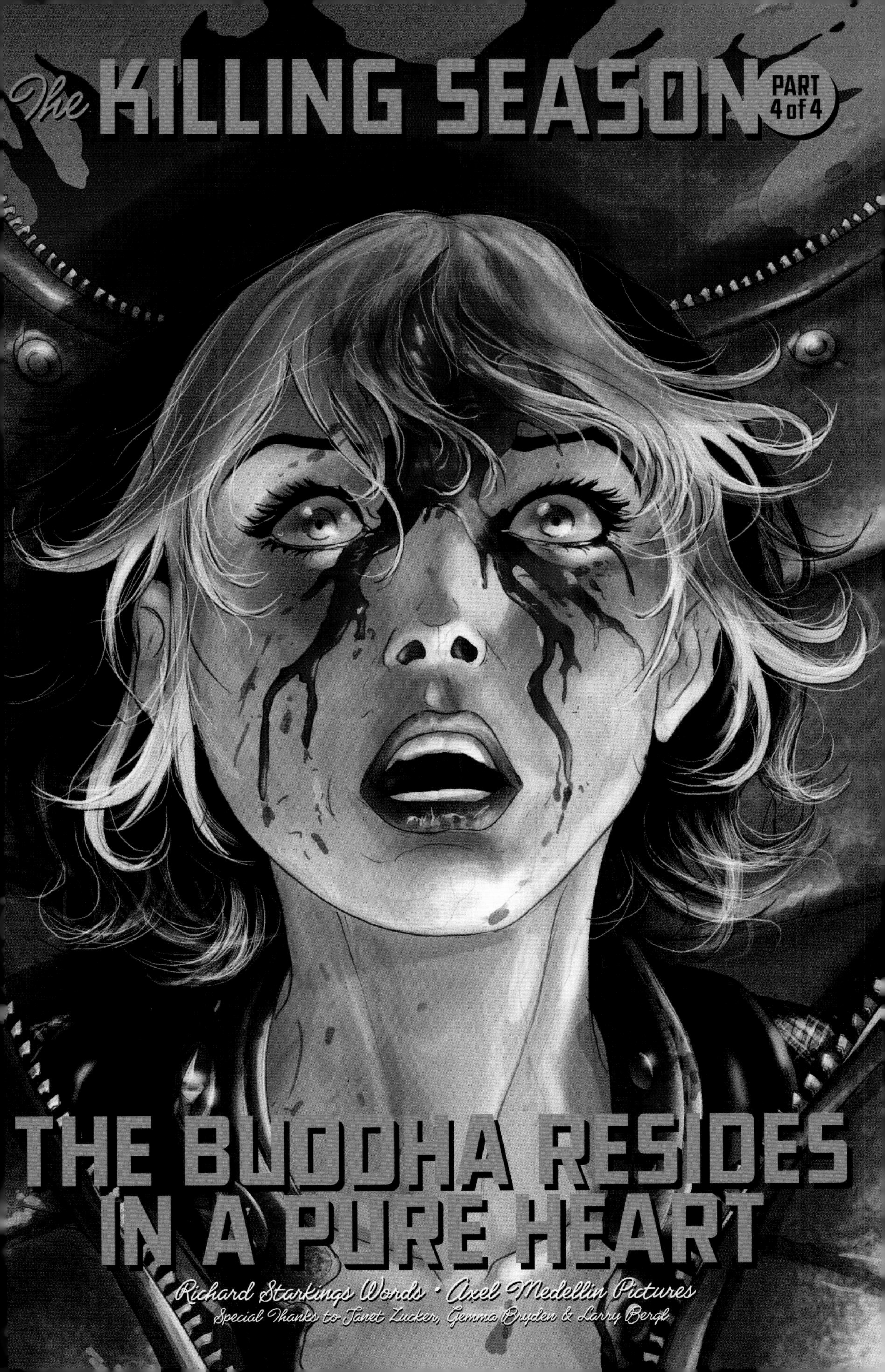
The KILLING SEASON
PART 4 of 4
THE BUDDHA RESIDES IN A PURE HEART
Richard Starkings Words • Axel Medellin Pictures
Special Thanks to Janet Zucker, Gemma Bryden & Larry Bergl

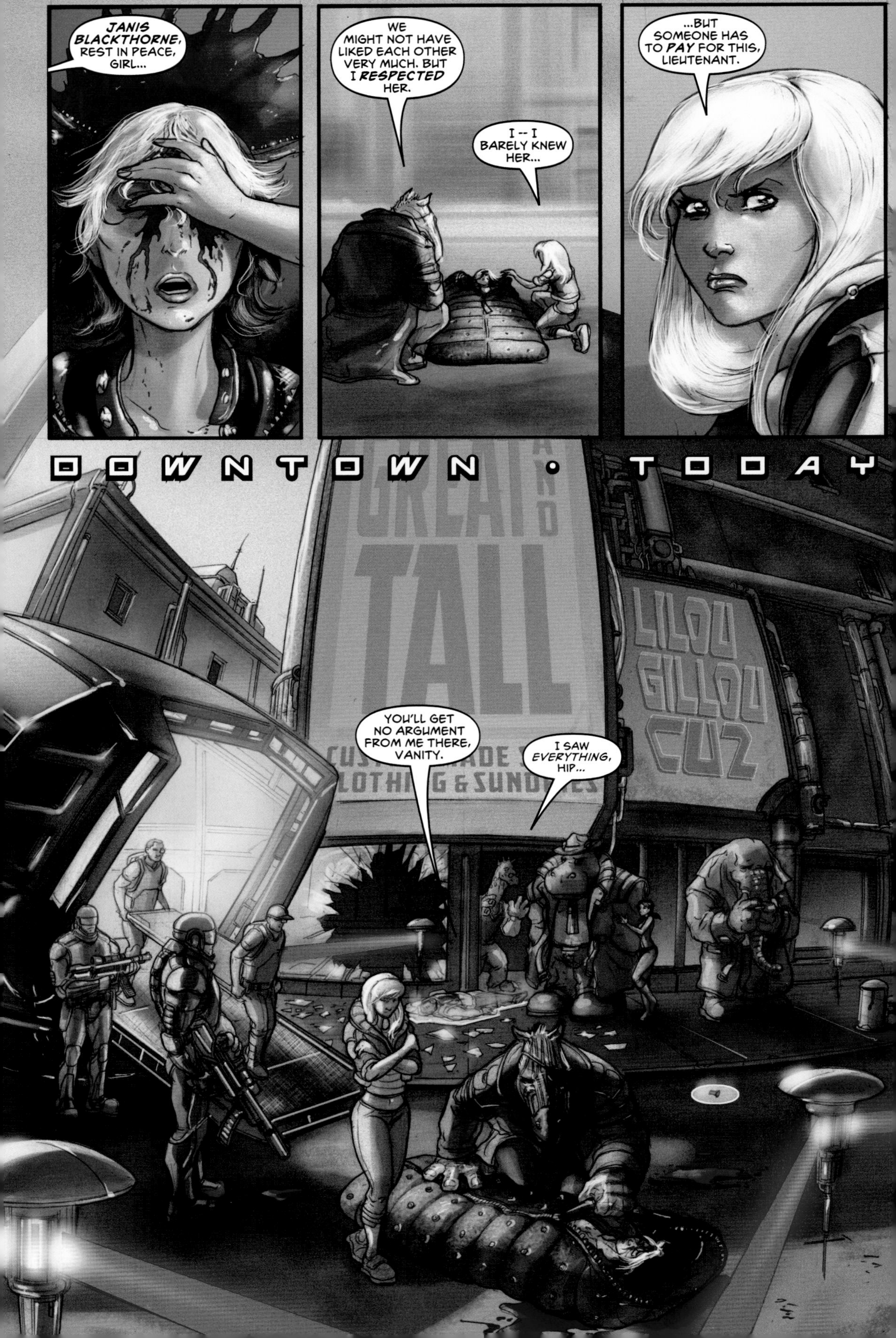
JANIS BLACKTHORNE, REST IN PEACE, GIRL...
WE MIGHT NOT HAVE LIKED EACH OTHER VERY MUCH. BUT I RESPECTED HER.
I -- I BARELY KNEW HER...
...BUT SOMEONE HAS TO PAY FOR THIS, LIEUTENANT.
DOWNTOWN • TODAY
GREAT AND TALL
CUST MADE
LOTHING & SUND
LILOU GILLOU CUZ
YOU'LL GET NO ARGUMENT FROM ME THERE, VANITY.
I SAW EVERYTHING, HIP...

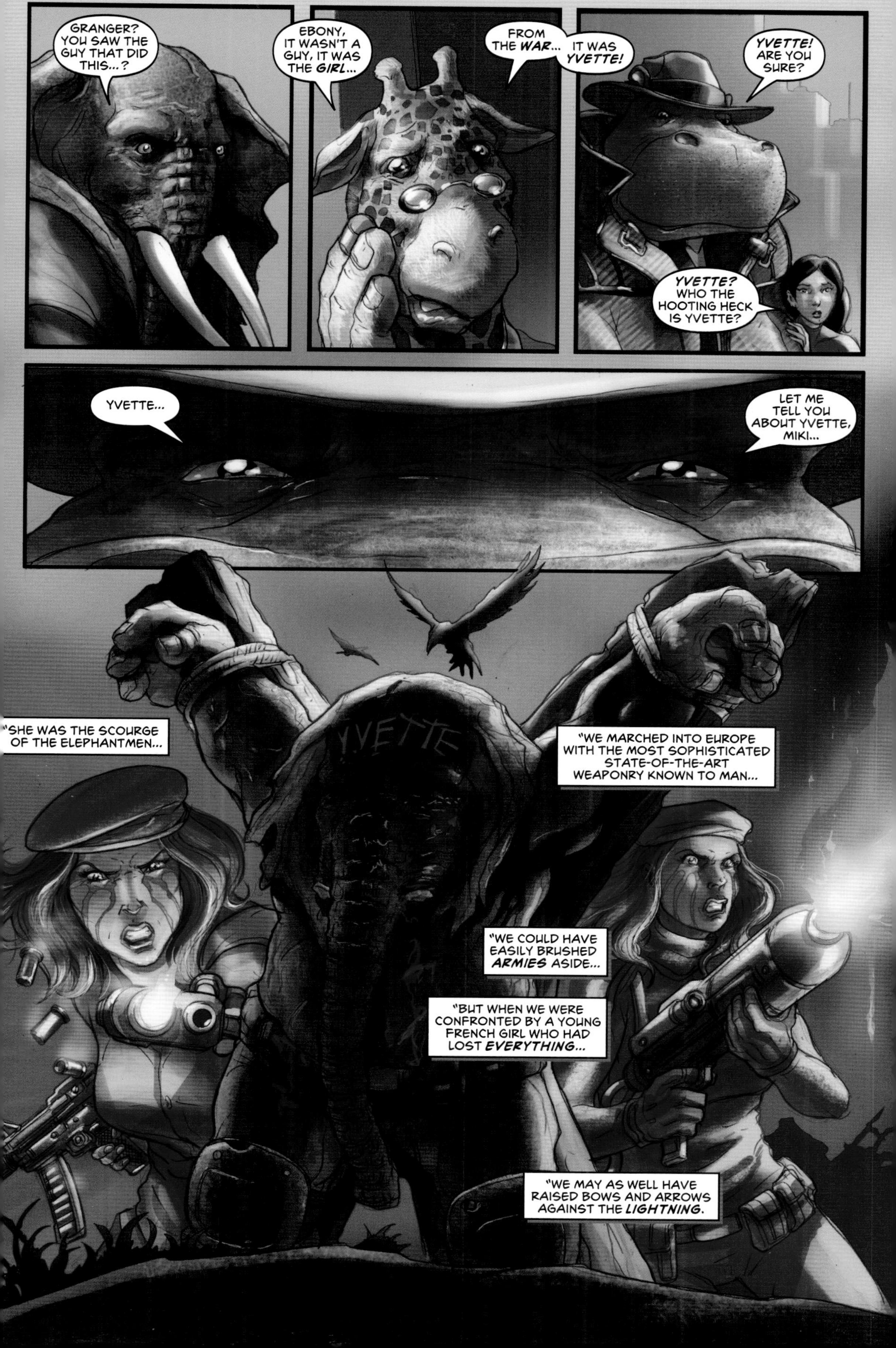
GRANGER? YOU SAW THE GUY THAT DID THIS...?
EBONY, IT WASN'T A GUY, IT WAS THE *GIRL*...
FROM THE *WAR*...
IT WAS *YVETTE!*
YVETTE! ARE YOU SURE?
YVETTE? WHO THE HOOTING HECK IS YVETTE?
YVETTE...
LET ME TELL YOU ABOUT YVETTE, MIKI...
"SHE WAS THE SCOURGE OF THE ELEPHANTMEN...
YVETTE
"WE MARCHED INTO EUROPE WITH THE MOST SOPHISTICATED STATE-OF-THE-ART WEAPONRY KNOWN TO MAN...
"WE COULD HAVE EASILY BRUSHED *ARMIES* ASIDE...
"BUT WHEN WE WERE CONFRONTED BY A YOUNG FRENCH GIRL WHO HAD LOST *EVERYTHING*...
"WE MAY AS WELL HAVE RAISED BOWS AND ARROWS AGAINST THE *LIGHTNING*.

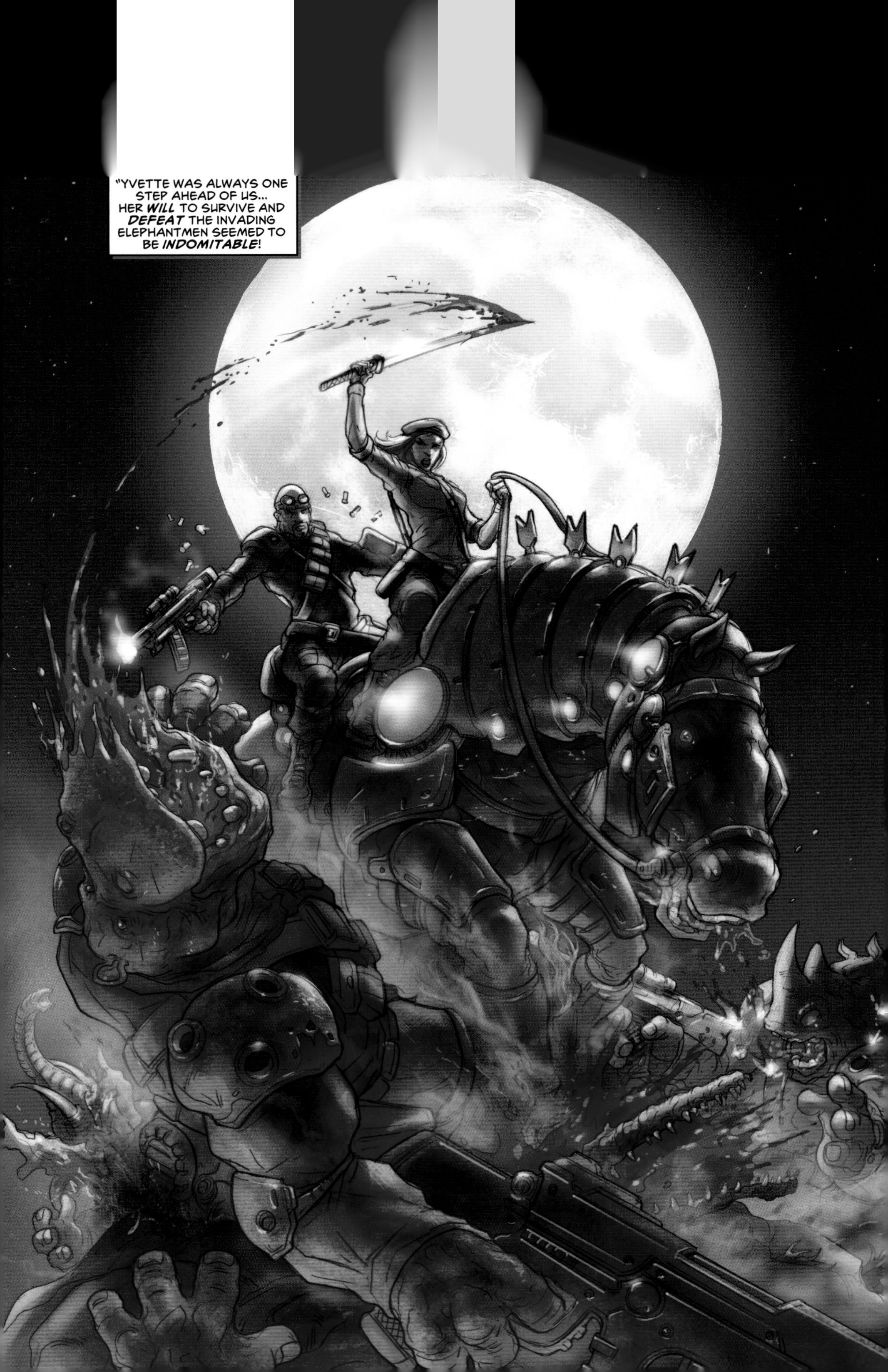
"YVETTE WAS ALWAYS ONE STEP AHEAD OF US... HER WILL TO SURVIVE AND DEFEAT THE INVADING ELEPHANTMEN SEEMED TO BE INDOMITABLE!

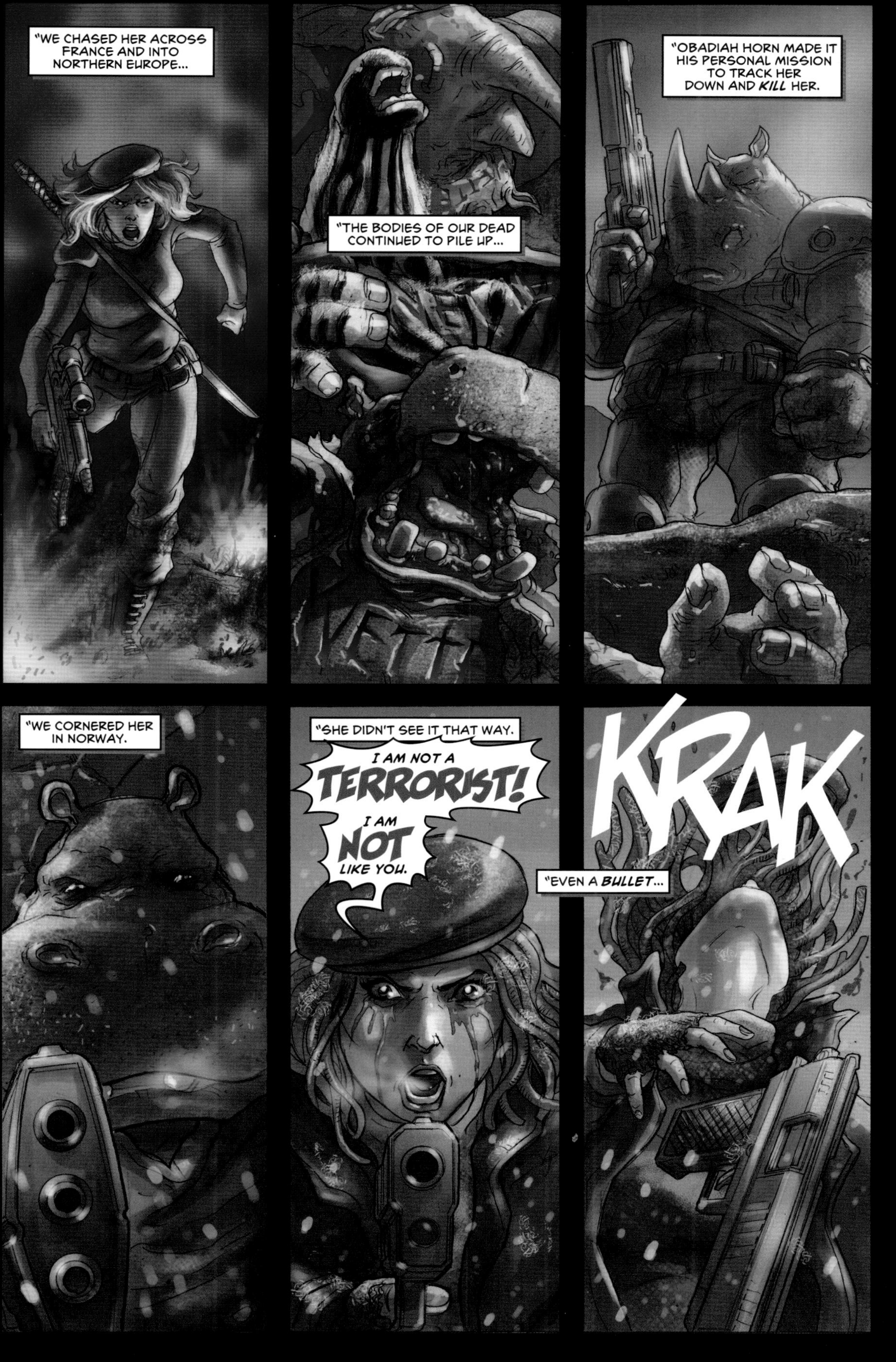
"WE CHASED HER ACROSS FRANCE AND INTO NORTHERN EUROPE...
"THE BODIES OF OUR DEAD CONTINUED TO PILE UP...
"OBADIAH HORN MADE IT HIS PERSONAL MISSION TO TRACK HER DOWN AND KILL HER.
"WE CORNERED HER IN NORWAY.
"SHE DIDN'T SEE IT THAT WAY.
I AM NOT A TERRORIST!
I AM NOT LIKE YOU.
KRAK
"EVEN A BULLET...

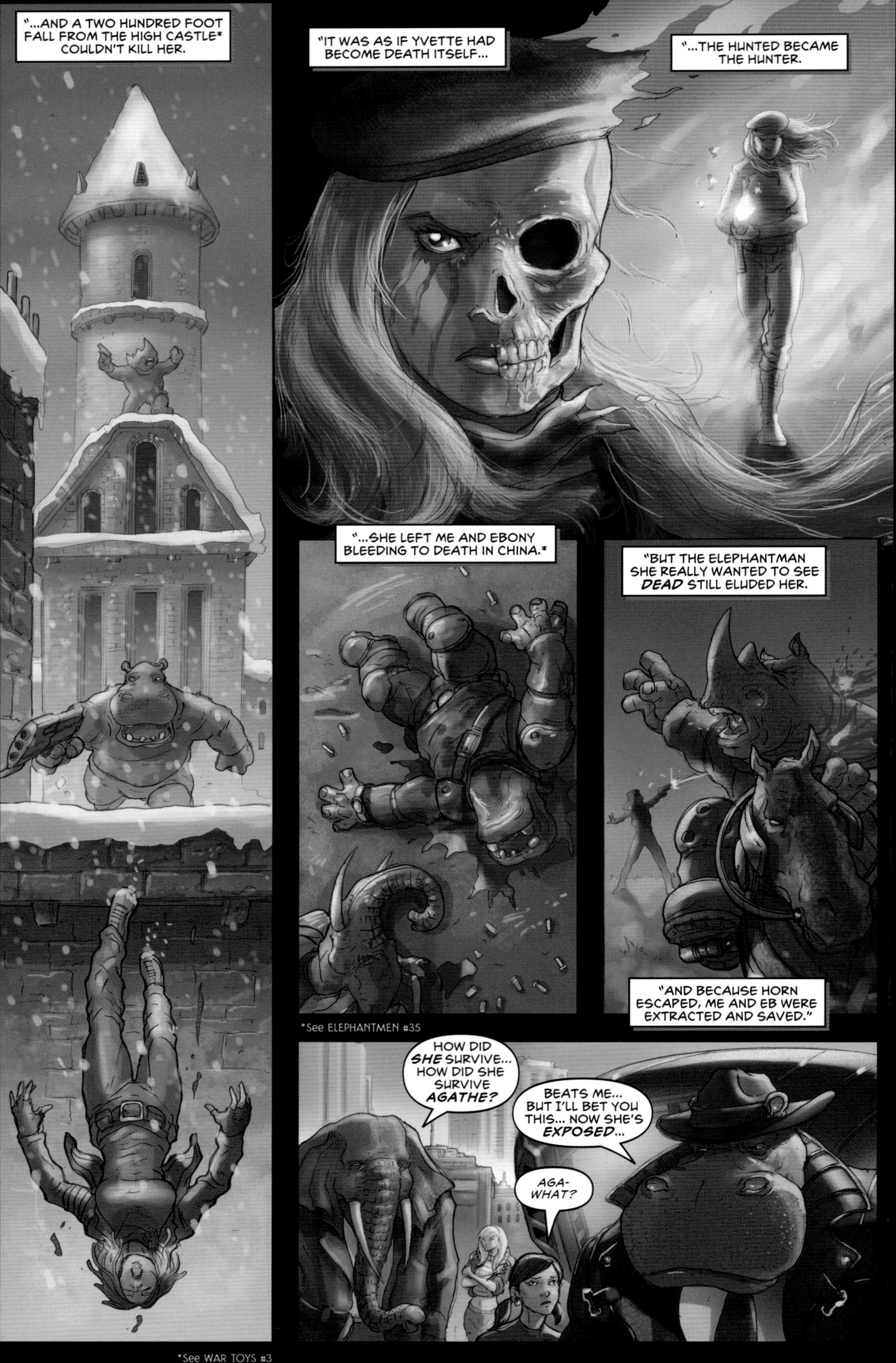
"...AND A TWO HUNDRED FOOT FALL FROM THE HIGH CASTLE* COULDN'T KILL HER.
"IT WAS AS IF YVETTE HAD BECOME DEATH ITSELF...
"...THE HUNTED BECAME THE HUNTER.
"...SHE LEFT ME AND EBONY BLEEDING TO DEATH IN CHINA.*
"BUT THE ELEPHANTMAN SHE REALLY WANTED TO SEE **DEAD** STILL ELUDED HER.
"AND BECAUSE HORN ESCAPED, ME AND EB WERE EXTRACTED AND SAVED."
*See ELEPHANTMEN #35
HOW DID **SHE** SURVIVE... HOW DID SHE SURVIVE **AGATHE?**
BEATS ME... BUT I'LL BET YOU THIS... NOW SHE'S **EXPOSED**...
AGA- WHAT?
*See WAR TOYS #3

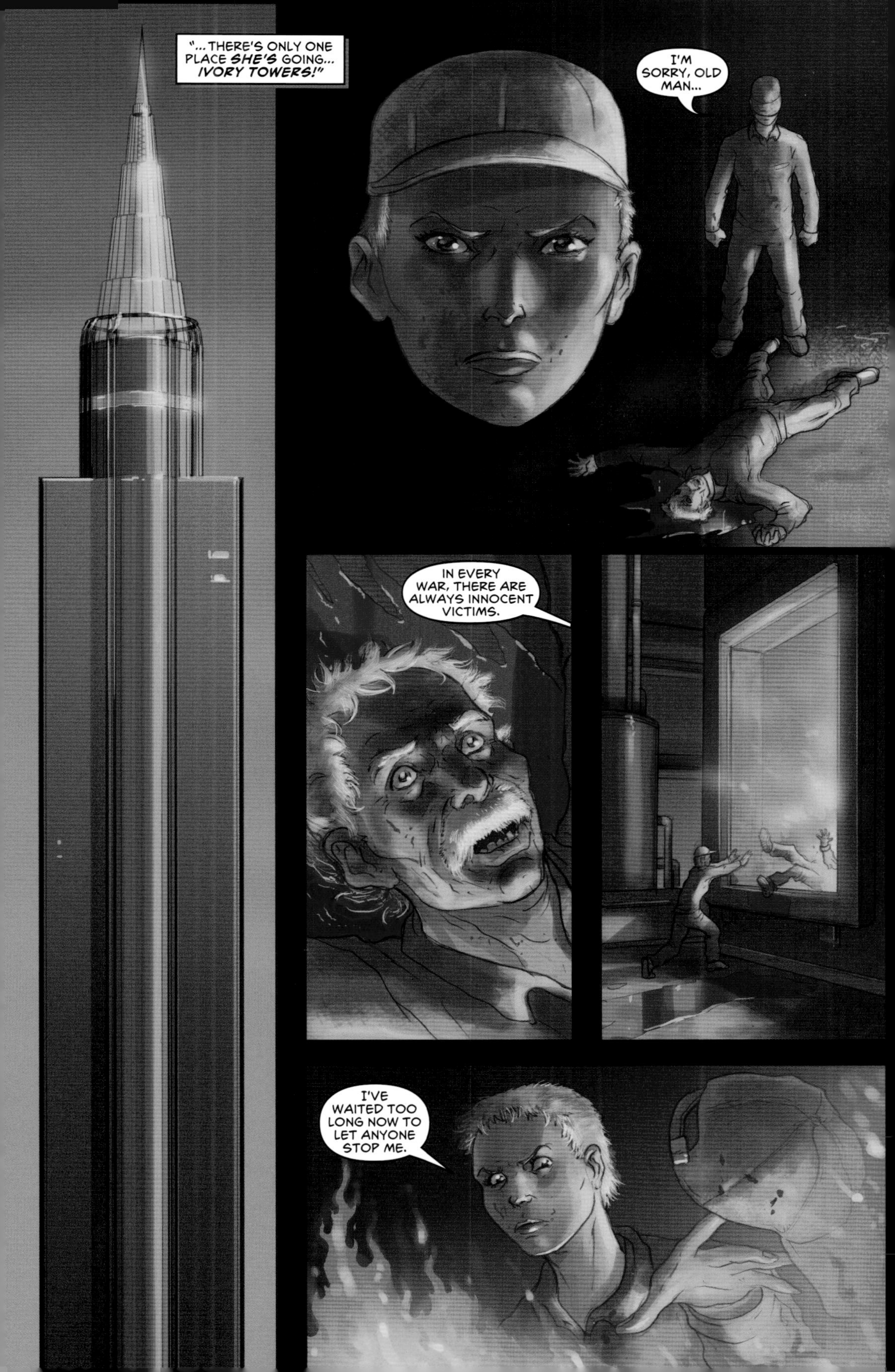
"... THERE'S ONLY ONE PLACE *SHE'S* GOING... *IVORY TOWERS!*"
I'M SORRY, OLD MAN...
IN EVERY WAR, THERE ARE ALWAYS INNOCENT VICTIMS.
I'VE WAITED TOO LONG NOW TO LET ANYONE STOP ME.

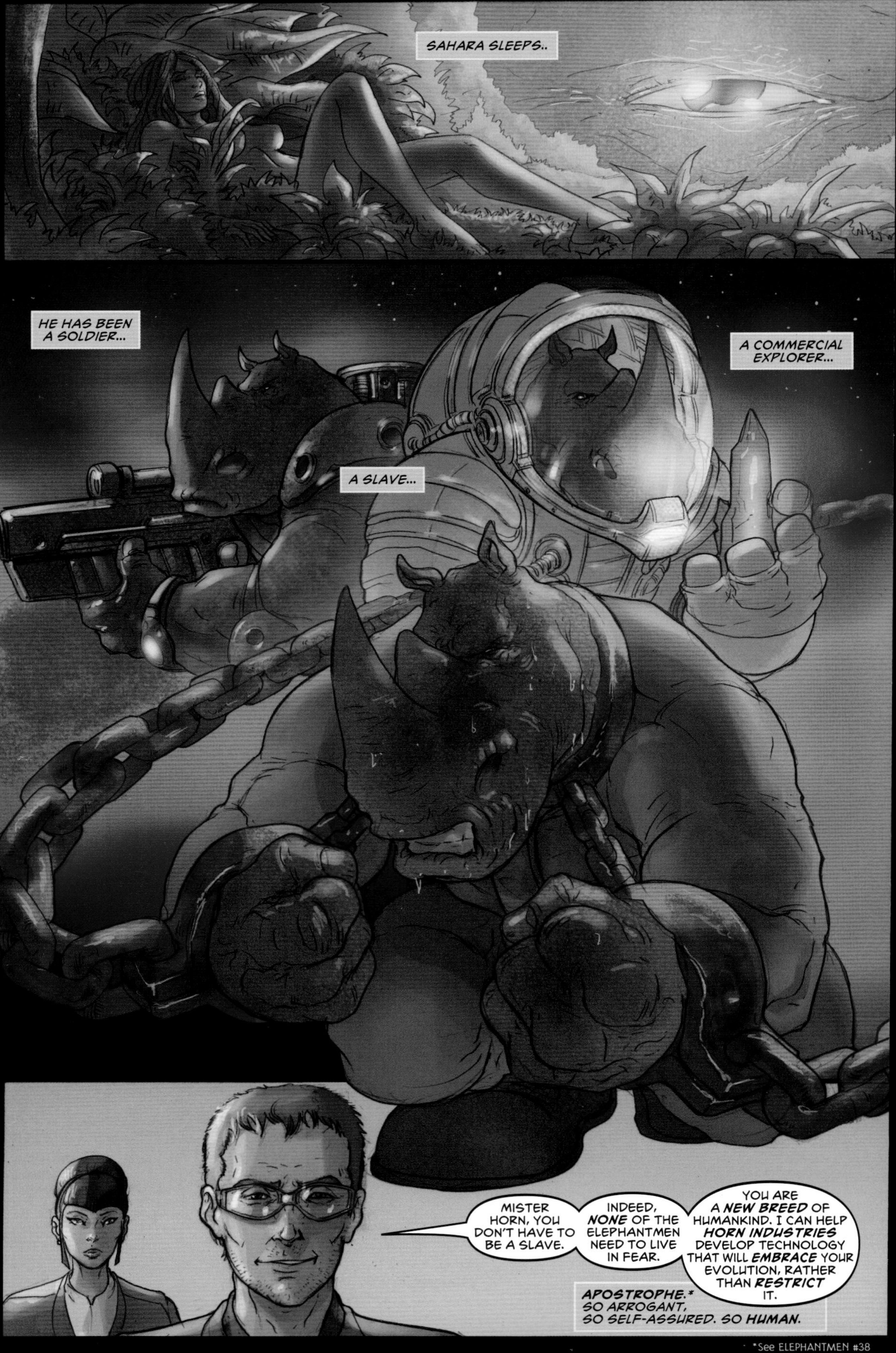

SAHARA SLEEPS..
HE HAS BEEN A SOLDIER...
A COMMERCIAL EXPLORER...
A SLAVE...
MISTER HORN, YOU DON'T HAVE TO BE A SLAVE.
INDEED, NONE OF THE ELEPHANTMEN NEED TO LIVE IN FEAR.
YOU ARE A NEW BREED OF HUMANKIND. I CAN HELP HORN INDUSTRIES DEVELOP TECHNOLOGY THAT WILL EMBRACE YOUR EVOLUTION, RATHER THAN RESTRICT IT.
APOSTROPHE.* SO ARROGANT, SO SELF-ASSURED. SO HUMAN.

*See ELEPHANTMEN #38

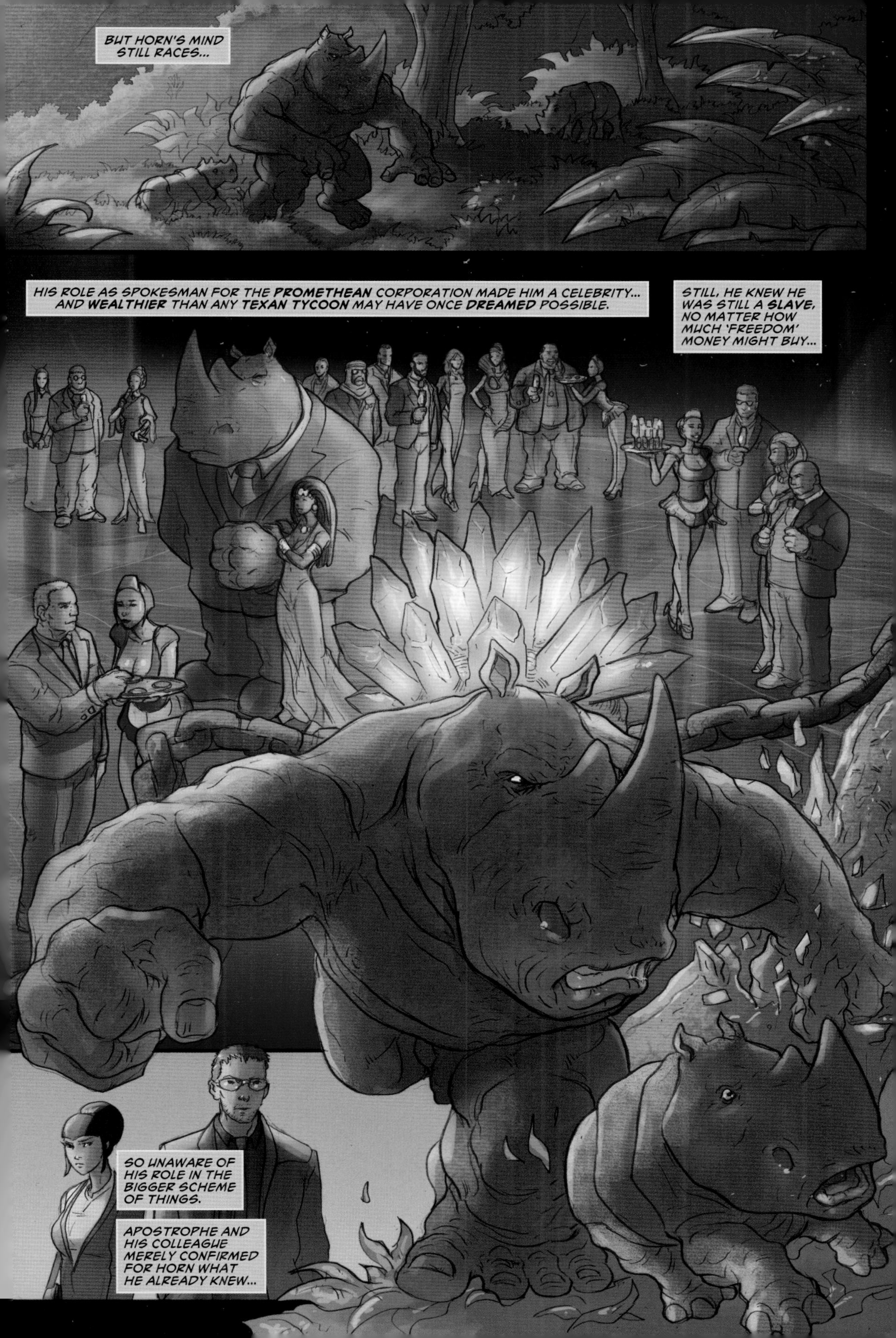
BUT HORN'S MIND STILL RACES...
HIS ROLE AS SPOKESMAN FOR THE PROMETHEAN CORPORATION MADE HIM A CELEBRITY... AND WEALTHIER THAN ANY TEXAN TYCOON MAY HAVE ONCE DREAMED POSSIBLE.
STILL, HE KNEW HE WAS STILL A SLAVE, NO MATTER HOW MUCH 'FREEDOM' MONEY MIGHT BUY...
SO UNAWARE OF HIS ROLE IN THE BIGGER SCHEME OF THINGS.
APOSTROPHE AND HIS COLLEAGUE MERELY CONFIRMED FOR HORN WHAT HE ALREADY KNEW...

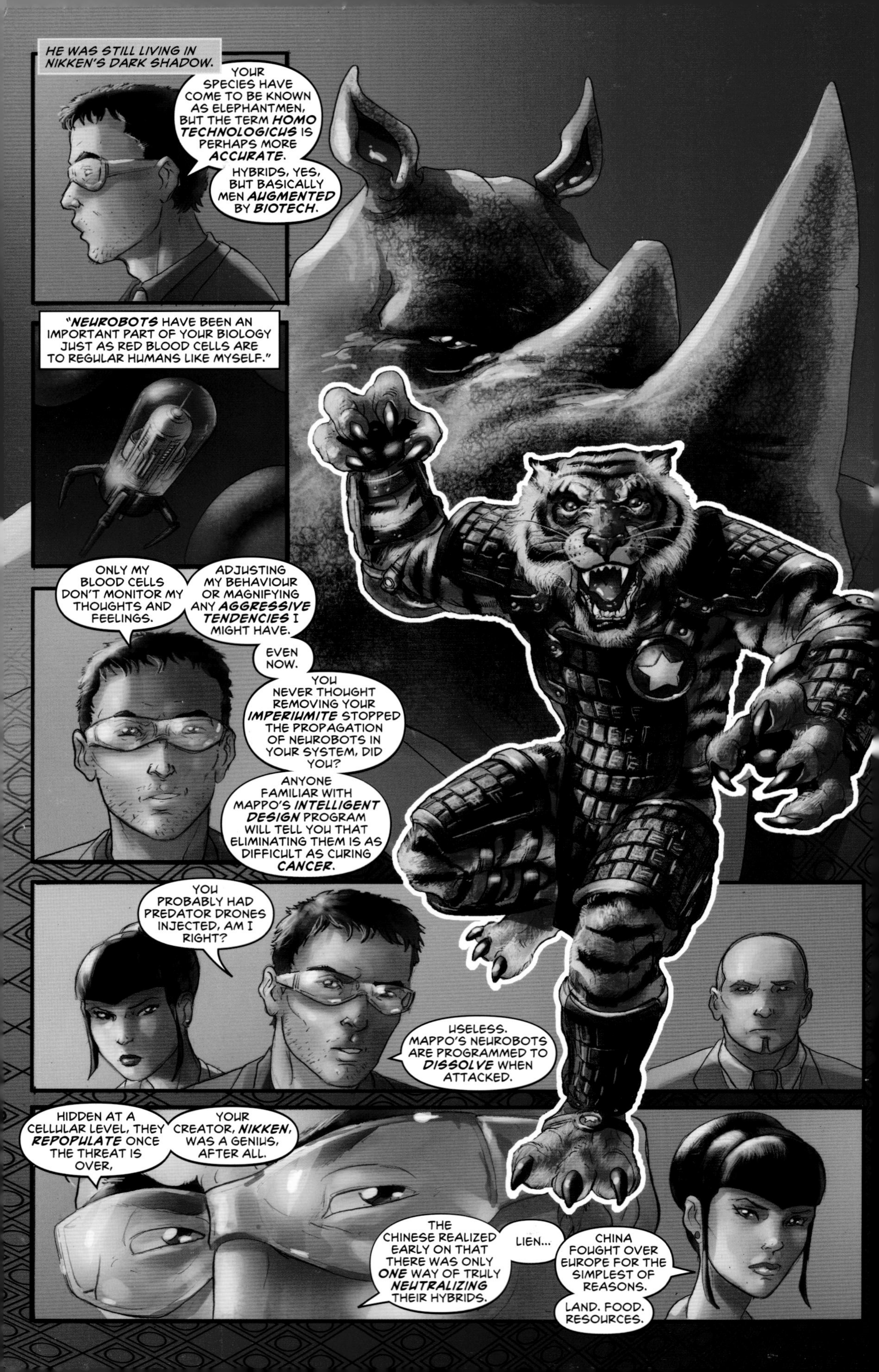
HE WAS STILL LIVING IN NIKKEN'S DARK SHADOW.
YOUR SPECIES HAVE COME TO BE KNOWN AS ELEPHANTMEN, BUT THE TERM HOMO TECHNOLOGICUS IS PERHAPS MORE ACCURATE.
HYBRIDS, YES, BUT BASICALLY MEN AUGMENTED BY BIOTECH.
"NEUROBOTS HAVE BEEN AN IMPORTANT PART OF YOUR BIOLOGY JUST AS RED BLOOD CELLS ARE TO REGULAR HUMANS LIKE MYSELF."
ONLY MY BLOOD CELLS DON'T MONITOR MY THOUGHTS AND FEELINGS.
ADJUSTING MY BEHAVIOUR OR MAGNIFYING ANY AGGRESSIVE TENDENCIES I MIGHT HAVE.
EVEN NOW.
YOU NEVER THOUGHT REMOVING YOUR IMPERIUMITE STOPPED THE PROPAGATION OF NEUROBOTS IN YOUR SYSTEM, DID YOU?
ANYONE FAMILIAR WITH MAPPO'S INTELLIGENT DESIGN PROGRAM WILL TELL YOU THAT ELIMINATING THEM IS AS DIFFICULT AS CURING CANCER.
YOU PROBABLY HAD PREDATOR DRONES INJECTED, AM I RIGHT?
USELESS. MAPPO'S NEUROBOTS ARE PROGRAMMED TO DISSOLVE WHEN ATTACKED.
HIDDEN AT A CELLULAR LEVEL, THEY REPOPULATE ONCE THE THREAT IS OVER,
YOUR CREATOR, NIKKEN, WAS A GENIUS, AFTER ALL.
THE CHINESE REALIZED EARLY ON THAT THERE WAS ONLY ONE WAY OF TRULY NEUTRALIZING THEIR HYBRIDS.
LIEN...
CHINA FOUGHT OVER EUROPE FOR THE SIMPLEST OF REASONS.
LAND. FOOD. RESOURCES.

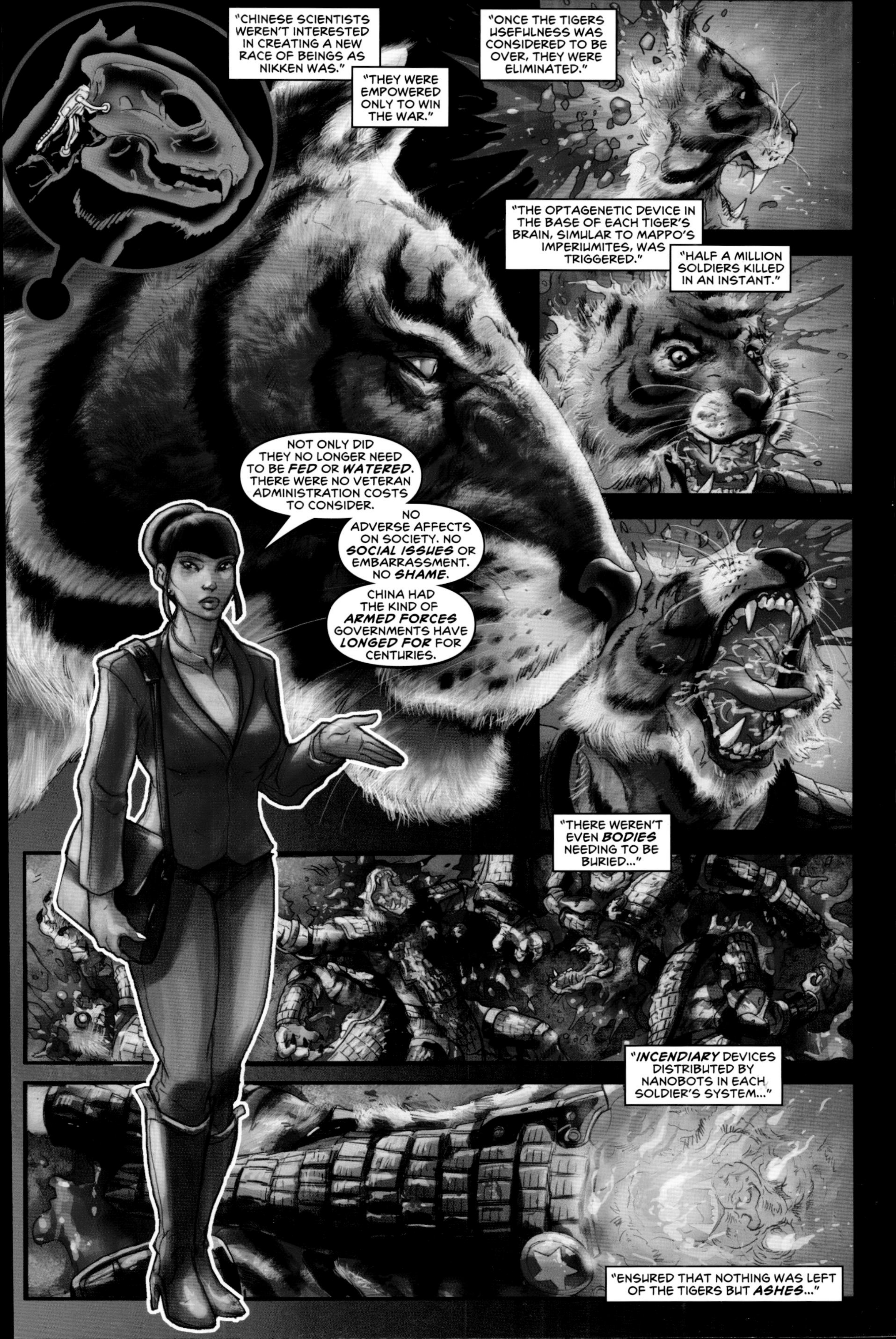
"CHINESE SCIENTISTS WEREN'T INTERESTED IN CREATING A NEW RACE OF BEINGS AS NIKKEN WAS."
"THEY WERE EMPOWERED ONLY TO WIN THE WAR."
"ONCE THE TIGERS USEFULNESS WAS CONSIDERED TO BE OVER, THEY WERE ELIMINATED."
"THE OPTAGENETIC DEVICE IN THE BASE OF EACH TIGER'S BRAIN, SIMULAR TO MAPPO'S IMPERIUMITES, WAS TRIGGERED."
"HALF A MILLION SOLDIERS KILLED IN AN INSTANT."
NOT ONLY DID THEY NO LONGER NEED TO BE FED OR WATERED. THERE WERE NO VETERAN ADMINISTRATION COSTS TO CONSIDER.
NO ADVERSE AFFECTS ON SOCIETY. NO SOCIAL ISSUES OR EMBARRASSMENT. NO SHAME.
CHINA HAD THE KIND OF ARMED FORCES GOVERNMENTS HAVE LONGED FOR FOR CENTURIES.
"THERE WEREN'T EVEN BODIES NEEDING TO BE BURIED..."
"INCENDIARY DEVICES DISTRIBUTED BY NANOBOTS IN EACH SOLDIER'S SYSTEM..."
"ENSURED THAT NOTHING WAS LEFT OF THE TIGERS BUT ASHES..."

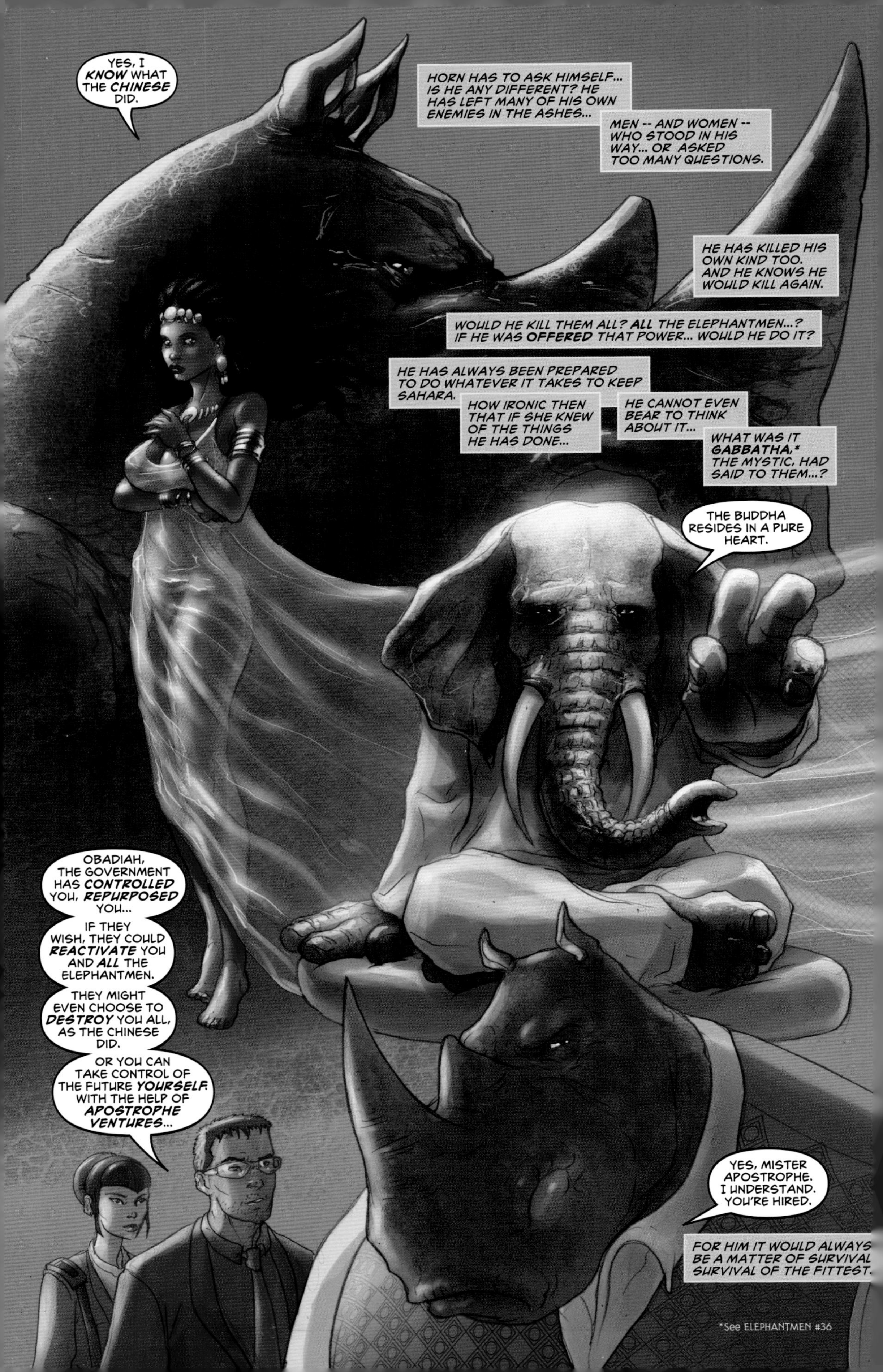
YES, I KNOW WHAT THE CHINESE DID.
HORN HAS TO ASK HIMSELF... IS HE ANY DIFFERENT? HE HAS LEFT MANY OF HIS OWN ENEMIES IN THE ASHES...
MEN -- AND WOMEN -- WHO STOOD IN HIS WAY... OR ASKED TOO MANY QUESTIONS.
HE HAS KILLED HIS OWN KIND TOO. AND HE KNOWS HE WOULD KILL AGAIN.
WOULD HE KILL THEM ALL? ALL THE ELEPHANTMEN...? IF HE WAS OFFERED THAT POWER... WOULD HE DO IT?
HE HAS ALWAYS BEEN PREPARED TO DO WHATEVER IT TAKES TO KEEP SAHARA.
HOW IRONIC THEN THAT IF SHE KNEW OF THE THINGS HE HAS DONE...
HE CANNOT EVEN BEAR TO THINK ABOUT IT...
WHAT WAS IT GABBATHA,* THE MYSTIC, HAD SAID TO THEM...?
THE BUDDHA RESIDES IN A PURE HEART.
OBADIAH, THE GOVERNMENT HAS CONTROLLED YOU, REPURPOSED YOU...
IF THEY WISH, THEY COULD REACTIVATE YOU AND ALL THE ELEPHANTMEN.
THEY MIGHT EVEN CHOOSE TO DESTROY YOU ALL, AS THE CHINESE DID.
OR YOU CAN TAKE CONTROL OF THE FUTURE YOURSELF. WITH THE HELP OF APOSTROPHE VENTURES...
YES, MISTER APOSTROPHE. I UNDERSTAND. YOU'RE HIRED.
FOR HIM IT WOULD ALWAYS BE A MATTER OF SURVIVAL. SURVIVAL OF THE FITTEST.

*See ELEPHANTMEN #36

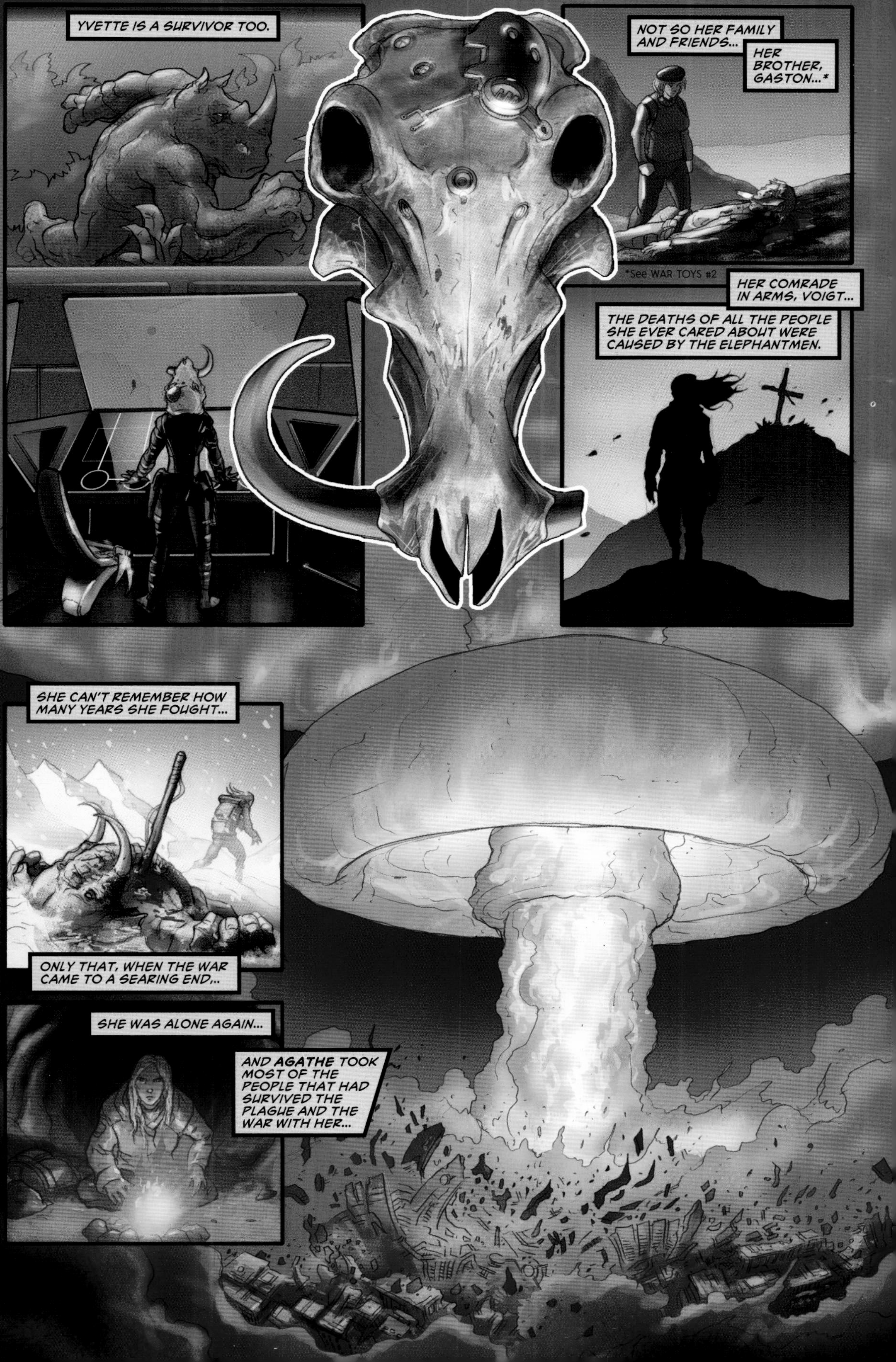
YVETTE IS A SURVIVOR TOO.
NOT SO HER FAMILY AND FRIENDS...
HER BROTHER, GASTON...*
*See WAR TOYS #2
HER COMRADE IN ARMS, VOIGT...
THE DEATHS OF ALL THE PEOPLE SHE EVER CARED ABOUT WERE CAUSED BY THE ELEPHANTMEN.
SHE CAN'T REMEMBER HOW MANY YEARS SHE FOUGHT...
ONLY THAT, WHEN THE WAR CAME TO A SEARING END...
SHE WAS ALONE AGAIN...
AND AGATHE TOOK MOST OF THE PEOPLE THAT HAD SURVIVED THE PLAGUE AND THE WAR WITH HER...

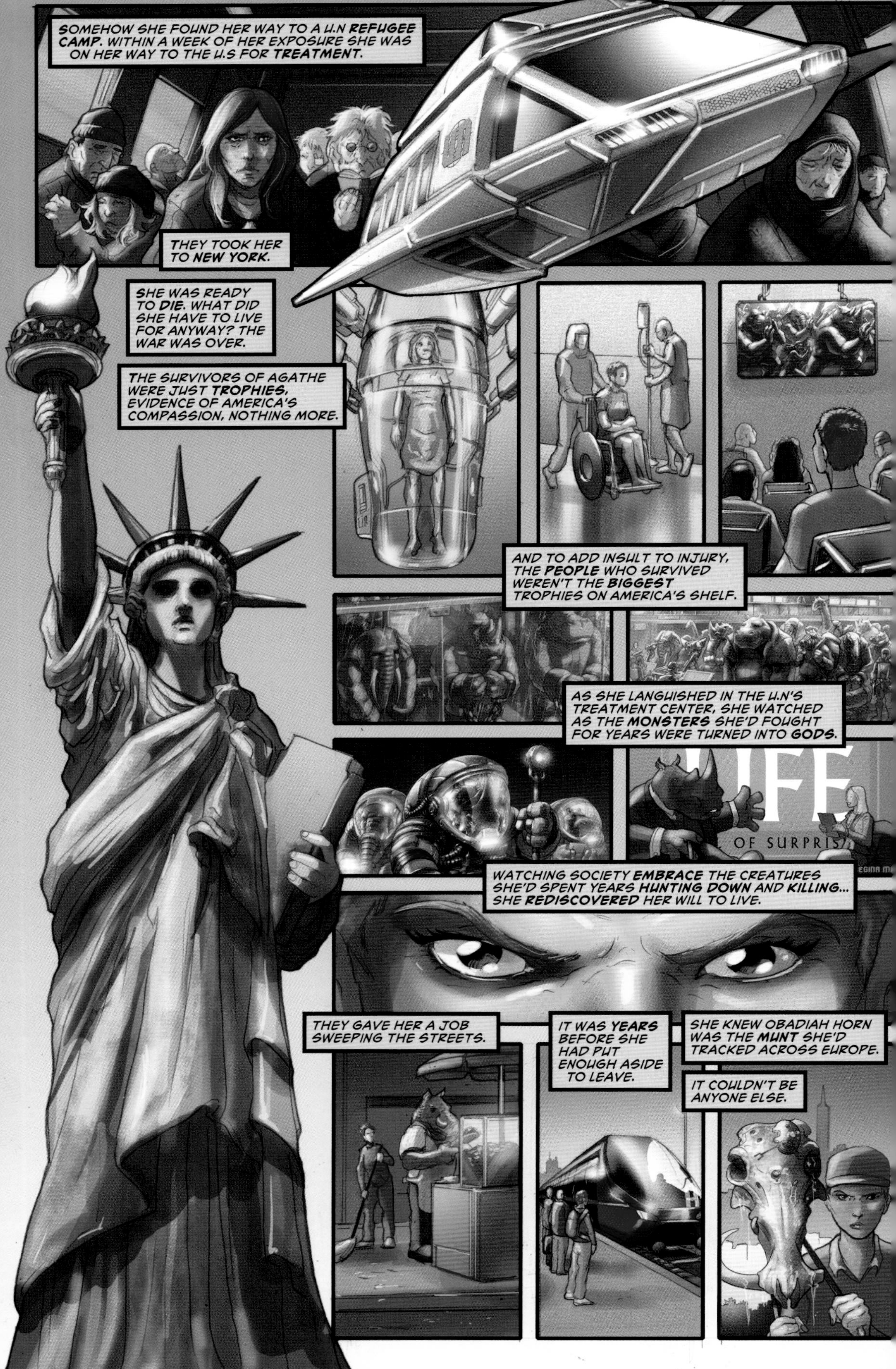
SOMEHOW SHE FOUND HER WAY TO A U.N REFUGEE CAMP. WITHIN A WEEK OF HER EXPOSURE SHE WAS ON HER WAY TO THE U.S FOR TREATMENT.
THEY TOOK HER TO NEW YORK.
SHE WAS READY TO DIE. WHAT DID SHE HAVE TO LIVE FOR ANYWAY? THE WAR WAS OVER.
THE SURVIVORS OF AGATHE WERE JUST TROPHIES, EVIDENCE OF AMERICA'S COMPASSION, NOTHING MORE.
AND TO ADD INSULT TO INJURY, THE PEOPLE WHO SURVIVED WEREN'T THE BIGGEST TROPHIES ON AMERICA'S SHELF.
AS SHE LANGUISHED IN THE U.N'S TREATMENT CENTER, SHE WATCHED AS THE MONSTERS SHE'D FOUGHT FOR YEARS WERE TURNED INTO GODS.
OF SURPRIS
WATCHING SOCIETY EMBRACE THE CREATURES SHE'D SPENT YEARS HUNTING DOWN AND KILLING... SHE REDISCOVERED HER WILL TO LIVE.
THEY GAVE HER A JOB SWEEPING THE STREETS.
IT WAS YEARS BEFORE SHE HAD PUT ENOUGH ASIDE TO LEAVE.
SHE KNEW OBADIAH HORN WAS THE MUNT SHE'D TRACKED ACROSS EUROPE.
IT COULDN'T BE ANYONE ELSE.

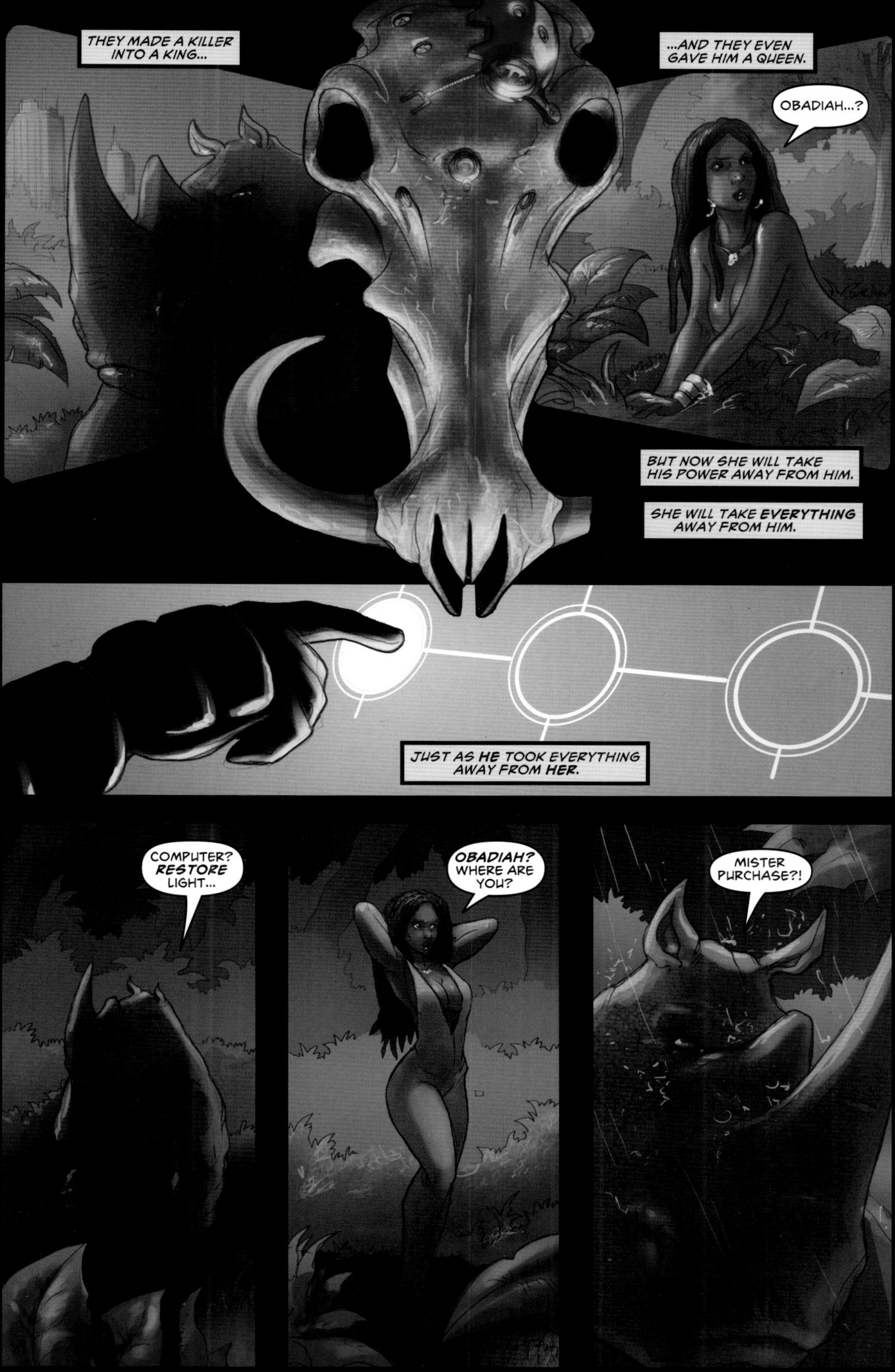
THEY MADE A KILLER INTO A KING...
...AND THEY EVEN GAVE HIM A QUEEN.
OBADIAH...?
BUT NOW SHE WILL TAKE HIS POWER AWAY FROM HIM.
SHE WILL TAKE EVERYTHING AWAY FROM HIM.
JUST AS HE TOOK EVERYTHING AWAY FROM HER.
COMPUTER? RESTORE LIGHT...
OBADIAH? WHERE ARE YOU?
MISTER PURCHASE?!

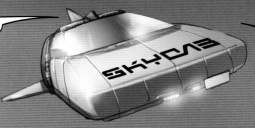

LOOK, GUYS, I'M JUST PLAYING A *HUNCH* HERE...

IF WE'D LET TRENCH IN ON THIS, HE'D SEND IN HALF THE *L.A.P.D* AND KEEP *US* OUT...

WHEN THERE'RE *OFFICERS DOWN*, HE'S GONNA KEEP HIS *BLINKER* ON...

AND IT'S NOT AS IF HORN IS GOING TO TAKE A *CALL* FROM *ME* AND TAKE IT SERIOUSLY.

HE'S USED TO *DEATH THREATS.*

TAKE US TOWARD THE *TOP* OF THE SPIRE, MIKI... HORN'S LITTLE *WILDLIFE PARK* THERE HAS *ATMOSPHERIC WINDSHIELDS*...

HIT THEM HARD AND *FAST* ENOUGH AND WE'LL SAIL RIGHT THROUGH!

WE'LL *SPLIT* INTO TWO TEAMS. JUST FIND *HORN* AND *SAHARA* AND GET 'EM *OUT.*

GOTCHA, HIP... FAST AND HARD, THE WAY I *LIKE* IT!

PROBABLY NOT THE BEST TIME TO BE HAVING A *MIRROR** FLASHBACK...

WE HAVE TO LOOK OUT FOR OURSELVES...

*See ELEPHANTMEN #32

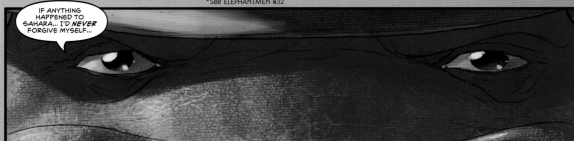

IF ANYTHING HAPPENED TO SAHARA... I'D *NEVER* FORGIVE MYSELF...

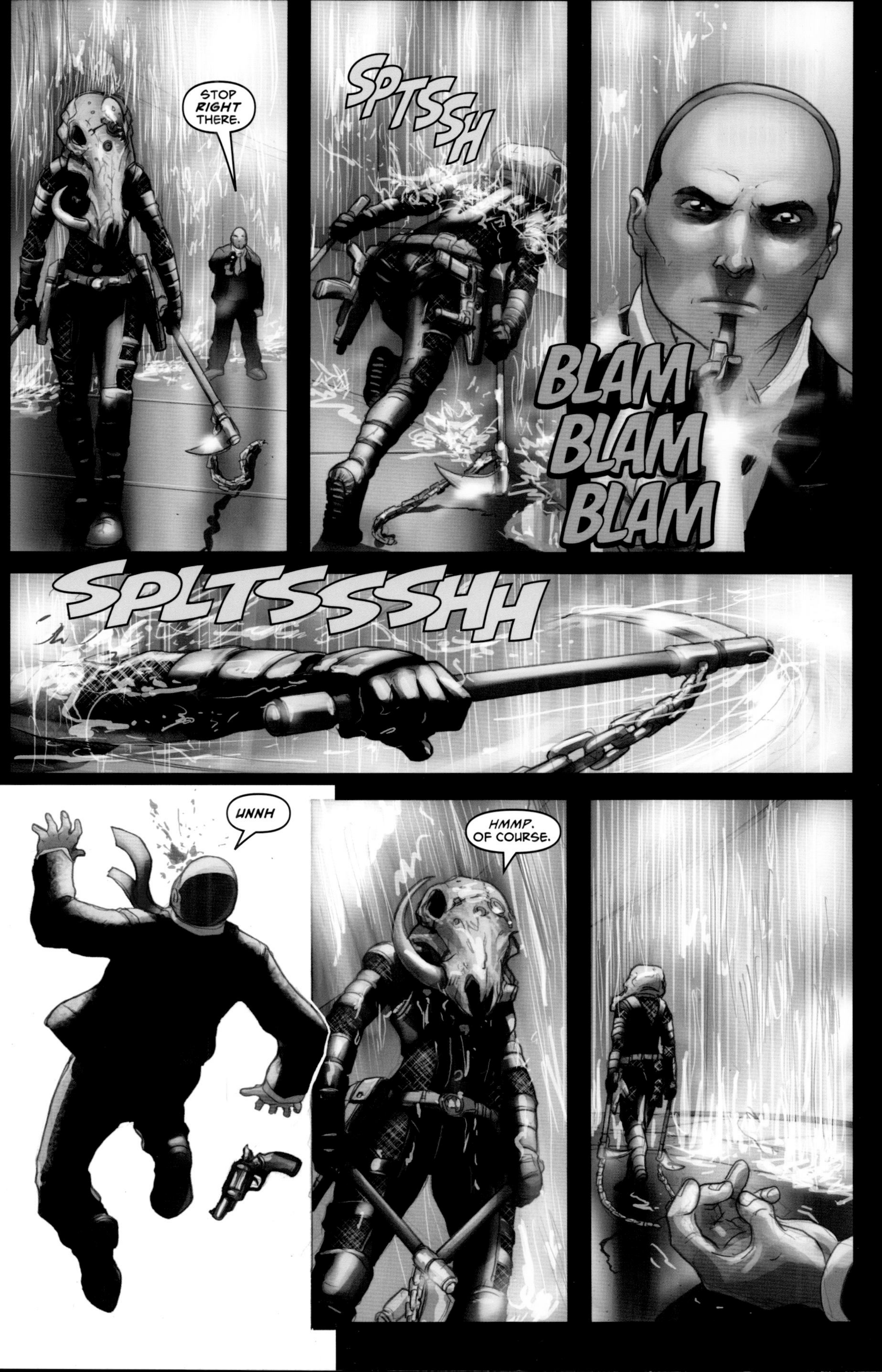
STOP RIGHT THERE.
SPTSSH
BLAM
BLAM
BLAM
SPLTSSSSHH
UNNH
HMMP. OF COURSE.

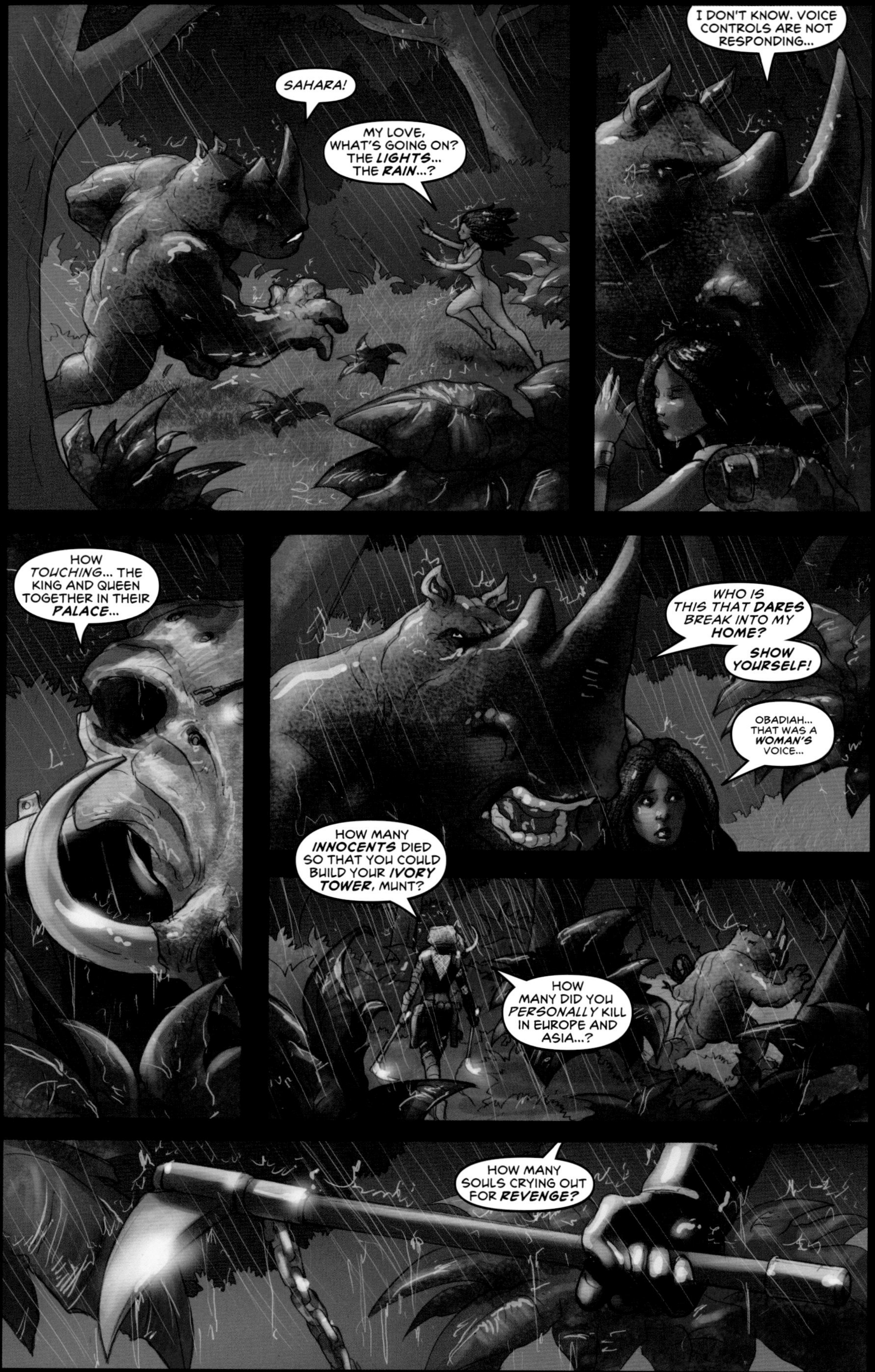
SAHARA!
MY LOVE, WHAT'S GOING ON? THE LIGHTS... THE RAIN...?
I DON'T KNOW. VOICE CONTROLS ARE NOT RESPONDING...
HOW TOUCHING... THE KING AND QUEEN TOGETHER IN THEIR PALACE...
WHO IS THIS THAT DARES BREAK INTO MY HOME?
SHOW YOURSELF!
OBADIAH... THAT WAS A WOMAN'S VOICE...
HOW MANY INNOCENTS DIED SO THAT YOU COULD BUILD YOUR IVORY TOWER, MUNT?
HOW MANY DID YOU PERSONALLY KILL IN EUROPE AND ASIA...?
HOW MANY SOULS CRYING OUT FOR REVENGE?

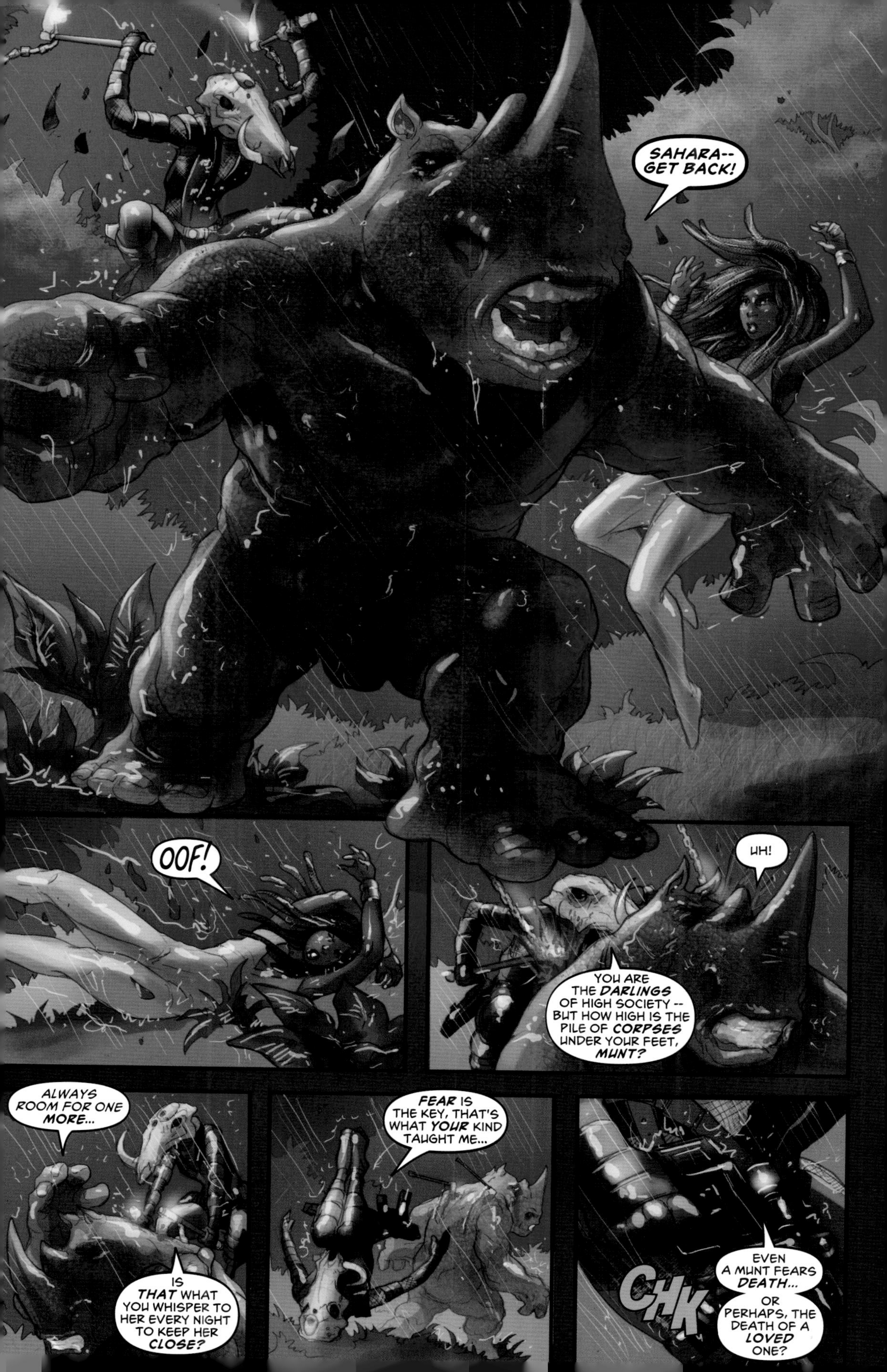
SAHARA-- GET BACK!
OOF!
UH!
YOU ARE THE DARLINGS OF HIGH SOCIETY -- BUT HOW HIGH IS THE PILE OF CORPSES UNDER YOUR FEET, MUNT?
ALWAYS ROOM FOR ONE MORE...
IS THAT WHAT YOU WHISPER TO HER EVERY NIGHT TO KEEP HER CLOSE?
FEAR IS THE KEY, THAT'S WHAT YOUR KIND TAUGHT ME...
CHK
EVEN A MUNT FEARS DEATH...
OR PERHAPS, THE DEATH OF A LOVED ONE?

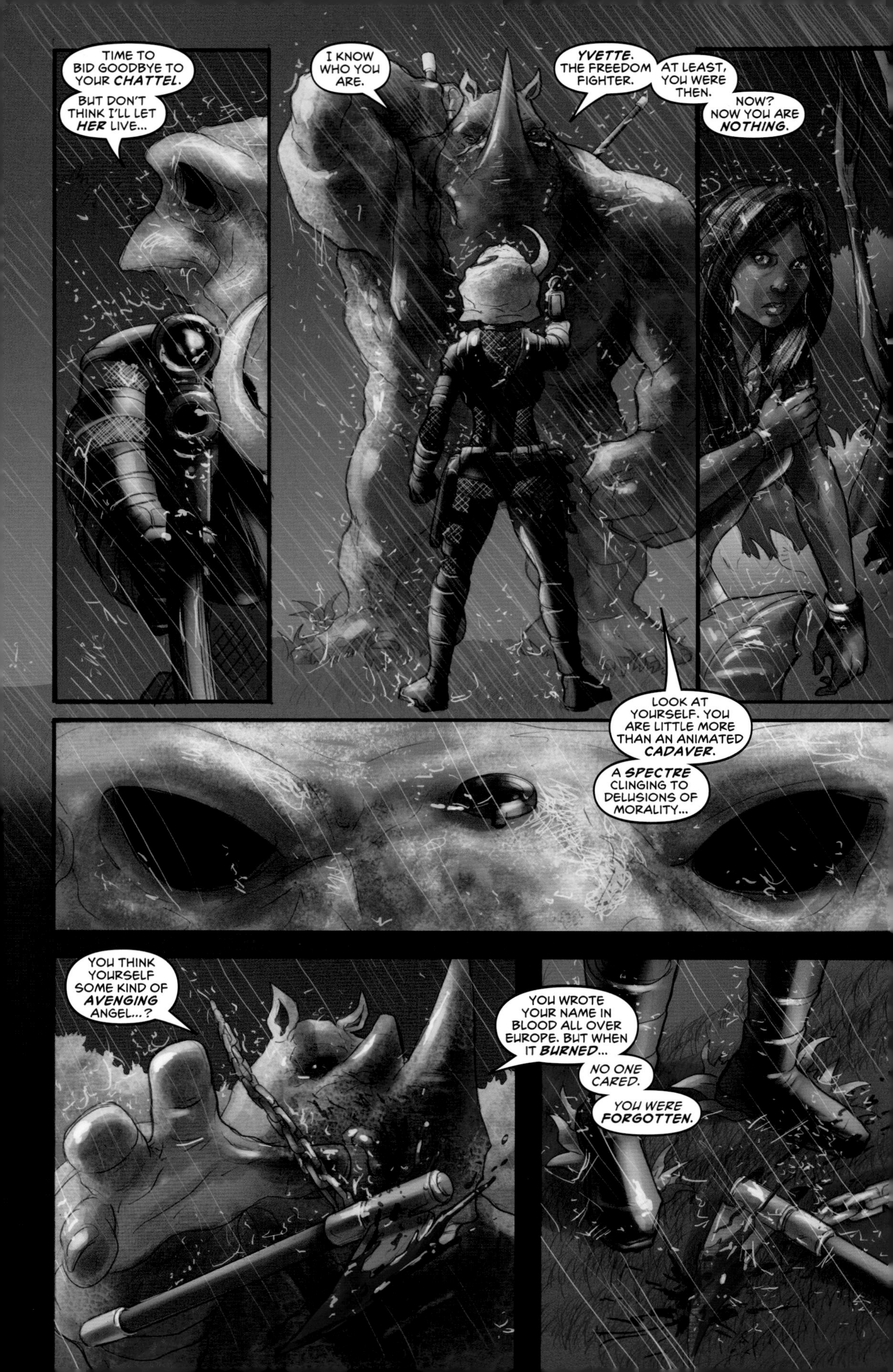
TIME TO BID GOODBYE TO YOUR CHATTEL.
BUT DON'T THINK I'LL LET HER LIVE...
I KNOW WHO YOU ARE.
YVETTE. THE FREEDOM FIGHTER.
AT LEAST, YOU WERE THEN.
NOW? NOW YOU ARE NOTHING.
LOOK AT YOURSELF. YOU ARE LITTLE MORE THAN AN ANIMATED CADAVER.
A SPECTRE CLINGING TO DELUSIONS OF MORALITY...
YOU THINK YOURSELF SOME KIND OF AVENGING ANGEL...?
YOU WROTE YOUR NAME IN BLOOD ALL OVER EUROPE. BUT WHEN IT BURNED...
NO ONE CARED.
YOU WERE FORGOTTEN.

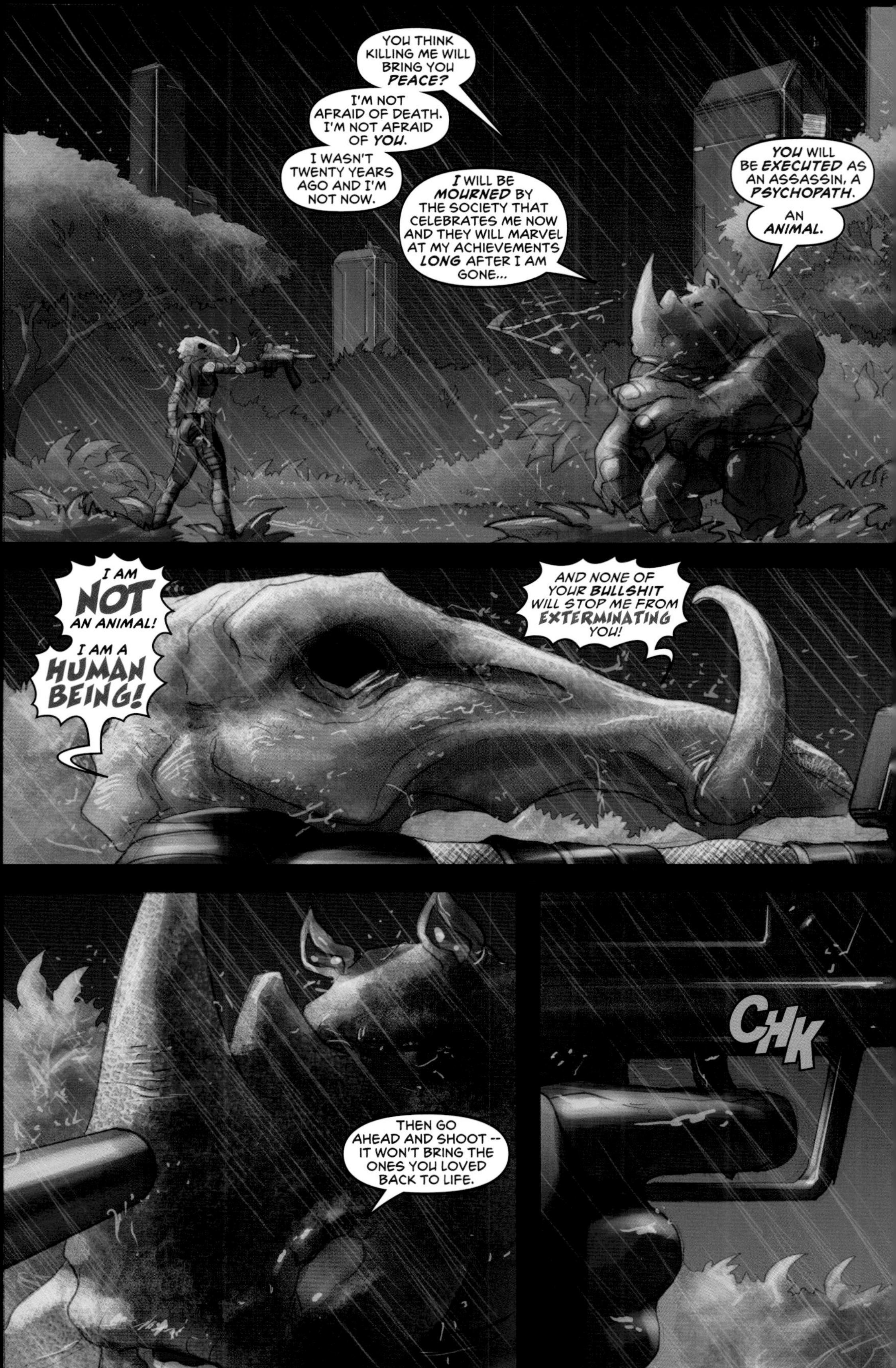
YOU THINK KILLING ME WILL BRING YOU *PEACE?*
I'M NOT AFRAID OF DEATH. I'M NOT AFRAID OF *YOU*.
I WASN'T TWENTY YEARS AGO AND I'M NOT NOW.
I WILL BE *MOURNED* BY THE SOCIETY THAT CELEBRATES ME NOW AND THEY WILL MARVEL AT MY ACHIEVEMENTS *LONG* AFTER I AM GONE...
YOU WILL BE *EXECUTED* AS AN ASSASSIN, A *PSYCHOPATH*.
AN *ANIMAL*.
I AM *NOT* AN ANIMAL!
I AM A *HUMAN BEING!*
AND NONE OF YOUR *BULLSHIT* WILL STOP ME FROM *EXTERMINATING* YOU!
THEN GO AHEAD AND SHOOT -- IT WON'T BRING THE ONES YOU LOVED BACK TO LIFE.
CHK

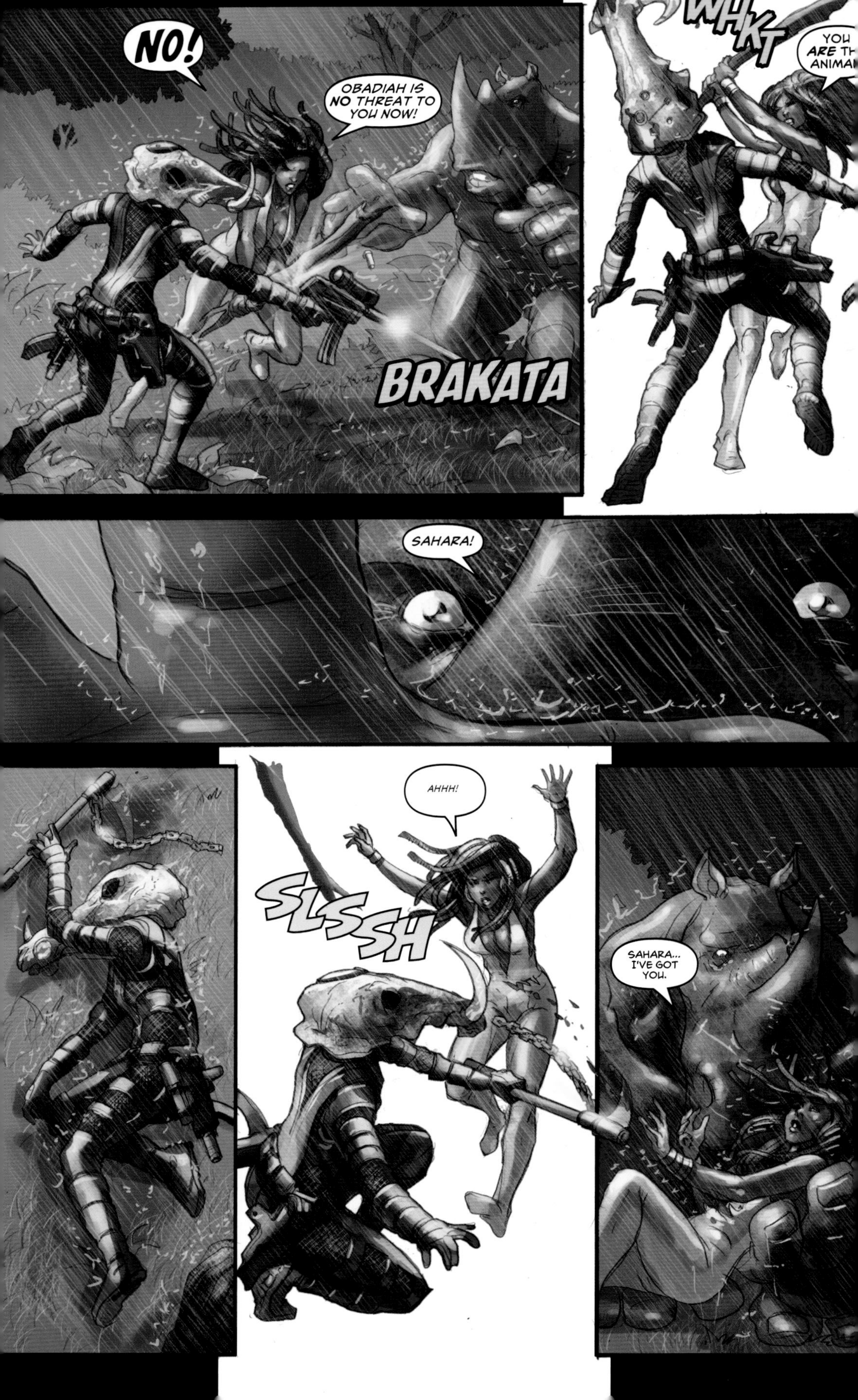
NO!
OBADIAH IS NO THREAT TO YOU NOW!
BRAKATA
WHKT
YOU ARE TH ANIMA
SAHARA!
AHHH!
SLSSH
SAHARA... I'VE GOT YOU.

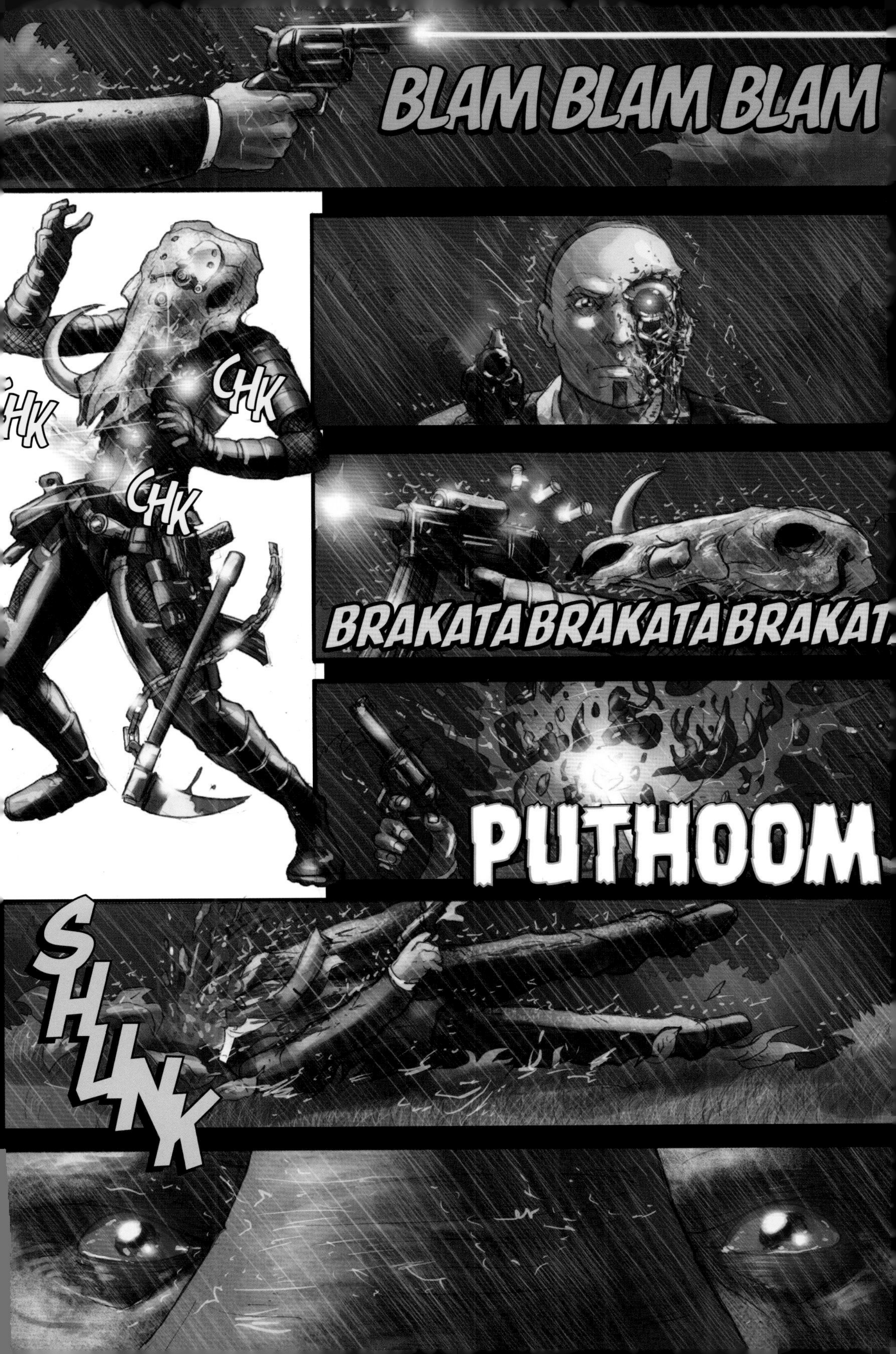
BLAM BLAM BLAM
CHK
CHK
CHK
BRAKATA BRAKATA BRAKAT
PUTHOOM
SHUNK

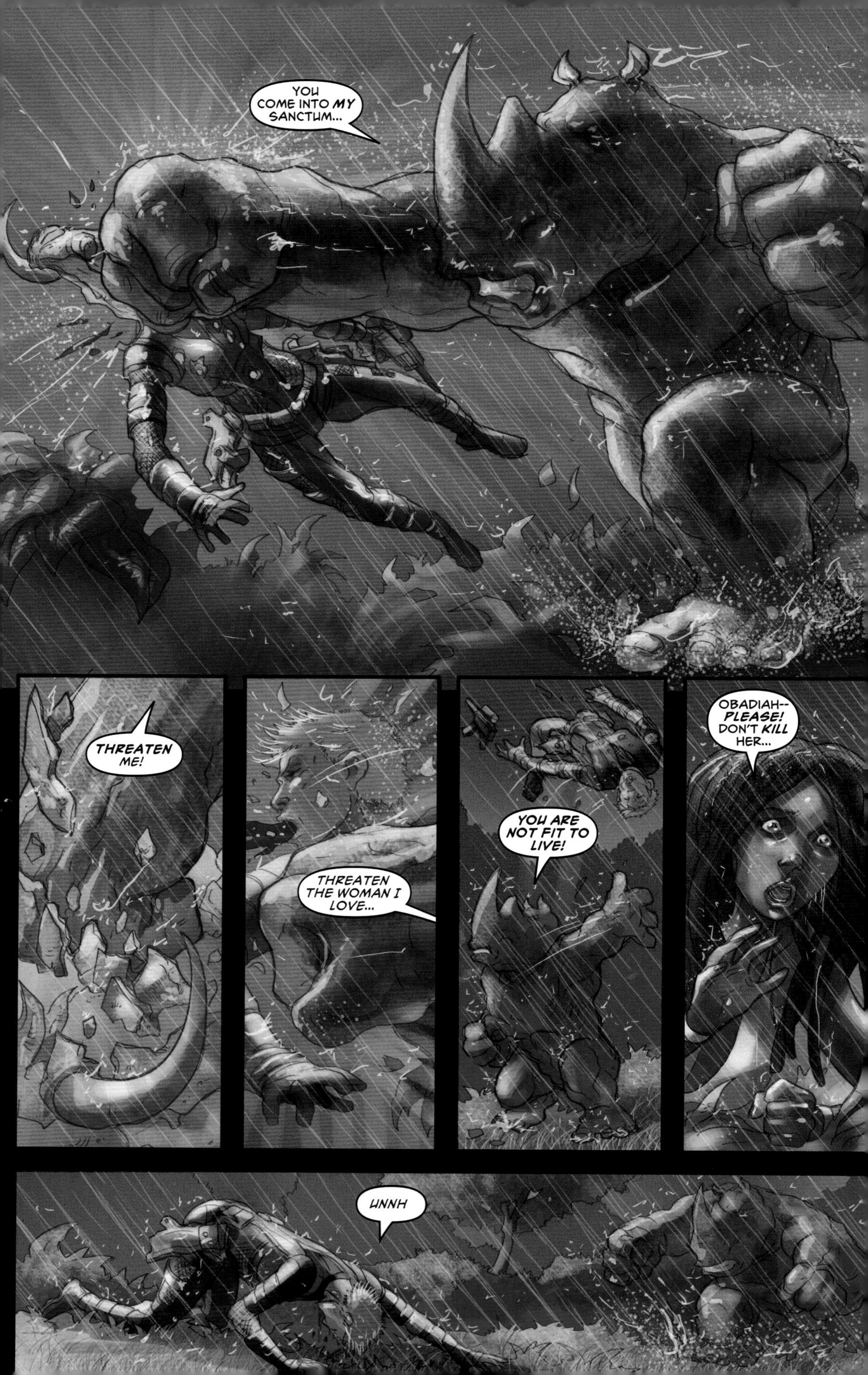
YOU COME INTO MY SANCTUM...
THREATEN ME!
THREATEN THE WOMAN I LOVE...
YOU ARE NOT FIT TO LIVE!
OBADIAH-- PLEASE! DON'T KILL HER...
UNNH

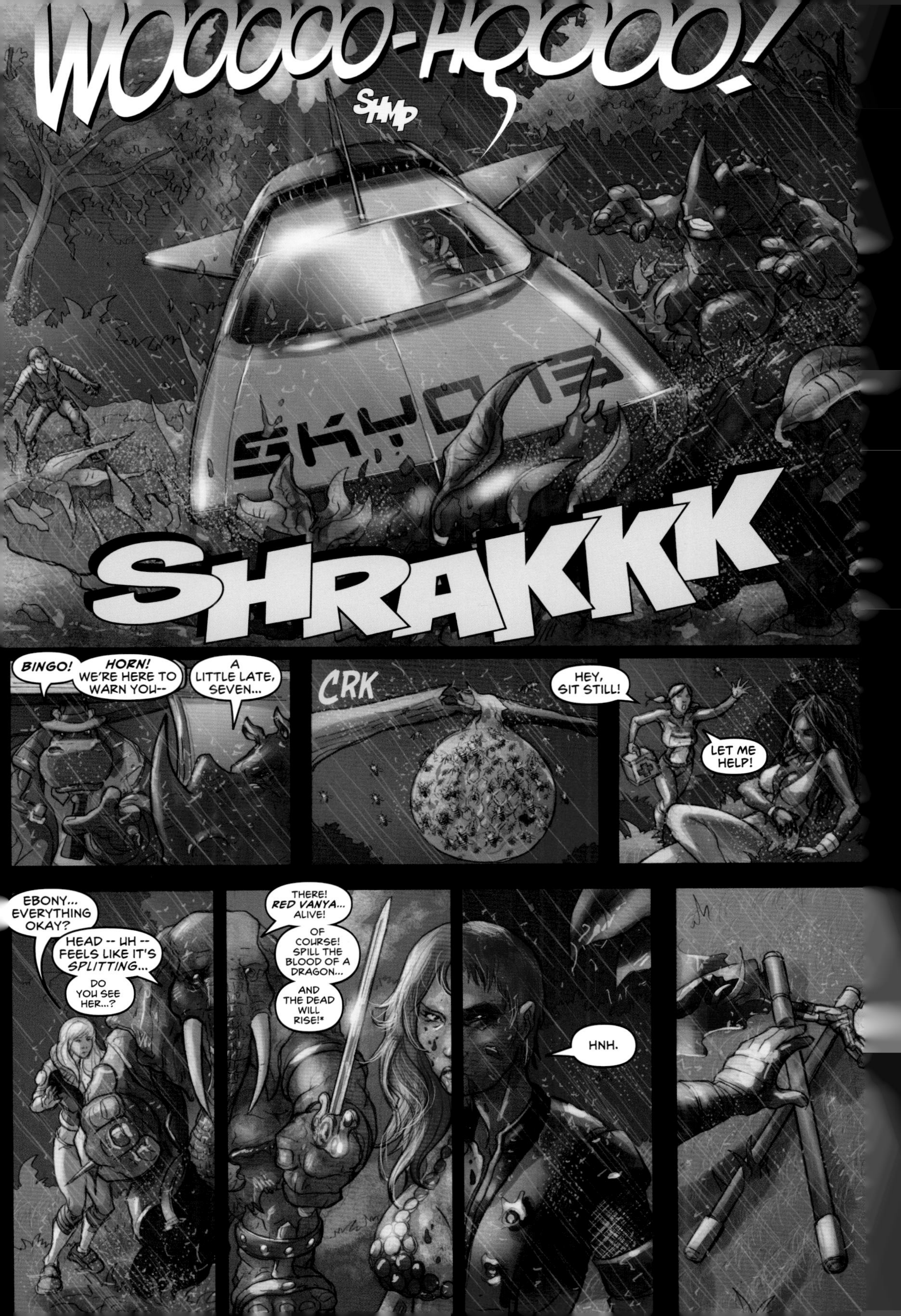
WOOOOO-HOOOOO!
SHMP
SKYO 13
SHRAKKK
BINGO!
HORN! WE'RE HERE TO WARN YOU--
A LITTLE LATE, SEVEN...
CRK
HEY, SIT STILL!
LET ME HELP!
EBONY... EVERYTHING OKAY?
HEAD -- UH -- FEELS LIKE IT'S SPLITTING...
DO YOU SEE HER...?
THERE! RED VANYA... ALIVE!
OF COURSE! SPILL THE BLOOD OF A DRAGON...
AND THE DEAD WILL RISE!*
HNH.

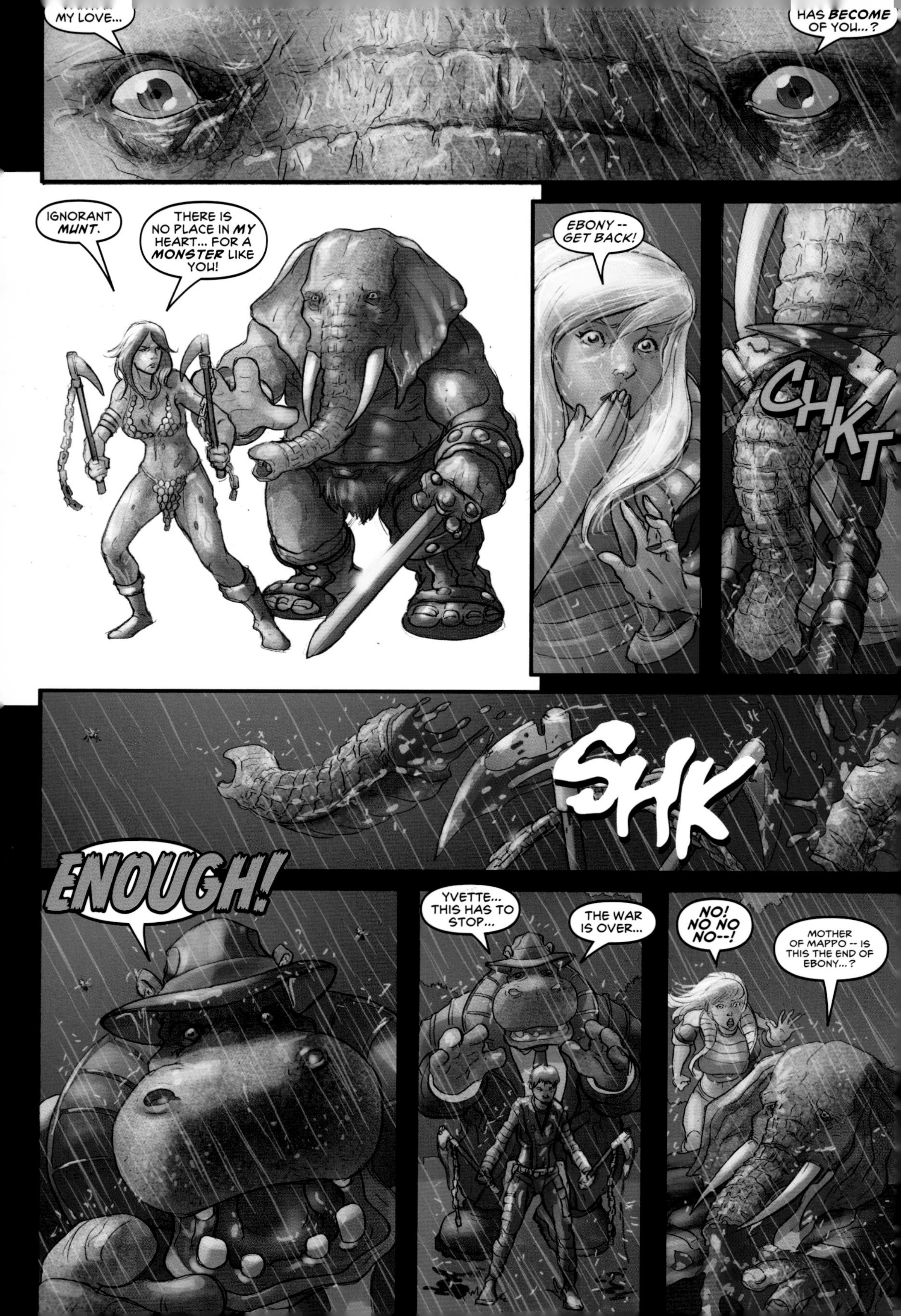
MY LOVE...
HAS BECOME OF YOU...?
IGNORANT MUNT.
THERE IS NO PLACE IN MY HEART... FOR A MONSTER LIKE YOU!
EBONY -- GET BACK!
CHKT
SHK
ENOUGH!
YVETTE... THIS HAS TO STOP...
THE WAR IS OVER...
NO! NO NO NO--!
MOTHER OF MAPPO -- IS THIS THE END OF EBONY...?

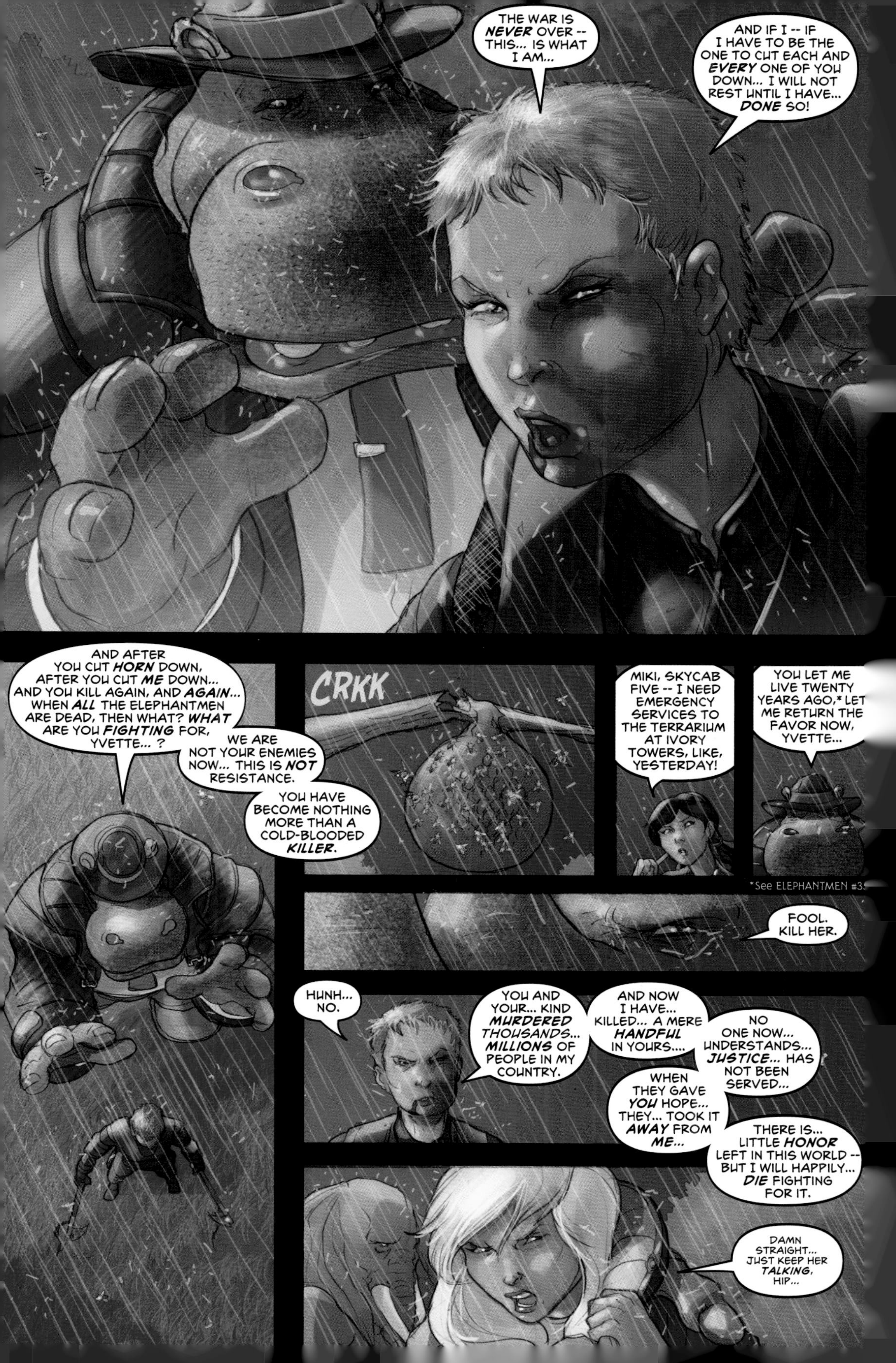
THE WAR IS NEVER OVER -- THIS... IS WHAT I AM...
AND IF I -- IF I HAVE TO BE THE ONE TO CUT EACH AND EVERY ONE OF YOU DOWN... I WILL NOT REST UNTIL I HAVE... DONE SO!
AND AFTER YOU CUT HORN DOWN, AFTER YOU CUT ME DOWN... AND YOU KILL AGAIN, AND AGAIN... WHEN ALL THE ELEPHANTMEN ARE DEAD, THEN WHAT? WHAT ARE YOU FIGHTING FOR, YVETTE... ?
WE ARE NOT YOUR ENEMIES NOW... THIS IS NOT RESISTANCE.
YOU HAVE BECOME NOTHING MORE THAN A COLD-BLOODED KILLER.
CRKK
MIKI, SKYCAB FIVE -- I NEED EMERGENCY SERVICES TO THE TERRARIUM AT IVORY TOWERS, LIKE, YESTERDAY!
YOU LET ME LIVE TWENTY YEARS AGO,* LET ME RETURN THE FAVOR NOW, YVETTE...
*See ELEPHANTMEN #3
FOOL. KILL HER.
HUNH... NO.
YOU AND YOUR... KIND MURDERED THOUSANDS... MILLIONS OF PEOPLE IN MY COUNTRY.
AND NOW I HAVE... KILLED... A MERE HANDFUL IN YOURS....
NO ONE NOW... UNDERSTANDS... JUSTICE... HAS NOT BEEN SERVED...
WHEN THEY GAVE YOU HOPE... THEY... TOOK IT AWAY FROM ME...
THERE IS... LITTLE HONOR LEFT IN THIS WORLD -- BUT I WILL HAPPILY... DIE FIGHTING FOR IT.
DAMN STRAIGHT... JUST KEEP HER TALKING, HIP...

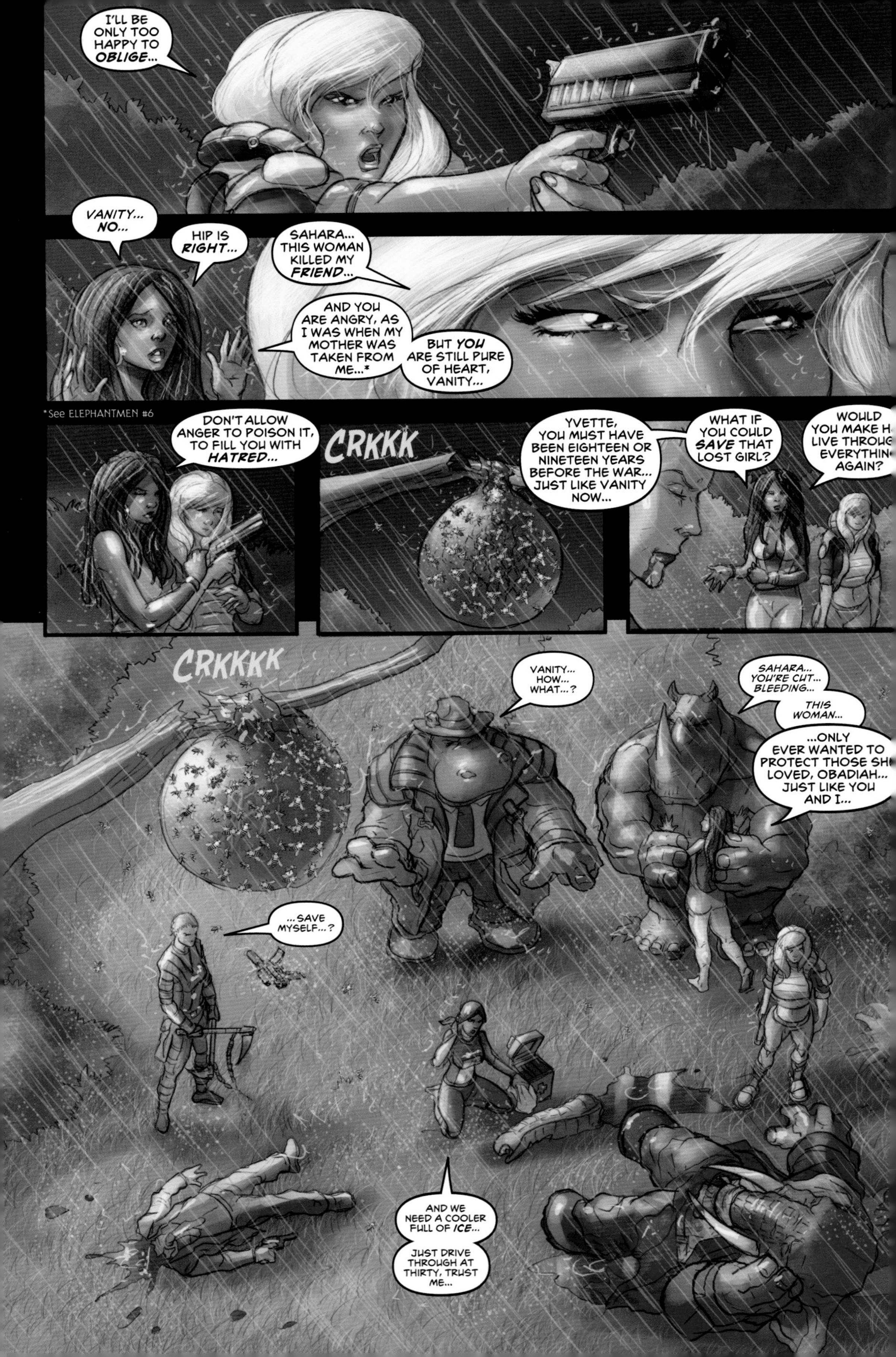
I'LL BE ONLY TOO HAPPY TO OBLIGE...
VANITY... NO...
HIP IS RIGHT...
SAHARA... THIS WOMAN KILLED MY FRIEND...
AND YOU ARE ANGRY, AS I WAS WHEN MY MOTHER WAS TAKEN FROM ME...*
BUT YOU ARE STILL PURE OF HEART, VANITY...
DON'T ALLOW ANGER TO POISON IT, TO FILL YOU WITH HATRED...
CRKKK
YVETTE, YOU MUST HAVE BEEN EIGHTEEN OR NINETEEN YEARS BEFORE THE WAR... JUST LIKE VANITY NOW...
WHAT IF YOU COULD SAVE THAT LOST GIRL?
WOULD YOU MAKE H LIVE THROUG EVERYTHIN AGAIN?
CRKKKK
VANITY... HOW... WHAT...?
SAHARA... YOU'RE CUT... BLEEDING...
THIS WOMAN...
...ONLY EVER WANTED TO PROTECT THOSE SH LOVED, OBADIAH... JUST LIKE YOU AND I...
...SAVE MYSELF...?
AND WE NEED A COOLER FULL OF ICE...
JUST DRIVE THROUGH AT THIRTY, TRUST ME...

*See ELEPHANTMEN #6

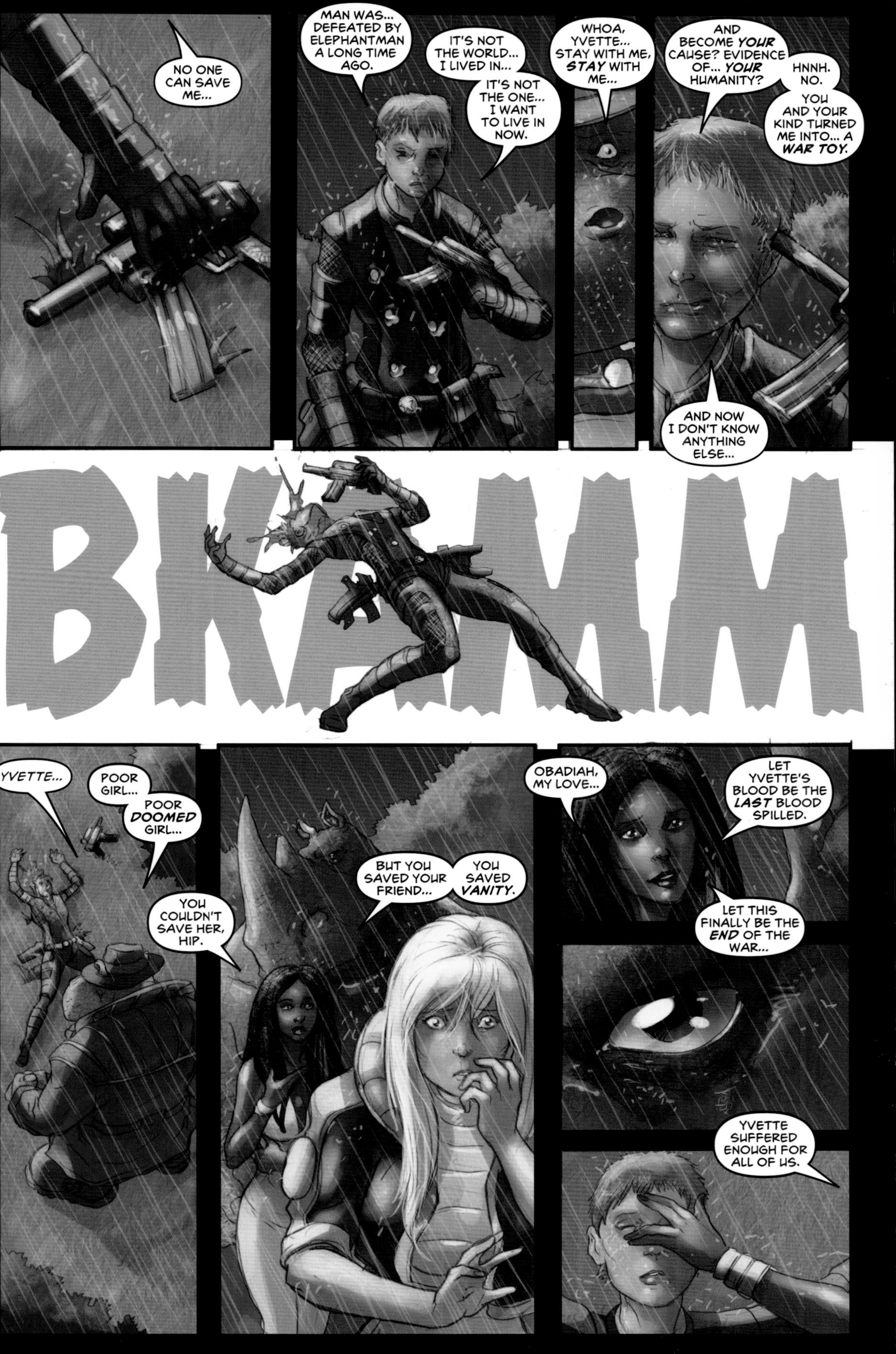
NO ONE CAN SAVE ME...
MAN WAS... DEFEATED BY ELEPHANTMAN A LONG TIME AGO.
IT'S NOT THE WORLD... I LIVED IN...
IT'S NOT THE ONE... I WANT TO LIVE IN NOW.
WHOA, YVETTE... STAY WITH ME, STAY WITH ME...
AND BECOME YOUR CAUSE? EVIDENCE OF... YOUR HUMANITY?
HNNH. NO.
YOU AND YOUR KIND TURNED ME INTO... A WAR TOY.
AND NOW I DON'T KNOW ANYTHING ELSE...
BKAMM
YVETTE...
POOR GIRL...
POOR DOOMED GIRL...
YOU COULDN'T SAVE HER, HIP.
BUT YOU SAVED YOUR FRIEND...
YOU SAVED VANITY.
OBADIAH, MY LOVE...
LET YVETTE'S BLOOD BE THE LAST BLOOD SPILLED.
LET THIS FINALLY BE THE END OF THE WAR...
YVETTE SUFFERED ENOUGH FOR ALL OF US.

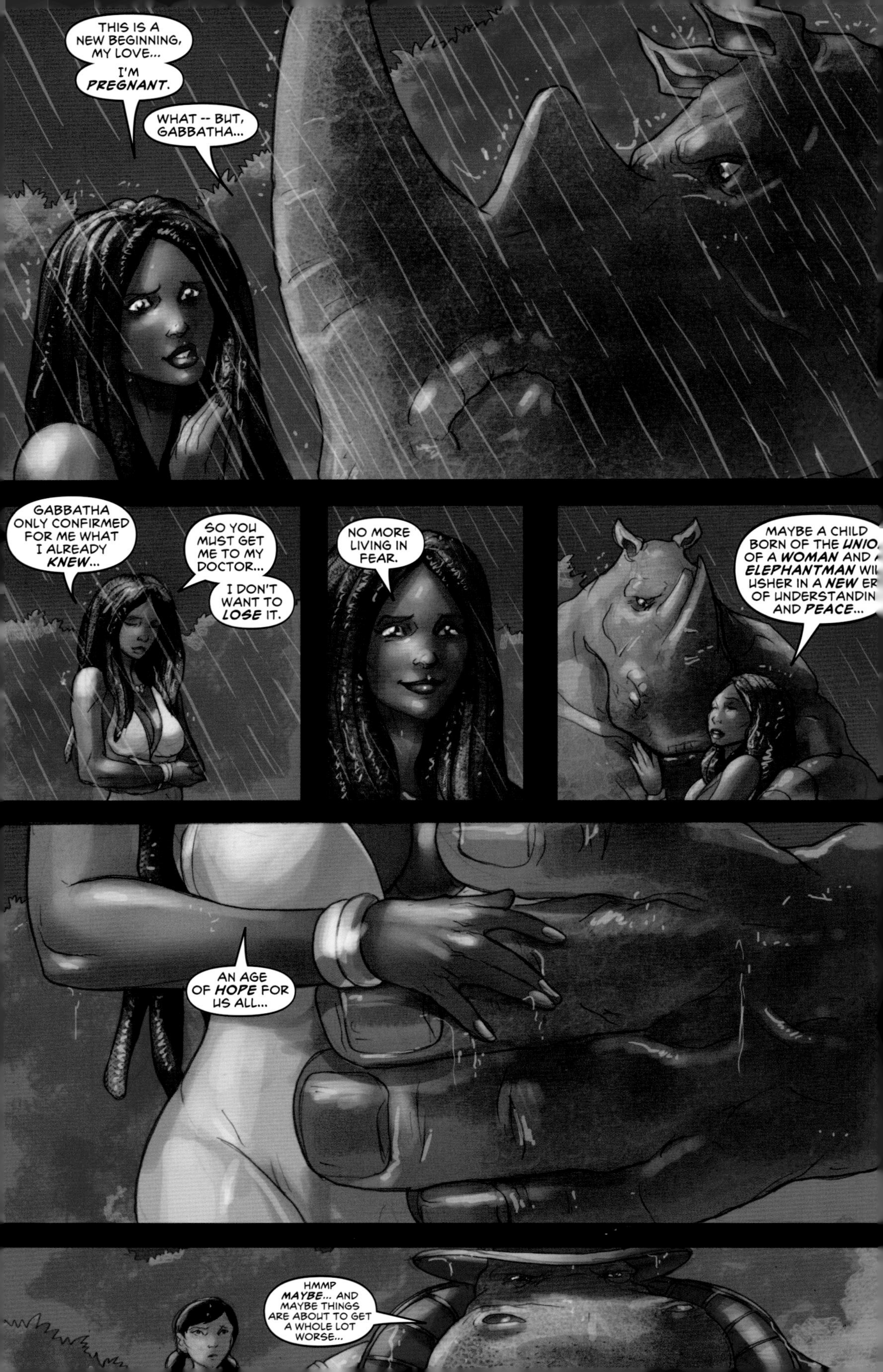

THIS IS A NEW BEGINNING, MY LOVE... I'M *PREGNANT*.
WHAT -- BUT, GABBATHA...
GABBATHA ONLY CONFIRMED FOR ME WHAT I ALREADY *KNEW*...
SO YOU MUST GET ME TO MY DOCTOR...
I DON'T WANT TO *LOSE* IT.
NO MORE LIVING IN FEAR.
MAYBE A CHILD BORN OF THE *UNIO* OF A *WOMAN* AND *ELEPHANTMAN* WI USHER IN A *NEW* ER OF UNDERSTANDIN AND *PEACE*...
AN AGE OF *HOPE* FOR US ALL...
HMMP *MAYBE*... AND MAYBE THINGS ARE ABOUT TO GET A WHOLE LOT WORSE...

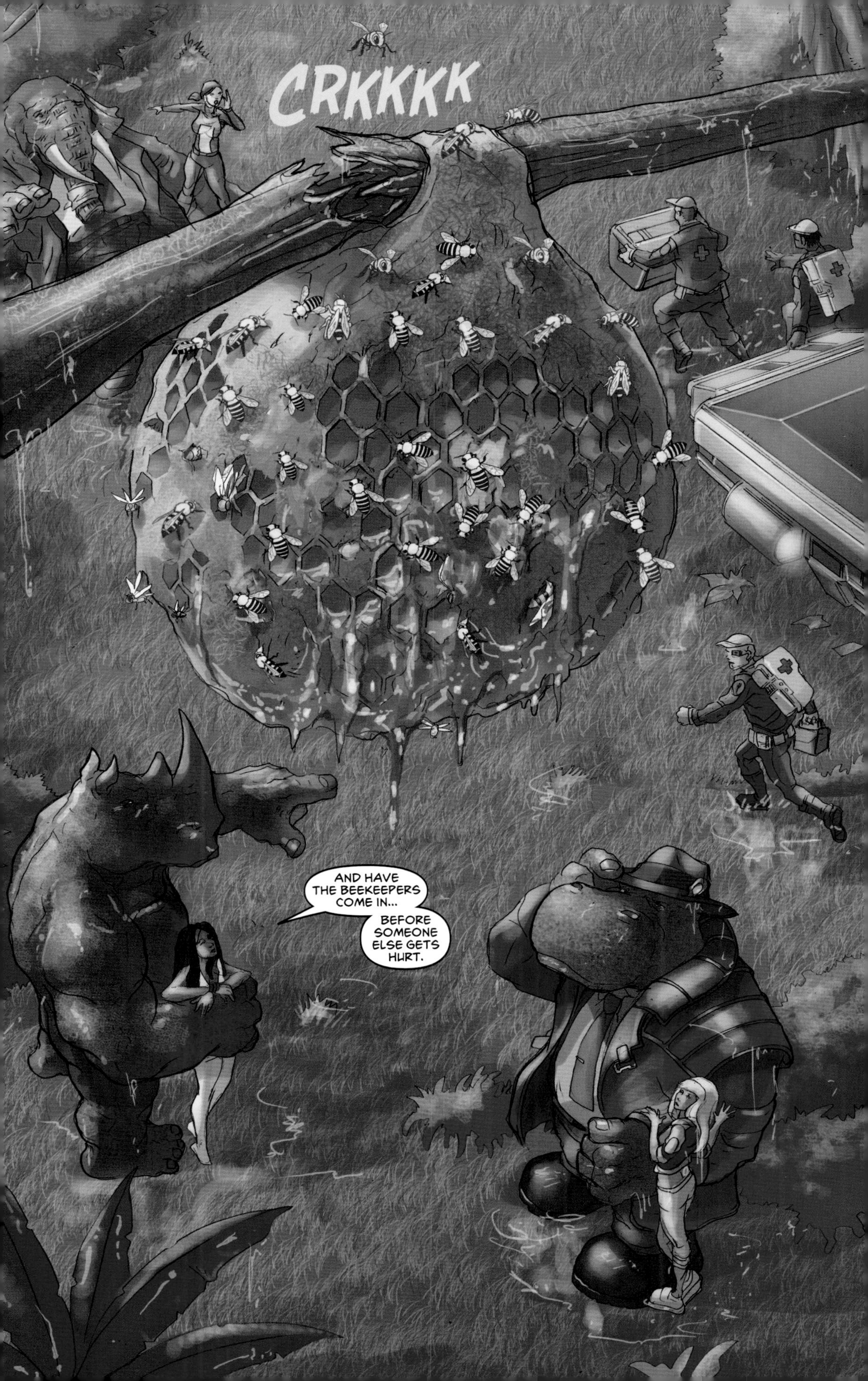
CRKKKK
AND HAVE THE BEEKEEPERS COME IN...
BEFORE SOMEONE ELSE GETS HURT.

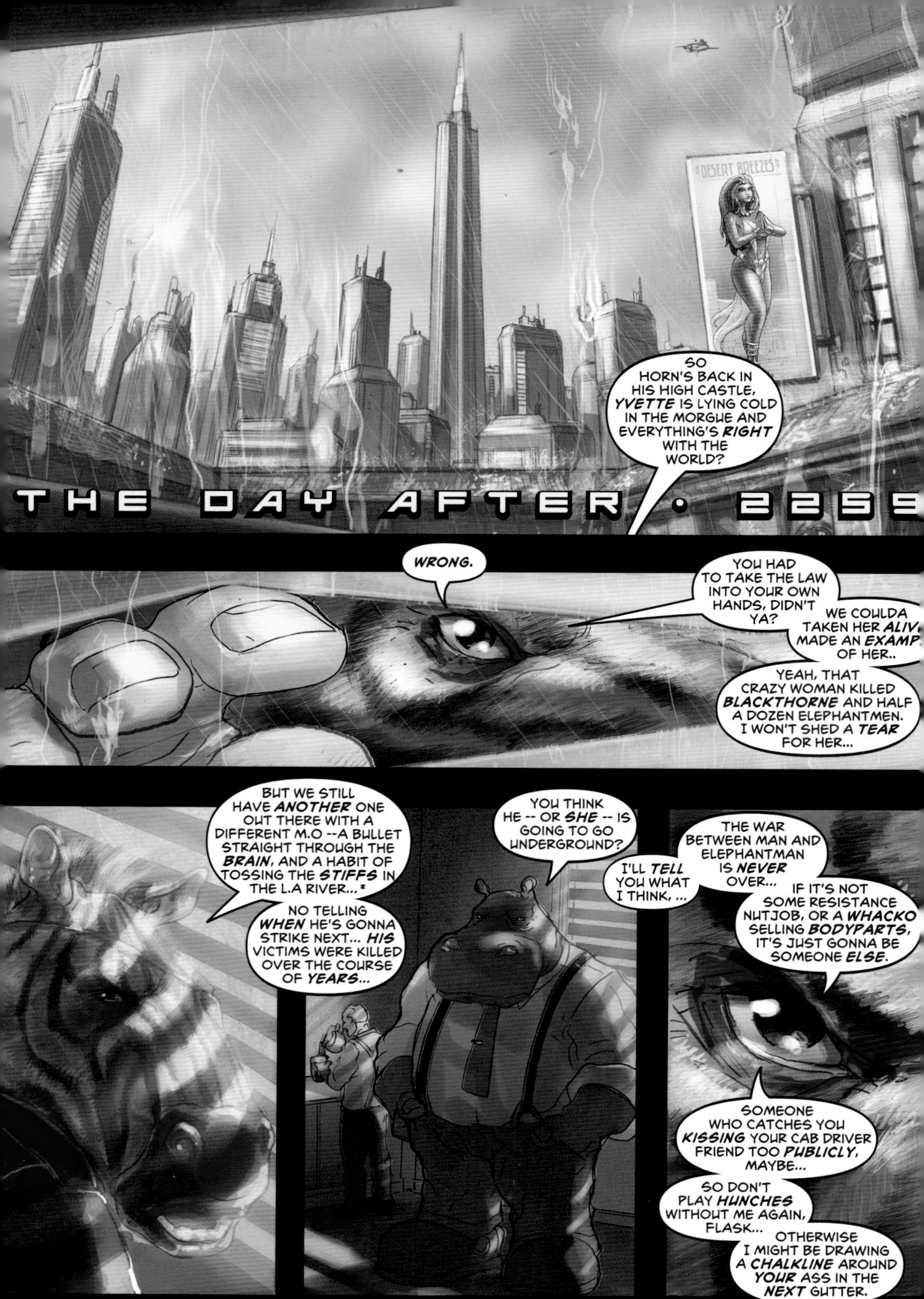
DESERT BREEZES
SO HORN'S BACK IN HIS HIGH CASTLE, YVETTE IS LYING COLD IN THE MORGUE AND EVERYTHING'S RIGHT WITH THE WORLD?
THE DAY AFTER • 2259
WRONG.
YOU HAD TO TAKE THE LAW INTO YOUR OWN HANDS, DIDN'T YA?
WE COULDA TAKEN HER ALIV MADE AN EXAMP OF HER..
YEAH, THAT CRAZY WOMAN KILLED BLACKTHORNE AND HALF A DOZEN ELEPHANTMEN. I WON'T SHED A TEAR FOR HER...
BUT WE STILL HAVE ANOTHER ONE OUT THERE WITH A DIFFERENT M.O --A BULLET STRAIGHT THROUGH THE BRAIN, AND A HABIT OF TOSSING THE STIFFS IN THE L.A RIVER...*
NO TELLING WHEN HE'S GONNA STRIKE NEXT... HIS VICTIMS WERE KILLED OVER THE COURSE OF YEARS...
YOU THINK HE -- OR SHE -- IS GOING TO GO UNDERGROUND?
I'LL TELL YOU WHAT I THINK, ...
THE WAR BETWEEN MAN AND ELEPHANTMAN IS NEVER OVER...
IF IT'S NOT SOME RESISTANCE NUTJOB, OR A WHACKO SELLING BODYPARTS, IT'S JUST GONNA BE SOMEONE ELSE.
SOMEONE WHO CATCHES YOU KISSING YOUR CAB DRIVER FRIEND TOO PUBLICLY, MAYBE...
SO DON'T PLAY HUNCHES WITHOUT ME AGAIN, FLASK...
OTHERWISE I MIGHT BE DRAWING A CHALKLINE AROUND YOUR ASS IN THE NEXT GUTTER.

*See ELEPHANTMEN #16 & 36

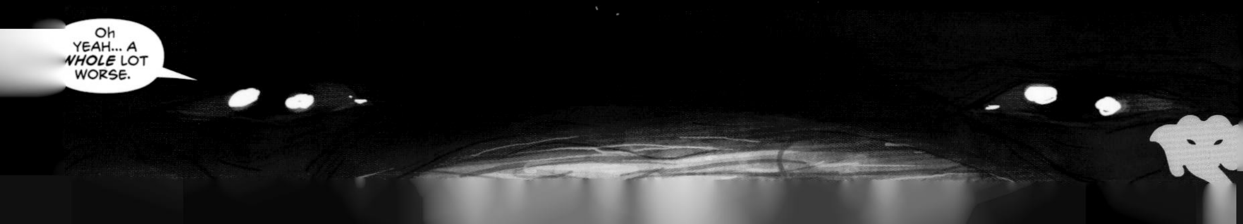
Oh YEAH... A WHOLE LOT WORSE.

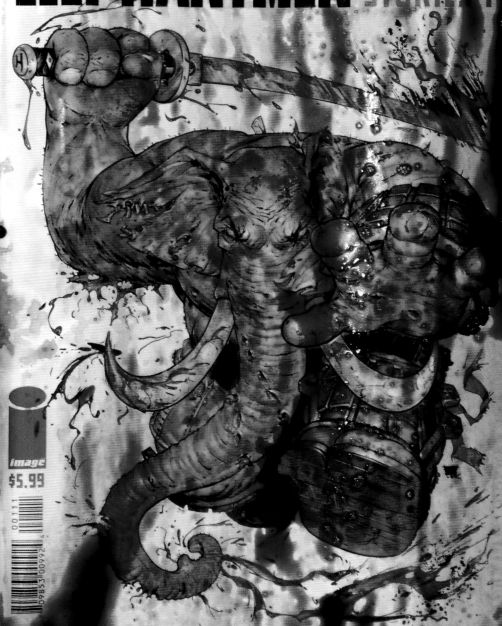

ELEPHANTMEN COVER STORIES

$5.99

image

LARROCA · BOO COOK · ROSHELL · STARKINGS

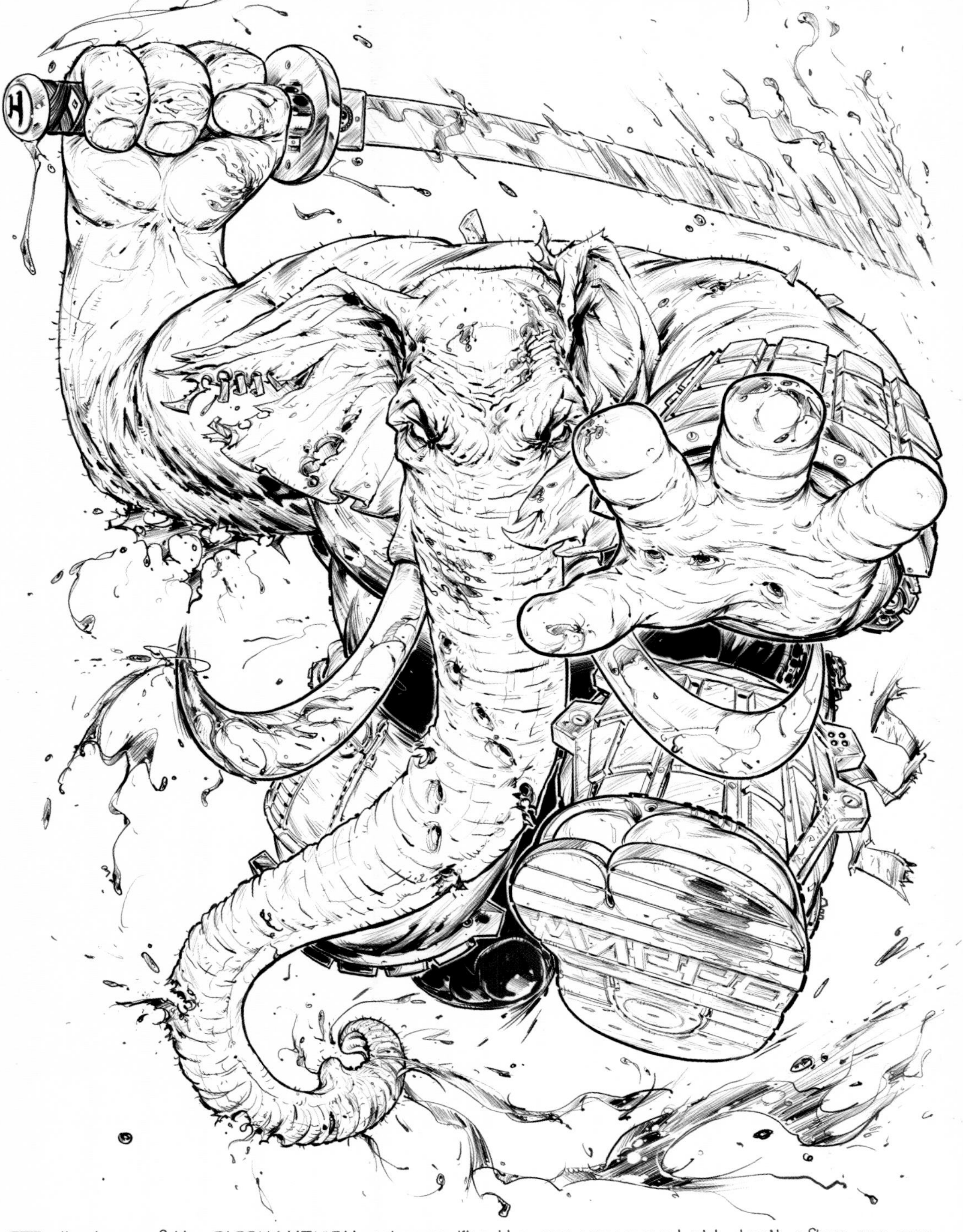

Collectors of the ELEPHANTMEN volumes, like the one you now hold, don't often see our covers as they were originally intended... thanks to the zealous efforts of Comicraft's Secret Weapon, John "JG" Roshell! His mission, which he always chooses to accept, has been to make every cover a part of the overall design of each package. JG has rubbed our covers with sandpaper, soaked them in water, floated them on oil, burnt them to a crisp, splashed blue goo on them and now, um, well, let's just say that no actual Elephantmen were hurt during the making of this edition! But for those of you who wanted to see the complete, unadulterated art, we've put together a collection of graphics-free covers and peeks-behind-the-scenes, some of which were featured in our COVER STORIES collection, and some that have never been seen before...

Ladrönn, Eisner award winner for HIP FLASK, created the first dozen covers for ELEPHANTMEN -- and you can find most of them in the hardcover edition of HIP FLASK: CONCRETE JUNGLE -- but as of #13 I realized I'd need a new artist... serendipiditiously, the following letter appeared in my emailbox...

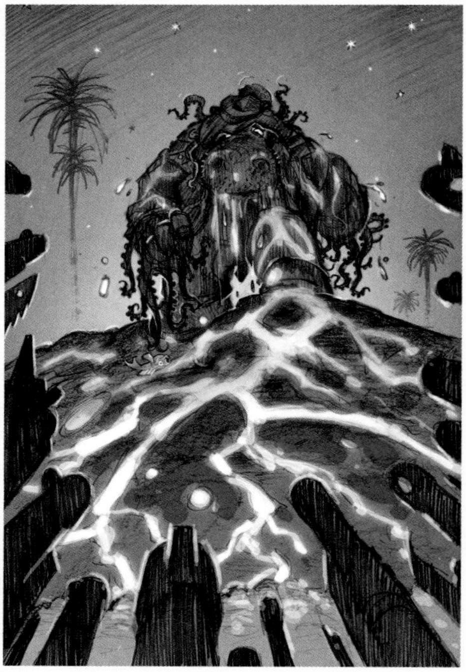

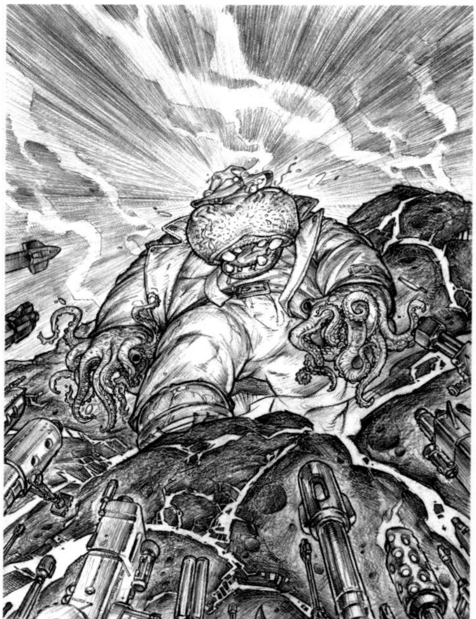

BOO COOK

2000 AD ARTIST SEEKING WORK...

HI RICHARD, THIS MIGHT NOT BE THE CORRECT AVENUE FOR SUCH THINGS SO I'LL KEEP IT SHORT AND SWEET : I'VE WORKED FOR 2000AD FOR 7 YEARS, DRAWING DREDD, A.B.C. WARRIORS, AND HARRY KIPLING TO MENTION A FEW - I LOVE HIPFLASK/ELEPHANTMEN , AND HAVING SEEN THE SUPERB MR. FLINT GET A SLOT IN THE MONTHLY, I BASICALLY JUST THOUGHT I'D SAY 'HELLO', AND IF YOU ARE EVER CONSIDERING ANY MORE GUEST SLOTS FROM OL' BLIGHTY I WOULD BE HONOURED IF YOU WOULD CONSIDER USING ME.

CHEERS FOR YOUR TIME!

BOO!

FEBRUARY 9, 2007
1:37:26 AM PST

BOO! Ye Gods...! I was just reading over 2000AD prog 1526, saw your DR & QUINCH piece and remembered your letter. Then I remembered that I FORGOT to reply to your letter!

Y'know, I was already familiar with your work, and have been keeping an eye on you... so was very happy you got in touch. Please forgive this tardy reply!

I actually created HIP FLASK and ELEPHANTMEN as the kind of strip I'd have created for 2000AD, if I'd had the chance. Look at it closely and you'll see elements of ROBO HUNTER, ABC WARRIORS, ROGUE TROOPER, JUDGE DREDD, STRONTIUM DOG and even HALO JONES. I'm not sure if you realize that I'm a Brit, by the way...

Here's the good news -- I'd LOVE a cover!

Cheers!

Rich!

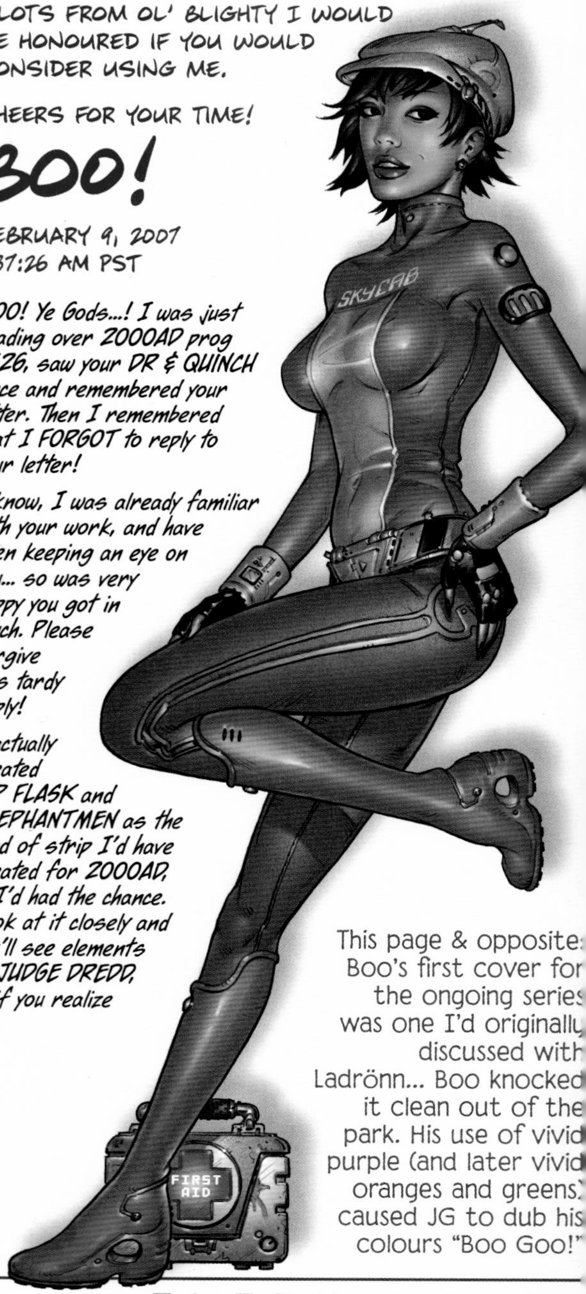

SKYCAB
FIRST AID

Right: Boo's Miki for the back cover of ELEPHANTMEN volume 1

This page & opposite: Boo's first cover for the ongoing series was one I'd originally discussed with Ladrönn... Boo knocked it clean out of the park. His use of vivid purple (and later vivid oranges and greens) caused JG to dub his colours "Boo Goo!"

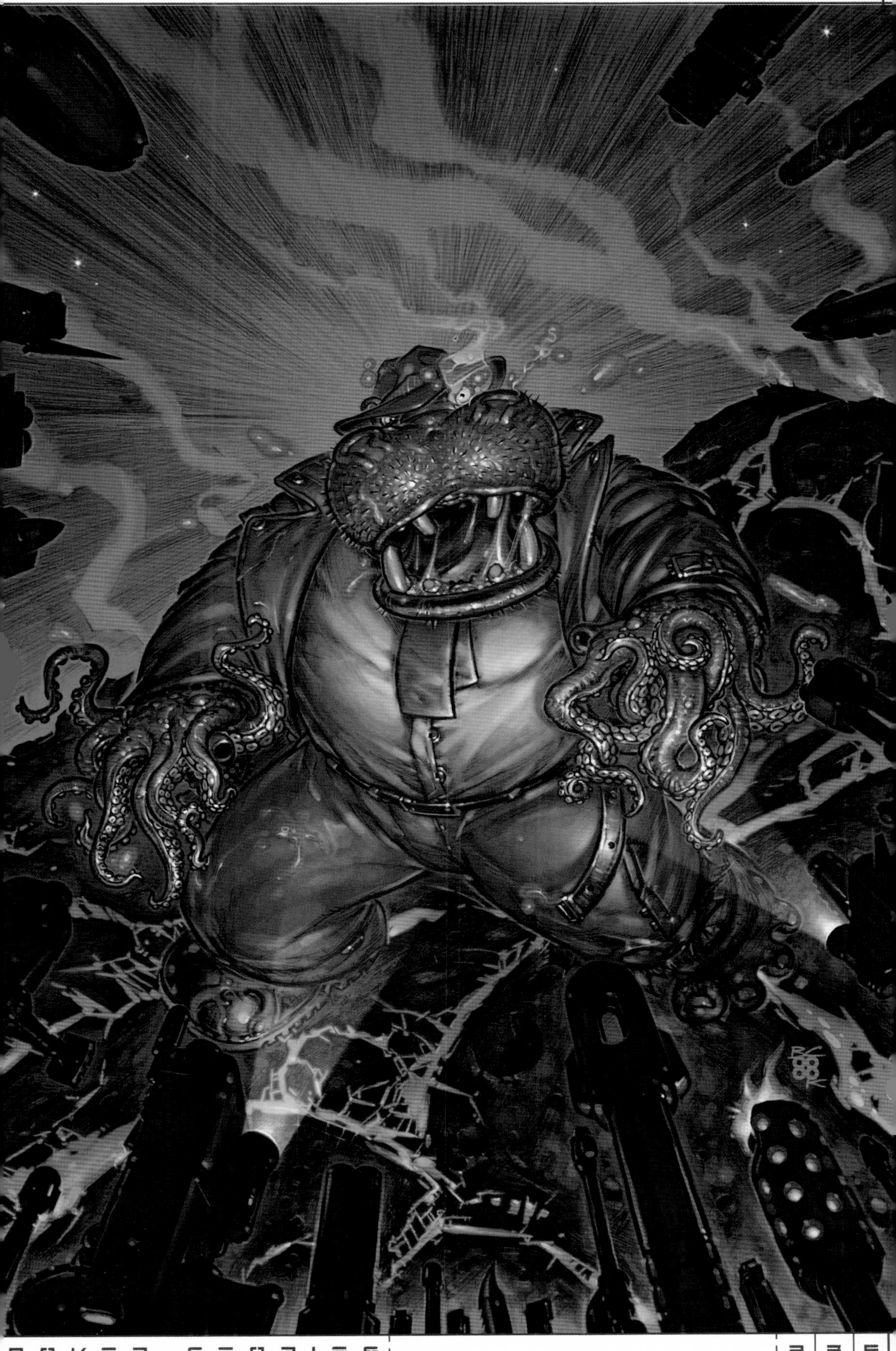

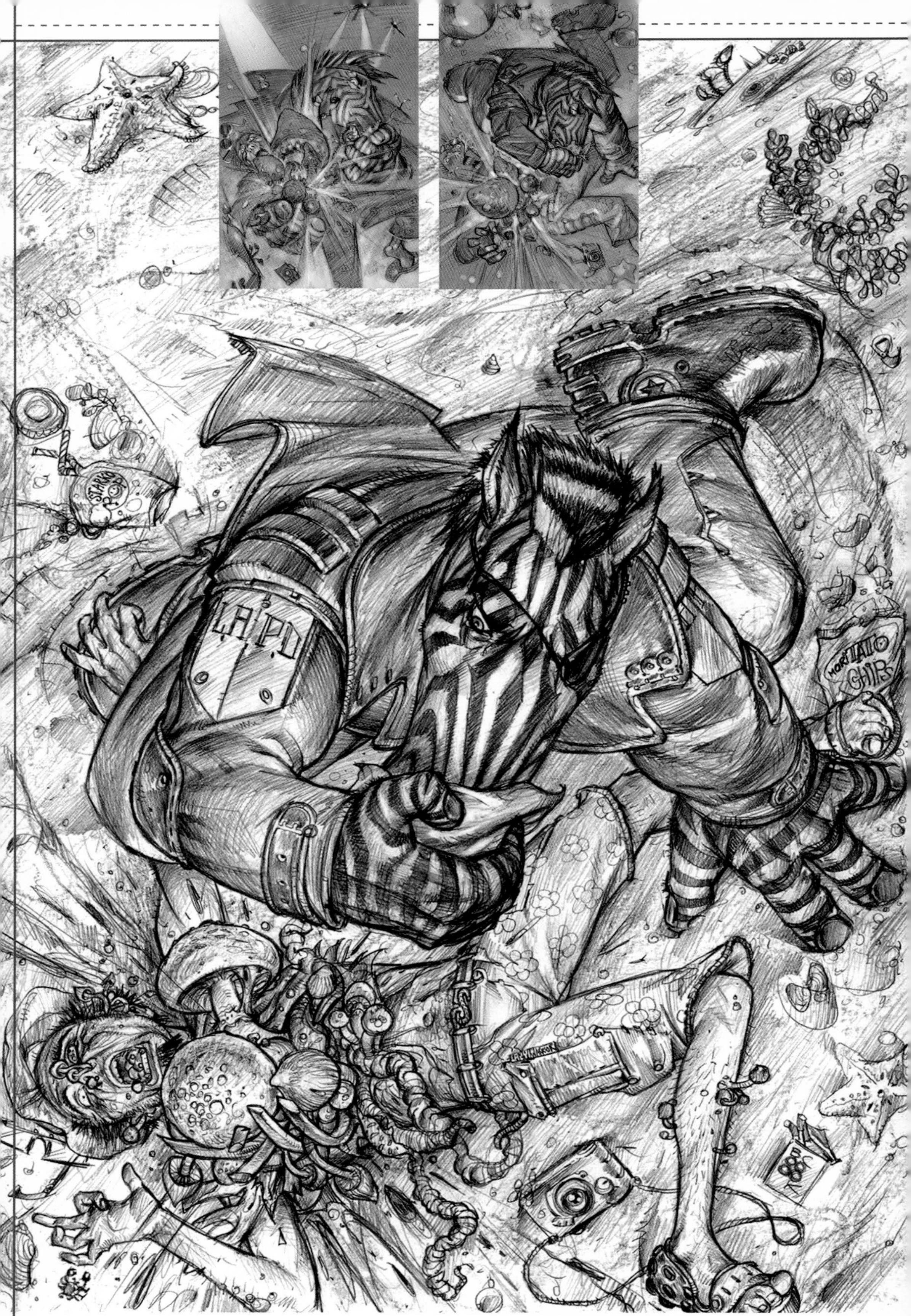
LAPD

Without doubt it was THIS cover, for ELEPHANTMEN #14, that made me realize I was barely scratching the surface of what Boo was capable. It encouraged me to scratch more! Poor Boo.

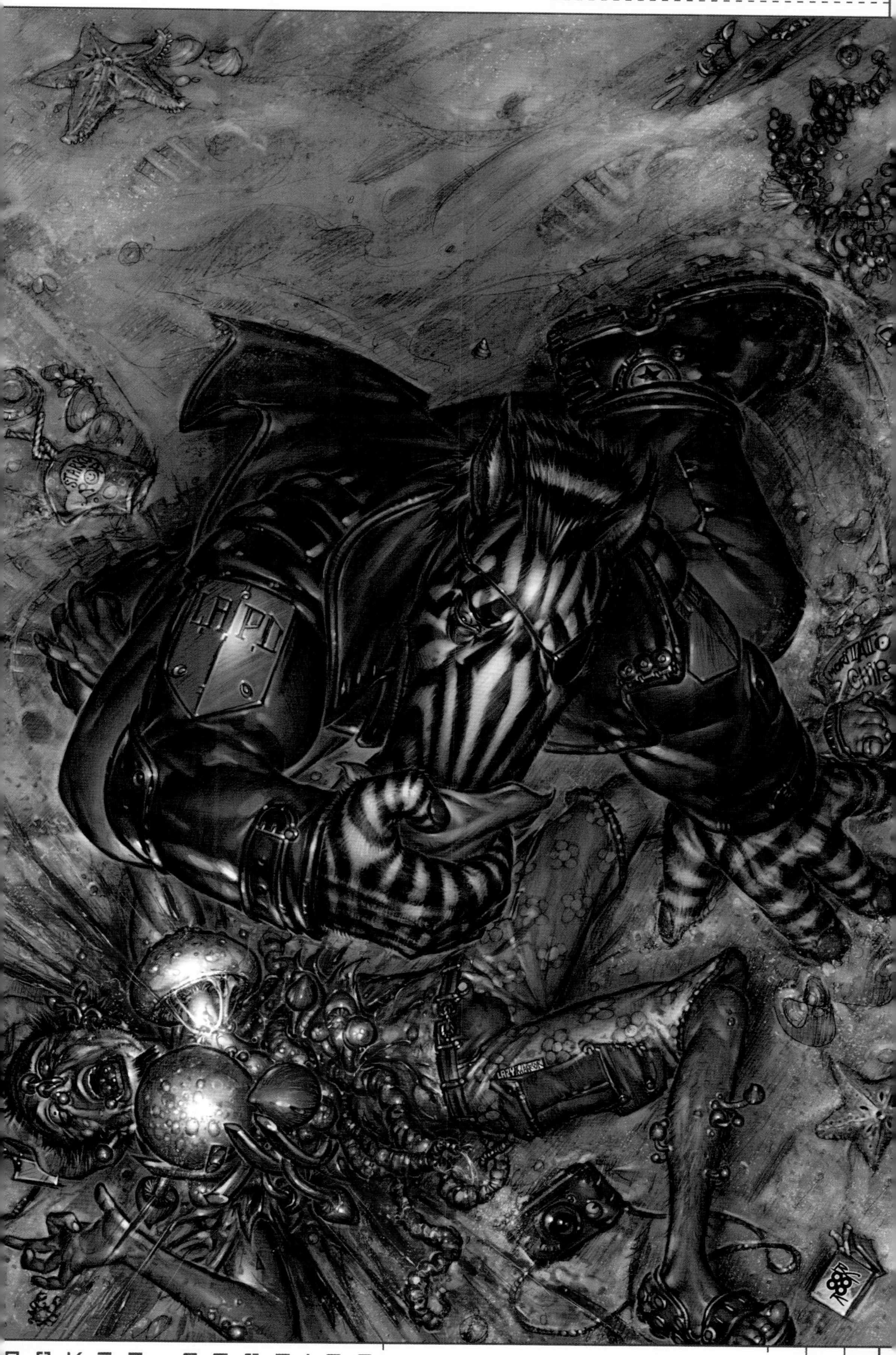
L.A.P.D.

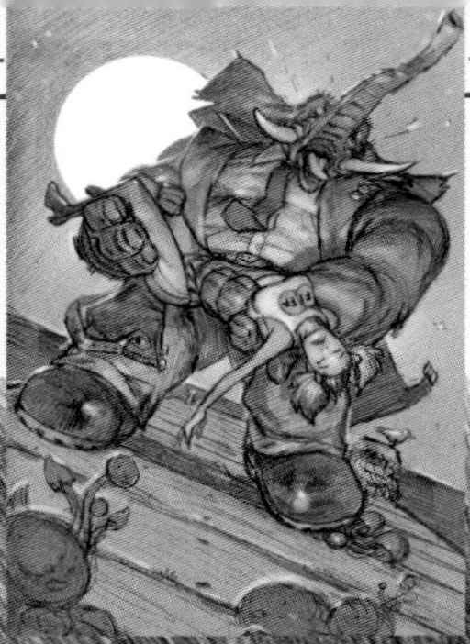

I've always loved the grieving hero cover, ever since Conan held the lifeless body of Bêlit in his arms on the cover of CONAN THE BARBARIAN #100... the fact that most covers like this feature characters who have actually died helped us mislead readers on this one. For now.

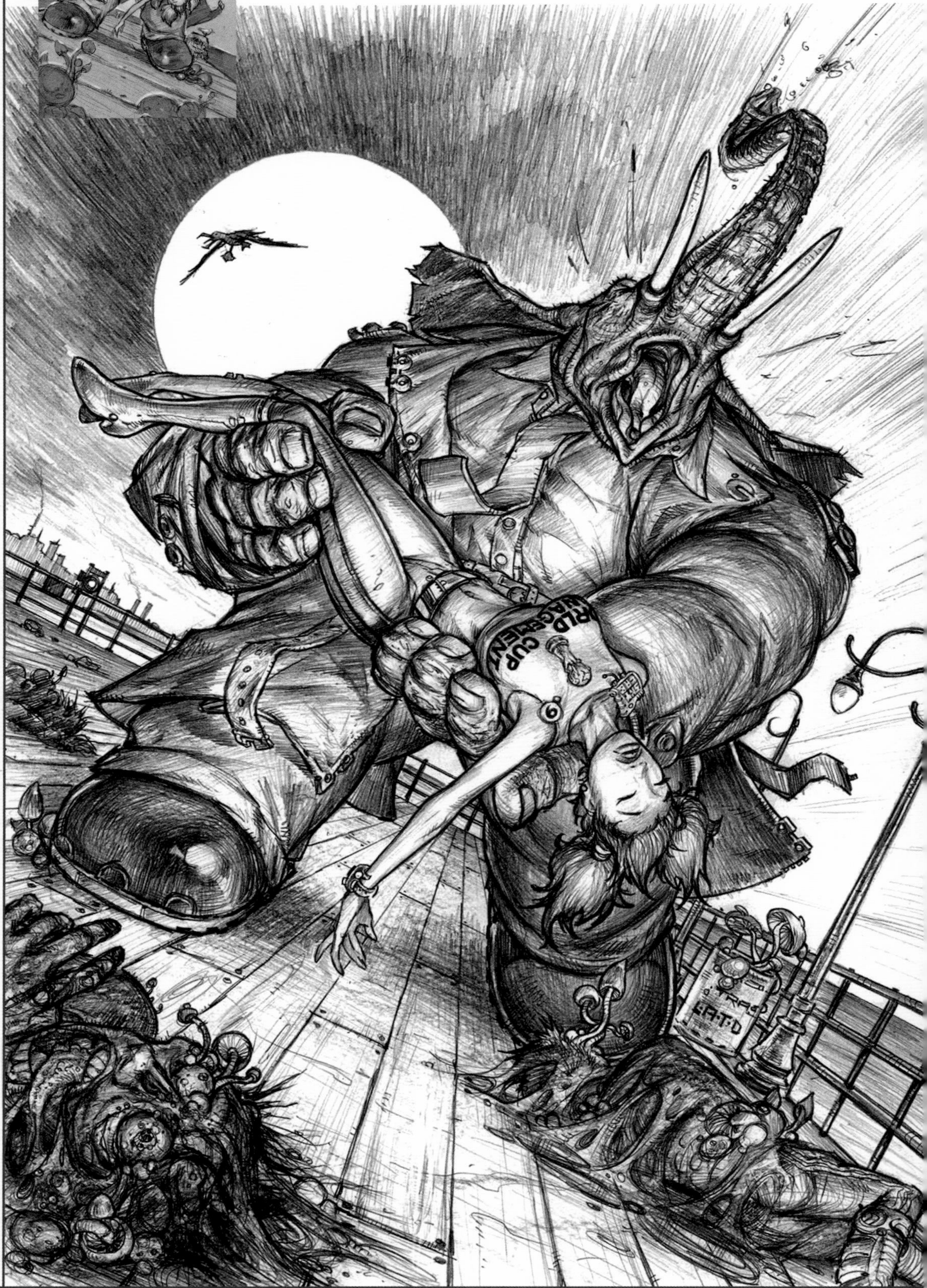

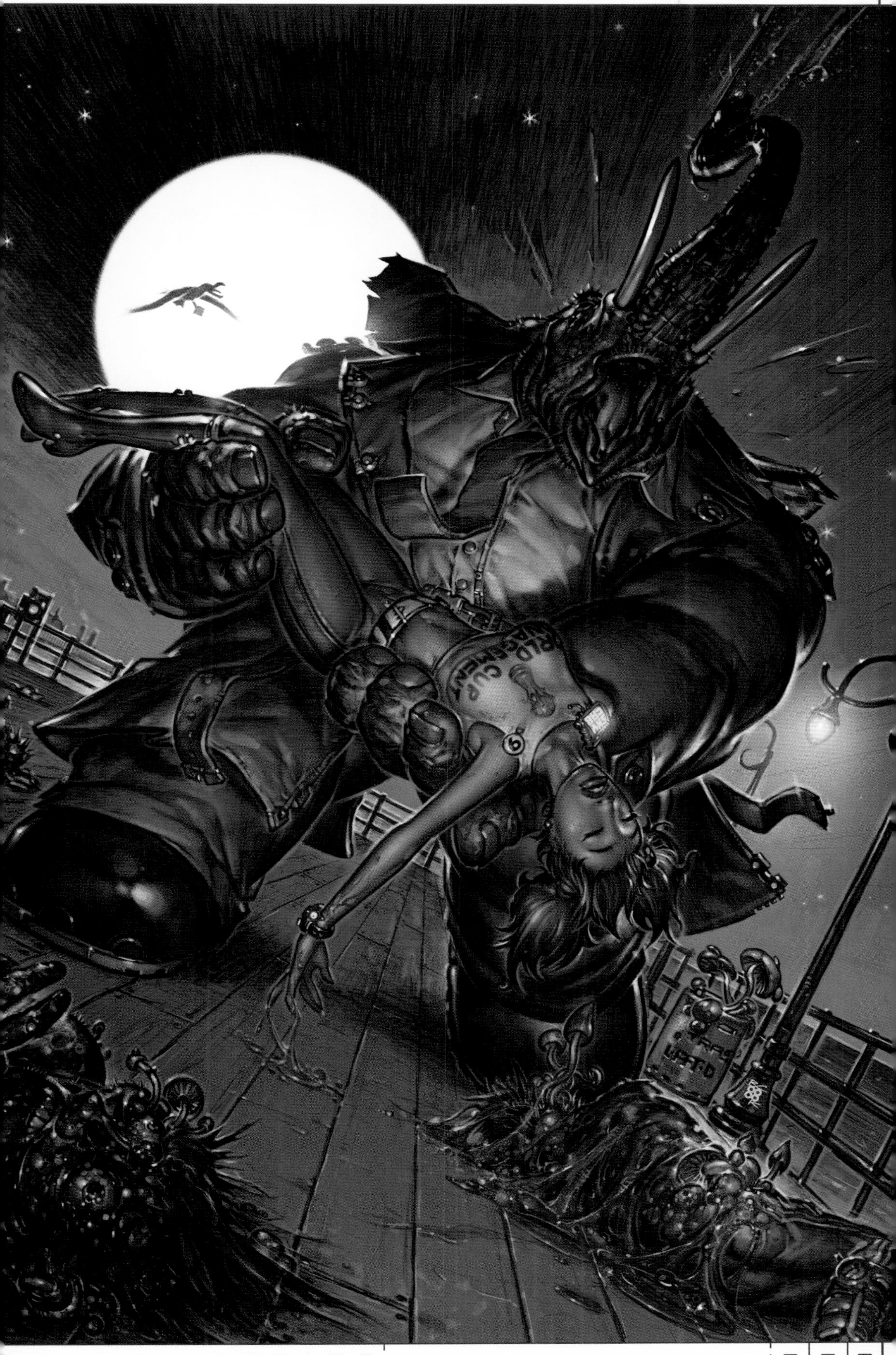

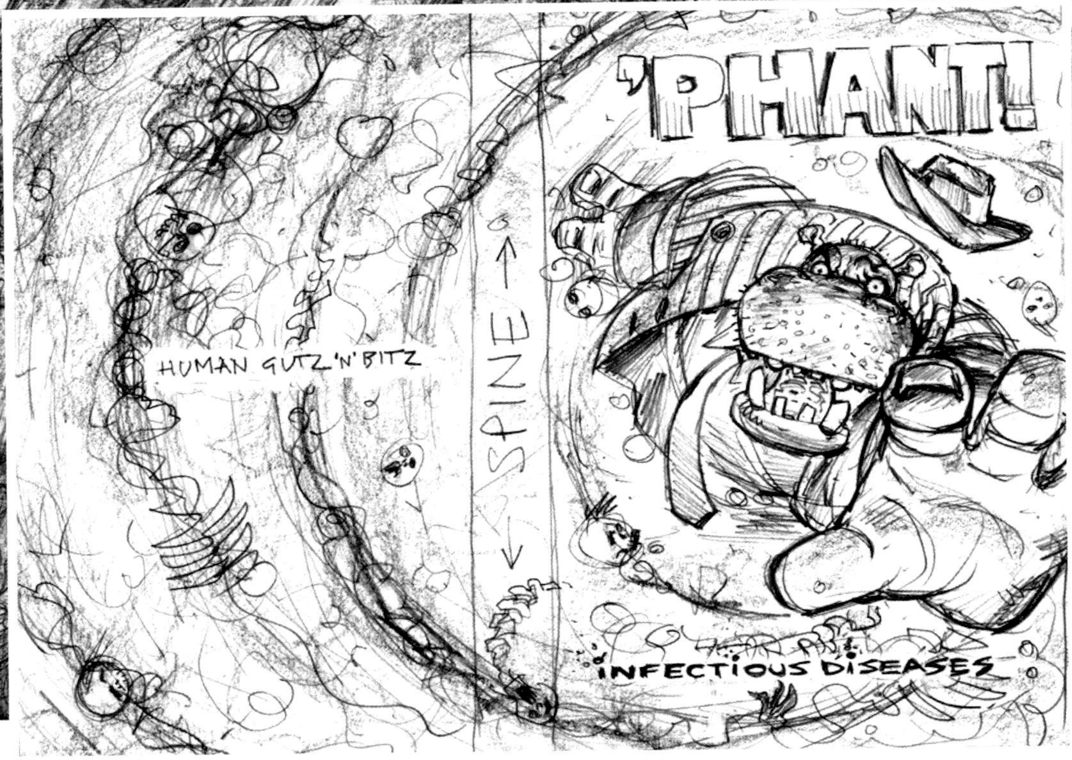
'PHANT!
HUMAN GUTZ'N'BITZ
SPINE
INFECTIOUS DISEASES

For the first edition of ELEPHANTMEN volume 2, FATAL DISEASES, I wanted to see Hip and Miki together again on a cover for the first time since issue #3! I think I asked Boo for an illustration that would make me feel ill just looking at it, and I think during its creation, Boo succeeded in making himself nauseous several times over. We now refer to this kaleidoscope of detritus as the whirlpool of vomit cover!

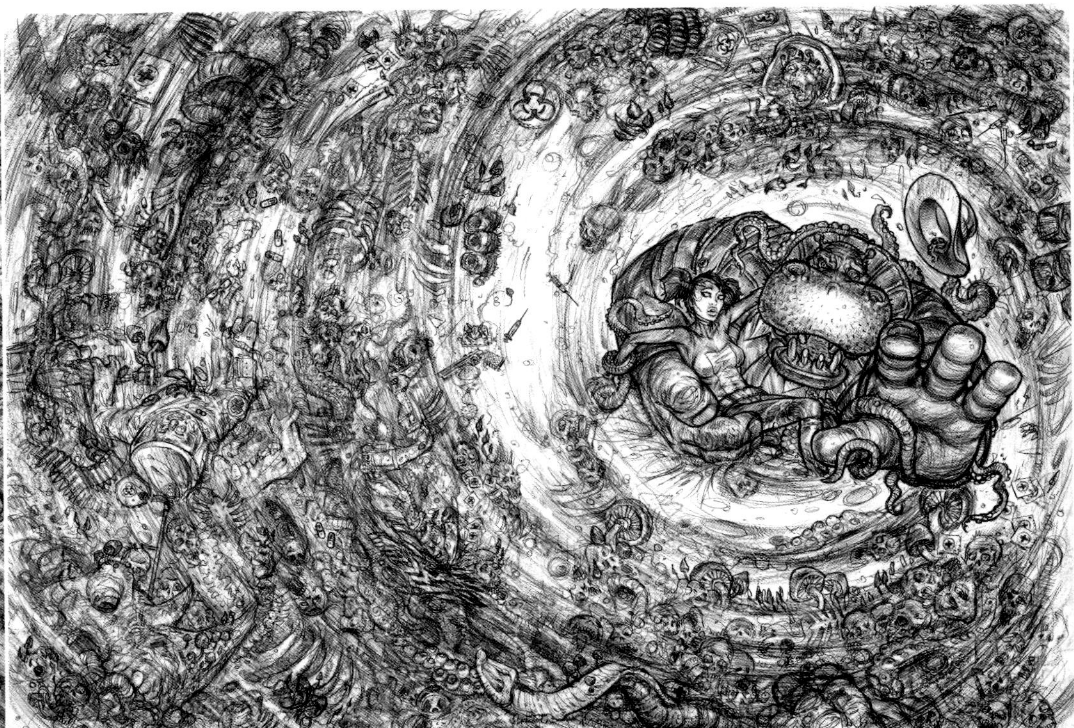

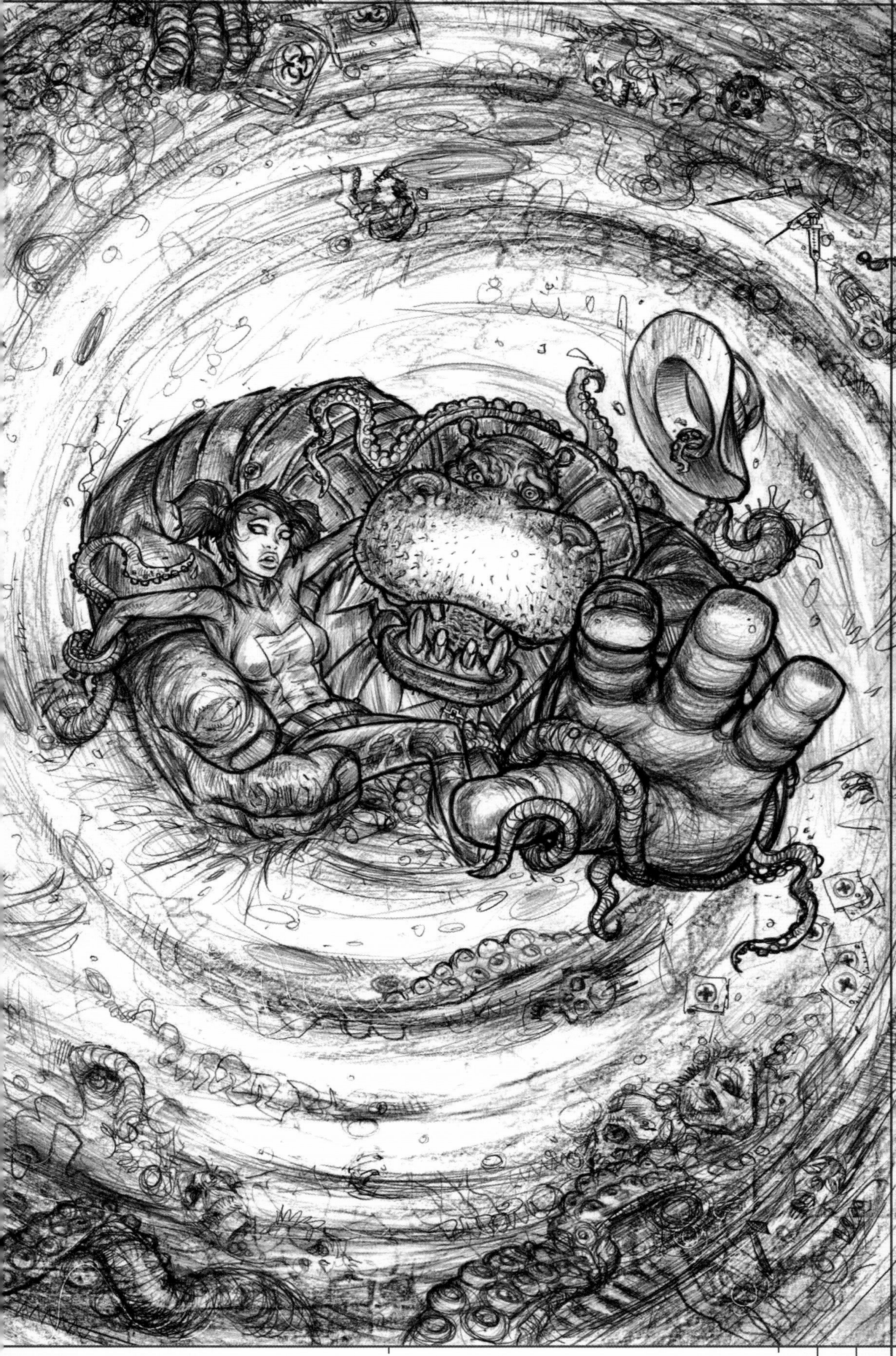

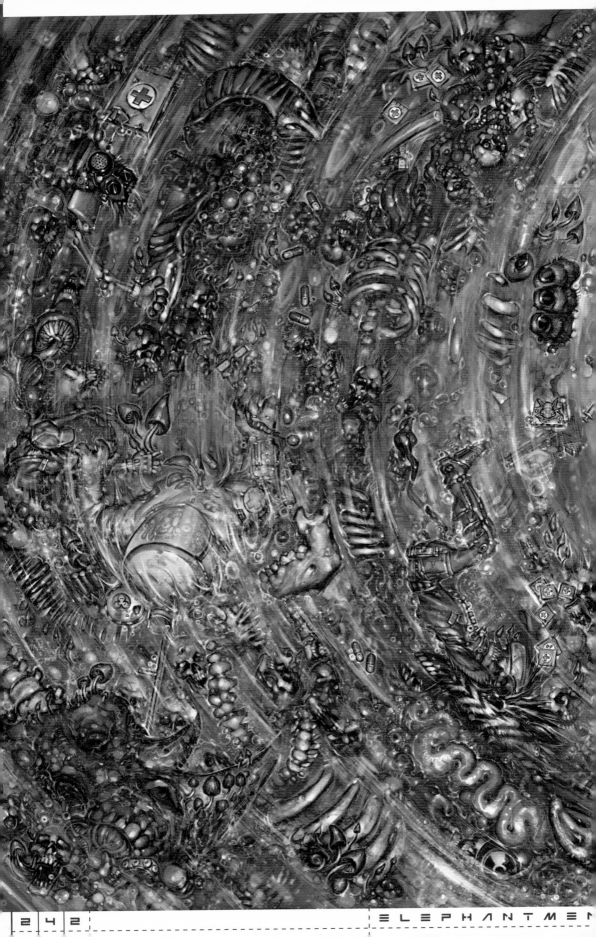

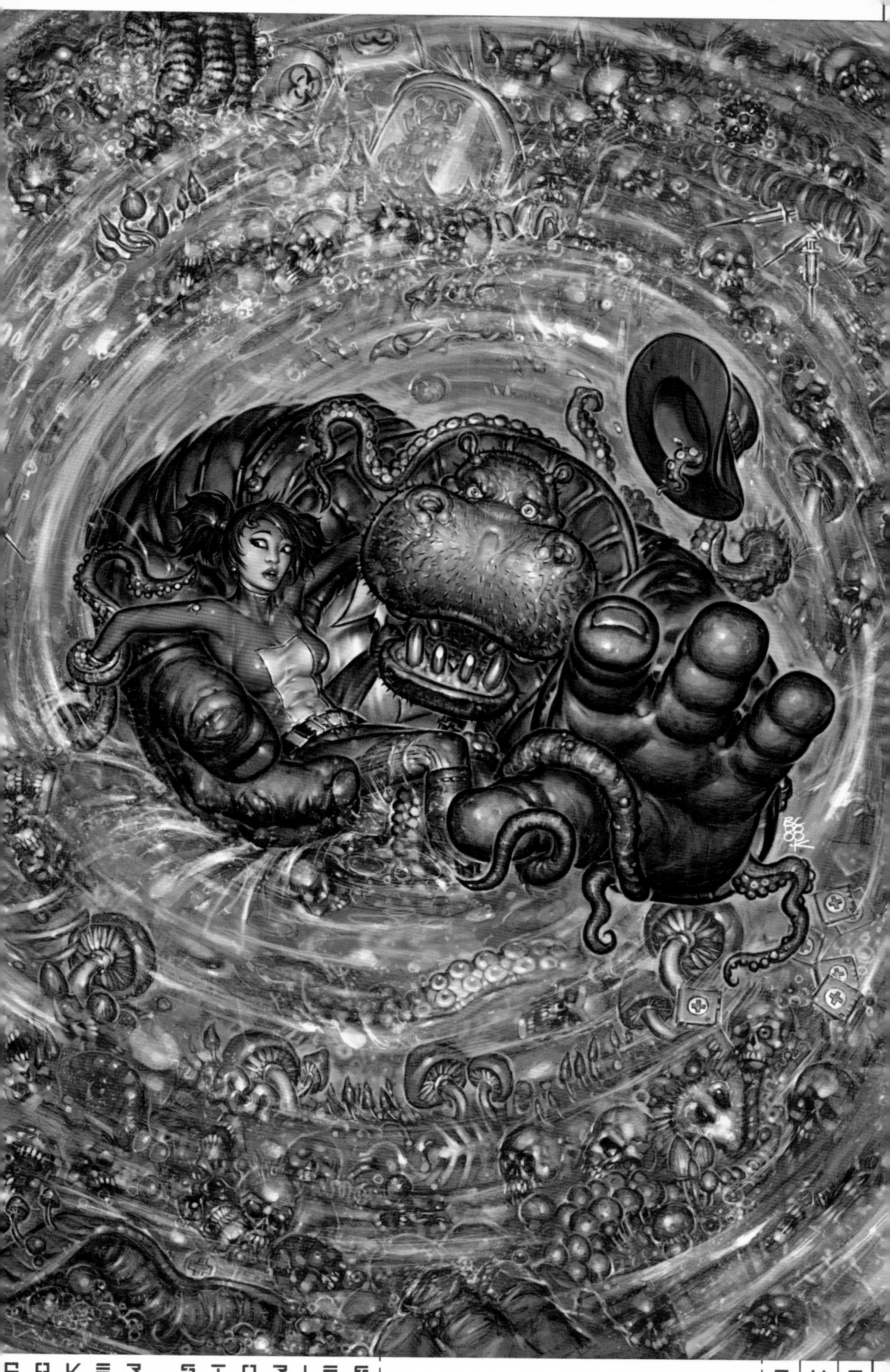

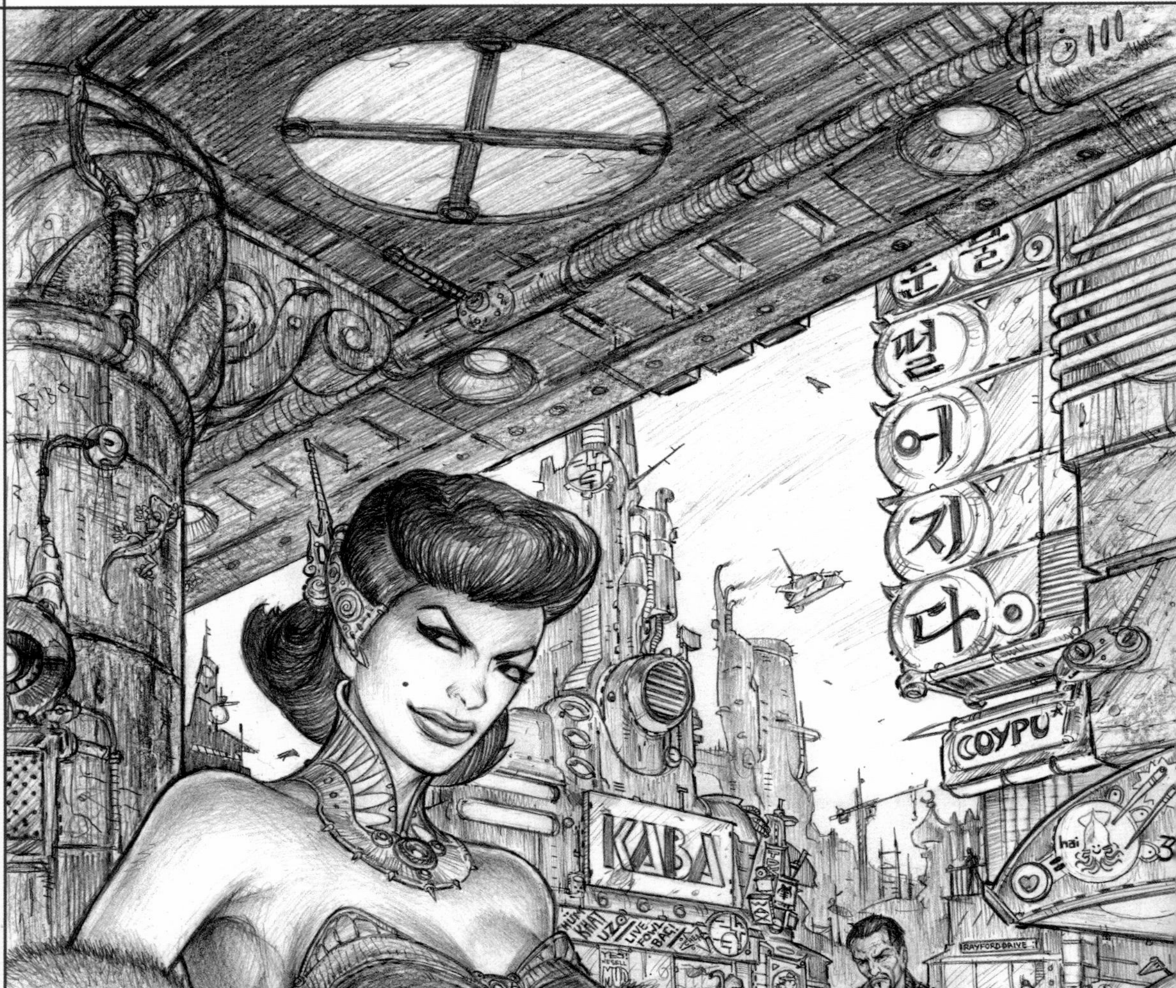
펄
어
지
다
COYPU
KABA
RAYFORD DRIVE

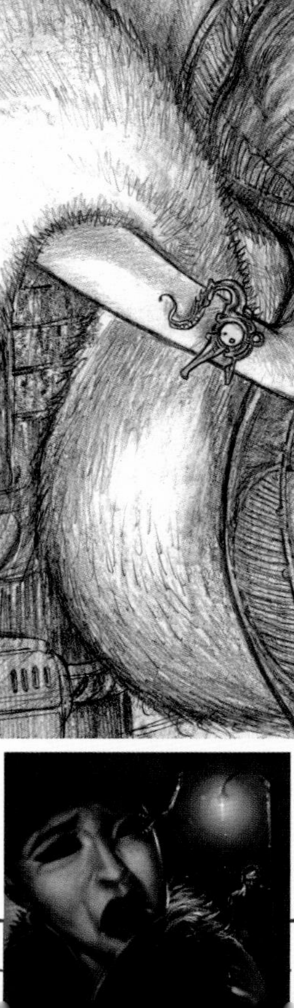

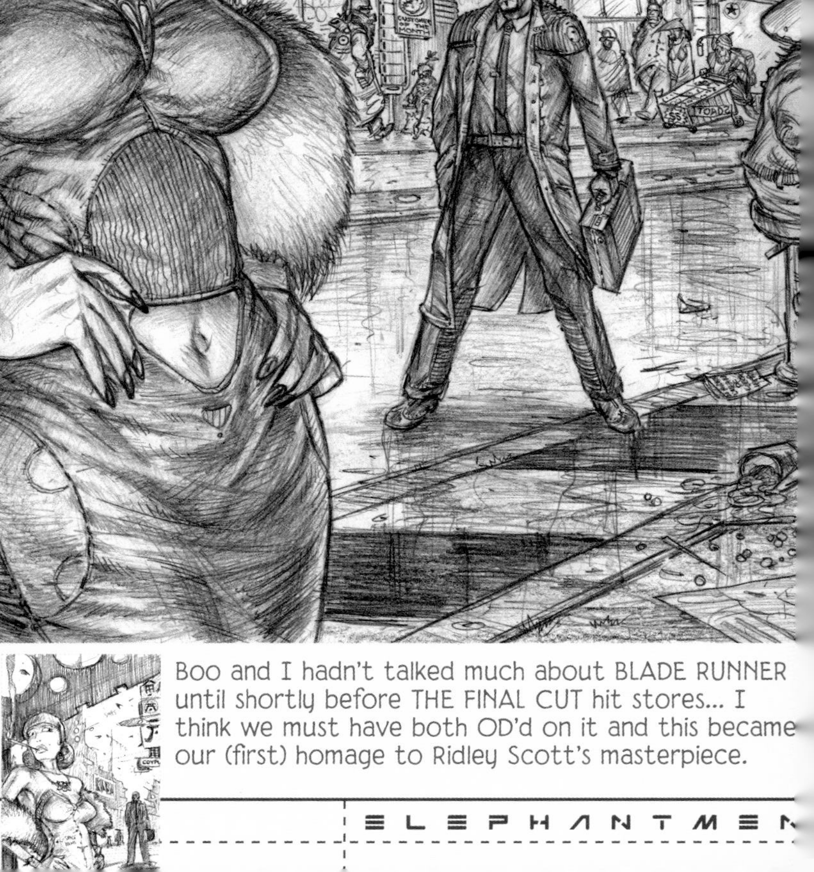

Boo and I hadn't talked much about BLADE RUNNER until shortly before THE FINAL CUT hit stores... I think we must have both OD'd on it and this became our (first) homage to Ridley Scott's masterpiece.

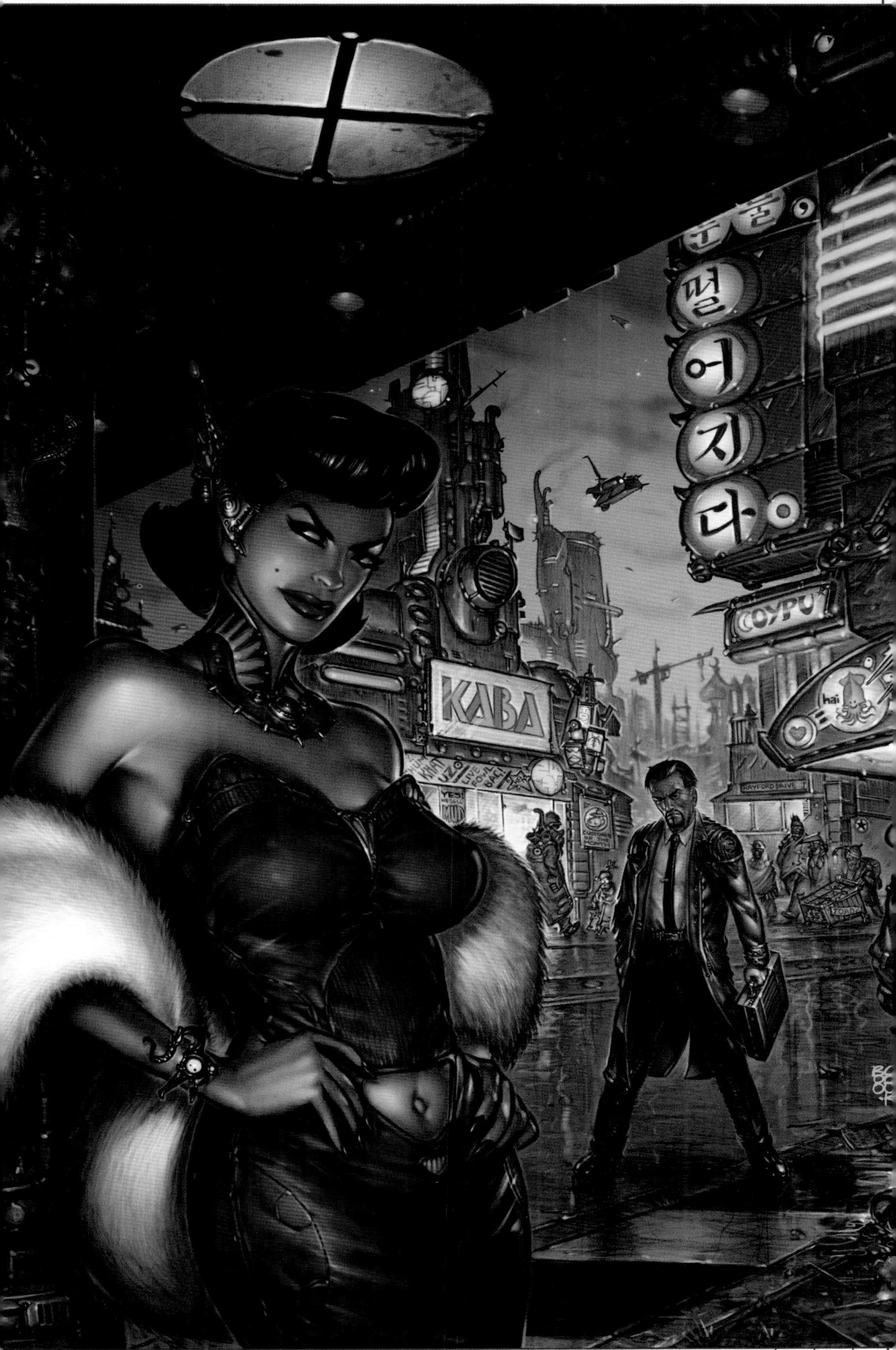
KABA
COYPU
hai
LIVE FOWL
YES!

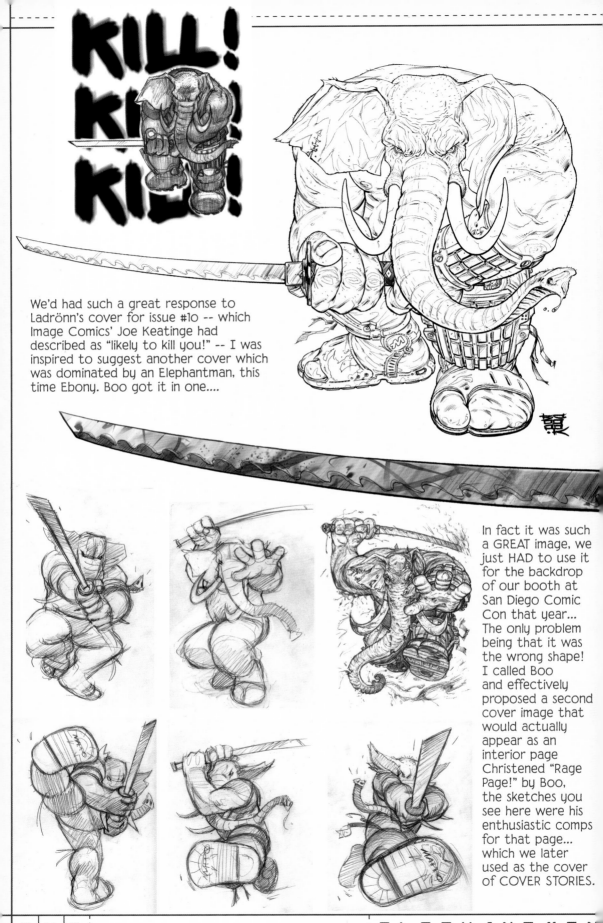

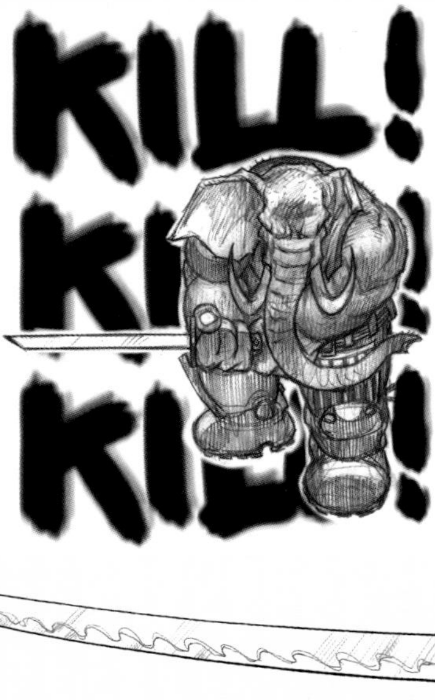
KILL!

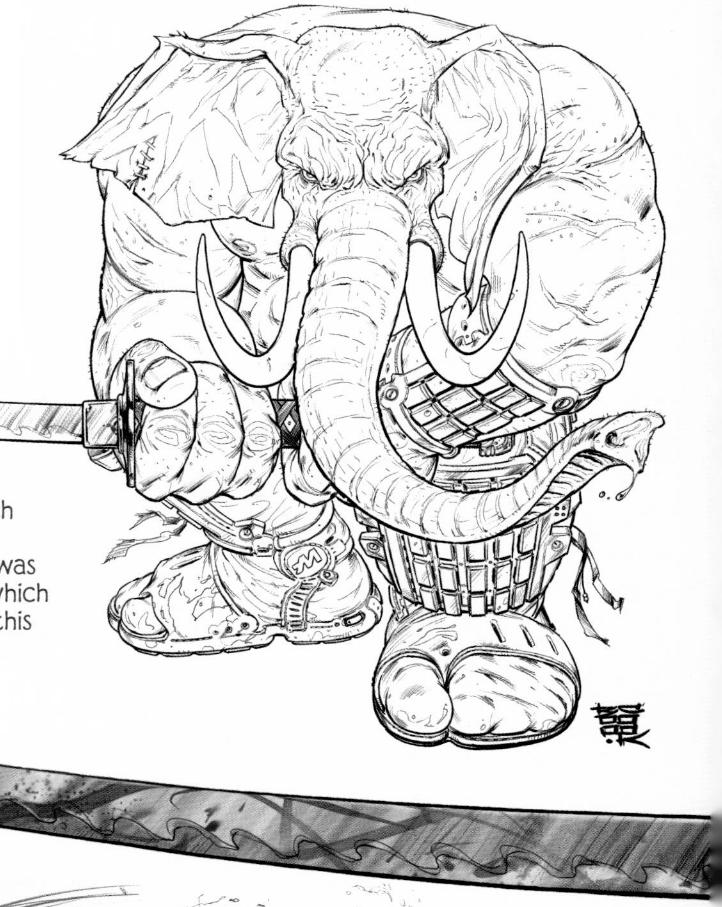

We'd had such a great response to Ladrönn's cover for issue #10 -- which Image Comics' Joe Keatinge had described as "likely to kill you!" -- I was inspired to suggest another cover which was dominated by an Elephantman, this time Ebony. Boo got it in one....

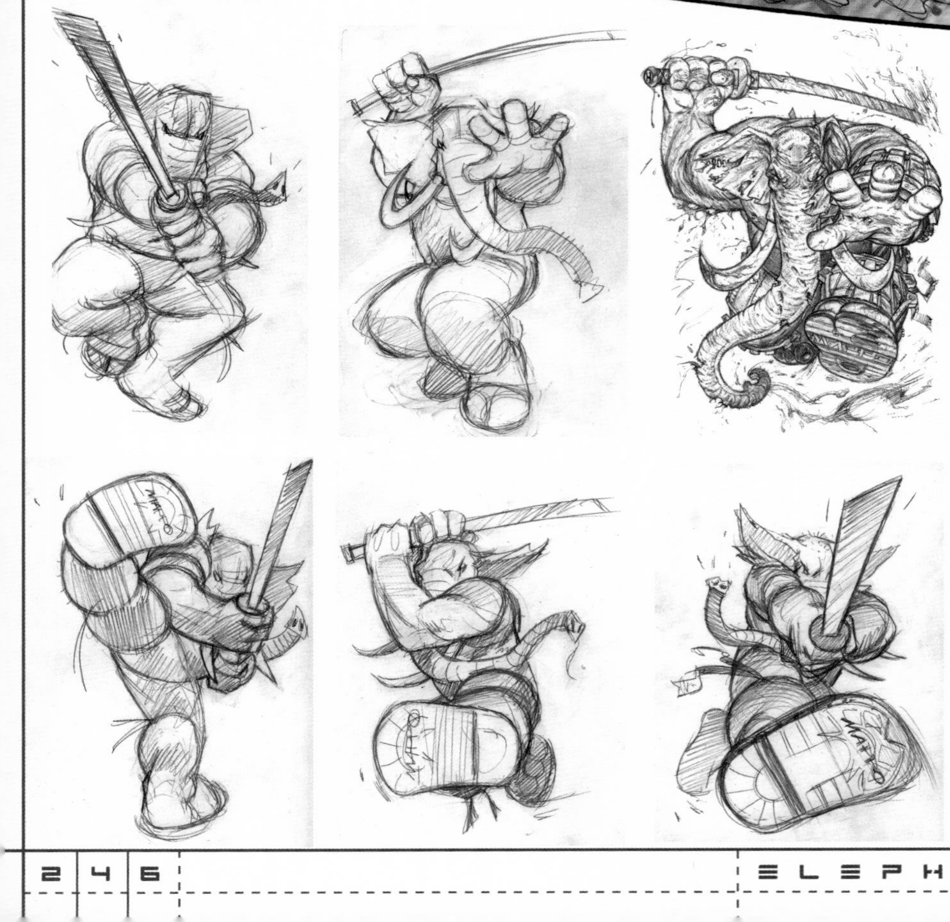

In fact it was such a GREAT image, we just HAD to use it for the backdrop of our booth at San Diego Comic Con that year... The only problem being that it was the wrong shape! I called Boo and effectively proposed a second cover image that would actually appear as an interior page Christened "Rage Page!" by Boo, the sketches you see here were his enthusiastic comps for that page... which we later used as the cover of COVER STORIES.

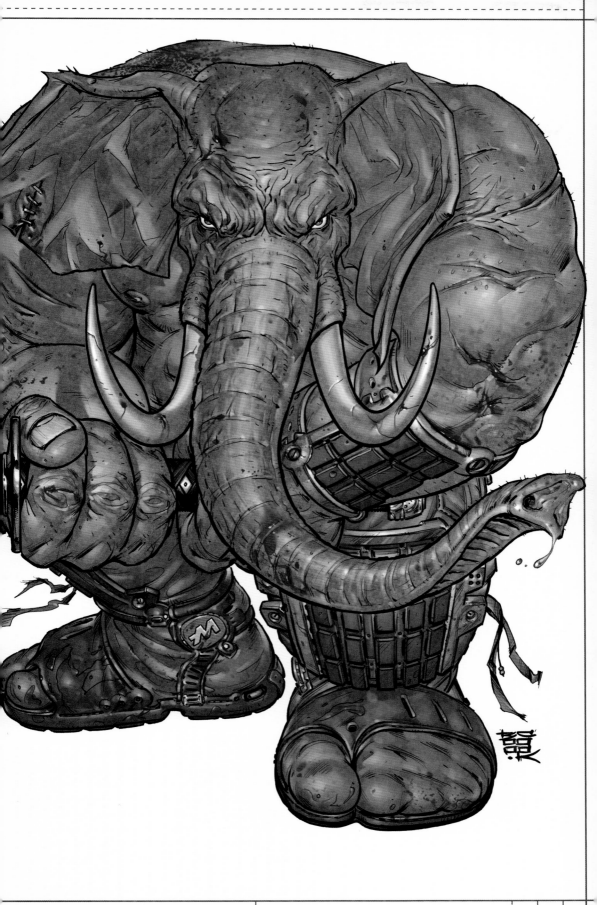

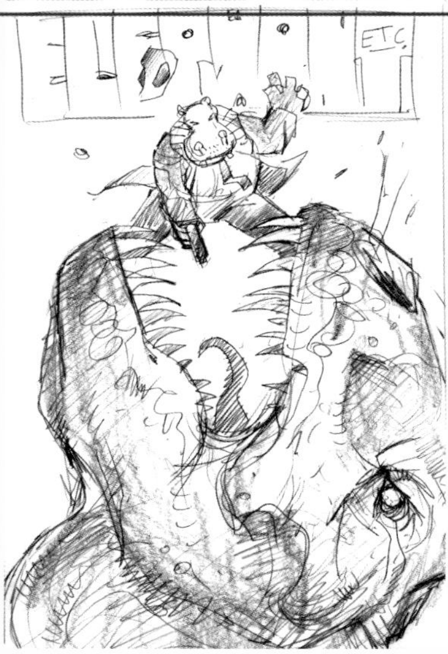
ETC.

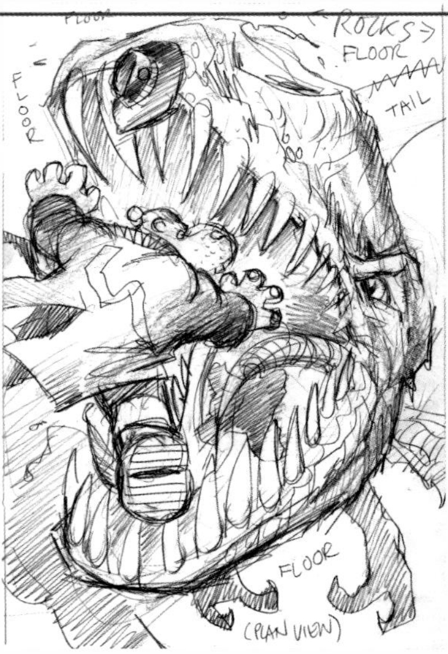
FLOOR
<ROCKS>
FLOOR
TAIL
FLOOR
FLOOR
(PLAN VIEW)

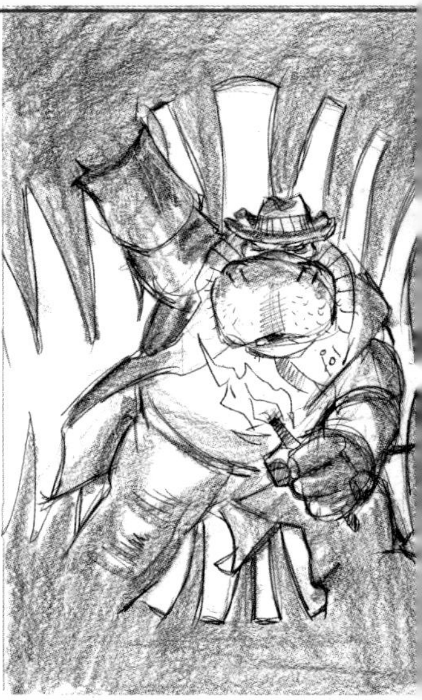

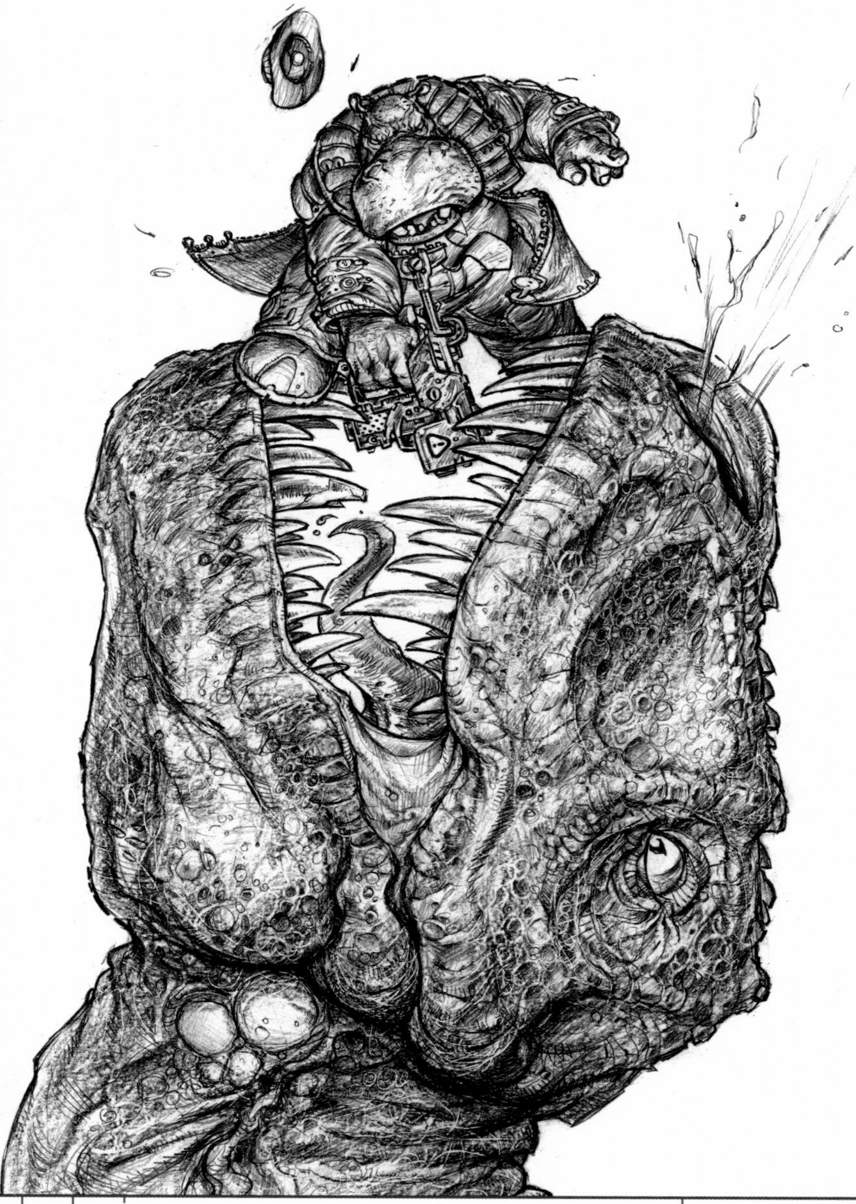

HIPPOPOTAMUS REX

I think it's fair to say that at this point, Boo and I were officially having Too Much Fun... all three of the comps you see above would have made great covers, but I went with the one that showed Hip looking the most heroic. The snot coming out of the T-Rex's nostrils is Boo Goo of the highest order.

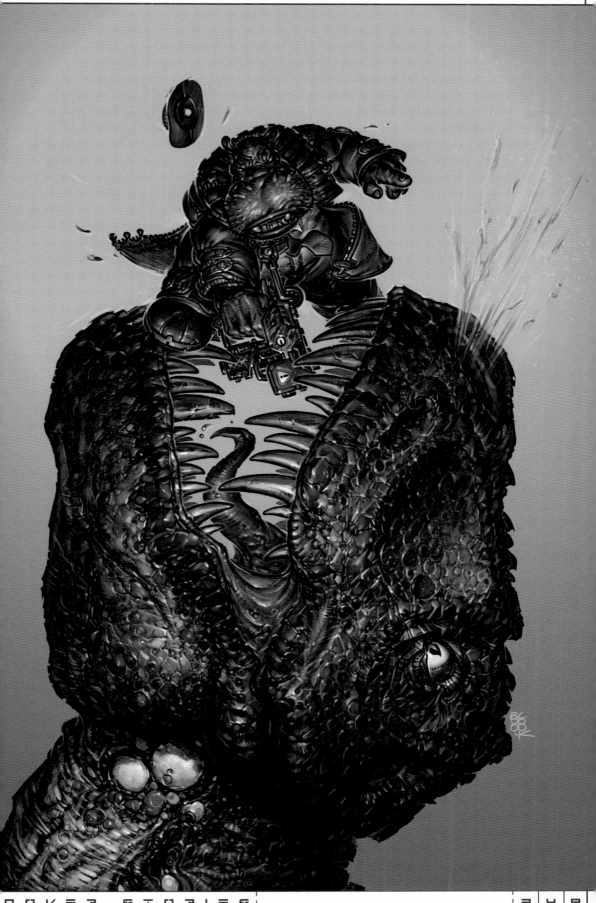

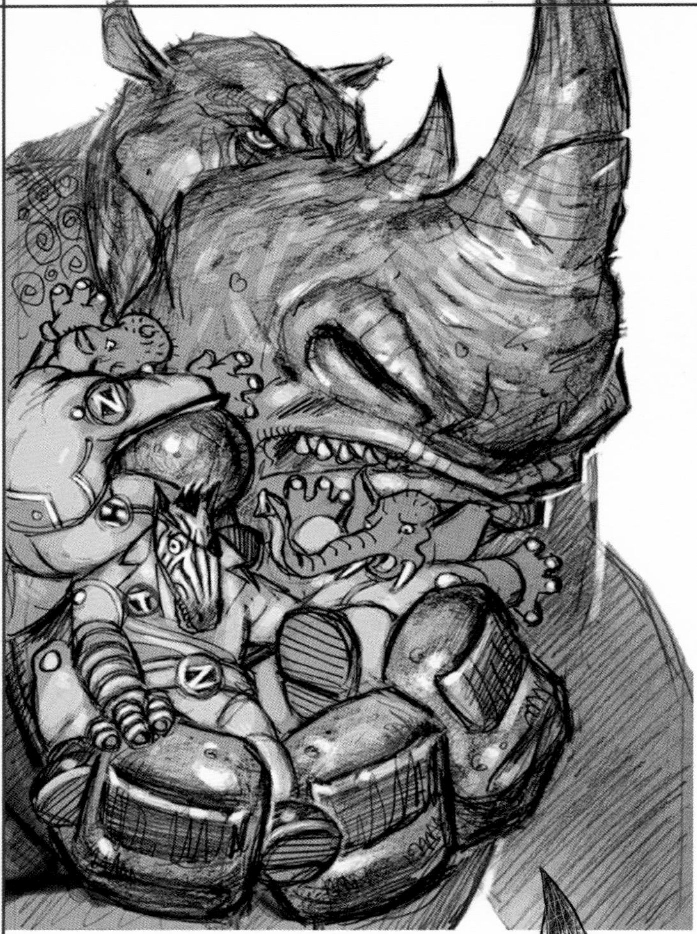

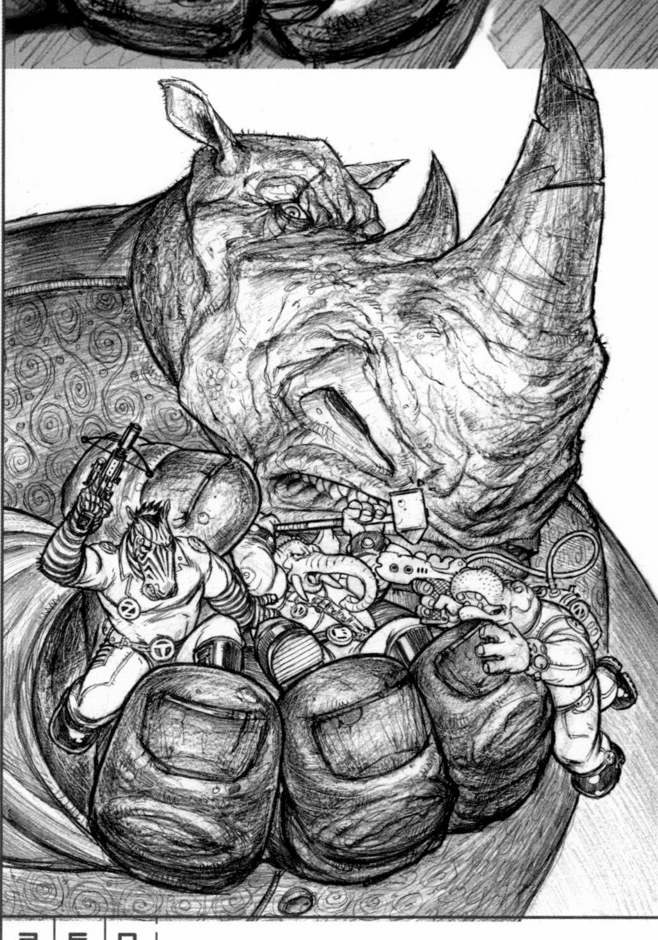

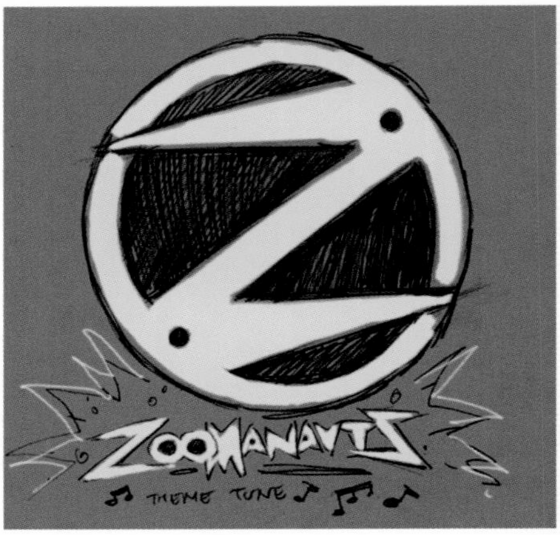

ZOOMANAUTS
THEME TUNE

This rich illustration and the previous one (Hippopotamus Rex) were originally planned to cover issues #16 and #17... but our regular interior artist, Moritat, was finding the strain of putting the book out on a monthly schedule -- while holding down other jobs in advertising and storyboarding -- too great. Chirpy Chris Burnham, a legend in his own mind, had been waiting in the wings to draw a full issue, so it was easy to pull his DARK HEART out to launch the next story arc (collected in ELEPHANTMEN volume 3: DANGEROUS LIAISONS). But then we also decided to pull Rob Steen's Tusk story forward, and then Marian Churchland's three issues forward too... and suddenly even Boo Cook's very own KILL KILL KILL issue was in print before the original covers for #16 and 17. They finally found homes on #22 and #23... issues which featured the brief return of Moritat to the series (ably assisted by André Szymanowicz) before DC snapped him up to illustrate THE SPIRIT.

Horn's handful was inspired by a cover I commissioned for THE REAL GHOSTBUSTERS ANNUAL over 20 years ago... THAT cover depicted the StayPuft Marshmallow Man holding the Ghostbusters in his big white hand. The story in #23 reveals that the Elephantmen have inspired a cartoon series in their own world, THE ZOOMANAUTS. Boo created the logo you see above just for fun and, between his first rough, top left, and the final pencils, bottom left, we imagined unique weapons for each of the Zoomen... However, if you're waiting for a spinoff, don't be holding your breath.

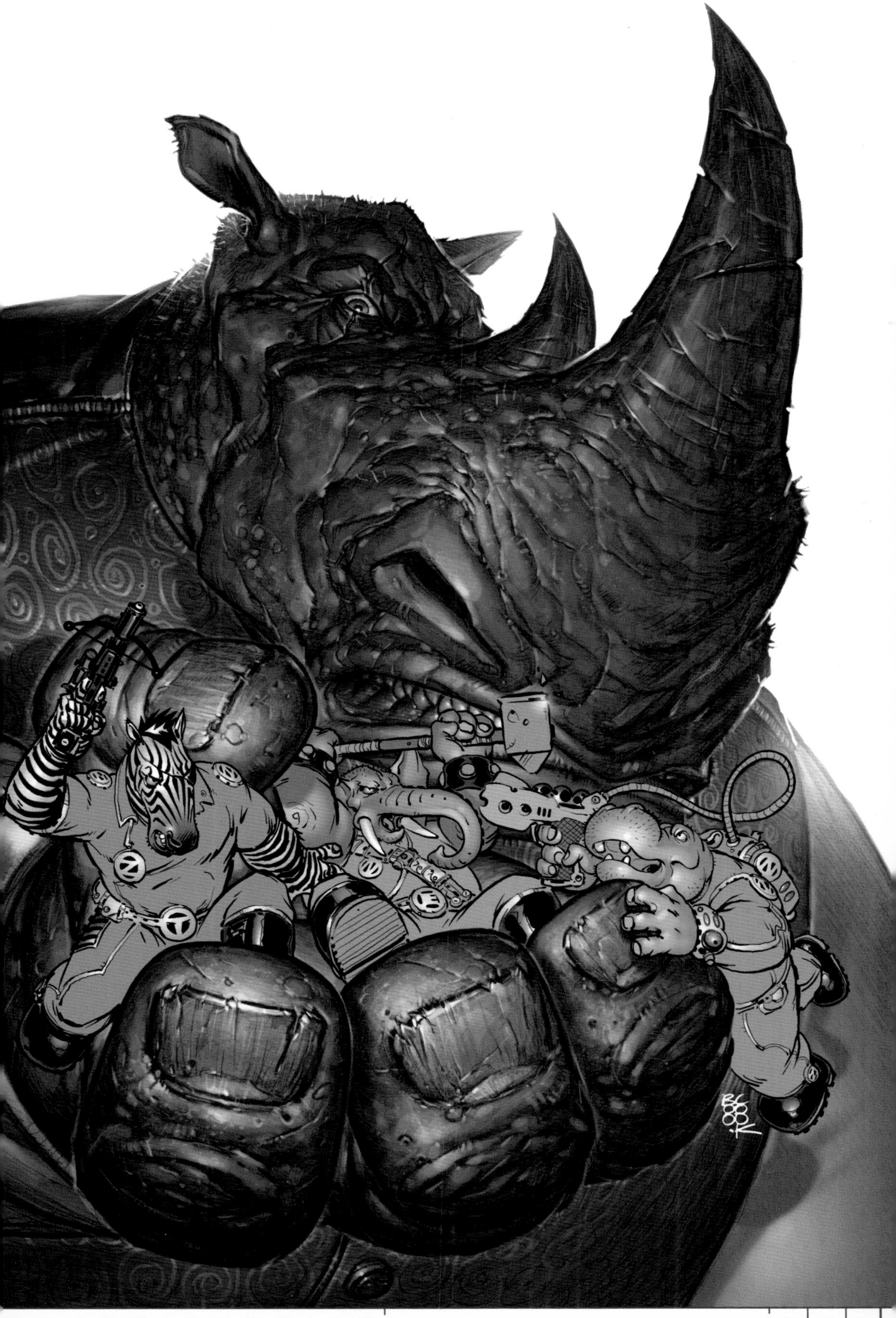

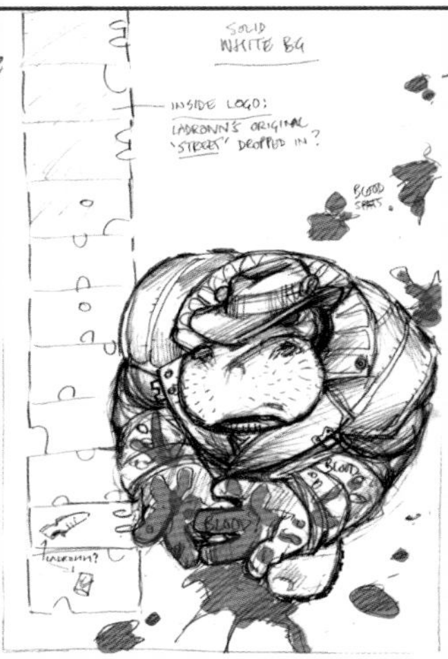
SOLID WHITE BG
INSIDE LOGO: LADRÖNN'S ORIGINAL 'STREETS' DROPPED IN?
BLOOD SPATS.

"QUESTIONABLE THINGS"

Left: SPOILERS! Although I loved Boo's shot of Hip looking up at us, eye glowing red, I felt that it gave too much away for solicitation purposes... the downshot here works just as well and brings to mind Ladrönn's shot of Hip in the Alley which graces the very book you hold in your own bloody hands!

Or is that ketchup?

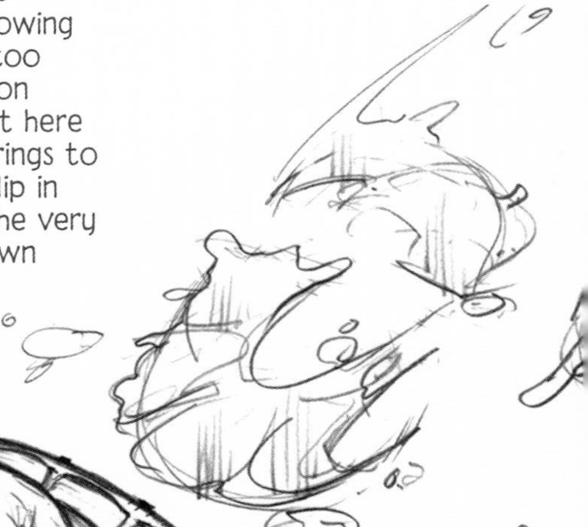

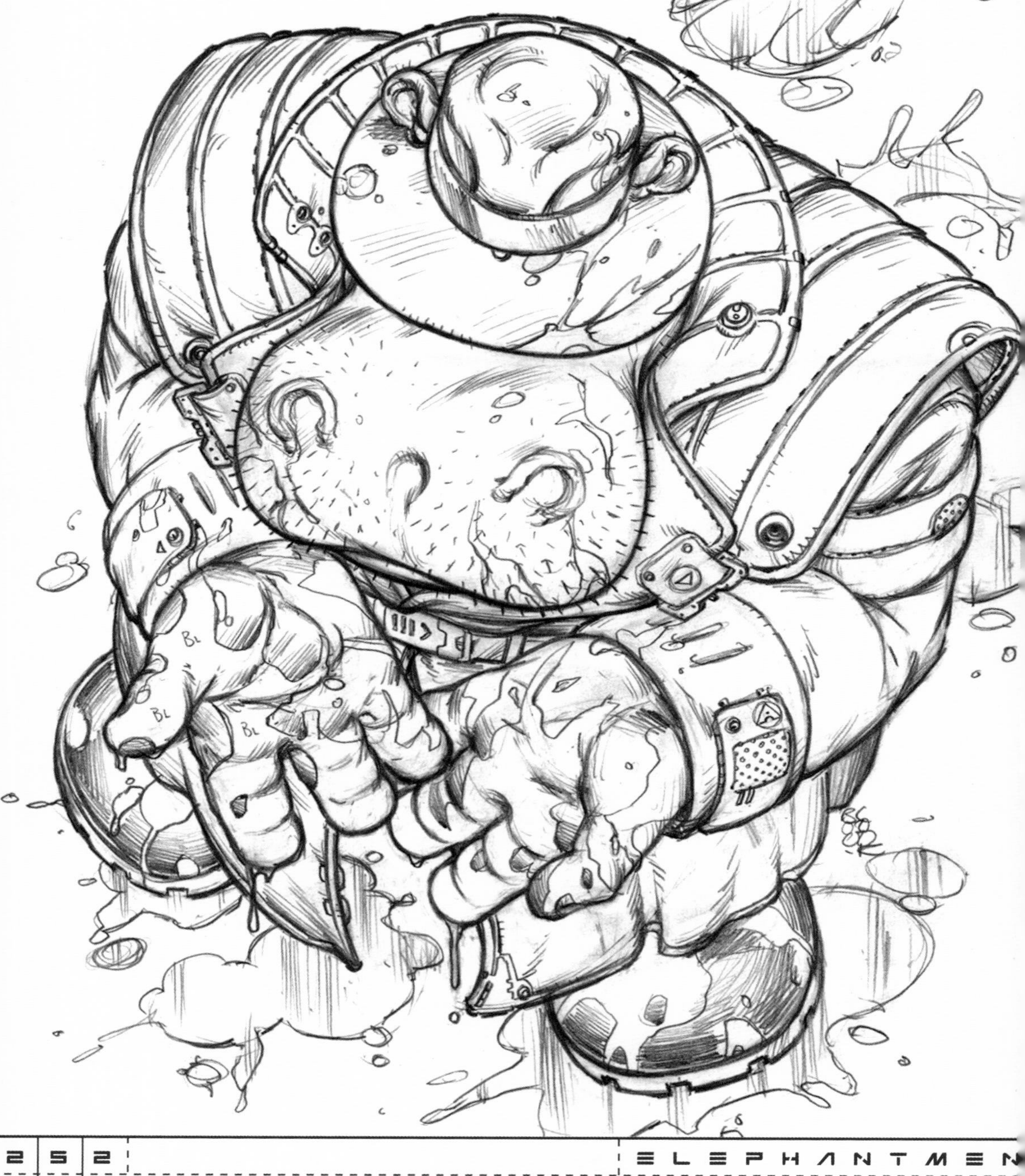

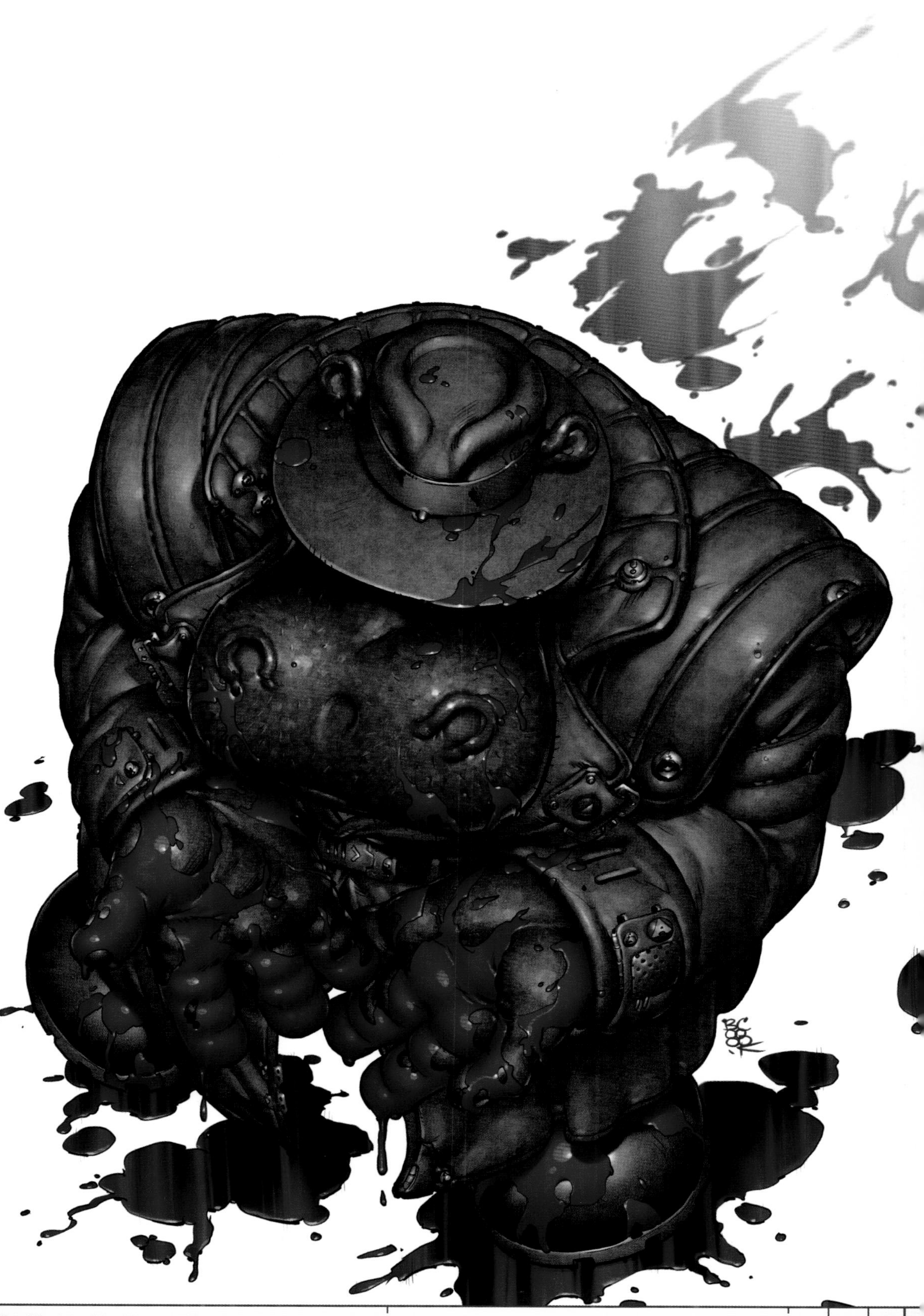

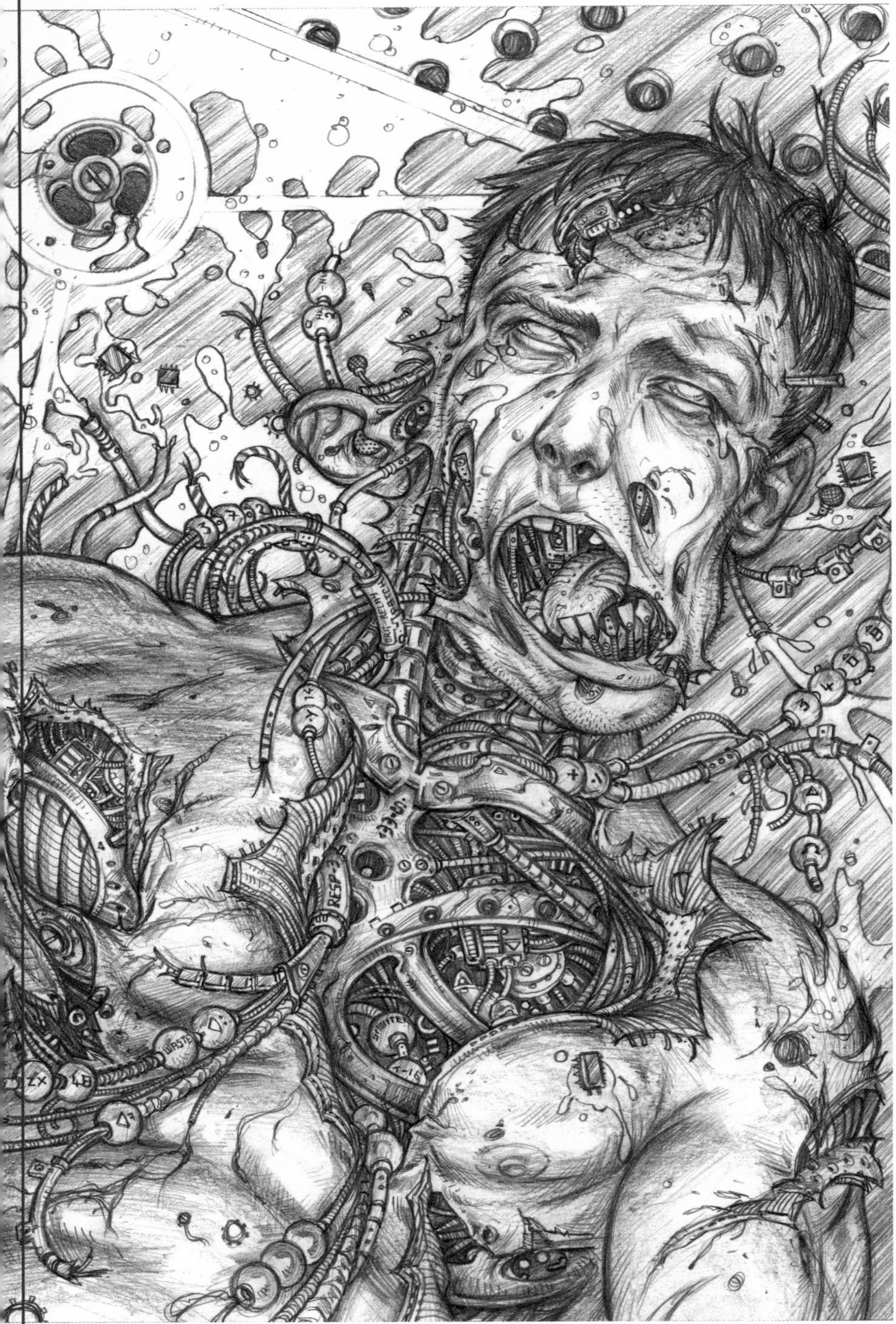

The cover of #25 was a labour of love on Boo's part... and a major spoiler for readers of the series who were under the impression that Simm was a regular guy.

If I'm honest, even I thought Simm might be human when one of him made an appearance in issue #15, but as soon as I saw his name in print, "SIMM!" I realized he could easily turn out to be an android.

Of course, after seeing Boo's amazing cover art, I was absolutely convinced that SIMM was really an android.

Mama Starkings dint raise no idjuts.

Below: We looked at different hair colours before settling on blonde to distinguish the SIMM on the slab from the SIMM who was still on the streets stalking Vanity.

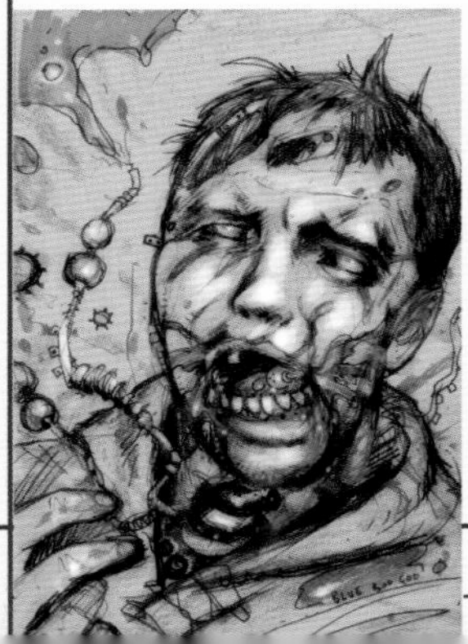

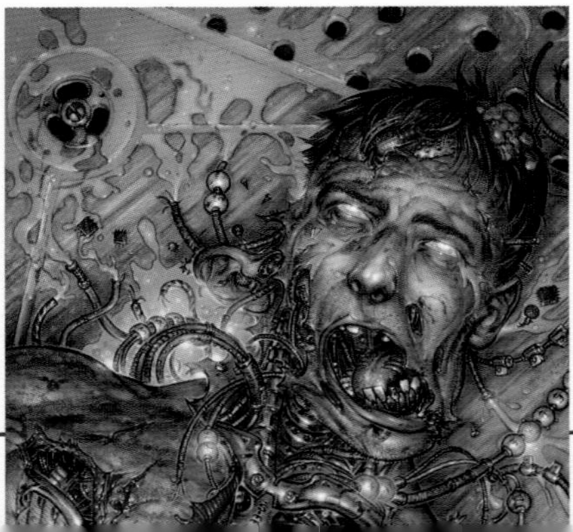

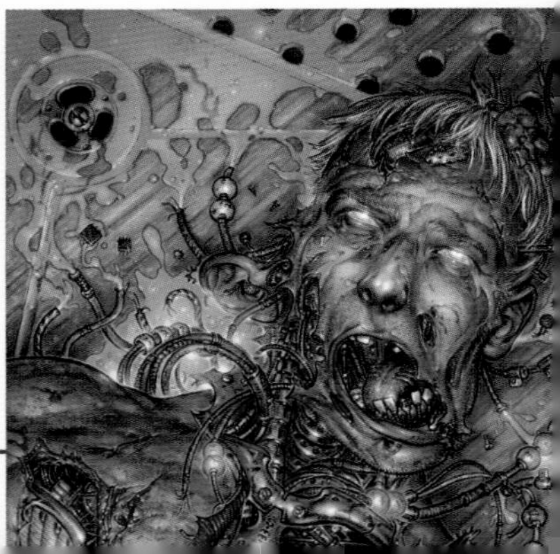

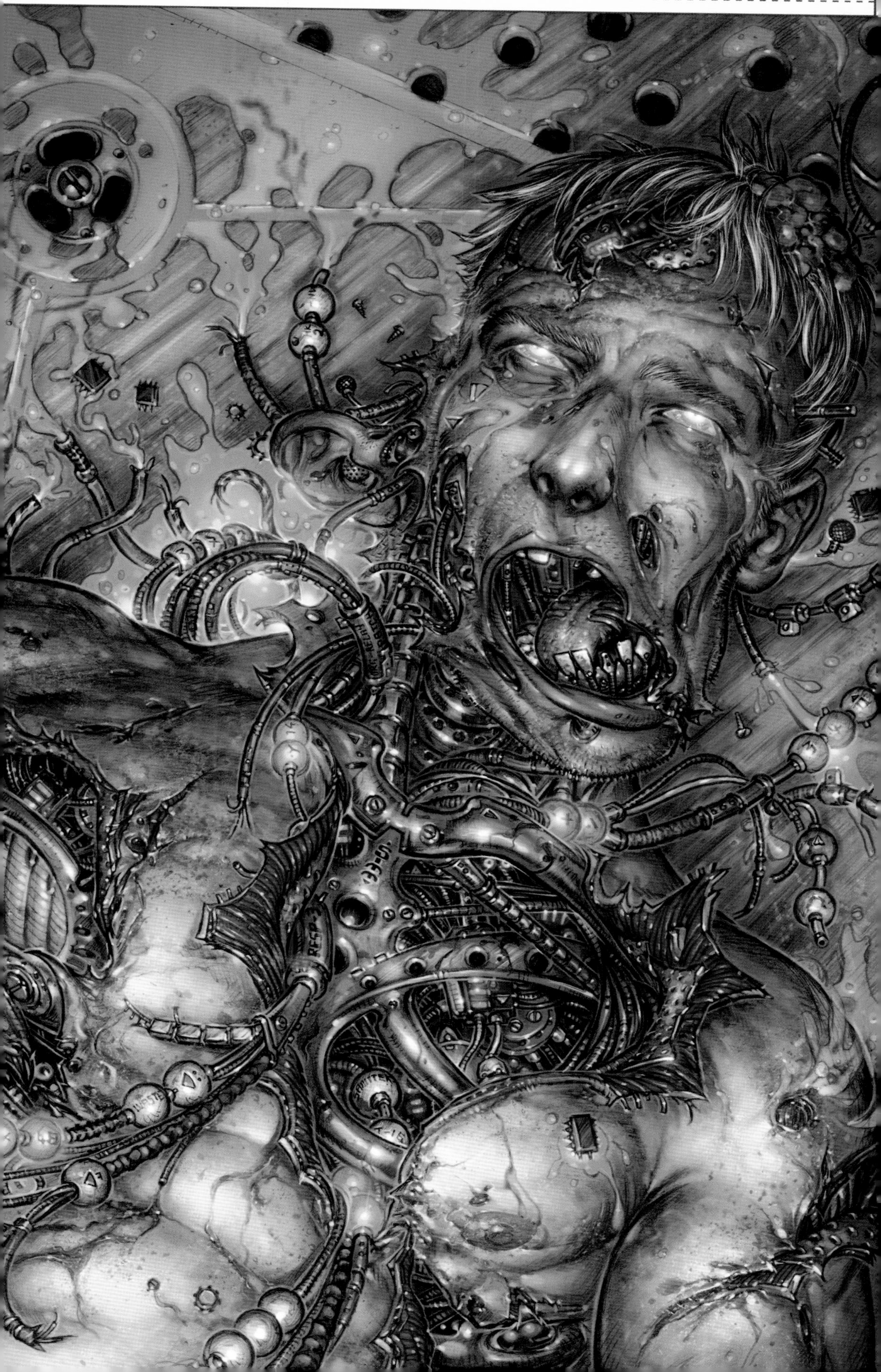

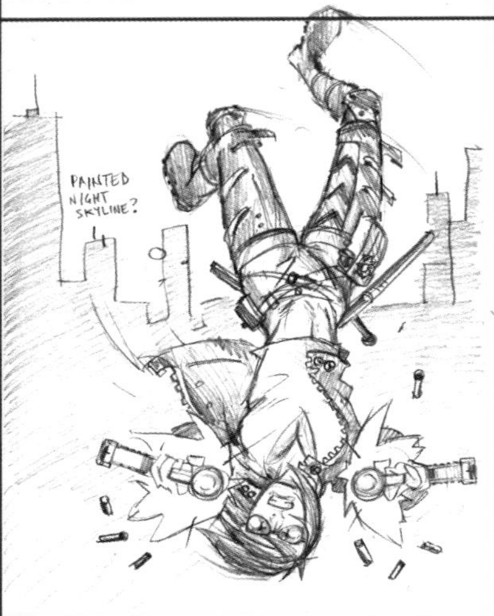
PAINTED NIGHT SKYLINE?

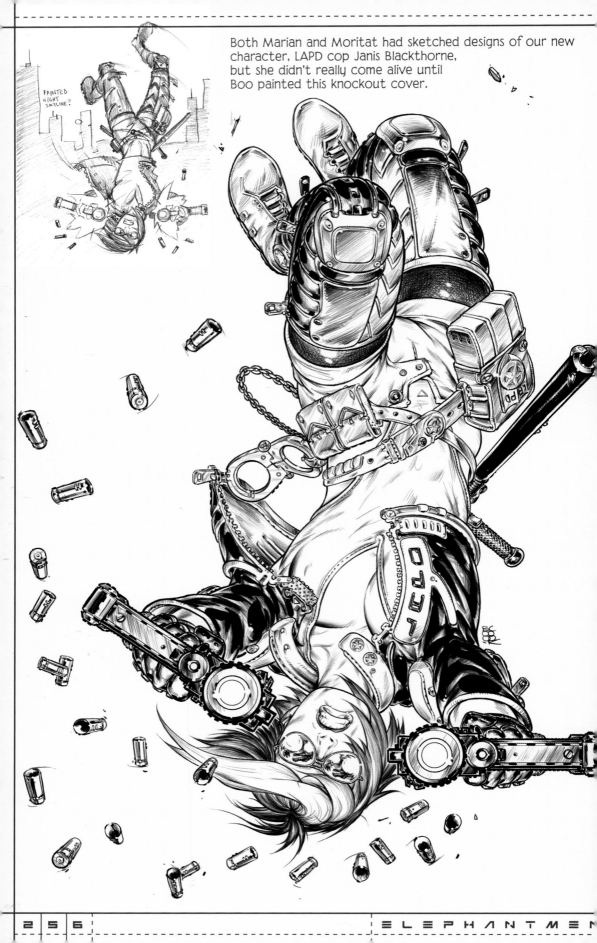

Both Marian and Moritat had sketched designs of our new character, LAPD cop Janis Blackthorne, but she didn't really come alive until Boo painted this knockout cover.

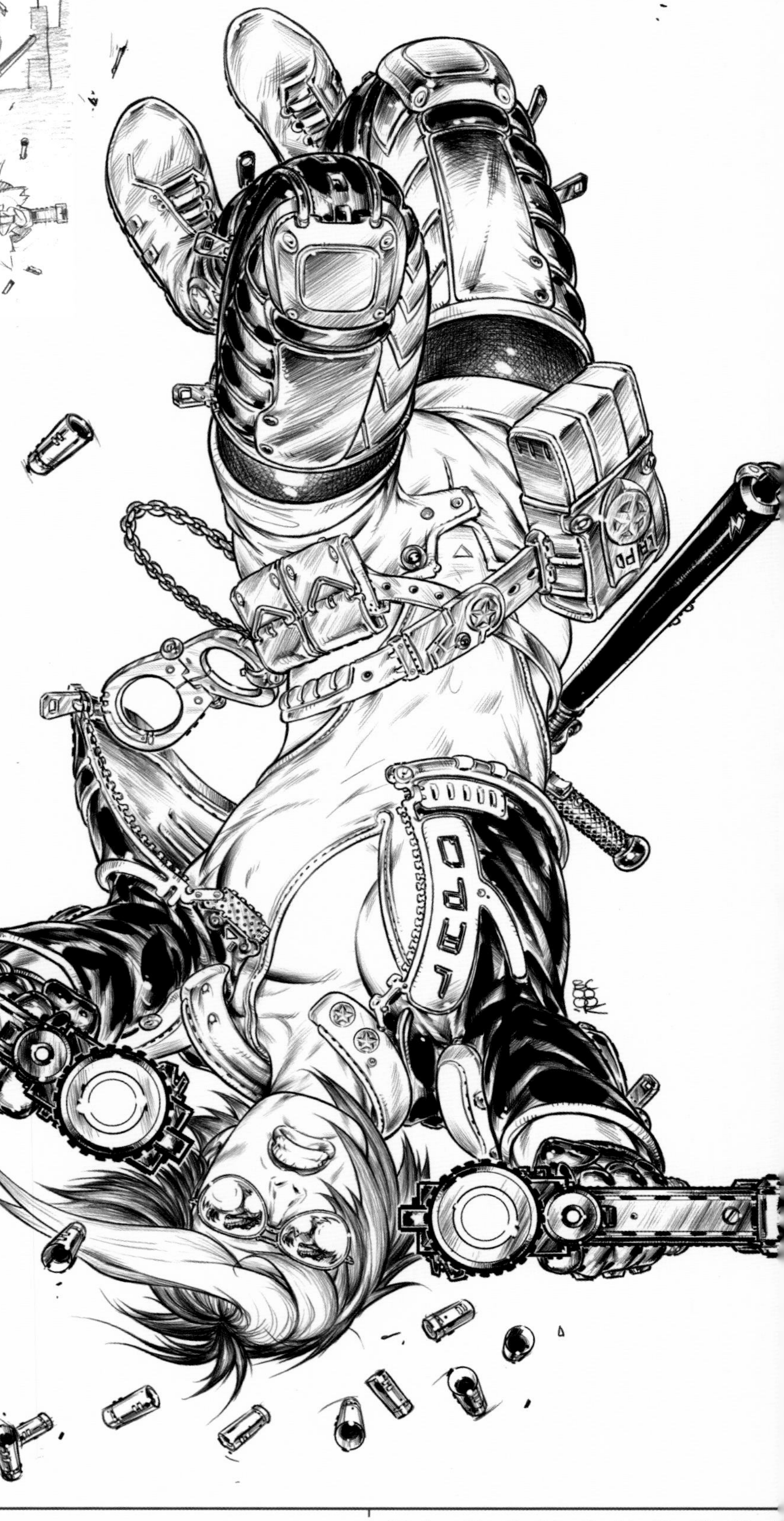

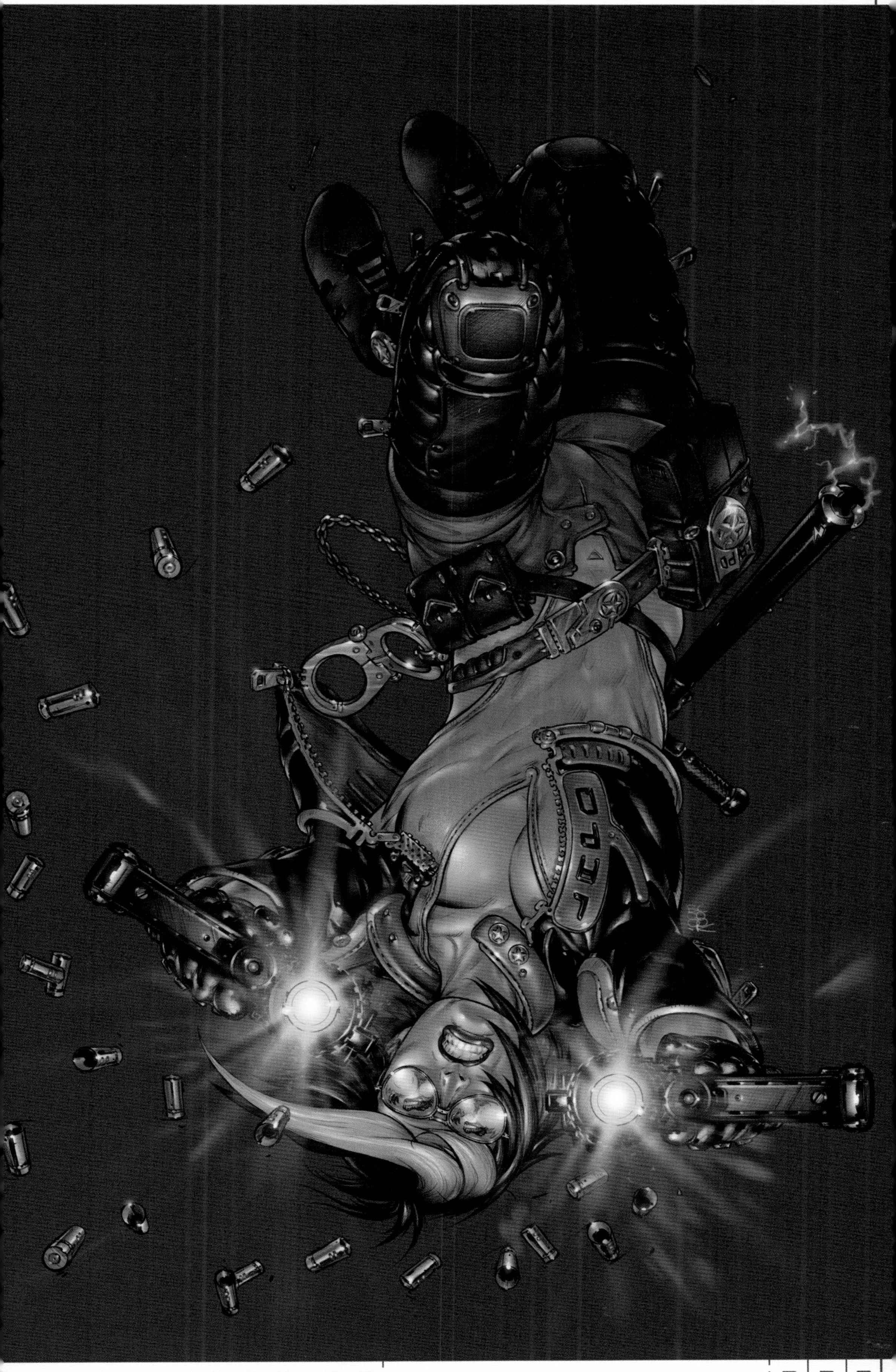

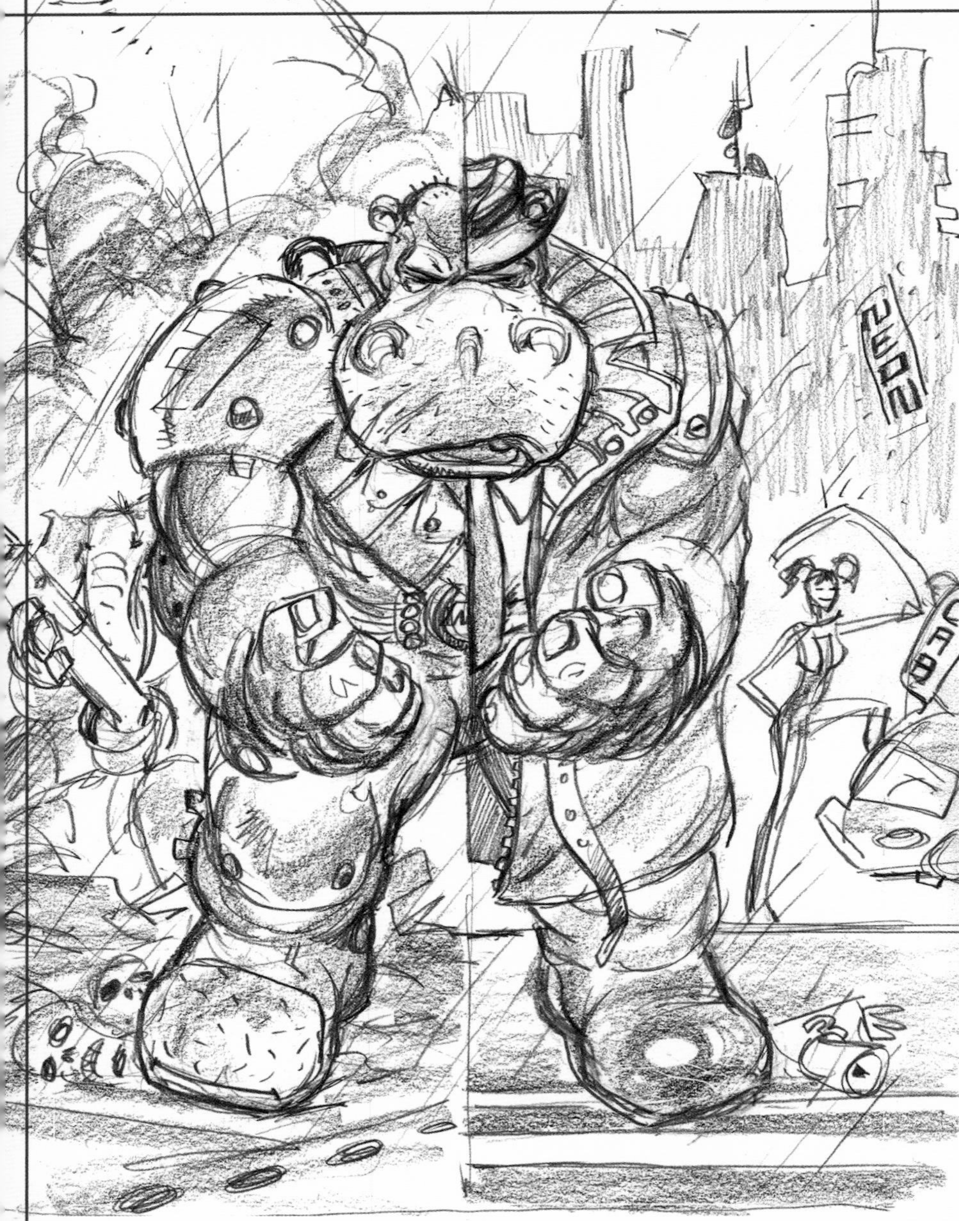

The four regular variant covers of ELEPHANTMEN: MAN AND ELEPHANTMAN were all intended to be pastiches of covers that comic book readers would readily recognize... thereby encouraging new readers to pick the book up and try it out.

The inspiration for Boo's cover was FANTASTIC FOUR #51: "This Man, This Monster!"

However, as we went through one rough after another, the cover took on new life and became something wholly its own. The finished painting opposite is not even the finished cover, which features a silhouette of Hip in human form, perhaps wondering what happened to the original idea.

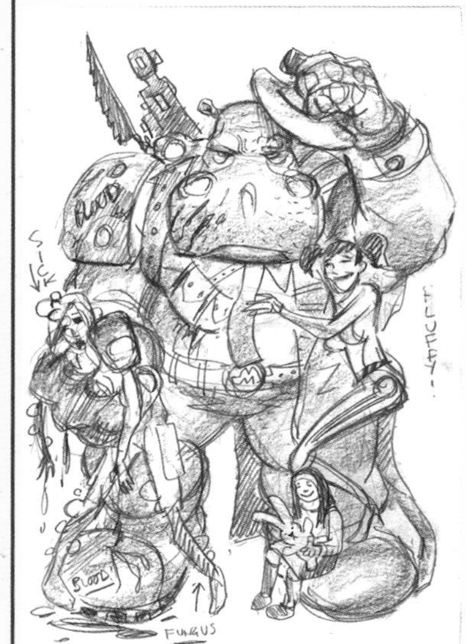
BLOOD
FUNGUS

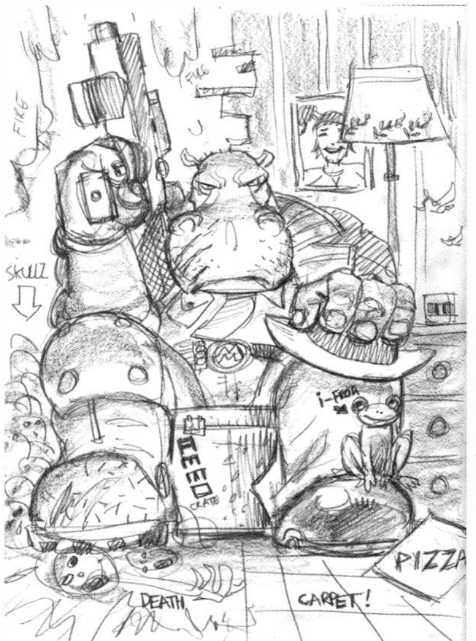
SKULL
PIZZA
DEATH
CARPET!

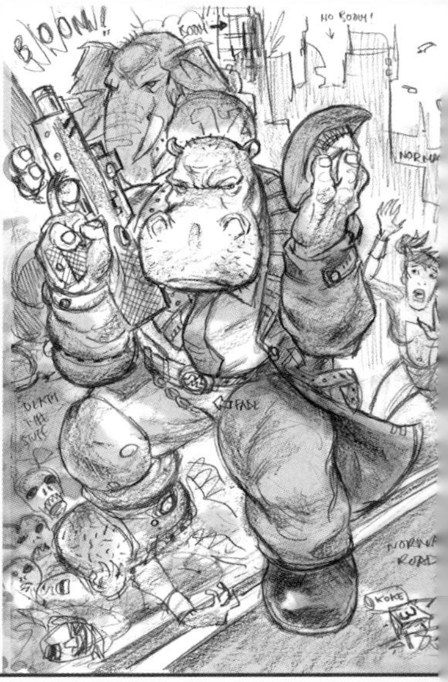

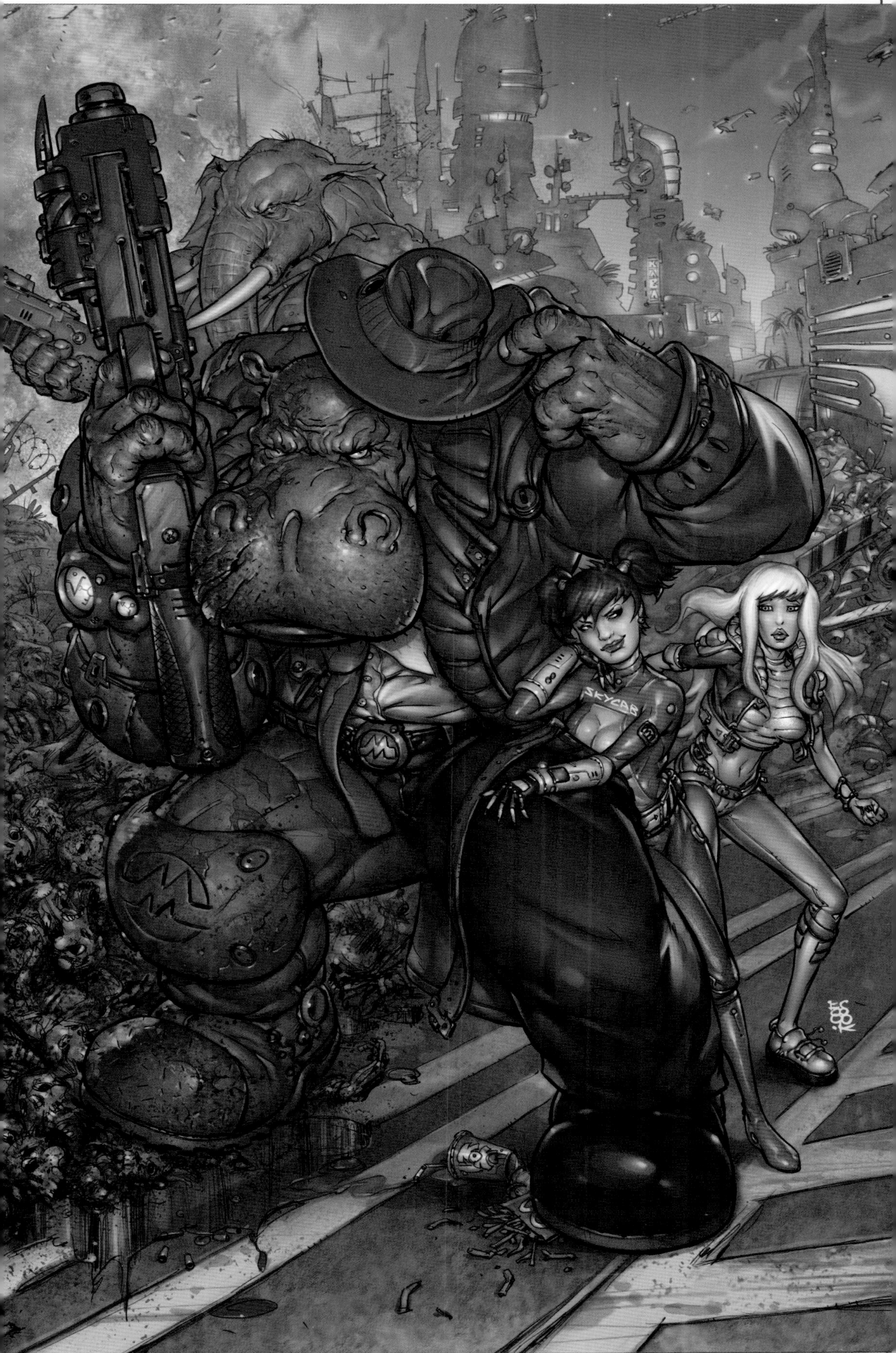
SKYCAB

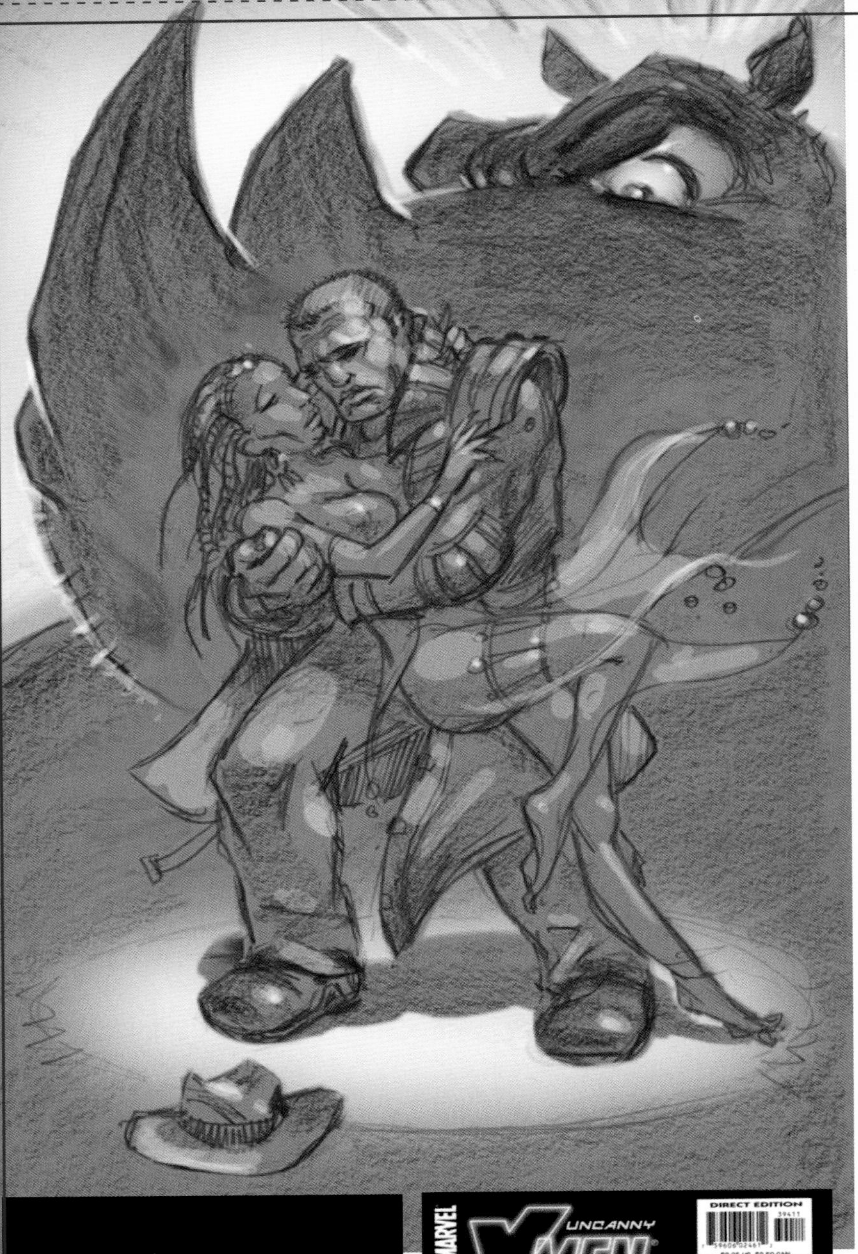

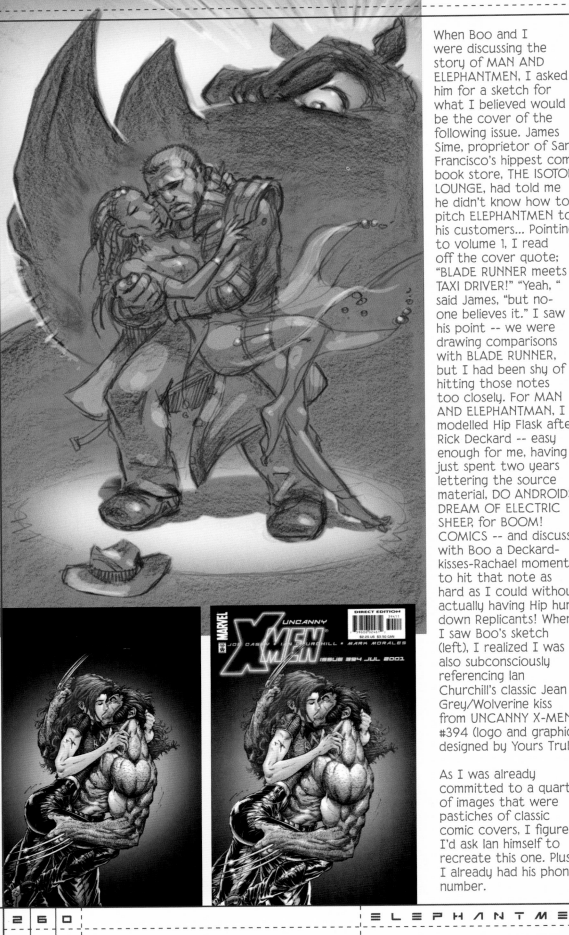

When Boo and I were discussing the story of MAN AND ELEPHANTMEN, I asked him for a sketch for what I believed would be the cover of the following issue. James Sime, proprietor of San Francisco's hippest comic book store, THE ISOTOPE LOUNGE, had told me he didn't know how to pitch ELEPHANTMEN to his customers... Pointing to volume 1, I read off the cover quote; "BLADE RUNNER meets TAXI DRIVER!" "Yeah, " said James, "but no-one believes it." I saw his point -- we were drawing comparisons with BLADE RUNNER, but I had been shy of hitting those notes too closely. For MAN AND ELEPHANTMAN, I modelled Hip Flask after Rick Deckard -- easy enough for me, having just spent two years lettering the source material, DO ANDROIDS DREAM OF ELECTRIC SHEEP, for BOOM! COMICS -- and discussed with Boo a Deckard-kisses-Rachael moment to hit that note as hard as I could without actually having Hip hunt down Replicants! When I saw Boo's sketch (left), I realized I was also subconsciously referencing Ian Churchill's classic Jean Grey/Wolverine kiss from UNCANNY X-MEN #394 (logo and graphics designed by Yours Truly).

As I was already committed to a quartet of images that were pastiches of classic comic covers, I figured I'd ask Ian himself to recreate this one. Plus, I already had his phone number.

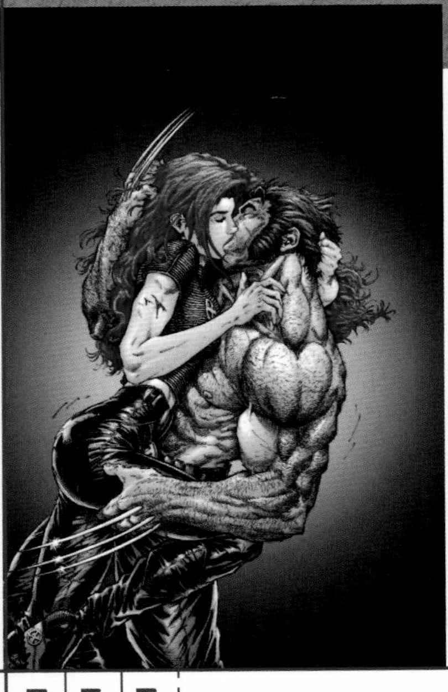

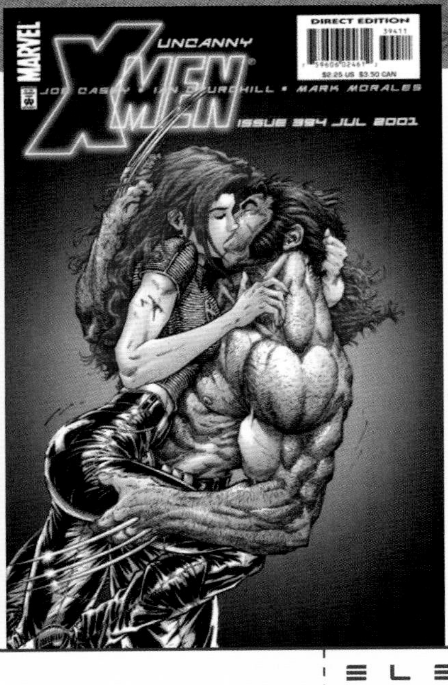
MARVEL
UNCANNY
X-MEN
DIRECT EDITION
$2.25 US $3.50 CAN
JOE CASEY • IAN CHURCHILL • MARK MORALES
ISSUE 394 JUL 2001

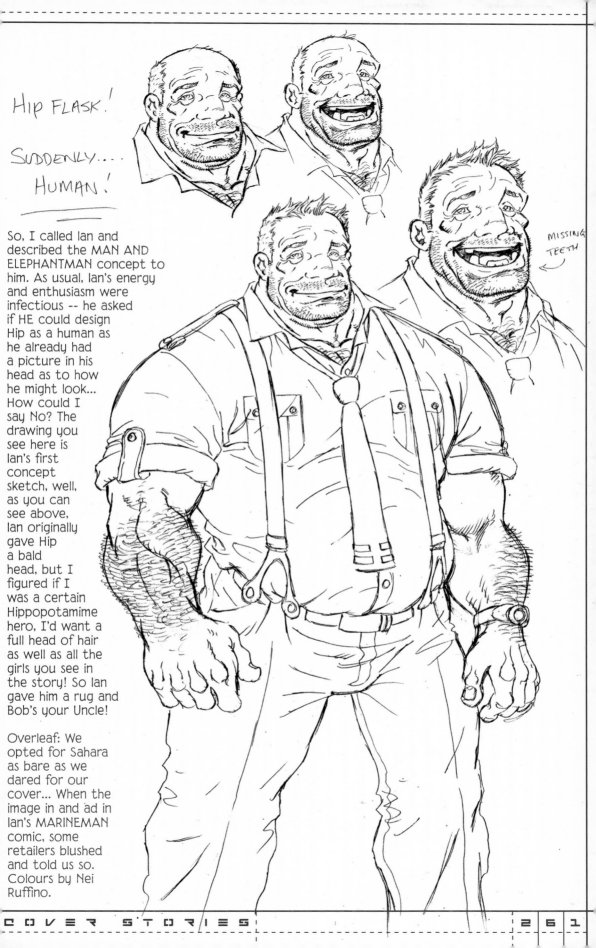

HIP FLASK!

SUDDENLY....
HUMAN!

MISSING
TEETH

So, I called Ian and
described the MAN AND
ELEPHANTMAN concept to
him. As usual, Ian's energy
and enthusiasm were
infectious -- he asked
if HE could design
Hip as a human as
he already had
a picture in his
head as to how
he might look...
How could I
say No? The
drawing you
see here is
Ian's first
concept
sketch, well,
as you can
see above,
Ian originally
gave Hip
a bald
head, but I
figured if I
was a certain
Hippopotamime
hero, I'd want a
full head of hair
as well as all the
girls you see in
the story! So Ian
gave him a rug and
Bob's your Uncle!

Overleaf: We
opted for Sahara
as bare as we
dared for our
cover... When the
image in and ad in
Ian's MARINEMAN
comic, some
retailers blushed
and told us so.
Colours by Nei
Ruffino.

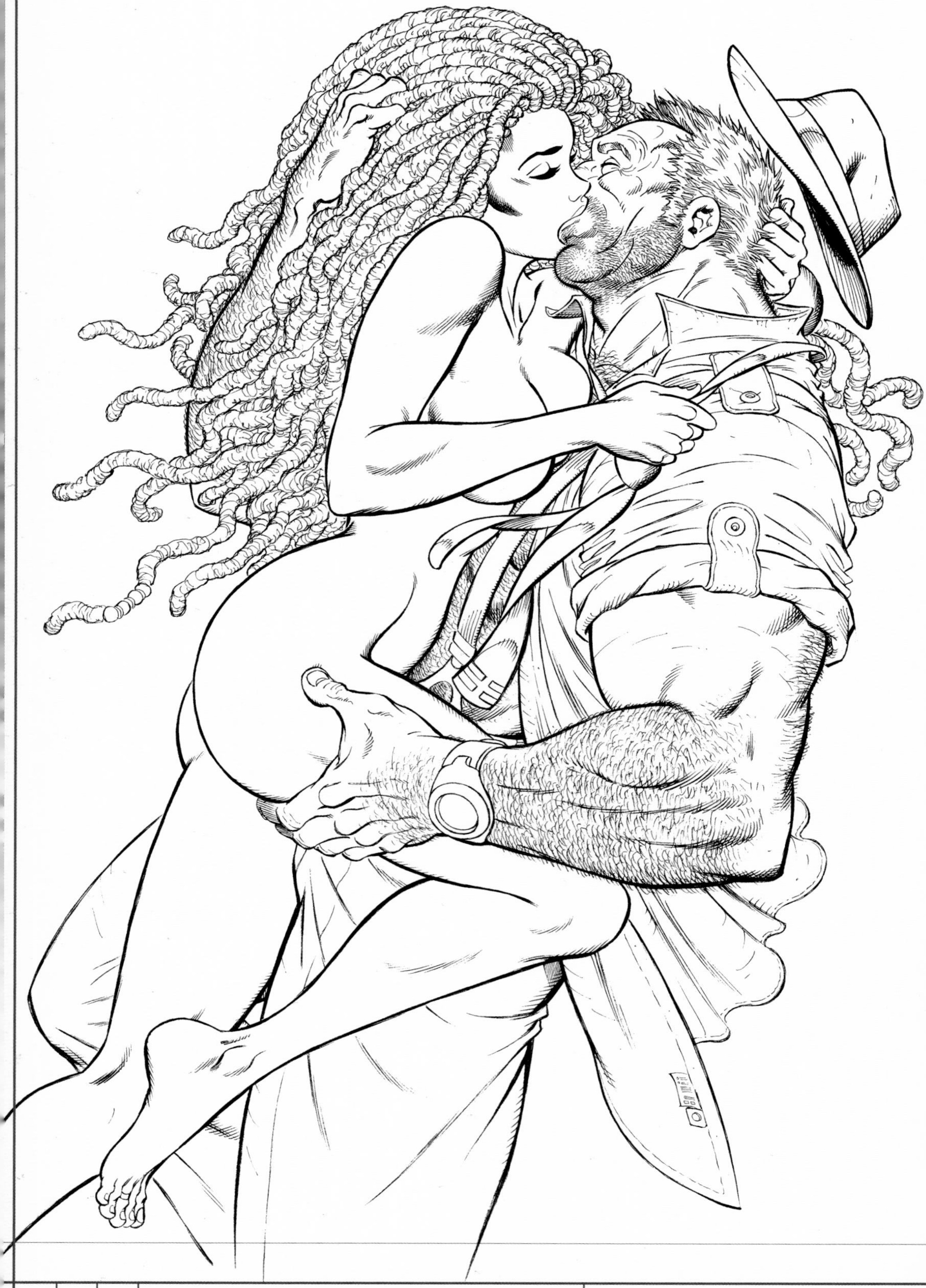

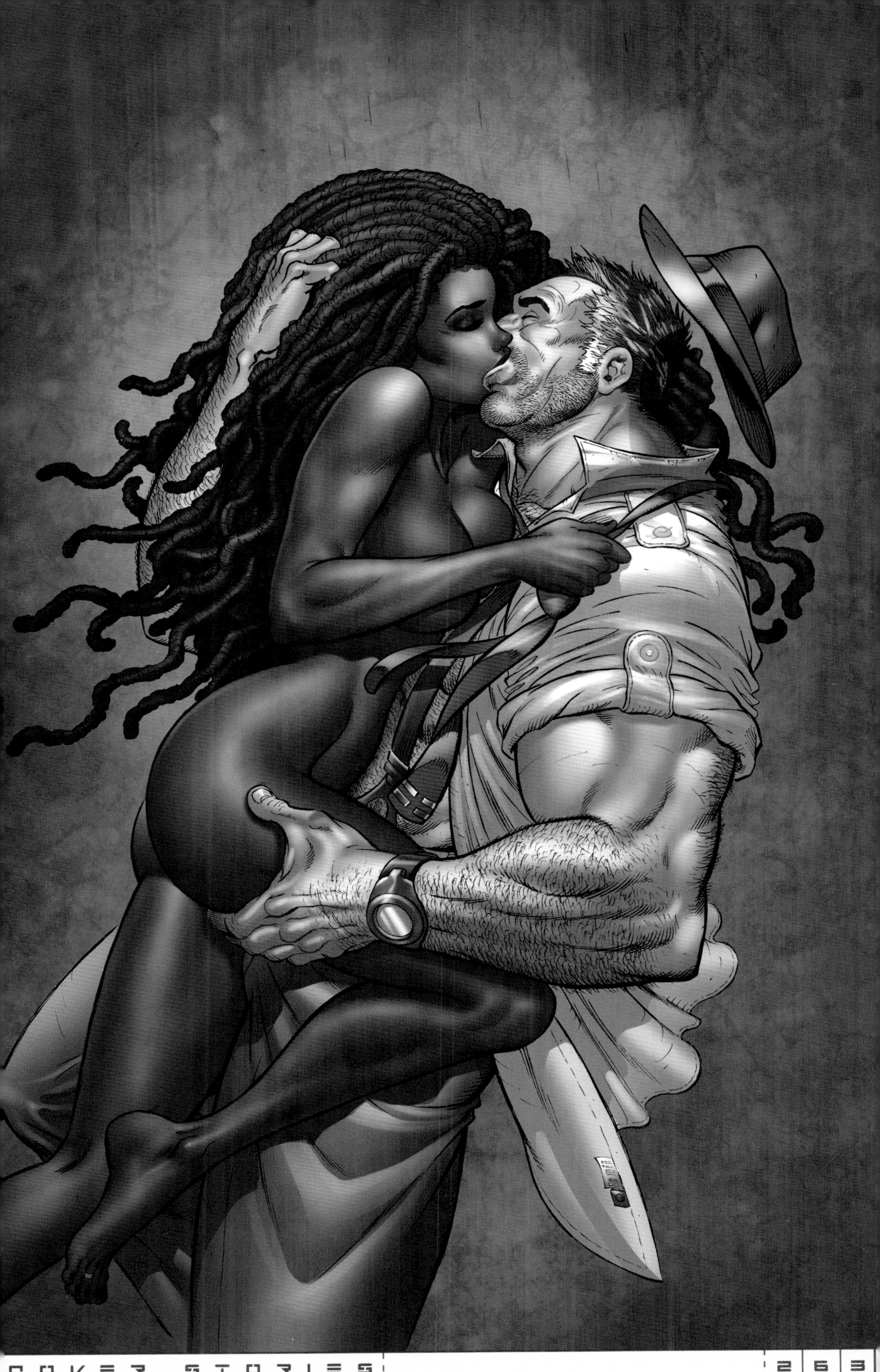

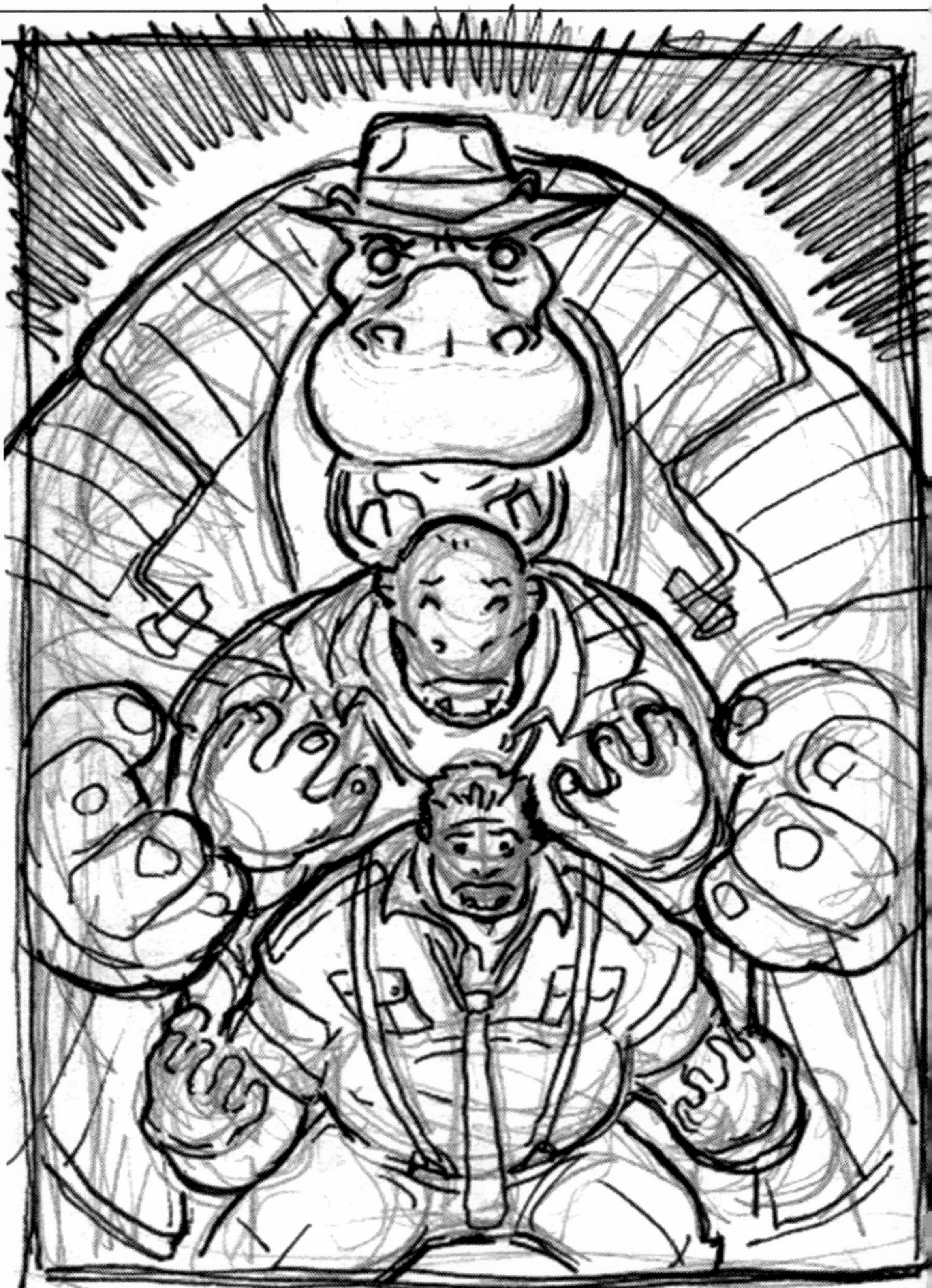

Ed McGuinness had promised me a cover for ELEPHANTMEN stretching back to the HIP FLASK days... and it seemed to me that Hip's metamorphosis from Man back to Elephantman was perfect for Ed, who was completing his run on Jeph Loeb's RED HULK series. Marvel gave special permission to Ed to create this piece -- a nod to the very first HULK cover -- and Boo Cook coloured it up so lovingly that Ed requested Boo colour his next three HULK covers.

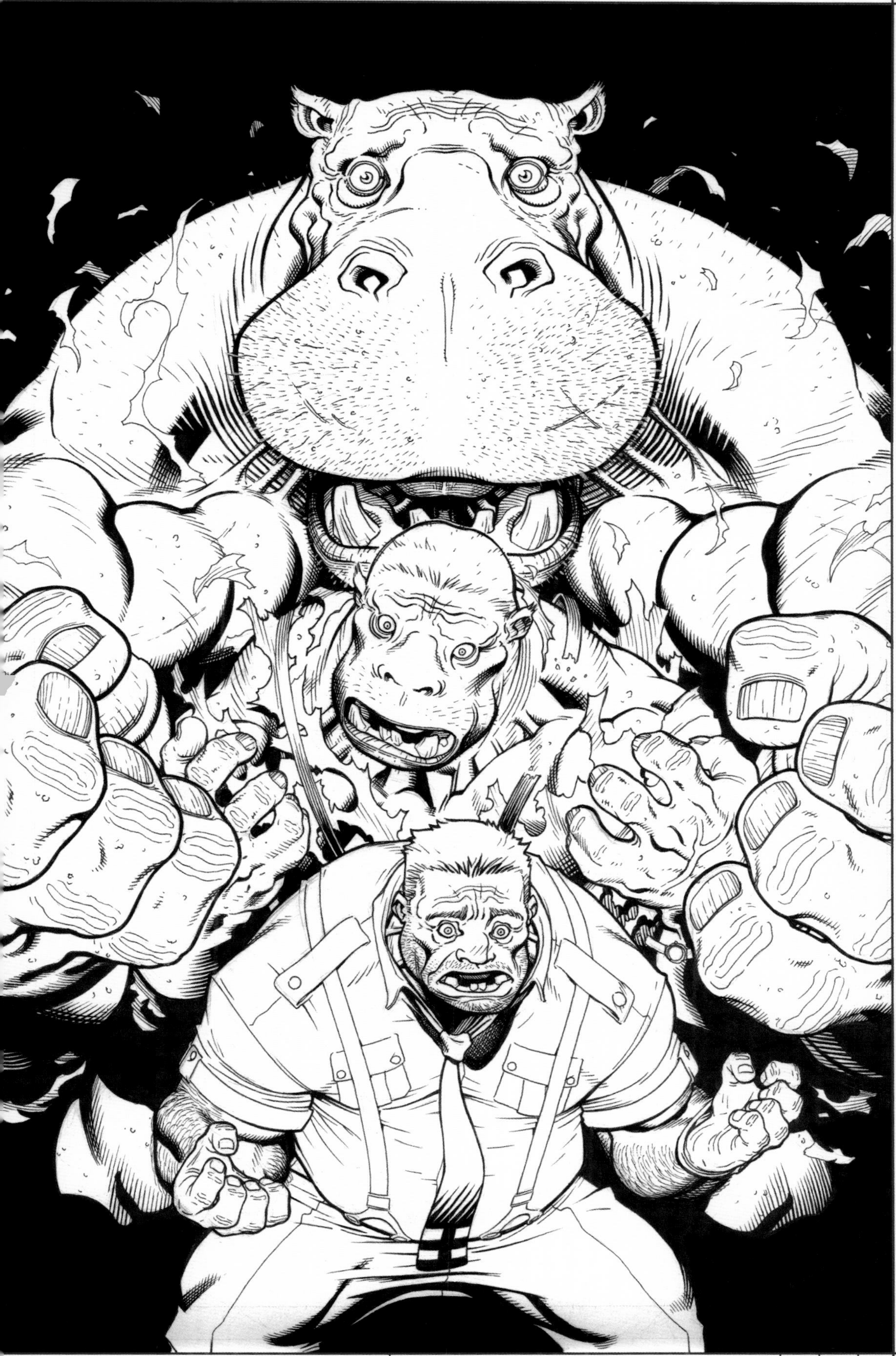

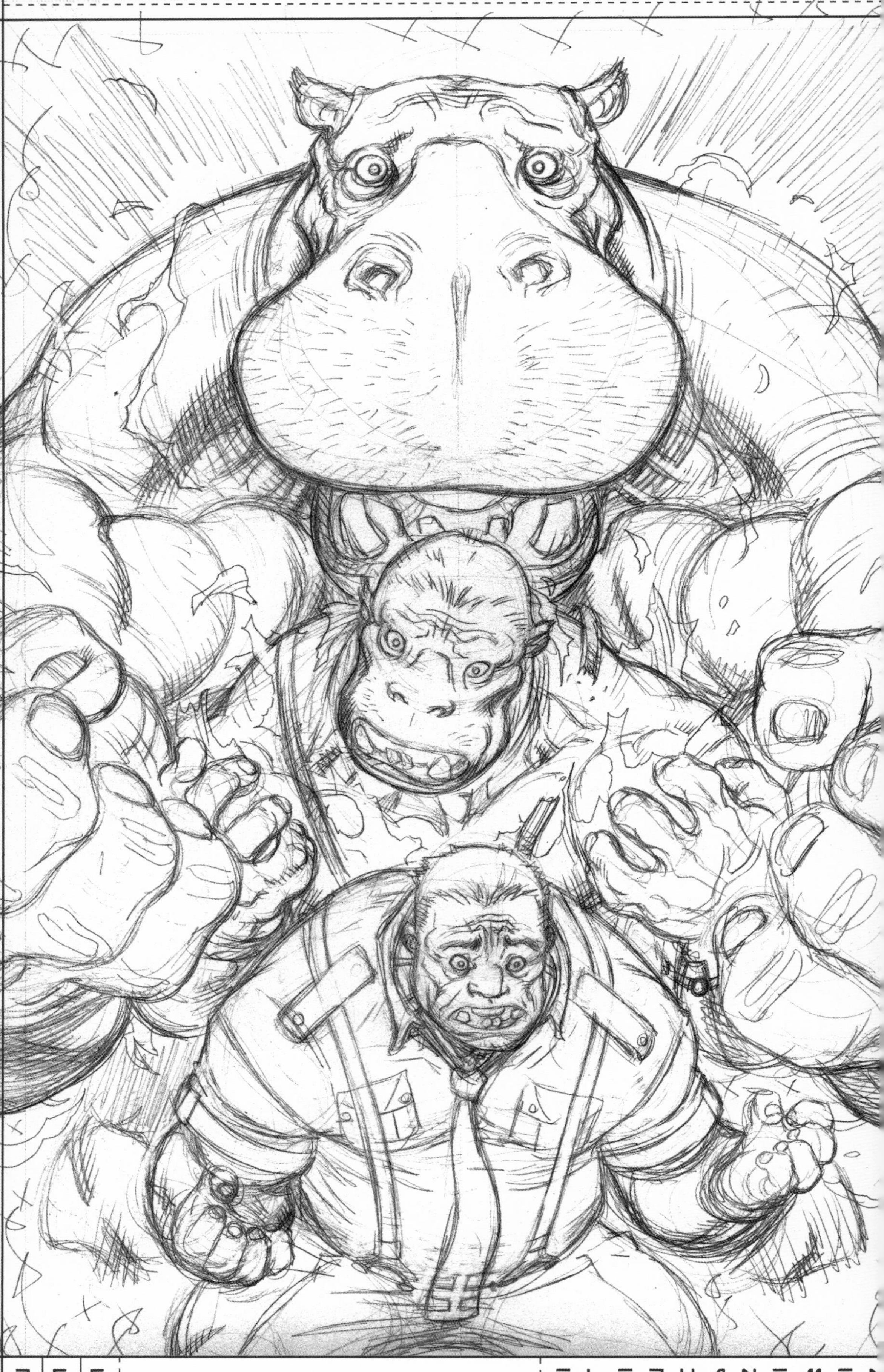

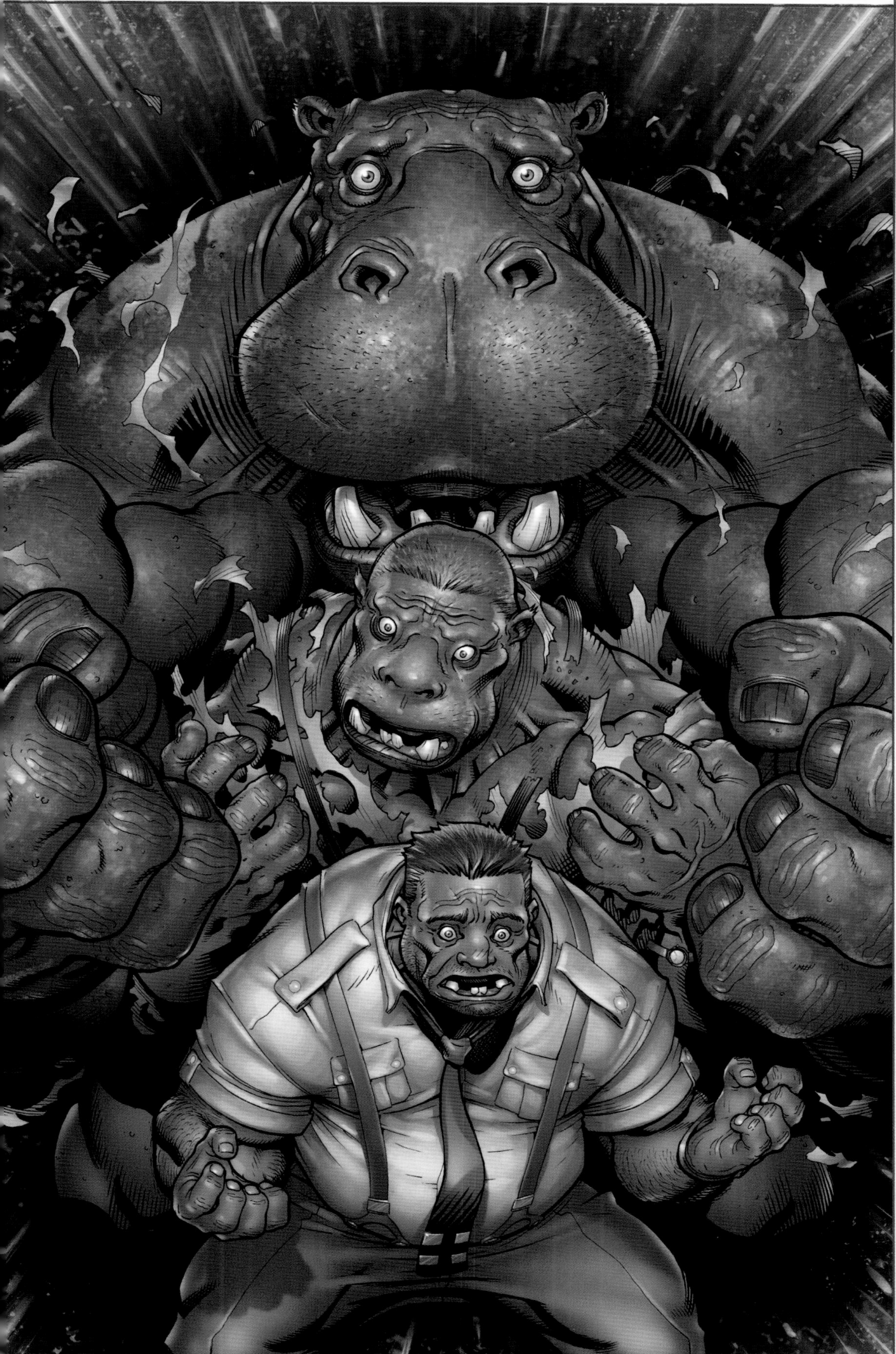

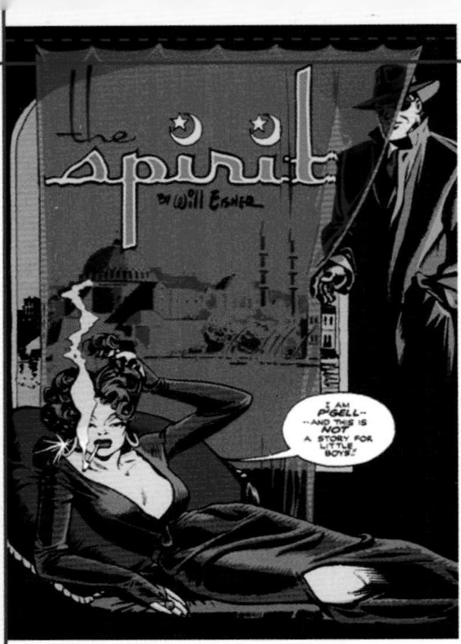
the spirit
BY Will Eisner
I AM P'GELL-- AND THIS IS NOT A STORY FOR LITTLE BOYS!

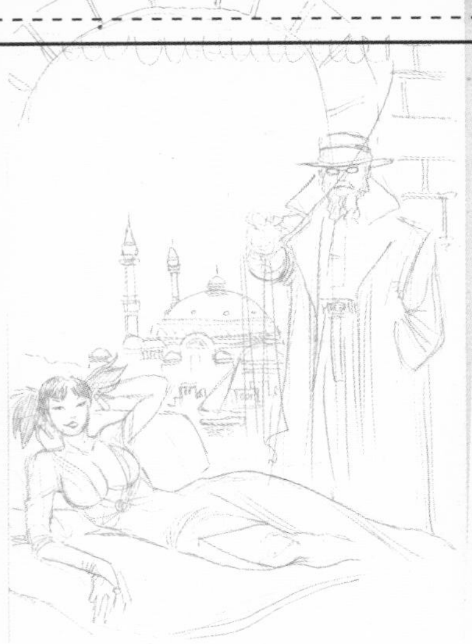

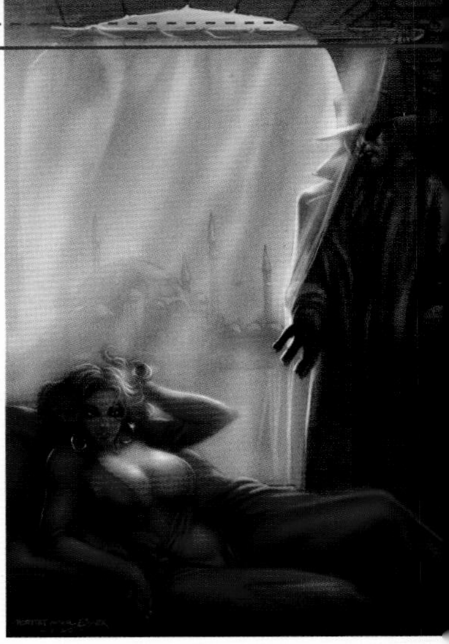

I've always loved THE SPIRIT title pages by Will Eisner, and the one you see top left has to be my favourite. Moritat had promised me he'd draw the pastiche I wanted for the cover, but when he finally sat down, he drew me as Hip instead (center). "Draw it yourself!" he challenged! So, with help from his own versions, and gorgeous colours by Boo Cook, I did!

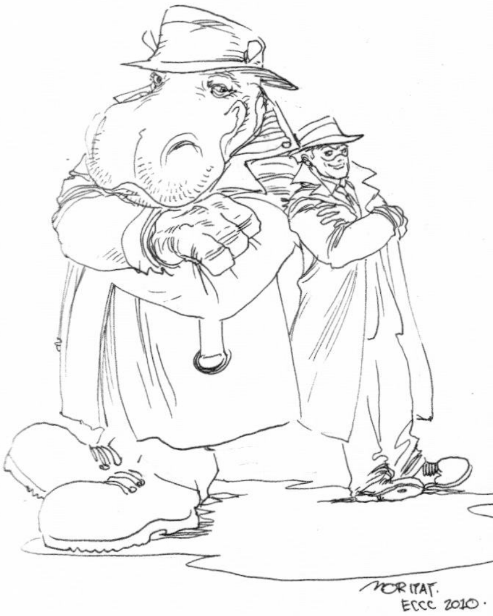
MORITAT.
ECCC 2010.

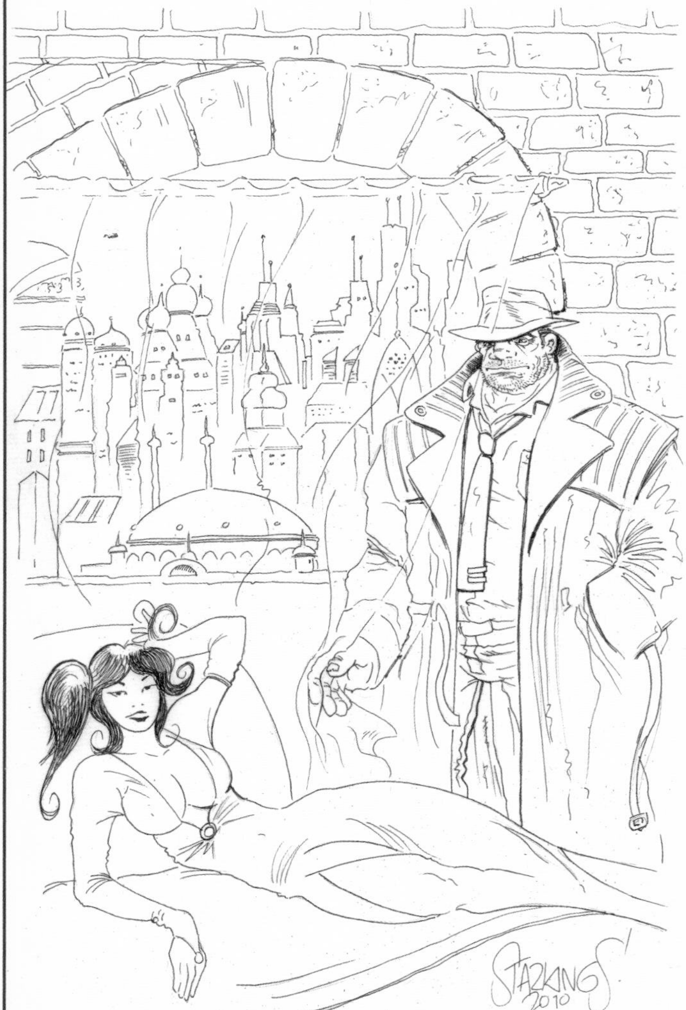
STARKINGS
2010

Below: I visited this cover once before, when Will Eisner passed away, with FATALE's Sean Phillips

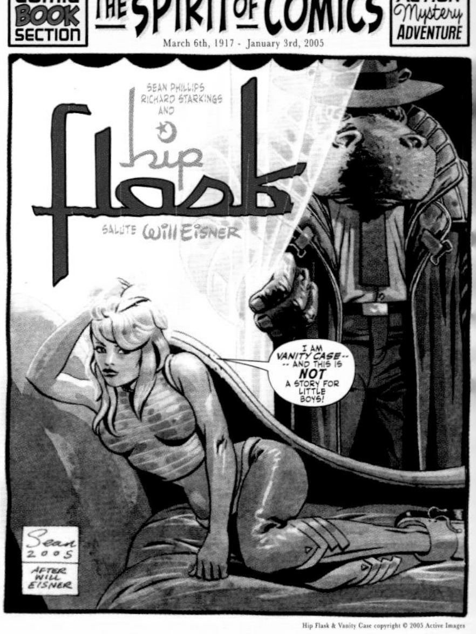
COMIC BOOK SECTION
THE SPIRIT OF COMICS
ACTION Mystery ADVENTURE
March 6th, 1917 - January 3rd, 2005
SEAN PHILLIPS
RICHARD STARKINGS
AND
hip flask
SALUTE Will Eisner
I AM VANITY CASE-- AND THIS IS NOT A STORY FOR LITTLE BOYS!
Sean 2005
AFTER WILL EISNER

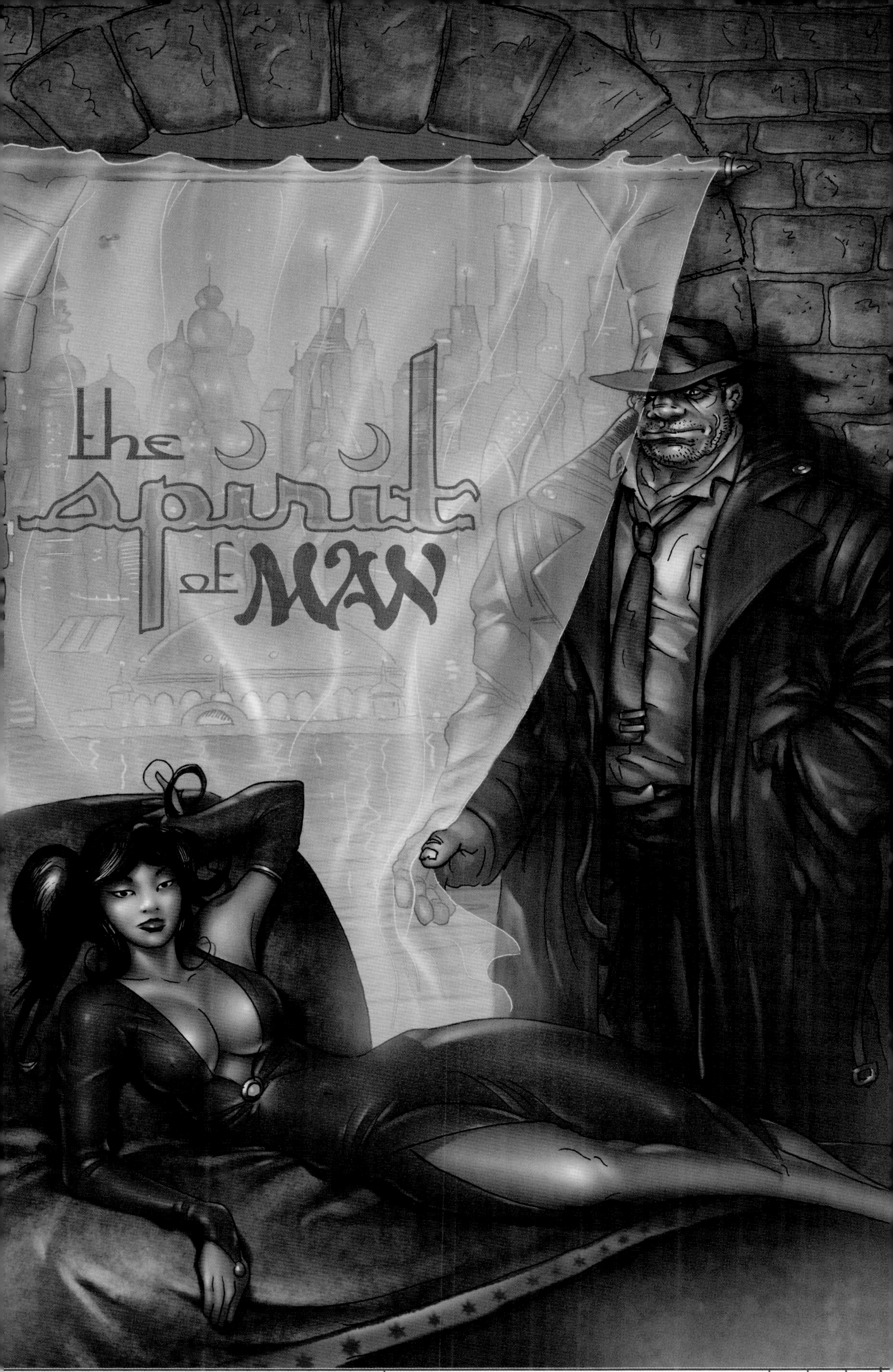
the spirit of MAN

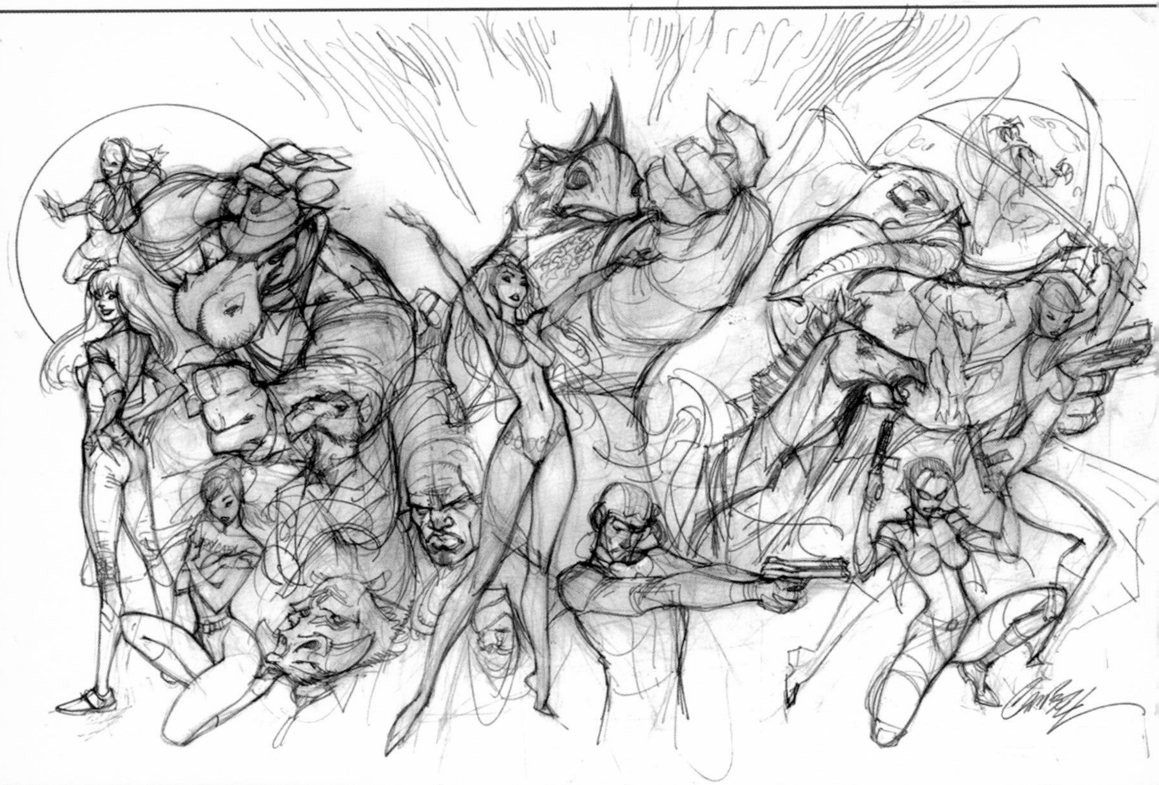

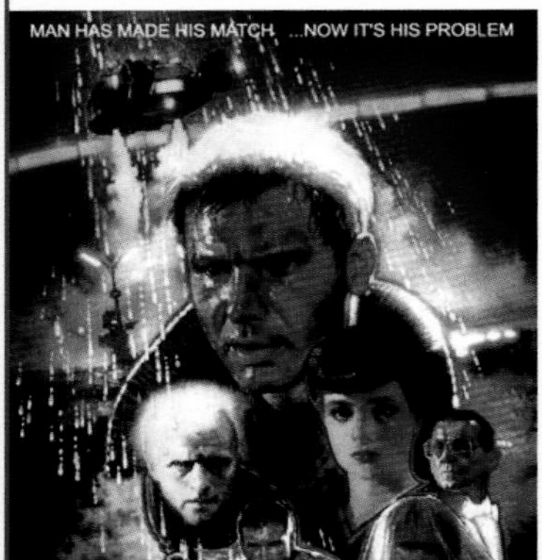
MAN HAS MADE HIS MATCH ...NOW IT'S HIS PROBLEM
HARRISON FORD
BLADE RUNNER

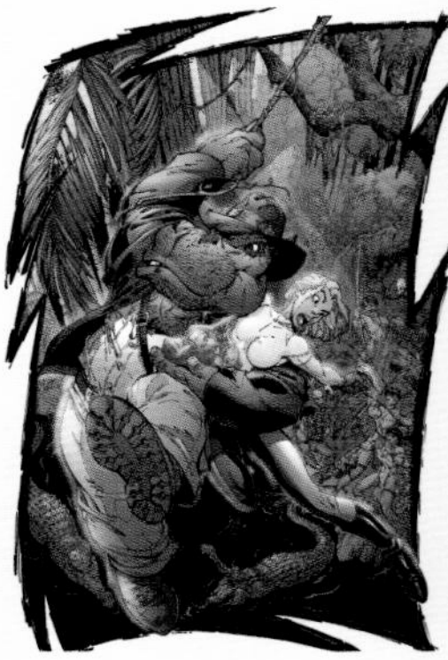

I'm often asked how I get so much great work out of J. Scott Campbell... and the truth is, I LOVE Jeff's art and I think I know how to get him excited about covers... I always seek to play to his strengths and consider his own interests when I put him to task. Amazingly, the triptych of retailer incentive covers for MAN AND ELEPHANTMAN, ELEPHANTMEN #31 and #32 were suggested BY Jeff! The very first piece Jeff created for me was a tip of the hat to INDIANA JONES (see right), which we had both loved as teenagers... for this piece, I proposed covers in the style of our favourite STAR WARS and BLADE RUNNER posters... part montage, part group shot and All Awesome! Jeff sent me the rough sketches above and overleaf to show me what he was thinking... grouping the characters from light to dark at my suggestion, but adding the sun and the moon as a way of creating light and mood for each of the three pieces so that they be distinct as separate covers.

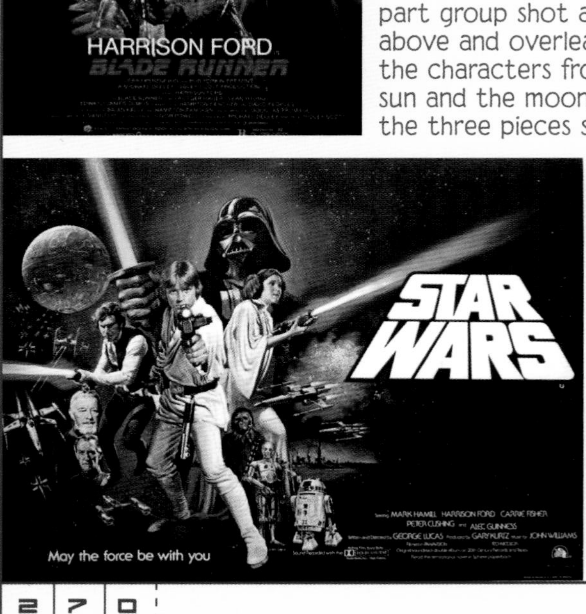
STAR WARS
MARK HAMILL HARRISON FORD CARRIE FISHER
PETER CUSHING and ALEC GUINNESS
May the force be with you

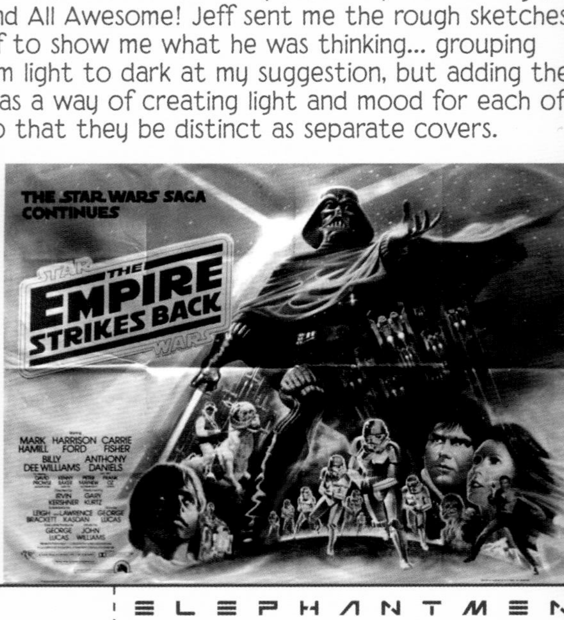
THE STAR WARS SAGA CONTINUES
STAR WARS
THE EMPIRE STRIKES BACK
MARK HAMILL HARRISON FORD CARRIE FISHER
BILLY DEE WILLIAMS ANTHONY DANIELS

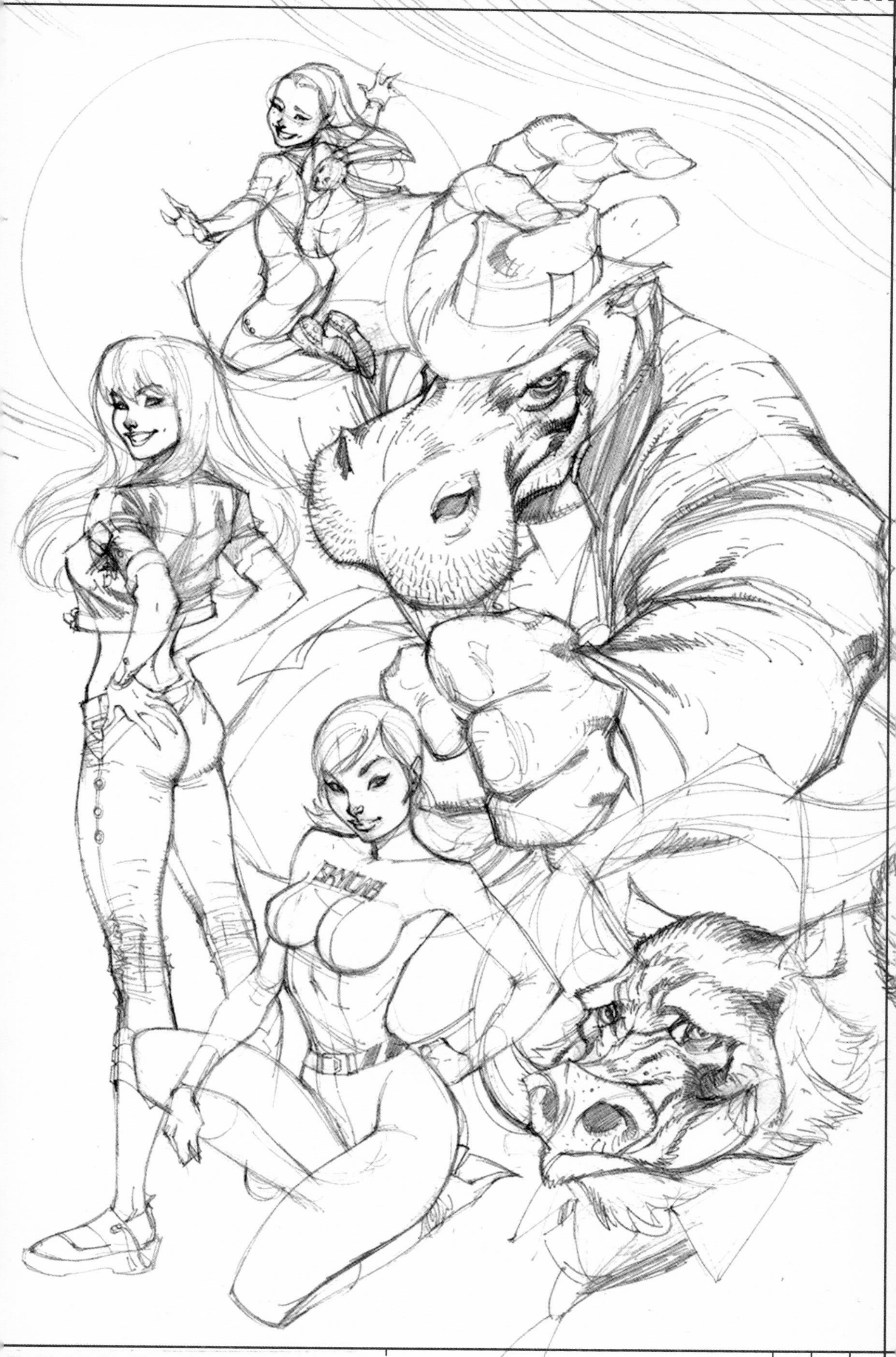

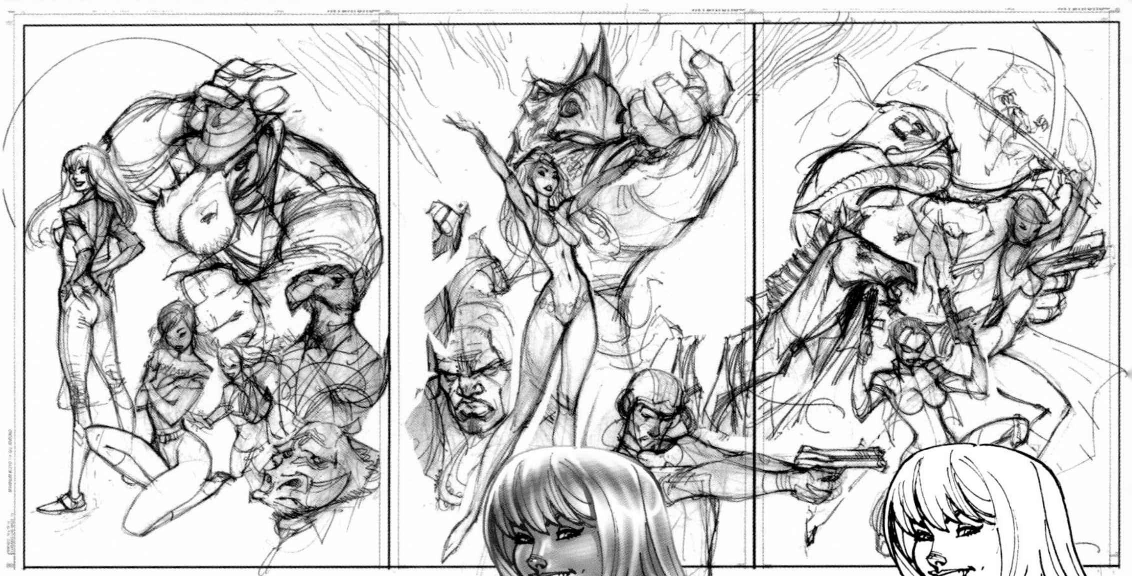

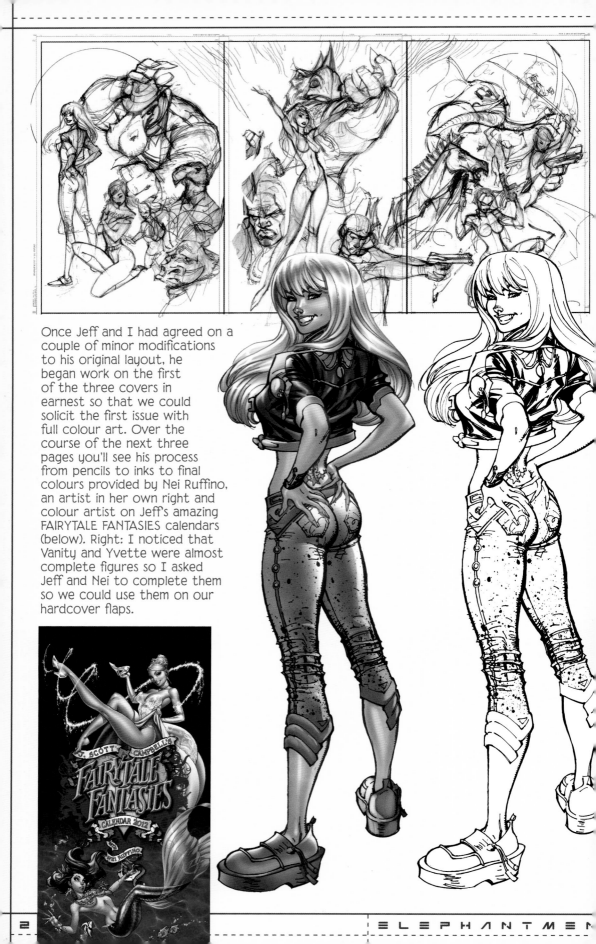

Once Jeff and I had agreed on a couple of minor modifications to his original layout, he began work on the first of the three covers in earnest so that we could solicit the first issue with full colour art. Over the course of the next three pages you'll see his process from pencils to inks to final colours provided by Nei Ruffino, an artist in her own right and colour artist on Jeff's amazing FAIRYTALE FANTASIES calendars (below). Right: I noticed that Vanity and Yvette were almost complete figures so I asked Jeff and Nei to complete them so we could use them on our hardcover flaps.

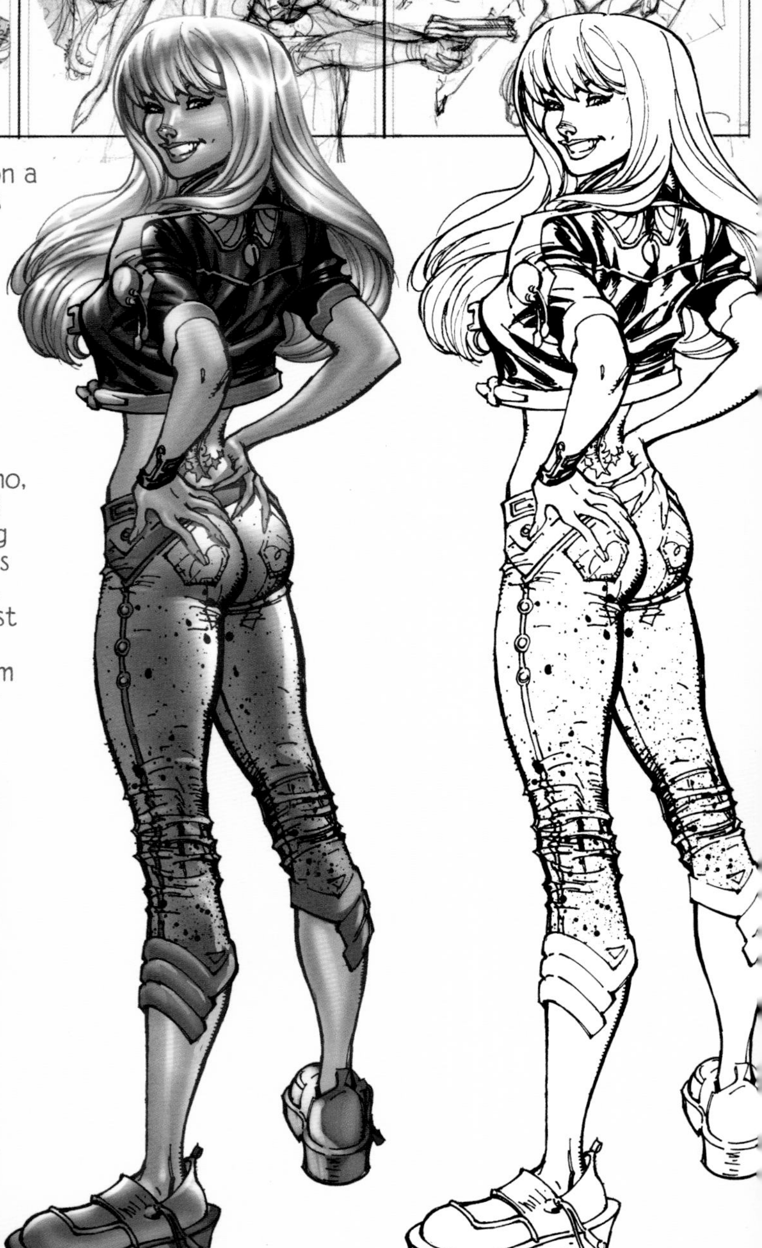

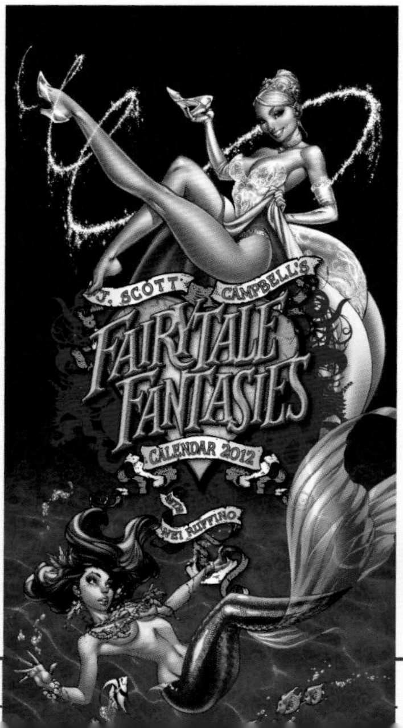
J. SCOTT CAMPBELL'S
FAIRYTALE FANTASIES
CALENDAR 2012

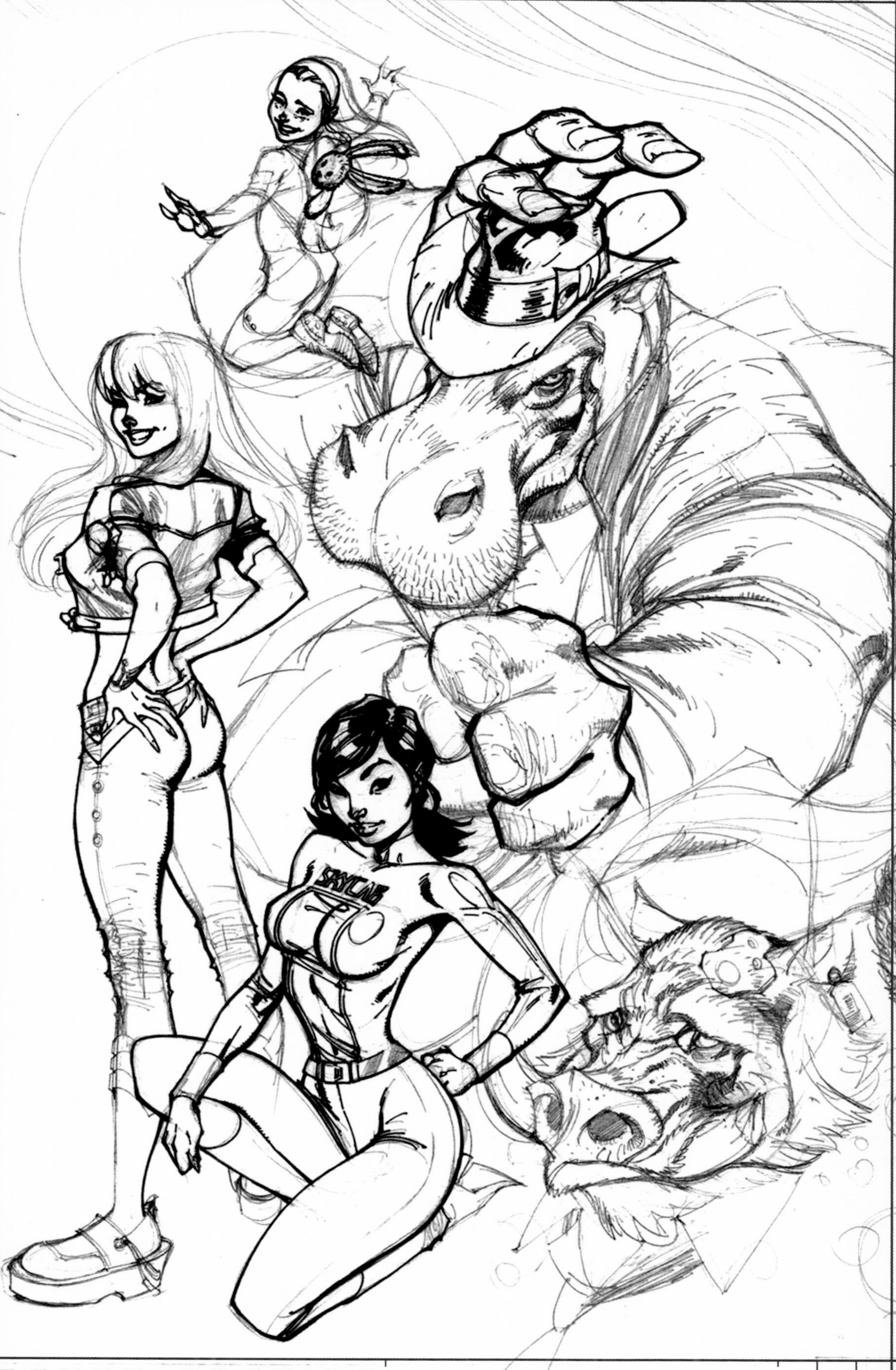
SKYCAB

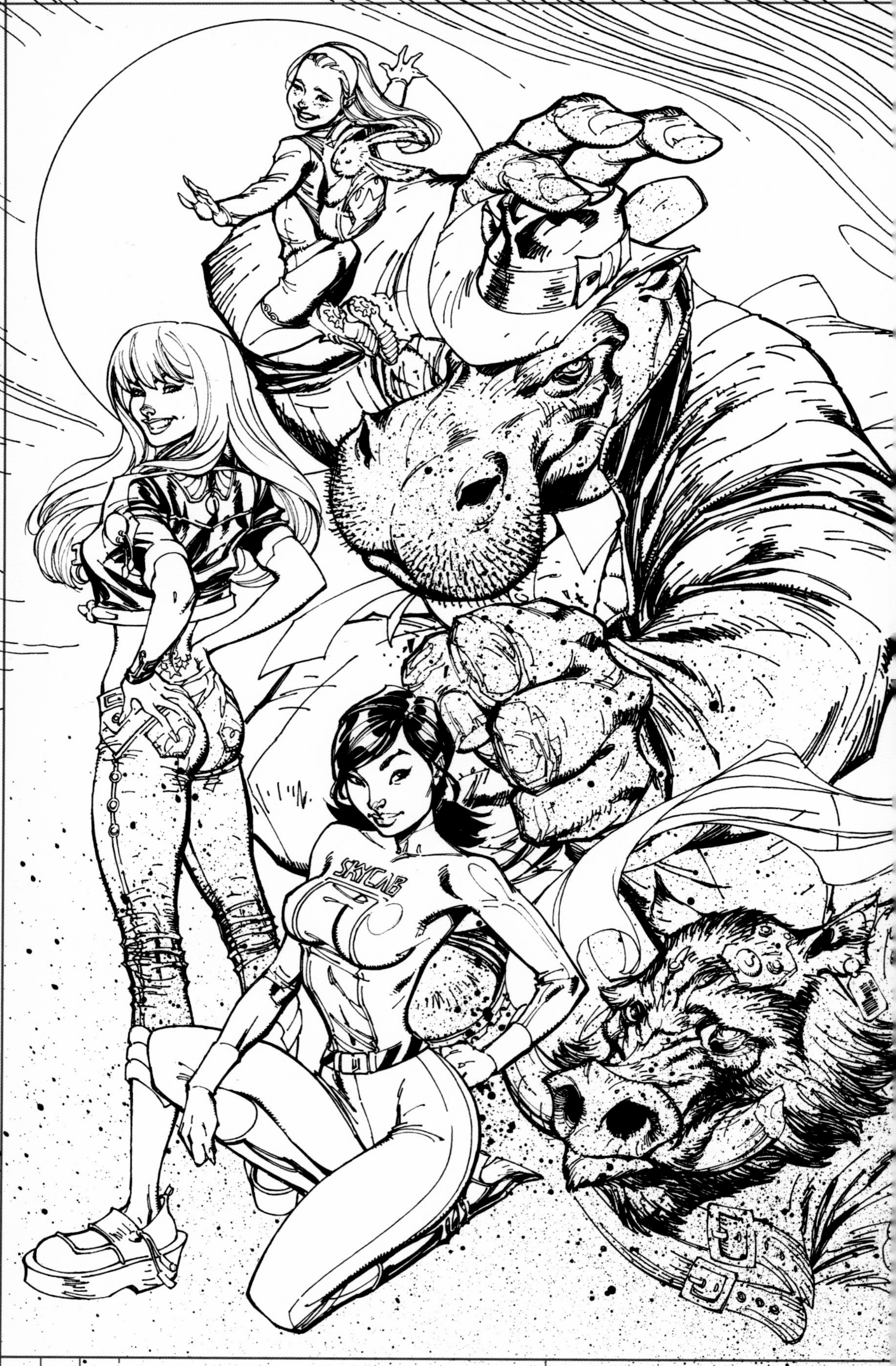
SKYCAB

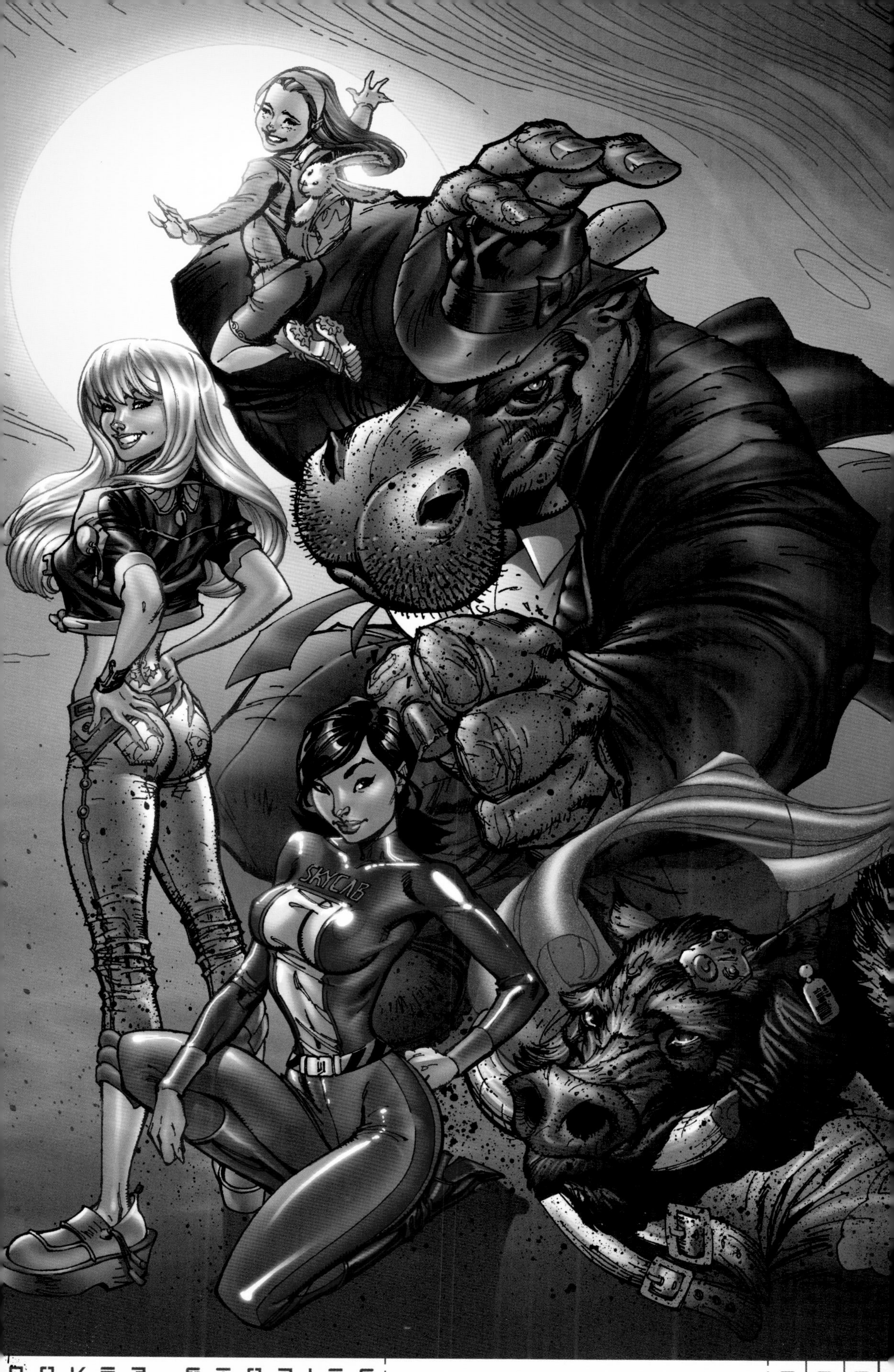
SKYCAB

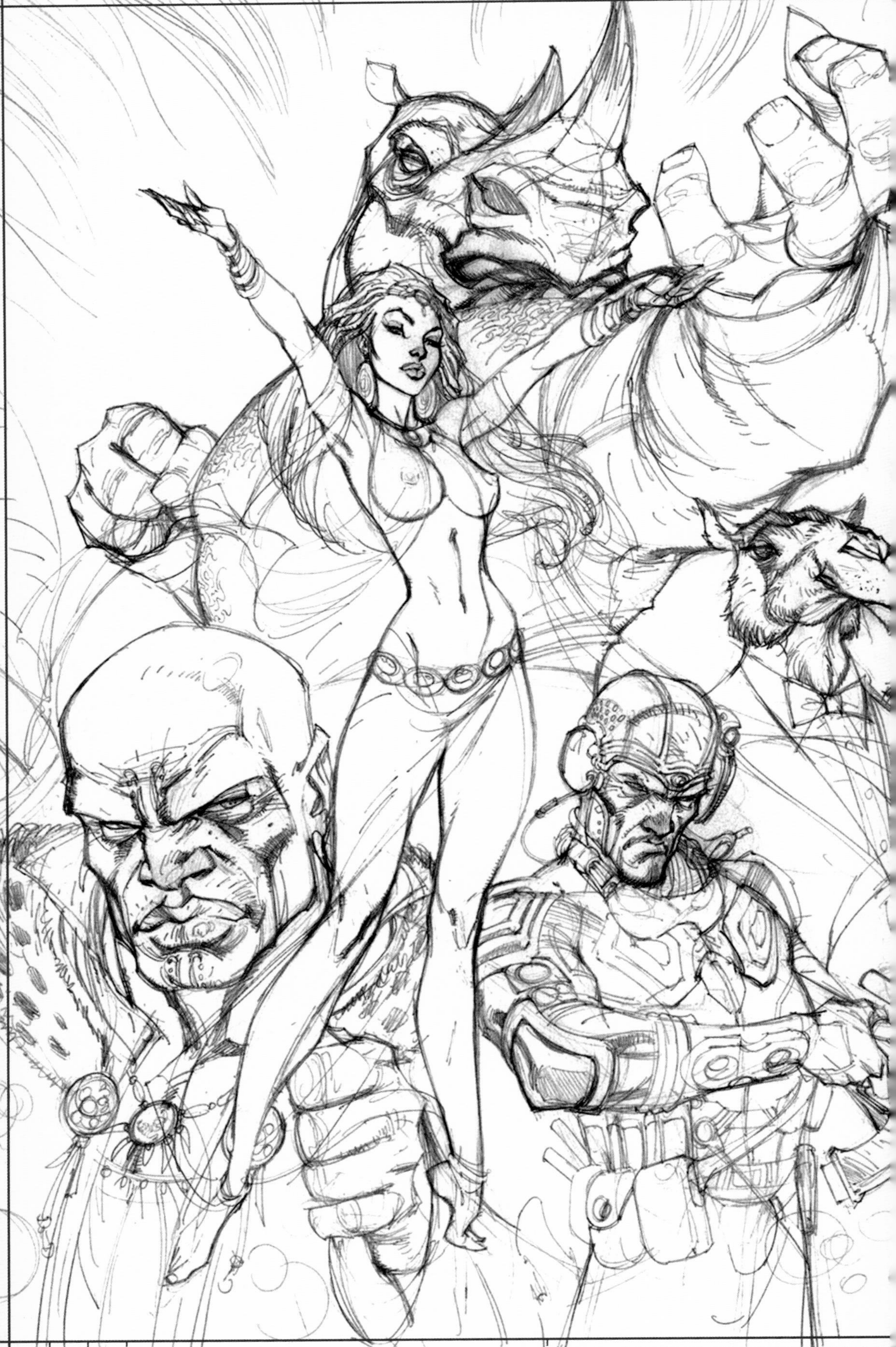

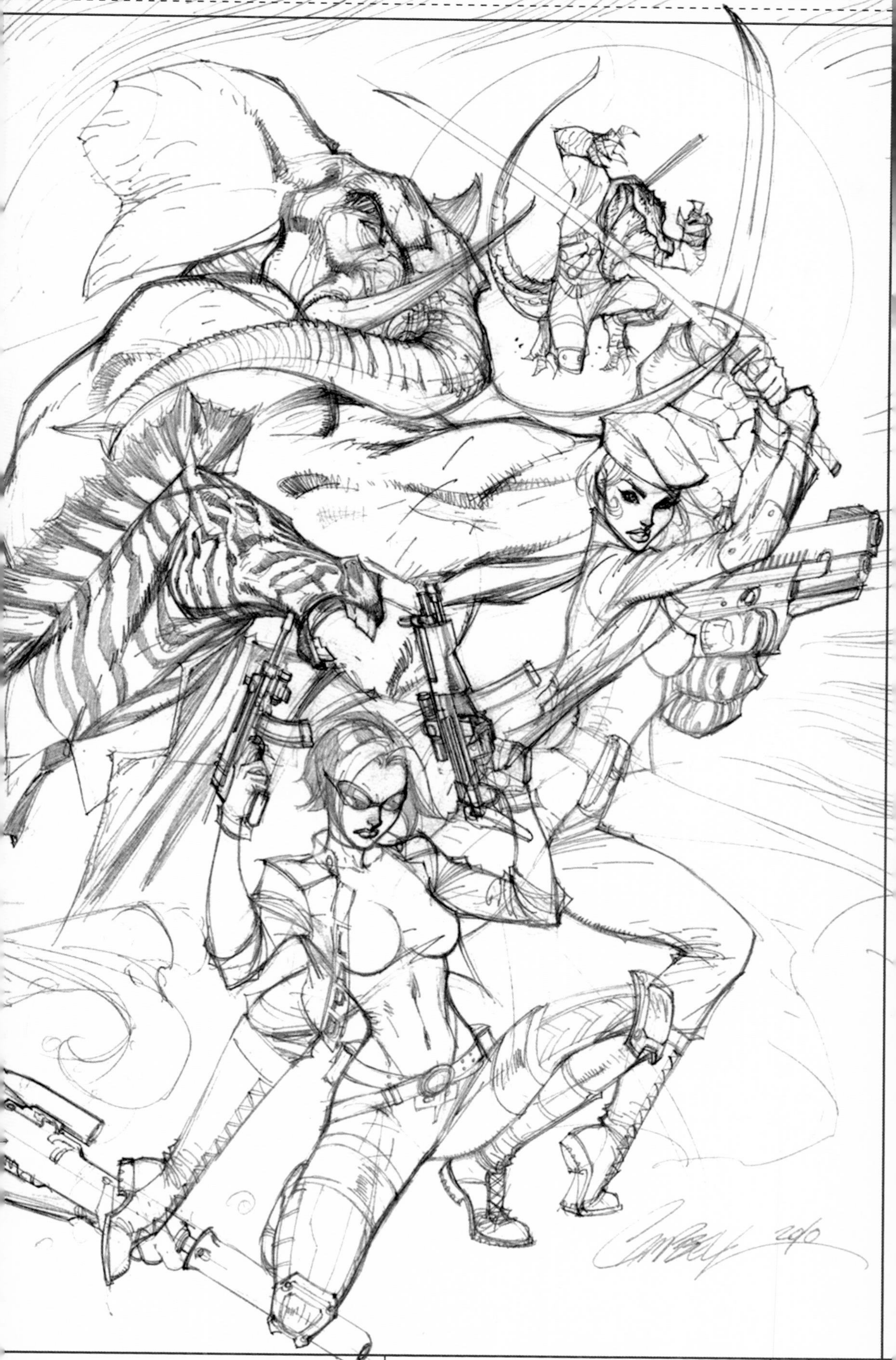

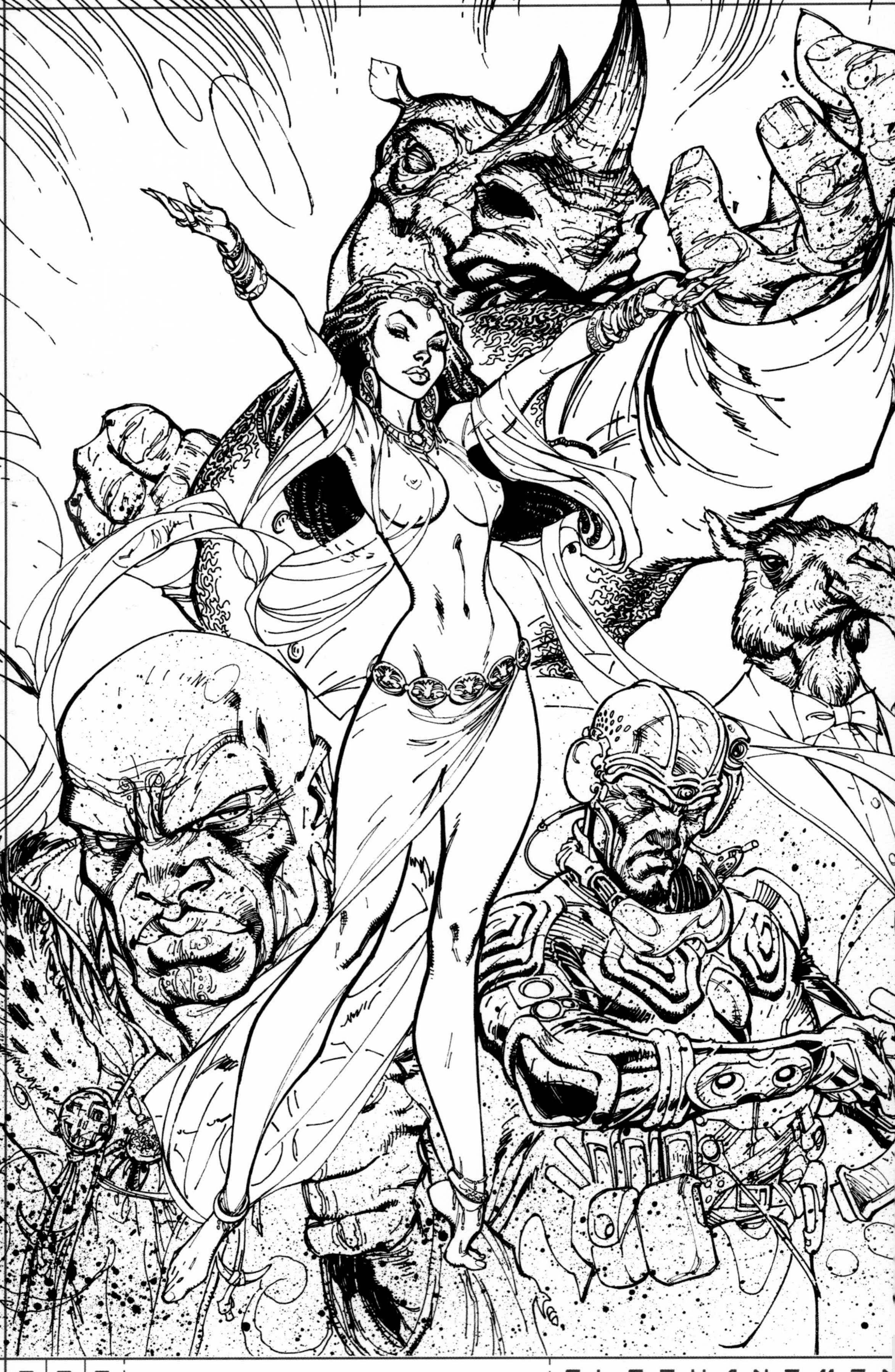

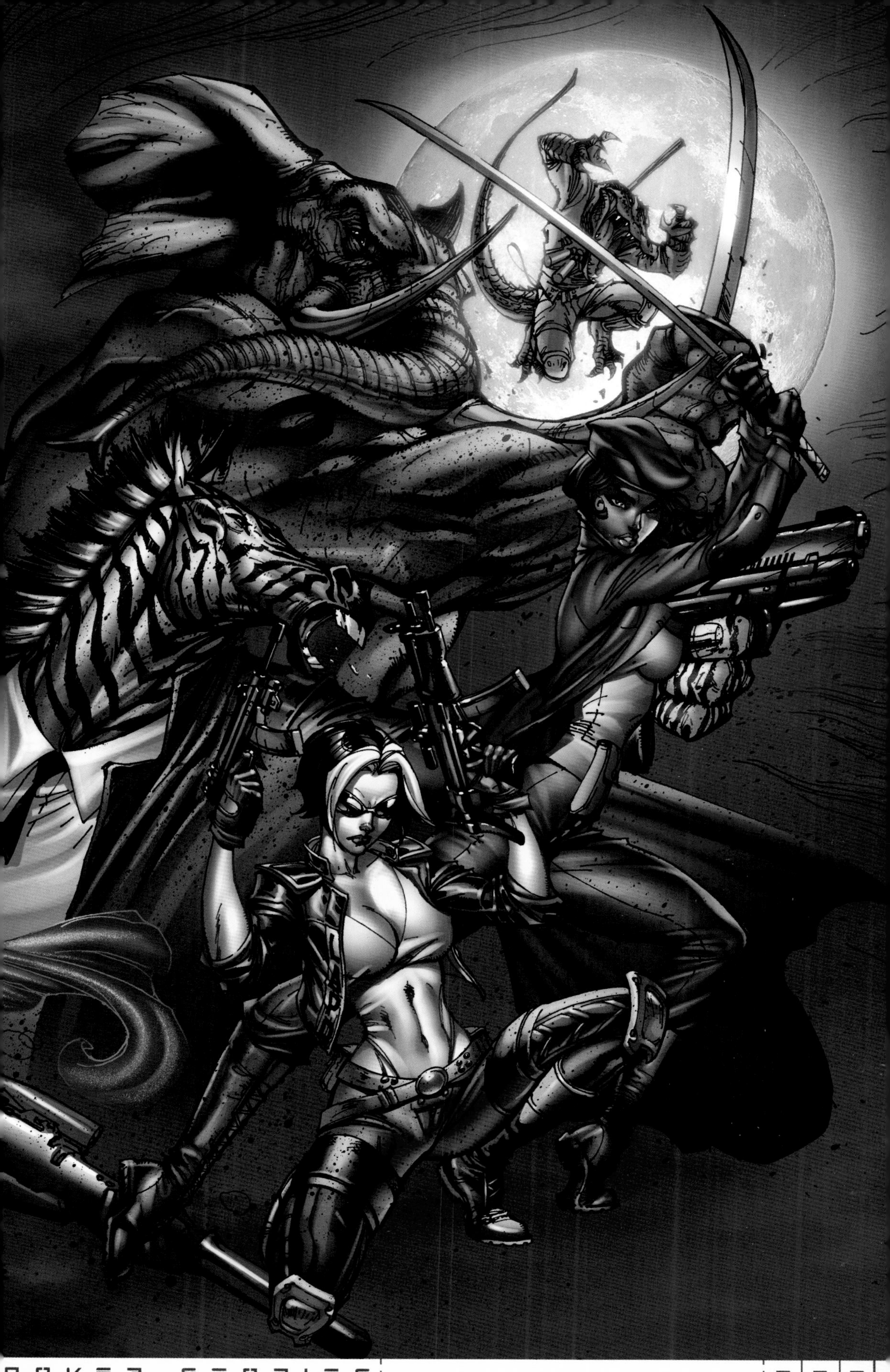

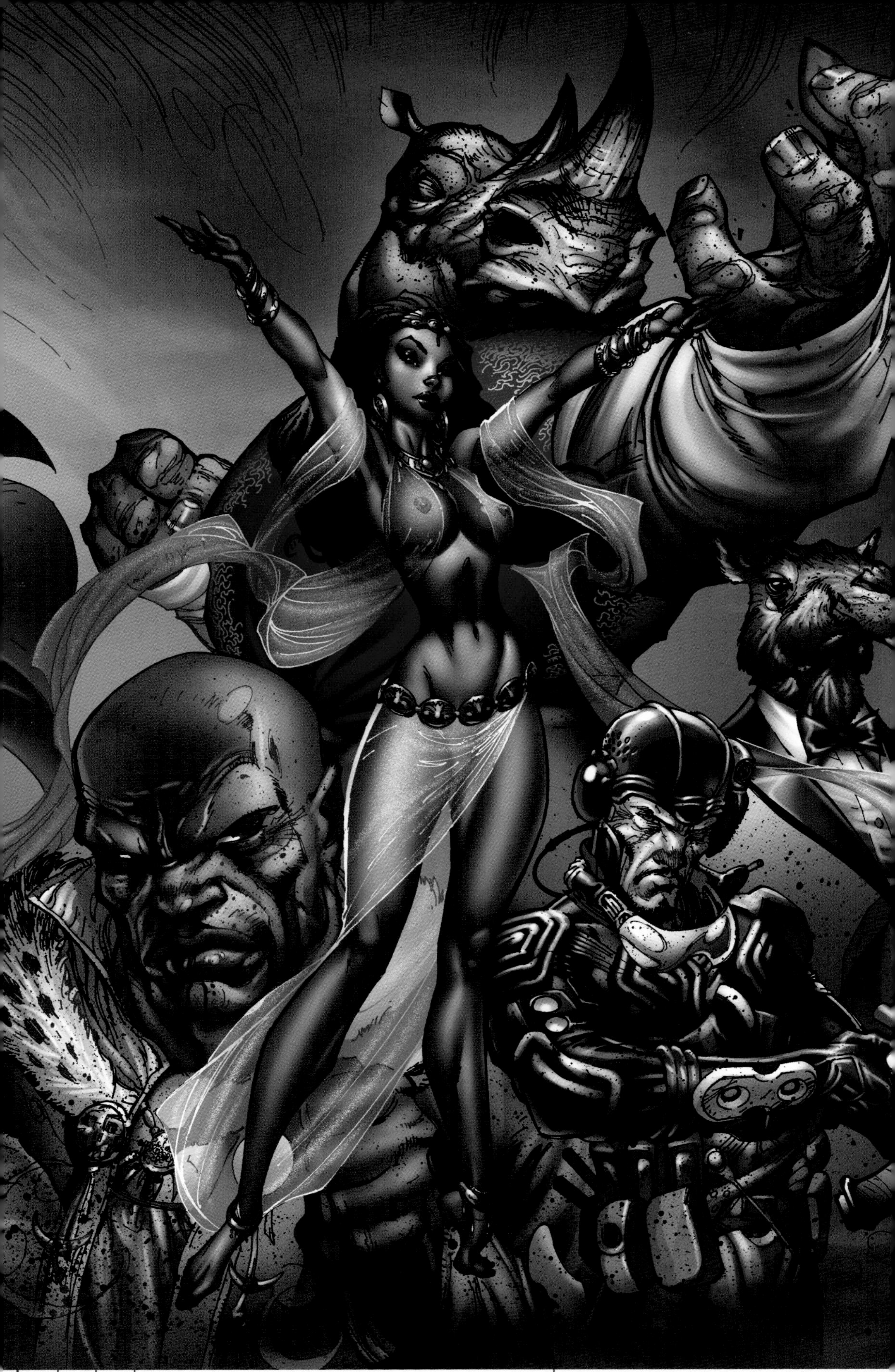

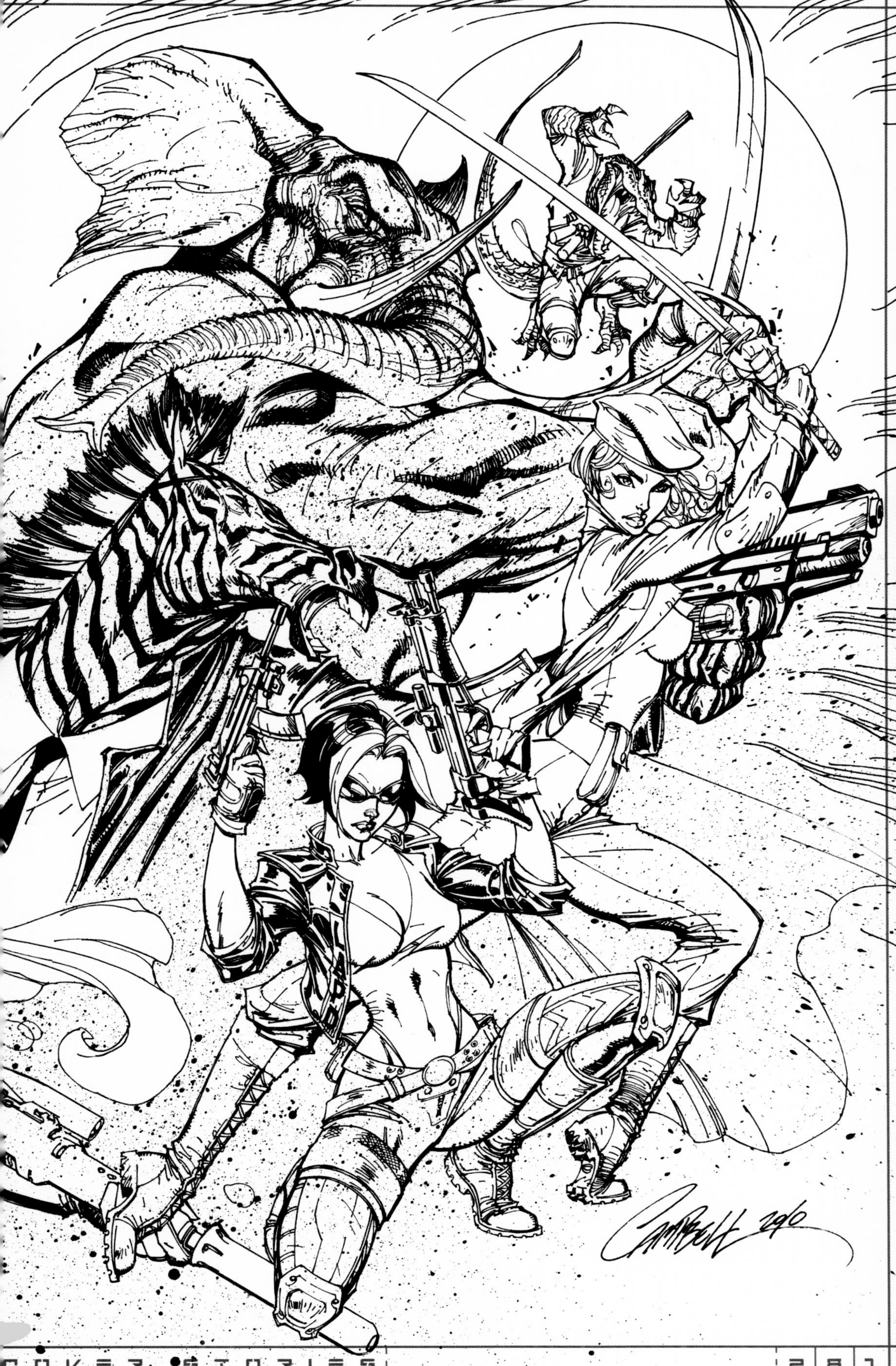

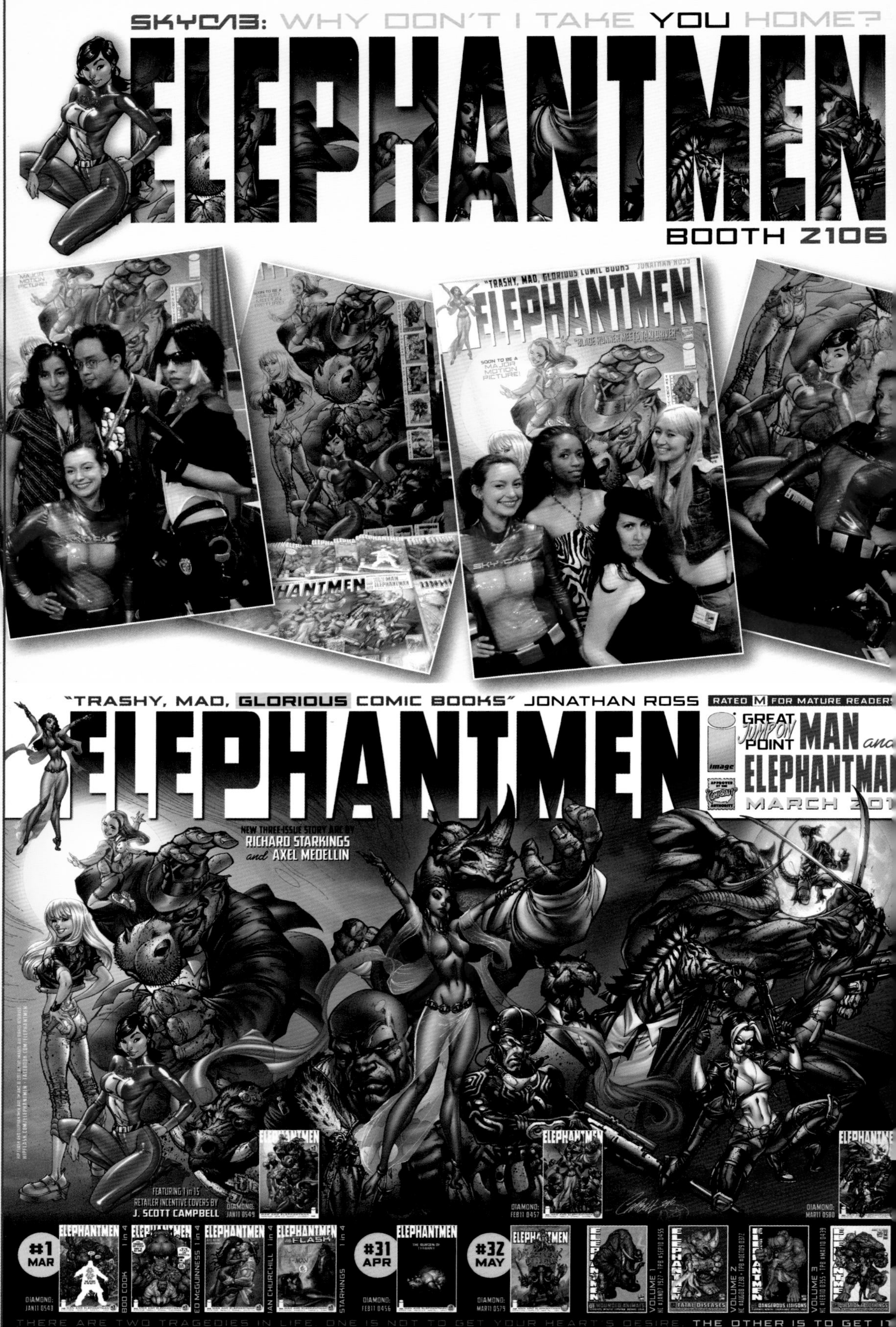

SKYCAB: WHY DON'T I TAKE YOU HOME?
ELEPHANTMEN
BOOTH Z106
"TRASHY, MAD, GLORIOUS COMIC BOOKS" JONATHAN ROSS
RATED M FOR MATURE READERS
ELEPHANTMEN
GREAT JUMP ON POINT
MAN and ELEPHANTMAN
MARCH 201
NEW THREE-ISSUE STORY ARC BY
RICHARD STARKINGS
and AXEL MEDELLIN
FEATURING 1 in 15
RETAILER INCENTIVE COVERS BY
J. SCOTT CAMPBELL
DIAMOND: JAN11 0549
DIAMOND: FEB11 0457
DIAMOND: MAR11 0580
#1 MAR
DIAMOND: JAN11 0548
BOO COOK 1 in 4
ED McGUINNESS 1 in 4
IAN CHURCHILL 1 in 4
STARKINGS 1 in 4
#31 APR
DIAMOND: FEB11 0456
#32 MAY
DIAMOND: MAR11 0579
VOLUME 1 HC #JAN07 1927 • TPB #SEP10 0455
WOUNDED ANIMALS
VOLUME 2 HC #AUG08 2238 • TPB #OCT09 0372
FATAL DISEASES
DANGEROUS LIAISONS
VOLUME 3 HC #FEB10 0355 • TPB #MAY10 0439
QUESTIONABLE THINGS
THERE ARE TWO TRAGEDIES IN LIFE. ONE IS NOT TO GET YOUR HEART'S DESIRE. THE OTHER IS TO GET IT

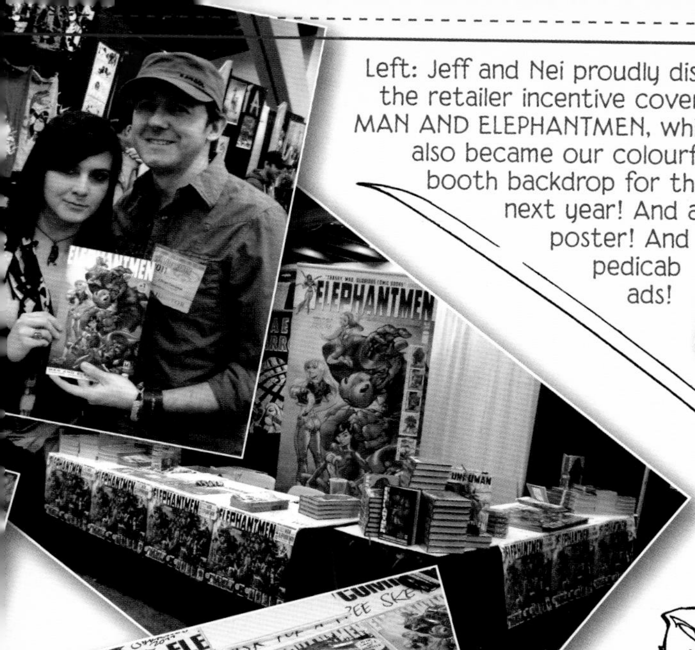

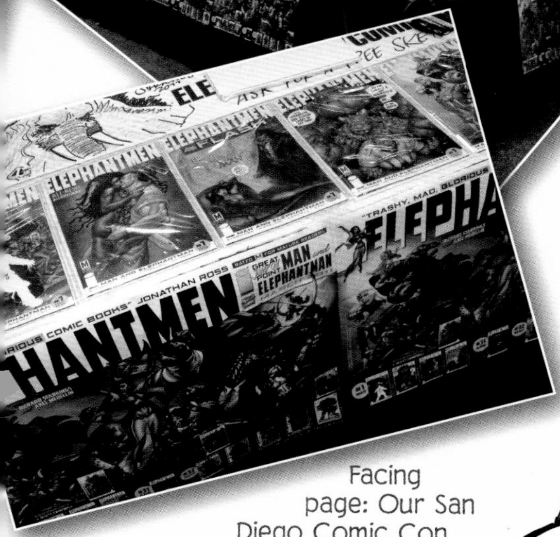

Left: Jeff and Nei proudly display the retailer incentive cover of MAN AND ELEPHANTMEN, which also became our colourful booth backdrop for the next year! And a poster! And pedicab ads!

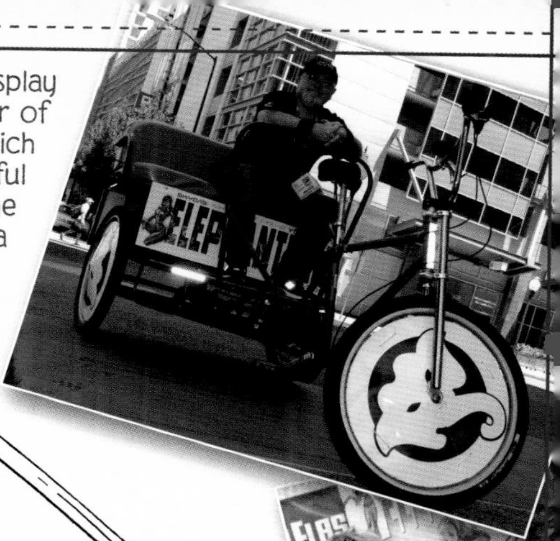

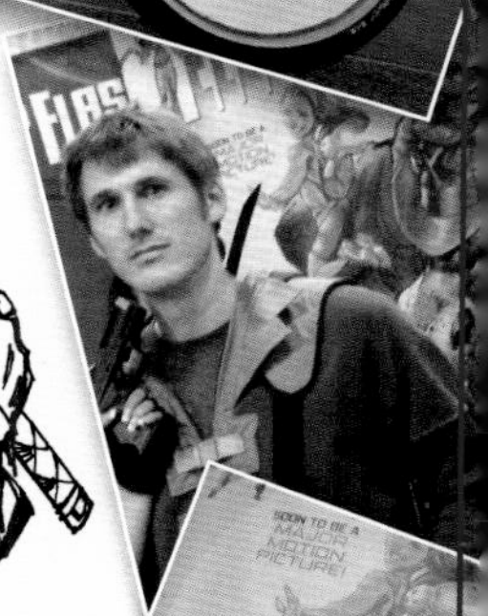

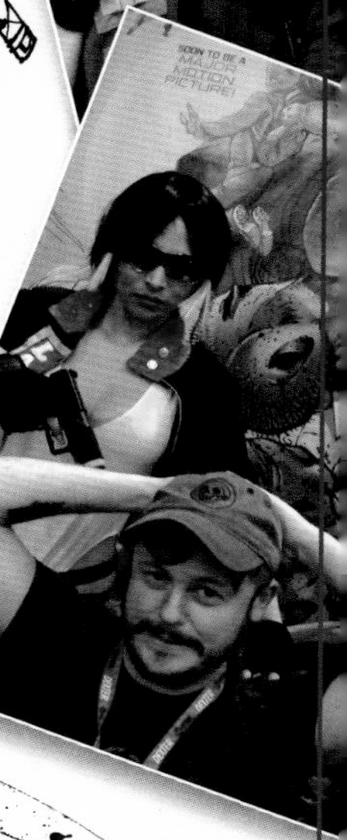

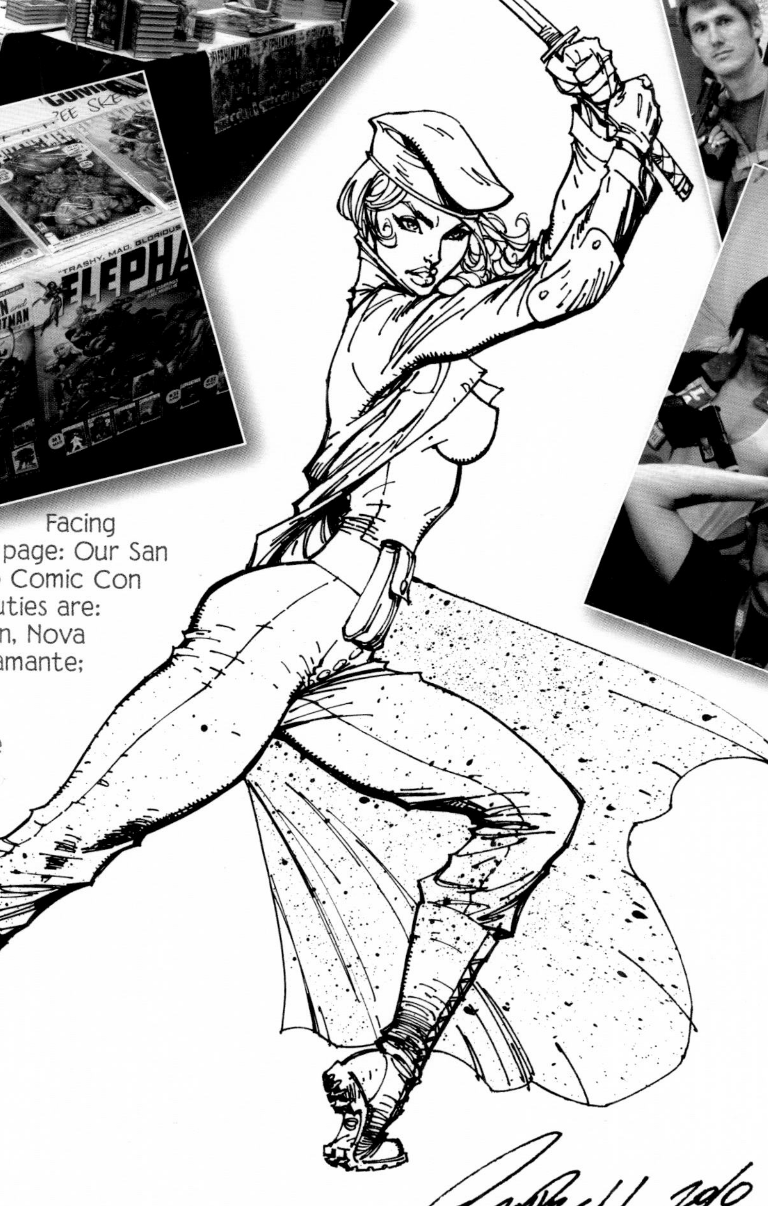

Facing page: Our San Diego Comic Con booth beauties are: Aurora and Axel Medelllin, Nova Parrish and Rosana Bustamante; Nova, Monifa Aldridge, Kathryn Renta and Jen Louie... Top Right: To the ELEPHANTMENmobile! Middle: Jake Freytag is SIMM! Bottom: Rosana gets ready to cuff our cover artist, Boo Cook!

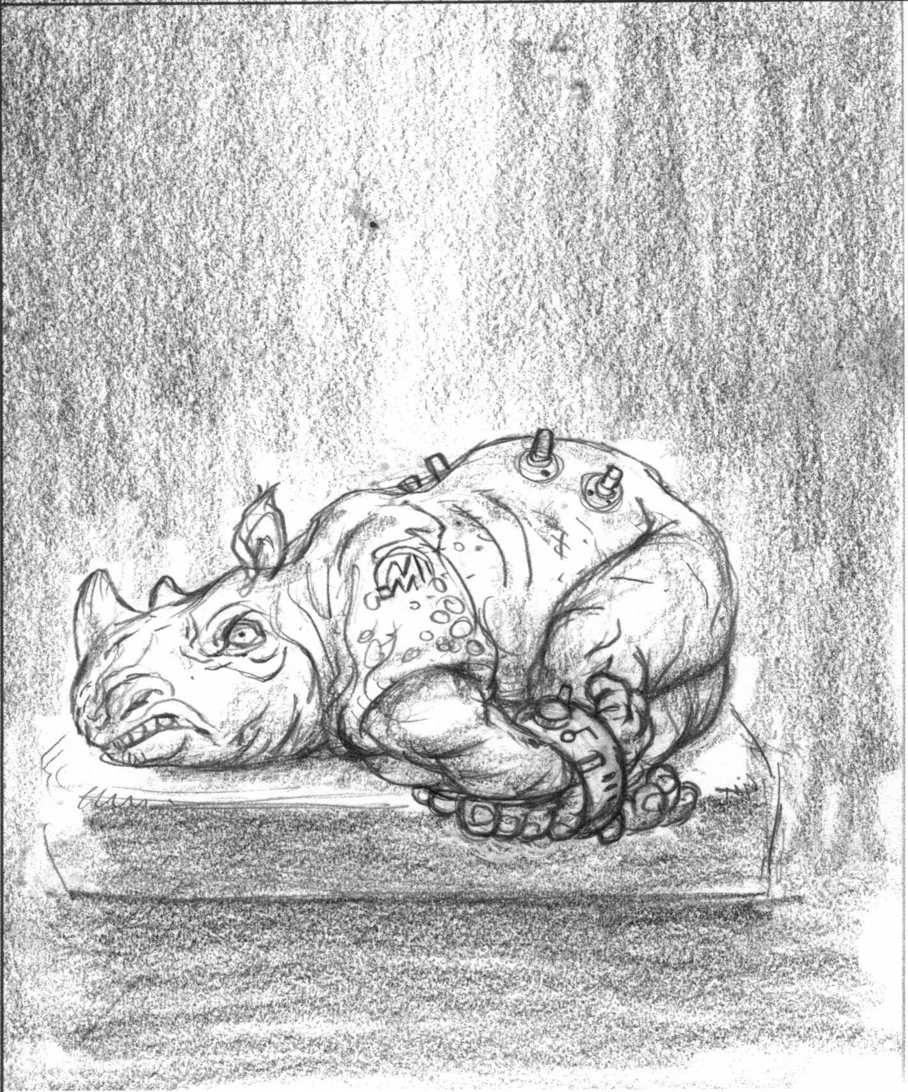

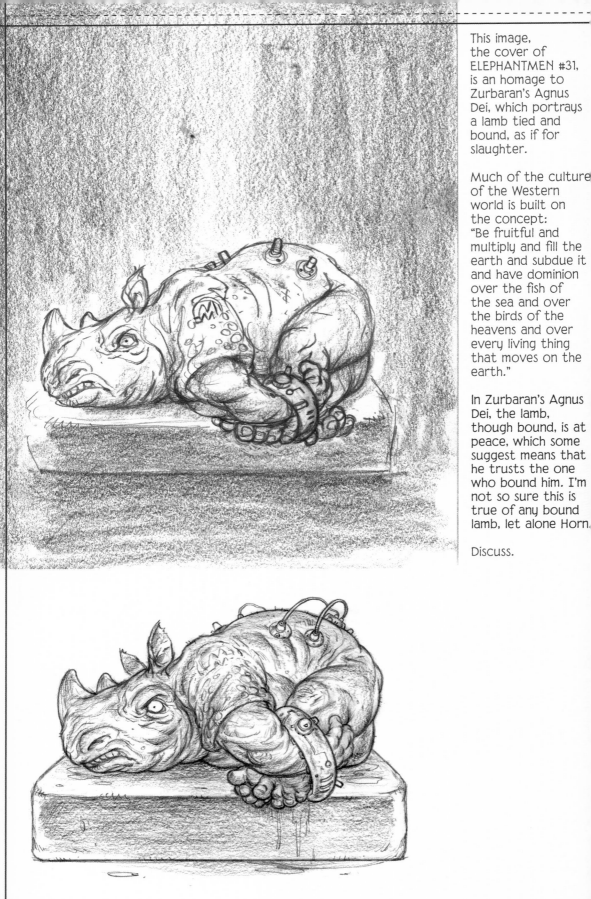

This image, the cover of ELEPHANTMEN #31, is an homage to Zurbaran's Agnus Dei, which portrays a lamb tied and bound, as if for slaughter.

Much of the culture of the Western world is built on the concept: "Be fruitful and multiply and fill the earth and subdue it and have dominion over the fish of the sea and over the birds of the heavens and over every living thing that moves on the earth."

In Zurbaran's Agnus Dei, the lamb, though bound, is at peace, which some suggest means that he trusts the one who bound him. I'm not so sure this is true of any bound lamb, let alone Horn.

Discuss.

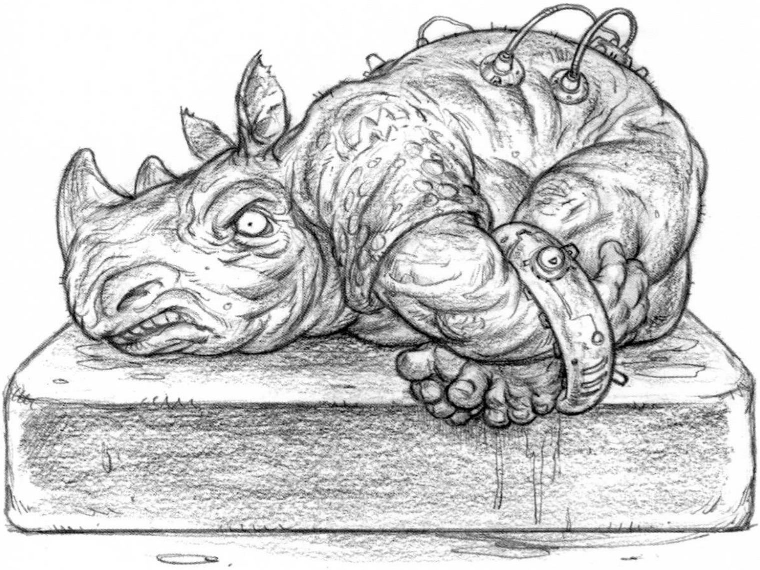

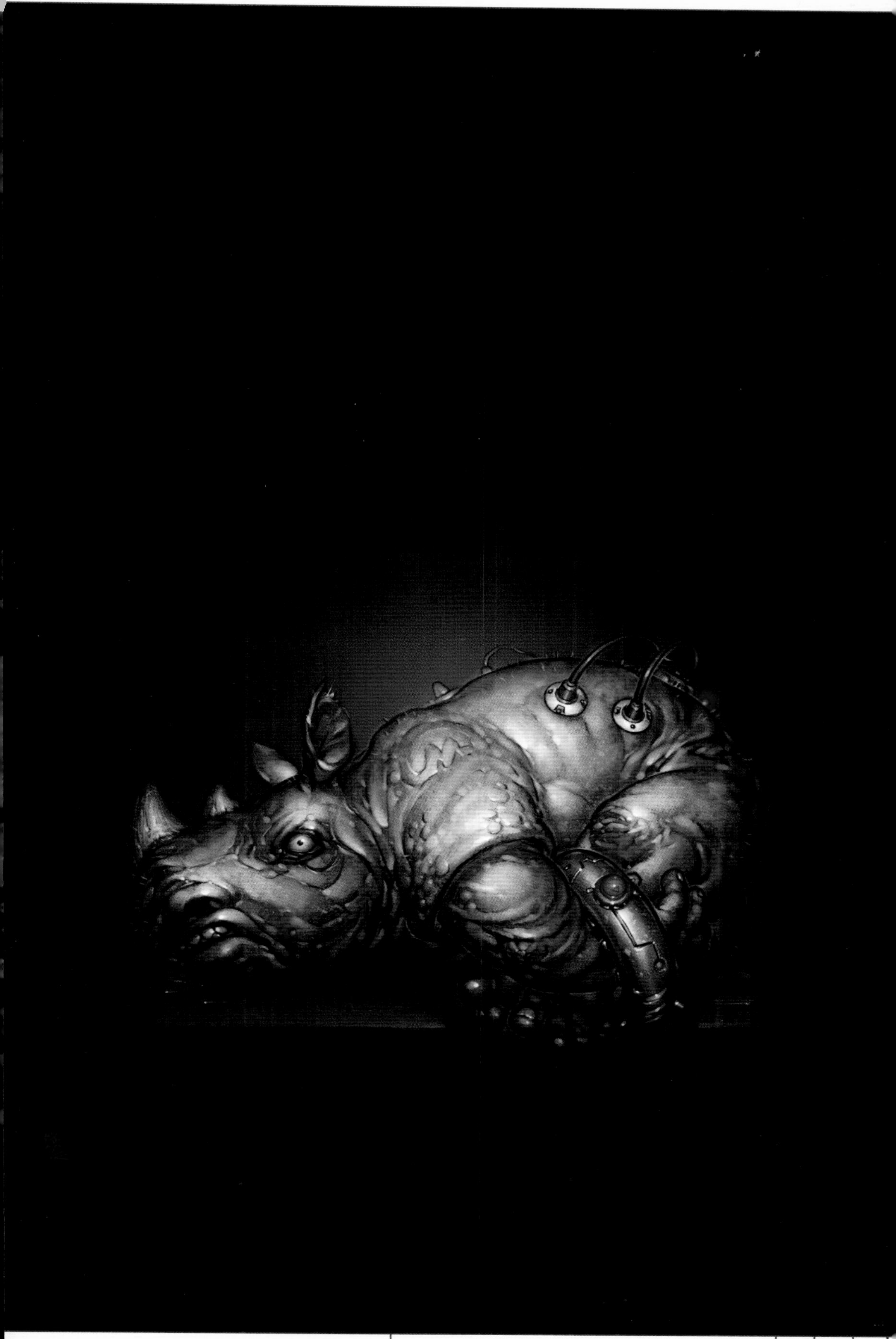

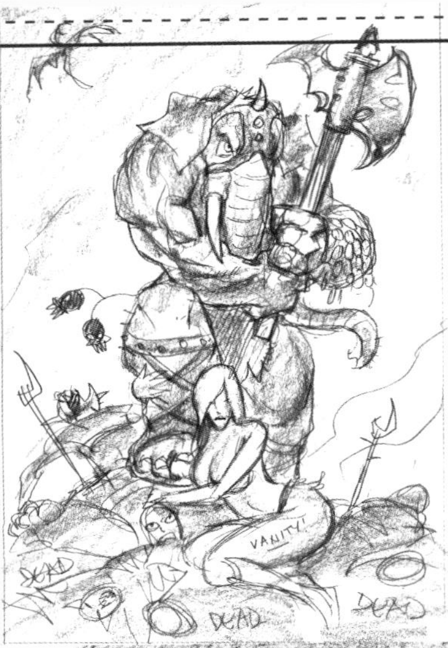
VANITY!
DEAD
DEAD
DEAD

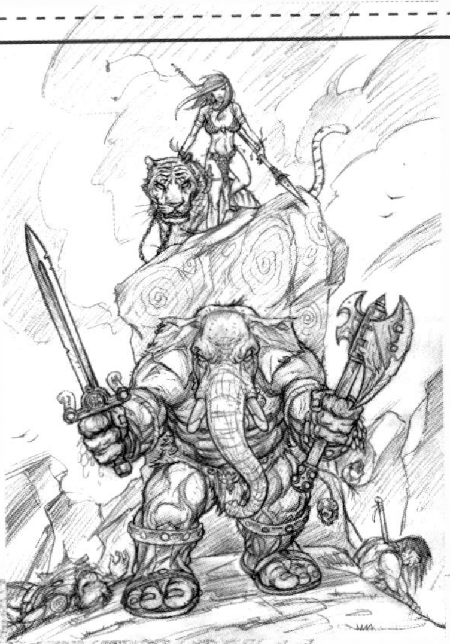

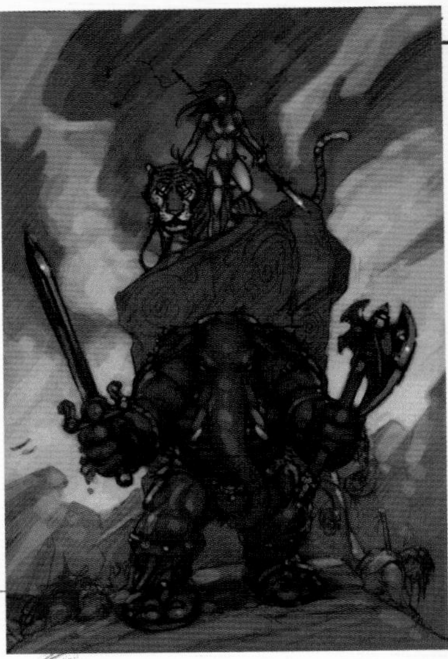

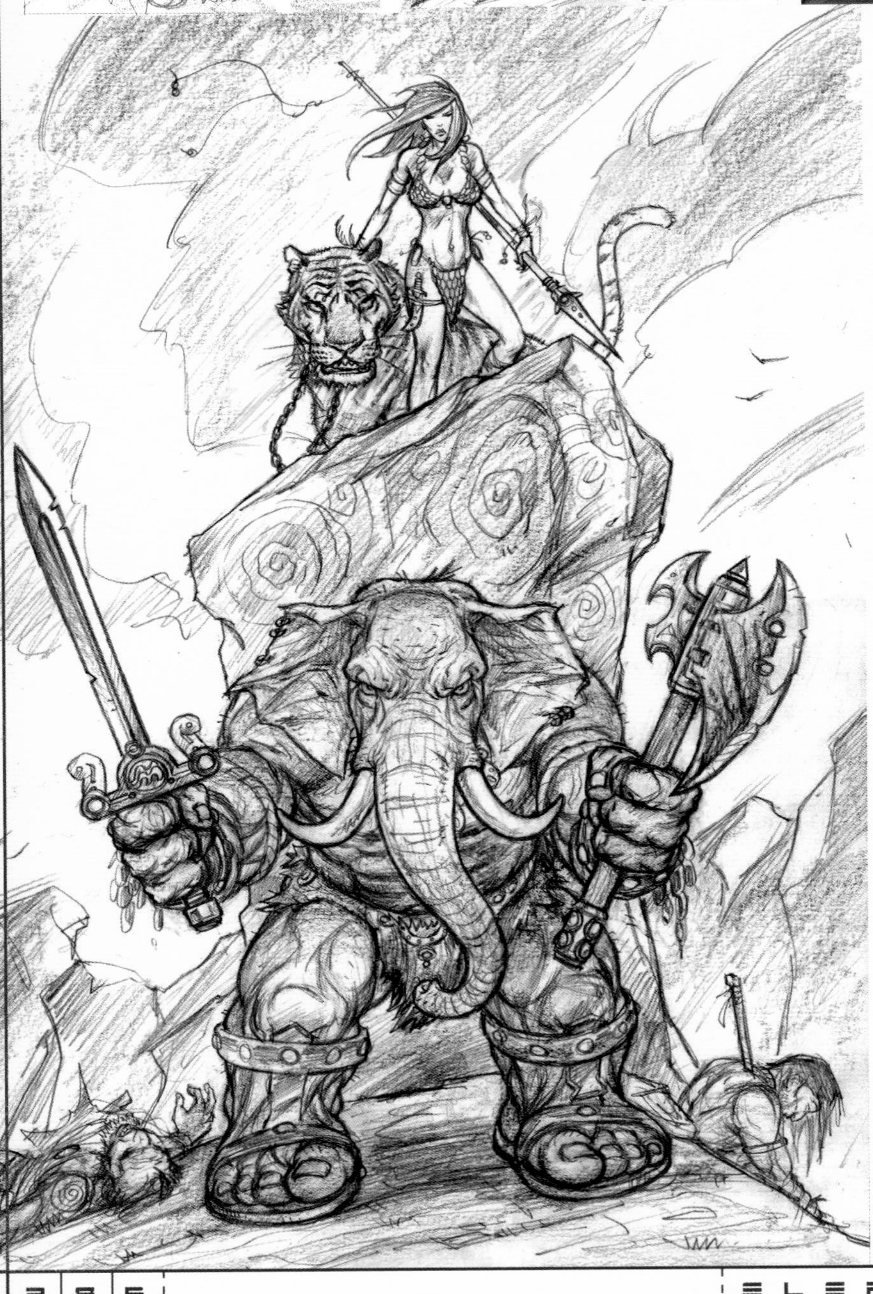

Boo, Axel Medellin (the current resident artist on ELEPHANTMEN) and I are all huge fans of CONAN THE BARBARIAN, so why wouldn't we want to create our own little homage to Robert E. Howard's favourite Cimmerian?

When we first discussed this cover, Boo rattled out the sketch you see top left, but I had a very specific story idea in mind, and sent him a mockup which I'm too embarrassed to show here. Boostah the Barbaric summoned up the drawing on the left like some Stygian Sorceror summoning something up sorcerously.

Opposite:
Look at that sky!

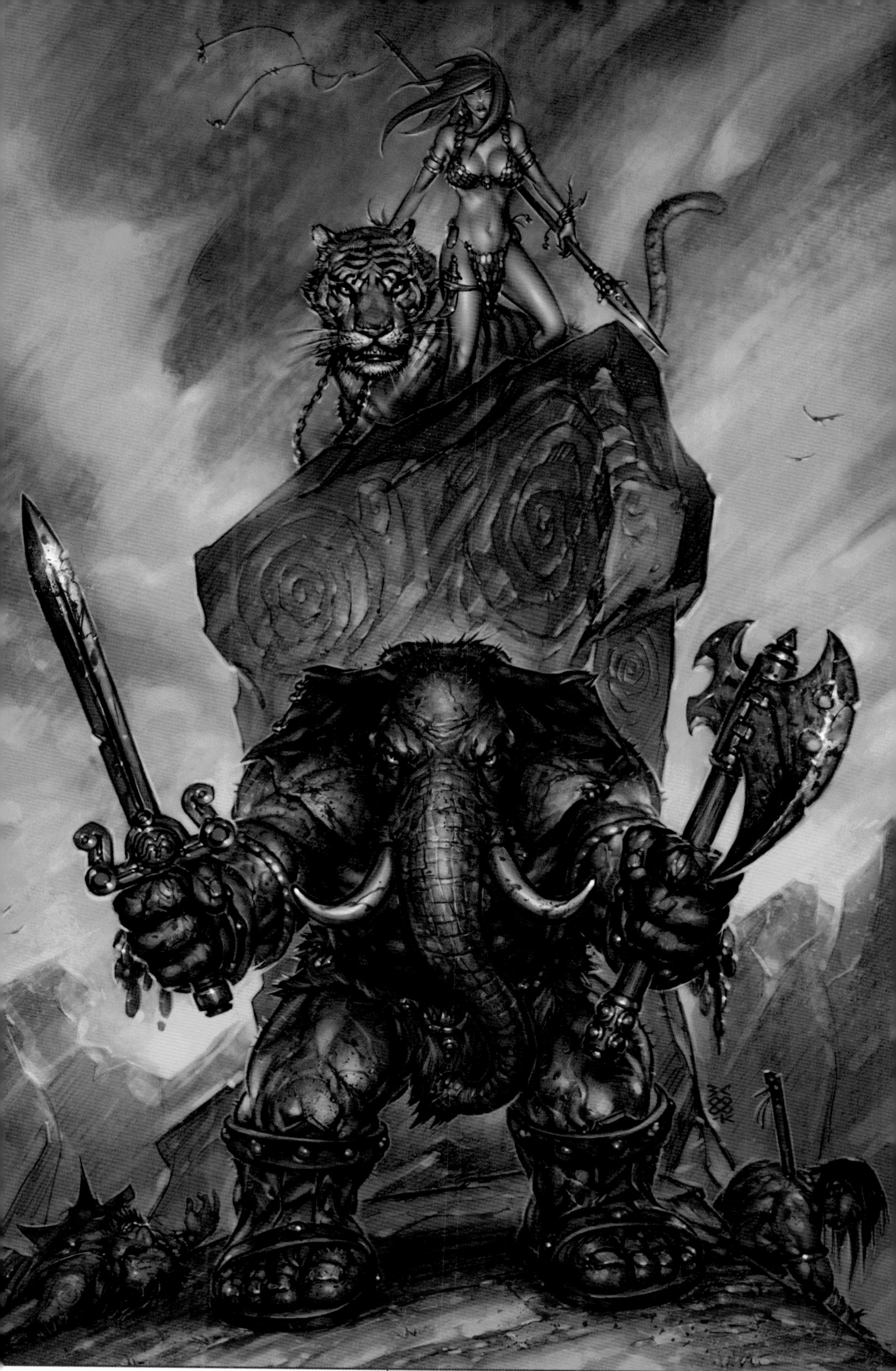

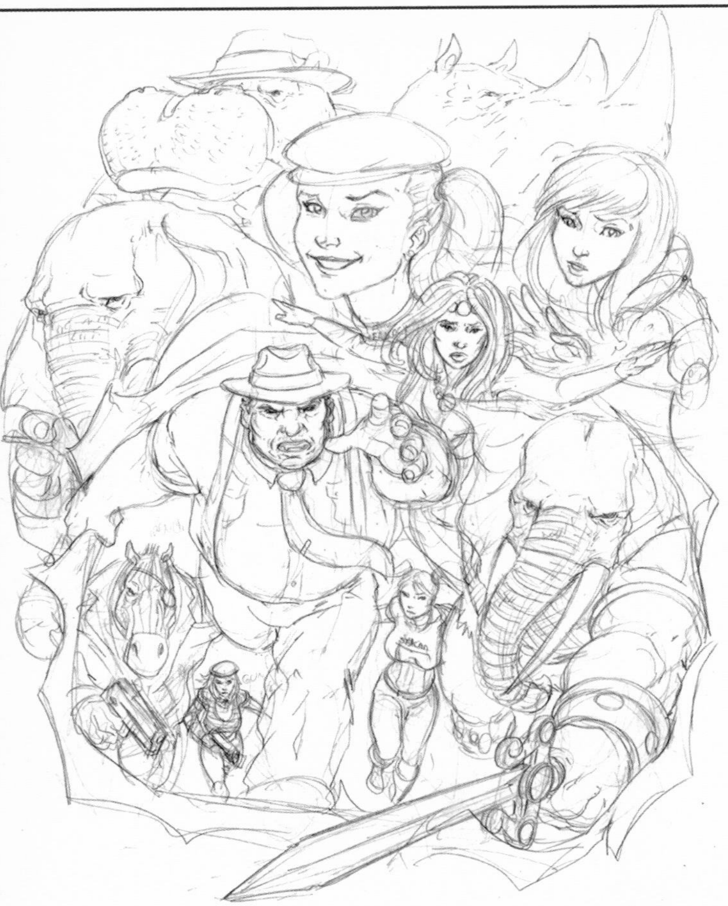

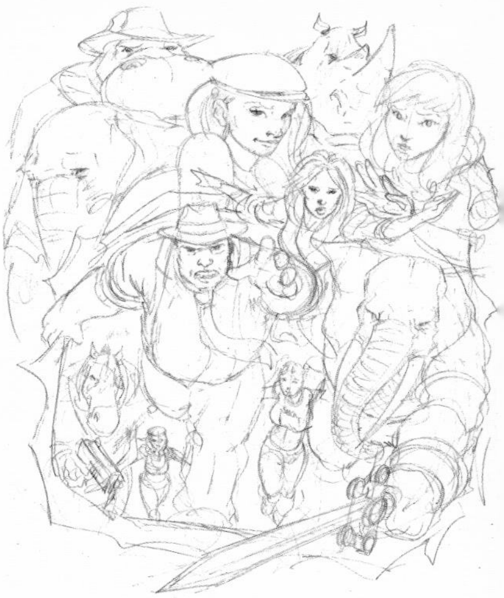

Our last pastiche was suggested by Image Publisher Eric Stephenson after I proposed a catch-up collection of MAN AND ELEPHANTMAN for readers who'd read the first installment on the flipside of THE WALKING DEAD #86. I suggested calling it GIANT-SIZE ELEPHANTMEN after Marvel Comic's best known "JUMP ON" issue (hard to believe now that Marvel had to re-start what is now regarded as their most popular superhero team) and so Eric proposed a cover by our regular artist, Axel Medellin, in that style. It was just a matter of matching up characters as per Dave Cockrum's original layout -- and, um, making more room for our slightly stockier leading men...

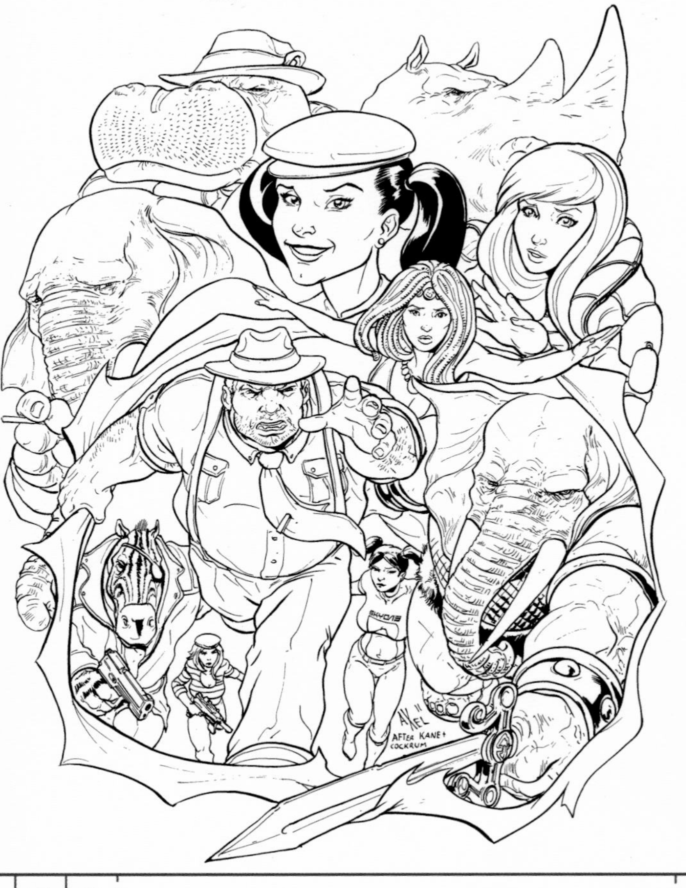
AXEL
AFTER KANE + COCKRUM

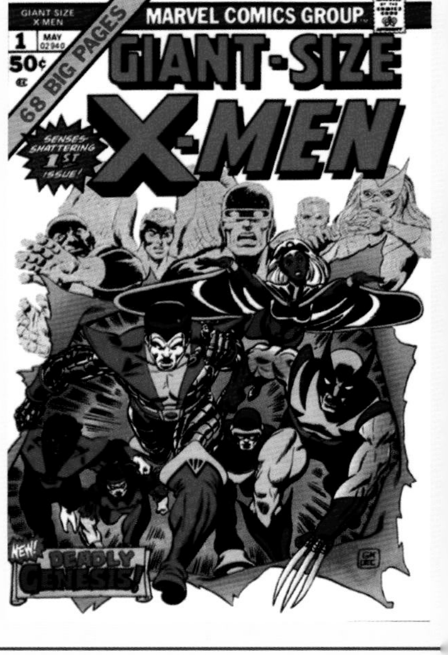
GIANT SIZE X-MEN
MARVEL COMICS GROUP
1
MAY 02940
50¢
68 BIG PAGES
GIANT-SIZE
X-MEN
SENSES-SHATTERING 1ST ISSUE!
NEW!
DEADLY GENESIS!

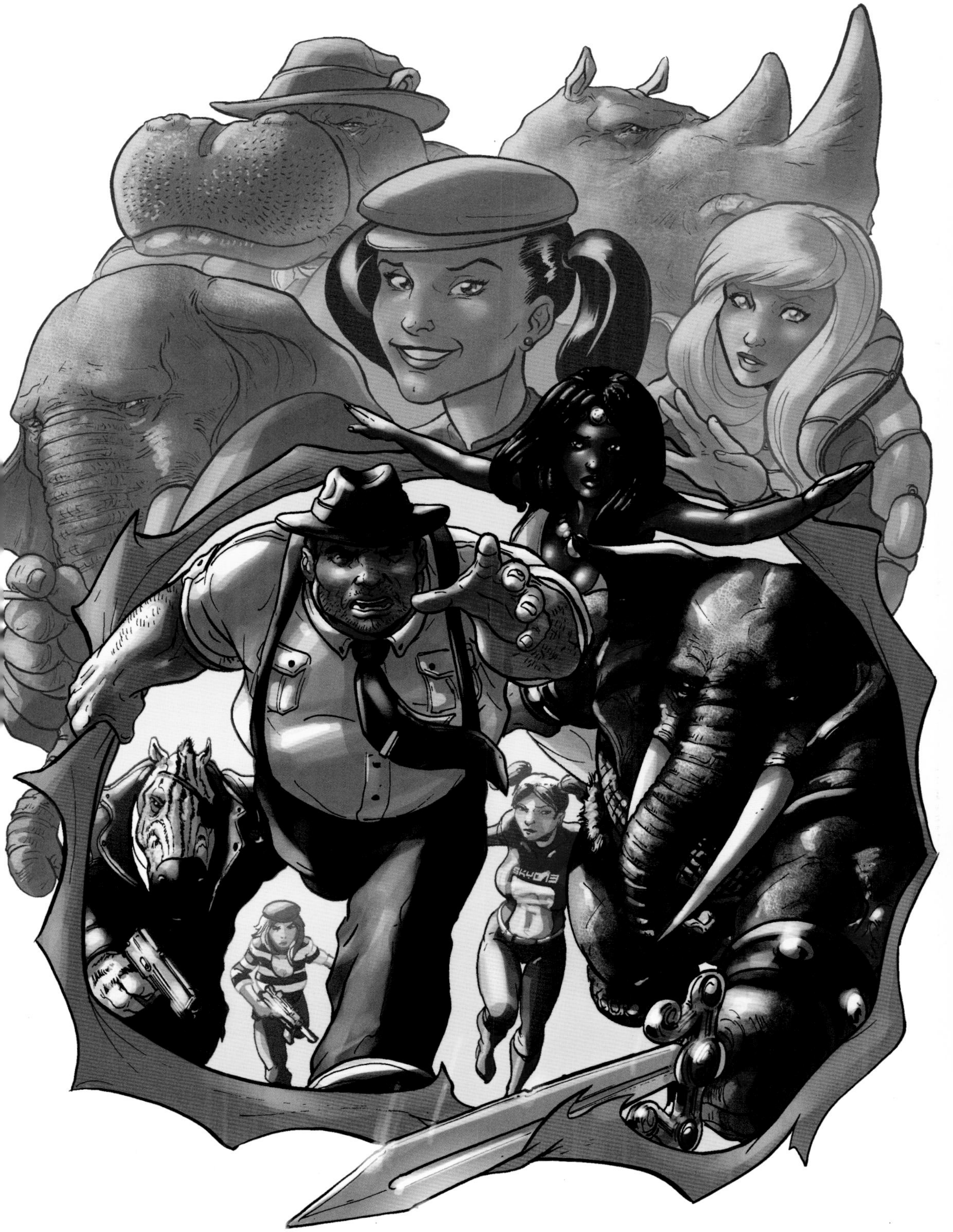

For the cover of perhaps the freakiest issue of ELEPHANTMEN yet, I asked Shaky Kane to combine elements from my favourite panels in the story... We went through some costume and colour changes, but the essential figures were just perfect...

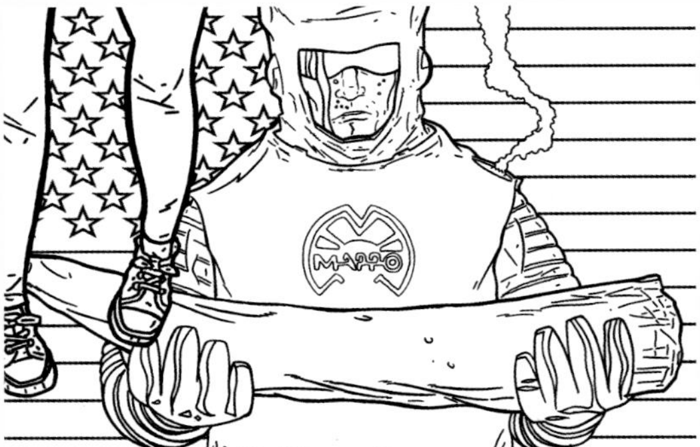

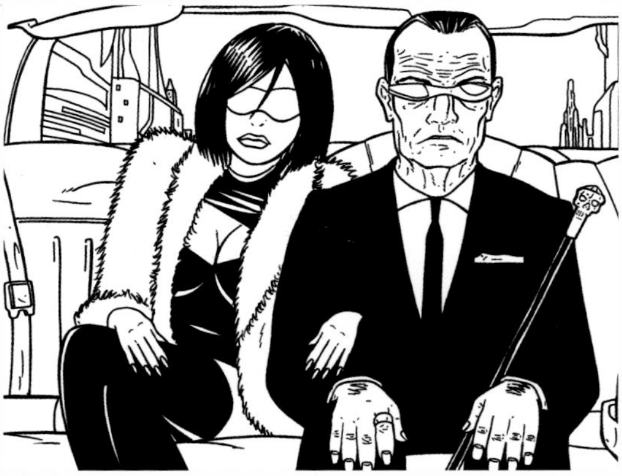

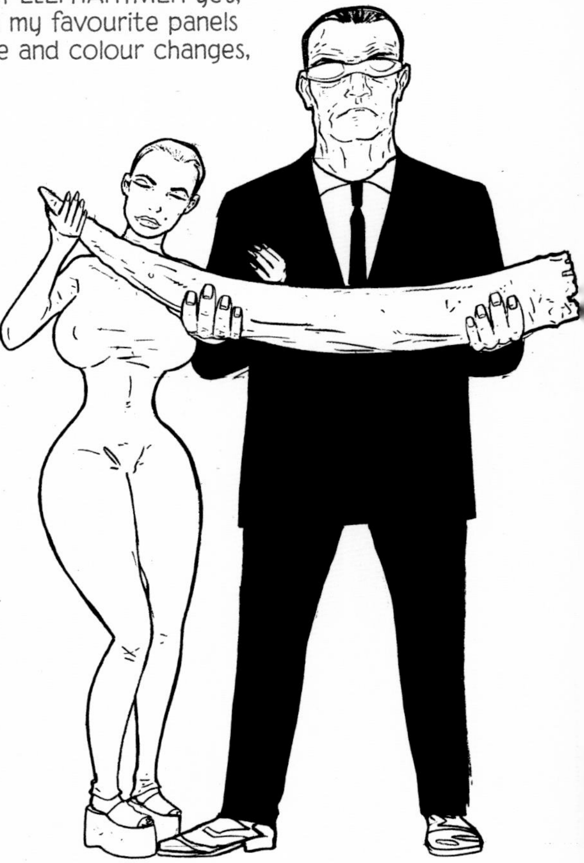

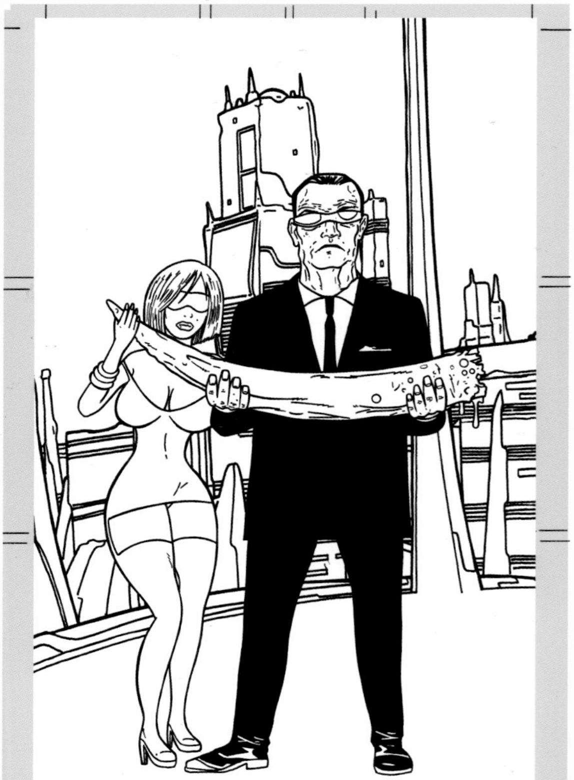

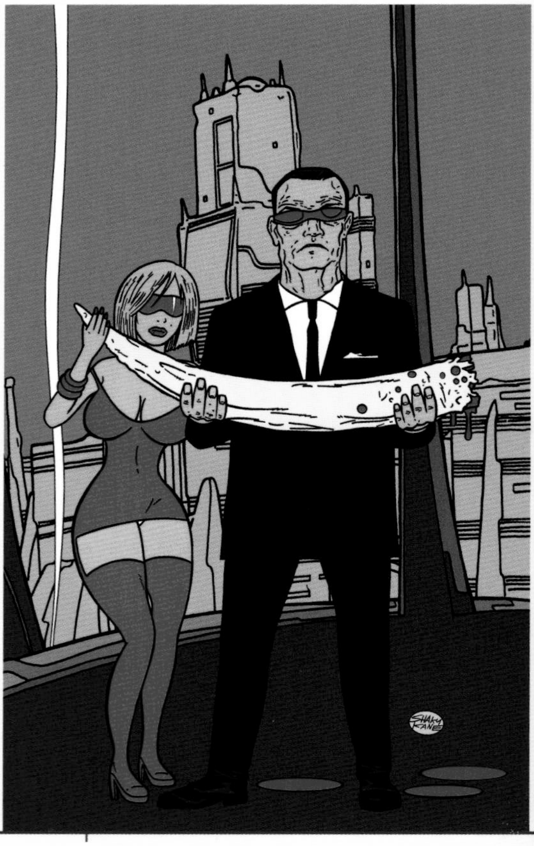
SHAKY KANE

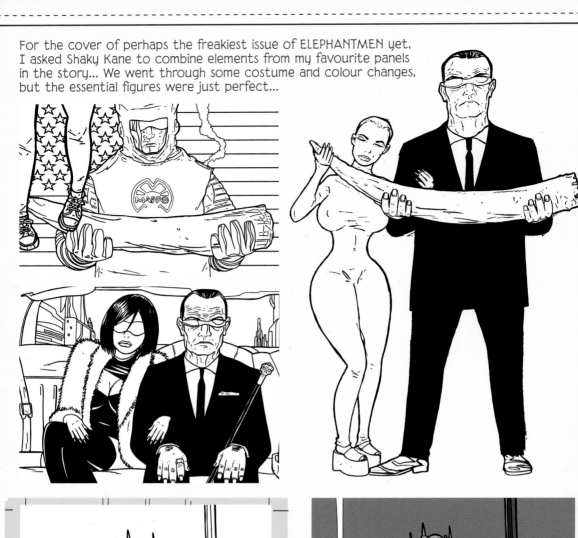

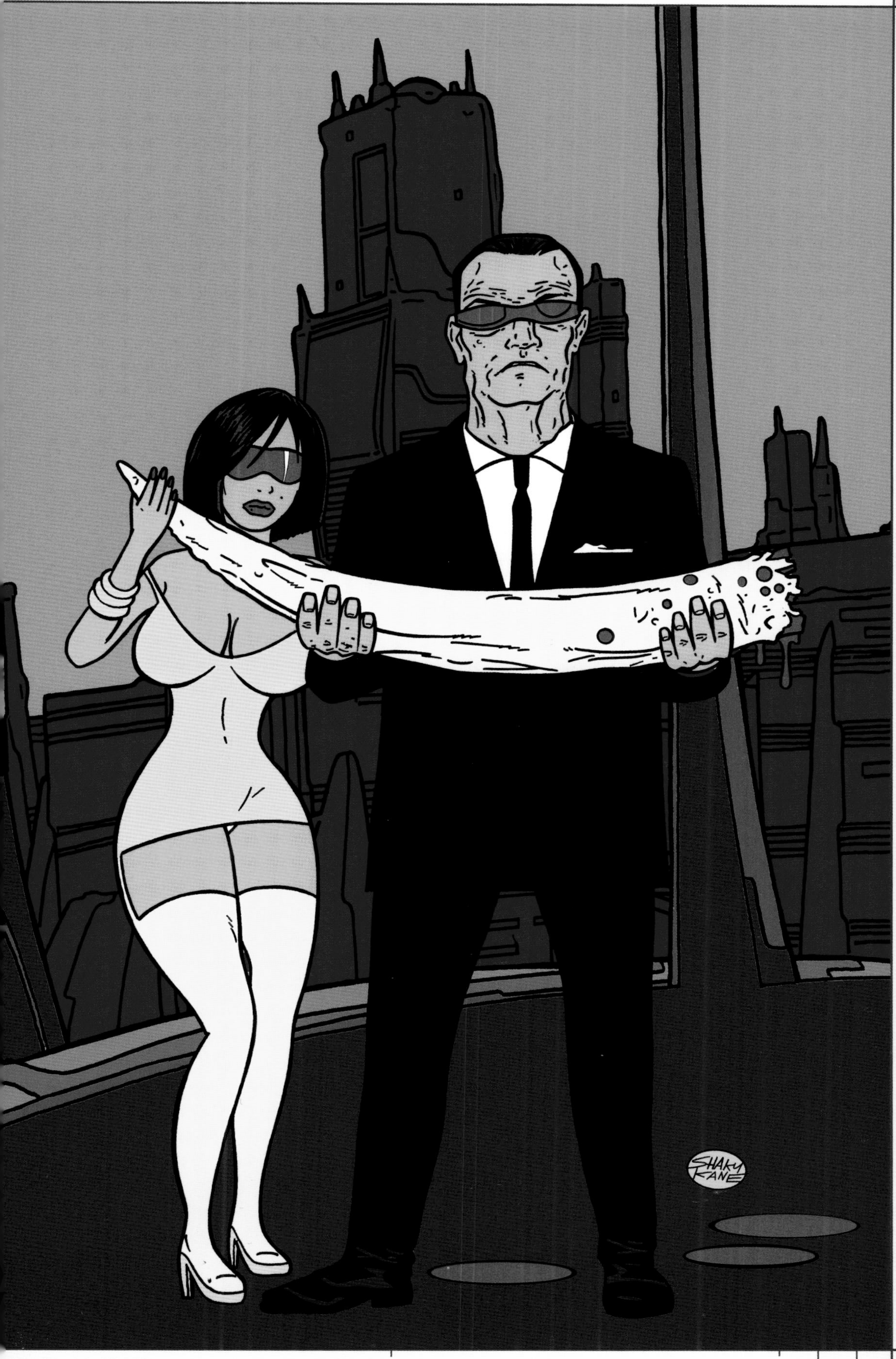
SHAKY KANE

Moritat created this moody, noir illustration of Hip Flask for a fan at my favourite North American show, the EMERALD CITY COMIC CON, in 2011... Seeing it, I realized we hadn't shown Hip mean and moody on the cover before and so, with Moritat's permission, I sent the piece to Axel Medellin to add his own unique touch. The result is perhaps one of my favourite covers of the entire series... it says everything an ELEPHANTMEN cover needs to say without a single word.

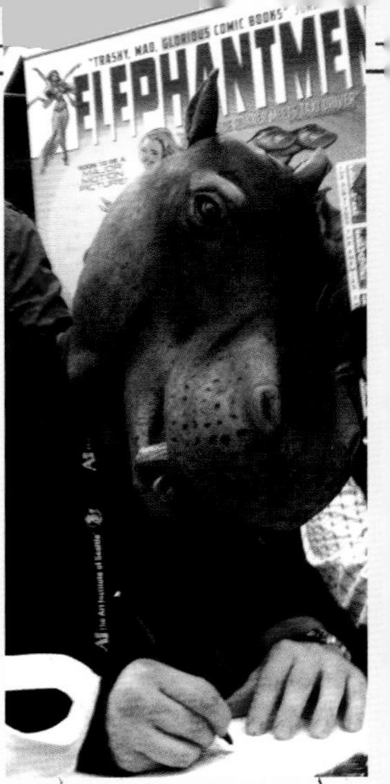
"TRASHY, MAD, GLORIOUS COMIC BOOKS"
ELEPHANTMEN

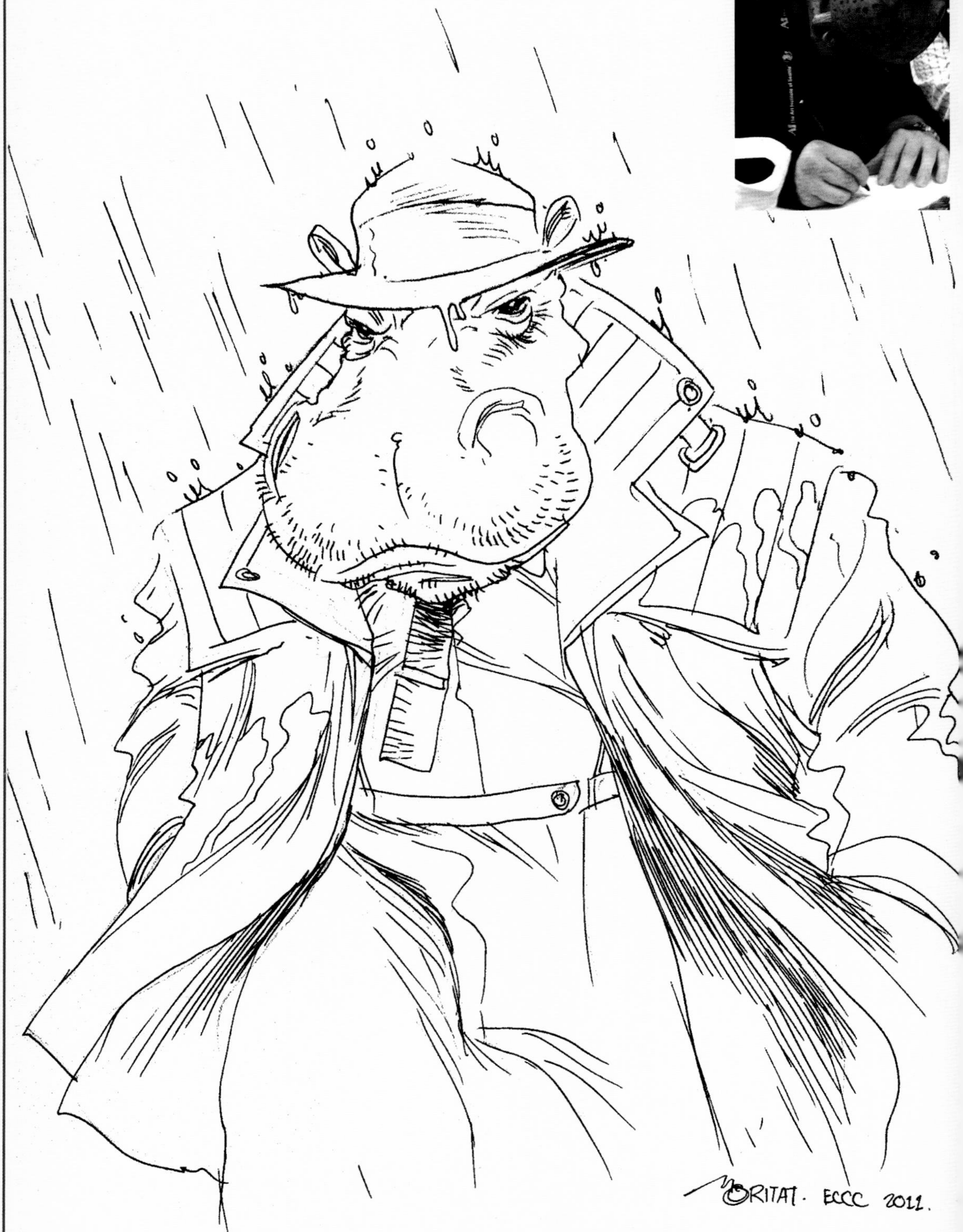
MORITAT · ECCC 2011.

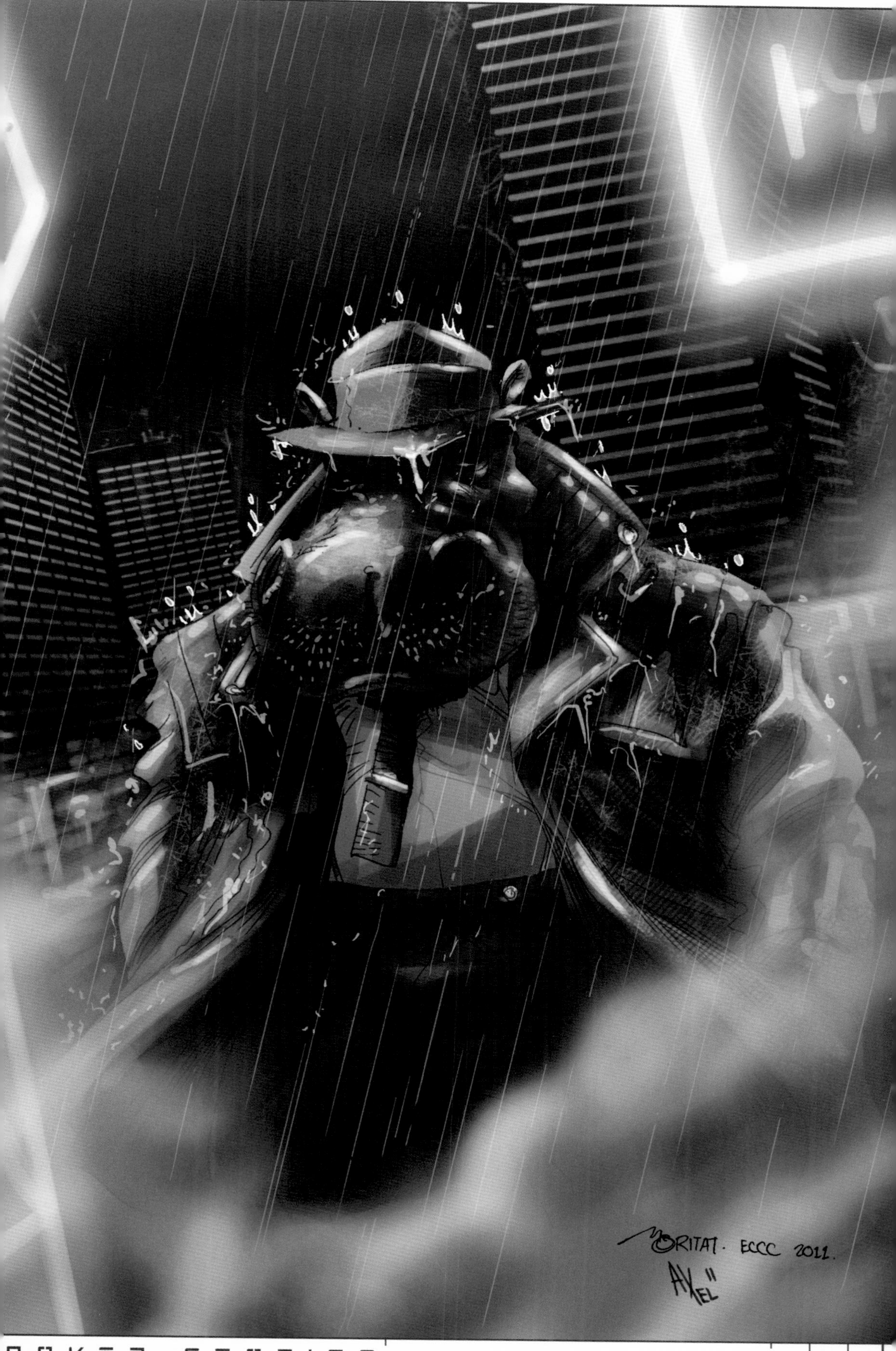
MORITAT. ECCC 2011.
AXEL"

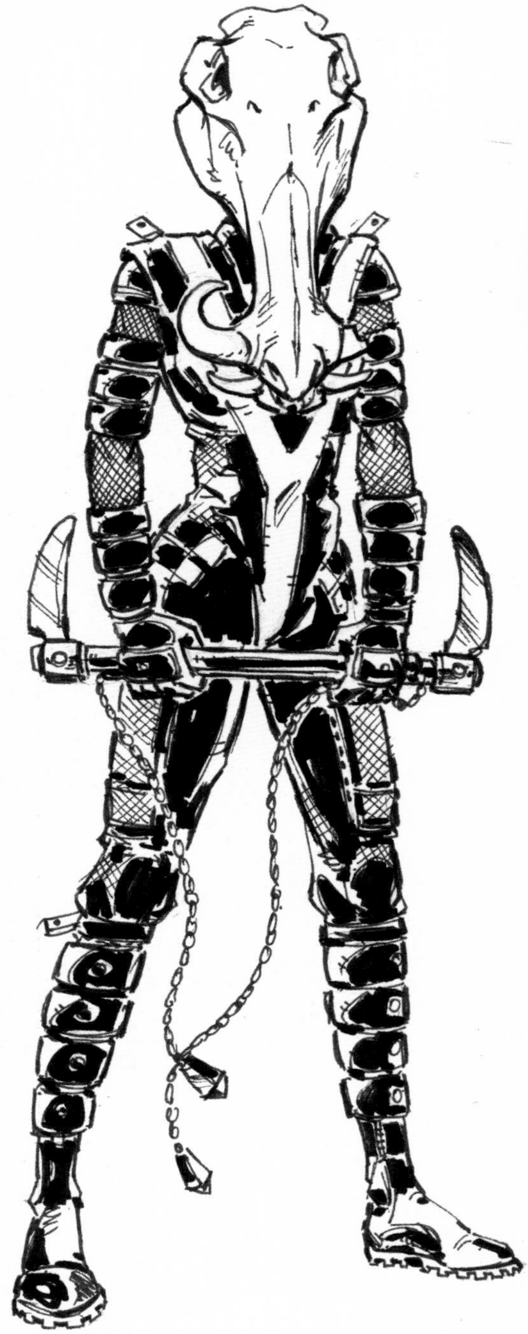

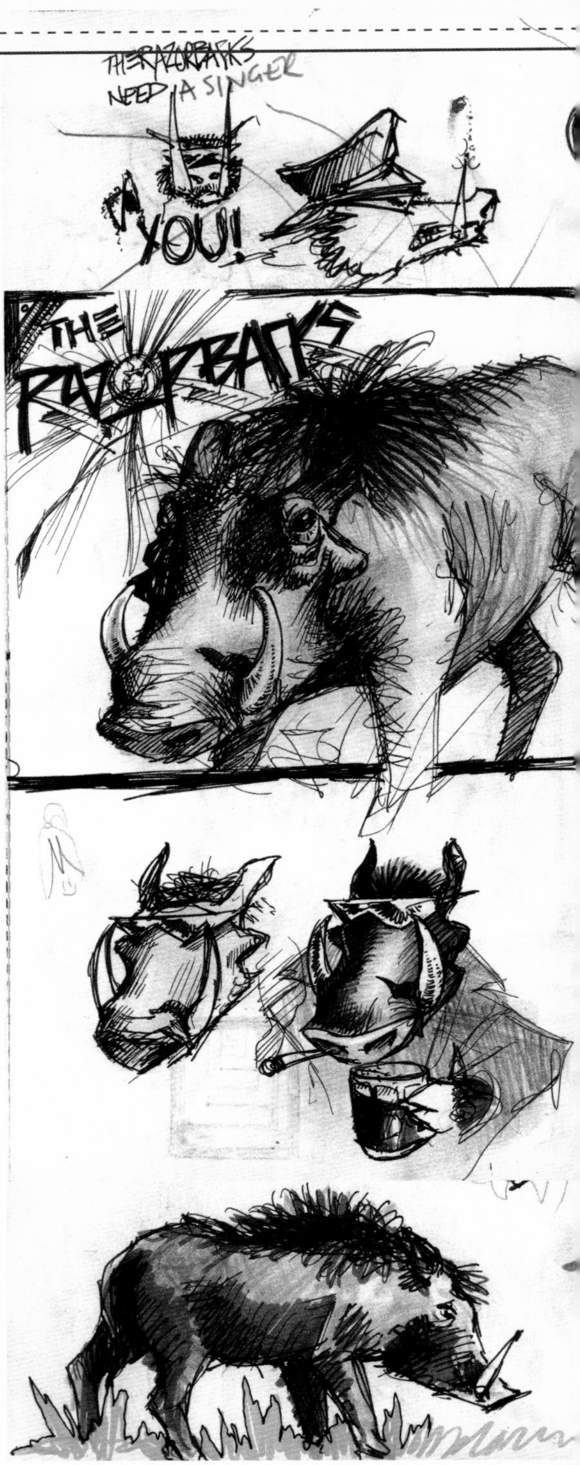
THE RAZORBACKS NEED A SINGER
YOU!
THE RAZORBACKS

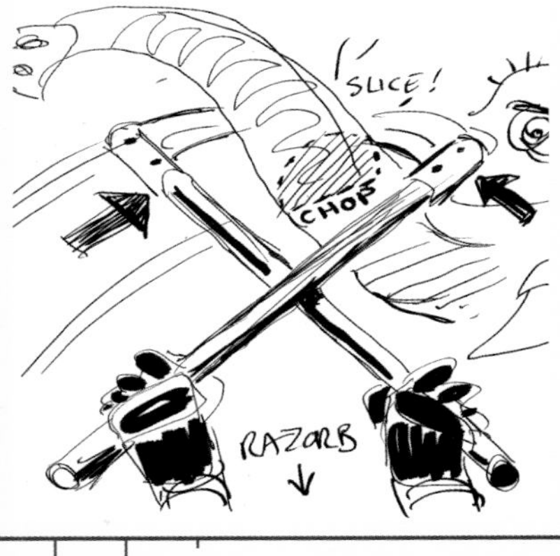
SLICE!
CHOP
RAZORB

I had first talked to Boo Cook about a vigilante killing Elephantmen when I was working with Kevin Eastman on THE MELTING POT. I imagined a harder hitting story that would fit in Kevin's HEAVY METAL -- bloodier and sexier and with some real consequences. Boo worked up the full figure sketch you see here when I was visiting him in Brighton in 2010 and he suggested the name RAZORBACK after a band he had played in many years ago. The drawings above are from his sketchbook at that time.

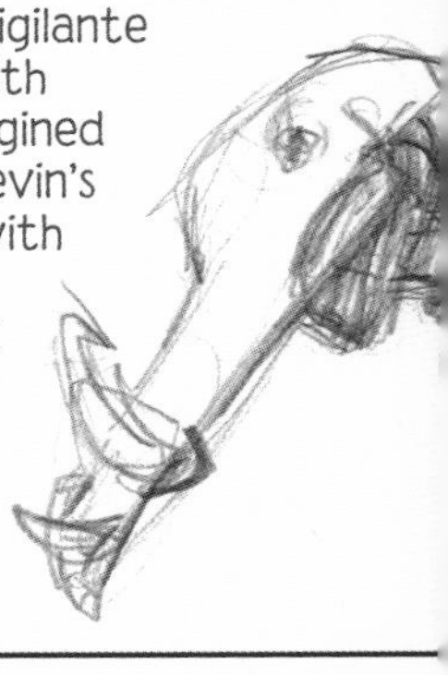

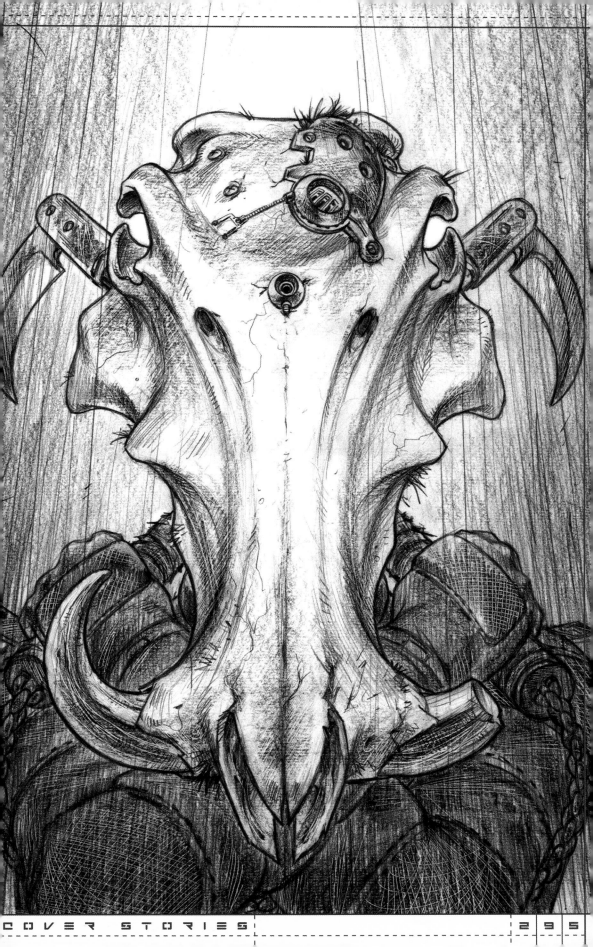

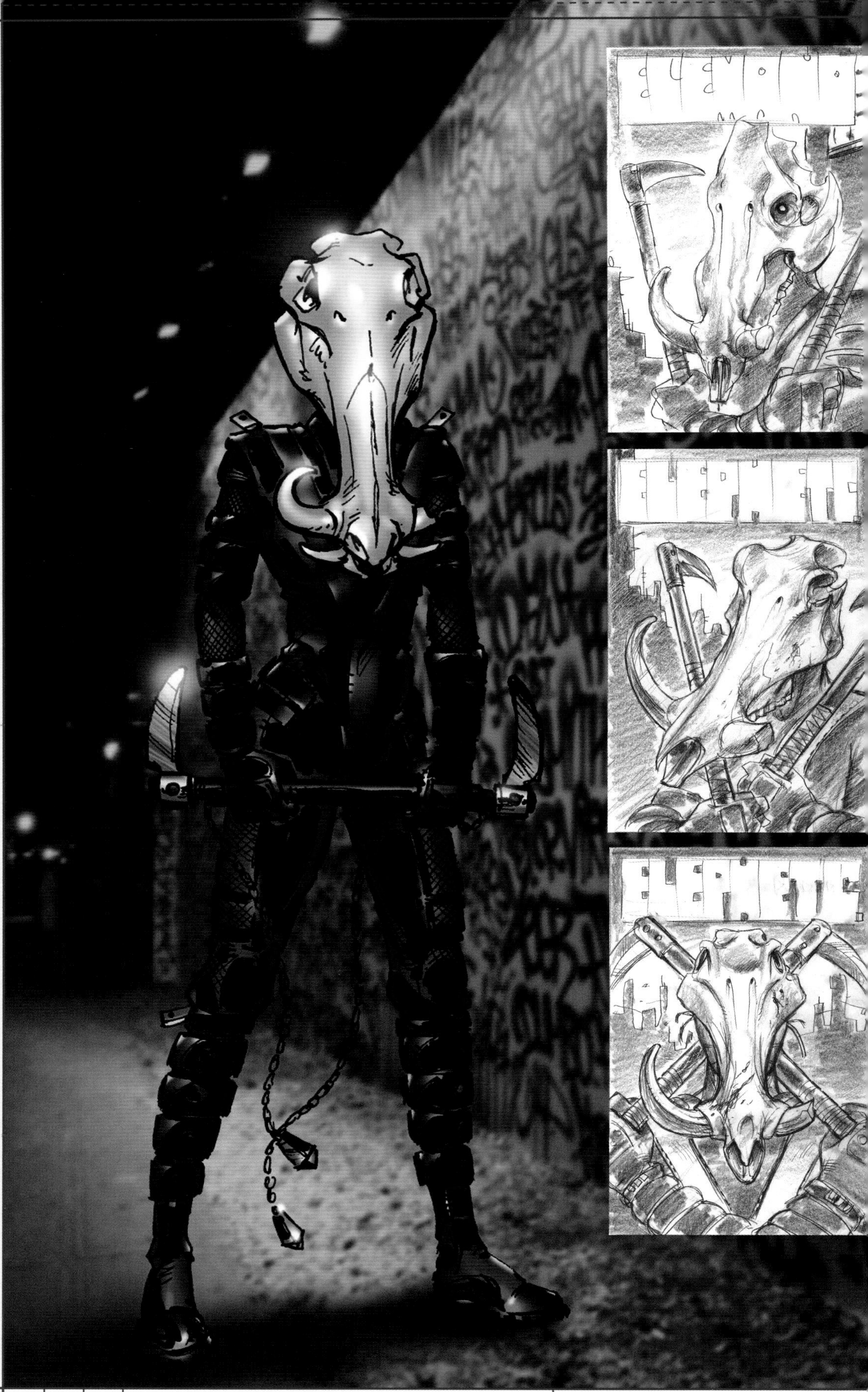

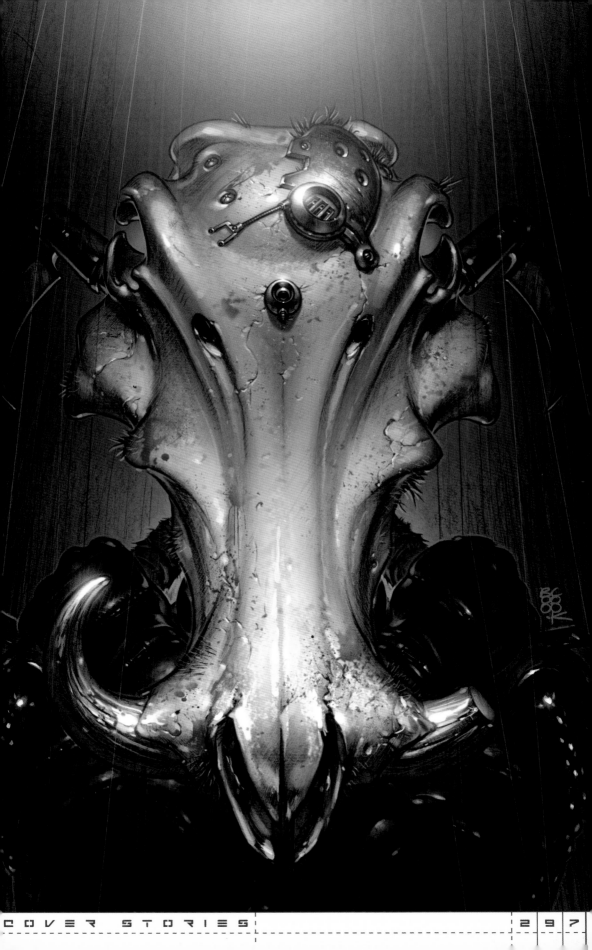

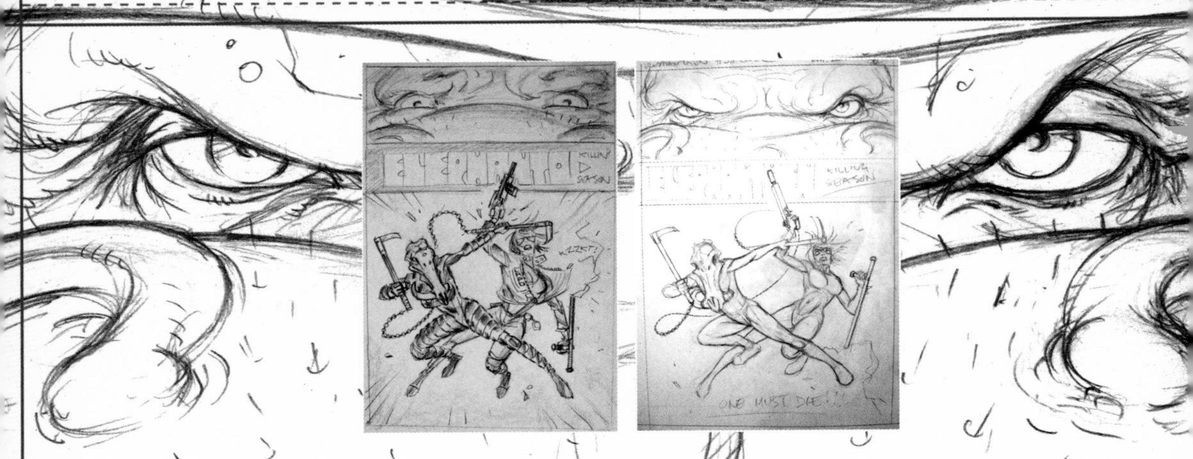

Not the cover for the finale, but the closest I could get to a climactic, FINAL BATTLE scene without giving away Razorback's identity and ultimate goal... Boo delivered this kickass piece with real style -- AND managed to conceal the sex of our vigilante even though the initial of the character is displayed in plain sight!

We ran this cover with the legend: ONE LIVES! ONE DIES!, as a tip of the hat to one of my all-time favourite comic books, DAREDEVIL #181 by Frank Miller; BULLSEYE vs ELEKTRA -- ONE LIVES, ONE DIES! All comic books should have slutty cover lines once in a while!

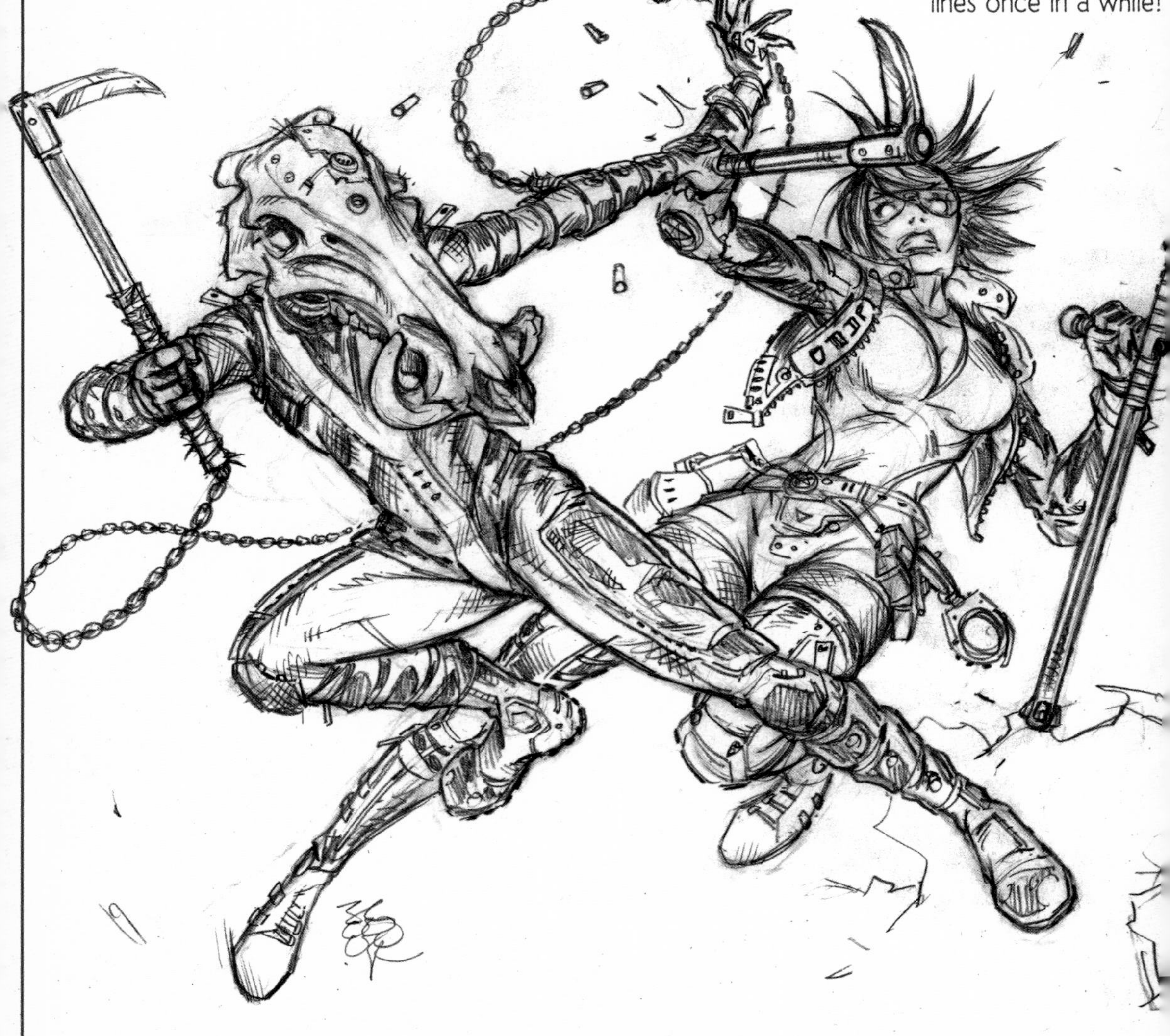

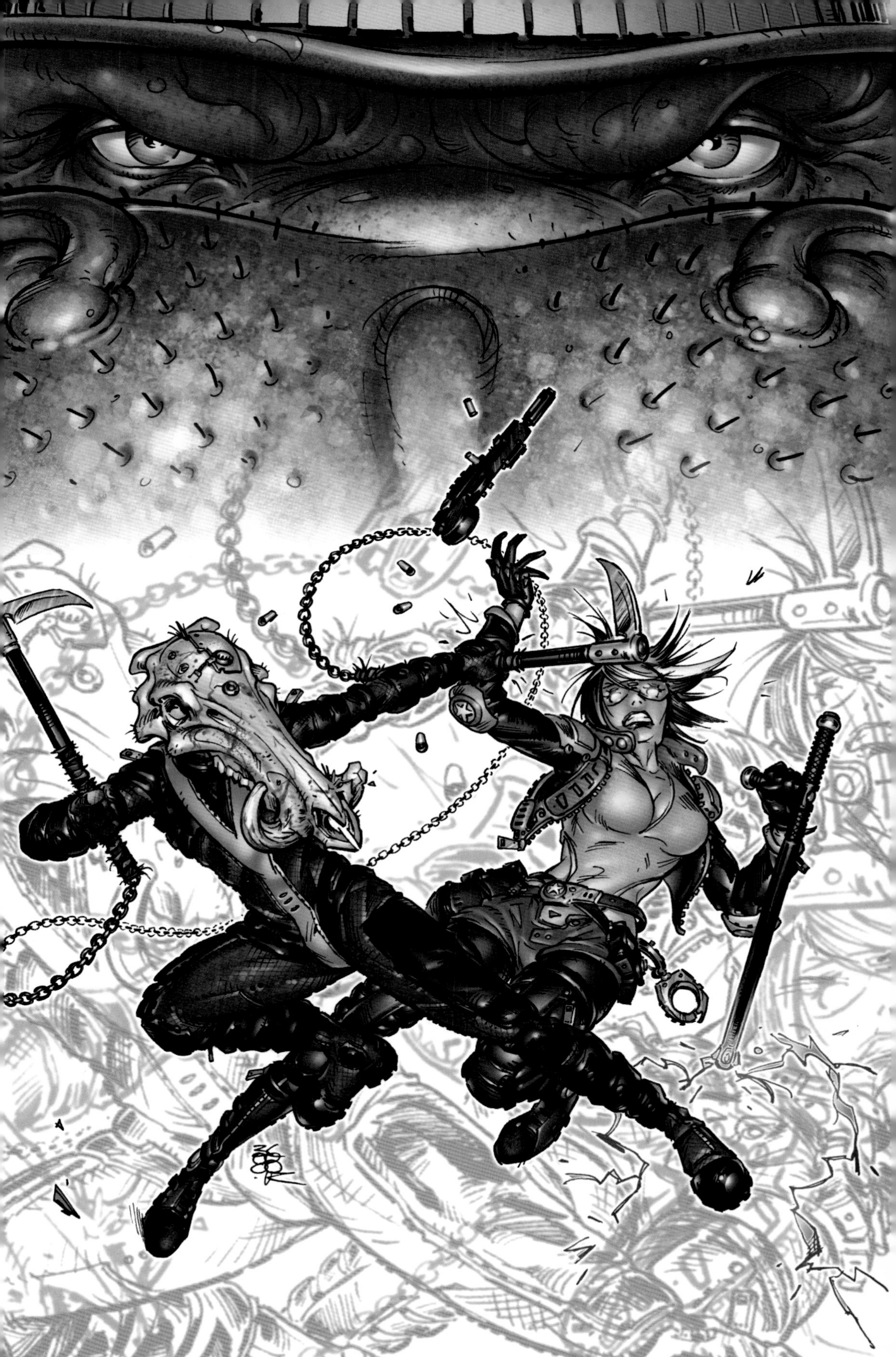

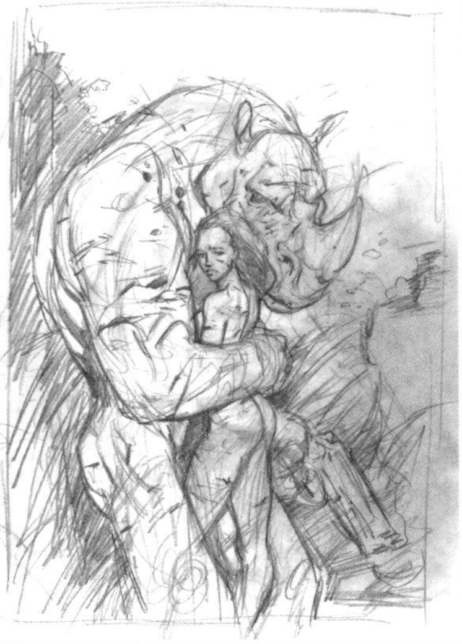

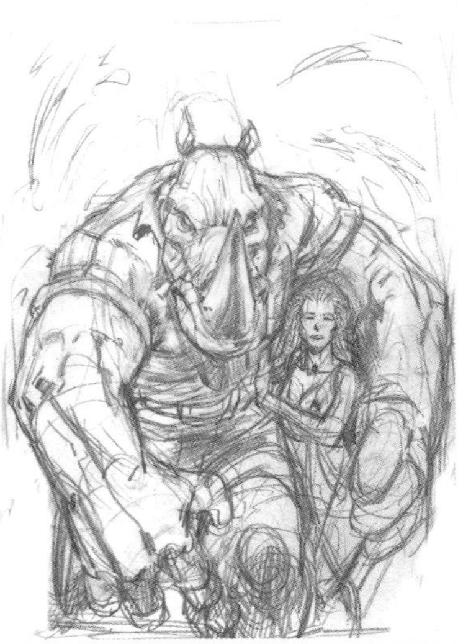

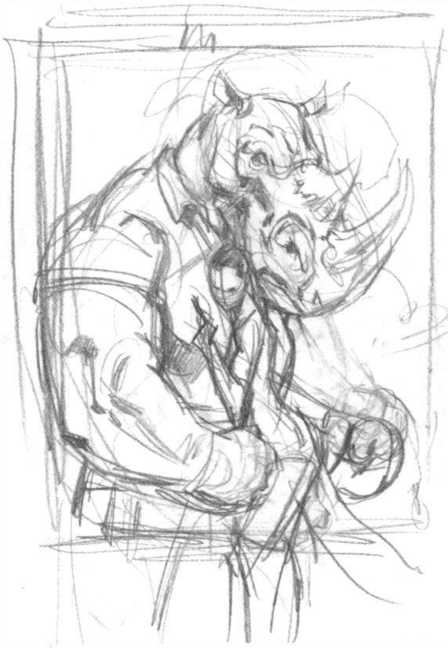

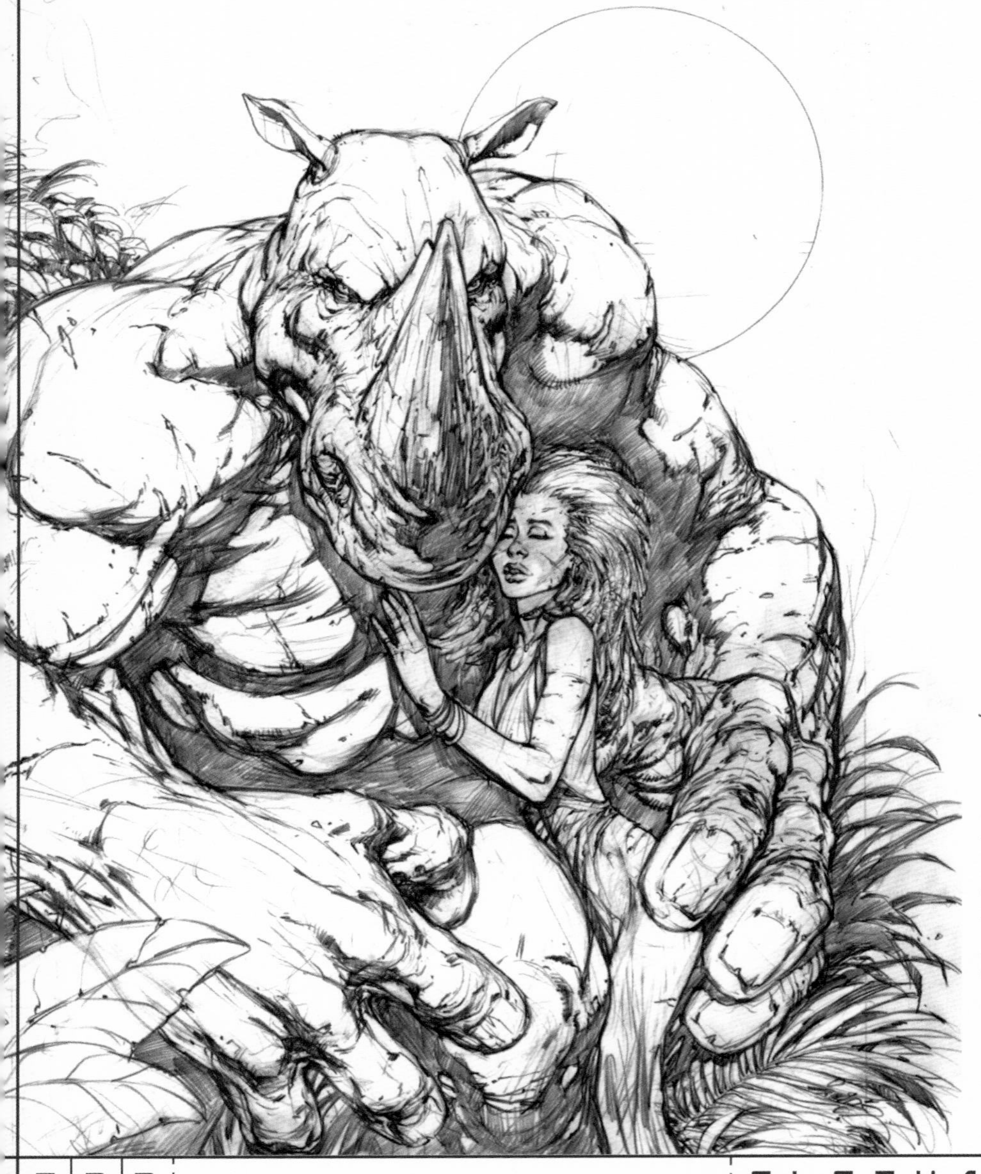

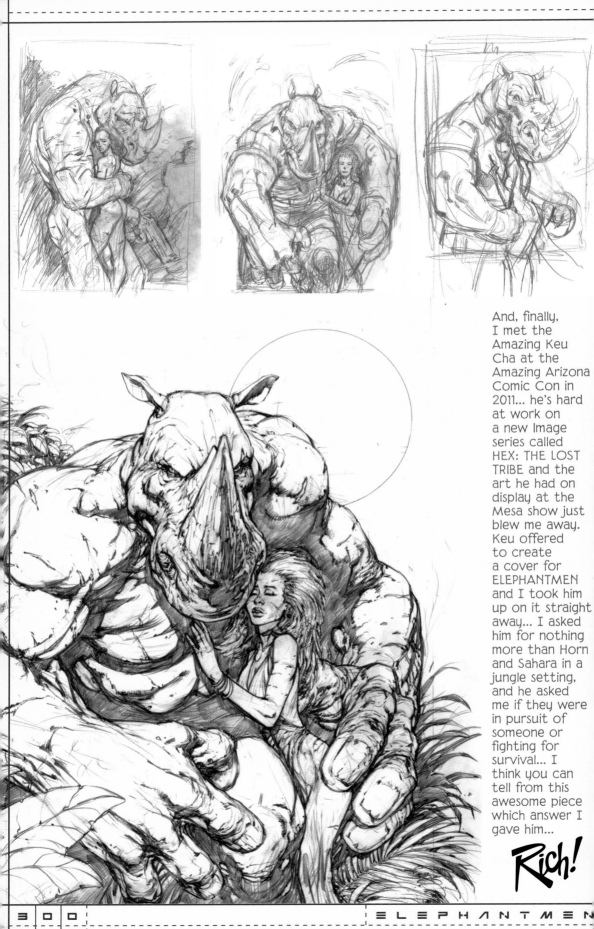

And, finally, I met the Amazing Keu Cha at the Amazing Arizona Comic Con in 2011... he's hard at work on a new Image series called HEX: THE LOST TRIBE and the art he had on display at the Mesa show just blew me away. Keu offered to create a cover for ELEPHANTMEN and I took him up on it straight away... I asked him for nothing more than Horn and Sahara in a jungle setting, and he asked me if they were in pursuit of someone or fighting for survival... I think you can tell from this awesome piece which answer I gave him...

Rich!

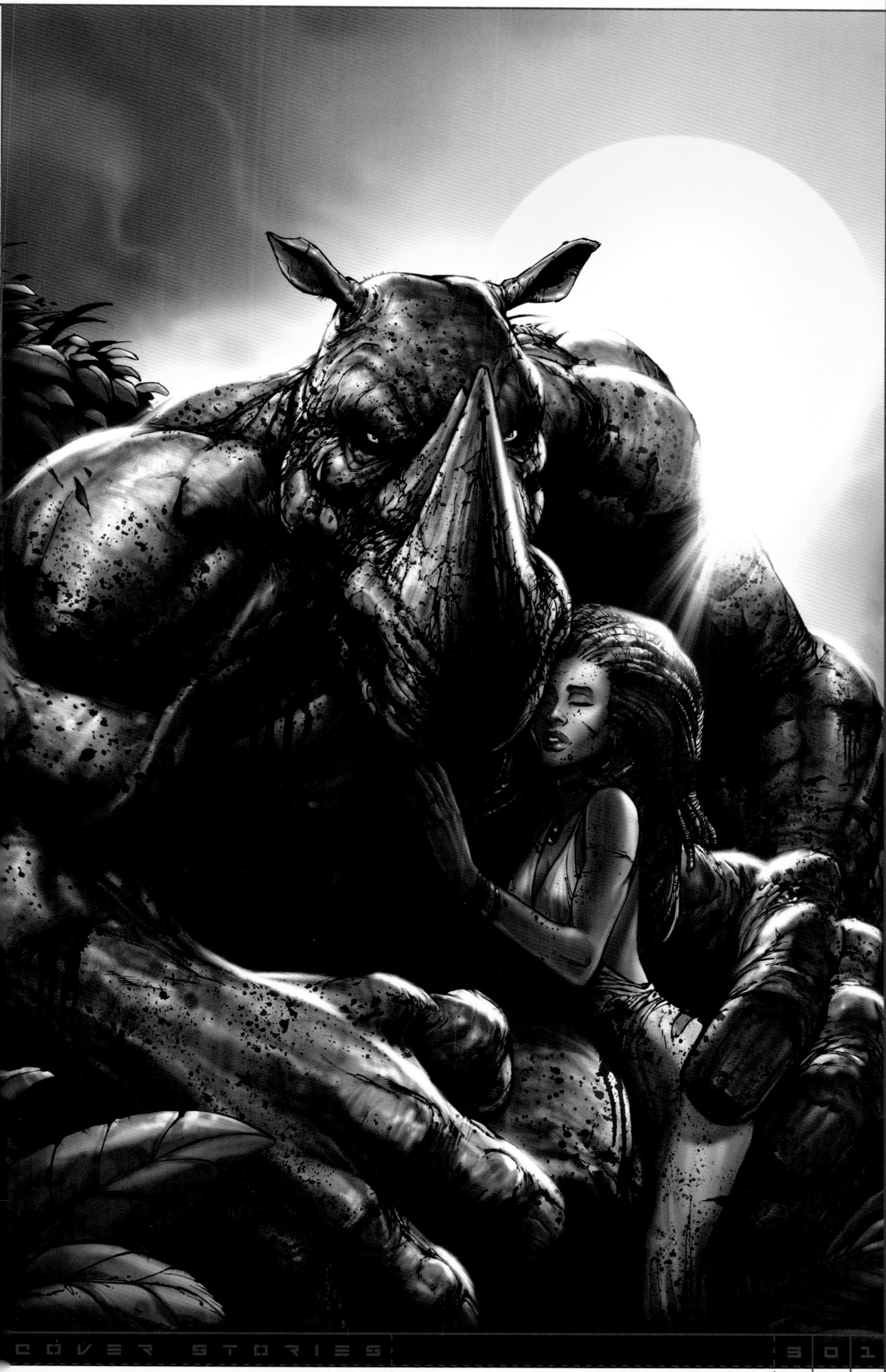

IN OUR DEFENSE

ELEPHANTMEN contributor and round-headed Rob Steen [look for his **ELEPHANTMEN** stories in volumes 0, 2 &3] gave me the drawing by his **FLANIMALS** co-creator Ricky Gervais seen here as a birthday present a couple of years ago. When the **COMIC BOOK LEGAL DEFENSE FUND** asked us to contribute a short strip for that year's **LIBERTY ANNUAL**, Ricky's drawing was probably lurking at the back of my mind. I contacted Shaky Kane with my idea, but he protested that he was too busy working on **THE BULLETPROOF COFFIN DISINTERRED** [another fine Image Comic, this one co-created by David Hine]... However, when I described each page to him over Facebook, he put aside the All-Seeing Eye and, cackling, swiftly delivered the disturbing drawings that follow, expertly coloured by boisterous Boo Cook. We do suggest that you leave this volume at home when you travel through international security checkpoints. Otherwise, please follow the directions in the text and recognize our disclaimers.

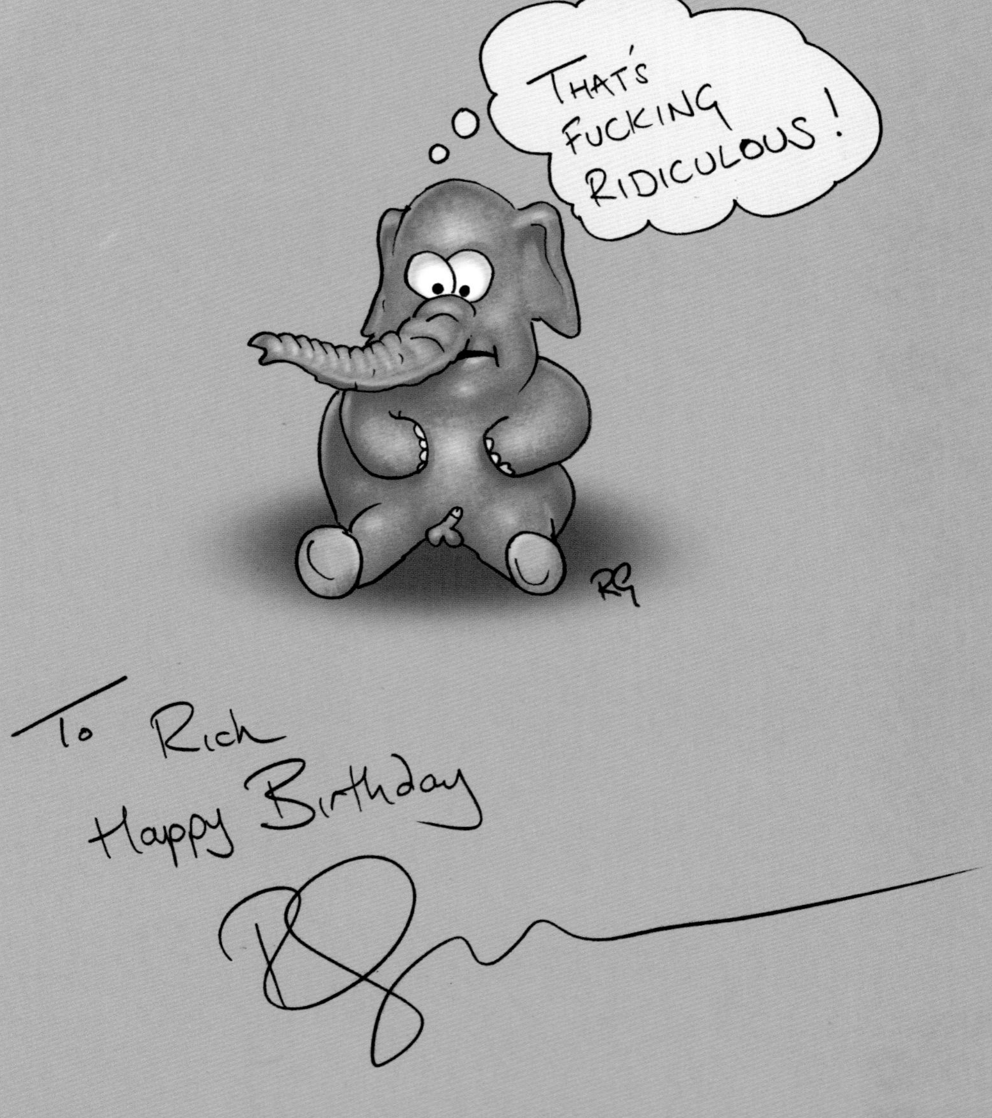
THAT'S FUCKING RIDICULOUS!
RG
To Rich
Happy Birthday

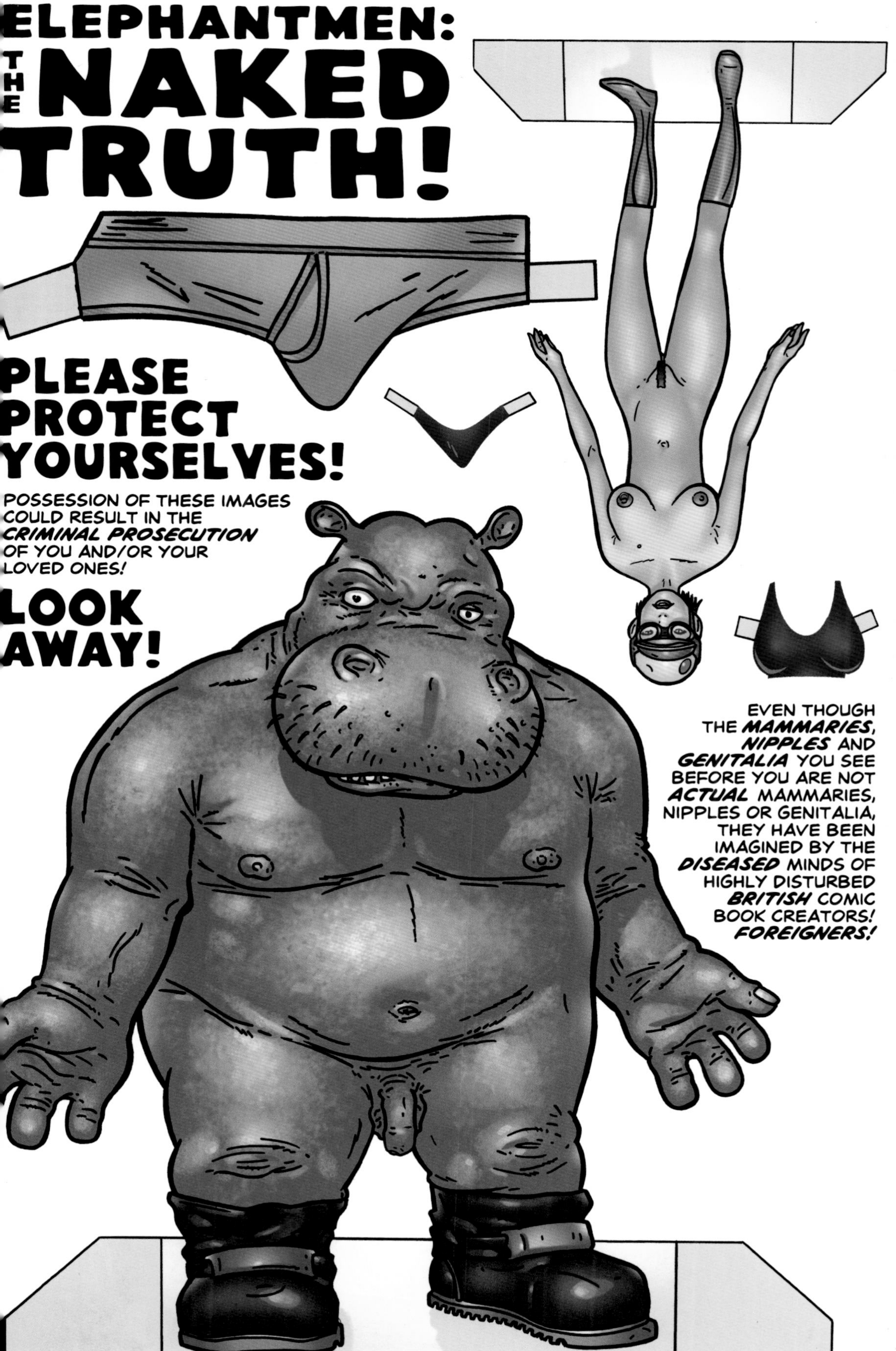
ELEPHANTMEN: THE NAKED TRUTH!
PLEASE PROTECT YOURSELVES!
POSSESSION OF THESE IMAGES COULD RESULT IN THE CRIMINAL PROSECUTION OF YOU AND/OR YOUR LOVED ONES!
LOOK AWAY!
EVEN THOUGH THE MAMMARIES, NIPPLES AND GENITALIA YOU SEE BEFORE YOU ARE NOT ACTUAL MAMMARIES, NIPPLES OR GENITALIA, THEY HAVE BEEN IMAGINED BY THE DISEASED MINDS OF HIGHLY DISTURBED BRITISH COMIC BOOK CREATORS! FOREIGNERS!

IT'S NOT TOO LATE!

CLIP OUT THE FIGURES AND THE UNDERWEAR YOU SEE HERE AND ***COVER UP*** THE UNFORTUNATE ELEPHANTMEN AND THE WOMEN THEY LOVE!

ANY ***DISGUSTING*** THOUGHTS YOU ARE CURRENTLY ENTERTAINING IN RESPONSE TO THESE IMAGES ARE ***NOT*** THE PUBLISHER'S RESPONSIBILITY. NO ONE AT ***IMAGE COMICS*** OR THE ***COMIC BOOK LEGAL DEFENSE FUND*** HAS ENJOYED LOOKING AT THESE DRAWINGS OR DESCRIBING THEM TO OFFICERS OF THE LAW!

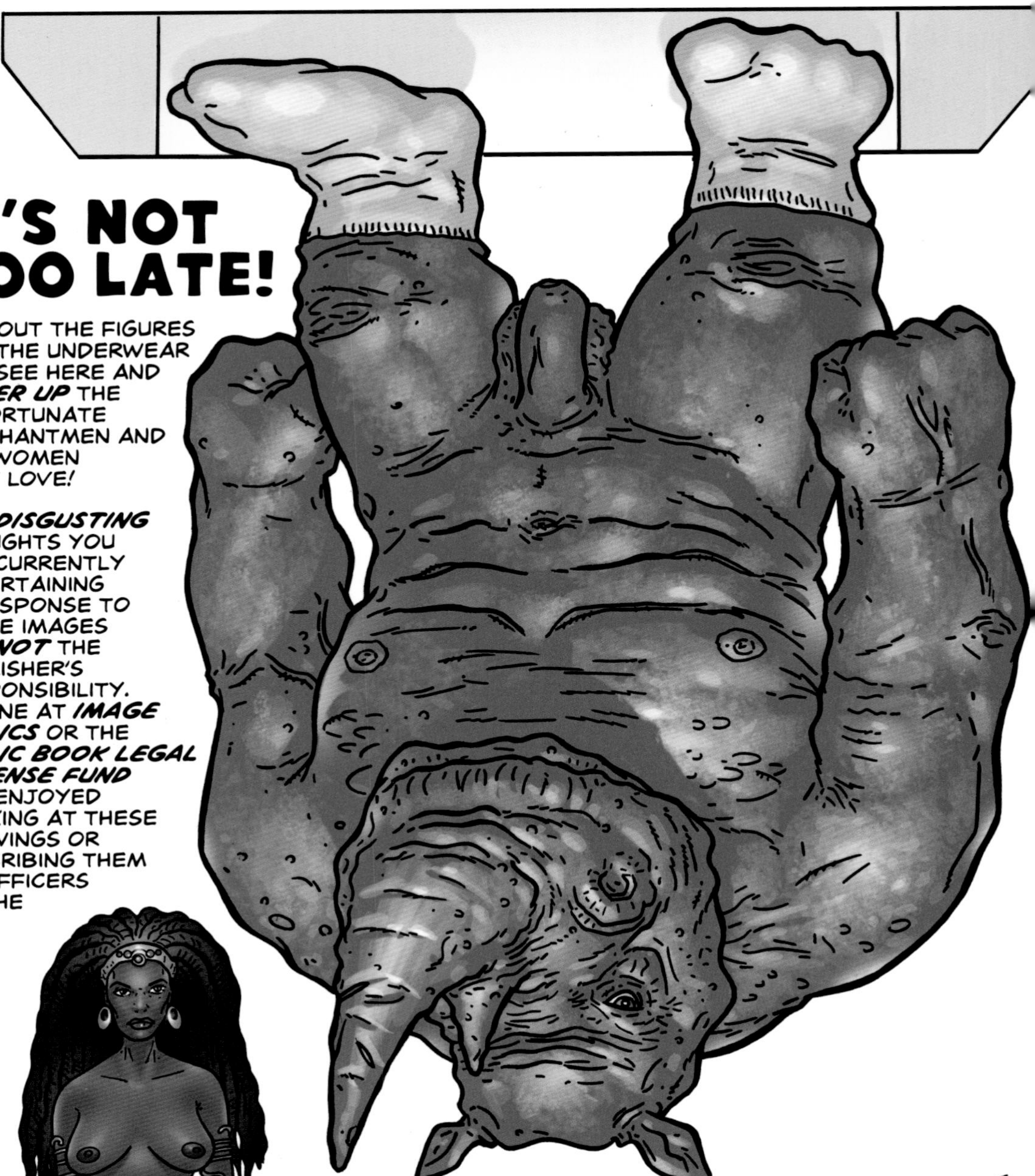

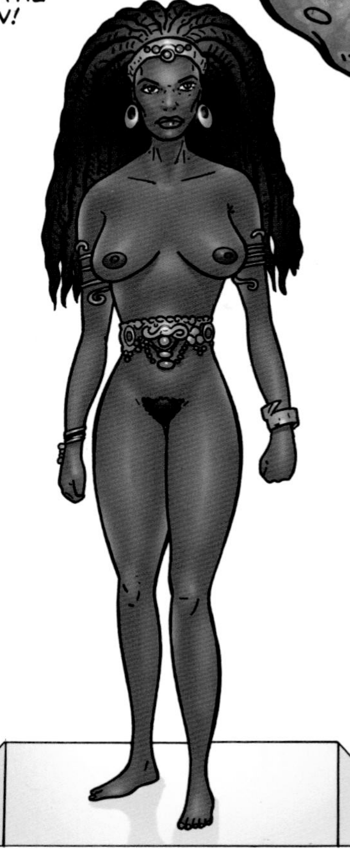

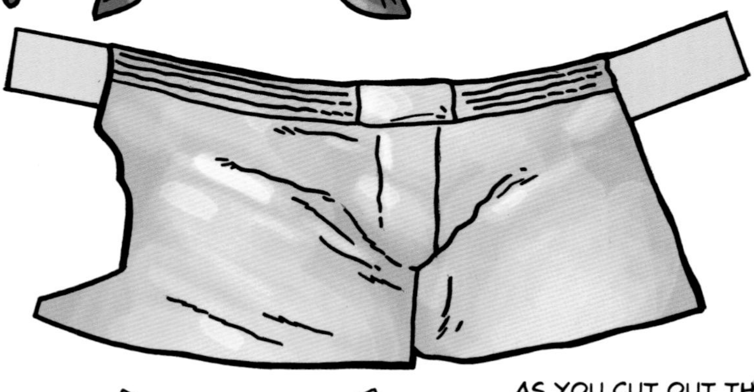

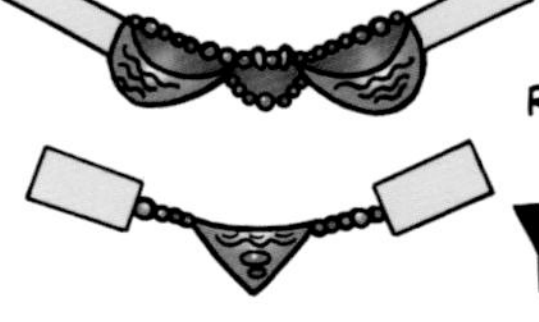

AS YOU CUT OUT TH
FREAKISH CHARACTER
SHOWN HERE, WE STRONGL
RECOMMEND THAT YOU **CLOS**
YOUR EYES

"SHAKY KANE" AND "BOO COOK" HAVE BEEN PULLING OFF ELEPHANTMEN DRAWINGS LIKE THIS FOR SOME TIME. IF THEY EVER SEEK TO ENTER A CIVILIZED COUNTRY, THEY WILL HAVE TO BE *LOBOTOMIZED* FIRST BECAUSE THEIR MINDS ARE FULL OF THESE KINDS OF *VULGAR* AND *SEDITIOUS* IMAGES AND IDEAS!

YOU HAVE BEEN WARNED!

DRESS UP THESE INNOCENT CHARACTERS *NOW!*

FIRST PRIZE

HUNH?

IF YOU FAIL TO COMPLY,

CHILDREN ALL OVER THE WORLD WILL SUFFER AND MAY EVEN DIE!

DO NOT APPROACH CARTOONISTS OR WRITERS LIKE ELEPHANTMEN CREATOR *RICHARD STARKINGS* IF YOU SEE THEM AT AIRPORTS OR OTHER *POINTS OF ENTRY!* THINKING ABOUT TALKING TO COMIC BOOK CREATORS OF THIS KIND CARRIES A MINIMUM OF ONE YEAR IN PRISON!

WE IMPLORE YOU:

DON'T THINK OF AN ELEPHANT'S PENIS!

HEY, KIDS, HERE'S HOW SHAKY DOES IT!

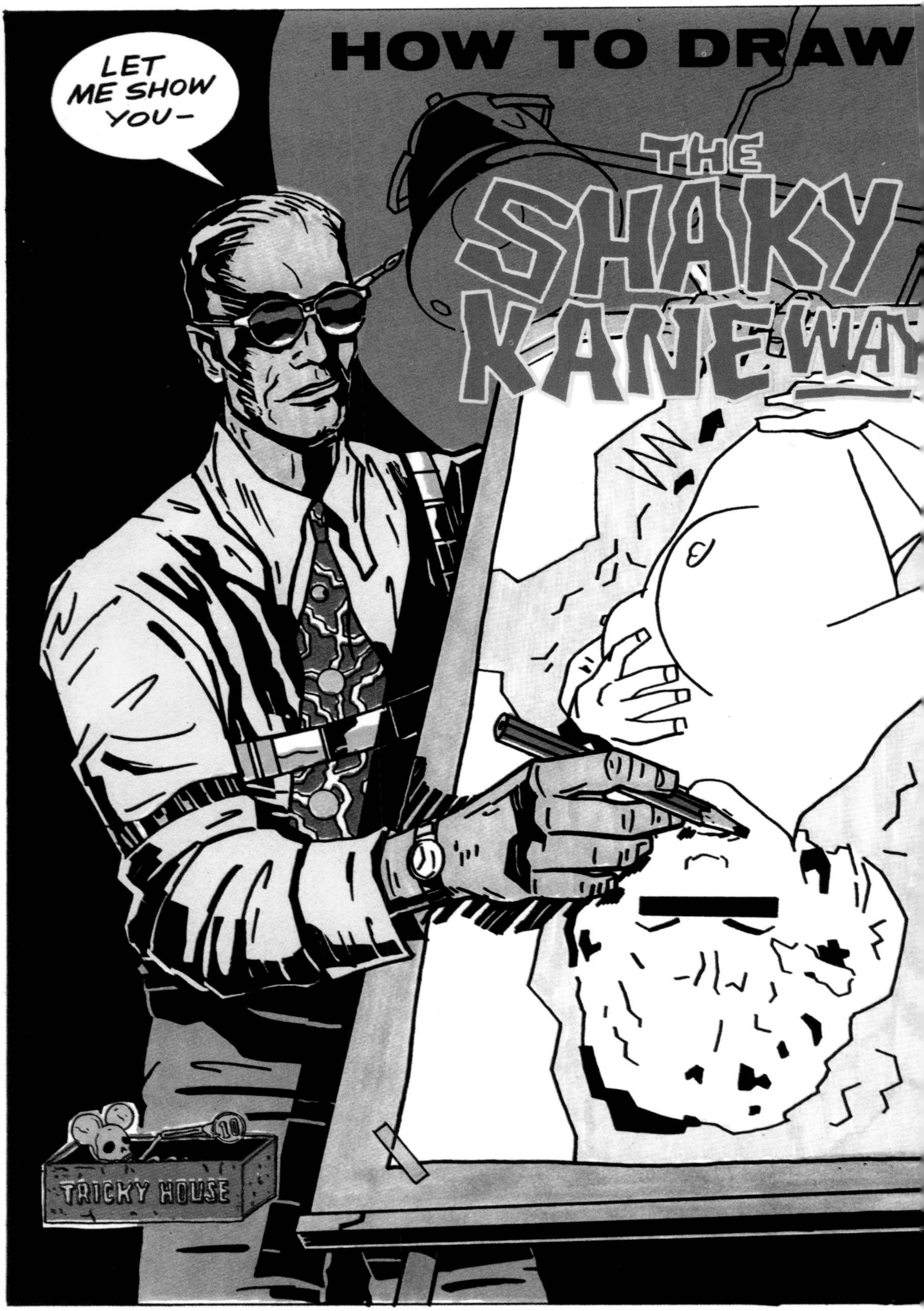
LET ME SHOW YOU-
HOW TO DRAW
THE SHAKY KANE WAY
TRICKY HOUSE
10

BUT REMEMBER, HE'S A PROFESSIONAL!

TEP 1: FINDING THE INSPIRATION

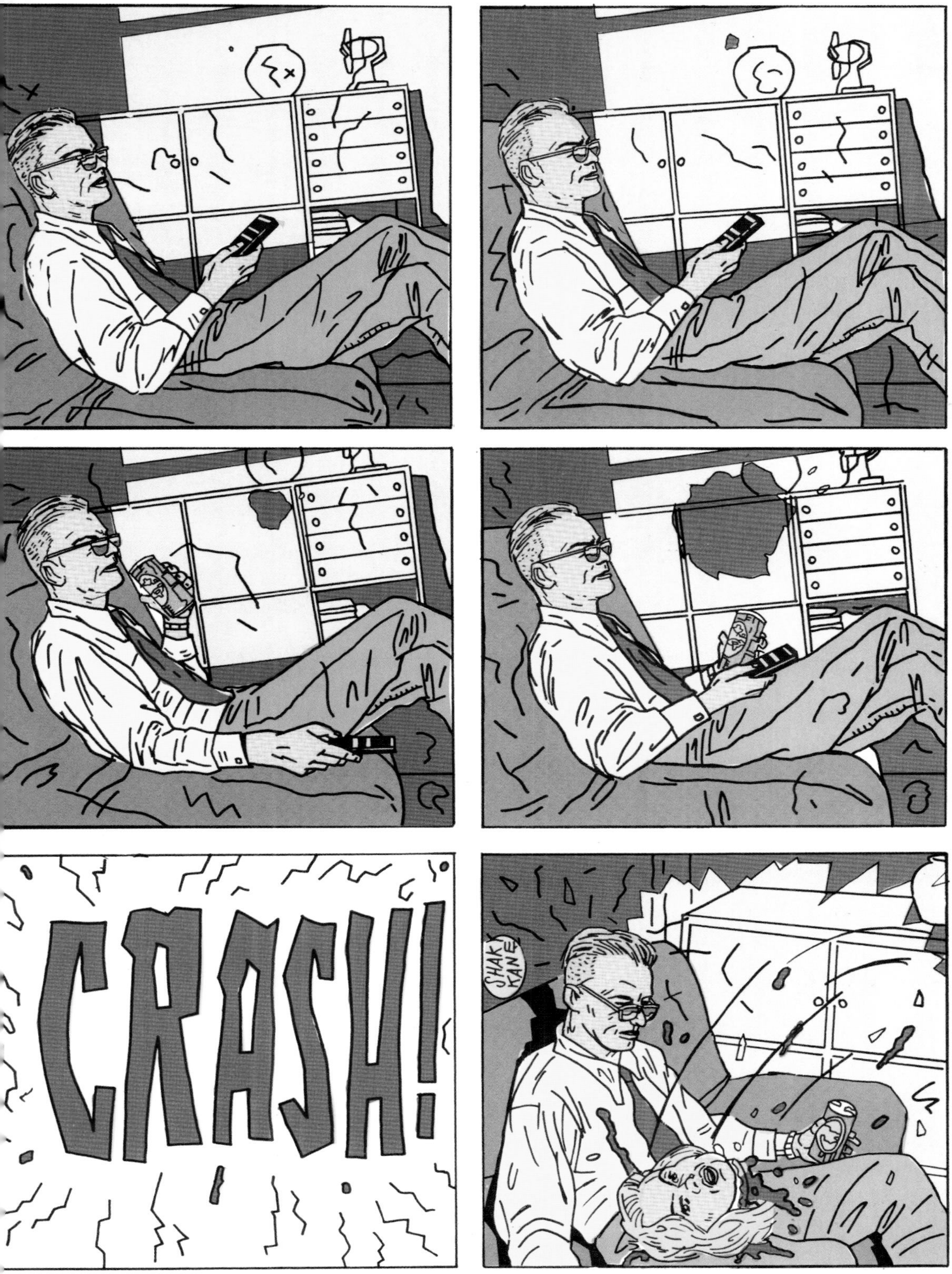
CRASH!

NEXT: who to buy drinks at conventions

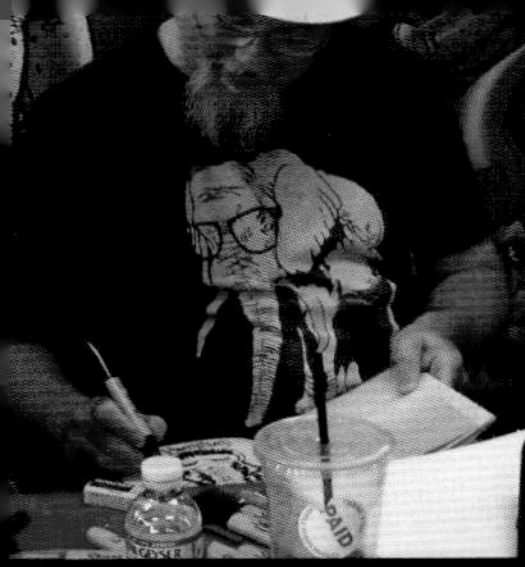

RICHARD STARKINGS is the creator of HIP FLASK and ELEPHANTMEN. Born and raised in England, Starkings worked for five years at Marvel UK's London offices as editor, designer and occasional writer of ZOIDS, GHOSTBUSTERS, TRANSFORMERS and the DOCTOR WHO comic strip. He is perhaps best known for his work with the award-winning Comicraft design and lettering studio, which he founded in 1992 with John 'JG' Roshell. Starkings & Roshell also co-authored the best-selling books COMIC BOOK LETTERING THE COMICRAFT WAY and TIM SALE: BLACK AND WHITE.

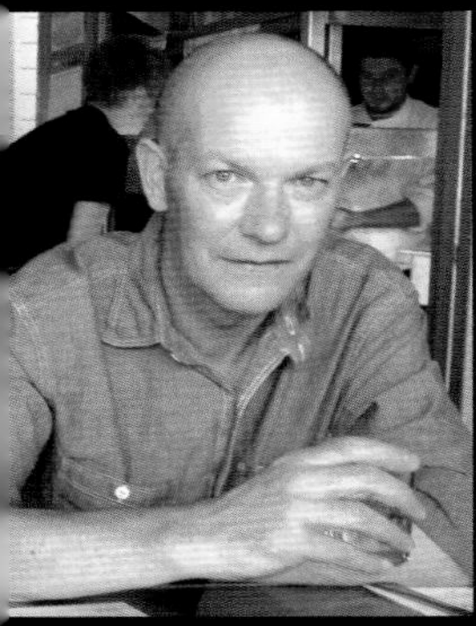

SHAKY KANE has applied his special form of psychedelic dementia to strips ranging from his own MONSTER TRUCK from Image Comics to THE A-MEN to JUDGE DREDD and SOUL SISTERS in the Galaxy's Greatest Comic ZOOOAD. His latest, hatest work is the surreal Image comics BULLETPROOF COFFIN and BULLETPROOF COFFIN DISINTERRED, a gem unearthed by David Hine. Look for new issues of ELEPHANTMEN drawn by Dave or Shaky in your LCBS soon!

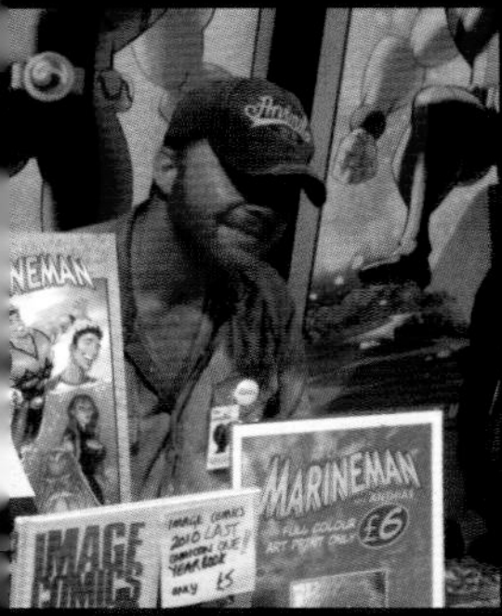
MARINEMAN

IAN CHURCHILL left a career in graphic design to work professionally in comics in 1994, when he was hired on the spot at a London comic convention by Marvel's editor-in-chief at the time, Bob Harras. Alongside Jeph Loeb, Churchill took Marvel's X-Men title, CABLE to new heights shortly before Joe Casey and Ladrönn created their memorable run on the book. Before launching his own creator owned series with Image, Churchill illustrated THE AVENGERS, UNCANNY X-MEN SUPERMAN, COVEN and a certain character by the name of HIP FLASK - Huzzah!

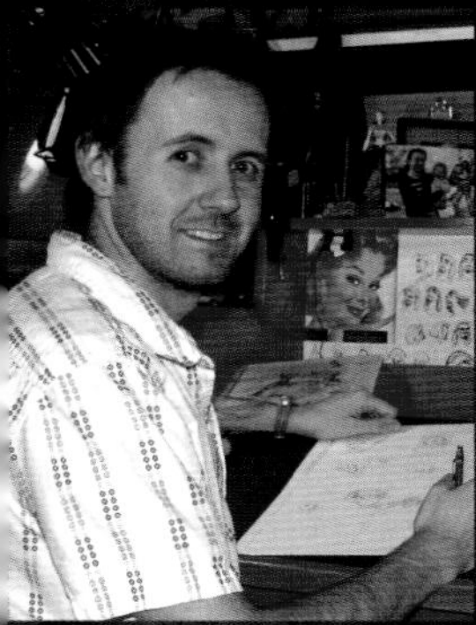

J. SCOTT CAMPBELL was initially discovered in the first Homage Studios talent search. His dynamic storytelling and animated style lent themselves perfectly to the smash-hit series GEN13 and his own DANGER GIRL. Campbell resides in Colorado where he's currently drawing a highly anticipated SPIDER-MAN project for Marvel, with some guy named Loeb, and finishing the final two issues of his creator-owned series WILDSIDERZ for DC Comics.

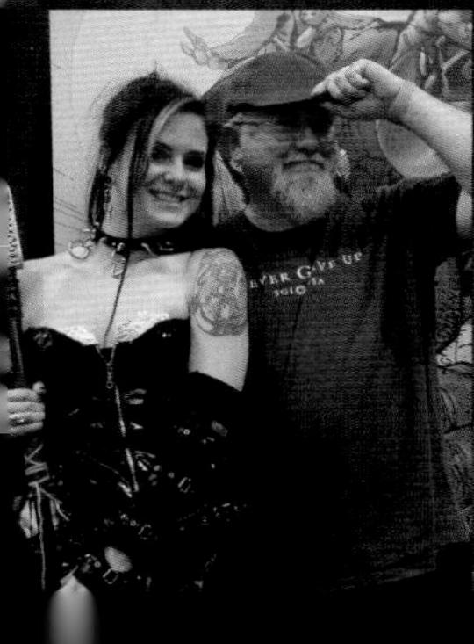

NEI RUFFINO is not only an incredible artist in her own right, producing comic book covers for companies like Zenescope and Big Dog Ink, she also works as a professional colour artist for DC Comics on titles such as BIRDS OF PREY, GREEN LANTERN and SUPERGIRL. She provided cover colours for Ian Churchill's MAN AND ELEPHANTMEN cover as well as J. Scott Campbell's latest four covers for ELEPHANTMEN, and she hooks up J. Scott's FAIRYTALE FANTASIES calendars with mind blowing colours every year. AND she's a sweetheart!

CREATORS

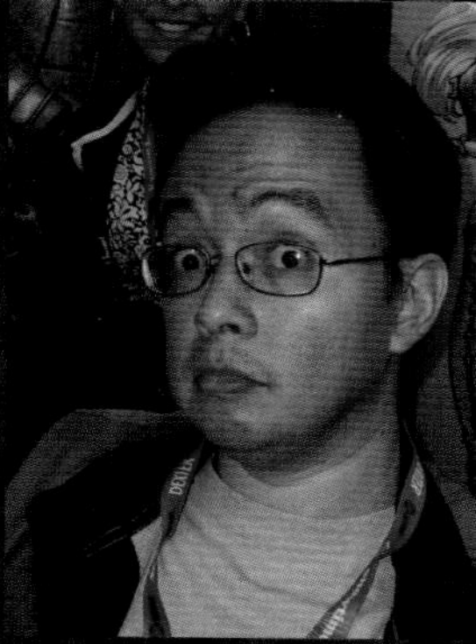

AXEL MEDELLIN was born in 1975 in Guadalajara, Mexico. Axel was a straight A-student until he graduated as an industrial designer and decided he wanted to draw comic books for a living, which in Mexico is like signing a suicide note. After working in advertising, llustration, storyboards and comic books in Mexico, Axel's first J.S. work appeared in METAL HURLANT, followed by stories for HEAVY METAL, FABLEWOOD, Zenoscope's GRIMM FAIRY TALES and Boom! Studios' MR STUFFINS. Before becoming the regular artist on ELEPHANTMEN, he completed Image Comics' 50 GIRLS 50.

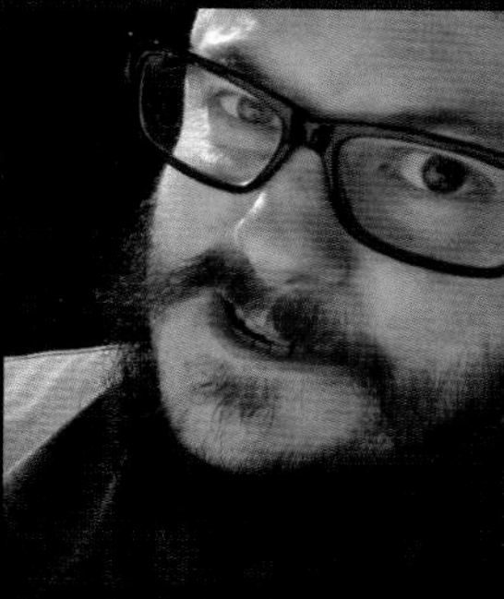

BOO COOK lives in Brighton, England with his lovely wife Gemma. He has worked on ZOOOAD for Tharg the Mighty in Blighty for eleven years now, drawing favorites such as JUDGE DREDD, JUDGE ANDERSON, A.B.C WARRIORS and a basketcase of covers including a run on Marvel's X-FACTOR series. If you want to track down a big chunk of Boo, look for the ASYLUM collection, and f it leaves you begging for more, ask him about BLUNT.

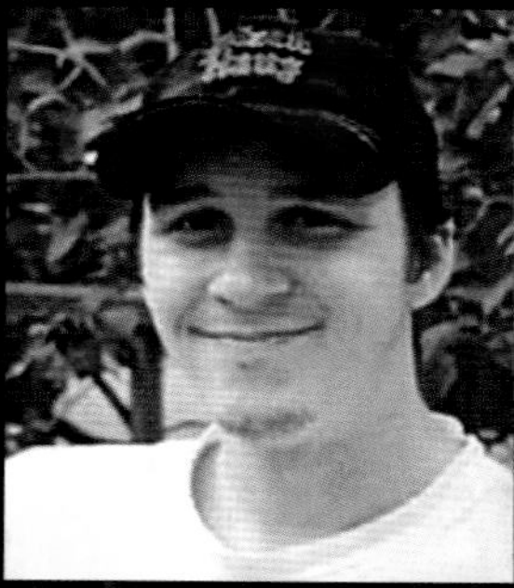

ED McGUINNESS came to prominence with his work on Harris Comics' VAMPIRELLA and Marvel's DEADPOOL. At Awesome comics, McGuinness participated in a FIGHTING AMERICAN revamp with writer Jeph Loeb, who would become a longtime collaborator. A short run on Wildstorm's MR. MAJESTIC led to a longer one on DC Comics' SUPERMAN and the launch of SUPERMAN/BATMAN with Loeb. Back at Marvel, McGuinness reunited with Loeb for FALLEN SON: THE DEATH OF CAPTAIN AMERICA, HULK and AVENGERS: X-SANCTION.

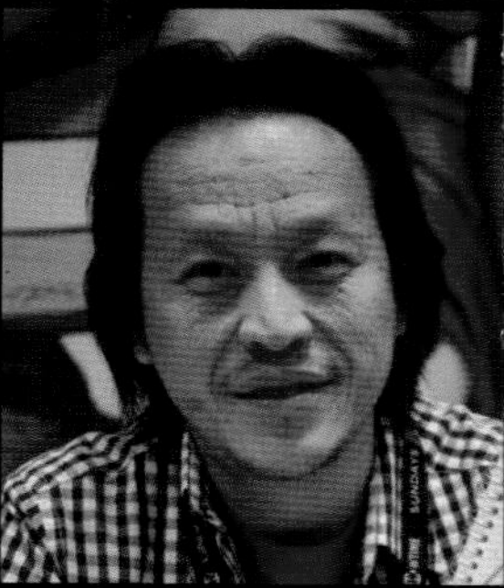

KEU CHA started drawing at a very young age, influenced by comic book and fantasy artists such as Marc Silvestri, Jim Lee, Todd McFarlane, Boris Vallejo and Frank Frazzetta. With almost no formal art training except for the encouragement of one caring art instructor, Keu bypassed art school for a job in comic books, honing his skills as a penciller on such titles as RISING STARS, WITCHBLADE, TOMB RAIDER and DARKNESS for Top Cow Productions. He is currently working on his own series for Image Comics, HEX THE LOST TRIBE.

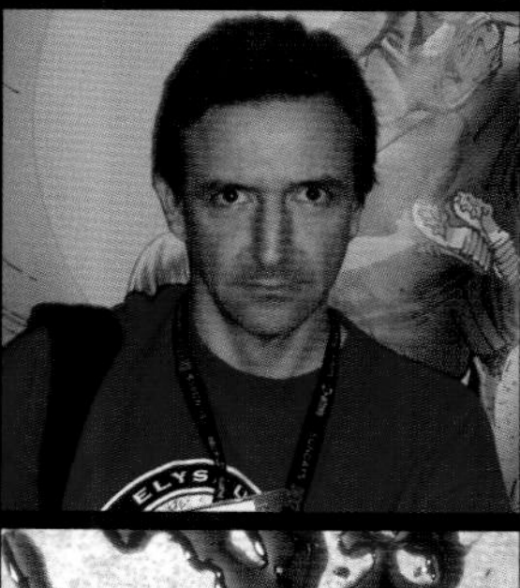

GREGORY WRIGHT's origin began on staff at Marvel comics. A Marvel/Epic Comic editor known to wield a small bat when discussing deadlines, he found that freelance writing and coloring was much less stressful and far more fulfilling. Greg has worked on everything from SPIDER-MAN to BATMAN to ROBOCOP to DEATHLOK and SILVER SABLE. His favorite color work is BATMAN: THE LONG HALLOWEEN.

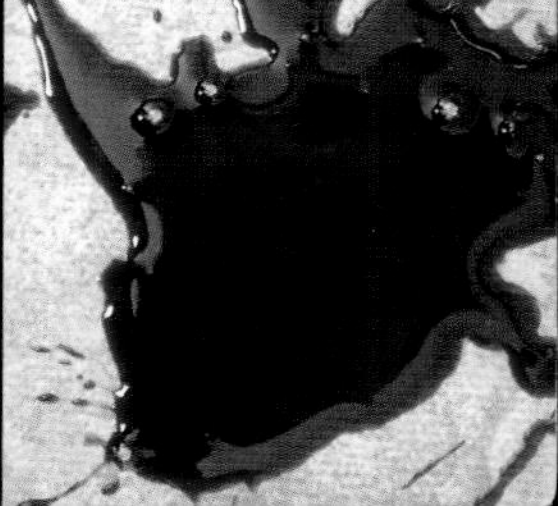

JOHN ROSHELL a.k.a. "JG", a.k.a. "Mr. Fontastic", a.k.a. "Comicraft's Secret Weapon", grew up nary an iPod's throw from Apple in Northern California. These days he uses the Mac to create fonts and design books, logos and websites, including the official ELEPHANTMEN site at HipFlask.com. He also writes CHARLEY LOVES ROBOTS and plays a mean guitar.

THE ORIGIN

STARKINGS · CASEY · LADRONN
HIP FLASK
UNNATURAL SELECTION

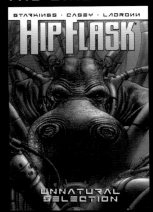

HIP FLASK VOL. 1: UNNATURAL SELECTION

2218: The birth of Hieronymous Flask and the Elephantmen, and their eventual liberation from the torturous world of MAPPO.

ISBN 0-97405-670-7
Diamond #STAR19898

THE MYSTERY

STARKINGS · CASEY · LADRÖNN
HIP FLASK
CONCRETE JUNGLE

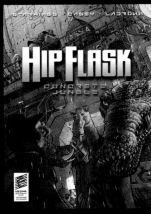

HIP FLASK VOL. 2: CONCRETE JUNGLE

2262: The broken and bloody body of an unidentifiable man sets Hip Flask and Vanity Case on a trail that leads them to Casbah Joe and The Eye of the Needle.

ISBN 1-58240-679-0
Diamond #NOV06 1859

THE WAR

ELEPHANTMEN
INTRODUCTION BY DAN ABNETT
00 ARMED FORCES
STARKINGS · MORITAT · MEDELLIN · ROSHELL · COOK

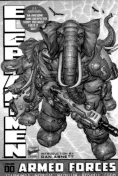

ELEPHANTMEN VOL. 0: ARMED FORCES

2239: Africa and China are at war. Enter: MAPPO's soldiers, the Elephantmen! Collects WAR TOYS #1-3, WAR TOYS: YVETTE and ELEPHANTMEN #34-35.

SOFTCOVER:
ISBN 978-160706-514-2
Diamond #MAR12 0426

HARDCOVER:
ISBN 978-1-60706-468-8
Diamond #SEP11 0394

THE SURVIVORS

ELEPHANTMEN
01 WOUNDED ANIMALS
STARKINGS · MORITAT · LADRÖNN · ROSHELL · COOK

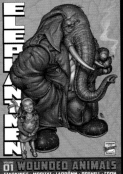

ELEPHANTMEN VOL. 1: WOUNDED ANIMALS

2259: Nikken's creations struggle for survival and acceptance in the world of man. TPB collects issues #0-7.

SOFTCOVER:
ISBN 978-160706-337-7
Diamond #SEP10 0455

HARDCOVER [#1-7]:
ISBN 978-1-60706-088-8
Diamond #JAN07 1927

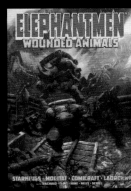

ELEPHANTMEN
WOUNDED ANIMALS

THE ENEMIE

ELEPHANTMEN
02 FATAL DISEA

ELEPHANTME VOL. 2: FATAL DISEASES

A meteor falls i Santa Monica B with far-reachi consequences f all. Collects issu #8-15 and PILOT

SOFTCOVER:
ISBN 978-1-60706-3
Diamond #MAY11 0

HARDCOVER:
ISBN 978-1-60706-0
Diamond #AUG08 2

ELEPHANT
FATAL DISEA

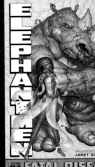

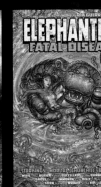

HE DARKNESS

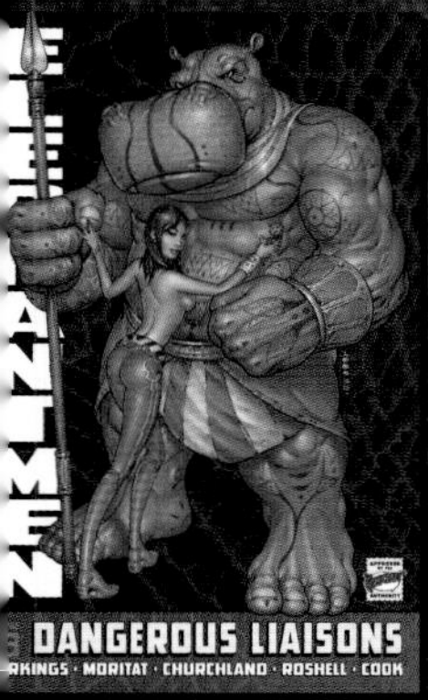
DANGEROUS LIAISONS
RKINGS · MORITAT · CHURCHLAND · ROSHELL · COOK

LEPHANTMEN
VOL. 3: DANGEROUS
IAISONS

ip Flask, Ebony Hide
nd Obadiah Horn go
bout their business
n Los Angeles, 2259,
naware a MAPPO
leeper cell has plans
or them. Collects
ssues #16-23.

OFTCOVER:
SBN 978-1-60706-268-4
iamond #MAY10 0439

ARDCOVER:
BN 978-1-60706-250-9
iamond #FEB10 0355

THE CASUALTIES

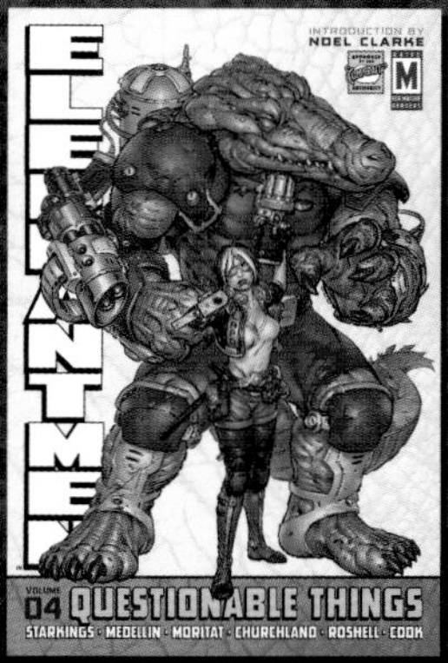
INTRODUCTION BY
NOEL CLARKE
ELEPHANTMEN
VOLUME 04 QUESTIONABLE THINGS
STARKINGS · MEDELLIN · MORITAT · CHURCHLAND · ROSHELL · COOK

ELEPHANTMEN
VOL. 4: QUESTIONABLE
THINGS

A MAPPO sleeper
cell has been
reactivating
Elephantmen.
Collects issues
#24-30

SOFTCOVER:
ISBN 978-1-60706-393-3

HARDCOVER:
ISBN 978-1-60706-364-3
Diamond #JAN11 0550

THE FANTASY

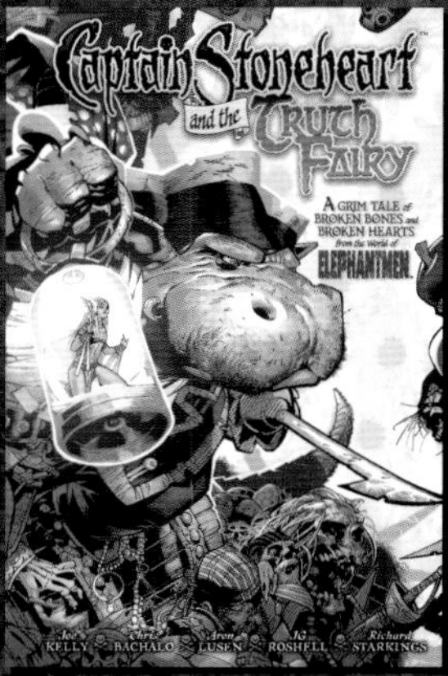
Captain Stoneheart and the Truth Fairy
A GRIM TALE of BROKEN BONES and BROKEN HEARTS from the World of ELEPHANTMEN
Joe KELLY
Chris BACHALO
Aron LUSEN
JG ROSHELL
Richard STARKINGS

CAPTAIN
STONEHEART AND
THE TRUTH FAIRY

Joe Kelly and Chris
Bachalo craft a grim
but beautiful fairy
tale of broken bones
and broken hearts.
Includes the full
script, pencil artwork
and audio CD.

ISBN 1-58240-865-3
Diamond #JAN07 1927

THE REALITY

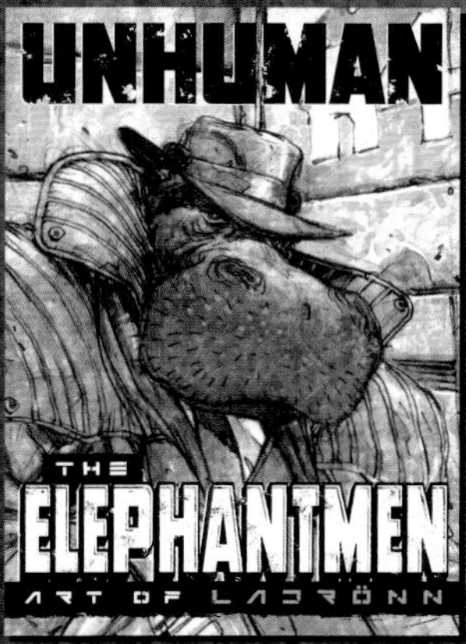
UNHUMAN
THE ELEPHANTMEN
ART OF LADRÖNN

UNHUMAN: THE
ELEPHANTMEN
ART OF LADRÖNN

Unpublished art,
sketches and drawings
by Ladrönn show the
development of the
HIP FLASK universe in
a beautiful oversized
hardcover volume.

ISBN 1-58240-882-3
Diamond #SEP07 1961

ALL-NEW DUSTJACKETS FOR VOLUME 1 & 2 HARDCOVERS AVAILABLE AT COMICRAZY.COM!

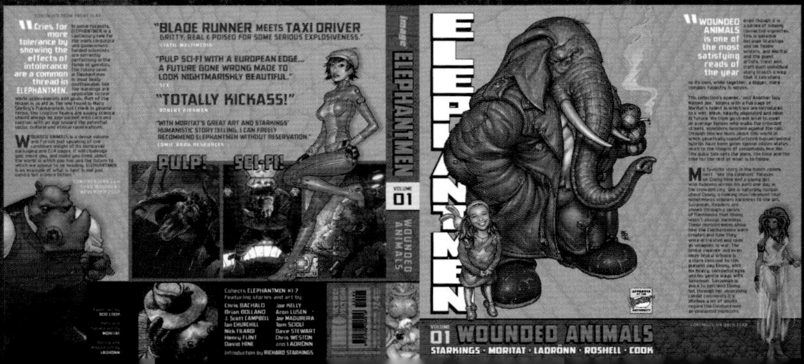
"BLADE RUNNER MEETS TAXI DRIVER
GRITTY, REAL & POISED FOR SOME SERIOUS EXPLOSIVENESS."
"PULP SCI-FI WITH A EUROPEAN EDGE... A FUTURE GONE WRONG MADE TO LOOK NIGHTMARISHLY BEAUTIFUL."
"TOTALLY KICKASS!"
PULP! SCI-FI!
ELEPHANTMEN
VOLUME 01 WOUNDED ANIMALS
STARKINGS · MORITAT · LADRÖNN · ROSHELL · COOK

50
GIRLS
50

50 GIRLS 50
VOL. 1: SHAKEDOWN

ISBN 978-1-60706-469-5
Diamond #SEP11 0390

HINE AND KANE'S
THE BULLETPROOF COFFIN

BULLETPROOF COFFIN

VOLUME 1
Diamond
#JUN12 0447

VOLUME 2
Diamond
#JUN12 0446

SHAKY KANE'S
MONSTER TRUCK
WISHBONE
AUTOMOBILES MONSTERS AND MAYHEM

SHAKY KANE'S MONSTER TRUCK

ISBN #978-1-60706-470-1
Diamond #JUN12 0448

ELEPHANTMEN
HIP FLASK AND ELEPHANTMEN ARE TM AND © 2007 ACTIVE IMAGES
ELEPHANTMEN JIGSAW PUZZLE 1000 PIECES

HIP FLASK 1000 PIECE JIGSAW PUZZLE BY LADRÖNN

Diamond #JUN07 1880

COMIC BOOK
LETTERING
THE COMICRAFT WAY!

COMIC BOOK LETTERING THE COMICRAFT WAY

ISBN #0-97405-673-1
Diamond #JUN12 0450

STEVEN T. SEAGLE
JUSTIN NORMAN
solstice
The shortest day of the year...
The longest day of their lives

BY STEVEN T. SEAGLE AND JUSTIN NORMAN

ISBN #0-97667-611-7
Diamond #APR05 2512

ALSO FROM IMAGE COMICS

STRANGE EMBRACE
1-58240-914-5

BULLETPROOF COFFIN
978-1-60706-368-1

MONSTER TRUCK
978-1-60706-470-1

CHEW VOL. 1
978-1-60706-159-5
CHEW VOL. 2
978-1-60706-260-8
CHEW VOL. 3
978-1-60706-335-3
CHEW VOL. 4
978-1-60706-398-8

PROOF VOL. 1
978-158240-944-3
PROOF VOL. 2
978-1-60706-017-8
PROOF VOL. 3
978-1-60706-134-2
PROOF VOL. 4
978-1-60706-285-1
PROOF VOL. 5
978-1-60706-348-3
PROOF VOL. 6
978-1-60706-391-9

REED GUNTHER VOL. 1
978-1-60706-462-6 $14.99

GIRLS VOL. 1
978-1-58240-529-2
GIRLS VOL. 2
978-1-58240-608-4
GIRLS VOL. 3
978-1-58240-703-6
GIRLS VOL. 4
978-1-58240-753-1

JACK STAFF VOL. 1
987-7-58240-335-9
JACK STAFF VOL. 2
978-1-58240-392-2
JACK STAFF VOL. 3
978-1-58240-719-7

POPGUN VOL. 1
978-1-58240-824-8
POPGUN VOL. 2
978-1-58240-920-7
POPGUN VOL. 3
978-1-58240-974-0
POPGUN VOL. 4
978-1-60706-188-5

THE SWORD VOL. 1
978-1-58240-879-8
THE SWORD VOL. 2
978-1-58240-976-4
THE SWORD VOL. 3
978-1-60706-073-4
THE SWORD VOL. 4
978-1-60706-168-7

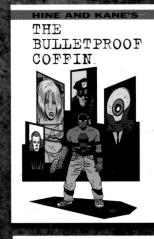